CALL HOME THE HEART

Olive Tilford Dargan, 1912

CALL HOME THE HEART

A Novel of the Thirties

Fielding Burke

With an Introduction by Alice Kessler-Harris and Paul Lauter
and Afterwords by Sylvia J. Cook and Anna W. Shannon

THE FEMINIST PRESS
Old Westbury
New York

Published in the United States of America by
The Feminist Press, Box 334, Old Westbury, New York 11568.

Library of Congress Cataloging in Publication Data
Burke, Fielding, 1869–1968.
    Call home the heart.

    (Novels of the thirties series)
    Originally published: London; New York: Longmans,
Green, 1932.
    Includes bibliographical references.
    I. Title. II. Series.
PS3507.A6C3 1983   813'.52   83-5606
ISBN 0-935312-15-3 (pbk.)

First Feminist Press edition
Manufactured in the United States of America at BookCrafters, Inc.

Cover design: Marta Ruliffson
Covert art: Sketch of "Tennessee Woman," 1885–86 by Elizabeth Nourse.
Reproduced by permission of Patricia Niehoff.
Frontispiece and back cover photographs: The Olive Tilford Dargan
Papers, the Southern Historical Collection, University of North Carolina
Library, Chapel Hill, North Carolina. Reproduced with permission.

CONTENTS

INTRODUCTION

Alice Kessler-Harris and Paul Lauter

The first phase of the women's movement, so the historical tradition goes, ended in the twenties. Its passion spent in the successful campaign for the vote, its remnants torn apart by divisions between those who wanted equality at once and those who insisted on retaining hard-won protections, the movement was stifled finally by a depression that mocked individual ambition. But if one kind of feminism ended in the twenties, another emerged in the thirties. Largely overlooked by historians, its existence is documented by the literature of the period.

The old movement that ended in the twenties declined in the affluence of that decade. After the vote was won, activist women set out to translate their political success into the economic equality it seemed to promise: Alice Paul's Women's Party pushed for an Equal Rights Amendment; coalitions of women's groups supported the Sheppard-Towner Act to provide maternal and well-baby care; the Women's Bureau successfully defended the rights of wage-earning women to minimum wages and shorter hours. The prosperity of the twenties made room for ambition, nurturing the talents of such writers as Edna St. Vincent Millay, Katherine Ann Porter, Zora Neale Hurston, and Anzia Yezierska. For a while it seemed as though the women who flooded into arts and letters as well as into banking and insurance were merely the vanguard of a new generation of self-confident and fulfilled womanhood.

Then came the depression, and widespread unemployment put an end to illusions of economic equality for women. The crisis of the thirties revealed the extent to which women's ambitions had relied on the opportunities offered by an expanding economy. With 25 percent of the work force unemployed by 1933, the picture changed dramatically. State and local governments tried to drive women, especially married women, out of the work force. Private industry took advantage of socially sanctioned discrimination against women to undercut the wages of poorly paid men. Opportunities for promotion and advancement shriveled.

To return to the home was no answer for most women. Families doubled up. Husbands and fathers lost their jobs. The home reflected the poverty and insecurity of unemployment as women and their children coped with the psychic tensions of maintaining family life and the economic pressures of insufficient incomes. Young women postponed marriage to help their parents survive, and they avoided pregnancy for fear of its economic consequences.

But women did not abandon the search for women's rights. Rather, as the crisis exposed their vulnerable positions, they began to question the degree to which the ambitions of the twenties were circumscribed by social reality. There would be no freedom for women at work while millions were unemployed; no genuine partnership in the home while clothing and food remained luxuries; no equality of opportunity for male or female children who grew up without medical attention or education. To women of the thirties, poverty and the social conditions that fostered it seemed as much women's issues as individual advancement had seemed in the twenties. To fulfill their own thwarted ambitions, women were required to connect themselves with the larger struggle for social justice. They would rise or fall with it. In this new generation, women who might earlier have been called feminists became social activists of a broader stamp.

As the old individualism gave way to concern for eliminating unemployment, preserving home life, and collective survival, women began to turn to available political movements for answers. Some moved into New Deal agencies, hoping to find a cure for despair in government social programs. Others chose to organize workers into the newly militant trade union movement. Many turned to the socialist and communist parties of the Left. Here, in an atmosphere of revolutionary possibility, they introduced questions of equality between the sexes, of women's education, and of reproductive and sexual freedom.

Left-wing groups like the Communist Party, USA, welcomed women into their ranks. They provided increased opportunities for women to act in the political arena, but they remained ambivalent about specifically women's issues. Though leftist ideology in the 1930s recognized the "special oppression" of women and formally espoused sexual equality, in practice, the Left tended to subordinate problems of gender to the overwhelming tasks of organizing the working class and fighting fascism. Both ideology and practice opposed feminism, fundamentally on the ground that it drew working-class women away from their male working-class allies and into the orbit of bourgeois women. Women constituted a formidable proportion of most left-wing groups, and Unemployment Councils, neighborhood groups, and even the emerging CIO relied heavily on them for leadership and support. By the end of the decade perhaps 40 percent of the membership of the Communist Party, USA, was female.[1] If the Communist Party did not provide a comfortable haven for women, if it subordinated women's questions and often refused to challenge sexual segregation on the job or rigid gender roles at home, its language of equality provided women with opportunities for debate, and its political programs opportunities for organizing and leadership experiences. The Left offered a forum and more serious attention to women's questions than any other group of the decade. It also provided women with a community of shared experience.

Female voices, primed by the rhetoric of equality, resonated on the printed page. A remarkable number of politically active women wrote. Their poems, stories, and songs, as well as their novels and essays, give us access to some of the issues seldom addressed in political practice, even on the Left. If the nature of women's participation in political action limited the issues about which they wrote, it also provided depth and insight into the critical social and personal conflicts that underlay activism. Their political views help clarify why most of the women writers of the thirties and in this series worked in a variety of forms: each form had both an artistic and political motivation as well as a particular audience. Fielding Burke, for example, had published many volumes of verse under her real name, Olive Tilford Dargan; Josephine Herbst was an active reporter throughout the thirties, as well as a critic; Mary Heaton Vorse, whose novel about Gastonia was a rather crude and obvious effort, wrote some of the decade's best books and articles about the developing labor movement. These writers strove not only to perfect the forms in which they wrote but to choose the forms most appropriate for the various political tasks in which they engaged.

We have chosen in this series to begin with fiction because it seems to reflect most closely the unfettered consciousness of women in the decade. The books in this series are part of a long tradition of literature about working-class life. Because they are written by women, these novels do not sit comfortably inside most accounts of that tradition, nor do they conform precisely to theories of "proletarian fiction" produced in the thirties. Yet the ways in which this women's fiction differs from that of men alert us to the particular qualities of some of the best female writers of this century, including Agnes Smedley and Meridel Le Sueur, and provide the most important reason for The Feminist Press to undertake this series.

In the 1920s, literary rebellion, in the words of Jack Conroy, "was directed principally against the fetters of form and language taboos."[2] By the thirties, literary theory had provided a systematic alternative to the modernist emphasis on formal experimentation, ironic distance, and linguistic complexity. Its major breakthrough, particularly for the work of left-wing and working-class writers, was to validate the experiences of working people. In her speech to the 1935 American Writers' Congress, Meridel Le Sueur made the point this way:

> It is from the working class that the use and function of native language is slowly being built. . . . This is the slow beginning of a culture, the slow and wonderful accumulation of an experience that has hitherto been unspoken, that has been a gigantic movement of labor, the swingdown of the pick, the ax that has hitherto made no sound but is now being heard.[3]

"Proletarian Realism," Mike Gold's widely adopted phrase, would thus deal in plain, crisp language with the lives and especially the work of the proletariat, optimistically urging them on "through the maze of history toward Socialism and the classless society."[4]

Though this is in fact a rich and complex aesthetic, it presented immediate problems for women who took their own experiences seriously. Less than a quarter of all women and fewer than 15 percent of married women worked outside the home during most of the

1930s. If the workplace was to be a major focus for art, as it was for Communist Party organizing, then, as "workplace" did not include work done in the home for the support of the family, only small fractions of women's lives would find their way into art. The rest would be ignored, subordinated once again to the demands of male politics. More important, since proletarian fiction, by the definition of the times, rested upon the central distinction between the experiences of the working class and those of the bourgeoisie, it would underplay, even deny, the relevance of other distinctive group experiences. Blacks, Hispanics, women—as groups suffering their own persecution—would have no place in it. In denying the commonalities of female experience, the vision of the proletarian aesthetic undermined such crucial issues for women as the uneven division of household labor, the sexual double standard, and male chauvinism within the working class or the Party itself.

Women writers who perceived such problems were placed in a certain dilemma: theory maintained that their work should be based upon the experiences of the working class; yet the experiences of one half of the working class—males—were clearly of more significance than the experiences of the other half of the working class. Where did that leave distinctly female experiences, like childbearing, or those, like the nurturance of children, which continued to be primarily women's tasks? And where in that theoretical framework could one find a place for the strengths and ambiguities of love, of rearing children, of family life, of the problems of control over one's body, the struggle to find emotional and sexual fulfillment?

Women writers of the Left chose to flout male convention and to write about themes that fell outside the frameworks of their male peers. But so strongly masculinist was the cultural theory and practice of the Left that it remained virtually immune to the feminist implications of their themes. The cultural apparatus of the Left in the thirties was, if anything, more firmly masculinist than its political institutions. It is not that women writers were ignored. Josephine Herbst was a "guest delegate" to the Kharkov conference of the International Union of Revolutionary Writers in 1930. Tillie Olsen and Meridel Le Sueur were among the (few) invited women speakers at the American Writers' Congress in 1935. The Communist Party's book club, the Book Union, selected as its representative "proletarian novels" Fielding Burke's *A Stone Came Rolling,* Clara Weatherwax's *Marching! Marching!,* and Leane Zugsmith's *A Time to Remember.* Herbst, Le Sueur, Zugsmith, and Grace Lumpkin, among others, were active reviewers for *The New Masses* and certain other Left journals.

But women were often, in fact, tokens at major conferences. Accounts of the John Reed clubs (the Communist Party's cultural associations), of the editorial boards of magazines like *The Anvil, Blast,* or *The Partisan Review,* and of other Communist Party and Left cultural organizations hardly acknowledge the existence of women—though many did, in fact, work in such groups. The hitch-hiking Wobbly style of life extolled by writers like Jack Conroy left room only for the rare Boxcar Bertha, while the hairy-chested polemics of left-wing critics like Mike Gold placed women's issues squarely in a male context. The worker-poet was inevitably male, his sexuality "evidence of healthy vigor"; his comrades, cigar-smoking talkers, in from the wheat fields or the Willys-Overland plant. In a *New Masses* editorial announcing the advent of "Proletarian Realism," Gold pictures the new writer as "a wild youth of about twenty-two, the son of working-class parents, who himself works in the lumber camps, coal mines, and steel mills, harvest fields and mountain camps of America. . . . He writes in jets of exasperated feeling. . . ."[5] Women writers were recognized on the Left, indeed occasionally puffed, just as women's issues were recognized. But the values and outlooks *institutionalized* in magazines, editorial boards, conferences, and theories of the Left were decidedly masculinist.

At the same time, there appear to have been few distinctly female cultural groups or networks of support among women writers on the Left. Meridel Le Sueur mentions in her American Writers' Congress speech a group of "a hundred and fifty women from factory and farm" who "wrote down their great proletarian experience." Myra Page, novelist and reporter, recalls the way experienced women took newcomers under their wings, but notes that women "felt that the general issue was the most important thing: depression and unemployment."[6] Support among women was directed at achieving the larger goals. Women intellectuals in books like Tess Slesinger's *The Unpossessed* and Josephine Herbst's *Rope of Gold* seem, from the perspective of the 1980s, strikingly isolated from one another. While there were female-centered cultural institutions during the 1930s—the YWCA, for example, supported a Women's Press—they were not of the Left. In fact, they were likely to be noted by the Communist Party, if at all, with suspicion. In short, there was little institutional support on the Left that might have validated any distinctly female culture, and much that discouraged it. Not perhaps by design, but effectively for all that, any female—much less feminist—tradition was submerged.

Within a few years, the entire world of left-wing culture was ploughed under by the attacks of McCarthyism. It is not always easy now, thirty years later, to perceive how successful the campaign was in silencing and burying writers on the Left. One good indicator is that copies of books by the writers with whom we are concerned are absent from libraries and used book shops. After the thirties, some of the women turned away from "political" subjects; some fell into silences; others continued to write but could find no publisher; many, like Tillie Olsen, were subjected to public attack. That happened, of course, to men as well as to women. But, in addition, women were confronted with that hostile ideology we have come to call "the feminine mystique." More profoundly, perhaps, the concern for working-class life and for understanding the relationship between gender and politics was suppressed in the fifties as anti-communism, suburbanization, and consumerism controlled the environment. As the cultural soil dried up, writers lost their audience. The run of stories, novels, poems, and songs that had established for an audience certain expectations, artistic conventions, and ideological perspectives, came to an end.

When the writing of the thirties began to be re-discovered twenty-five years ago, critics persisted in denying its feminist proclivities. In his comprehensive book, *The Radical Novel in the United States,* for example, Walter Rideout suggests that "the explicit linking of political revolution and sexual freedom rarely appears" in left-wing novels of the thirties "as it did in *Daughter of Earth.*"[7] In fact, however, sexuality, personal liberation, and radical politics are closely intertwined in Fielding Burke's *Call Home the Heart;* sexual politics are at the center of conflicts described in Tess Slesinger's *The Unpossessed;* personal and sexual relations provide the critical counterpoint to emerging political differences in Josephine Herbst's *Rope of Gold.*

Female writers who accepted the central class division of socialist realism nevertheless paid attention to women-centered issues. In Tillie Olsen's *Yonnondio,* as Deborah Rosenfelt argues, "the major transformation is based on human love, on the capacity to respond to beauty, and on the premise of a regenerative life cycle of which mother and daughter are a part." For feminist proletarian writers, these issues are not separable from the capacity to effect a successful political transformation. As Rosenfelt tells us, "Women's work in preserving and nurturing that creative capacity in the young is shown in *Yonnondio* to be an essential precondition to social change."[8] Such themes, ignored by male critics, are not peculiar to Olsen. Both in her story "Annunciation" and in her novella *The Girl,* Meridel Le Sueur focuses on the regenerative power of pregnancy and birth. The action in Leane Zugsmith's *A Time to Remember* concerns a department store strike, but the emotional conflict that constitutes the dynamic tension of the novel comes from the attempts of strikers and their families to cope with the social reality of women's subordinate positions.

The books in this series demonstrate the substantial and vigorous tradition of women-centered literature. We find in these books women of intellect and strength—like Victoria in Herbst's *Rope of Gold*—seeking work that is politically meaningful and yet consonant with their need for personal independence. We encounter in Slesinger's *The Unpossessed* many of the same conflicts between ostensibly progressive politics and real chauvinist behavior that helped generate the women's liberation movement of the late 1960s. With Ishma in Fielding Burke's *Call Home the Heart* we experience the contrary appeals of full-time, heroic but often grubby, work in a movement for social change and of the rich, green pastures of the hill country. These books present women (and men) in varieties of workplaces—including the home—participants in strikes and demonstrations, observers and reporters of what seemed a growing, international revolutionary movement. Their steady grasp of sexual politics illuminates the inner contradictions and struggles of movements for change. These writers are the sisters and comrades of Agnes Smedley, Meridel Le Sueur, and Tillie Olsen: their work asserts the richness, as well as the continuity, of the traditions of left-wing feminism in the United States.

Certainly all the female authors of the thirties did not write in ways that distinguished them from men. But some of the best works written by women addressed the distinctive experience of both working-class and female lives. Women in that decade produced a body of writing with qualities that overlap but are not identical with those of the male writers of the period. This literature—we might now call it "socialist feminist"—is only beginning to be explored by scholars with an eye to what it tells us about the complex factors that encouraged women to write both as activists and as critics. In presenting these books as part of a series, The Feminist Press hopes to underline the need to reconstruct the cultural context that helped shape them.

That process will require us to re-examine questions around which debate swirled in the thirties. What is the function of art in a revolutionary movement? Do we cast aside as merely absurd the notions of some socialist critics, who suggested that art was a "weapon" in the class struggle, that writers must under all circumstances convey a sense of "proletarian optimism," and that they must write only in language plain enough for plain people? Or are we to understand the criticism of the Left in that period as a creative effort to confront issues with which the artists themselves were struggling? Are there ways to resolve the tensions between the slow, sustained discipline which the artful rendering of experience demands and the more immediate requirements of writing hitched to the needs of a political movement? How can a writer bring alive the vision of a triumphant socialist future, which no one has seen or fully imagined, with anything like the power to evoke the struggles and devastation of capitalism in decline? Just who is one's audience? And if the audience for socialist art should, at least in part, be working-class people, what functions does art serve in their lives, and are these different from its functions in the lives of the traditional audience for writers?

The writers in this series largely avoided the more formulaic demands of thirties criticism. Their endings are not always unambiguous and hopeful as "socialist realism" theoretically required. Their heroines, like Ishma in *Call Home the Heart,* share both the virtues and the profound limitations of their class origins. They portray retreat as well as triumph; confusion and ambiguity as well as possibility. But struggle was never simple. Together these books provide another piece of the puzzle that illustrates how women have come to consciousness over the years. In publishing this series, The Feminist Press calls attention to the varieties of feminism and its expressions. The fiction of the thirties is part of our common heritage. We hope it will be useful in conceiving of our future lives.

Alice Kessler-Harris
Hofstra University

Paul Lauter
State University of New York,
College at Old Westbury

Notes

1. See Robert Shaffer, "Women and the Communist Party, USA, 1930-1940," *Socialist Review* #45 (May-June 1979): 90 for this and for additional information on women and the Communist Party.

2. Jack Conroy, "Introduction," *Writers in Revolt: The Anvil Anthology* (New York, Westport: Lawrence Hill, 1973), p. ix.

3. From "Proceedings of the American Writers' Congress," New York, 1935, reprinted by West End Press, Minneapolis, 1981.

4. Edward Seaver, "Socialist Realism," *The New Masses* 17 (23 October, 1935): 24.

5. "Go Left, Young Writers," *Mike Gold: A Literary Anthology,* ed. Michael Folsom (New York: International Publishers, 1972), p. 188.

6. Interview with Alice Kessler-Harris, December 1, 1982.

7. Walter Rideout, *The Radical Novel in the United States* (New York: Hill and Wang, 1956), p. 219.

8. Deborah Rosenfelt, "From the Thirties: Tillie Olsen and the Radical Tradition," *Feminist Studies* 7 (Fall 1981): 398.

CALL HOME THE HEART

CALL HOME THE HEART

CHAPTER I

HER FAMILY

BEFORE she was seven, Ishma, the youngest child of Marshall and Laviny Waycaster, had joined the class of burden-bearers. By the time she was thirteen there was little rest for her except on Sunday. That day she kept for herself on the hill-tops. This was after Granny Starkweather's bright, detaining spirit had gone forever from the house. Six days of the week Ishma was merely a family possession, giving herself so effectually that no one suspected she was giving; so entirely that she did not suspect it herself. But channels of being that open so readily outward must, more than those whose gates are tight and rusty, protect their reservoir. With no intuitive hint that she had chanced upon a law of salvation, Ishma found a way of replenishing her fount.

On Sunday morning she would be up early, put some scraps of food into a paper bag, and set off for the high woods. Up there no one came. The travelled trails lay lower down, most of them intersecting at her mother's cabin, making it a popular Sunday rendezvous. All who passed felt that they must stop for friendly speech, if they didn't stay to dinner. But too often they stayed.

High on Lame Goat Ridge Ishma had earth to herself. This was the eastern and highest part of Dancer Ridge, the long line that meandered and dipped and curved between Dancer and Wimble counties. The top of Lame Goat gleamed bonily with cliffs and rocks, but the sides were thickly wooded, enclosing her in a world of tumbling waters and wild odors. In summer there were strange flowers trembling higher than her head, and birds innumerable; creepers, warblers of all kinds; thrushes, chewinks, wood-doves; and sometimes an unknown visitor with a cry thrillingly new. If she went far enough around the mountain on the north-east side she would come to a "bench" big enough for the dashing stream to gather itself into a great pool before creeping to the edge of the bench and shooting a thousand silver arrows downward. She could sit by this pool for hours without wanting to move, feeling within herself a leisurely flow of activity that made her both contented and eager. The fount was filling up.

Her mother, Laviny, had a distorted sense of justice, but could be fair at times, and never remonstrated with Ishma over her Sunday defection. But once when the child came rushing in towards night, saying she had been to Moonfeather Falls, her mother grumbled. "Fer the land's sake, Ishmalee, the strenth ort to be dreened out o' ye, cruisin' so fur, but you look like you could heave a hoss."

Bainie put in a complaint, since Laviny had opened the way. She was Ishma's older sister, and the wearily incompetent mother of four small children. "You shore got out o' work today. I never seen so many folks on the mountain, an' they must 'a' left home 'fore breakfast, measurin' up the way they et. The baby 's ailin' too, an' cried till I didn't have no sense."

It was easy to arouse remorse in Ishma's gay heart. "I'm sorry, Bainie," she said. "Maybe I'll stay at home next Sunday."

"Maybe! You know you won't, less'n it's rainin' go-devils! An' if it is, there won't be no company to wait on. I ain't got the pull of a tow string, an' the wash-tub set fer tomorr'."

"I'll do ever' bit of it, Bainie. You needn't wet your hands!"

Bainie knew the child would keep her promise, and her stream of complaint changed somewhat to concern. "Some o' these days you're goin' to plop yer foot down on a rattler an' get bit. You'll lay up there in the woods an' swell till you bust. I don't know what mommie 's thinkin' about to let you traipse off thataway." And this set Ishma to laughing again.

Sometimes she would come home late enough to find the tired family in bed. Slipping to the kitchen, she would clean up the supper things, always left for her, then creep into her own little bed which she had made out of split rails and rabbit wire discarded by Jim Wishart, Bainie's husband. This was her happy alternative to sleeping with three of her sister's younguns. A thick layer of "coker" sacks, rescued from the mud around the barn and washed clean in the branch, made her mattress. Over the bed, as a final cover, was spread the pride of her life; a quilt

2

made fifty years before by Granny Starkweather's own hands. Granny had taken it from her hog-hide trunk and given it to Ishma on her tenth birthday. It tinged with glamour the moment of going to bed and the time of getting up. Bainie had never received such a present from grandmother. "She's dauncey an' she's sloven," said candid Granny. "Ishma is clean always, an' she's well always. She'll keep that quilt sweet. It'll last her fer weddin' bed."

The old lady would have sighed then if she hadn't been so determinedly opposed to the sign of dejection. So many marriages and dowerings in her life had left her little to give. Seventeen sons and daughters, going out with this keepsake and that; and here in a bare house was Ishma, whom she would have loved to shower with treasures. Not even John Stark, her wonderful youngest, had been more dear to her than this child who had so surprisingly filled her heart at the end of her time.

A bare house it was; struggling bravely, with crumbling tenacity, to shelter the descendants of Frady Starkweather, its pioneer builder. For ninety odd years the mountain winds had tested their teeth on its big hewn logs. They had held together because so many of them were of winter-cut oak and chestnut. Time and sun had turned the oak to iron, and dried the chestnut to a light, aluminum staunchness. But here and there were logs of poplar, dustily dropping away from the chinking, and yearly widening the cracks in the walls. "No use tackin' boards over doty poplar," Jim Wishart excused himself. "The nails 'll ease right out."

Frady, the great-grandfather of Ishma, had been a young man of twenty, and only two weeks married, when he climbed the unharried slope of Cloudy Knob mountain, his bride and his dog loyal at his heels, and built himself a one-room dwelling with as proud a precision as he could attain with a broad-axe, a giant auger, and huge locust pins. As his family grew, so did his house. Finally there were three rooms, each with its large door and latchstring, opening on the porch that fronted the building its full length, making of it a home with no hint of the decrepit days when again it would be a cabin. The big room on the west became the kitchen, the bigger room toward the east was full of beds, and the middle room evolved into a living centre for the household. This room had windows. Frady put them in for his second wife, so that the light would fall on her loom. Nancy, the first little bride, had succumbed after twenty years of pioneering and child-bearing. Sarah, his second — Ishma's own Granny Stark — was a widow of forty when she married handsome Frady. She was trim, slim, wise and witty, with a talent for housewifery that she kept burnished as her own tea-cups. The inadequate fumblings of his gentle first mate had been accepted by Frady as the way of a wife, and it was some time before his astonishment at the competence of Sarah relaxed into surety.

When this desirable woman had been only fifteen, but weirdly mature, she had married a widower with nine children. She wanted a family, she said, and her "druthers" were for a ready-made one. The husband and father died, and she carried on the farm work with more success than masculine direction had attained. When the last of her nine step-children married, she handed over to him her comfortable valley home, and joined Frady on Cloudy Knob, where she found plentiful material, including seven new "steps," for exploiting her restless talent. But Frady himself was her chief reason for ascending the mountain. The union was a love-match, though neither confessed it until after the birth of their son, John. With all of Sarah's preference for ready-mades, and her long escape from maternity, after a year with Frady she became a dubiously delighted mother. Then their love became shyly communicative. Frady had paid in none of his good looks for the privilege of living so long on the fringe of a wilderness, and Sarah was as piquant as the air of early morning after a sun-drenched frost. This spicy freshness was still with her when she died sixty-seven years later, at the age of one hundred and seven. In her last years she liked to talk of the seventeen sons and daughters she had so earnestly mothered, married, and set on their way. But only John was the actual fruit of her flesh.

This unexpected son of Frady and Sarah became a very promising six-foot youth who married before he was twenty. The following winter was so cold that not even old Gaby Jones ventured to say that he had seen the earth more deeply frozen. "It

4

would shiver the soil to Chiny, an' be a power o' help to next year's crops," the people said, encouraging themselves. But silence fell on them after pneumonia began to pick off its victims. John Starkweather and his young wife, Lindy, were both stricken.

"Too much winter," said the old doctor who came out muleback from Carson. Mrs. Frady tried to mention the new freshair cure, but was suppressed with as much ire as anybody dared exhibit before her. Under the old doctor's stern eyes and direction, the two invalids were placed in the middle room, which was smaller than the others and could be kept sweating warm with a big fire in the fire-place. The windows must be clamped down, and the door opened only for hurried passage.

Lindy's baby was barely a month old. The youthful mother, further weakened by the heat of the room and heavy air, soon gave up her life. Young John's six feet of vitality surrendered to ignorance and grief, and he followed her within twenty-four hours. It did not lessen his mother's sorrow to hear the doctor say, "We have all done our best, my good woman. Let us remember that it is the Lord who has sent this bitter season upon us, and his wisdom is infinite." For the first time in her life she had failed to follow her own lead, and she had forty-seven years of regret before her.

Laviny, the month-old baby of John and Lindy, was left to the care of her grandmother. She grew up quickly, and at seventeen was a slender, sharp-tongued young woman, pretty enough and pert enough to bring the roving feet of Marshall Waycaster to a standstill. Little was known of Marshall except that he was a "roamin' feller" whom everybody liked. Frady was not there to start an investigation. He had died a year before his son. Grandmother didn't start anything, because she liked Waycaster just as he stood in his boots, and felt that perky little Laviny was in luck to get him. "When Laviny wizens up," she had said, "there'll not be much left of her but her tongue." A true prediction. The girl's beauty was very different from her grandmother's which remained vivid long after Laviny's was an incredible memory. Ishma could remember hearing the old lady counsel Laviny after a burst of temper, "Go ahead, my gal. If you make yer face any sharper you can use it to cut yer kindlin' with."

Ishma had the joy of knowing that she pleased grandmother. Children had come rapidly to Marshall and Laviny. Six had preceded Ishma, but only two had lived, Bainie and Steve. Granny detected in the last little girl a strong resemblance to herself. "What ain't me is Marshall," she reflected. "That ought to be a fair mix."

Ishma learned to read by stumbling through the Bible under the old lady's eye, beginning with the chapters that Granny knew by heart. The attentive Frady had read them to her through many rainy day hours, as she sat industrious or idle at her loom, and from memory she could correct the little girl almost to the letter. But Ishma was easily a scholar, and Granny, to her zest and delight, soon found herself led on to less familiar chapters. In fair recompense, she made the child her companion on out-door ventures, and so it was that Ishma learned the way of a wind on the mountain, of water around a rock, of a goat on Devil's Spur.

The last three years of Sarah Starkweather's life she had a "burnin' under her feet" that made walking painful. When she insisted on her periodical visits to her neighbors two and three miles distant she sat in a split-bottomed chair and was carried by any two young men who happened to be available. One on each side, they grasped the rounds of her chair and bore her smoothly up ridge and down, in cove and out, to her chosen destination. Anyone picked for this service was inwardly proud of the honor, but it was the habit of the boys so conscripted to complain about it among themselves. "Come jedgment, Granny Stark 'll send Gabe about his business an' go livin' right on," they said. "She ain't ever meanin' to die."

After grandmother stopped "cruisin' the cliffs" because of her burning feet, Ishma had little time for the low seat at her side. Marshall Waycaster had proved to be a willing worker, but no farmer. "It would be better," said Granny, "if he didn't go at things so hard, sence he goes at 'em back'ards." And she rather encouraged his whistling, dancing, and swapping jokes with the countryside. But Marshall, in the pride of his dancing years,

6

was stricken with paralysis. He who had insisted on an upright position almost day and night throughout his life, spent his last three years supine and speechless.

Laviny's boy, Steve, who, like his grandfather John, was six feet tall at the age of fifteen, ran away in his sixteenth year, and had no trouble in joining the army. Bainie's husband, "coon-huntin' Jim Wishart," was pleased to become the head of the house and master of Cloudy Knob farm, but he saw to it that his honors in no way laid extra duties upon him. Every year his wife presented the tolerant household with a new baby; and every year saw the family scale of living running lower. Granny could stand no longer at her wheel; no longer could she sit treadling at her loom; no more was her voice heard in the big kitchen where she had so long and capably presided over the filling of cans, kraut-tubs and bean-barrels. More and more the family became dependent on Gaffney's store in Beebread, at the foot of the mountain.

Ishma was thirteen when Granny Stark died. The death of her much loved father three years before had been a more bear-able sorrow. Hundreds of valley folks climbed the mountain to see the old lady carried to the family graveyard where Frady Starkweather lay, three coves east of the dwelling. Long-faced and conspicuous among the mourners, were the boys who had been so often commandeered to bear Granny Stark's chair.

Ishma had heard that the spirit of the dead sometimes hovered over the grave of its body on the first night after burial, and that night she slipped out of bed to lie in the graveyard with her head on the fresh dirt. But Granny gave no sign. Laviny was awake when the girl came in at dawn, her cheeks wet with tears of disappointment, and later in the day she took her to the spring-house and heckled her until Ishma told where she had been. Then Laviny looked strangely on her daughter, and begged her, for God's sake, never to tell another soul. Of all afflictions that could come to a mountain mother the worst was that of having a child who was not right in the head. It had been hinted that Mrs. Frady had conversed from her early years with invisible coun-sellors; but this rumor inspired awe rather than fear or aversion. Sarah Starkweather had been superb enough to carry off anything. Poor Laviny couldn't be so sure about her daughter. Sometimes her secret worry would break out in an irritable desire to punish Ishma, but she couldn't forget a scene at Granny's bedside when the dying old lady commanded her never to drop a heavy hand on that child. "If you do, Laviny, I'll not lay quiet, an' you needn't expect it. I'll be hoverin' right over ye." This was merely a threat, for Granny certainly expected to go to Heaven and stay there, but the warning was effective with Laviny.

"In the first place," thought the mother, "the gal knows too much. That sort always dies, er goes wrong, give 'em time." She would slant her eyes disapprovingly on Ishma sitting down to teach the younguns their lessons when she'd never poked her head inside of a school-house. Ever since Sam, Bainie's oldest, had started to school in Beebread, on the outward side of the mountain where the railroad and the new highway ran, Ishma had taken charge of his "home-work." She studied his books carefully, and kept with him through the first, second, third and fourth grades. When he reached the fifth he became stubborn and she had to pull him through. Vainly she drilled him in speech-mending ways according to the rules and examples laid down in his language book. Figures he could endure, and geography was easy, but he couldn't see any sense in learning to talk a new way when the old was just as good. "Pop an' mom an' all the neighbors got along with it." With Ishma's help he memorized enough of the book-stuff to pass examinations, because, he reasoned, he was on the junior basket-ball team, and he'd rather go to school than work anyway, and he hated to let Ish down, but he was going to quit and get a man's job in Carson before long. He was getting too big to wear rags. He wanted *clo's*. The last time that welfare woman frowned at his split shoes he had wanted to sock her one.

Ishma did not share Sam's aversion to the language book. It was a way to power and larger life. She sometimes carried it with her on her days in the woods, and studied the fascinating pages over which Sam would be led the following week. But she found it was pleasanter to do this on her way out to the ridge, stopping to rest for an hour or so. The book was not so en-

trancing on the home-coming road when her mind was full of
the joys of the day.

Her reading was not confined to school matter. She had, indeed, books of her own. In the hog-hide trunk which Granny
had left to her she found three volumes that had belonged to
Frady. Granny had kept them concealed from the ravaging
hands of Bainie's children, who held nothing too good for destruction except the big book on the lamp-table, which they
thought had power in itself to avenge any disrespect. One of
Ishma's inherited volumes was *Pilgrim's Progress,* inscribed with
the name of Frady's father and a town in Virginia. Evidently
it had trekked with him across Hickory Nut Gap to the wilderness. She read this faithfully, though she thought that the pilgrim
was rather stupid. Another volume was Jeremy Taylor's *Holy
Living and Dying,* which she liked to read aloud to herself, listening to the words running smoothly along like an endless brook.
When they were big and difficult she practiced them until she
could read without tripping. And it was true that she was more
concerned with her performance than with the matter she fed
on. A third book was a thick, small, calf-bound volume in very
fine print, entitled *Alonzo and Melissa.* This was a novel, romantic beyond any modern daring, and full of thrills as breath-
taking as could be devised out of such material as an under-
ground tunnel, inhuman parent, and the resurrection of the
heroine after the hero had wept hours away on her grave. Ishma
read it with abandon; incredulous, but grateful for the debauch.

Under the three books when discovered by her, lay something
that looked like old magazines with the backs off. Unpromising,
but the greatest find of all; a history of England, most bravely
illustrated, and told as if the listeners were all men of great adventure and the teller must prove worthy of his famous audience.
It had been printed serially, and the missing numbers made
aching gaps in Ishma's thrilling advance.

Besides these treasures there was a collection of recipes, which
Granny could not read but which she had carefully preserved
in the handwriting of numerous and long dead friends. She had
been a notable cook, and Frady, under her leading, had become a
notable provider. He could bring a ham into her kitchen, a ham

cured by himself in hickory ashes, wash it carefully and leave it, knowing it would be boiled in cider, tenderly skinned and given a new covering of baked sugar with just the right number of cloves. He liked to help her can tomatoes. She boiled the sun in them, he said. Long before the Mexican culinary invasion, Granny would cook her tomatoes down to a crimson puree and add a sprinkling of fresh, chipped peppers before applying the tin covers and sealing-wax. In her Frady period, of course, she had the best covers and rubbers obtainable, and in her garden grew every kind of seasoning known to her day. Nothing remained of it but one basil bush in the back yard. Instead of the foresighted Frady with his pungent cellar and full barn, they had Jim, whose idea of providing was limited to fat-back, corn-pone and coffee. Supplementary dishes were entirely the concern of the women, if they cared about such inessentials.

Ishma already knew many of the recipes which she found in the collection, for her grandmother had often consigned them to her verbally; but the books were a different matter. In her struggle with difficult words, whose meaning she had to guess, she received unexpected help. Sam brought home a dictionary which his teacher had compelled him to buy. It had consumed his hoard for cartridges, having cost the price of five 'possum skins. The imposition made him growl and swear, and kick the book into the yard. Ishma picked it up, and finding it so helpful, she paid Sam for it and added it to her treasures.

In time the lock to the trunk was enterprisingly broken, and after that her books gradually disappeared under the brigand hands of Bainie's brats. The English history with its brave pictures was the first seized upon and the first to pass away. Ishma forgave and forgot. Her hunger for reading was appeased from another source. One of the teachers in Sam's school wandered up the mountain. He had thought of staying over Sunday at the farm-house, but revised his plan after casting his eye over sleeping probabilities and sharing a supper served for the entire family, in interlapping relays, with seven pie-tins, two cups and saucers, a few pint cups, three earthen bowls, a broken pitcher, and here and there a knife, fork, or spoon. The food was palatable, for Ishma had cooked it; but his eye became dreamy and a little later he filtered down to Beebread. He was a nice young man, and had been horrified to learn that Ishma had never been in school.

"How could she go?" asked Laviny, virtuously. "She's took keer o' Baine's younguns sence she's five year old."

"But the law —" began the young teacher.

"The law don't come up the mountain an' do our work. When it does, I'll send 'em all. Ishmalee don't need larnin'. She's got too much sense now. If she had any more she'd be top-heavy. She'd teeter tryin' to walk."

"The other children go."

"Yes, that's why Ishmalee stays at home mostly. So they can go. They need ever'thing they can git, looks like. An' let me tell you, young man, it's too late to go hornet-huntin' over Ishmalee. She's past fourteen."

The teacher went away with regret brooding in his eyes. That was his last year at Beebread; but for three years thereafter Ishma received a monthly magazine, *Woman at Home,* which may have been an unworthy substitute for the reflecting Jeremy, or the tale of daring souls building the greatest of modern empires, one's own always excepted; but it opened gates to a way of living so enticing in comfort, so engaging in form, so ravishing in color, that it seemed nothing short of celestial to Ishma. Those doorways, those halls, those vistas of bed-rooms, those shimmering bath-rooms, those gleaming floors, those radiant nooks and corners of beauty, with the graceful beings from another world, curving, bending, smiling, always smiling! They took her breath. But the most miraculous of all were the laden eating-tables. Surely they were waiting for angels to sit down at them! Ishma clutched the page to her heart. "He has prepared me a table in the midst of mine enemies," she whispered, with daring mis-application. Sometimes the angels were visible. True they were usually twirling or smoking cigarettes, but how gracefully they did it! How clear-minded and clean of life they looked! Their souls must be as pure as their bodies or they couldn't shine like that.

Once little Nettie came from school trying to tell how a teacher had taken some of the older girls into the 'mestic science room and set a table, then made them do it all over after her. From Nettie's report, Ishma thought that the set-out must have been a very drab affair.

There were times in the woods when she practiced arraying such a table as was in her heart. With a stick she would trace an oval on a bit of mossy ground and mark the line carefully with tiny fern-leaves. Her service set would be of galax. Flattened, the leaves were plates, and she could have them in any size; but she could twist them and pin them with their own stems into cups, bowls, dishes of whatever kind she wished. The food would be made of wild-flower petals and the tender rosy and red-hued baby oaks and maples that had pushed a few inches above the ground.

One Sunday she took her pet rabbit, Dock, with her, a cabbage leaf in her pocket for his dinner. She intended to lose him somewhere, because he had been bothering Laviny's garden. Up by the big pool she prepared her table and looked at it with satisfaction. Never before had she made one so pretty. Dock was invited to be a guest, and very willingly nibbled the cabbage leaf. Ishma was pleased and tired. The night before, neighbors had gathered in for singing and she had been up late. Leaning back against a tree whose roots had been her chair, she slept for a moment. When she opened her eyes a strange little bird was keeping Dock company. It had eaten all of the berries in a galax bowl, and with a whirr of thanks to Dock, flew away. Ishma never set her table again. Nothing nicer than that could happen, she thought.

At eighteen she was tall and strong, with no droop of the shoulders to hint of the burden they carried. Nothing in her face or figure suggested the wiry little Laviny. She had Granny's broad forehead and delicate eyebrows that were almost horizontal until their sudden ending in a down-flung curve. The eyes, too, of twilight grey were direct from grandmother Starkweather. No day had so worn on Granny, guiding the lives of her two families, that her eyes could not keep faith with solitude and deep woods. Ishma's face was open, true to sun and sweet air, but her eyes, with all their level honesty, guarded reserves unknown to herself. Her head was by no means small, though it looked so because of its perfect rondures hugged by short, dark curls. She held it with the light grace of a deer. Derry Unthank, in later days, said that when she looked at him straight and full, he could sniff the woods and see the parted leaves framing her lifted head and neck. At eighteen there was no one around her who could tell her that, though Britt Hensley might have felt it with all of his lithe, happy body.

From Marshall Waycaster Ishma had her correct nose with its thin, breathing nostrils, her large mouth, tenderly curved and marked with an aloof humor, and her straight figure, built for strength; smaller and gentler of mould than his, but larger than the body of most women. "An' well enough," said Laviny, "with all the load she's got to tote."

The girl was almost single-handed in her struggle to make the farm keep them all decently alive. Laviny, bitten and pinched with rheumatism, found it more than she could do to keep up with the garden and patches near the house. Bainie slumped along with the cooking and mending, making occasional gestures toward redding up the rooms. Jim aside from his ploughing, was more of a hindrance than a help, with his chronic mismanagement, his weakness for mastership, and his incurable laziness. During vacation, the children helped uncomplainingly under Ishma's direction, but her busiest times — the seasons of planting and harvest — fell upon her during the school term. Frady's ghost, if ever it hung over the scene of his earthly endeavors, must have found it hard to recognize the briery, outcast fields and the crumbling house with little inside to remind him of his reign of glory. The big corner cupboard of curly maple, which he had lovingly fashioned for Sarah Starkweather, still stood in the kitchen, but Jim, pushed to activity by a cold snap, had threatened to use its doors for kindling. "What's the use o' doors? A curtain is all you want." Laviny had stayed his hand and given him a piece of her bitter mind. "There's dead wood all over the hill, waitin' fer the axe, an' you've kindled up the fence-rails till I kain't find enough fer a calf-pen. You'll be burnin' up the beds next an' put us all on the floor. That's yore idy o' livin', but it ain't mine, Jim Wishart. A body 'ud think you's raised on 'taters an' salt!"

When Laviny finally got through with him, Jim picked up the axe, went up the hill, and brought down enough wood for a Christmas fire. He sat by it, talking of the things he was going to do to make Cloudy Knob a show to the world, but his resolution faded with the fire, and the children picked up chips and brush to cook the next day's dinner.

As Ishma toiled through her crop, she tried to believe that every year was the last for her in the field. She intended to get a little ahead and go away where she could make enough to keep herself and her mother. Jim and his family must shift for themselves. But she loved the children. They were almost her own. On the verge of leaving them she always paused, and every Spring found her back in the field making sure of their bread. She had less time for her forest playground; less time for refilling her fount; and she felt the drouth within her.

But her dream of a more embellished life persisted. She tried to improve her speech by reading aloud and accustoming her ears to something different from the lazily uttered, half-finished words and twisted syntax of those about her. She noticed that visitors in the mountains, who sometimes found their way to Cloudy Knob, and commented on the native speech as "quaint," or "really Shakespearean," were careful to use nothing resembling it. She liked Miss Eller much better. She was a teacher in Beebread who brought the children up the mountain one Autumn day on a chestnut hunt. Miss Eller had shown surprise when she found that Ishma had taught herself. "You talk as well as I do," she said, and promised to send up some books from the library that was having its feeble beginning in the school. She forgot her promise, but Ishma did not forget her encouragement. Attempts to drill the children had been given up, rendered futile by Bainie's sniffs and Laviny's open scorn. For harmony's sake she spoke at home more or less in the family fashion, but she exulted in knowing better. On stormy, cold Sundays she read and practiced in the barn loft, and in bright weather her hills awaited her. Fortunately she did not try to mend her voice; a voice that belonged with her eyes, and bore her words in its flow like a cool, forest brook dripping over shadowy ledges.

We have noted her eighteenth birthday. Radburn Bailey was

14

looking at her with greed and longing in his pleasant blue eyes; but Britton Hensley looked at her with the thrill of ownership. Though she had given him no promise he couldn't imagine any future for himself apart from Ishma Waycaster. Neither of the lovers saw much of her. She had never shared her high trail with anyone. Britt once hardily attempted to follow her, but with lively indirection, dodging and sheltering herself, she outwitted and outclimbed him utterly. When he came in at night he found that she had reached home an hour before him. Both boys felt aggrieved because they had to do their courting in the bosom of the family, but they had no choice except to leave her altogether, which seemed impossible for either of them.

One April day Laviny and Bainie sat on the perilous porch discussing the prospects of the suitors. It was nearing sunset, but Ishma was still in the field getting the land ready for the plough. Ploughing was the only part of the farm work which she refused to do. Jim had become convinced that this perversity must be accepted, and was usually on hand to take hold of the plough when Ishma announced that a field was ready. He felt that this supreme service established him as master of the place and controller of its output. Such trivial work as grubbing, planting, hoeing and harvesting, gave Ishma no special rights as he could see.

"Rad Bailey would make Ish a good livin'," said Bainie, shifting the overalls in her lap to reveal another hole, and threading a big needle. "Nothin' but shoe-thread 'll hold this together, an' they ain't a needleful on the mountain."

"Hit won't be Rad," said Laviny. "Hit'll be Britt."

"Shorely you ain't fer Britt, mommie. His hand is as weak as Jim's in a crop."

"He's a sight better lookin'. Hit'll be Britt."

Laviny reserved her aspirate for emphasis. It's omission showed that her mind had relaxed. It might even indicate resignation. She sighed as if giving up her last bit of energy to the problem of life, then became aggressively alert. "Where's my snuff, Bain' Wishart?" Bainie reached to the window ledge behind her, picked up a box of snuff, and handed it to her mother.

"You've shore been in it! I kain't keep snuff fer ever'body an' only three hens a layin'." Taking a sweet-gum brush from her apron pocket and swabbing it in the box, she placed it far back in her mouth where her lost molars should have been. Her next sigh was resigned, and her third reached contentment. After a few moments she was ready for effort.

"Might as well start the fire an' git the kittle to goin'," she said, entering the house. "Ishmalee 'll be here d'reckly."

Bainie went on patching, not once looking toward her children playing in front of the cabin. Ben, Andy and Nettie had come from school, and were quarrelling about the proper way to build a chimney with rocks they had brought from the branch that ran through the yard. Ellie, three years old, went into the kitchen and, after a consultation with her grandmother, came out nibbling a large piece of corn-bread. She jumped off the porch, and a liver-spotted hound dashed from under it, snapping at the bread. Ellie fought him off with only partial loss of her prize, but she was still insecure in possession. A yellow rooster with a flourishing red and black tail darted to her and pecked at her hand. She screamed, and Ben became interested. The rooster was his.

"Give him a bit, kain't you ?" he commanded. Ellie made a careful division and resumed nibbling. But there was a third assault. A very dirty white pig rubbed up, knocked little Ellie over, and ran away with the bread. The fall angered her more than her loss. She scrambled out of the sour-smelling mud and began a determined cry that partially aroused her mother. Without looking up she told Ellie to stop her racket. "I've had enough out o' you fer one day."

At that moment Ishma came around the western end of the porch. She was carrying her field tools — pitchfork, grubbing hoe, and briar scythe. Dropping them all, she went to Ellie.

"Don't cry, honey. I'll wash your dress for you."

"An' what'll she put on while you're washin' it ? Tell me that," said Bainie, her eyes still on the patching.

"She wouldn't have got so muddy if you hadn't thrown so much dishwater out here. You promised me you's goin to quit that, Bainie. Looks like shame 's not in you."

Bainie looked and felt too weary to protest. Seven children

before she was thirty, and life that had never known a single enthusiasm, had given her a patience more defensive than real. She asked nothing better than to be let alone, with freedom to whine and mutter to her soul's content. Her younger sister's ambitious strength seemed only another oppression.

Ishma took an old sweater from a nail in a porch post. "Here, Ellie, you put this on." She stripped the child of her dress and swathed her in the ragged garment. Ellie flapped her sleeves delighted. "I'm as big as you now, Ishma !"

Ishma was holding up the muddy dress. "I'll do Nettie's too, while I'm washing this — an' Ben's an' Andy's overalls. I was plumb ashamed for them to start off to school this morning fair dripping the dirt."

"What'll *we* put on ?" Ben asked doubtfully.

"O, get in there and find something," Ishma ventured with a confidence that Bainie knew was unwarranted. "I've got to have your clothes right now if I do them before slap dark."

The children ran into the house, delighted to have high authority for a rampage. Ishma sat on the floor and began to take off her patched shoes. "Is there a fire in the stove ?" she asked.

"Yes, mommie started it, an' the kittle's full, 'cause I didn't wash up after dinner."

Ishma was taking rags off her feet. "You got a flour-poke I can make me some fresh toe-rags out of ?"

"No, I hain't. It takes ever' poke I can git aholt of fer the patchin'."

"There !" said Ishma, getting up. "My feet are out of jail and they're not going back till morning. I'll wash at the branch."

She went down to the stream that ran a little distance from the eastern end of the house. There was another, smaller stream on the west side, running from the spring from which they carried water. Between this branch and the house lay a few poles representing a woodpile. Laviny came out, went across to the poles, picked up the axe with grunting effort, and began to cut wood. Bainie protested. Jim would be home in time to get breakfast-wood. *She* wasn't going to do his work. She'd said it and she meant it.

"Takes you a long time to larn you're nothin' but a woman,

Bainie. I never seen one, 'scusin Granny, that didn't have to cut wood, if she et her meals halfway reg'lar."

"I'll show Jim !" said Bainie, her voice lifted out of its whine.

"You'll show him like you're doin' this minute. Him out with his gun an' hit ploughin' time ! Takin' little Sam at his heels too ! Sam could 'a' hacked wood, if he didn't want to go to school."

"You wait, mommie, an' let Ish do it. She's as strong as Sampson's steer. Hit pulled the wind out o' March."

Laviny dropped the axe and gave her words to Bainie straight.

"Ishmalee went to the field 'fore clear daylight this mornin'. She's been cuttin' an' pilin' briers ever sence. Nothin' but a cold snack up by the Birch spring. If she wants to set down, her cheer is bought an' paid fer. But she ain't fer settin' down. She's goin' wash yer brats' clo's."

Laviny returned to the axe. Bainie rolled up the overalls. "Eh-ay," she said, undisturbed, "you're always fer Ish. It's gittin' too duskish to thread a needle."

Ishma came slowly up from the branch on the opposite side of the house. Her head was turned, and she was looking back over her shoulder. West of Cloudy Knob the sun was already hidden, but between it and the south-east where the valley wound along the river, there were no intervening ridges. Reflections from the western sky colored the slow curves of the Little Tennessee as it flowed errantly and golden from its source in the Nantahalas, whose distant peaks were a panting radiance above their dark, blue bodies. When Ishma came up the steps at the end of the porch she turned again and stood looking down on the long stretch of valley, and on out to the horizon where the rolling transparency of the mountains was inundating earth with dream. Her whole body seemed caught in an intent gaze.

Laviny stared across the yard at her daughter. Bainie stared too, but she wasn't silent. "What you seein', Ish ?" Her voice was loud enough, but Ishma didn't hear.

"You shet up, Bainie," said her mother. "It *is* a purty sunset tonight, dog-gone ef it ain't !"

A little ashamed of her concession to beauty, she resumed her hacking, and Ishma turned at the sound of the axe.

"Mommie !" she called, "I've told you and told you not to do

18

that *!* Now you'll be hurting all night with your arm !" She crossed to her mother and took the axe. "You go sit down now. Mommie, you *go sit down !*"

Laviny went to a chair on the porch and seated herself, protesting but relieved. Ishma began to cut the wood skillfully, with a man's swinging blow. Andy put his head through the window of the middle room where a pane of glass should have been. He was careful to be visible only from his waist up, being all the way naked. To his complaint that he could find nothing, his mother replied, "Git them overalls I'm usin' fer patches. They's a smart bit of 'em left. In the barrel behind the kitchen door."

"Ben's got *them* on," said Andy.

"You'll have to git yer poppie's best uns then. But don't dirt 'em er he'll tan ye bloody." She ended with a mumble to herself. "Looks like Ish could a let 'em alone till Sat'day."

Nettie, Andy and Ben flopped out of the house and into the yard. Ben's only garment was an unbelievably stripped and tattered pair of overalls. Andy was swallowed in a pair of respectable entirety, the legs rolled into wads about his knees, and the braces tied around his neck. Nettie wore a checked apron pinned over her shoulders and a small red tablecloth for a skirt.

"Now you'll ketch it, Nettie," screamed her mother. "That's the new lamp-table cover Ish bought."

Ishma was coming in with an armful of wood. "Keep out of the mud, Nettie," she said, "and you may wear it till bed-time. Bring me the big tub, Ben." Ben dashed around the house. Ishma left her wood in the kitchen, and came out. Laviny was staring at Nettie, despair mapping her wrinkled face. "Is that youngun scratchin' her head agin ?"

"It's nothin' else. That's all school 's fit fer," said Bainie. "To give 'em boogers in the head."

"She's got a power o' hair, an' hit curly. A booger 'd swim a river to git to a head o' hair like that."

Bainie's voice in reply was several depths more disconsolate. "It was jest last week that I bridled the comb an' redd her hair good."

Ishma felt sick. "O, Bainie, stop it !"

"Come ten year you'll have four er five o' yer own to clean up. You won't be so sugar-mouth then."

"Ten years ? Ten thousand is more like it !"

Bainie laughed, a silly, vulgar laugh. "Time's the truth-teller," she said.

Ben came back without the tub. Bainie thought the children might have dragged it to their new playhouse above the barn. Ishma set off hastily to find the tub, Ben hurrying after.

"That Ishmalee's a mixtry," said Laviny. "I kain't git aholt o' her. But she's a sight o' help, that's shore. You got to quit throwin' off on her, Bain Wishart. She might up an' leave, an' I reckon we'd all starve without her hand in the crop."

"She'll leave anyhow if she gits married."

"That would be nater. We kain't hep that. 'A gal she must marry, an' a wife she must carry.' "

Ishma returned with Ben, bearing a large wooden tub which she placed on the edge of the porch. "We'll have these rags out in a sawed-off minute," she said to the boy. "I've got a pot full, a kettle full, and a dishpan full of water." She went into the kitchen and swiftly reappeared with a steaming supply. Ben ran to the branch and came back with a bucket of cold water.

"Fine ! We'll hurry, Ben. Night sha'n't catch us. Moonlight's not good soap, Granny used to say."

They did hurry, rubbing, wringing, fetching, and in a short time the clothes were ready for rinsing in the branch.

"Eh-law, you never stop," said Laviny. "But you'll stump yer toes some day, like I did."

When the garments were on the fence, Ishma came back, picked up the tub of water and started off with it.

"Why'n't you have decent mercy on yer back ? You turn that water out," called her mother.

"I'm not makin' a hogwaller," she answered. "Bainie 'll see to that."

At last she was ready to stop, and sat down on the porch near Laviny's chair. There was no longer any glow in the sky, nor on the distant mountains.

"You be dead tired, I reckon," her mother said.

Ishma accepted the awkward form of speech without a wince.

for with her mother "be" was the verb of intimacy and affection.

"No, I'll go help with supper in a minute."

"Let Bainie wrassle it. She's been settin' sence twelve. You're gittin' too much like yer daddy, Ishmalee, goin' ever' minute."

"Tell me about daddy, mommie."

"Law, child, what fer?"

"You never talk about him."

"Well, ain't he dead?"

"You've got children dead too, and you talk about them."

"Yes, I've got four dead, an' they don't give me a minute's trouble."

"Daddy didn't beat you."

"I reckon he didn't! But he was a fidgety man. A fidgety woman is hard to put up with, but a man takes all the peace out o' life."

This was a new picture of her father for Ishma. "But every-body liked him, mommie."

"Yes, he come inter the mountains with the biggest pack o' jokes that anybody ever brought in. He had to have 'em 'cause the only times he could set still was when he's tellin' one. He never got tired. I used to wish he could know what it wuz to feel dog-tired jest onct. He wuz never ready fer bed. Looked like it never come night fer him. If there was a dance, er any kind o' shindy doin's, in ten mile of us, he'd walk to it, ay he would, ten year after we's married, an' me with a pack o' younguns. He wore me bone sore. It was a lot easier after he got a stroke an' couldn't leave his cheer. I could make a livin' easier'n I could keep up with him when he wuz goin'. He wuz always beggin' me to leave here an' set out roamin' same as if there wuzn't any younguns to feed."

Ishma looked at the big chair pushed back against the wall and used as a catch-all for corn-baskets, old harness, school books and caps, Laviny's shoe-mending outfit, ragged quilts, and mail order catalogues. Her father had hired Abe Willis to make it, and the back could be lifted up and let down. Nowadays it was always down so that more things could be piled on it. Ishma's heart bled as she thought of her father lying on that chair for three years.

"Ay, he wuz never satisfied," her mother continued. "Always seekin', an' no name fer it. When he had his stroke the doctors said he'd be gone in three months, but he took a year fer ever' month they give him. I knowed he'd do that. I've wondered sometimes why he didn't put out an' leave when he wuz able to walk off. But he thought a sight o' you younguns, pertickly Steve. He wuz a plumb fool about Steve. I reckon that's why he stayed around. Twa'n't me keepin' him."

Ishma was still looking at the chair. She had been six years old when her father was struck down, and nine when he was buried. His prostrate years she tried to forget, and remembered him walking about, singing gay songs, and teasing her mother.

"I've quit blamin' him," said Laviny, following Ishma's eyes, "fer ever'thing 'cept Steve leavin' me. The only livin' boy I had, an' a grown man at fifteen."

Ishma had proud memories of Steve. "I'll never forget him," she said.

"You ortent. You's eight when he left out. An' you'd mighty nigh see him agin ef you'd look in the bottom of a new dish-pan. You're powerful like him, only you've got a gal counte-nance."

"What did daddy have to do with Steve's leavin' out? You've never told me that."

"I ain't goin' to nuther."

Ishma didn't try persuasion, and Laviny sat in silence, licking old wounds and seeing the past only through her injury. With no intention to speak, her story, as her daughter expected, began to pour through her lips.

"I didn't know his daddy had anything to do with it at first. Steve had been fussin' an' squirmin' fer about a year, like any boy when he's growin' up too fast, an' I'd ketch his daddy lookin' curious at him, like he wanted awful to speak, but his tongue wuz so nigh dead by that time he could only choke an' blow red when he tried to talk. Steve would git out o' bed of a mornin' lookin' holler-eyed an' sayin' he hadn't slep' none. Course the farm was purty heavy on a boy's back, an' him only fifteen. Bainie an' Jim wuz married, an' Jim —"

Laviny stopped loyally, but Ishma took up her words. "And Jim was piling everything on Steve."

"Jim wuz doin' fair enough. But I could see yer daddy had Steve on his mind. An' fust I knowed my boy was clear light gone. There I was with a fam'ly an' a farm an' a half-dead man, all waitin' my two hands."

"You had Jim," said Ishma, ashamed of the dig and her suppressed smile.

"Jim ! — He had his hands full, you might know, with his own fam'ly, an' Bainie not stout." Again she became silent, nursing her bitterness.

"But what did daddy *do*, mommie ?"

"It was about two months after Steve left, I's cuttin' up a pair o' his old overalls that I'd sort o' kep' away from the scissors, 'cause they's the pair he had on the last day he's at home, an' in one o' the pockets, I found a piece o' paper with writin' on it. Pencil marks, mighty shaky, but I made 'em out. *'Go, Steve,'* that's all it said. An' Steve went."

"Daddy wrote it?"

"Ay, he did. An' I didn't know he could move his fingers then. I figgered that he'd looked beggin' at Steve, an' twitched his fingers, an' Steve give him the paper an' pencil. I kain't think of any other way fer it."

"He never found out you knew, did he ?"

"I took keer he did ! I went right to him an' bust loose. He could hear like a cat to the last, an' I let him have it. There wusn't nothin' I left out. I give it to him on a shovel. An' all at once it come over me that he wuz a laffin'. I wuz plumb beat. Yes, sir, he lay there an' beat me plumb out. I couldn't say another word. My mouth wuz jest sewed up. Him a laffin' !" Laviny paused for a response from Ishma, but no sound came. "An' all I've got left o' my boy is that telegram sayin' he died in the Philippines."

Suddenly she was through with self-pity. "Bainie, why'n't you light the lamp ?" she called sharply, and Bainie answered from the kitchen, "Lamp-oil 's out."

"Jim's been usin' it in his huntin' lantern then. We got a

whole half a gallon last time. Ishmalee, I saw where some limbs offen that dead chestnut back o' the barn wuz blown down today. They's bone dry, an 'll make a blaze fer us to eat supper by."

Ishma said she would get them, and went off by the path that led around the eastern end of the house then veered north up the hill to the barn. Bainie poked her head out of the kitchen door, and seeing no one but her mother, came out, heavy with mystery.

"Mommie," she whispered, with unnecessary caution, "I've found where Ish keeps her money. I's pullin' splinters off the wall to make a light an' a board come off. There was the money, in the crack. I knowed she's hidin' it. Dimes, nickels an' quarters. There's one fifty-center too! She must a been savin' up fer a year, an' makin' us believe she spent ever' cent! It was tied up in a rag, an' layin' in this little tin box, tight as could be. Fourteen dollars! You reckon she's goin' to buy weddin' clo's?"

Laviny's face had turned a more unhappy grey. "Bainie, you put that board back quick, an' the money behind it! Ishmalee's as much like Steve as a gal child dare to be. You kain't go too fur with her. You put it back right now."

Bainie went in, but there was not time to replace the money before Ishma came up to the porch steps with her arms full of broken sticks. Laviny hurried to meet her.

"Give 'em here, an' I'll start the fire, Ishmalee. You git the younguns things off the fence an' we'll dry 'em by the fire, seein' we've got to have a blaze goin'."

Ishma transferred her armful and started for the fence. A few steps off, she turned back her head. "He was laffin', mother?"

"As I'm standin' here he wuz. An' him nothin' but eyes."

Laviny hastened in and started the fire in the kitchen fireplace. Bainie was still fumbling at the wall.

"Lord, Bainie, lick yer fingers!" warned her mother, hearing Ishma's returning step.

"It's about fixed," said Bainie; but Laviny met Ishma at the door. "I'll spread 'em out," she said, taking the garments, knowing that Ishma would turn back. She never stayed in the

24

house when she could be out of it. A moment later, when Laviny came out on the porch, she was standing at the west end looking at the sky.

"There's a light," she said, "that looks like it might be above Copper Creek. Maybe a fire has started up in Dark Moon Cove."

"Lord hep us, if it's so! I kain't fight fire any more," her mother protested. But Ishma's heart was leaping. She could remember one great forest fire that she had seen when she was five years old. Her father was fighting it. He fought till he fell. The fire got past him and burnt up all of Granny Whitt's hay. Nobody was permitted to forget that fire as long as Granny Whitt lived. But Ishma had not been concerned with the hay. She had broken away from her father and the other men, and had run to a high knob. From there she could see an ocean of flame rolling and twisting in the valley below. That was when Dark Moon had been burnt over. She thought that she had floated high in the air above that fire. Night after night her ecstasy was repeated in her dreams, making it harder to doubt that she had flown over that flaming ocean.

"There's nothing I'd rather see tonight than a big fire," she said, "only I hate for the woods to get burnt up. If they've got to burn though, I want to see it."

"My sakes, child, you'd better be wishin' fer bed an' sleep!"

Ishma came back and stood in the wide kitchen door, watching the blaze made by the dry chestnut in the fire-place. Nothing could be more beautiful than fire, she thought, but what she said was, "I want to write a letter, and that fire's too hot to sit by."

Bainie looked up from the stove, her face crinkled unpleasantly. "If you want lamp-oil fer a light you'll have to pay fer it yersef. I'm not goin' to spend another brownie till I buy Nettie a dress. That'n you washed 'll drop offen her 'fore another week. Mommie, if you'd lend me a dollar I'd pay it back soon as we shear the sheep."

"You know that wool money is done took up at Gaffney's store. If I had a dollar I'd know something better to do with it. I'd git me another bottle of that Indian Bone Cure fer this rheumatiz."

Ishma felt besieged. "You'll poison yourself with that stuff some day," she said to her mother, as she went out the door and off the porch. Laviny called to her to bring the milk and butter from the spring-house. When Ishma reached the spring, she sat down for a moment on the rock wall that guarded it, wondering why she felt cramped and hot when it was so sweet and cool all about her.

Bainie, in the house, was still whining about the money. "She wants to write a letter. I bet she's goin' to order her a dress out o' that new order book. She took it with her to the field yister-day."

"Ain't the bread nearly done ?" asked Laviny, uneasy with Bainie's talk.

"No, I made a thick pone." It had grown uncomfortably warm in the kitchen and Bainie had stepped to the door. "I b'lieve that's Aunt Cynthy Webb comin'," she said, peering through the dusk. "This time o' day !"

"Pore Cynthy !" said Laviny. "I reckon Zeke's on a drunk an' she'll stay the night. Howdy, Cynthy !" she called, sending her welcome into the yard. Cynthy Webb, fat and breathless, came on the porch before she returned the salute. She always climbed the steps in terror, expecting them to give way under her two hundred pounds. Laviny put a chair for her guest on one side of the kitchen door, and one for herself on the other side. "Set right down, Cynthy, an' tell me how're y'all."

"Crawlin', crawlin'. Reckon y'all afoot ?"

"Ay, about an' about."

Cynthy's affliction was a quarrelling, tippling husband, as every-body knew, but she loyally went through the form of keeping it a secret. She now craned her neck and looked into the kitchen, then drew it back and asked Laviny to let what she was going to tell her go with her to her last bed. Laviny declared that it should freeze in her dead body, and Cynthy disclosed that Zeke had come from Copper Creek drunk.

"I say !" exclaimed Laviny, duly astonished. "They'll make that stuff over there to the end of time, I reckon."

"Long as the mountains don't rock, they will. But the moun-tains *air* goin' to rock, Laviny, ef folks don't quit peekin' inter hell. Some o' these days they won't git the door shet quick enough, an' the whole lake o' brimstone 'll roll out. I was settin' at home peaceable, readin' my Bible, an' waitin' fer Julie to come up from Beebread. She's helpin' Lu Gaddy down there, puttin' out her garden. An' I looks out an' sees Zeke jest a rockin' the trail. When he got in, ever' side o' the house was hisn. I'd prayed my knees sore astin' the Lord not to let him come home drunk, but looks like my prayers don't git no higher 'n my head. Zeke was rantin' so fierce, I up an' lit out. When Julie comes she'll figger where I am an' come after me."

"You're stayin' right here, Cynthy. Don't you worry more'n a flea can tote in its weskit pocket."

Ishma came from the spring carrying a bowl of butter and a jar of milk. "Howdys" were passed, and the girl added, "You'll stay the night, Aunt Cynthy ?"

"Law, child, I got to git home. Zeke might come in an' me gone."

"You let Uncle Zeke take care of himself for one night."

"You won't talk thataway when it's yore man around. That won't be long, I'm thinkin'."

"About as long as never !" Ishma went into the kitchen, her shoulders high. Cynthy watched her put the milk on the table, then go out the back door.

"Tetchy ! That means something. Ain't her an' Rad got it fixed up yit ?"

"I ain't shore it's Rad. Not gospel shore, I ain't."

"You don't mean she'll take Britt when she can git a steady worker like Rad ?"

"I've come to think I don't much keer which un it is. If it's Rad, he'll take her away. But I reckon Britt would have to live right here. He ain't got nothin' but a gittar, an' that's a leetle less than nothin'. He wouldn't take Ishmalee away, an' she's a sight o' help on this place."

"You know how to find the good grain in a sack o' hulls, Laviny. I'd better be startin' down. I know I'll meet Julie, an' save her a step."

"Don't you move, Cynthy. Bainie, lay Aunt Cynthy a plate."

"I've done laid it," called Bainie from the kitchen.

"What's the matter with yer supper?" asked Laviny, starting up and falling back with a groan, saying that her pesterin' knee was stiff again. Cynthy assured her that it couldn't be worse than the stinging she'd had around her neck all the week, an' was botherin' her crazy that minute. Laviny nursed her knee, declaring that it was like an auger borin' in yer bones.

"Mine," insisted Cynthy, "comes jest like a swarm o' sweat-bees settlin' on my neck."

Laviny crowed over her. "A hammer crackin' my bones to the marr' couldn't be wuss," and Cynthy met that with, "A thousand needlepints wouldn't tell it fer *me*!"

They had turned their chairs and faced each other in a duel of ailments, their profiles in hostile outline against the light that poured through the broad door of the kitchen. Ishma, under the apple tree in the front yard, began to laugh softly, listening to their interjections.

"Screwin' right inter the jint —"

"Skin smartin' like it wuz whipped with nettles —"

"Fire a-borin' —"

"Wasps —"

Their voices, growing shriller and running together, were cut off by the sound of a guitar loudly picked by Britt Hensley. He was standing in the path at the western end of the porch. Ishma, when she heard him, slipped around the house at the other end and went into the kitchen by the back door. He might stay to supper, and Bainie always forgot to wipe off the oil-cloth.

Britt came up the steps, singing boldly to the tune of "Rattler."

> *Two old women talkin',*
> *Night a creepin' round,*
> *Make a jay-bird squawkin'*
> *A mighty pleasant sound.*
>
> > *O, where you goin', Bobby?*
> > *O, where you goin', Bill?*
> > *Goin' to drown my troubles*
> > *At a good old mountain still!*

CHAPTER II

BRITT laid his guitar on the porch floor, carefully against the wall, and came up to the women. They were in a high huff from the invasion, but he cheerily ignored their scant welcome.

"Howdy, aunt Laviny! Howdy, aunt Cynthy! Why'n't you keep it up? I'll be referee an' get the winner a Christmas present."

"You'll have to see the sawder-man, Britt, 'bout that leak in yore mouth," said Laviny. "Hit's gettin' bad."

Aunt Cynthy was more gentle. "Wait till ol' pappy Time gits holt o' yore red hair, boy. Then you'll do yore share o' frettin'."

"No, aunt Cynthy. I was born without a worry bone. But my wishbone 's workin' all right." He took a seat inside the kitchen door, where he could continue his banter and cast his eye about for Ishma. "An' I'd like to know what you mean callin' my hair red. That good-lookin' little teacher down in Beebread says it's sunset brown."

His eye roved, but he didn't see Ishma. She had slipped out again to the front yard, and stood unseen in the dusk, watching Britt as he sat in the light of the chestnut blaze. Her mind was made up. She would not marry him. She had commanded her heart to be still whenever he came into her presence, but out there in the dark she let it flutter ever so little, and generously appraised what she was casting away. The kindly firelight gave beauty to the features that within the last year had grown strong and mannish. A gentleness lay on them that was dangerous to her resolution. His hair — there was almost too much of it — was full of bronze shadows and restless light as he threw back his head and sent his laughter rolling like an upward wave. That hair was safely fire-brown, but to his grief it crinkled like a mop, and the cow-lick that interfered with the line of parting curved

29

much too prettily. Teasing girls called it his dimple, and more than one had given it the kiss that it seemed to ask for.

"You wouldn't take a prize at ballit-makin', Britt," said aunt Cynthy, still chafing a little over having been be-rhymed in the midst of a highly pleasureable set-to. "You ort to hear Si Welch turnin' out a good un."

"Ay, he's quick at ballits, but *you* ought to heard me an' my guitar in Carson today."

Laviny became eager. "You been to town, Britt ?"

"Sure, ain't it court week ?"

"Law, I fergot. You been in trouble agin ?"

"No, but the judge was. He didn't know what to do with me. Said I was too mean to turn loose an' not mean enough to go to jail. Talked about finin' me fifty dollars, but he 'lowed it would be just as hard for me to skeer up five as fifty, so he made it five."

"What you back fer then ? You know you didn't have five dollars on ye. Why'n't you in jail ?"

"The good old jury made up the fine. They said I'd helped 'em that much decidin' a poison case they's settin' on."

"You know you wa'n't on the jury !"

"I wasn't. But ol' Dick Medlin was. He 's foreman. An' you know there's nothin' he'd ruther hear than a guitar picked by a picker that can pick."

"I 'lowed that thing wuz in it somers." Laviny's opinion of the guitar, the jury and Britt, was scathingly evident, but her scorn brought more laughter from Britt.

"I sat outside the window an' picked fer 'em all night. When I'd stop they'd knock on the wall an' I'd start up again. I picked, I'll tell the mountains ! I knew my case was comin' up t'day, an' I picked the shine off the stars. They told me they couldn't kep' awake without me."

Cynthy was trying, with little success, to make her fat face look austere. "Whad the jury mean, payin' you out after con-victin' ye ?"

"Well, they had to convict me. They couldn't get around that. You see I did kill Lem Weaver's cow. I've never de-nied it."

30

"What got inter you, Britt? You allers liked Lem Weaver."

"I liked his cow too. I wasn't easin' no grudge against her. It was her own fault I killed her, an' I told the judge all about it today. I couldn't get it out before, but I got where I had to speak up for myself, an' not let an' old cow put it over me."

"What she do, Britt? She wuz a mighty peaceable cow."

"Peaceable she was. She 's lyin' down right in the middle of the road when I come along one night. The moon was shinin' an' I could see her a long ways off. I thought she 'd get up an' not keep sprawlin' all over the right o' way, but she laid there an' chawed like she was goin' to chaw right on into judgment. It riled me to see anything that knowed her own mind like that cow did. But it was the white spot that finenchally got me."

"Ay, she had a white spot."

"Right in the middle of her forehead — about as big as a marble. An' I had my sling-shot. It was a case o' puttin' two an' two together, as I told the judge. I couldn't a kept from sendin' that shot at that white spot if Golier had been aholt o' my hand. An' it killed her stone dead. I'll never get over bein' surprised at the way she dropped her head right down an' never picked it up. It wasn't my fault. I just couldn't help it. An' the judge looked at it my way after I'd explained ever'-thing, an' picked him a few pieces when they's takin' recess."

"Where does Lem come in?" Cynthy asked anxiously. "Ain't he goin' to git nothin' fer his cow?"

Britt assured her that Lem was taken care of; in fact, he, Britt himself, was going to help Lem put in his crop, and harvest it too. He would have done that anyway, he declared, even if the judge hadn't made him promise.

"Hep him?" rasped Laviny. "You mean you'll eat his rations an' keep the fam'ly up nights with that gittar. Lem 'ud better bury the debt where he buried his cow."

"Aunt Laviny, I'll tell you it's worth something to play to Lem Weaver's fam'ly. Ain't one of 'em can tell Dan Tucker from a pig a-gruntin'."

Cynthy softened. She was afflicted with a sensitive ear herself.

" 'Course you'll do fair, Britt, jest like yer daddy larnt ye."

Britt grinned affectionately; showing firm white teeth that almost sang of health. His father had taught him in childhood to keep them clean by rubbing with a rag and salt. This father, dearly loved, and eight years dead, had been a preacher who rode about the settlements and knew a thing or two. The thing or two did not include a knowledge of how to save money or get himself a toe-hold on earth, even in the days when a few hundred dollars would buy a mountain side with two or three trout streams thrown in. Why should he care, when every trout stream in the land was his for good pleasure ?

Britt had known his mother only through his father's memories, recounted on fishing trips, usually after camp supper, when they could talk with no household ears about them. A child of the coves, she had battled her way to a "C" certificate, and after a year of teaching had married the "ridin' preacher," much older than herself. A baby, and death, came with another year, her bright hair and cow-lick passing on to the child. Motherly hands reached out for little Britt, but the father would surrender neither his wanderings nor his baby. Was not every house a home to the bringer of salvation ?

When Britt was old enough for school his father found that he must stay in one community throughout the term; but the next year would find the pair in another vicinity. From week-end visits to distant pulpits, the elder Hensley brought home "collections" sufficient for clothing, a full pipe, and school necessities. Britt, unaffected by his father's restlessness, accepted the yearly change of bed and roof as if it were a boy's normal life, though aunt Cynthy's home was perhaps his choice. Contrary to what might have been expected, he made good progress in school and finished the sixth grade in his twelfth year; the year of heavy rains and his father's last week-end. Horse and rider were swept away by the Little Tennessee at high flood. Hensley's body was taken ashore near Beebread and that community had the honor of burying it, though bids for the distinction came in from all the neighboring townships. Abe Willis made the coffin of wide, poplar boards, planed and glistening, and three weeks after the burial a preacher came all the way from Franklin to deliver the funeral sermon. The people assembled with heavy dinner baskets and made a great day of it; a day worthy of so good a man.

Little Britt sat in the high place, his mouth tragically twisted out of its laughing curves. Women wept over him till he longed to get away and go fishing. But he wouldn't have his father to go with him, and this thought twisted his mouth again and set the women weeping anew over his bright head. Passing days lightened his grief, and sympathy became more embarrassing. Before a month was gone he was stealing away to the woods where he could weep in pleasant peace, or throw back his head and try a gently daring laugh on the sailing clouds. He had loved his father, but the world was still fine.

When all was over there was no more school for Britt. He was only a farmed-out boy working for board and clothes. But he could change his working place with every season if the County Commissioners gave him permission. And Britt always got what he asked for. The loss of school didn't worry him. His father's sister, up in St. Louis, sent him a guitar as a consolation present. He had played the "frensharp" from babyhood, and soon learned, by making himself a head-guard, to play the two instruments together, thus fitting himself admirably for an unanchored life. His first surprising thought of settling down came on the long night when he had tried to reason his heart out of his love for Ishma and failed utterly and forever. Now, while he sat in the firelight, his glance darting here and there in search of her, she was hungrily taking leave of him.

Bainie's younguns came racing back from the barn. They had learned that Britt had been to the county-seat, and as they bounded onto the porch their cries and questions merged into one intelligible query.

"You got any candy?"

"Well," Britt hesitated, "I did have some, but I forgot" — his face lengthened — "I forgot which pocket I put it in."

He was assailed, pounded and pawed, until the candy appeared. Bainie came out and told him he was spilin' the brats till she couldn't whip it out of 'em. For answer he handed her a box of Old Mill snuff.

"A twenty-five center!" she exulted. "But you needn't be throwin' yer money away on me, Britt. Ish won't listen to a word I say."

"Let him throw it," said Laviny. "He'll never have enough anyway to keep hissef in sassafrac tea an' rabbit terbacker."

Britt's smile became particularly joyous. "Looky what I brought for you, aunt Laviny!" Before her eyes was a big, red-flowered handkerchief, held out in the fire-shine. Laviny jerked her chair farther into the door, took the handkerchief, and began gently smoothing it out on her lap.

"Hit's shore purty, Britt. But where in the world did you git all the money?"

"Why, after the fellers made up enough to pay my fine, the judge come back after dinner an' 'lowed he'd let me off payin' it. He was eatin' at the Freeman House, an' I went round there at dinner time an' picked a few pieces just to keep busy."

"You'll git into Heaven pickin' that gittar, Britt," said Cynthy.

"Guess that's my best chance, aunt Cynthy. The men wouldn't take the money back, an' there I was with five dollars burnin' my pocket."

The children began to shout again. "There he was!" "An' he got us candy!" "An' a present fer mommie!" "An' fer gran-mommie!"

"Shet up!" cried Ben. "I got to ast him something."

"Shoot, son," said Britt.

"Whad you git fer Ishma?"

Britt was now outside, and at that moment Ishma appeared on the porch. Ben waited for his answer. "'Tain't fair to tell you first," Britt declared. "You bantlin's get into the kitchen — ever' one of you! It's bread an' milk time."

Bainie began to drive them in. "He's shore right! Y'all git in there! Ain't one of you fitten fer a buzzard to look at."

"We'll all go," said Laviny. "I ain't goin' to wait a minute on Jim. We'll eat while the pone's fresh. I churned today, an' there's plenty o' cold buttermilk. Come in, Cynthy. Come along, Britt."

34

But Britt had "done been." He had stopped at Si Welch's coming up.

"I reckon Ishmalee's ready to eat. She'd orter be."

Ishma was not ready. "Suit yersevs then," said her mother, and the next moment Ishma and Britt were alone. They moved together to the farther, eastern end of the porch.

"What you reckon I brought you, Ishma?"

"I'm not good at guessin'."

"Guess something you want then, an' next time I'll get it, if I've missed it now."

"I'd like something I never heard of. Something from way off. Just anything, so I'd never heard of it."

"I've got it! I've got it exactly!"

He went to the kitchen end of the porch and returned with his guitar. Then he sat down on the floor's edge, with his feet on the ground.

"There was a little Jew feller in Carson," he began, looking up through the shadows at the tall girl above him. "O, say, why don't you sit down?"

He tried to be careful of his speech when with Ishma, because he knew it pleased her. But sometimes he forgot the right form, sometimes he didn't know it, and sometimes he thought, "Heck! she oughtn't to mind, if she keers fer me!"

Ishma sat down by his side, as a courted lady should, telling herself that it was the last time. Warm, hazel eyes, under brown lashes that curved with appealing distraction, and the proud lift of broad shoulders, could be too thrilling at close quarters.

"Yes," he said, "I met a little Jew feller yesterday. He was from way off — New York, or furder — an' he grabbed holt o' my guitar an' played a piece he called Sebastopol. I made him spell it out. Awful name, but the prettiest music you'd want to hear. I made him keep pickin' till I learnt it myself. I knew you'd like it. I knew it belonged to you, an' that's why I brung it. It keeps tryin' to tell you something, an' you mighty nigh guess it, but not quite."

He began to play, and when he had finished, waited eagerly for her approval. She said nothing, and he leaned over, looking closely into her face.

"You cryin', Ishma ?"

"O, Britt ! I never heard anything like that before ! You play it again."

"No. I'm not goin' to make you cry."

"I've been wanting to cry all day, and nothing seemed worth it. You play it, Britt."

Before he could begin, a scream came from within the house. Ishma sprang to her feet. "It's Ellie ! She's spankin' her ! Bainie 's spankin' that little un !"

"Don't you mix, Ishma. Let's go to the spring. When hearin' bothers you, go furder, that's what I say."

Ellie came flying through the middle room door and stood uncertain.

"Here, Ellie !" called Ishma. The child ran to her, the old sweater tangling her feet. Ishma sat down, and Ellie was snuggled in her lap when Bainie came out.

"There you go pettin' her !" cried the mother. "She'll drive me out o' the house 'fore she's six year old. Got mad 'cause I wouldn't tell her that bat an' cat stuff you made up fer her last night. 'S if I could harbor sech craziness !"

"I'll say it, Ellie," comforted Ishma, "if you'll promise to shut your eyes and not open them until morning."

Ellie hastily shut her eyes, and nodded with vigor.

"There was a bat—" Ishma began, and feeling Britt's presence, she became timid. "O, shucks ! It's just fool stuff."

"Just what I like. Fool stuff !" said Britt happily.

"I'm waitin'," Ellie reminded her.

"You'll go to bed right now," said Ishma.

The finality of her voice brought a scream from Ellie. She had been cheated. That was as bad as a spanking.

"S'pose I say it, Ellie ?" Britt volunteered.

"You don't know none."

"I can make one."

"New one ?"

"Bran' new."

"Must I shut my eyes ?"

"Yes. An' not open 'em till mornin'."

Ellie closed her eyes, still doubting, and Britt began.

36

There was a bat — flew in a house.
There was a cat — thought it 'uz a mouse.
The mouse — I mean the bat — crawled on the floor.
The cat she thought she had him shore.
The bat jumped up an' out he flit.
That cat's a lookin' for him yit.

Ellie opened her eyes wide. "It's better than Ishma's," she announced judicially.

"Shh! you go to sleep!" Britt admonished, and with new respect for him, she cuddled down, her infant mind at peace.

"She's a cute youngun," said Britt softly.

Ishma pulled the ragged sweater about the perfect little form. "She's gone right to sleep. Bainie, you ought to be ashamed o' yourself for spankin' her."

Bainie was still in the door. They couldn't see her nose go up, but they could hear her sniff. "You wait till you git haf a dozen o' yer own. You'll knock down an' drag out jest like I do." With that she vanished. Ishma leaned back against the post, making her first confession of weariness. "It's good to have a restin' spell."

Britt hovered toward her. "You're workin' too hard, Ishma."

"No, I'm not." Her stout negative was almost resentful. "Wish I could work hard enough to make something happen."

"Something *is* goin' to happen, Ishma. We're goin' to get married."

He had not meant to say it, but the sight of her relaxed grace, and the child breathing softly in her lap, brought an emotional rush that was too swift for him. The words out, he held his breath and waited. Ishma wasn't thinking. She already had decided. But the gift life offered was dear and bright. She breathed on it gently before she let it go.

"No, Britt. That is one thing that will *never* happen."

"But, Ishma —"

"You think I'm going into that with Bainie and her kids right before my eyes?"

"My Lord, Ishma! You an' Bainie are two things!"

"We are, that's a fact, Britt. I couldn't put up with her kind

37

of life noway — noway at all." She got up with the child in her arms. "I'll put Ellie to bed."

As soon as she was gone, Britt went to the other end of the porch and took out the small package which he had slipped between the floor and a sleeper when he had come in. It was a little pasteboard box containing a cluster of tiny, artificial roses. As he came back he stooped and stuck the bunch into one of Ishma's flower-buckets that were set in a row along the edge of the porch between the two middle posts. When Ishma came out again, Britt was sitting where she had left him, his guitar in hand, pursuing a runaway tune.

"Play that pretty one again, Britt. If it's mine I ought to have it when I want it."

"Sure you ought! An' I'll be right here if you want it ever' minute." But he was up and moving toward the flowers. "How's your bucket-purties comin' on?" Instantly she was eager.

"The snow-carpet 's got little buds, an' there's three bunches of love-lies-bleeding about ready to bloom. I kept them in the kitchen a whole month, and I'll have blossoms before Eve Copp will this Spring. I'm not trying to have anything in the yard, just for Jim's hogs to root up. I've been afraid they'd kill that little balsam you set out for me, snoutin' around it. That's about all I've got left in the yard. There's a sow an' pigs under the floor right now."

"When we get our little home, Ishma — "

"We'll never get it. Don't talk about it, Britt."

"Wouldn't you like it?"

"Maybe I would, but what I'm saying is we'll never get it."

Britt was standing by the buckets. "Which is love-lies-bleedin'?"

She bent down to show him. "Why — what — you got your flash, Britt?" He whirled the flashlight on the flowers, and she began to laugh. "Pink roses! Tee-niny pink roses! You brought 'em, Britt."

"For your hat, Ishma. The one you been fixin'."

"It's spoiled now." Her voice was doleful. She had tried unsuccessfully to paint an old straw with Jim's shoe-blacking. An-

38

other look at the roses still shining in the flashlight, and she brightened. "I'll take a dollar and buy a new frame at Gaffney's."

"And wear it to meetin' next Sunday with my flowers on it?"

Then she remembered that she couldn't take a day off. She had to keep fighting briars if they were to have any crop at all. "The dogwood blossoms have done dropped off," she said, "and it scares me to think maybe we won't get the corn in the ground before the next rain sets in."

"What's Jim doin'?" Britt asked, with as near an approach to a growl as he could make.

"He'll do the ploughin', but he's got nothin' to hitch up but a rack-o'-bones that Alec Craig put on him. He brought it home yesterday, and I thought it would fall down before we could get it to the pasture."

"I'll work a day fer ye, an' you go to Gaffney's. I'll work all next week fer ye."

"What about you workin' out Lem Weaver's cow?"

Britt's head went down. He had promised the judge he wouldn't lose a day. They both stood silent, feeling nearer each other; united in the troubles of youth. Ishma began to think aloud.

"I'm goin' away before long. Clean away from here, and send mother and the children all I make. I'll go down to the mills —"

"Not if I can hep it! I know about the mills. All a girl can make is her board and clo's. You wouldn't have a thing left to send back."

"I'm strong. I could make more than most girls. But it would be hard to leave mommie and the kids with only Jim to look after them. Ben's getting a fine start in school, and he's more willing than Sam. And — my Jersey heifer — she's so pretty." She smiled, acknowledging her idolatry. So far, the Jersey heifer was her great experience.

Britt smiled with her. "I heard Jim was tryin' to sell her, but don't you let him."

"That's one thing he'll not get away from me. Eve Copp gave me that heifer when she thought it was going to die, and I 'tended it night and day till it got well. I wouldn't sell her for any money. My own mommie couldn't beg me out of her."

39

"Ay, she's a thoroughbred."

"She's *registered,* Britt! Since I've had her on the farm, the whole place seems different."

"She's the purtiest thing on the mountain, leavin' you out, honey. That hide o' hern shines like a lookin'-glass. Where you keepin' her now? I ain't seen her lately."

"She's at Alec Craig's. He's got good tame pasture. We've got nothing fit for a Jersey calf. Coarse, wild stuff. I'm going to pay Alec a dollar a month for her. That's cheap, and he said I could work it out hoein' for him this summer. He'll 'low me a dollar a day, same as a man. That'll be only one day a month to give her good eatin'. I miss her though. The place seems all run down without her. Such a neck an' eyes she's got! And her little cream-colored hoofs! I'll be proud when I get to milkin' her!"

He could feel her warmth, her excitement, and all for a Jersey calf. What if a man could prove himself a thoroughbred in her eyes? A man she loved? What would the days — the nights — be like for him? The thought drove the blood from his face. He could scarcely hear her for the roaring in his ears.

"When I look at that heifer, Britt, I don't mind rags, nor old split shoes, nor anything! She's a sign to me, a sign of what's coming. Next year I'm goin' to have a setting of ordered eggs, Buff Orpingtons, or Rhode Island Reds maybe, and not waste my time on onery chickens. I'll be milkin' Jersey Belle, and I'll have butter and eggs to take down the mountain, an' fryers by March, Britt. Orps an' Reds grow fast. I'll have a little to go on with, an' can keep the younguns decent for school —"

"Jim's younguns!"

"They can't help that. They're good kids, ever' one of 'em. And maybe I can take a trip off sometime — where that little Jew feller came from — or farther. Play my piece again, Britt. Looks like I've got it an' not got it. I want it right now, with the moon comin' up. Look yonder over High Swamp Willows, how it's frostin' ever'thing!"

Britt started to play, but after the first few bars the melody was broken by a voice ringing up the hill. "Tum-tum-tumpty!

Hello, Britt !" It was Rad Bailey, approaching with aunt Cynthy's daughter, Julie.

"Hello, Rad !" Britt flung out. "You're as welcome as frost on an early bean patch."

"What about me ?" Julie asked, nearing the porch.

"O, you're a medder lark singin' in January."

"Are you for sitting down, or going into the house ?" welcomed Ishma.

Rad made his answer known by seating himself as near to her as possible, and Julie showed hers by placing herself at the side of Britt. "Out here is good enough," she said. "The moon's not clear, but it's pushin' soft. Mother's in the house, I reckon ?"

"Yes," said Ishma, moving quietly away from Rad and sitting down by the corner post.

"I come up from Beebread an' found dad on a tear, so I 'lowed she's up here. I'll take her back home if you'll stay the night with us, Britt, an' keep dad from splittin' the roof."

"Sure I will, Julie !" He gave her shoulder an assuring pat. "Don't you worry."

Julie was small and plump and sweet, with brown eyes, brown hair and brown face. She and Britt had been friends since the first day that his father, riding up the hill with his two-year-old son strapped behind him, had alighted at aunt Cynthy's gate. It was easy for anyone except himself to see that the girl's thoughts of him sprang from a warmer fire than friendship. Ishma knew that Julie would gladly take up the prize she was laying down. She knew, too, that Britt's companionable soul would find it hard to endure life unmated. There was no tinct of jealousy in her blood or spirit, yet a sickening throb troubled her heart as she thought of him possessed by another — perhaps Julie.

Bainie, on the porch, bucket in hand, was asking Ishma to go to the spring for water. Injury whined in her voice. Two girls on the porch courting, and she with everything to clean up !

"I ain't got a drap fer the dishes. An' when you git back, Ish, you go fetch some more o' that dry chestnut. The light 's dyin' down.till I kain't see."

Rad grabbed the bucket. "Ish an' me fer the spring! Julie an' Britt fer the wood!"

Ishma moved over to Britt. "I'll have to go for the wood. Don't any of you know where it is."

The bucket fell from Rad's grasp. "All right, gal! They can have the spring."

Ishma picked up the hat which Julie had laid on the porch floor and hung it on a spike in the porch wall. "You don't want your hat tromped on, Julie. It's a new one too!"

"Yes, I wore it jest to show you."

"It suits you bodily."

"That's what ever'body says. But I b'lieve I'd like blue flowers better."

"O, no! Nothing 's sweeter than tiny, pink roses."

Bainie was waiting. "I don't want that water fer the baby's weddin'," she said. "I want to git to bed sometime tonight."

"Come on, Ish," called Rad, making a leap off the porch and tripping on one of the little buckets. In his sprawl they were all tumbled to the ground. Ishma's body curved in silent lament over the scattered and bruised flowers. Britt was aghast, but Rad was unconscious of tragedy. Julie tried to be comforting.

"You can re-set 'em, Ishma, an' they'll live. Though they won't bloom early, an' that's what you nussed 'em so long fer."

"Don't you keer, Ish," said Rad. "There's nothin' to them things. One o' my sows come in from the mountains yesterday with seven pigs. I'm 'lowin' to bring you one — not the runt either. That'll be wuth more'n this truck."

Ishma looked at Britt. "A pig! He'll bring me a pig! As if we didn't have too many mountain rooters round here now!"

The flush on her cheek meant fire within. She started abruptly for the wood. Rad followed, unhumbled and protesting. When they were gone, Julie tried to pick up the flowers.

"All broke off," she said pityingly. "They'll never bloom now. Why — here are some artificial ones — down in the dirt. How'd they get here?"

"I brought 'em to Ishma, an' stuck 'em there, like a smooth idiot."

"Jest like mine. Guess they're from Leroy's too."

"That's where I got 'em. Say, Julie, what'll you take fer your flowers ?"

Julie promptly got her hat and took the flowers off. "I jest pinned 'em on. You can have 'em, Britt. I'll put the spiled ones on my hat, an' she won't notice 'em in the dark."

"I'll pay you, Julie."

"No, you won't. I want blue ones anyway."

"I say, you're awful good, Julie."

"We'd better go fer that water."

Britt picked up the bucket and they were barely out of hearing when Ishma and Rad returned, amity only partly restored.

"I'm shore sorry I made ye mad, Ish."

"You couldn't help falling, I reckon, but I didn't like you offering me a pig when I could have a whole yard full of flowers if it wasn't for the onery pigs. If you'd said a Red Duroc, or White Yorkshire, you'd been talkin'."

Cynthy and Laviny had come out and were seated by the kitchen door for their snuff-taking, always an essential after meals. Cynthy peered around and inquired for Julie. Rad was quick to say that she had gone with Britt to the spring some time back. "Give 'em a chance, aunt Cynthy," he laughed. "They'll come in 'fore mornin'." Ishma stood cold, pretending not to hear. Bainie, in the kitchen door, remarked with as much tartness as her whine would permit, "I'd a got to bed sooner by goin' after that water myself."

The innocents reappeared at that moment, and Bainie took the bucket jerkily from Britt, saying that he must have thought she wanted it for breakfast coffee. Julie advanced with the flowers in her hand.

"I found yer hat-flowers, Ishma. Not hardly teched."

"Oh, that's luck !" Ishma took the flowers and turned them to the firelight from the open door. But she looked up too soon, in time to see an exchange of glances between Britt and Julie.

"I don't want *your* flowers, Julie," she said, handing them back, "but you're good to offer 'em."

"My gracious !" cried Julie. She flounced over to the end of the porch and sat down on the steps. "Come over here, Britt ! We've got to study up something else."

"You do the studyin', Julie," he said, going over and sitting down by her. "Looks like I don't know my way about tonight."

Julie refrained from condolence. She knew something better. Reaching for the guitar, she brought it forward and laid it gently on Britt's knees. "They's a line in that 'twitter song' that's botherin' me. You pick it once an' I'll git it right. Then I can thump it on my banjo."

Soon they were talking about pitch and key, breaking into bits of song, and laughing softly. Rad looked at the pair, and felt that he was losing good time. He crossed to the opposite end of of the porch. "I've got something to tell you, Ish," he called, but she didn't move from her post near Cynthy and Laviny. "It's about yer Jersey Belle. I was at Alec's today." That'll fetch her, he thought.

"You've seen her ?" she asked eagerly, moving to him. "How's she looking ?"

He caught his breath as she came close, her eyes full upon him. "There's something else I've got to tell you first," he said.

"If it's the same old thing, Rad, please don't."

"You'd listen quick enough if Britt was out o' my way. Your ears would be sharp as a hungry cat's."

Rad was accustomed to the smiles of girls, and he felt that Ishma resisted him because he had failed to state his case clearly. He had too much simple vanity to suspect that, stripped of farm and goods, his drab hair and blue eyes would be only faintly attractive beside the vividness of Britt.

"He'll be off the track soon, mebbe, settin' up to Julie like Sunday night. She's a good girl too. Ought to do better'n take a loaferin' tum-tummer like that."

"You take her, Rad."

"You know there's only one girl for me, Ish. Britt 'll find second choice good enough, but not me. I'm steady hearted, an' you're the one I'm goin' to have, soon as I can make you see it, an' you stop lettin' a bag o' tow block a good road."

"You can lay off Britt, Rad. There's no danger of my marryin' him."

Rad hugged the air. It was the first admission that he had received from her. "You mean that, Ish ?"

44

"Not a smidgeon o' danger." But her eyes clung through the dark to the two figures humming and thrumming at the other end of the porch. With an effort she drew her eyes away, and lifted them to the western sky. Then her gaze swept on to the north. A haze, not moonlight, was reflected there, and everything else was forgotten in her thought of the fire. She meant to slip away by herself, up the ridge that sloped skyward between two coves for about a mile back of the cabin. She would go to the highest point, where she could look over Silver Valley and the masses of cliff and laurel that made Dark Moon Cove the stronghold of blockaders. She would have to wait until her guests were gone and the household was in sleep. She and her mother were sharing the same bed in the middle room, and she would have to lie down and make a pretense of sleep, if she avoided argument. Later she could creep from Laviny's side without awakening her. Then she would have the mountains, the fire, the world, to herself. She scarcely heard Rad's voice, her own thoughts were so busy and loud.

"I knowed you'd find the place where you left yer good sense, Ish. You're too smart to git caught by a feller that could walk round the world 'thout standin' one time on his own ground."

"What did you have to tell me, Rad ? You've not said anything yet."

His vanity crumpled, and he didn't care if he hurt her, not too much. "O, I reckon you know about Jim sellin' yer calf to Alec Craig."

Ishma turned a white face to him, trying not to believe. "You're hard up for a joke, Rad. Jim wouldn't dare do that."

"He's done it all the same. Three days ago, but I didn't hear about it until today when I's passin' Alec's an' got in a chow with him."

"Jim couldn't — he couldn't !"

"Alec's braggin' mighty big about the trade. He's goin' to take the heifer to the fair, he says."

Ishma began pleading with fate. "Jim couldn't treat me that way and me nigh makin' the living for his family."

She turned to the little group about the door, flecked with

45

firelight and shadows. "Mommie! Bainie! You heard anything about Jim selling Jersey Belle?"

"I swear to God," cried Bainie, fright in her voice, "I didn't know it! I tried to git Jim not to do it!"

The hysterical admission turned Ishma hot and cold. It was true. She was speechless. Rad began to fill the silence. "Alec give Jim an' old steer an' nine dollars to boot."

"Oh!" Ishma's hurt cry brought Britt and Julie over to the shadowy group. "That's where he got that thing he brought home to plough with. A stack o' bones you could see through like a ladder!"

"Sounds like it, 'cordin' to Alec," Rad corroborated, enjoying his position as chief informer. He thought he knew how he could comfort Ishma. But Britt knew that she could not be comforted. The women were amazed, not at her depth of feeling, but at her display of it. Laviny had liked to speak of her as "Indian-natered, she's that cyam."

"My Jersey Belle! My beauty!" she was crying. "He couldn't! He just couldn't!"

Laviny forced herself forward. "Now, Ishmalee, you jest quit takin' on. Ain't nobody dead. You go on scan'lous 'bout a calf an' the Lord 'll send you some shore enough trouble. You know Jim. An' you know you kain't do a pinched-off speck 'bout anything he does."

Laviny had made a mistake in tactics. The unsympathetic words turned Ishma's grief wholly to anger. She was standing where the wavering moonlight fell on the porch, and Britt wished that the light was stronger. She was like "a white rock afire," he told himself afterwards.

Turning quickly, she stepped off the porch, giving her back to all witnesses. Laviny was alarmed. If Ishma left the mountain, how could the family go on without her? Nine to eat from one meal barrel, and only Ishma to fill it. She stilled the quaver in her voice and tried to gather authority, edging away from disaster and drama.

"Fer the Lord's sake, don't git the sulks, Ishmalee! I thought we's goin' to have some enjoyment tonight. Here's enough folks come up to have some good singin'. Julie an' Britt kain't be

46

beat when they try, an' Rad an' Bainie air good enough fer Sunday, let alone middle o' the week. Ishmalee can drown out a pack o' fox-hounds when she wants to let go."

"Good idy, aunt Laviny," said Rad, helping her get the situation back to a matter-of-fact groove. Everybody began to feel more comfortable except Britt. Aching for Ishma, he thought that music might serve to pull the gang off her, and went back for his guitar.

"What'll we sing?" Julie queried, and a flood of suggestions rushed over her, from Bainie, Laviny, aunt Cynthy and Rad. Laviny wanted the new one folks had made up about Ben Ross killing Abe Snead's turkey.

"No," said Rad, "Ben's threatenin' to put the law on anybody that sings it. He's madder than ol' Heck in the rain."

"Well, let's have something 'sides talk."

"Ol' Joe Clark fer mine," said Rad, beginning to hum.

> i never liked ol' Joe Clark,
> An' I never, never shall.
> He wore a skillet fer a shoe,
> But he had a honey gal!

"I hearn that when I wuz a gal myself," said Cynthy. "Ol' Joe lived on the farm next ourn, an' he kep' a shot-gun fer anybody that sung it in passin'. Kain't you think up nothin' else?"

"Let's try dad's old song," said Bainie. "The one he larnt the winter he was in Alabam."

"Tombigbee River. Let's go! I can get a good cord on that," said Britt, making ready.

"It's about a Julie too, hey?" Rad announced. "Come on! It's Tombigbee River!"

"Hello, folks!" a voice called from the trail.

"Tim Wheeler! Who's he follerin'? Choke him off from the singin'. I d'ruther hear a hoot-owl on Friday."

"Hello, Tim!" called Julie. "We're goin' to sing."

"I'm fer it," said Tim, reaching the porch and seating himself on the edge of it, his long legs outspread.

"Lead off, Julie," Britt commanded, and her clear voice rolled out with the first line of the song. Bainie came in with the alto, and Rad took up the tenor. Britt was anywhere he chose to be with his voice, but he kept his instrument under discipline. And all the time he was thinking of Ishma, out there, dim in the moonlight, her back to the house, and her straight, broad shoulders held in challenging outline. He wanted to go to her, but she didn't need him. He was useless. She was gathering strength from the night. It was flowing to her. Strength for what ? Something apart from him, he knew.

The others were trying to make jolly work of the song.

> *On Tombigbee river so bright I was born,*
> *In a hut made of husks of the tall yellow corn.*
> *It was there I first met her, my Julie so true,*
> *And I rowed her around in my gum-tree canoe.*

> *Singing row away row, o'er the water so blue !*
> *Like a feather I float in my gum-tree canoe !*

> *I go to the field and the cotton I hoe;*
> *I think of my Julie and sing as I go.*
> *I catch her a bird with a wing of true blue,*
> *And at night sail her round in my gum-tree canoe.*

"Whyn't you come in on it, Ish ?" called Rad to the motionless figure in the yard.

"Let her be, Rad," warned Laviny. But he wouldn't. He got off the porch and came up behind her. "You ain't nosin' the ground yit about that calf, are you ?" he asked, over her resolute shoulder. "I've got three heifers. You can take yer pick of 'em. They're part Jersey."

"What part ? The bawl, I reckon," she said, and moved farther away. But Rad followed.

"Ishma, if you'd marry me, you could have ever'thing you want, right off."

"I won't marry you, nor anybody."

"That's fool talk. A girl's goin' to marry an' not wait fer her granny's ridin'-saddle nuther."

48

"Why does everybody think a girl 's got to marry ? I'm going to have something else."

"Have what ?"

"I don't know."

"Thought you didn't. You'll be all right with me, Ish. You don't know how easy I'll make it fer ye. My land is paid for now. That debt the old man left on it is smoothed right off. I've picked out a place fer our new house, down by the willer spring — "

"In that holler !"

"I'll let you pick yer own, Ish. An' you won't have to go the field at all, lessen the weather ketches me."

"And what 'll I do in the house ?"

"Why, you know — sweepin' — cookin' — piecin' quilts — an' — " Rad's voice stumbled, then rallied — "babies, mebbe."

"You needn't talk, Rad. I've got some money. Enough to buy me a dress and shoes, and a ticket to some place."

"You won't go away ?" Surprise lifted his voice. Laviny's cocked ear heard and her heart quivered and sank. Why didn't the fool let Ishmalee alone ?

"If I've got any sense I'll go, Rad. I've always heard I've got sense. Even mommie says that. I'll see if I can use it."

"You can't leave the mountains ! You've always been crazy about 'em. I never could see why, but I'm glad now. You can't leave 'em."

"It'll be hard. They're fine. Life ought to be like 'em somehow. It oughtn't to be all work and dirt and younguns." She could have laughed at his scandalized stare. "I've got just one word to say to you and the mountains, Rad, and that's goodbye."

She left him, going farther toward the fringe of woods, and sat down on the tongue of a battered wagon abandoned by Jim on its way to the barn. Rad didn't want to stand looking after her, revealing to everybody that she had shown him her heels. He came back to where Britt and Julie were again sitting together.

"What you twangin' at now, Britt ?" he asked jauntily. "Sounds good."

"Tryin' something of my own. But it needs the frensharp

49

with it, an' I've lost my head-guard." He held out the harmonica to Julie. "You hold it for me an' I'll try 'em out."

Julie jumped up, over-ready, and took the harmonica. Getting behind him she held it to his mouth. She could have done this with one hand, but she used both, circling Britt's head with her arms. Unexpectedly, Ishma was standing by them.

"Your guard 's here, Britt," she said, reaching up to a rafter and taking down the lost guard. "I found it up in Ellie's play-house, and put it out of the way."

"Nice gal !" said Britt, quickly putting it on and adjusting the harmonica. Julia sat down, her disappointment so obvious that Ishma turned her head away.

"I made words to this," said Britt, when he had played the piece through, "and I'm goin' to teach Julie to come in on it with her banjo. Then we'll go to Carson an' make a noise."

Julie's little brown face began to glow again, but Rad was scornful. "Yeah ! You'll skeer the rats out o' the corn-cribs. You'll git the farm vote shore."

"Julie could do her," averred Tim. "Julie's my bet !"

Noiselessly Jim Wishart slouched around the west end of the house and onto the porch. Still noiselessly he lifted his gun over his head and laid it on the crossbeams; then he kicked his dog back into the yard. The yelp of the dog announced his presence, and brought greetings from the other end of the porch.

"Howdy, fellers," he said, barely opening his mouth for the flattened exit of his words.

Little Sam, the lively antithesis of his father, bounced about, swollen with news. "They's a big fire comin' from Copper Creek side ! We saw it from the top o' the hill back o' the barn !"

"That so, Jim ?" asked Bainie.

"It's nothin' else. Lucky youah heah, boys. Ever'body an' the baby 's got to fight fire tonight. Sam, you go flyin' down to Alec Craig's, an' tell him an' Bert Wiggins to git up heah right now. Tell 'em not to wait to dig no well to drown the cat in, an' bring all the pitchforks they can lay hands on. Tell 'em to holler fer Si Welch an' Bud Wills. Highball now !"

Before he had finished, Sam was on the trail and Jim was talking to a disappearing streak.

"Shorely we don't all have to go," pleaded Bainie.

"Don't stand there talkin'." Jim was rising to leadership, and ludicrously attempting to look the part. "You an' Ish git up all the hoes an' pitchforks you can find. Hunt up ever' one. I'll take these heah." He shambled off the porch into the yard where the moonlight revealed Ishma's tools, and picked them up.

"We kain't find what ain't in the world," Bainie informed him. "You mighty well know all the hoes an' forks we got are right in yore hands now."

"You've lost 'em then. I kain't keep nothin' on this farm. I reckon the boys 'll have to cut y'all some good brush sticks."

Bainie made another bid for delay. "Ain't you goin' to eat nothin' ?"

"Eatin's got to wait this time." He assumed a virtue where he had it not, for he had stopped on Ivy Fork and supped with Ben Snead. "It looked fierce from up yander. Darn good luck you come up, boys, I say it is. Ever'body ready ? Mother, you an' aunt Cynthy comin' ?"

"I say we ain't !" Laviny snapped at the leader. "Forty year is long enough to fight fire. I begun when I's ten, an' I've quit. Cynthy ain't in no fix to git her skin het up. We're goin' to bed."

"Julie can go 'long with you an' Bainie, Jim," said Cynthy. "Ain't no better at battlin' fire than Julie."

"Come on then, ever'body that's comin'." There was a forward movement that didn't include Ishma. "Ish !" Jim called, "move yo'sef ! We got to hump it !"

She rose from her seat on the porch edge, came up to Jim, and looked him in the face. "Where's my Jersey heifer ?"

"At Alec's, o' course."

"You sold her ?"

Jim looked about for help, and saw that he was to get none from anybody present. "Why, you know I ast you about it, Ish."

"And what did I tell you ?"

"You didn't give me no satisfaction, but I 'lowed I ortent to let a good trade slip me jest 'cause you couldn't see it."

"Where's the boot ? You got some money. Where is it ?"

"Why, we had to have rations, Ish. We had to live. Don't go into onreason."

"And you had to have shells for your gun, so you could loaf in the woods, and the ground cryin' for the plough. And you had to have a new pair o' shoes, an' me without a hat to wear to meetin'."

"I never throwed away a dollar of it, Ish. I spent it right."

"Is it all gone?"

Jim turned his pockets inside out to demonstrate his veracity. "You can see fo' yo'sef. I ain't kep' a nickel. Come on now, les git up the hill. Ef that fire climbs to the ridge from t'other side, an' blows down that holler full o' dead leaves, it'll roar to our barn, an' Joshuway couldn't stop it."

"You can fight your own fires, Jim Wishart, now and ever!"

Jim was startled, but his eyes barely flickered. His expression could not scramble out of habitual grooves. "Well, you been workin' hard today, Ish, an' the ground 'll need you tomorr'. We'll make out tonight, an' let ye be."

"You'll make out without me for the rest of your life."

"You ain't goin' back on yo' mother an' the younguns? I kain't think that o' ye, Ish."

Ishma's voice was steady as she answered him, but its mellow depth was gone, and it flowed round a core of iron. No longer water dripping in dark woods, holding something fragrant and hidden.

"She's Bainie's mother too. This is her farm, not yours. It will take care of her if you will work it and give her what she ought to have out of it. The children are yours, not mine. I'm saying goodbye to you, Jim. You won't see me here tomorrow."

Laviny laid a hand on Jim's arm. "You go 'long, an' don't stand here pesterin' her out of her senses. Git on, all o' ye! Git right on!"

Her sharp tongue and flourishing hands got them started up the hill. She watched them until their footsteps ceased to echo; then turned and made two or three unsuccessful attempts to go towards Ishma. The way of conciliation was strange to her, and she decided not to walk it.

"Come, Cynthy, les git along to bed. It's all we can do, I reckon."

They went in, leaving Ishma sitting stolid on the porch, her bare feet on the ground. The moon was now almost golden bright, and that brought Laviny back to the door.

"I'll have to shet the door, Ishmalee," she said, finding relief in words that made life simple again. "The moonlight allers bothers my sleep."

"All right, mother."

Laviny hesitated once more, then went in and closed the door behind her. Ishma laid herself down on the floor, her head resting on her arms. She was alone and could think. And thinking must be swift and sure, with what was before her. But she was not to have even one minute for her own thoughts. Britt had not gone up the hill. He had fallen back, in the rear of the cabin, and waited for Laviny to go in. He now came softly up to Ishma and stood looking down upon her. He knew she was thinking, planning. She wanted to be alone. He could feel remonstrance in her hidden face, her still form, but it couldn't push him away. He had to speak.

"Ishma!"

"Go away, Britt!" Her head was not lifted.

"Ishma!" he repeated, in a voice that had lost the twinkle which she thought made it unlike any other voice in the world. She sprang up then, but before she could protest, he was talking.

"Don't leave the mountains, Ishma. You couldn't stand it away from here."

"I can't stand it *here*."

"It'll come easier after a little. You ain't made for the low country."

"I'm going out of this. I'm not going to live in Heck's woodshed any longer."

"Girls have it hard down there. I know about it. They come back with no health an' their minds sopped up with trashy clo's."

"I'm getting out, Britt. And you needn't worry about me. I'm strong."

"I'll make Jim pay you. He'll have to fight me."

"You'll make him pay when you know he hasn't a brownie. You've seen his pockets inside out, and you'll make him pay!"

"You can't go without some money, Ishma. You'll find you

look like a tramp if you get out there with what you got on."

"I've got a little money. Enough to do till I find work."

"S'pose you take Julie's place at Mis' Gaddy's. She's not goin' back."

She shook her head. "It's got to be farther than that."

"But why, Ishma ?"

"There's more 'n Jim pushin' me off. Something you don't know."

"Tell me, honey."

"I learned something about myself tonight."

"You'll tell me, darling !" He laid a hand on her shoulder, but she put up her own and moved it away.

"Stand off there then. I'll tell you, just for goodbye, Britt — if you'll promise to go right off and not stand here talking when you know how busy in my mind I've got to be."

No iron in the voice now; all water in dark woods, holding a hidden fragrance.

"For goodbye, Britt. I found that if I stayed here, I'd be Bainie all over again, and you'd be Jim."

Hot passion swept his face and left it white, all that was careless and gay burnt out of it, as he leaned toward her, yet held himself from leaning too much. "God, Ishma ! You'd marry me ?"

"When you were sitting by Julie, and when I thought you'd been so long at the spring — I knew what I'd do if I stayed around here."

"You do love me ?"

"I reckon Bainie loved Jim once."

How could she, in such a moment, think of beings so alien ? He was angry. "We're different — different as — as birds and goats. I'm not Jim. I'll work my arms off for you, Ishma."

"You think you will."

"You don't love me. If you did you wouldn't be studyin' how we're goin' to get along."

"I would too ! People don't have to go crazy just 'cause they're in love. We haven't got a thing. We'd have to live right here on mommie's place with Bainie and Jim. And you can't even

54

work for yourself this summer. If we had Jersey Belle for a start, I might — I *might* think about it. But we haven't got a hoof of anything alive."

Britt took up his guitar. His face had regained its color while she was talking. It was both misty and glowing, as if soft winds were passing over it. In his heart came a gay certainty.

"You reckon I could play a little 'thout wakin' the folks up ?"

She put her hands over her ears. "Don't you do that, Britt. It's not fair."

"I won't then. But that piece o' yours would sound mighty good right now." He rose and put his guitar back against the wall. "You lay that in the house for me in the dry 'fore you leave. You won't be startin' down till daylight, will you ?"

"Soon as it's bare light."

"I'm comin' back to go down with you."

"You won't either. I'm going off this mountain by myself."

"Well, I'm off. You won't kiss me, Ishma, seein' you're leavin' out ?"

His lips curved beggingly, and his shoulders curved too, though he stood apart. The moonlight was clear again, and she could see his eyes darken with pleading, going from hazel to their deepest fire-brown. Her body seemed pushing toward him. She braced her toes against the ground. A kiss would be fatal, she knew.

"No, I won't. But — thank you, Britt."

He looked at her silently, wondering if he might dare. She understood, and saved herself with effort, commanding him to get on to the fire. He shut his lips tightly over a great hope; but she only saw that he moved off too briskly.

A little way up the hill he turned back and went down on the other side of the cabin; went carefully so that Ishma would not discover him. She couldn't have seen him even if he had taken no care, so downcast she was, balanced on the rickety edge of the porch, with her eyes on her bare feet. She let her thoughts flow hurriedly, without form; trying to cover up the one throbbing thought of Britt, and of that other woman, somewhere in the world, who would not refuse his kiss.

55

She must get into the house and find her stockings. Bainie, no doubt, had been wearing them. She mustn't wake her mother. It had been years since she had seen her mother weep. She just couldn't bear that! Stooping, she took her shoes from under the floor and shook the field dirt out of them. They wouldn't more than take her down the mountain, but she could get a new pair at Gaffney's. The store would be open by six o'clock. She would have half an hour before train time. That was too long. She didn't want to answer questions. The Beebread people got up early to ask questions. It was hard enough to leave the mountains, without talking about it. She thought of the fire—her great, lost wonder on the ridge. Perhaps she would go yet. But the men would be whistling and singing and shouting all along the crest. She might find a spot on Lame Goat Ridge where she could be by herself. There would be no message, no comfort, no revelation for her in those tongues of fire unless she went to them holily and alone. She'd sleep a little first, and then go. Weariness was heavy on all her limbs, and once more she laid her full length on the porch, her arms her pillow. A moment later she was in deep sleep. Hours afterwards she was awakened by a happy dream, and opened her eyes to see Britt standing by her. She rose up, sleep clinging about her and making him vague.

"I declare I dreamed I heard Jersey Belle calling me. Britt! What you back for?"

"You didn't dream it, Ishma. She's out there in the lot, and wants to say 'howdy' to you. That's what you heard. Come on an' see her. Don't keep her waitin'. She knew all the time she was comin' to you, an' kep ahead o' me up the hill."

Ishma was still mistily uncertain. "You brought her back?"

"Sure I did! You reckon I'm goin' to let you be tromped on like that?"

"Jersey Belle?"

The heifer called again, and Ishma was not dreaming. Instantly her arms were around Britt's neck and he was giving her a long triumphant kiss; the kiss they had both wanted and which neither of them would ever forget.

"She's here!" Ishma was murmuring. "I've got her back!

56

Darling ! Darling !" Britt's arms mistakenly tightened, and she drew away.

"I didn't mean that, Britt," she whispered, in a fright.

"Let's see you get it back !"

"But you brought Jersey Belle ! My beauty ! Oh — do you think Alec will take her away from me ?"

"Let him try. You only got what belongs to you. He'll have to settle with Jim."

"He might take a warrant for Jim."

"No danger. I know Alec. That steer ain't worth a plough-line. He ought to paid Jim for drivin' it off. He ain't out but nine dollars, an' he wouldn't let himself be laughed at for that bit o' money. He'll say he found out the calf was yorn an' he let her come back. That's the way he'll talk. He'll be tellin' ever'body he let the fence down an' give her her choice. His ol' fence is fallin' to pieces anyway. Guess he'll think she got out by herself."

"O, Britt, he'll find out you brought her !"

"Let him. I'd like to tech him up a little if he wants a fight. It's due him."

"No, no ! You're not through with that Lem Weaver trouble, and looking for more ! You've got to keep out of trouble now."

"Why now, Ishma ? Why now ?"

"O — well."

"You do mean it ! You'll stay here and marry me ! O, honi-est in the world, I'll keep out of trouble the rest of my life ! I'll run from Alec if you want me to. I'll promise you anything, Ish-my-own !"

"Promise ? Yes."

"I'll keep my word. You never heard o' my breakin' my word, did you ?"

"No, Britt."

"And you never will hear of it. I'll settle down, an' I'll *work*. Folks think I can't stay in one place. What did I want to stay for when I didn't have you ? I'll show ever'body. I'll show 'em what settlin' down means. We'll get married right away — "

"As soon as you've worked out Lem Weaver's cow," she calmly reminded him, intending no cruelty.

Britt sat down as if struck. "Wish I'd never heard o' that cow." Feeling something under him besides the floor, he moved and dragged out a mail order catalogue. "What's this ? What you goin' to order, Ishma ?"

"Nothing. I'm not studying it. The younguns left it there. But I was looking at some dresses yesterday — just looking. O, there's one all white silk and lace that costs nine ninety-eight ! I'll show it to you."

They hastily turned the leaves and found the dress. "There's not enough moonlight for you to see it good. Turn on your flash, Britt."

He held the light close and they gazed together. "It's fine, Ishma," he decided. "But that girl ain't pretty as you. You could show her how to wear that thing. She's just a little scrap. You could *wear* it. Just wait till I get that cow worked out an' makin' my own money. You'll be so sweet there won't be nary bee left in a hive when you go walkin' out."

Ishma was feeling herself taken up into his eyes. "If you's me, Britt — and had the money — would you — would you buy that dress ?" A little fear hovered over her level voice and broke it. She was so unused to buying things.

"Would I ? The money would be in the Post Office 'fore sun-up. Lord, honey, what a stand-up dress that 'ud make !"

"I've got the money, Britt !" Her voice was mended now, and firm.

Awe crept into Britt's face. "And you'll get the dress ? You'll get it for the wedding ?"

"Listen to you ! And I haven't promised a thing."

"But you're not going away. You've promised that much. You're going to stay here with — with — "

"Jersey Belle," she finished for him, and they laughed together.

Ishma heard voices on the slope. Were the men coming down ? She sprang up. "They mustn't find you here, Britt ! And the calf back home ! You know what they'll say. You'll never get straight with Alec and Jim."

Britt was not disturbed. "O, you're just afraid they'll find me here with *you,* an' say we've got it fixed up to be married. That's

58

all right, honiest that ever was. I'll be playin' you a little sere-nade—"

"No, you won't. Let that guitar be! You go right off to the fire. Slip up quiet and get with the other men. They'll think you've been clearin' a fire-trail somewhere. You fix *that* up, Britt. I can't stand it if Alec comes on you, and things get mixed up more than they are now."

"I'll go if it's botherin' you. My time, it's sweet to be any concern o' yorn!"

He caught and kissed her—their long, second kiss, more fiercely sweet—and hurried off, up by the barn, to avoid who-ever it was on the trail. She watched him until he was hidden by the slim, moonlit poplars overgrowing the hill pasture. Then she sat down, drew the catalogue to her, and looked with fear-ful joy at the dress.

"There's lace here—and here"—she said, fingering her ragged frock at the neck and sides, and seeing herself "standing-up" with Britt in the little meeting-house on the forks of Ivy. They would rent a farm the first year. No, they would buy one, on time. That would be better, for Britt would never leave the mountains. He had spent two or three months one year in the low country, and had come back saying it "didn't suit him." That was final for Britt. But even here she would make their lives different. She knew she could. Such strength she had! There was no weariness in her limbs now. She would never be weary again. Happiness cured everything.

The voices on the slope dropped into silence. A little later the sound of violent weeping troubled the air near the cabin. Ishma recognized Bainie's wail. Instantly she was stoic, realizing calam-ity. How contemptible of Bainie to howl like that, whatever had happened! If she had to do it, why didn't she get through with it up in the woods and not wait until she was near the house, tearing mommie all up?

When Bainie, shaking and sobbing, followed by Tim Wheeler, came up the porch steps, Ishma stood before her in silence. She knew that in some way this was an attack on her happiness, and she intended to defend it with all the forces she could summon.

Her new life of burning joy and wonder — nothing could make her let it go!

She waited, and when Bainie saw that the first move must be her own, she sobbed out, "Jim's nearly kilt, Ishma. I reckon his back 's about broke."

And still Ishma said nothing. Tim was puzzled, and ventured further explanation. "A burnin' tree fell on him. He's purty nigh done fer. But maybe he'll pull up. I'm goin' fer a doctor."

Then Ishma spoke, and her voice was hard. "Doctor Stinnett?"

Bainie ceased sobbing. "Like to know who else they is to go fer?"

"You mean," said Ishma, "that he's the only doctor who'll climb these mountains — who'll drive all the way from Carson — to save folks' lives — and get nothing but thanks. Not always that much. You know that Jim never paid him a cent for coming when Ellie was born — nor for coming when Sam broke his leg — nor a cent when mommie had her turn. And you know what he said the last time. 'When you want me again, Jim, you send the money.' And he's right. A body can't blame him. Jim swore he'd pay him, and he never sent him a brownie."

Bainie flinched under Ishma's words, but she had a reason for not being hopeless. With the sob again in her voice, she said that Tim was going to Gaffney's and telephone Doc Stinnett to come anyhow. "But I know he won't," she wailed. "He meant them bitter words. He won't come. An' Jim 'll die! He'll lay up there an' die, pore feller!"

Tim felt there was something wrong. Ishma wasn't asking a thing about the accident. She just stood there, with her arms crossed, looking at Bainie as if she were a stump, instead of a pore, broken-hearted sister.

"They're makin' a stretcher to bring him down the hill," he said, "but he begs 'em not to tech him. He may have to lay up there till Doc gits here."

"An' he won't come! I know he won't!" rose Bainie's voice of despair, while she kept an eye slanted on Ishma.

"You'll have mommie out here in a minute. Looks like you could think of somebody besides you and Jim." She was hor-

60

rified at the coldness of her own voice, at her utter lack of sympathy. She wanted to shake Bainie.

"Kain't we tell Doc it's fer you, Ish ? He'll come fer you. He'll come in a trot. He needn't know it's Jim till he gits here."

"No ! None of your lies !"

Then Bainie shook and rocked and wept. "Stop that," Ishma commanded. "The doctor 's going to come."

She went into the house, and Bainie's cunning, greedy eyes followed her. She forgot to sob, and remained silent, hardly breathing until Ishma came out and laid some money in Tim's hand. "It's only fourteen dollars," she said. "Fifteen is the fee for coming up here, but this will bring him. You tell him Jim is sending it. Tell him it's in your hands waiting for him."

The relieved Tim averred that he wouldn't lose a minute 'twixt there and the telephone, and loped off down the hill. Bainie made no show of gratitude which she knew would not be welcomed. She waited for Ishma to speak, but the heavy silence was unbroken. At that moment Bainie did not exist for the half-stunned girl, wandering amid shattered dreams. She was seeing the face of Britt, far off, but coming towards her on her mountain. She watched his countenance that continually changed in the pause or drive of his spirit. She could tell when he looked at a bird, a cloud, a leaf, a gleam of water, a stab of color. She knew when he was near enough to look at *her*. His face leapt alive with an intense light that made the bright arrest of previous moments seem only a casual glow. Her man, out of all the world. Shadows fell, blotting him out, his eyes still seeking hers, her own straining to find him.

"I'll git back to Jim, pore ol' boy," said Bainie at last, and turning about she started up the hill. Laviny came out of the middle room, an old shawl hugged about her splintery body.

"I heard it all, honey. I heard ever' word. I's layin' there listenin'. Jim crippled, an' you goin' to leave."

"I'll have to stay now, mommie. You know that."

"You ort to have yer chance, Ishmalee. God knows you ort. There'll never be nothin' fer ye here. But it was hurtin' me awful. Jim gittin' kilt wouldn't be nothin' to yore leavin' out."

61

"I'm stayin', mommie." She said it mechanically, drearily unaware of Laviny's awakened tenderness.

"Looks like the Lord puts us where we kain't hep ourselves."

"You better go back to bed. We can't do anything but wait for Doctor Stinnett. Get some sleep while you can."

"I reckon I might as well." Laviny started in, but stopped to speak again, her voice heavy and beaten. "This 'll take a heap o' money."

Ishma said nothing. Her eyes fell on the catalogue lying on the floor. With a slow movement of her foot she pushed it off the porch. Laviny stood in the partly open door, her pinched figure a moonlit fragility held down by the weight of her shawl. The small criss-cross wrinkles were invisible on her softened face; a face that palely outlined a pathetic return of the brief beauty that had held Marshall Waycaster for the fatal moment of committal. If her daughter had looked at her then, she might have seen her mother, for once in her life, facing her with the eyes of youth and sympathy. But Ishma, more silent than the night, was not thinking of her mother.

"Course I can sell the hens," said Laviny, resuming age and defeat as she went wisp-like into the house and shut the door on the triumphantly riding moon.

Ishma had a belated sense of her mother's words. "And I can sell Jersey Belle," she said, taking the last glimpse of her joy and lifting her eyes, without reproach, toward the stars that had failed her.

CHAPTER III

"A GAL SHE MUST MARRY"

JIM, true to his natural pace, recovered very leisurely, his disablement absorbing everything on the farm that could be turned into money. Jersey Belle went first. Alec Craig saw her driven by his gate, and had nothing to say then or afterwards. He came up to see Jim, and the next day went to Carson, with Si Welch as accessory, and interviewed the judge who had passed sentence on Britt. It was made clear to the open-minded jurist that the neighbors would club in and give Lem Weaver help now and then, in the ratio of his need, if Britt could be free to take Jim's place on the Waycaster farm. When the judge learned that a wedding hung upon his assent, he gave them a smile rich in memories and delivered Britt from bondage. This was a bit of clever work on the part of Jim's neighbors. Helpless, the invalid had full claim on them for his crop, however meagrely he might contribute to it when in health. Britt was hardly more famous than Jim for throwing a steady arm, but they felt that if they got him on the job they could leave it to Ishma to put him through.

Ishma had steadily refused to see Britt. She didn't dare listen to him. If she listened, her heart would surely outride her head, and with things in such a tangle she must run no risk of making them worse. Love was a whirlpool, calling to something wild, sweet and unreasonable within her. If she went near it she would throw herself over the brink. But Britt rushed to her with the news of his freedom and made her hear him. When she understood that they could be married, that they could live and work together, that life was in their hands, and Fate an unreal shadow, she couldn't answer him for the sob in her throat, and covered her eyes because of the burning light in them. He pulled her hands away, kissed both of her eyes, her cheeks, her lips, and

63

hurried off to Carson for the license. He needn't have hurried, for when he returned Ishma made him wait three days longer, giving no reason that a man could understand.

The wedding was not a great to-do. There was no journey to the meeting-house, no dress of white silk and lace. The pair "stood up" on the uncertain porch as sure of themselves and each other as they were of the eternal hills about them. Ishma's short, dusky curls had been coaxed and rounded to her head, making its upheld beauty more than ever like a slim, sleek deer's. One might think her ready to dart away until met by her broad brow and level eyes, sea-grey in a cloister of dark lashes. And there was no hint of flight in the firm grace of her figure. Rising tall and unabashed in a much washed gingham, she looked as she felt, the mistress of her destiny. When her eyes turned to Britt, the airy distance between man and maid seemed bridged with security and joy.

Neighbors came in for the "tie-up," and Rad was among them. He had meant to show them all how little he cared, but he stumbled about, his face grey and his eyes incredulous, until Si took him by the shoulders and told him to "git home an' cuss it out."

Britt stood up in a suit that had been with him through two seasons of corn-shuckings when he had danced the nights through. He and Ishma together had cleaned and pressed it, laughing and loving each other as if poverty had no grip on their happiness. Nor did it have for at least one golden half year. They worked side by side in the fields, and not since the days of great-grand-father Frady had Cloudy Knob known such a crop. They planted two fields that had been untilled for several years and in that idle period had regained enough humus to make them gasp forth one more harvest. One of the fields Ishma had made ready before Britt arrived. With such eager reinforcement, and the Spring rains holding back, it was easy to add another. Not a weed was allowed to grow in them until the corn was "laid by." Laviny made the garden and worked the patches of beans and potatoes. Si Welch lent them a cow to milk, and after Laviny sold her hens the women roundabout made up an offer-

64

ing of six "settin' hens" with eggs to go under them. Bainie did the puttering in the house, going for days without whine or complaint, and taking all necessary care of Jim. She sat by his bed, darning and mending until, as she said, she had everything patched but their skins.

Ishma cooked the early breakfast before leaving for the field, and half an hour before twelve she would come in and give her efficient touch to the dinner. She was deft in a kitchen, and she remembered much of her grandmother's teaching. Long ponderings over the *Woman at Home* had made her daring with materials at hand. But the Sunday dinner was left to family incompetence and monotony. That was the day which she and Britt kept for themselves, and they usually spent it out on their hills, as Ishma had done in her maiden days. They were both church members, but they didn't belong to the village church down in Beebread. Their meeting-house stood in the forks of Ivy creek, at the western foot of Cloudy Knob mountain. It was a little, unpainted house of "boxin' an' battin'," but too big for the few who straggled into it on the third Sunday of every month. If the third Sunday happened to be rainy, Britt and Ishma made their appearance there, patched and clean. The walk of two miles in rough weather gave them a reputation among the faithful. They enjoyed the honor guiltily, knowing they would not have sacrificed a day of sunshine in such approved fashion.

"Sacrifice" was the right word for it. Ishma's familiarity with the Bible had not enslaved her mind. Granny Stark had taken care of that. From the time that Ishma had begun to stumble through the sacred chapters for Granny's pleasure, she had been interrupted with such comments as "That's not decent!" "I don't have to believe that, thank God!" "They've got things mixed up there, the heavenly an' the airthly." "Mark that fer skippin', darter. We'll not read that twict." But the old lady's most frequent dissent was, "They're tellin' lies on Him now. God ain't like that. *I know Him.*"

She was no less free with comments of approval whenever the text coincided with her own ideas of right and wrong, or induced an elevation of spirit. "That's the truth, darter. Don't fergit that." "Stop right now, darter, an' git that by heart." "That makes a body want to fly. I'd trade these ol' feet fer the wings right now."

Sarah Stark knew how to explain these contradictions. The word of God came from God, but men had to put it in a book. "It all had to be set down by men, here an' yan. An' they's jest human; they mixed it up, like humans always do. Sometimes they didn't know no better, an' sometimes they's mean-natered an' wanted an excuse for their meanness. A body has to know how to pick over it." And Granny knew.

So Ishma's mind had put out its tendrils freely, with no choking discomfort from Hebraic tradition. What was welcome to her spirit, she received; what would trammel it, she let alone. It was not always easy for her in a community where people were held more accountable for their belief than for their actions. Religion was a revered theory, apart from life and much too good for it, but never to be disputed. When sticklers for the word tried to heckle her, saying you had to believe all or none, she would answer, "Well, Granny didn't, and you daren't say she's in hell." They didn't dare, for Granny in her grave was still powerful, and Ishma's untroubled smile closed the question.

Britt's Biblical education had been different, but the result was about the same. While his father lived no night passed without his listening to a chapter of the Bible, carefully selected. He had never opened the book himself, and he had grown up with no knowledge of the human abysses contained between the revered covers. The Book had been given to man for his good and for his happiness; and he knew that he felt best and happiest the more certainly that he felt within himself the flowing tides of freedom. So, in the depth of his mind, he had a sort of holy sanction for his Sundays on the hills.

On the days when he and Ishma went to preachin' they would come home with a cheated feeling. They enjoyed the neighbors and the hand-shaking. They didn't care at all if their shabby clothes drew glances, curious or concerned; there were others present who were more shabby and hardly so clean. They didn't mind when someone asked Ishma if she thought she could make Britt "stay with it," having in mind his well-known aversion to feet "with roots to 'em." But they did feel emotionally run down and shoddy by the time they were starting for home; they didn't climb the long "two-mile hill" with hearts lifting their feet, as happened when they walked on Silver Ridge, or faced the cleansing wind that blew forever through Turkle Gap. By the time they were home, with another week of steady toil before them, Ishma would feel that something must be done to save the day. Perhaps she would go to the kitchen, and after a careful skirmish apply her wits and skill to contriving a more interesting supper than the buttermilk and cold pone which Bainie had intended to set before the family. She knew from the Health and Food bulletins which the children brought from school, that the corn-product and milk made a wholesome meal, and she and Britt could go to it with relish after a dinnerless day spent in scaling Whiteface, or some other rarely visited spur; but a drab, un-eventful preachin' day had to be enlivened. There was one rainy third Sunday in June, seven weeks after her marriage, that she long remembered. The garden beans were still too slim for plucking, and Laviny stood ready to check any grabbling hand reaching for her early potatoes. Ishma searched the cellar — old Frady's cellar — but it had been cleaned out, even of turnip kraut and pickled beans. She found a few handfuls of dried apples, which she picked over, scalded, and cooked to a healthy red. She would make tasty turnovers of them, if there was any flour left — and there was! While she was standing in the centre of the kitchen wondering what else, Nettie called out that they had found two little striped punkins in the hay in the barn. Ishma had them brought in. They might be — yes, they were — mountain cymlings. She would bake them by Granny's recipe. "A cymlin'," said Granny, "is as near to nothin' as a snowball on the forestick when it ain't properly cooked, but cook it right, an' there's yer barbecue!" It had to be cut a certain way, round and round, and baked with no more than a rain-drop o' water. The inside was smeared with molasses, if you were out of brown sugar, and a smidgeon o' sweet-basil. Her basil bush was still in the back-yard, protected from rooting pigs by Ishma's careful picketing. The middle of the cymling ought to be filled with rice and butter, but there wasn't any rice, and Laviny would not permit a raid on the breakfast butter. The dish was meant to be served with ham, but Ishma knew how to substitute fat-back by slicing it, rolling the slices in flour, and frying them a crisp brown. The baking of the cymling would take a long time, but they had reached home early and it could be done before dark. The children were gay through the hours of expectation, playing "peep granny" around Ishma and the table, or climbing over Britt who had piled up the wood in the corner of the kitchen and sat feeding the stove and looking at Ishma. They straddled his shoulders, and tried to balance on his head, but were shaken off and caught, with hands of iron, on their way to sudden death. Ishma specially provided for the younger children by wheedling Laviny out of a quart of new milk from her pail as she came in from the milk-gap, and pouring it over thin slices of corn-pone which had been heated through until they were daintily light.

All this gayety and invention kept Britt and Ishma from going to bed depressed, and in the morning they rose with good spirit to face six days of hard labor. But they missed the full elation that came from a day spent in the woods, or on a piny crest, or following sunny water to hidden falls. Those days, strung shiningly along from April to November, were set amid the others like the blue beads which the children put here and there on their strings of chinkapin.

Ishma's terror of marriage was utterly forgotten. Mated wholly, spirit and body, she and Britt harnessed their youth to the daily load and scarcely felt the tug of it. One morning Britt stopped in the furrow he was ploughing, looked about him, and halooed with all his might to the mountains, to the winding river valley, to the clouds of foaming pearl, and to all the happy spirits of time and eternity, who surely had nothing on *him*. Ishma, three hundred yards away with her grubbing hoe, stopped too, and answered him with lines from one of their favorite songs:

> *The world is round, and I'm going round it,*
> *The sky is high, and I'm going to climb it,*
> *With my dear love on my shoulder!*

Ishma's voice needed an unlimited horizon for its full, clear music. In the meeting-house, or around home, she had trouble in "smothering her notes down." Britt listened while she sang, then took up the plough-handles and went on, his heart swelling with happiness till it gave him a joyous hurt.

Another day he looked across the upturned ground at Ishma and saw her in one of her motionless moments gazing out over the farthest peaks as if she could see beyond the dimmest outline, the most feathery azure light. She looked so remote that he couldn't bear it. Hastily he fastened his lines to the plough-beam and went running over the pungent furrows, leaping two, three, sometimes four at a step. When she drew her eyes back until her gaze embraced him there was no break in their light; he was part of her vision. He stood there feeling safe again and a little sheepish.

"What you want, Britt?" She knew very well. He was staring at her his eyes clinging, and spilling a joyful warmth on the air. How could he help it? She was superbly lovely. A summer flush lit the transparent bronze of her cheek. Her short curls were burnished black in the sun. Her eyes, that could be so intellectually grey and detached, were warm and sheltering. The silver-green in their depth, that sometimes swam bewilderingly, was calm as faith. Their light flowed out steadily under the shading dark lashes; while the gleam from Britt's eyes was breaking in eager bits and tangling in his curving, bronze fringe.

"I thought you were going to run away," he said, throwing his head back the better to laugh at himself.

"Kid!" She mothered him in her arms, but gave him a bride's lips.

This sort of thing had a miraculous effect on the crop. The neighbors ceased their doubtful prophecies and began to brag on the way Britt was keeping at it. He read with Ishma the Farm Bulletins and the *Progressive Farmer*. They made great and many plans, that came to dreamy blossom and fruit. Next year they would put the old "top-field" in soy beans and begin their programme for a permanent pasture. When they got that they could put in a strain of Hereford or Durham for beef cattle, and

69

sell one off any time they needed a little money. Whatever was heavy enough for beef could be sold any day just by driving it to Carson. They couldn't ship anything, for shipping costs were too heavy. Prices were very low in Carson, but they were sure, and a little money would go far on the mountain. The prospect helped to console Ishma for the loss of Jersey Belle. Of course they intended to have Jerseys for the home dairy some day, but you couldn't count on selling milk-stock in a pinch as you could beef cattle. The Hereford strain would be better than Durham they finally decided, after weeks of happy debate, and it began to be talked about that Britt was going into the business of raising "White Hooferds," the local name for the red-colored breed, based with graphic adaptation on the bit of white above the hooves.

But prosperity lay in the future. Dream-fields were assuring, but their harvest couldn't be gathered. For the present they had to make a debt at Gaffney's, and part of the crop must go in payment as soon as harvested. In another year Britt would build a rat-proof crib, so they could hold their surplus until Spring and sell high. They were careful to keep their debt down to the lowest possible sum, and they put the same limit on Bainie that they did on themselves, though that required some watching.

"That debt will come out of our crop," Ishma informed her, "and you'll have to skimp the same as we do."

Summer went by in a whirl of toil and laughter, with only a few days for fishing, and those priceless Sundays when nothing shut them away from each other. Towards fall Ishma's step was not so light, though still sure and steady. Her figure was changing just a little. Britt had been so proud of her figure, with its strong, spare muscles, like his own, and not an ounce of useless flesh anywhere; just grace and strength. He wanted no change in it.

"You are not afraid, sweetheart?"

"No, Britt. Are you?"

They were lying on the sunny side of Blackspur, where chestnut trees abounded; their leaves a burnt yellow and their nuts falling ripe.

"I say I'm not! Listen, Ishma, there's another chestnut-burr

70

droppin'." It rattled through the tree, and the chestnuts flew out and tapped, tapped over the ground. "When I hear nuts fall in the woods like that, it makes me feel rich. The whole world is rich. Ever'body 's got enough. The Lord is looking out for his earth, and nobody is going hungry. That's the way I feel."

'It's a good feeling," she answered, thinking that a man had to do a pretty big part of the foraging. He had to get to the tree before the squirrels, and some years the nuts were all wormy when he got there. But she loved the happy mood in Britt too well to discount it with any thought of hers; so she repeated, "A good feeling, Britt. I'm not afraid our baby won't be taken care of."

Britt tingled joyously. It was the first time that she had said "our baby." Women, he found, didn't talk much about such things, if they were all like Ishma. For himself, he wanted to blab it to the heavens. His baby and Ishma's !

They were very comfortable on the great bed of brown leaves that he had piled up in the sunshine; so far away from Jim and Bainie, and Jim and Bainie's seven children; so far away from the crowded little house and Laviny's untiring curiosity. Laviny was very well satisfied as the days went, but there was no snaffling the unbridled habit of her tongue.

"Next year we'll be to ourselves," said Britt, after a long, full silence.

"Three of us." Her smile was so dear that he had to kiss her again, and he did it fiercely, as if his kiss must reach down to her heart.

"Look at the old sun," she said. "How unfair he is ! So many hollows down there with no light at all, and others full of blue gold. See Jabe Minson's house there to the east; it's been dark for half an hour. And over here on Turkey Creek, old Ans Brown's place is shiny and warm. Uncle Jabe is the best man in the valley, too, and old Ans is the meanest."

"Maybe the Lord knows more about 'em than we do, and parcels it out like it ought to be."

"It's not the Lord, Britt. It was just good sense that made Ans choose Turkey hollow, and bad judgment that put uncle Jabe over there in the dark. He won't even get the early morning sun, 'cause of that little mountain butting in there to the east of him."

Britt thought this over. "I'm going to let you pick our place, Ishma. Our house will set right where you say. I won't have a blasted thing to do with it, except to come along afterwards an' swear I couldn't a beat it."

"We'll pick it together, Britt." She moved over to him and dropped her head on his arm, her face turned to the sky. "That's the third flock of geese I've seen going South today. They're making straight for the Nantahalas. They'll have to fly higher or they'll bump. If one dropped now he'd come right down over High Lonesome. Then Judd Wimble would come out with his gun and kill it."

"He wouldn't get much. Blue strings an' bone. Funny how they stay north till they're nearly starved 'fore they set out flyin'."

"String and bone can fly better'n fat, maybe."

"Ducks are different. You can eat ducks."

"They're low fliers, and stop oftener to eat, I reckon."

"You've always got a reason for things," admired Britt.

"I guess my reason 's no 'count half the time. I don't know enough."

She was touching a sore longing, as Britt knew.

"You know what we're goin' to do sometime, Ish-my-own? We'll get us a flivver an' go down to the University. We'll camp in the flivver an' go to summer school."

"O, Britt! They wouldn't let us. We couldn't get into *anything*."

"They've got classes now that *anybody* can get into. That new school-teacher told me about it when she come up with Sam an' Nettie."

"I didn't see her. I left out when she 's there. Bainie had the house in such a fix I was ashamed to stay."

"You keer too much about things like that, honey. Let 'em mess up the place all they want to. We've got the mountains to be clean in."

She didn't hear him because she had heard it so often. Her mind was on that summer dream, trailing it, transfixing it.

72

"Britt, do you think we could ever go ? Just once, and I'd be satisfied."

"Sure we could go — and we *will !*"

She had lifted her head and shoulders, but now she sank back with an achieving sigh, as grateful to Britt as if his prophecy had been an actual gift.

Sunshine was still pricking out gold spots over the farther blue slopes and the nearer, scattered farms. On the river was one spot like yellow glass, and a blood-red maple dotting it. Some of the coves were filling with mist that dropped like silvery quilts, where young wood-things might tuck into bed, while the old-things prowled for a breakfast to bring home. Though the leaves were rusty and falling, up there where Ishma and Britt were lying, all of the lower ridges were swelling and flowing with color. Ishma turned her eyes to the sky to rest them. A flock of woolly little clouds were puzzling about in the north-east.

"It looks like they'd tear themselves to pieces on those peaks," she said, "but they don't. Soon as they hit one they wind about it and hug it as if that was what they were looking for. Watch that soft, little one now. It got its white breast split open, and there it is with two arms around the blue peak, not hurt a bit."

"Are you hungry, Ishma ?"

"No, why ?"

"I was thinkin' we wouldn't try to get home for supper."

"I was thinkin' that too. It's warm here in the leaves."

"We'll play hoot-owl. You can count all that holler on the west and south, an' I'll count all on the north and east."

"I guess so ! You know the big hoot-owl tree is north of us."

"But hoot-owl cove is down there in the south. We'll start about even. Hope you're not going to mind about supper. After dark we'll hear warblers an' swallers an' robins goin' south, twitterin' an' fussin'. Wonder why they travel so much more at night than in the day time."

"They have to eat in the day time. They're little and have to fuel up."

"We'll go home by the 'simmon patch an' get us a 'possum. There's been two or three big frosts. We'll shore find one. I'm sort o' hungry for a fat, baked 'possum, like you can cook."

73

"We haven't got the dog."

"I'll tree him myself. The moon 'll be shinin'."

"The moon won't be up for hours."

"That'll give you time to tell me some o' Granny Stark's old tales, when we get tired o' hoot-owl. What you lookin' at, Ishma ?"

"I've been watching that sumac down in that old field. It's the reddest one I ever saw. Maybe it's Sumaka herself standing down there."

"Sumaka ?"

"The Indian girl. I learned about her from old Mag Standing Deer."

"The Cherokee that lives in Bat Hollow ?"

"Yes. You want to hear about Sumaka ?"

"Sure I do !"

"She was so lovely that all of the Indian boys brought her gifts, but it was Firebird that she chose for her husband. He was the tallest and handsomest of them all. After she was married she liked to talk and laugh in the other wigwams, and run about as she had done when she was a maiden. Everybody made her welcome, though they knew Firebird didn't like it. Her smile was as bright as running water with the sun on it, and her eyes so black that they made a crow feather look grey. Firebird wouldn't look at her in company, because everybody could see in his eyes that he was a fool for love. Sumaka kept running away and hurting his heart until he couldn't bear it any longer. He went to Ojumpa, an old man who had skill in all things that can come between a man and his woman. Firebird begged his help, saying that his heart had turned weak as a maiden's. He wanted a man's heart again, so that he could go to the hunt when the bears were fat, and could go with the men when the moon was right for spearing fish in the big river. But most of all he wanted Sumaka to find her joy only in him and forget the wigwams of the tribe. 'That is easy,' Ojumpa told him, and made a brew of magic leaves which Firebird was to swallow before he lay down to sleep. Then he was not to speak to Sumaka for three days. On the third morning she would put her arms about him and vow never to leave the wigwam unless he bade her. It happened as Ojumpa said. On the third morning, when Firebird felt Sumaka's arms around him, he leapt up, took his gun, and set off into the woods. He forgot the hot drink and the meal-pone which she had made ready for him on the bread-rock. He had a man's heart again. When she saw him going from her, she stood for a minute watching him, not believing what her eyes told her. Then without waiting to eat or drink she ran after him. When she called to him he hurried faster, and was soon out of sight in the woods. She followed his track all day, and at night came upon him where he slept. When she knelt by him he woke in anger. 'Get you back to the wigwam,' he said, 'and see that you make me three willow baskets before I come.' She went aside and hid behind a tree. Next morning her arms were about him when he awoke. He threw her off, took up his gun, and set off, running swiftly. She ran too, but he went faster and faster. He came to the big river, swam easily across it, and began to climb the mountain on the other side. There was a little old field at the foot of the mountain, and a hut that was tumbling down. Sumaka swam the river, but she nearly drowned. She was so tired before she reached the other side that she could hardly pull herself up to rest on the grass. She called towards the old hut for help, but nobody lived there. Far up on the mountain side she could see Firebird, still climbing, and never looking back at her. She started to cross the field, but after a few steps she was unable to lift her feet. She stood there, looking at Firebird, and every minute feeling her heart grow bigger. At last Firebird looked back to see if she was climbing after him. He couldn't see her anywhere, but there in the bare old field stood a blazing sumac, red as a woman's heart. He never saw Sumaka again."

Britt turned his head and pressed his face against Ishma's shoulder.

"Why, Britt, what's the matter?"

He lifted his head. "I was just thinking. What would I do if you were to run away from me, Ishma? That poor little Indian girl, she'd know how I'd feel."

75

"More likely I'll be left and you'll run away, Britt. That's what everybody said when we were married. You know your feet loved the road, honey."

"Ay, they did. But I've forgot all about it now. That was a good story, Ishma. I could mighty nigh believe it. I hope old Firebird's heart got broke in two."

"He died, old Mag said, and made them bury him under the blazing bush. And the bush was named for Sumaka."

IT WAS nearly four hours later when they reached the persimmon patch in a castaway field. Britt began to creep along among the saplings, but Ishma hung back. "I'll stand out here by the fence," she said, and Britt went on with lowered enthusiasm.

Ishma never wanted anything killed. "What about lions an' catamounts an' rats an' fleas ?" he sometimes asked her. "They'd take the world away from us if we let 'em alone." And she had no answer except that she couldn't bear bloody work.

She knew that her man wasn't bad about hunting and killing, whatever he might say. He would join a fox hunt perhaps once or twice a year, and he liked an occasional 'possum. But when he caught one he killed it instantly by a stroke of his stiffened hand across the back of its neck, and never teased or tormented his catch as so many of the boys liked to do. At heart, she believed, he disliked bloody work almost as much as she did.

After a few minutes under the saplings he called out that he had his 'possum and was shaking it down. A few more minutes, and he came to the fence, but he was empty-handed.

"I thought I'd got a big fat one," he said, "but when I shook him down he turned out to be an' old mother 'possum with eight little 'uns in her bag. Beats me how she could climb around with that load. Looks like she'd leave 'em at home when she goes up to feed. Had me fooled all right."

"We can wait and get a young one, Britt. Doesn't make any difference how long we stay out."

Britt seemed rather solemn in the moonlight, and a bit ashamed. "No, that old lady looked at me so funny. Don't believe I can eat 'possim for a month or two." He put his arm

76

around Ishma's growing waist, and they moved silently down the hill.

When that first year's crop was harvested it proved as abundant as its promise. Britt walked among his neighbors feeling their commending eyes upon him. Gaffney shook his hand when he brought his first load of corn down to pay on the family debt. That debt was larger than Britt expected to find it. There were twelve in the household, not counting the company that Jim's affliction brought in, and four of the children were going to school. However inexorably they limited their spending, some needs had to be met. And Gaffney, always liberal of heart, had met them. Britt and Ishma decided to pay him in full, and do without any new winter clothes. They had to buy a cow, but cows were cheap that year, and Abe Marsh let them have one with a heifer calf for thirty bushels of corn. That was as far as the crop would stretch, aside from the part they must keep for bread and feed. But Jim was getting well, and wouldn't need any more money for medicine and liniment and invalid's kick-shaws. The doctor had told them two months before that he wouldn't have to come again, and that immense drain was stopped. Britt sold his gun and laid the money away for the time when Ishma would need it. They felt even with the world, and were not afraid to start a new debt at Gaffney's. This was necessary because Britt intended to put in most of the winter clearing new-ground. They knew that the old fields would not repeat their generosity another year. It wasn't possible to put all of the "stalk-land" in orchard grass and sweet clover as they had planned, for seed was too costly. Orchard grass would make good summer pasture, and when it died down there would be the green winter clover for the cattle. They expected to have their own ox-team to feed the next year, and not be dependent on neighbors for plough-brutes. But it would take fifty dollars to seed the land. That would have to wait.

It was February and bitter cold when Edward Britton Hensley was born. Ishma knew she would never forget how cold it was, and how cramped they were for room. She had wanted Laviny to give up her bed in the middle room and let her be sick there, but her mother said there was no use beginning to humor her,

she'd have to get used to things like any married woman. So
Ishma kept her own bed in the corner of the big room where Jim
and Bainie, with their two least ones, occupied another corner,
and Sam, Andy and Ben, another. Nettie and Ellie slept with
Laviny in the middle room. When Ishma's hour approached, the
children all were sent off to the neighbors for a day and night.
But they trooped back too soon for Ishma's peace.

"Can't you send them out a little while?" she asked Bainie,
feebly hopeful.

"They've jest been out. I kain't send 'em right back an' the
air hangin' with ice. They're all keepin' back there in the
kitchen. I reckon you don't want the whole house."

"Sounds like they're right on the other side o' the wall, banging
and yelping."

"You'll have to git aholt o' yersef, Ishmalee," said her mother,
"an' not let Britt make a fool o' ye."

Britt went up to the barn where he could swear unimpeded.
He wouldn't let Ishma sit up for two weeks, although Laviny insisted on her "comin' out of it" the ninth day. He and Laviny had
their first quarrel, but Britt suddenly became very quiet when he
saw tears pushing from under Ishma's eyelashes. He went to
her and whispered, "Next time we'll be to ourselves," and with a
vehemence that bewildered him she had answered, "There'll be
no next time!"

Ned was the finest baby that had ever come into the family.
Laviny admitted it, and when he was old enough to return her
attachment, she pushed Ishma aside and took possession of him.
"You'll have plenty more," she said. "I'll look out fer this'n."

Within a month after his birth, Ishma had regained her bloom
and her strength, though she was a little confused in her thinking. Life, the future, her plans, were not so clear as they had
been. She felt mentally clamped down, in the way that she had
felt physically cramped the night Ned was born. How she had
wanted room for her body! The walls had pressed in against
her, the presence of the people, taking up good space, smothered
her.

Jim, who could hobble about by February, came in one night
saying that he had fastened the cow in a stall where she couldn't

78

thrash around. She'd find a calf before morning, and if they left her out she'd go to the very top o' the pasture and they'd have a masterous time getting her down. Cows always wanted the whole earth an' sky too when they's droppin' a calf. He'd shore fixed this 'n until she couldn't more'n switch her tail.

That night, while Jim and Bainie were snoring, Ishma slipped from the side of Britt, climbed up to the barn, and let the moaning cow out of the narrow, unclean stall. Next morning the cow was found with her calf at the head of the pasture, and great was the stir over the trouble she gave them. Jim had a mind to give her one good lashing, but he didn't; and it was Britt who finally coaxed her down to the barn lot. Ishma sat by the fire, holding Ned, and smiling.

The second year passed more slowly and less goldenly. They had the new-ground, and they bought a yoke of oxen on time. Britt mended the old wagon and made it do. Now and then he hauled a load of wood to Beebread and got a little money for it. But there were others as needy, and living nearer than he, watching for a chance to supply the limited market.

Clearing the new-ground had been a continuous battle for Britt. He had selected a slope that rolled eastward in the sun, and furnished a pretty expanse for the plough. But the soil was full of concealed roots and snirls. For years that patch of woods had provided the family with fuel. Saplings were cut as fast as they grew, and rooty sprouts sprang from them until the soil was veined with the stubborn tangles. But much worse was the aftermath of a cut tree. Britt found it easy to grub a standing tree, for he could loosen the upper side and its own weight would lay it down the hill, its roots uptorn. But the cut-overs — old stumps with their dozens of healthy, determined sprouts — were a different problem. Some of them he reluctantly left with their sprangly clutch untroubled; but next year he meant to get some dynamite an' fix 'em ! A few giant poplars remained of the ancient woods. These he cut without help, but he had to call on Si Welch for aid with the sawing and rolling, before he could get the cuts down to the edge of the field. Some day he would log them to a sawmill. There was good money in sound old yellow poplar. Si offered to furnish one team and help take them out for half the profits. But Britt was cultivating foresight. Next year he would have a strong team of his own — he had his eye on the pair of mules he wanted — and he would hire another for a few days, pocketing all of the profits less the hire of one team. Si went off and advertised to the community that Britt was shore a surprise, the way he was layin' his mind to it, 'long with his shoulders.

On days when the ground was too deeply frozen for grubbing, Britt would pile and burn brush, or take the oxen and sled and bring wood down from the clearing. The woodpile grew high, and Ishma turned her head and smiled when she heard Laviny say, "If Granpap Frady could see that woodpile he'd think Britt wuz his own blood-kin."

Ploughing-time brought him to the most vexatious part of his task. The plough moved jerkily along among the too numerous stumps and the roots that had been left in the ground. In those days Britt began to swear a little. He had never been an oathy man, but he couldn't take *everything* dumb. His temper was most tried when Jim sauntered up to the new-ground to watch him labor. Jim's back was still strangely feeble, though Doctor Stinnett had assured him that it was in trim for work. Whenever he talked of the clearing he used the first person plural. "We burnt a lot o' brush today." "We're goin' to git at the big logs tomorr'." "We got the best o' seven stumps this morning." "I'd like fer Alec to come up an' open his eyes on what we're doin' to that ground." "Well, we're goin' to stick the plough in her tomorr'." Britt would get sore and his face grow cloudy.

"I reckon by next year," he said to Ishma, "Jim 'll be talkin' about *his* clearin'."

Ishma slipped an arm about his neck. "We won't be here more'n two years longer. We'll make enough out o' that new-ground this year and next to leave on."

But that year, even with the prolific new-ground, nothing could be saved. The corn grew high and strong, with two ears to the stalk. Jim invited all and sundry to come up and look at his oudaceous crop, and Ishma and Britt kept incessantly after the weeds. But when the harvest was in, and they had settled the

80

store-debt and finished paying for the ox-team, they looked blankly at each other. Britt clenched his scarred hands. "We'll try it another year, Ish-my-own, but I'll make Jim divide the fields. I'll take the new-ground, and leave him ever'thing he had when I come on the place."

"That's what you'll have to do, Britt," Ishma agreed. But they kept their plan a secret until the next Spring. Then Laviny came out in strong opposition. "Jim will do his part this year," she said, with groundless optimism. "No use cuttin' up the land like we's two fam'lies. You an' Britt air welcome to stay here, but you know what the Bible says about a house divided agin itself, an' I'm not goin' to have it."

She saw no injustice in Ishma and Britt casting all their strength into the family struggle. A family had to work together. "Some members was pushin', an' some had to be hepped along." She'd worked as hard as she could all her life, an' all she got was a living. They were getting that much, and ought to be satisfied. They'd have to be anyway, if they stayed on her farm.

After a panicky conference they decided that they must stay one more year. If they left they could take only enough corn for their bread. The implements, and work-oxen, must be left behind. They would have to ask credit for as much as one hoe.

"I'll tell you, honiest," said Britt, "I'll go to the lumber camps after the crop is laid by, and work out enough to get us a start. We can earn our keep on the farm, and what I get I'll put away."

They smiled at each other, but by this time there were reservations back of their smiles.

That third summer, in August, Ishma gave birth to twins, a boy and a girl. They were tiny things, but throve mightily, and Ishma watched their little bodies grow and tried to take joy in them. She had come to her time in the same bed and the same corner of the big room. There had been no money for the doctor, for Britt, before he received his first pay-check, had come out of the lumber camp with an excruciating case of inflammatory rheumatism. Rain had fallen every day while he was in the primeval woods on the slopes of the Smokies. The men working with the heavy timber, got excessively heated, the rain soaked their clothes through, and at night in the shacks there was no place for so many to dry out properly. They pulled on their wet clothes in the morning, saying that the rain or sweat one would soon have 'em wet anyhow, and went to work. But every few days a man would drop out with lumbago, or rheumatism, or "quare shootin' pains," and be hauled home, another winter burden on his penniless wife.

When Britt was struck down he was astonished and resentful. Never in his life had he been ill. At first he was more shocked than suffering, but after a few days the pain was great enough to usurp all other sensation. He was afraid that he would scream and cry like a baby. To forfend this he made up a funny song which he would shout on his highest possible note whenever he felt a pang coming. But when he got home he had to be quiet because of Ishma. Her nerves couldn't stand a fuss. He couldn't lie on her bed, and another had been borrowed for him from aunt Cynthy. It was set up in the fourth corner of the room, and there he lay, biting his lips and tongue, while his twins were coming into the world, and Ishma seemed to be going out of it. His darling, going out, and he couldn't reach her, couldn't put out one finger to hold her.

He had sent a letter to Doctor Stinnett telling him that he couldn't pay soon, but asking him to come — to come to Ishma. And the doctor was there, standing over her, trying to hold her back. But she was going. Her feet were in the river. Strong, laughing, invincible Britt fainted; and nobody noticed him.

But Ishma didn't go. Thirty minutes passed, and the doctor knew she was staying with them. Smiling, he came over to Britt's bed.

"Look here, boy, I told you to be quiet, but I didn't tell you to play dead on us."

Then he saw, and there was more flying around. Laviny, Bainie, and the neighbor women, jumped about under the doctor's orders, and Britt was brought to. He came back with a spasm of pain, but was too weak for the shriek that tried to escape his lips. He looked across to Ishma's bed. Her eyes were open, watching him. He could read what they were saying. "I'm not leaving you. Let's fight through." And Britt fought.

Within a fortnight they were both sitting up, looking life in the face; weak of limb, debt-heavy, and with three children swinging on their taut nerves. It had been two months since they had talked together with no one near, and they were hungry of heart and mind for each other. It was only through each other that they could find reassurance for their shaken foundations. But it was more than a week after they got up before they had their opportunity to be alone.

One afternoon Laviny was down at Cynthy's, and Bainie and Jim went to the field to gather a few rows of early corn which was ripe enough for the mill. All of last year's harvest had been fed out. They took the older children to help, and Nettie had the younger ones up at their playhouse.

It was a warm day in September. With chairs and pillows, Ishma had fixed a bed on the porch for the twins, where they were considerately asleep. They were ravenous, noisy, healthy babies. Ishma knew she would have to drink more milk and cocoa or she wouldn't be able to feed them. She loathed cocoa, and the cow was going dry. But she couldn't think of that now. She wanted to sit there by Britt and the babies, with Ned asleep on the floor, making a pillow of her adored feet. Laviny was his slave, but all of his admiration was reserved for his mother. Britt put his chair close to hers. He was nearly free of pain now; only one ankle kept him crippled, and that would soon be all right. They looked at each other, and Britt leaned over to kiss her solemnly, as after a long separation.

East, west, north, the hills rose about the cabin, but in the south-east the slopes parted, making a wide, downward lane through which they could see the valley with its winding, yellow river. Far away, where the river was lost to sight, rose the blue, mobile outlines of the Nantahalas, changing always with sun and cloud. At the foot of their own mountain they could see the railroad trestle that crossed the crystal water of the Nantahala where it merged with the yellow flow of the Little Tennessee. The children liked to gather and watch whenever a train puffed across the trestle. Very small it looked, a little toy train, and several times Ned had undertaken to knock it off with a pebble vehemently thrown. He was truly a robust youngster. Doctor Stinnett had remarked when he was born that he would be tremendous, and Ishma had told him that she hoped he would be fine, not big. "He'll be both," said the doctor. "No worry."

But now he was asleep with his head on her feet. She couldn't understand how she and Britt so quickly had knarled the smooth skein of their union, entangling it with three blameless children. There were times when she felt that they couldn't be her own. Surely that was impossible ! But they were lovely and sweet; and she found her heart wrapping about them like an inseparable sheath. By and by, she supposed, life would seem natural again. One thing she couldn't bear — for Britt to be apologetic about it.

"Never mind, my man," she said, "you can stand up to the job."

"This ankle looks like it."

"You'll be as well as ever in a week or two. And one thing is certain about the future anyway. You are not going into the Smokies again. Not ever !"

"But we'll have to get *some* money."

"Not that way. You see what's happened. Instead of a start, we are down deeper in debt. And Bainie and Jim are actin' up 'cause we've been sick, as if you hadn't earned the right to be sick a year, if it fell on you to be ! What you got on your mind, Britt ?"

"Ishma," he began, with lowered voice, though no one was there to overhear, "Bert Wiggins is goin' to the mills. That's what Si was talkin' about when we's settin' out there on that log yesterday."

"Cindy Wiggins has always wanted to do that."

"Their place 'll be for rent." He was almost whispering now. Ishma's heart thrilled and leapt.

"We'll go look at it soon as you can walk."

They were silent. All the little things they had intended to talk about were covered up with this one big thing. The store-debt, the unpaid doctor, the failing cow, the leak-all-over roof, Jim's domineering, Bainie's jealousy, Laviny's unfairness; all these bothers would be non-existent for them if they could get their own place. So why talk about them ?

Bert wanted somebody to take over his crop, his two cows, his hogs, and most of his household goods, and give him a third of everything made on the place each year. That's what Si said. It was a wonderful chance.

84

In one week, instead of two, Britt and Ishma were on their way to look the place over. Each of them carried a twin, for they might be gone all day. Ned was left with Laviny. The farm was nearly three miles away, about five coves west of old Frady's cabin, but much lower down the mountain. Before reaching it they had to pass the Jack Wiggins' place. Jack was a brother of Bert's, but a mighty different sort, folks said. He was out at his woodpile in front of his house when the homeseekers trudged up.

"Ef you're goin' to see Bert an' Cindy you might as well stop here," he told them. "They left ever'thing in my care."

"They're gone?"

"Started at daybreak yisterday. Cindy 'll be satisfied now, I reckon. She's been naggin' to go fer two year. Ef you're wantin' to rent the place, I'm the man to talk to."

"We'll go on and look at it," said Ishma. "Did Cindy leave her things?"

"She took most of 'em. They got a truck from Carson to haul 'em out. But you'll find some of her stuff over there. Enough fer young folks to begin with."

"What about the cows and hogs?" asked Britt.

"I got 'em, an' I'm ready to sell 'em fer cash to whoever wants 'em. I git a third fer my trouble. I'll put the price right, but it'll take cash to git 'em."

"Have you got the crop too?"

"I've got ever'thing, an' cash 'll git any of it."

They went on, their feet moving more heavily, until Ishma said, "It's fine to get a day off like this. Been a long time since we had one. Let's don't let anything spoil it."

"We won't," said Britt. "If the joke's on us, we'll not let the others do all the laughing."

They reached the desolate house. Its roof, peppered with holes, let the light through. No wonder Cindy wanted to leave it. There was a broken stove in the kitchen, propped up with rocks for three legs. Examination revealed that the fire-back was burnt out.

"I can cook on the fire-place the first year," Ishma declared valiantly.

"And I can roof the house," Britt grandly asserted. "The log-walls are good."

All the furniture left by Cindy consisted of a corner cupboard with the doors broken off, some rough shelves, and three chairs with the bottoms out. Shining pages of the *Woman at Home* flashed before Ishma, but she said bravely, "I can make furniture out of boxes and boards. Gaffney will give me all the boxes I want. It's only the crop that's bothering me. How are we going to live the first year ? We'll have our bread, but nothing else."

"I can get work by the day roundabout."

He couldn't keep back a flush as he said it. That was the lowest form of industrial life in the mountains — living by a day's work here and there. The pay was small, just what the neighbors could, or couldn't afford, and employment was uncertain as the weather.

"Count that out, Britt," she said sharply, the sharpness not intended for him, as he knew. The suspense left his eyes. "It'll take both of us working every day right at home to pull up this rundown place. We'll buy it on time. It won't do to put in a lot of work and let Bert sell to someone else. We'll do things here just as we planned for Cloudy Knob. I believe Gaffney will let us have a hundred dollars. Fifty now and fifty in the spring."

"That's our chance, Ishma."

"We'll go on to the forks of the road. I'll carry the twins home, and you go right down to Gaffney's. We'll have to know before somebody else takes the place."

They started back and found Jack Wiggins waiting for them.

"Think you'll take it?"

"If we can buy it," Britt answered.

"Course you can buy it. Two hundred and fifty down, an' three years' time on the rest is all Bert 's astin'."

"Two hundred and fifty down ?"

"That's mighty little. Bert says he don't want nobody comin' on his place, burnin' the wood an' haulin' it out, lessn they can show that much money."

"I'll write to Bert."

"No use. No use at all. He left orders with me. I've took

over the job o' lookin' after ever'thing, an' I'm goin' to do it."

"All right. Wish you luck !"

They started on, hope gone, their faces blown on by a dark wind. When they reached the forks of the road, Britt stopped and looked at Ishma. She shifted the baby she held, and took his arm.

"Come on," she said, and started up the hill. "We could get three hundred and fifty dollars about as easy as we could get a million."

They reached home tired and hungry; glad to sit down to the cold bread and beans left from supper. When Bainie heard how the trip had ended, she said she wasn't expecting them to find anything to suit their notions anyway. Jim was relieved to learn that the expedition had been fruitless. He asked nothing better than for Britt and Ishma to remain on Cloudy Knob sharing his work and debts while he retained his position as master of the place.

With Britt's return to health, life brightened for all on the farm. Ishma worked by his side in the harvest days. They carried the babies to the field, well wrapped, and made them comfortable on an old quilt spread over a pile of leaves, thick and dry. There they slept or cried as they chose, with little Ellie to guard them. Ishma's help was needed. The harvest was late and the ground-squirrels were ravaging the crop. Britt had planted the corn early, but the last working over had been left for Jim and the children, while he went to the lumber camp. As a consequence, the crab-grass had gone jumping and ramping down the rows, sucking the life out of the grain. And the gathering was late because Jim had waited for Britt's help. Between the ground-squirrels and the grass, they harvested a third less than the year before. Gaffney had to be satisfied with the debt not more than half covered; and Doctor Stinnett received a few bushels on his bill. With the remainder they could get through the winter, good luck and good health prevailing. They would have a large patch of turnip greens, and Ishma made two barrels of kraut from Laviny's big cabbage patch. Bainie had dried the apples. She liked to sit all day and peel, making Nettie carry out and in. The potatoes, both Irish and sweet, were no disappointment, and would last until Spring. Jim's hogs would provide meat. The eggs would cover small needs. But where would school-books and clothes come from ? And the farm itself was a voracious consumer. They would have to get a new plough, a new wagon, and a dozen other necessaries for work. With so much of the previous year's debt unpaid, they couldn't ask Gaffney for everything that they must have.

The merchants along the new highway were beginning to put delivery trucks on the road. Britt might get a job as driver. If he did it would be by favor only, for there were three or four applicants for every job. Before anything was decided, the "flu" came along and disorganized business and labor all over the county. Everybody had his work cut out under a master fate. The well nursed the sick until their turn came. Cloudy Knob seemed safe from infection, but Britt and Ishma were both skillful in nursing and Doctor Stinnett sent up a plea that they could not ignore. They went down together and did what they could. The disease was fiendishly fatal to young wives in childbirth, and Ishma's heart was hot with insurrection. A score of mothers died that winter in Wimble County. Ishma and Britt went among the neediest and most inaccessible families. At Jabe Minson's there were seven little children. An eighth child and the mother lay dead on the bed. The father, in another bed, could scarcely speak. The eldest girl and boy, eleven and twelve years old, were out picking up wood. The other five sat on a long bench against the wall, each with head dropped on the shoulder of the next child, like chickens in a row before a cold rain, and they were all asleep. Ishma pointed to them and began to cry, clinging to Britt.

When they reached home at midnight, Laviny and Bainie were up doctoring the twins for the croup. Laviny told of how she had kept them closely wrapped in their box before the fire. They were in a good, warm sweat when she lay down, she said. She had to lay down because she'd been awake with her rheumatism the whole of the night before. An' that Bainie stayed in the kitchen an' let the fire in the middle room go smack out. Not a spark when she woke up an' heard the twins a chokin'.

Bainie was loud in self-defense. "I couldn't be in two rooms at

88

onct. I had an awful washin' an' was finishin' up by lamp-light. I was doin' yer babies' things too, Ish. Nobody can say it was my fault if they've got the truth in 'em." She went on and on, with Laviny's tongue slashing into her protest, until Ishma begged them to hush. "I'm not blaming anybody. We've got to save them, that's all."

Useless to send for a doctor. They had tried for half the night to get one for Jabe Minson. Every doctor in the county had ten times more calls than he could answer. Laviny had been busy with home remedies, all that she knew, but the croup had fastened too tightly on the little throats before it was discovered. Bainie stood in helpless horror, still muttering in her own defense. Ishma was hearing nothing but her babies' hoarse struggles; seeing nothing but their clutching hands and little, twisted bodies. Her agony had a brief watch. Friendly death came in less than half an hour after the return of the parents.

They were buried in the same graveyard with Sarah Starkweather. Ishma walked towards home with Britt, chattering immoderately. He hurried her along, hoping that the few neighbors who had been at the burying ground would not hear her. She talked and talked, her cheeks a fiery red and her hands burning. Britt was in a daze himself, but it dawned upon him that she had fever. He got her home and tried to make her go to bed, but she went into the kitchen, saying that she was going to cook something to eat. She would make all sorts of good things, and he must go to the barn and look for eggs. She wanted to make a custard. The babies could eat custard.

"The babies !" cried Britt.

"Yes, our little babies — the twins, you smooth idiot ! They like custard."

Britt grabbed her in his arms and carried her, struggling, to her bed. He had to force her to lie down. He had to be cruel.

"If you don't lie still, I'll get a rope and tie you."

She believed him, and began to cry; but she was very still. He laid himself by her, his arm across her chest, and wondered how in the world he was going to get a doctor up there. Stinnett was sick, done out with overwork. Ishma had pneumonia, Britt felt sure, and he had nursed several cases of that. If it wasn't very bad, he could get along without a doctor. He'd have to, no doubt, whatever the need for one. The fever turned out to be not so bad. He soon had it under control; but Ishma remained in bed with no desire to get up. Her mind was on her babies, so suddenly taken from her.

"Hit's a sin to be questionin' the Lord's will like you do, Ishmalee," remonstrated Laviny.

"The Lord ? Why didn't he take care of my babies when I was out in the night doing his work ?"

Laviny shook with fright. "Now you jest shet up. Nobody's goin' talk thataway in my house."

"I'll not, mother. I'll just think it."

But a change came. One day she called Britt to the bed and told him that she intended to get up. She felt much better, she said.

"You look it too, honey. Honest, you do !"

"I thought of something last night, and I've been hovering it all the morning. Just suppose, Britt, that I'd been taken, like Ann Minson, and the twins left here ?"

"That's what I've been tellin' you, sweetheart."

"Have you ? I don't reckon I heard you. It came on me last night, right out of the sky, and I wouldn't let it go. I've been lying here bein' thankful. It's almost enough to make a body believe in God."

"Why, honiest, you do believe in him !"

"Do I ?" She laughed, and her voice, to Britt, seemed hard and pert. But he knew he would soon have her back — his gentle love who had been long away. That day she let Ned clamber over her, and played with him for hours. The next morning she went about her work in the house and on the farm.

Laviny had assumed entire charge of Ned, and was shameless in her partiality. If Bainie didn't like it, she could sulk it out. At the same time, she nagged at Ishma for neglecting him. She was eating her cake and keeping it too. Ishma maintained peace by not opposing her mother, and smiled softly at her unreasonable grumbling. She was going to be hard driven for time now, and at least she could cut out the bickering.

Cold weather was over, the epidemic was in retreat, and the

country people, mentally staggering from the shake-up, began to think about crops. Britt and Ishma knew they must face another year on Cloudy Knob. But Ishma had a plan, which she began to develop in a talk with Jim.

"What you goin' to do with the top-field this year, Jim ?"

"Nothin'. It wouldn't bring nubbins big as yer little finger."

"Well, if you don't want it, you let me and Britt put it in soy beans."

"That truck ! You'll be throwin' away yer muscle. You kain't cure that heavy hay in these mountains. Weather's too wet."

"If you'll let us have what we can make off it, we won't look for another place this Spring."

"Shore you can have it. I don't want to see you leavin', Ish. Though I don't keer so much about Britt. An uppity man like him ort to be on his own place."

Ishma smiled. "I suppose you feel about Britt like Bainie does about me."

"Bain feels same as me about you, Ish. She likes to jower. 'Tain't nothin' else."

"You sure you don't want to come in with us and work the top-field ?"

"Lord, no ! I'd make more a sleepin'."

"We'll stay this year then, and give you two good hands in the main crop. Your back has been hurting you some, I notice. Maybe you'd better go light on it this year."

Jim tugged at his ears to see what was wrong with them. Finding them as usual, he assured Ishma that she was perfectly welcome to the field. All he'd want fer it would be a little help when he was under the weather. But Ishma knew she had agreed to make Jim's crop. Well, they'd have to make it anyhow, and this time they'd get something for it.

"All right, Jim. You tell mommie about it. She'll take it better from you."

The master went to Laviny. He told her that Britt was going to leave unless he could have that good for nothin' top-field fer some crazy experimentin' on his own. Laviny came on Ishma.

"You an' Britt leavin', air you ?"

"We'd like to stay if you'd give us the top-field, mommie."

"I reckon you can have what nobody but a fool 'ud want. You'll not hurt anybody but yersevs. I'll make a hen's nest out of all you git off that field. An' I'm fair to say, Ishmalee, I don't want you to leave the mountain. If you an' Britt ever git yer little house built up by the Birch spring, like you wuz talkin' onct, I'll set over half the farm to ye. But I ain't goin' to have a house divided, an' while we eat together we're goin' to work together. My givin' you the top-field ain't meanin' I've let down ary speck on my principles."

Ishma felt triumphant. Soy-bean hay would bring a good price. They would cut it when the beans were in milk and it would answer for both corn and roughage. They would sell it in the Spring when the farmers were fed out, and had to have something for plough horses and oxen while putting in their crops. At last they would get their "start." But how were they to buy the beans for planting ? It would take seven bushels for the seven acre field.

Wimble County possessed a farm agent with headquarters at Carson. Ishma heard that he was to be in Beebread on a certain day, and without consulting Britt, she was there to see him.

Allan Beck, the agent, was seated in Gaffney's store with a circle of interested farmers around him when Ishma appeared in the store door. Her grey eyes seemed larger than usual in their hedge of dark lashes, and her hatless curls glistened softly about her very pale face. The men stared, and one of them said, "Howdy, Ishmer !" She stood waiting till her cheeks flushed, wondering how she could see the agent alone. She could never put herself forward so much as to call him out before all those eager eyes. Then she was put at ease by the agent walking over to her and shaking hands. He had been wanting to visit Cloudy Knob, he said, and was glad to have an opportunity to find out how things were going up there. Did they have any farm problems he could help them out with ? He had ordered a car load of soy beans, and hoped he could get enough of the farmers to use up the load. Nothing like soy beans for making over old land, and if you inoculated them properly they would give you a good paying crop at the same time.

"Soy beans !" Ishma was excited, but she kept her voice level. "That's what I've come for."

They had passed out of the store and were standing on the little porch in front. "Let's sit down on these boxes," said Beck, "and you can tell me about it."

It was almost too easy then, and Ishma told more than she intended. Allan Beck was the son of a mountain farmer. A few words would open a book for him, and Ishma, with soft, steady measure, spoke more than a few. She didn't have to wait for his answer.

Yes, he assured her, he had a fund which he could draw upon for just such needs as she had described. The price of the seed beans could be returned when the crop was harvested. But he would ask that she and her husband keep the matter between themselves. The fund was very limited, and he didn't want to get more appeals than it would cover. Ishma promised, not suspecting that the money was coming from Allan Beck's not too full but sympathetic pocket. He carefully explained the process of inoculating the beans with nitrogen bacteria, and gave her seven cards, one for each bushel, each card to be signed by a different member of the Cloudy Knob household and mailed to the Department of Agriculture. At the right time she would receive material for treating the seven bushels of seed beans. The result, he was sure, would be a heavy crop of hay, and the land would be made rich enough for permanent pasture. Grass and clover seed were costly, but he hoped she and her husband could buy enough next year for seeding the land.

Ishma's heart sang as she went up the mountain. Maybe they would stay on the farm after all. There was a point in the road where she could look up from the valley and see the "top-field." It was a dull abandoned grey. What if some day she could look up there and see it green against the sky, with specks of red and white on it that meant fat, young Herefords ready for the market ? There was a wonderful place for a cabin up by the Birch spring; and plenty of slim chestnut trees just right for the logs. If they had their own house she knew her mother would keep her word and divide the fields. The neighbors would come in and help with the house-raising. If they got the logs up, Britt could

93

do everything else himself. There were two fine board trees at the head of Grapevine Cove, next to Rad Bailey's land, that would make a good roof. They wouldn't have to buy anything but floor lumber and windows. She'd be glad to live on a dirt floor and do without windows for a year or two, to get their own place. She loved Cloudy Knob, with its peaks, its cold, bubbling springs, and its ferns waist high. She knew where a pair of cardinals built every year. They never left the mountain even in the coldest winter. She had seen Mister Cardinal flashing over snow. She guessed she loved Cloudy Knob as much as he did.

When Ishma came to the cabin she didn't stop to rest after her climb, but went on to the field half a mile farther, where Britt was grubbing sprouts and getting the new-ground — no longer new — ready for its third year of corn. There they sat down and rebuilt their future on the slender basis of seven bushels of beans.

CHAPTER IV

"AND A WIFE SHE MUST CARRY"

GAY DAYS on the mountain. Ishma had never felt such strength in her limbs, such surety in her heart. The first summer of her married life had been a happy one; but this later happiness had in it the bouyancy of triumph. She had known hopelessness, grief, and the dismay that flows from an enfeebled body. Now that they were gone, joy rose in their wake with the zest of a conqueror.

At daybreak one morning she and Britt set off for the top-field. They would have a mile to walk if they went by the sled road that dipped into three coves and picked its way around the ridges that divided them. But they disdained its easy length and took the "straight-up" trail through the pasture, over the face of a cliff and up through the "climbin' holler" whose declivitous sides kept a strip of "big woods" safe from the axe. Coming out at the upper end of the hollow, they faced seven acres of rolling, open land, all their own. It was thickly overgrown with persimmon bushes, locusts and briars. They pushed forward through the growth until they came to the uppermost edge of the field. One step more would have taken them into Dancer County. The boundary line of the farm, according to old records, followed the "meanders" of the ridge, and this was also the dividing line between the two counties. The north face of the mountain was in Dancer, and the south face in Wimble. The latter sloped amiably downward, wrinkled with coves that mostly were arable, and streaked with penetrable woods; but the Dancer side was precipitous. It required a knowledge of the carefully picked out trails to take one safely down to Silver Valley and the Dark Moon region. The ridge of separation was about three miles long, and varied gracefully in height, its flowing rise and fall broken by only two or three abrupt, rocky knobs.

The young farmers stood with their backs to Dancer and looked down over their field. There would have to be a masterous cleaning-up, Britt said, and they would do it together. But Ishma had a better plan. They would clean off one acre together, then he could put the plough to it and she would keep ahead of him with the remainder of the grubbing and cleaning. If she fell behind, he could help her for an hour or two. In this way they would get through sooner, and he would not have to spend a single day ploughing alone in the field. Again they were lovers first, and the bitter winter a fading dream. So swiftly blood rushes in youth, and buries time.

The sun would be up in a moment, but before they began work they had to stand together and look over the mountain world, feeling the air whose balm though sweet with promise was not wholly free of winter. In the hollow below the field the tall poplars had begun to "cloud"; which meant that the high boughs were tipped with misty, yellow buds. Down under the poplars they could hear the tinkling hesitations and onrush of the stream that had its beginning in the Birch spring and was fed from the ferny sides of the hollow. At the other end of the long valley stretching away from the foot of their mountain, the hills began to climb again, and on their slopes lay a dark-blue cloud like a meadow lake. Soon the sun would be upon it, and heavy with gold it would sink down, pinning itself in the tree-tops. The far, circling peaks lay almost black in the east against a peach-blow heaven; violet-tipped in the south and west, and gold-green in the north. Looking upward, they saw a sky creamy white, and tender as a blessing.

"We'll never leave Cloudy Knob," said Ishma, and Britt's echoing "never!" was as certain as her own.

At noon they went down to the spring, where they washed and drank before eating their cold lunch. They each had a pint of milk, for the heifer had "come in" a month before; and biscuits split open and shut again on a spread of blackberry jelly. The previous summer Ishma and the children had carried berries to Beebread and exchanged them for sugar which she had used to make jelly for the school-lunches. This morning Bainie had scowled at her when she helped herself to the jelly. "You'll shore make it sca'ce if you're goin' to take it to the field, an' you know you've got the younguns too uppity to take 'lasses to school." Ishma laughed, remembering the remark, and ate happily. Fom now on she was going to have her rights in everything, and see that Britt got his. Britt had to know what she was laughing at, but he didn't kindle with her over the prospect of independence.

"What about our agreein' to mighty nigh make Jim's crop for him ?"

"You won't have to do a lick more than you would if we hadn't agreed about it. Jim's back would give out in ploughin' time, no matter what. And it was that agreement that got him to put it over mommie and get all this land for ourselves. Jim can't be bossy over *this* field."

"Well, that's all I want — for Jim to quit high-hossin' me. I don't mind a little extra ploughin'."

She was leaning to him over the spring that held deep under its clear surface the fluttering green of a bent, young willow.

"Your eyes are like that," he said, pointing to the shadowy water with its buried silver-green, and leaning until their lips met.

They climbed the hill. Half way up he slipped an arm about her shoulders. "I'll get you a pretty sweater the first thing I buy," he said, out of his rich, new life.

In less than ten days the land was ready for the beans, but they were not to be broadcast until June. During the interval Britt and Ishma were engaged with the corn-crop. Jim had some wild hogs ranging over on Dancer side, and they had to be looked after about the time that Britt had the corn land ready for the plough. "We'll shore miss the meat on our table next winter," said Jim, "if I don't look after them shotes." He carried his gun while on this pleasant duty, and never failed to bring back several squirrels, however unsuccessful with the shotes. Ishma made pot-pies of the squirrels, which were the big, sandy, fox kind. Sometimes she boiled them with dumplings, or, if they were specially fat and young, braised them in the hearth-oven. Jim enjoyed them mightily, but more than that he en-

97

joyed estimation as a provident male. Britt, hungry from hard work, ate with appetite, and Ishma saw that an extra hind-quarter, or plump saddle, fell to his share, ignoring Jim's proprietorship and Bainie's accusing glance.

"Some men can eat fer two," said Bainie one day. "Yes," assented Ishma, "but Britt is the only man I know of who can plough for two." Britt, who had flushed at Bainie's remark, threw a laugh to the rafters and passed his plate again.

In the month of May Bainie was brought to bed with her eighth child. This kept Ishma out of the field, and Britt had only the children's help in getting the corn planted and covered. School closed in April that year, but Sam, the oldest boy, was working in a grocery store in Carson for two dollars a week. "That's all school done fer him," growled Jim, "made him too upheaded to stay at home an' hep his fam'ly."

Bainie had refused to have a doctor, saying she always had it easy and that the money for her last youngun had been "hung on a fodder limb." The truth was, the doctor had received nothing, but poor, hard-pressed Bainie found much comfort in her improvised record for honesty and bounty. In retrospect, at least, she was always even with her creditors. This time her boast for having it easy was refuted. After the birth of the baby boy she became dangerously ill. The doctor had to be called, and Laviny was kept at the bedside. Ishma was swamped with all of the housework and cooking to do for the large family. There was washing, churning, milking — and when she could get a few hours away she would slip up to the field and help Britt. It was during these days of rush and strain that the beans had to be planted. The seven bushels had duly arrived in Bee-bread, and Britt sledded them up the mountain. The wagon had given out, and needed several parts which they didn't want to buy, hoping to put the money on a new one. Laviny, Jim and Bainie, treated everything connected with the bean-field as a joke, except when such preparations clashed with other work. Then their jokes became complaints.

Ishma read over and over the directions for inoculation. What gave her most concern was the injunction to get the beans into the ground without the sun striking them after they had been treated. They'd have to pick a shady day, and they were in no position to pick their time. And it would take more than one day to get through.

"I'll tell you what we'll do, Britt," she said finally. "We'll work at night. We'll begin at sundown, and we'll get in two bushels by late bed-time."

"Lordy, why'd'n't I think of that ? We can get through in three or four nights, an' it won't take me a minute from the crop in daytime."

They waited no longer for a shady day. The next afternoon Ishma went up to the field two or three hours before sundown, leaving the supper and milking to her mother. Julie had come up to watch by Bainie. Ishma took with her a big tarpaulin which she had pieced together out of fragments of an old army tent. This she spread out in the shade of a large walnut tree standing in the edge of the field, and poured on it as many of the beans as she thought they could plant that day. These she treated with the miraculous, jelly-like substance which the Government had provided. She tossed and rubbed and stirred the beans until they were all moistened with it, then continued to lift and toss and stir, and by sundown they were dry enough to go into the ground. Britt came over from the corn-field, walking along the Dancer ridge, and driving the oxen. Ishma had brought their supper to the field, and as soon as they had eaten they began to work. They were too interested, too full of the adventure to feel weary. Ishma began broadcasting, and Britt covered. But he found that the home-made harrow, fashioned of long rail-road spikes, was putting the beans too deep in the loose soil of the old field. Half of them would rot after the first heavy rain. Ishma had brought the axe, intending to cut poles and mend a breach in the fence if she had time. Britt took it and cut the tops from several bushy saplings. Ishma, just as quickly, found some spindling little hickories, and using Britt's knife, stripped them for withes. With these the sapling tops were bound together, a small short log was fastened across them, and their covering instrument was made. The oxen made no objection, and dragged the big brush along with their usual dignity. It covered more ground than the harrow, and by the time the moon had replaced the daylight, half of the inoculated beans were in the ground. By ten o'clock they had finished with the lot.

The two following nights saw the work completed. But they had no time for triumphant breathing. The larder was crying for flour, sugar, coffee, and other supplies. Eggs, which were all applied to Jim's credit at the store, were few in number. Most of the hens were hovering chickens too small for the market. Luckily the children, released from school, could run wild and ragged, with no continual cry for pencils, tablets, books, and this and that decent necessity.

While Britt and Ishma were putting in the beans, Laviny nagged them persistently for being "dumb-headed," and on every opportunity repeated the list of daily needs. Mrs. Bowers, who kept the boarding house in Beebread had promised to take three loads of wood if Britt could find time to cut it for her kitchen-stove. As soon as they were through in the top-field, he jumped into the job, prepared the wood and sledded it down, fearful that someone would get ahead of him. Jim offered to help cut the wood, but his work would have been feeble compared with his hand on the spoils. Britt advised him not to risk his back too far, and did the work himself. The net result was eleven dollars which was immediately laid out in necessaries and stopped Laviny's nagging and Bainie's whine for a whole month.

One morning in July they went up to look at their bean-field. They had not seen it since planting time. But others, passing through the gap, had looked at it and indifferently admitted that they'd get a piece of a stand anyhow, but maybe it wouldn't hold out. Wimble was a pea country, and planting this "furrin' truck" had been an affront to the elders.

Ishma and Britt waited a moment in the woods, wondering what they should see. Then they caught hands and came out to the field. A fluttering, tender green that seemed to cover every inch of the seven acres dazzled their eyes. Ishma gasped and sat down. Britt gave a shout and sprang to the top of the fence. Balanced on a rail, he surveyed their handiwork. Theirs and God's. Then he leapt back to Ishma and laid his head in her lap.

"We'll make it, Britt," she whispered. And he wouldn't answer, afraid his voice would jerk with a sob. They stood up again, and looked. It was part of themselves — that green abundance — flowing out of their bodies.

Britt had never entirely recovered from the rheumatism that he brought with him from the Smoky woods. Sometimes, after a hard day's work, when perhaps he had spent twelve hours or more in the field, his ankle would keep him in agony through the night. Usually the pain subsided by morning, and a bare snatch of sleep sufficed him for renewal. A little pale of face, he would rise ready for a bound up the hill to the waiting furrows.

Late in July, when the time came for the last ploughing of the corn-rows, he borrowed a cultivator from Si Welch, and also Si's young mule, for a day's work. The usual prolonged rain of summer was expected. If it should find the crop "filthy" with grass and weeds, there would be no hope for it. Days of rain would foster the invading growth and leave the corn too "stalky" for another ploughing. Si loaned the cultivator for a day only. His crop, too, needed a last going over before he could resign it to the gods of the weather. Britt determined to get over all of the corn-ground that day. With a four-footed implement he could clean a corn-middle every time he went across the field. The mule was a lively youngster and filled Britt with a longing to possess him. One of the least tolerable things in farming was the annoyance of having to slow his gait behind oxen. The mule seemed to recognize a swifter spirit than Si's at the plough, and together they made fine play of covering several acres in a few hours. Britt stopped at noon to eat the lunch that Ishma brought him. Five minutes served to dispatch it, but he gave the mule twenty more to eat his hay and corn. Britt shelled the corn for him, and received nosey riffles of thanks. They ploughed on, not stopping for supper. A full moon rose early and the last acre was covered by its light. Britt gave the mule a fine feed, petted him proud and took him home. Coming back, his ankle pained him until he could scarcely make the last furlong up the mountain. He got home at ten o'clock and dropped into bed. Ishma applied hot cloths to the ankle until ease came and he went to sleep. At one o'clock she went to bed. The moon was gone, leaving the earth black, and swept by a rainy wind. She had been sleeping lightly for an hour when the faint ting of a far away bell made her leap out of bed. No creature on the farm wore a bell. It had happened at last! Dancer county had no stock law, and cattle had wandered up the mountain. She listened until she was certain that the sound was made by a cow-bell and that it came from the direction of the bean-field. Britt was in a deep, restful sleep. If she waked him, he would try to climb to the field, and she mustn't let him do that. It would be useless to ask aid of Jim. His back would be giving him "down the creek, I 'clare to jiminy, Ish!" Ben was spending the night with the Craig boys. She would have to go alone, and of course there was no oil for the lantern. She tried to take some out of the lamp, but that, too, was exhausted. Perhaps it was only one cow anyway, and maybe she hadn't got through the fence yet. She put on her shoes quickly, snatched up her dress, and was slipping it over her head as she ran through the upper yard. She took the shortest, steepest trail, and at first had no trouble in keeping it, though the thick darkness left nothing visible.

But her haste made more delay. She climbed so rapidly that her breath left her — a stupid thing for a mountain girl to do. She sat still for painful minutes, upbraiding herself, before she could go on. When she came to the cliff she couldn't keep the cork-screw track with only her blindly exploring feet to help her, and had to pull up by saplings and roots that pushed out of the rocky crevices. Above the cliff was a narrow bench with its big trees still standing, and here she tried to walk through the middle of a giant poplar. This threw her to the ground, and she scrambled about, feeling the earth with her hands, until she found the trail. From that point the way was not so steep and she began running once more. The bell-sound was loud now and the clang of it sickened her through all of her body. Would she ever get there? What if it were uncle Ben Snead's bell-cow that led a herd of yearlings over the grazing lands around Dark Moon? They would trample down the bean-field in one night.

The sound came from the middle of the field. It was a shade

lighter there than in the woods, and she could distinguish vague forms moving, huddling, and scattering in the darkness. The sickness in her limbs vanished, consumed by the rage that seized her. They were trampling more than the bean-field; they were destroying her foundations. The largest vague figure threw up a head, and the bell rattled. She advanced on the marauders. The younger ones jumped about and scattered. The big bell-cow tossed her head and ran, not up the hill as she should have done, but to the eastern side of the field. The others followed, gathered about her, and waited in silence.

Ishma, knowing that she would have to locate the gap where the cattle had entered, went to the top of the ridge and felt carefully along the fence until she discovered where the brush had been torn away and the rails thrown down. The gap was about midway between the east and west ends of the field. She had to be accurate or she could never drive them through it, so she counted her strides until she again reached the invading group. They were not huddled now, but slightly scattered, voraciously tearing and munching the young vines. Going behind the leader, she began to shout and wave her arms. The waving may have been futile in the darkness, but the shouting was not lost. The cow rushed off, kicking and prancing, sending back bits of dirt and clods in Ishma's face. Every print of the hoof's seemed set on her heart, but she dashed on after the cow, hoping to turn her up the hill towards the gap. The creature sped on to the extreme western side of the field. Ishma stopped for breath, then ran to a gully which she and Britt had filled with persimmon saplings, locusts, and briars, when they were cleaning off the land. She felt around in the dark, scratching and wounding herself on thorns and briars, until she secured a stick as thick as her wrist and about six feet long. She would have to beat that cow inhumanly. Nothing else would make her go through the gap. Ishma knew that if her rage cooled she couldn't be cruel, and she was glad that her blood was still hot and racing when once more she came up to the cattle. She peered through the blinding dark until she could see that the cow had her head turned up the hill as she munched and devoured. Lifting her stick, and augmenting the gesture with a great shout, she let a murderous blow fall on the animal's rump. There was a snorting bawl and a wild dash up the hill, with Ishma following fast on her victim. When the upper fence was reached the cow ran along the side of it and Ishma kept running guard below her until they came to the gap. With a lunge she managed to reach the flying rump with another blow, and the cow leapt into Dancer county.

Ishma sank down inside the field, kneeling close against the fence where she would be out of the way of the yearlings that were bounding up the hill to the sound of the bell. In two minutes all of them had passed through the gap, and Ishma was up repairing the fence. She knew what had happened. Two nights before she had heard fox-hunters running over the mountain. No doubt they had torn away the brush that was piled on top of the fence, and against it on the Dancer side. This had begun a breach which the cattle were able to finish. She laid up the rails without trouble, and began to search for the scattered brush to pile against it. A cow could lift rails with her horns, but she couldn't get at them through a brush barrier. She and Britt had worked for days "brushing" the Dancer fence, to provide against just this hap.

When her blindfold task was done she sat down to rest. The cattle had taken a westward trail around the shoulder of the mountain. Cattle must see better than men in the dark, she thought, or they wouldn't be able to keep that trail and avoid the precipices that made the Dancer side so dangerous. She heard the tinkle, tinkle of the bell growing lower and farther. Well, if they broke their necks they couldn't come back ! Suddenly she leapt to her feet and listened. Was that sound lower ? Farther ? With a clear ring it burst around the upper end of the mountain shoulder, and the next moment seemed to be tearing down into the field. She rushed to the western side. The clouds were thicker above, and the night was blacker, if possible, but she heard and saw. It would have to be done all over again. No need to look for the gap. It must be in the upper west corner of the fence. She hurried down below the vague, demonic group, and again came behind the bell-cow with her stick. Before she could strike, the cow discovered her, wheeled, and made a wildly destructive dash across the field, with the yearlings after her. There wouldn't be a bean-vine left! Ishma ran too, her hot tears flying into the dark. When the cattle reached the eastern fence they stopped and huddled. Ishma halted. She would have to be cunning this time if she got near enough to strike the cow and make her believe that death was at her heels. It was, if Ishma's rage could have killed. She dropped to the ground and crept up as softly as she could, hugging the stick under her arm. The fence, with its corners filled with briars and weeds, helped to conceal her approach. The wind helped too. It was blowing down the hill, and away from the cow, which was facing the west, no doubt believing that the fence proctected her rear. Ishma was able to launch a mighty blow, and by making a great leap, followed it with another. Bellowing with fright and pain, the cow raced across the field to the gap. She didn't stop until she was through, and Ishma had no need to hasten after her. The yearlings had torn along after the cow, and passed through at her heels. Ishma was stumbling, trembling, falling, and when she reached the broken fence she had to sit down a moment before she could get to work on it. When she had finished she made her way carefully along to where she had repaired the other breach and found no more weak spots.

She was ready to go down. Slowly she moved over the broken vines. No need to be careful now. She and Britt had never gone into the field, even to verify its luxuriance, fearful that they might break down a few stalks. And here was utter destruction. When she came to the lower fence she climbed up and sat on top of it, hesitating to go into the woods. To her, so exhausted, they seemed strange and forbidding. She didn't know where the trail began. She might fall over a cliff. Coming up was much safer than going down, when one couldn't see. The wind carried more rain now, and her clothes were moist. She was so weak that she could throw up no mental barriers, and all the little foxes that lurk about the corners of one's life rushed in and tore at her with their keen, stinging teeth.

How hard she had worked! How hard Britt had worked! It was no use to fight any longer there on the mountain. They ought to have gone long ago. Britt ought to have found a way out. She ought to have found a way out. They had let everything roll over them. They had taken trouble by the hand and fed it, when they ought to have kicked it out like a bad dog. Jim, a lazy liar. A houseful of children that were no better than a million other housefuls of children. A jealous, unreasonable thing like Bainie, with the life drained out of her, bringing another life into the world. Farming — without tools, stock, seed. Nothing to pour into it but their strength. What had it brought them ? Debt, sneers, injustice. Nothing to wear. The crudest food, and no time to prepare it. Nothing for study — books — trips. Just bare life. And now Dancer county had come against them. They would never be through with those cattle. Why didn't she let them alone ? Let them have every bean in the field ? She was tired, sick. If she couldn't get out and leave it all, she would just sit down and quit work. Sit down, and see what would happen.

She slid to the lower side of the fence, because she was too weak to stay on top of it, and leaning against it gave her body up to tears and sobs. Then she slipped lower and rested on a log. She thought of Britt, and wanted to get down. He might wake and begin to worry. By and by she felt stronger, and began to be a little ashamed of herself.

Poor old cow ! How she had beaten her ! When, by all cow standards, she had been doing her duty in a splendid way. Through dark night she had led her herd to green pastures. She had left stony ground and leapt barriers to set her feet in the midst of milk-making plenty. And she had been nearly killed for her courage and good sense. "I had to beat her, but I didn't have to get so mad. I'll never get mad again," she resolved. The field was ruined, but it might mean freedom for her and Britt. They might have to get out now. Go somewhere down to the towns and find work. She thought of a saying of Granny Stark's. "Don't you fret, darter. The worst trouble may be the best luck." The words seemed to sound on the air. She sat very still, and heard Granny telling again the pioneer version of a tale that was probably old three thousand years before her.

"A man had to go on a far journey. He was a good man, and that was his name, Goodman. He had a fine rooster that had made a big name fer himself, and the king of the far country sent Goodman word that he would give him a kegful of money fer the rooster. So he started out, an' took a lamp along fer dark nights, an' rode a little donkey. When he come to some big woods it got night, an' he ast to stop at a house. Nobody was in the house but an' old man an' old woman. They had a nice big feather bed they wa'n't usin', but they said he couldn't stay. So he went into the woods an' it was terrible dark. It was quaky dark, fer a fact. He tried to light his lamp, but the grease was all gone. In them days they put grease in lamps, an' laid a wick in the grease, an' when the rag was lit it made a right peart light. Goodman minded that when he set his lamp down on the steps o' the house an' was talkin' to the old woman, her cat come an' licked up all the grease. He minded how the cat had rubbed around his legs. Well, he laid down in the big woods an' went to sleep. While he was sleepin, a fox came along an' got his rooster. When he woke up he reached out to make shore it was there an' it was gone. He felt so bad about it he couldn't sleep no more, an' went over to where he'd tied his donkey, an' a painter had jumped down on it an' clawed it to death. 'This is bad,' he says. 'I reckon I must a slep' awful sound.' But he couldn't git out o' the woods till daylight, so he laid down again. He didn't go to sleep though, knowin' they's painters about. An' after a while two men come along, tippin' easy like. They stopped right close to him an' he heard 'em talkin'. One of 'em says, 'I reckon thet house an' thet ol' boy an' gal air burnt in their beds.' 'But we didn't git the traveller,' says t'other man. 'An' we burnt 'em up fer nothin'.' 'Tain't no matter,' says the fust one. 'Serve 'em well right. They's born to be burnt in their beds.' 'Maybe we won't find that traveller,' says the second man, 'an' he's carryin' gold shore. He wouldn't be ridin' ef he wuzn't carryin' gold.'

"'We'll git him yit,' says the fust feller. 'He's got a lamp with him, an' when he lights it we'll walk right on him.'

"'Maybe the lamp won't hold out in this wind,' says t'other one, who was a sort o' doubtin' feller.

"'Well,' says the fust one, 'that rooster 'll crow, er that don-key 'll set in an' bray. A rooster an' a donkey air what kain't keep their mouths shet.'

"The men went on a lookin', an' Goodman lay there right still, prayin' hard an' thankin' the Lord fer havin' saved him with trouble. But that wa'n't all of it. Next mornin' when light come, he could see on the mountain side right ahead of him a big blue an' white flower, sech a flower as he'd never seen be-fore. I'll take that to the king, he says. But there was a big rock in the way. It had four straight-up sides. Goodman he sweated an' he scrambled, but he couldn't git over it. He had to go way down below a cliff an' way round on t'other side an' come up agin till he's on a level with the flower. Then he come along back to it, an' when he got there he looked over it at the big rock jest a little ways off, an' there was a big di'mond back rattler quiled up agin it. Ef he'd got over that rock he'd a jumped right down on that rattler."

Ishma could hear herself asking, "Did he get to the king, Granny?"

"I don't know, an' it don't make no difference. He'd larnt a sight more'n a king could tell him. Don't ever fret, darter. Yer worst trouble may be yer best luck."

Ishma rose up, but where was the trail? Nothing to do but make a plunge for it. She went a few feet into the woods, and stood still. Then something happened. A falling meteor lit up the woods and turned all the black night into a trans-parent cool flame. She had often seen a star shoot across the sky and drop over a distant horizon; lighting the heavens, but never the earth. She had never known anyone, not even Granny, who had breathed in the very flaming light of one. It had seemed to fall down in the tree-tops that rose from the ravine not a hundred yards away. A few seconds afterwards another one had fallen over beyond the Snowbird mountains in the north-west. But this one was hers. Her meteor! Right at her feet from millions and millions of miles away. It had come so suddenly, winding her in such wonder that at first she didn't know what it meant. When she understood, her exaltation leapt higher. She had seen every leaf and twig and rock about her, every fern and bit of moss, every rain-pearl like a tiny seed in the air. It had been a cool light like the moon's, but it had seemed brighter than the sun; and it had bathed everything; the trees, the gathered rain-clouds, her face, her hands, and the blueberry bush at her knees. She had seen the little printed flower of her dress and the gleam of her finger nails by a light from another world. She would never tell anyone about it. Who would believe it ? How could she have seen so much in a few seconds ? There was the old chestnut tree with the squirrel hole in it; the pine that had been struck by lightning, pointing to the sky with three black fingers; the big white oak with the scraggly buzzards' nest in the highest fork. So strange and sudden, the light had kindled its own response, a response like the power one had in dreams. In a single brief dream she could live a lifetime, roam over many countries, be several people all at once. Why couldn't she have a little of that power when awake ? She could. For the tenth of a minute she had been all-seeing. Now she could believe that some day a light would come into the world of her mind making everything clear. Just as clear as this in her woods. From somewhere, another world it might be. If a stone, a rock could come, how much more easily a thought ! She needn't worry about not being ready for it. With its power it would kindle hers.

The worn earth of the trail had shone bare in the light. She stepped into it and went down. She was young, she was strong, and her veins were warm with a strange, new joy.

THEY went up the next day to look at the wreck, and found that half a crop might be saved. Britt was the downcast one, Ishma the comforter. "Half a crop will get us out," she said, thinking that it would be easy to walk off without anything. Britt looked at her a little puzzled, but happier. "Lord, you take it fine, Ishma !"

Going down, his spirits revived still more, and he took up their old game of spying out trees that would make good logs for their house. "There's one we've never counted, up there between that black-oak and sweet-gum. Ain't he a long, slim feller ? We'll put him over the door. He'll reach from one corner to the other an' not gain more'n two inches in width."

Ishma seemed uninterested. "That makes forty-nine," pursued Britt. She said nothing, and with hurt lips he asked, "You're not wantin' the house ?"

"It doesn't matter much, Britt. Maybe we'll not stay. We can make it through anywhere — anywhere in the world."

"We'll make it through here," said Britt, setting his teeth on a decision.

THE summer passed, a time of breathless toil. Britt got out his poplar logs, but he had to get Si's help after all, paying him half. And when the logs were at the sawmill, the lumberman to whom he sold them declared that they were partly doty and worm-eaten, though Britt's strong eyes could detect nothing wrong with them, and Si swore and stormed his protest. They barely made wages out of the logs, and Britt's share was immediately turned in on Gaffney's account. The ox-team would have to jog through another crop. He bought himself overalls, two work-shirts, shoes and socks; for Ishma print stuff for two dresses, and shoes and stockings. Then he went up the mountain to face the scowls of Bainie and the recriminations of Laviny, which ceased as soon as he gave Laviny the other half of his money — her pay for her logs.

Ishma was taking care of the "patches" that summer, for Bainie kept feeble and Laviny was needed in the house. With the children for aids, she fought weeds early and late. She knew what a winter would mean on the mountain if they didn't save the potatoes, cabbage, tomatoes, beans, turnips, and the cane patch. Thirty-nine meals a day, not counting the baby's, couldn't be paid for out of Gaffney's store.

Britt had planned to cover the barn as soon as he was through logging. The great loft was almost open to the sky, and he wanted to put his hay there for the winter. But as soon as the logs were down he had to begin cutting his hay. Heavy rains interfered, until at last he had to go after Milt Slagle and get him to come up with his mowing machine. This cut him down to one-quarter of a crop, as Milt took half for his pay. But he helped Britt cure and shock the hay. Ishma, too, worked with them, neglecting the house and accepting such food as Laviny chose to prepare. They couldn't take any more risks with what was left of the hay. They put it up in well-cured stacks, protected the outside with hay that had been ruined by the rain, and decided to leave it in the field until Spring. That would be better than letting it rot under a leaky roof. There was no time now to cover the barn. Britt had to get out and find work for the interval between hay-making and harvesting the corn. Allan Beck had been promised his money by December, and it couldn't come out of the hay. They would have to hold that until Spring for a profitable sale. After a week's search, Britt found work twenty miles away, near Raccoon Springs, where a lumber company was putting a road through to their timber. He got on the force because they were working negroes, and very few mountain men were willing to work with a black gang. He was to receive two dollars a day, but he proved himself such a handy good fellow with negroes and mules that his pay was secretly raised fifty cents before a week was out. The hands were not paid "solid time." Rainy days were lost days, but one dollar a day for board was demanded of them rain or shine. When Britt left for home to gather the corn, he had twenty-five dollars in his pocket. He had not spent a penny for good-fellowship, having found that his music acceptably replaced offerings of tobacco and liquor. When he reached Carson he hunted up Allan Beck and paid him seventeen dollars. Then he bought guitar strings for himself and banjo strings for Julie Webb; a harmonica for Ned, and a box each of very popular snuff for Bainie and Laviny. All of the remainder he put into a sweater for Ishma; the prettiest he could find, which was a soft, smoky tan, with borders of amber and green. Penniless, he would have had to walk the ten miles to Beebread if he hadn't run up on Jed Stone who gave him a ride for his company.

Britt was happy. The month away from home had lessened the irritations of Cloudy Knob to the vanishing point. Wife, child and home filled his mind and his heart. How had he ever been content to shift about for so many years ? He would plant his feet on Cloudy Knob and conquer right there.

Ishma had been treated to no vacation from work and monotony, but her face was bright when she saw him. She had walked halfway down to Beebread to meet him, leading Ned. They had gathered some hazel-nuts and were sitting on a rock above the road eating them when they heard Britt shout. He was waving his hat, and looking altogether handsome, his wife thought. There was no other man in the mountains so good-looking as hers. Britt ran up, and Ishma and Ned ran down, until they met. It was sweet to kiss with abandon, while no one saw. They had been married over three years, and married folks had to hide their kisses or be laughed at. Ned danced and blew his harmonica, but when Britt kept on kissing Ishma he thought he was missing something and fought for his share. The sweater was exhibited and she had to put it on.

"It's beautiful, Britt, and soft as a dog's nose !" She stood against a grey rock where a partridge vine scrambled, covered with red berries. Laurel framed the rock, and it was all a frame for Ishma. Britt looked at her silently. He couldn't speak his joy and pride. "I'll get you what you ought to have some day," he said, trying to be brusque and offish.

On their way up the hill she kept him talking of the camp, the work, the men, of everything that had happened to him during their separation. She was glad to think of something besides her heavy labors and the tense atmosphere of home.

Laviny and Bainie were sitting on the porch looking grimly down the road. " 'Tain't no use fer you to act like you's still a courtin'," Bainie had said to Ishma when she started down the mountain. "It don't fool nobody." Ishma knew that Bainie was speaking from a starved heart, and would have parted with some of her own happiness to ease it. Years had passed since Jim had given his wife an affectionate word. But the children kept coming just the same. How horrible it must be ! Ishma couldn't picture it. The thought of it brought a blank terror to her mind.

The sweater was admired, with tense reservations. Britt

handed out the boxes of snuff, and still they waited. Surely that couldn't be all, their eyes cried out. The sweat started up around Britt's neck. He tried to talk to Ned, but Ned was blowing the harmonica in little Jim's ears and making him cry for it. Ishma took the harmonica and handed it to little Jim. "Now you let him play it." Her act precipitated one of Bainie's sniffs. "There'll be a steady fight from now on, if you didn't bring home but one o' them things."

Britt was burning in his shoes. Why had he been so owdaceous dumb? There he was, without a dollar to turn over, and not a gift to make his peace with. Bainie was handling her box of snuff as if it were a fire-coal. Suddenly she flung it as far as she could, out into a clump of laurel. Her eyes marked where it fell, and she would go out after dark and retrieve it. But she'd showed that Britt something. Laviny began to scold her. In her nagging way she loved Britt, and knew in her heart that he was her best prospect for support in her old age. Ishma had stepped into the kitchen, after a glance at Britt's pale face, and now came out with a large piece of bread wrapped in a clean apron. She took Britt by the arm.

"There'll be a full moon up in half an hour — a big harvest moon. Let's go to the field and look at the corn."

Britt picked up Ned, but Laviny took hold of the boy. "You're not goin' to take that youngun out tonight. *He* ain't got no warm sweater."

"You want to stay with granny, son?" his father asked him. Ned threw a belligerent eye on little Jim who was still in posession of the harmonica, and decided to stay. Britt, who guessed the deciding factor, put him down with no twinge of jealousy, and went off with Ishma. He was glad to be alone with her, and she wanted only Britt.

The family were all in bed when they returned. Next morning they were out early, on their way to the corn-ground with sled and ox-team. Laviny had prudently relented overnight and called after them, "Yer dinner 'll be hot at twelve!" Then she began to putter about in the effort to make good her promise. She snubbed Bainie, and told her she'd better act decent till the corn was gathered, if she couldn't hold out no longer. "When

113

you ain't got but one feather in yer pillow, don't pizen yer geese," she advised her.

For a time the mountain seemed to heave with labor, and heart-burnings slept. The busy Autumn passed. Cold weather came on swiftly. The laurel leaves began to cradle early. It would be a bitter winter. December froze the earth, and January brought an unmelting snow. Even the faithful cardinals flew away. Ishma shivered, and a paralyzing pall settled down upon her when she discovered that there was to be another child on the mountain, not Bainie's but her own.

CHAPTER V

THE middle South was again under the spell of April. Ishma Waycaster and Britton Hensley had been married four years. Four years since that night of fragrance and a wan moon, of disaster and aching joy.

Ishma sat on the cabin porch, looking over some scraps of print and gingham which she had taken out of a tow bag. Far to the left sat Laviny, sorting beans, with aunt Cynthy Webb in a chair near her. Against the wall back of them was the big, invalid's chair, piled high with farm miscellany and household clutter. On the house and its surroundings the four years had left no sign of alteration for the better. The cabin roof wore a more mottled and mossy coat, the walls had lost more chinking, and the long porch sagged and rallied on its faithful locust pillars. The only thriving thing in the yard was the blue balsam. It had struggled upward and outward, and now exhibited an almost portly beauty. Everything else in the unkempt place advertised poverty and indifference. Ishma, sitting stolid, with listlessly moving fingers, seemed a corporate part of her environment. Laviny, who usually hopped about galvanically all through springtime, betrayed no answering thrill to the call of resurrection.

"There," she was saying, "that'll be as many beans as I'll want to plant in the up-cove. It's so fur, an' I'm past my time fer trapsein' up an' down. Ishmalee ain't goin' to be no hep this summer, the way she's started out. Law, law, when her an' Britt got married you ought to a heard him makin' promises. He fair run over with 'em. 'Aunt Laviny,' he says, 'you're goin' to take yer rest now. An' it'll be fer life. You've done got yer sentence. You ain't even goin' to know where yore bean-patch is.' Law, law !"

"I'll take what you got left, Laviny," said Cynthy. "I'm a little short o' seed beans this year. It's nearin' Good Friday an' they ort to be in the ground. The sign 's in the arms next week."

"You're shore welcome." She tore some leaves out of a catalogue lying on the big chair and began to wrap up the beans for Cynthy.

"You tearin' up that new order book from Philadelphy?"

"Nobody 's got any use fer order books round here, an' never will have, I reckon. You shore it's in the arms next week, Cynthy? Ishmalee, git me the almanac."

Ishma rose and went into the house. Cynthy leaned guardedly toward Laviny. "How long 's she got to go yit?"

"I kain't git it out o' her. An' you kain't tell from her looks, fer she never shows big. Not even with the twins she didn't. But I kinder b'lieve it won't be more'n two months now. They's like they'd jest got married when Britt came home last fall. S'pose you try to find out, Cynthy. 'F I ast her her mouth 'll glue up. She ain't like herself, ner hain't been all winter. She wouldn't mind jumpin' on me nary bit, if I went too fur."

Ishma came out with the almanac, which she gave to her mother, and went back to her scraps and silence. Cynthy rose and moved toward her, casual as a slow breeze.

"How you gittin' along with yer baby clo's, Ishmer?"

More silence. Laviny was eagerly tense. Ishma didn't look up.

"Haven't started yet," she answered, as if she had used the pause to choose the fewest words possible.

"My! you'll be late with 'em, won't you? Be keerful, er you'll be as bad as Jane Ludd wuz last week. Hern come an' not a stitch to put on it. They wrapped it in her man's Sunday shirt, an' when he come home he swore till the roof cracked."

"You wouldn't ketch Britt doin' that," shot from Laviny. Cynthy turned to her and grinned. "No, but I reckon Britt ain't got no Sunday shirt nohow." Again she fixed her twinkling brown eyes on Ishma. "Britt's been talkin' to Zeke like you an' him air goin' to move to yersevs soon. Goin' to have a house-raisin' an' build up by the Birch spring."

The answer came from Laviny. "Talk is all it is. They ain't got the scrapin's of a dough-pan to take inter a house."

"Don't be too pertikler 'bout settin' up, Ishmer. The fust year I's married we didn't have nothin' but one skillet to cook in. I'd bake my pone, then I'd fry my meat. An' ef I wanted to cook any sass I'd have to walk a mile to sister Lu's an' borry a pot. Beginners can git along most anyways ef they want to. Nowadays they don't want to. They've got to have ever'thing — two beds, an' a stove an' dishes, er they won't start at all. Don't you git upheaded, Ishmer, an' wait too long."

Ishma might or might not have heard her. Cynthy chose another topic. "Them's mighty purty quilt pieces. Wonder where'd you git 'em, Ishmer ?"

Civility was again rescued by Laviny. "Eve Copp sent 'em over to Ishmalee. I'm glad to see her gittin' at 'em like she meant it. She can piece up a lot 'fore next winter, settin' round like she does, an' she'll shore need kiver."

The last three words were uttered in a way that made Ishma bundle the scraps back into the bag. Cynthy's fat face beamed peace and good-will. "Ef you've got a check piece like my apern, Ishmer, wisht you'd give it to me. I've got a spark-hole in it, an' nary a scrap."

"Take them all," said Ishma. "You're welcome." She put the bag on a chair and walked to the right as far as she could without leaving the porch, and stood there looking down at some plants in a box, not seeing them at all. Cynthy looked at the bag and at Laviny, then pursued Ishma and asked how her tomato plants were coming on. Getting no answer, she made her own investigation. "They're a little for'd o' mine," she said. "Mine's jest puttin' out second leaves. Better set 'em inside tonight. Hit's frosty lookin' an' no wind."

Ishma turned her head toward the valley, and Cynthy went back to Laviny.

"Quare enough, but time 'll cure it. I'll be goin' now, Laviny. I told Julie I'd be right back."

"I hearn Julie had broke off with Tim Wheeler."

"My, yes ! 'Pears like she kain't git her mind fixed on Tim. An' her weddin' dress made. Gals air gittin' quare, Laviny. 'Tain't only wives."

She began to get off the porch, with slow, balancing care.

"You come down to Webb holler, Ishmer. It'll hep ye to walk about some. Make it easier when you'll be wantin' ease, I'm tellin' ye."

Ishma made no reply, and Cynthy went off down the hill. As soon as she was out of hearing, Laviny turned courageously on her daughter.

"You ain't as civil as a barn-cat."

"Barn-cat? I'd like to live in a barn for a while."

"Nobody's astin' you to live here. I don't know what's got inter you, Ishmalee. You've changed a sight more 'n nater 'll account fer. Used to be nobody could stop you at anything. Now you kain't git started at nothin'. Britt's tryin' a heap harder 'n you."

"What's he doing today? Gone to the Swimmin' Bald for ramps."

"It's Sat'day, an' he worked till twelve."

"Ramps!" She put intense disgust into the word.

"They's mighty healthy in the spring o' the year."

"I can't abide the smell, and he knows it."

"A man's stomach is more cravin' than a woman's."

"He doesn't want ramps. He won't touch one. He only wants to lie out. I can't blame him for that though. I'd like to be on the top of the Bald myself. You can see into three States from the top. And there's a lake up there. The wild geese stop to feed. If I could 'a' gone — "

Her voice dropped with heavy longing.

"You look like it!" cried her mother. "Go an' 'tend to them diddlies! That grey hen 's comin' off."

"I told you if we didn't get started with a good breed of chickens this year I wouldn't 'tend to 'em."

"You want them big yaller hens like Eve Copp's got, an' if you tried feedin' 'em fer a while you'd be through with 'em."

"I'd like to try. I'm sick of scrubs, of all sorts."

She didn't see little Ned as he came around the house and began to climb the steps at the left end of the porch, stumbling, and dragging a large stick with both hands. There was no sign in Ned of the general surrender that affected Cloudy Knob. His parents might quail before life, but his little body spoke stoutly of confidence and vigor.

"Mommie!" he shouted. At the sound of his voice Ishma gave a start, then flushed as with guilt. Why did she have to feel surprised, as if she were continually learning of his existence ?

"Careful, son. You'll fall with that stick."

"For granny ! Bake me cake !"

"Lord love it !" said his grandmother. "They ain't a speck o' flour in the house."

Ned tossed his head covered with shiny, crinkled hair like Britt's, and dragged the stick into the kitchen. "Daddy get some fower," he said with assurance.

"If I could see to thread a needle," said Laviny, "that child 'ud have something to put on. Britt got some stuff when he took that last load o' wood to Beebread — 'nough to make him two aperns. Whyn't you git at 'em, Ishmalee ? Nobody 'ud know he belonged to you."

"Bainie 's going to make them. I've swopped work with her. I'm going to do the milking all the time."

"I thought them scrub cows wuzn't good enough fer you to tech."

"It's warm enough to do the milking up at the gap now. You can see clean over the Smokies from there, almost."

"That heps fill the bucket, don't it ? You got through, Bainie ?"

Bainie was coming from the upper yard carrying a battered washboard and bucket. Dropping them on the porch, she sat down and wiped her face.

"Yes, I'm done at last. Cleanin' them overalls was like scrubbin' the ground. I don't see why Ish kain't be more hep. She won't tech a thing but Britt's clo's an' Ned's an' her own duds. I allers do anything that comes, right up to my time."

"No, you don't, Bainie. You're fergittin' the days Ishmalee put in fer you when yore younguns was comin' along."

"Where's the rest o' ye ?" Bainie's sharp question was addressed to Andy, who had come up the road, books under arm, and stood undecidedly in the yard.

"You said Ben an' Nettie could stay down at uncle Bill's to-

night, an' Ellie stopped at aunt Cynthy's. Said she's tired."
Laviny entered her usual protest. "She's too little anyhow to
be pullin' up an' down the mountain jest fer schoolin'."

"You come here, Andy," said his mother. When he went to
her, she examined him anxiously. "You got that hurtin' in yer
head yit?" He nodded, bashful under sympathy. "Mommie,
I wish you'd take a look at him. He's been punyin' fer two er
three days."

Laviny gave the boy a close scrutiny, then turned a superior
look on her daughter. "Kain't you tell worms yit, Bainie?
Don't you see how white he is round his mouth, an' he keeps
botherin' his nose?"

"It's worms? I'll have to make some droozly-moke syrup
then."

"For goodnes' sake, Bainie," said Ishma, "can't you say Jerusalem Oak? I've told you fifty times."

Laviny scolded. "What you breakin' out fer? It was droozly-
moke in my mother's time, an' droozly-moke in my time, an' it
might as well be droozly-moke in yore an' Bainie's time."

"Will you git me some, Ish?" asked Bainie.

"Some what?"

"You know."

"Say it! Say it!"

"I'll git it mysef." Bainie started up angrily. Ishma held her
back.

"No, I'll get it."

"There's plenty up by the hog-lot," said Bainie, quickly pla-
cated.

"It smells awful. Makes me sick."

"You'll git used to it by the time you've got eight younguns
to doctor, like I have."

"Eight! God-a-mercy!" Ishma turned to go off the porch.
Passing Ned, she snatched him up and held him high above her
head, staring at him and giving him a slight shake. "How'd
you get here? How'd you get here?" she asked, of herself.
Putting him down as suddenly as she had lifted him, she hurried
off. Laviny's puzzled look met Bainie's.

"Whad she mean, mommie ? Poor little feller ! Whad she mean, you reckon ?"

"She's shore a sight," said Laviny, venturing no explanation.

Ned, a little frightened, hid his face in his grandmother's lap. "You ort to git Steve to talk to her, mommie. A good bawlin' out might hep her, an' she'll never git it from Britt. Maybe she'd listen to Steve. Reckon he's comin' in tonight ?"

"What you astin' me about Steve fer ? He don't tell me nothin' about his comin' an' goin'."

"I seen you lookin' down the road."

"Well, ain't it Sat'day ? He ain't likely to stay up in that lumber camp over Sunday. 'Tain't much I'll see of him though, if he does come home."

"Julie said he ast her to go to a dance at Carson tonight, but she couldn't git ready."

"I don't keer if he takes her an' goes furder."

"Yes, you do, mommie. You're powerful set on Steve."

"I wish he hadn't come back, that's what I wish."

"Lordy, mommie, ain't you skeered to say that ? You wish he'd been dead like that telegram said ?"

"I never said nothin' about wishin' him dead. You're talkin' keerless, Bainie. What I meant was that I kain't see as his comin' back was anything fer me to pray fer. He ain't no hep to anybody but hissef."

"He's promised to help with the crop this year."

"An' I'm jest a waitin' to see what his promise is wuth. About time he took holt, if he's goin' to." She looked wistfully down the road, stiffening her shoulders towards Bainie. "I reckon we'd better kill that pided hen fer Sunday dinner. Maybe Ishmalee 'll feel like makin' a good dressin' fer it. Steve can eat a sight o' dressin'."

Ned's face was still buried in his grandmother's lap. He wouldn't cry. No, he would *not* cry. But he wiggled his head to make granny notice him.

"I know what Neddy wants," she said, getting up. "That apple in the crack behind the cupboard. Then we'll go take off the diddlies."

She went into the kitchen, Bainie looking after her sulkily. "Don't let little Jim see yer apple," she called, "less'n you divide it." Laviny pretended not to hear, and left for the barn by the back door, with Ned trailing her happily. They were barely up the hill when Britt appeared with his gun and dog.

"Thought you wasn't in seven miles o' home," said Bainie. "Ain't you goin' to the Bald ?"

"No. When I got well up on Tiry Knob I could see the smoke boilin' out o' Dark Moon, an' I knew we's in for a fire-fight. I'll have to go down the mountain an' let the fellers know. Hope Steve will get in. We may have to be up all night."

"An' me plumb beat out !"

"We'll get along without you. Jim got back from Gaffney's ?"

"You know he always makes it dark."

Britt was looking around inquiringly, and Bainie answered his eyes. "Ish is up by the hog-lot."

He looked relieved. "Bain, I don't want Ishma to know about the fire, if we can help it. She might want to go."

"Shorely she wouldn't ! She ain't that crazy, Britt."

"Don't tell her anyway. You stay home an' say nothin'. I'll go gether up the men, an' I'll ask 'em to go up the mountain by Broke Yoke ridge, 'stead o' this way. I'll come back here myself, but I'll tell Ishma I just changed my mind about going to the Bald. Maybe I can get uncle Zeke to round up the men for me, an' I'll hurry back."

He lifted his gun and laid it carefully on the cross-beams. "She won't notice it up there 'fore I get back, an' I'll take the dog with me."

"Land sakes, Britt, why'n't you up an' tell Ish she jest ain't a-goin' ?"

"I don't mean to cross her noways at all, long as I can help it. Where's Ned ?"

"Up at the barn with mommie."

"Well, I'm hurryin' down. If that fire gets to Dancer ridge it'll take the haystacks. Jed Stone says he'll need all three of 'em an'll pay me cash. It's no joke my needin' money."

He stepped off briskly. Nowadays he often moved briskly

for a few minutes, then dropped back into his most careless step, humming a new phrase of music or perfecting an old one. But this time he remembered not to sing. Ishma might hear him and ask Bainie questions. And Bainie always blundered when she attempted diplomacy.

She went into the house to jerk Jimmie away from the churn, and when she came out again Laviny was in front looking searchingly down the trail.

"That kain't be Steve come home an' gone down again ?"

"No, it's Britt. He come back 'cause he saw fire risin' from Dark Moon. He's gone for help, an' he don't want Ish to know about the fire. 'Fraid she'll go."

"She might. There's no handlin' her lately."

"Lately ? They never was. But Britt makes me sick, easin' around 'fraid he'll hurt her feelin's."

"Shet up ! She's comin'. Look out for them shaky steps, Ishmalee. You don't want no mishap now."

Ishma came on the porch with her arms full of a pungent, green plant that grew rank and early in the rich ground by the hog-pen. Bainie took the stuff and carried it into the kitchen. Ishma sat down, feeling the unusual quiet of the place, and thankful that three of the children had not come home. She had been dreading their return, each with his or her particular little world of noisy wants. "Eight !" she said to herself, her mind on Bainie's prophecy.

A sound of violent scuffling came from within, and angry screams from Ned and little Jim. Bainie came out, dragging Ned by the arm.

"Keep yore brat out here ! He's scratched Jimmy all bloody."

Ned, though not hurt, was trying, with some success, to howl louder than Jimmy. Ishma put her hands over her ears. Ned hopped to her lap and pulled her hands away, still screaming. She ought to listen, he was doing it so bravely.

"Ain't you goin' to spank him ?" asked Bainie, and Ned paused to hear the answer.

"She jest ain't," Laviny broke in. "It was Jimmy's fault. I's watchin' through the winder. He hit Neddy first."

" 'Course you'll take up fer Ned."

"Who will if I don't ? Britt's gone, an' Ishmalee's about as consarned as a door-post."

"Better not git so set on him, mommie. You'll have to do without him when Britt an' Ish move off."

"They ain't gone yet."

"I see they hain't !"

"Now looky here, Bainie, you know Ishmalee's done yore turns time an' time agin. She's been a power o' hep to ye, first an' last. Give you all her money onct — "

"Fourteen dollars ! An' I've paid it back twenty times in rations, an' waitin' on her when she was in the straw with Ned an' the twins — "

"You sew that mouth up ! Didn't she give you her heifer ? Let 'em drive it off, an — "

"Please stop, mother," said Ishma, white and quivering. "I'm not asking her for anything."

"No, you're jest takin' it !" Bainie's flashing eyes and pink-spotted cheeks came near giving distinction to her uninteresting face. She had choked back her fancied injuries till she felt she must strangle or speak. But Ned had rushed back into the room, and a despairing howl from Jimmy made her postpone her verbal onslaught and dart to his rescue. Again she came out dragging Ned. "I'll spank him myself !" she cried. Laviny flew at her, tearing the child from her grasp.

"I dare you to lay a finger on him, Bain Wishart !"

Ishma covered her eyes and sat immobile. Laviny glanced at her and subsided. Her voice became natural again. "If Jim wuz half as good as Neddy they'd play peaceable. Bainie ort to know that."

Ishma looked up, her eyes dark and glistening as with water, though they were burning dry. "It's not Ned she's sore on, mommie, it's me. She'd treat him the same as her own if I wasn't here. Wouldn't you, Bainie ?"

"Anybody 'd be good to a kid without a mommie. But he *has* got a mommie, an' — "

"An' I'm *her*," said Laviny. "If Britt an' Ishmalee move off, I 'low to keep Neddy."

That helped Ishma, and brought the tears. "It wouldn't be

fair to ask Britt to give him up. He thinks there's nothing like Ned."

"Shucks, he'll git used to younguns, an' won't keer if one is missin'."

Ishma sprang up with a hysterical start and leapt off the porch.

"Mind what you're doin' !" Laviny cried out. "Stop right there now ! I'm goin' to talk to ye."

Ishma turned to her mother and waited, standing in fire.

"You act like Harret Smith when she didn't want her last youngun. I couldn't blame Harret much, 'cause she'd had eight, an' Lem Smith was allers dauncey an' ailin'. But you ain't got no cause to complain, Ishmalee. You ain't been hurried birthin' younguns. You've got a roof over ye, an' if it leaks there's allers a dry spot you can shift yer bed to. You ain't starvin' ner goin' naked. An' you've got a man that thinks you're the pot o' gold in the rainbow. What more do you want ?"

"Hush, mommie !" warned Bainie. "Somebody's comin'."

Laviny looked hopefully down the mountain. "Steve, I reckon." But it was only Tim Wheeler. After greetings, Bainie said she was starting to the barn to take in some wool she'd put on the shed to dry.

"Need me to hep ye ?" asked Tim.

"No, thank 'e, Tim." But Laviny said she was going along. "I've got to see that she don't draggle it an' dress up ever' locus' bush on the mountain with fribs. Make yersef at home, Tim. Sorter surprised to see you this fur up the mountain sence you an' Julie broke up. I reckon it's so ?"

"Looks thataway, aunt Laviny."

The two women left for the barn, Ned holding fast to Laviny's skirt. When left alone with Ishma, Tim looked at her and dropped his head dismally.

"What's the matter with you and Julie, Tim ?"

"That's what I've come about — the matter with Julie." He got up and brought his chair nearer to Ishma. "I b'lieve I know what it is. I've knowed a good while now, but I kep' thinkin' she'd git over it."

She waited, wondering how she could help him and why he had come to her.

"You know, Ish, I ain't a man fer makin' trouble 'twixt folks."

"Why, no, Tim."

"You an' Britt have always thought a sight of each other."

"Yes — and we're likely to keep right on that way."

"I know that — but, 'fore you's married — Julie, she sort o' liked Britt. She likes him now."

"Not the way you're thinking about, Tim."

"What's she lettin' him hang round her fer then ?"

"What you sayin', Tim Wheeler ?"

"He's goin' there all the time."

"Yes, aunt Cyn is forever asking him to come down and settle Zeke."

"Aunt Cyn stays half her time over at her sister's on Larky, an' Britt hangs 'round jest the same."

"He can't, for he hasn't got time. Britt works !"

"Zeke lays drunk, an' Britt an' Julie sing an' play the guitar an' banjo."

"I tell you, Tim, that Britt is only friends with Julie, like they've been since he was two years old. He's got to have a little time away from home. This place is no sugar-tree camp nowadays. I don't sing any more myself, and Britt's bound to have music of some kind. He couldn't live without it. If Julie helps to satisfy him, I'm thankful to her."

"His guitar jest stays there, hangin' up waitin' fer him."

"It's in the box under my bed right now."

"You go look, Ish."

"Just to show you, I will."

She got up and went into the big room full of beds. Tim peered after her.

"Find it ?" he asked, as Ishma came out.

"It's not there. But it makes no difference to me. Britt is not after Julie the way you think."

"It's not Britt I'm bothered about. It's Julie. It's what she keers fer him that's troublin' me. I've tried to swing off to other girls, but I kain't somehow. Looks like you'd have some feelin' fer me, Ish. You know what it is to love hard."

"But what can I do ?"

"You can tell Britt to keep away from Julie. He'll do what-

126

ever you say, an' I'll quit losin' sleep. Ef he didn't see her ever'
day — "

"It's not every day !"

"I bet he's there right now, settin' under the tree by the spring,
tum-te-diddlin', an' Julie singin' that song he made up. They
don't ever git done with that song."

She wanted to know about the song, but she wouldn't ask.
Britt ought to have told her.

"They're always at it — that corn-drappin' song. You know it
goes thisaway." He began to sing, ludicrously out of tune.

> *Mountain men, it's time fer hoein'*
> *When you hear the ring-dove mourn;*
> *Time to ask—*

"Don't, Tim," she said, trying to keep her fingers out of her
ears. He stopped, not in the least taken aback. No one ever
had been able to convince Tim that he was not musical.

"I'm too heavy-minded to sing anyway," he said. "I bet they're
together right now."

"Tim, I'll tell you where Britt is, then you'll know what a fool
you are. He's gone to the Swimmin' Bald for ramps. He took
his gun, and some bacon and meal for camping out."

"Well, I reckon you know. But Julie 's heard a lot o' stuff.
They're startin' a tale down in the valley 'bout you not bein' satisfied. They say you've jest set down. An' they say Rad Bailey
is still waitin' fer ye, hopin' you an' Britt are goin' to break up."

"Tim, I was sorry for you, but if you are going to carry tales like
that around the country, I don't care how miserable you are."

"Don't Rad ever come about you? Folks say he does."

"He was here when we had singin' on the mountain about six
months ago. That's the last time. I'm ashamed of you, Tim. I'm
most too ashamed of you to be mad at you."

"Well, Lizzie Welch says she could git Rad quick enough if it
wasn't for you."

"Tim, you want me to tell you to shut your mouth ?"

He was sitting with his chair turned so that he could see down
the trail.

"Looky yander, Ish !"

She looked and saw Julie and Britt coming up the hill. Britt was carrying his guitar and Julie had her banjo. Ishma felt her blood quicken, but she clutched the back of her chair and sat very still. She had not a pang of jealousy, but she was very angry. Britt ought to have told her he was going to Julie's, and not let her make a fool of herself to Tim. And here he was, calling "Hello, Tim !" in his gay, easy way, as if he were all right with the world and his wife. Tim gave him a sulky reply, and Julie, without speaking to Tim, began talking to Ishma.

"I didn't bring Ellie. She wanted to stay, an' I hope Bainie won't keer."

"She'll be glad to have one more out of the way. You changed your mind about going to the Bald, Britt?"

"Yes, I got to thinkin' that home an' music was good enough. I'd left my guitar down at uncle Zeke's, so I went after it, an' made Julie come along with her banjo. We'll try out some pieces, an' when Steve an' Jim come in, we'll go see if we can trail that fox that's ramblin' over Dark Moon."

"You're not speakin' to me, Julie ?" appealed Tim, unable to keep the silence he had meant to observe.

"Jest waitin' fer you to look like you wanted me to," said Julie, laughing. *"I've* got no hard feelin's."

This was enough to draw Tim's heart from the depths. He jumped up and seated himself by Julie's side. Britt was listening for small feet pattering on the hillside, and went to meet them. When he re-appeared a moment later, with Ned on his shoulder, Tim called to him, "Me an' Julie 's goin' to the spring," and was answered with a "Good luck !" from Britt as they disappeared.

Ishma wanted to talk to Britt, but could think of no way to begin. He was playing with his son as happily as if there were not a care or problem in the world. He wasn't clean either, wearing the clothes he had worked in all the week, instead of shining from his usual Saturday wash-up. "No use," he had said, "to dress up for the Bald." He would change when he came in Sunday night. His hair was getting too long, but that was her fault. It was her job to cut it, and she hadn't mentioned it lately. When too long the curly circlets seemed to fasten into one another, making a

128

forbidding tangle and giving his head an overlarge stolidity. Very often now she missed the mental mating which had been so perfect in the early days of their marriage. He wouldn't listen any more to talk of leaving the mountain. "My hand 's on the plough right here, honey, an' I'm not goin' to take it off. You jest wait !" It was harder on him than on her, yet he could be cheerful about it and talk of waiting. In January he had cut the logs for their house, having been unable to find work away from home. The road job was finished, and Ishma would not let him try the lumber camp again. So he cut his logs, kept good fires, and made roof-boards. Made them endlessly. Laviny had told him that he could have all the board-trees he wanted for himself, if he would turn out enough to cover her house and the big barn first. In high spirits Britt had set in on the job, but Ishma had felt a little bitter. All that work for board-trees that could be bought for a few dollars standing ! Britt said he wasn't counting it in money. He'd do that much for her mother anyhow. He'd put the boards on for her too, if ever he got time. They couldn't go into a tight new house and leave mother to the weather. Ishma didn't believe they would ever get into a tight new house, but she gave him a hug and said if she were as good as he was, maybe they wouldn't have to take so much punishment. He held her tight then, kissed her tears, and said, "You just wait, honey !"

Wait ! The word stung like a lash. All she wanted now was to get away. They could never get an inch further without a little money, and they would have to go where the money was and find work. When they had saved up two or three hundred dollars they could come back and begin right. There was the bean-field now all ready for grass, and it would take sixty dollars to buy good seed for seven acres. "A dead man can't walk." She resented Britt's hopefulness in the face of intolerable facts; but more than she suspected, he too was feeling the heavy hand of circumstance. More and more he was falling back on his music, or rather on his ability to create it, as help towards softening life and moulding it in the fashion of his modest vision. But the air about Laviny was corroding to music. She wanted him to play only when there was company to be entertained. What he most enjoyed was playing for himself, and inventing new little phrases for old pieces, or sometimes making an entirely new song. This was why he liked to slip off to Julie's, though he never thought of it as "slipping off." Julie was so quick to catch any new thing, and the next minute would be playing it on her banjo. His mind and courage would warm up in her company. With a whistle cheery enough to liquidate all misgivings, he would go back to whatever job might be uppermost. But a bold whistle, and the careless sling of shoulders, easily could be interpreted as indifference to anything that required taking thought. Actually he had merely donned armor against the disintegrating power of worry.

Ned was another renewing factor in his life. He could forget everything doubtful in the presence of that vivid little body. Ishma's support had become less reassuring. Love was still warm at the centre of their lives, but it had lost its power to shine through. In a fog of uncertainty they wound painfully about each other, pushing and tugging their burdens. But when Britt looked at Ned, life seemed justified and sure, directed by a power not in his hands. Ishma felt differently in the presence of her son. He was another and stronger reason why they should break away and get a start. Gone from her were the hours when her love for Britt, and his for her, had made mere living luminous and enough. For Ned's sake, if not their own, they *had* to get a start.

Ned, on his father's knee, was hearing about the trap. It had been set on the trail of a weasel that made a nightly visit to suck the blood of their few indispensable hens. Yes, daddy had gone to the trap, but there was nothing in it. A ground-hog had been there but it had got away. The mystery of its escape had to be explained to Ned.

"The trap caught his leg, and he took his big, front teeth and sawed it off." Ned looked dolefully at his stout little legs. "Him own leg?" he asked with such fearful awe that Britt burst into laughter. "I reckon he figgers this way, son. It's better to lose a leg than for his whole body to go to the cook-pot and be et up."

Ishma, without intending it, dropped a vehement "Yes!" Britt looked at her inquiringly, but she stepped aside and he turned again to Ned, whose mind had teed from cook-pot to cake. He told his daddy of the stove-wood so proudly brought in, and what

130

granny was going to bake for him as soon as daddy got some flour. Britt was asked pointedly when this would be.

"Just as soon as Jed Stone pays me for the haystacks."

Suddenly Ishma knew what to say. "Britt, I want that money."

"All of it?"

"Every dollar. I haven't touched money for a long time, Britt."

"All right, you can have the handlin' of it. I'll tell Jed to pay it to you if you want me to."

"I don't mean it that way. I want it to do as I please with. I want it to be *mine*."

"You'll get what we need, I reckon." He was puzzled, and tried to show no reluctance.

"No, I don't even promise that much."

"I was expectin' to use a little of it on a project o' my own, but that can wait a bit. Seems to me though we ought to put in some rations with part of it, for I'll not be makin' any more till the crop is in. Let's ask mother about it. Maybe she can get along."

He went into the house, and a minute afterwards Laviny came flurrying out with him. "What you after now, Ishmalee? What you want with all that money?"

"All? There can't be much for three haystacks."

"It'll be twenty-one dollars. Them beans is wuth twice as much as common hay."

"Oh! You've changed your opinion since we planted the field."

"Of course she has," said Britt. "She's not goin' to let Jim corn it to death either. She's goin' to let it stand till we can buy seed and grass it down."

Laviny kept on the track. "What yer wantin' with it, I'm astin' you?"

Ishma was stubborn. Britt's eyes plead with Laviny. "Can't we let her have it, mother?"

"You can do as you please. There'll be a doctor to pay 'fore long."

"I'll go to the camps and work out enough for that."

"In crop time? You goin' crazy too, Britt?"

He was bewildered. Of course he couldn't leave the farm;

and if he could, Ishma wouldn't consent for him to go back to the big woods. They needed that money. But Ishma wanted it. She was planning something, just as *he* was. He hadn't told her about it, and he didn't intend to tell her until it came to something. Now he'd have to give it up for a while. He couldn't refuse her. But what was Laviny saying ? He couldn't believe his ears !

"You're honeyin' her too much, Britt. It's bad fer her an' you too. Ef you'd take a stick to Ishmalee onct or twict she'd soon be so's a body could do something with her."

Britt's veins turned to running fire. Words fell from his lips as from a furnace. "If a man said that to me, he'd be peckin' on his box !"

"Be makin' his coffin, would he ? Well, I'm not makin' mine, an' I'm sayin' what I please in my own house."

Britt tried to cool down. "I reckon you've got a right to lay me out, mother, but I d'ruther you let Ishma alone."

"An' if that ain't jest what I'm doin' I'll larn how over the river."

"B'lieve I'll go feed the steers," said Britt, ashamed of his outbreak, and wanting to get himself away. "Looks like Jim's goin' to be late."

When he was gone, Laviny began again. "You tell me what you want with that money ? How can I know to let you have it, if I don't know what you're doin' with it ? Britt ain't got no sense about it."

"I know I want it, that's all."

"Ishmalee, you ain't too old fer me to slap yer jaws. Britt gives you yer pick o' d'ruthers an' then you kain't please yersef. You're my own gal, an' I don't reckon yer man'll ever own the roof his younguns air born under, but he's wuth more in his tracks than your air over the whole place, you're gittin' that triflin'. Maybe Jed won't take that hay."

"Oh, he's got to ! He's got to !"

Laviny looked closely at her daughter and saw she was trembling. "Now don't be actin' a fool, Ishmalee. I'll make you some snake-root tea tonight. That'll put you in a sweat an' you'll sleep good. I see Ben comin' in a trot, up hill too. Jim kain't be fur behind him."

Ben ran up, threw his cap on the porch floor, and handed some packages to Laviny.

"Dad told me to run ahead with the coffee an' fat-back, an' tell mommie to double up on the bread. He's bringin' the fellers to fight the fire, an' they ain't had supper."

Laviny went in with the packages. Britt would be mad because Ishma had heard about the fire, but how could they keep it from her when the whole country knew about it ? "A fire is something nobody ain't hid yet," she said to Bainie in the kitchen.

Ben, on the porch, was giving Ishma further information. "Dark Moon's lit up already. We could see the smoke from top o' the hill the other side o' the river, an' poppie got ever'body he could to come along."

When Britt came down from the barn he was confounded by the sight of men gathering in the yard. There was Si Welch, Jed Stone, Alec Craig, Milt Slagle, Rad Bailey, and four or five others. Rad was keeping back in the edge of the crowd, and looking at Ishma when he thought no one was watching him. Several voices hailed Britt, and Jim asked him if Steve had got in. "There'll be a great old fire tonight," he said. "Come on, boys. Pick you out a nice seat on the floor. There'll be no settin' down places up on the ridge when we git there."

Britt asked if anyone had seen uncle Zeke Webb. He had sent him down to tell everybody about the fire. No one had seen him. "He's under a tree sleepin' it off," said Si. "Whyd'n't you lend him a team o' crawfish, Britt, an' maybe he'd a got around ?"

And so, thought Ishma, Britt knew all about the fire. That was why he didn't go to the Bald. He thought he'd keep it from her. But she was no baby, and he'd better be careful about treating her like one.

Jim was calling to Bainie, "Crowd the pans in that oven ! Any o' that ham left ?"

There had been no ham in the house for months, but Bainie knew her part. "Not a sliver left," she called back. "Fat-back 'll have to do ye, an' I'll make the coffee strong enough to stand up."

Ishma went to tell her mother that she would set out the dishes she had won with soap coupons, carefully saved over three years. She had meant to keep them packed away until she and Britt had their first meal in the house by the Birch spring. But she couldn't believe any more in that new house. After unpacking the dishes, she went to the cellar and brought out some canned tomatoes and her last half-gallon can of peaches. Then she returned to the porch and sat down.

"Let's go to the spout an' wash up, fellers," said Jim, leading the men off. Jed Stone was the last to follow. Britt held him back, and asked if he'd brought up the money for the hay.

"No," said Jed. "Thought I'd wait till the fire was over. A feller might buy haystacks up there tonight an' have nothin' but ashes in the wind tomorrow. If they last through it, I'll be up in three days with the wagons an' the money."

Jed went along after the men, and Britt returned to Ishma. "You'll get it," he said. "How you feelin' tonight, honey?"

"I'm all right, Britt, and I'm going to the fire."

He began to plead. She hardly listened. He caught her by the shoulders and came very near shaking her. "You know you can't climb that hill now. You'd get all out of breath. You've got to think of the baby."

"That's what I've got to forget. I have to go, Britt. You know I didn't get to that one four years ago."

"Ain't you never going to forget that fire, Ishma?"

"No. And I'm not going to miss this one. That can't happen twice to me. If I'd seen that other one —"

"Oh, I know! You think everything would have been different. But it wouldn't."

"Yes, it would. What I feel is no lie. And I'm going tonight."

Bainie, who had come to the door to listen, broke in before Britt could answer. "Listen to that thing! Jest clear light crazy." But Bainie had something more exciting on her mind than the fire. She had to find out what Ishma was up to, wanting that money and not telling what for. "You're not goin' to let her have all of Jed's pay, are you, Britt?"

"Yes, I am," he said, wanting very much to tell Bainie to keep her tongue out of his business.

"Well, I reckon you'll git it back, in a way. She'll be buyin' house-fixin's. You goin' to git that white iron bed at Gaffney's, Ish? I'm goin' down tomorr', an' I'll speak fer it."

"No. I don't want a bed."

"It's what you're goin' to need anyway. I won't put Ned in the truckle-bed with my younguns when you git another 'n here. He'd kick an' scratch till they'd be out in the floor."

Laviny called Bainie into the kitchen. "Don't let her bother you, honey," said Britt, as soon as she was gone.

"She can't bother me any more." Ishma was seeing clear. She was going away. She could forgive Bainie her bitterness. She could be sorry for her. Poor Bainie could never get away.

"Soon as the crop is in, I'll find something to do. There's bound to be something waiting for me, an' I'll find it."

"If you do, we owe more than you'll make."

"Gaffney won't push us. He's a good feller."

"I don't see you coming clear here ever, Britt."

The men shambled back from washing-up. Julie and Tim were herded with them.

"Looky, Britt," called Si, pushing Tim. "Here's a big spring lizard we found."

"Aw, quit it," said Jed, "an' let's have a tune 'fore we start. What about it, Britt ?"

"Not playin' tonight, Jed."

Tim had found Britt's guitar, and said he would try one fer the fellers. "Hand her over," said Britt hastily. "I'll play." And Si informed all and sundry that Tim could play about as well as a jaybird could sing.

Rad was keeping very quiet, and that could not be permitted on a gala fire-fighting night. Jed Stone dragged him out, and under a fire of epithets he was made to do a clog. The effort was so feeble and brief that he was advised to try it standing on his head, since his feet had gone no 'count. When Rad sat down he chose a place close to Ishma's chair. The deepening shadows where they sat gave him courage to remark, "Well, it's crop time again." She had replied, without turning her head toward him, "Yes, it's crop time." And the sound of her voice, for him only, mellowed the air for Rad.

His chair might have been vacant for all Ishma felt of his presence. Over and over, one thought was rolling through her mind. She was going away ! She would go just as soon as the baby was

born and she was well again. She would go, and Britt would follow her. Why hadn't she done it long ago? She could recall
nothing of the allurements, the plans, the entanglements that had
kept them on the mountain. She had stayed on simply because
she had forgotten that her feet could carry her away. How easy
things were if you didn't look at too many at the same time!

"Ain't you never goin' to git tuned up, Britt?"

"What'll it be, boys?"

A torrent of suggestions was at last reduced to Si's choice, "Sourwood Mountain." He agreed to dance, and being an expert at
the buck an' wing, won a majority.

"Lick yer fingers, Julie! We got to have the banjo with this."

Julie and Britt began to play, and soon all of the men were
singing except two. Tim was promptly choked off, and Rad kept
very still, as if movement might break some sort of desirable charm.
Each man had his own method of keeping time — shuffling, wriggling, pounding or dancing, as he sang.

> *I've got a gal on Sourwood Mountain,*
> *That gal's mine till the jedgment day!*
> *I've got a gun an' it ain't no quitter,*
> *Boys, boys, you'd better git away!*

> *One man killed on Sourwood Mountain,*
> *Jest when the chickens was crowin' fer day!*
> *Devil's a rantin' on Sourwood Mountain,*
> *Tell all the boys they'd better git away!*

> *Two men killed on Sourwood Mountain!*
> *Come an' see who's layin' in the hay!*
> *Tech my gal ef you want to see yer Jesus!*
> *Boys, boys, you'd better git away!*

Britt's fingers were flying. His hair, that bushed large around
his young face, sparkled with health. The railroad lines that had
begun to perplex his forehead were entirely gone. He was smiling, and Ishma knew that just behind him Julie was smiling too.
How little it took to make some people happy! Why did it take

136

so much for her? She could get no pleasure out of the rough singing and thumping, though Britt was trying to make it interesting by putting in the wildest shakes and quavers wherever he could. She liked music when Nature helped to make it. She liked to sing above the winds, or against a waterfall, or throw her voice over the tree-tops to the rising sun. These wriggling, perspiring men, with their whoops and steady pat-pat, made her feel like a chained animal.

A smothered crash from the kitchen told of a shattered dish. "Break them all," she said to herself. "I'm going away."

Three men killed on Sourwood Mountain!
Ol' mammy cryin' fer wild Jim Ray,
Layin' on his back a lookin' at the angels,
Boys, boys, you'd better git away!

Wild Jim's dead on Sourwood Mountain,
Layin' on his back with his head again a tree.
No little gal a cryin' on his bosom,
But a forty-four Colt they say belongs to me!

The men were tireless. The verses, with their piled up dead, were innumerable. Britt's fingers raged over the keys. Raged, relented, crept and seized. Julie, playing hard, leaned to his shoulder. He threw back his head and her face was in his bush of hair. "Take him," was Ishma's voiceless cry. "Take him, for God's sake, and let me go!" She was shaking so visibly that her chair made a little pecking noise on the uneven floor. The sun was down behind the mountains, and the shadows grew deeper on the swaying porch. There was no one to notice her but Rad, and pity was mixed with the greed and hunger in his eyes.

"Lucky that ol' Frady put locus' sills under this here porch," he said at her ear. "Some o' the boys will bust through the floor boards in a minute."

Ishma didn't know that he had spoken. Her heart was bursting, and her thoughts were tumbling crazily in her head. The noise and the music suddenly ceased. Laviny was in the door. "Come to supper, an' welcome," she was saying. " 'Tain't much but it's yorn." There was pride in her voice. She had managed to set out a plentiful meal, and by tomorrow every housewife in the township would know about the new dishes. She was feeling kindly toward Ishma. "Maybe the gal be takin' a turn back to herself," she had said to Bainie in the kitchen. "She'll have a long way to go," Bainie had sulkily responded.

The men rustled in. Britt propped his guitar against the wall, and Julie laid down her banjo. Neither of them wanted supper. Julie had made Britt take a bite with her before they started up the hill, she told Ishma. "I had a fat hen baked fer tomorr', an' some apple pies. We jest went into 'em."

"I know you're a fine cook, Julie."

"She kain't beat you, Ishma," Britt was too anxious to declare.

"Don't yer fingers hurt, buddy ?" asked Julie.

"No. Calluses are too hard."

"Let's see."

He held out his hand and Julie rubbed the tips of his fingers.

"Britt," said Ishma, "I want you an' Julie to do something for me. I want you to sing your new song."

He assumed ignorance. "Which un's that, honey ?"

"The corn-dropping song."

"You've heard about that ? It's not finished yet. I was goin' to play it for you soon as I got it like I want it."

"It's good enough for me now. I want to hear it tonight. Hear you and Julie play it together."

"All right ! Julie thinks it's fine, but it wouldn't be nothin' without her."

Julie's clear, moving soprano mingled perfectly with Britt's heavier tone. They needed each other musically. "That's all it is," thought Ishma. "A good and happy thing. People oughtn't to talk mean about it." She could feel sorry for them, and the unjust talk, as they began to sing.

> Mountain men, it's time for hoein'
> When you hear the ring-doves mourn.
> Time to ask the moon so knowin'
> When to plant the corn.

Corn ! . . . corn ! . . . corn ! . . .
When the bell-bud 's turnin' pink,
And the moon gives us the wink,
Then we plant the corn.

Flaxbirds watchin' from the tree-tops,
Waitin' for the dinner horn,
Yellow wings all in a flutter,
Golden like the corn.

That's my girl, a stream o' sunshine,
Singin' 'fore me in the row.
If she don't quit laughin' backwards
Down I'll drop my hoe !

An' her lips I'll be a kissin',
Sweeter 'n honey in the gum.
There'll be twenty stalks a missin'
When the tossels come !

Ishma was a girl again, back in the spring-time field with Britt, and love, beauty and song filled the earth and the heavens. Julie was waiting for her comment, but Britt knew the meaning of her silence and closed eyes. He leaned towards her. "You know who my girl is, Ishma ?"

"I reckon I do, Britt."

"Lord, it'll be fine when you can get out on the hills again and I can hear you sing. She makes the mountains listen, Julie."

The men came crowding out of the kitchen door, clamoring their approval. "You shore hepped my appetite," said Jedd. "Whyn't you an' Julie go to Knoxville an' make some phonygraph records for that company what's combin' the mountains fer musicianers ?"

"We're not that far along, Jed."

"Shucks !" said Si, "they only have to hear you onct."

"Once would be all, I reckon."

"Say, boys," Jim called to his subject troop, "that fire ain't holdin' back fer us. We've got to shove up the hill."

With whooping and stirring they got in file on the trail leading up to the ridge that overlooked Dark Moon. They had decided that their force was strong enough without the women, and Julie went in to help Bainie clean up. Britt waited by Ishma in the porch shadows. She must promise him that she wouldn't come up to the fire.

"But, Britt, if Dark Moon burns you know what a wonder it'll be. I've told you about seeing it when I was little, and all my life I've wanted to see it again. If I could, I b'lieve — "

"What, honey ?"

"I can't just say it. But I'd rather go to that fire than go to New York. There's something here" — she touched her breast — "that would burn loose."

"I wish you could go. You know I do. But you mustn't. You know that too."

"Well, you go on, Britt."

"I will when you promise."

"I'll try to stay away."

"Good girl ! You always do what you try." But still he hesitated. "Ishma, there's something I'm going to tell you when I come back from the fire. I wanted to be plumb shore about it first, but maybe it will chirk you up."

"Oh, what is it ?"

"It'll take time to explain. But I've got a plan."

He couldn't see the light die in her face. A plan ! She was so weary of plans. Something must be *done.*

"Maybe before you know it we'll have our house-raisin' an' get to ourselves."

She failed in an attempt to smile. "We've thought that before, Britt."

"But this is goin' to work. I'll tell you all about it soon as I get back." He started off, running to catch up with the men. Hot tears rolled from Ishma's eyes. "He thinks it'll work. Wish I could fool myself just for a minute. That much would rest me a little." But why had she dropped back to her old despair when she knew she was going away ?

Laviny came to the door. "Ishmalee, you come an' take holt in here. I've got to put Neddy to bed. Julie went to milk fer ye,

an' left Bainie to clean up. Ever' pot an' pan 's got to be washed."
"Three of 'em ! That's a killing job."
Laviny moved closer to her. "You hain't been cryin' again ?
We never broke but one of your dishes."
Dishes ! Oh Lord ! "I don't care about the dish."
"What air you cryin' about then ?"
"I'm not cryin'."
Laviny peered closer. "You ain't hearn what they're sayin'
'bout Britt an' Julie, hev you ?"
"Yes, and it doesn't bother me."
"That's sensible. Britt'll never keer about anybody but you."
"I know it. But if I were dead, or out of the way somewhere,
he might marry Julie, an' be sort o' satisfied. Britt can't stand
being lonesome."
"You ain't goin' to die, Ishmalee. The women in our fam'ly
don't go thataway. I never hearn o' one that did. You git up
from there an' come an' hep Bainie. 'Tain't safe to git notions in
yer head when you're waitin' yer time. I been too easy on ye.
You come along now !"
Laviny went in, but Ishma made no movement to follow her.
Instead, she shoved everything off the big chair and got on it.
The back of the chair was lowered, and she could lie there at full
length. "I wonder how daddy felt," she thought, "lying here for
three years, and nothing ever happening except to lose Steve."
Her father had been helpless; but she had feet to walk with,
hands to work with. She needn't wait. They thought she had
changed, but she hadn't; not a bit. She was as ready to work as
ever, but she had to know that it was getting her somewhere. She
couldn't go on this way, sliding back a little every year instead of
getting out. As soon as the crop was in, Britt would go off, and
if he could find work he would come back with a few dollars to
put on debts. There would be no time for house-building before
the harvest. Next winter he would have to make a new clearing
if they had any place for corn. This year they were putting the
"new-ground" in corn for the fourth time without a single cover
crop, and that would ruin it entirely. It had been thin, acid land
to begin with, not like oak and hickory coves. They had decided
on it because it lay fine to the sun, and they thought they could

clover it in winter and make it richer every year. Now it would hardly bear a crop, and Britt was supplementing it by grubbing up an old field covered with little poplars. They ought to let the poplars stand and grow for pulpwood. But of course they had to have bread from something. And bread was about all they would make this year, in spite of Britt's hard labor. With no surplus, what would they do? This was why Britt would have to go away again, and she'd be left there, sick with nobody but Bainie to help her. She wouldn't even have a quiet place to sleep.

She thought of aunt Nancy Barton's home on the Little Tennessee, in a curve of the river. Aunt Nancy and uncle Bill Barton lived there by themselves. It was a sweet place, with flower-beds around the door and everything clean. The walls inside were white-washed, and there was one little room with a sunny window and blue curtains looped back, that they kept for their girl whenever she came home. Nanny Barton had "broke away" and gone to college and studied law. She was about thirty-five now, and had never married. Abe Winston had wanted to marry her, and he was still a bachelor. He proposed to her every time she came home, and didn't care who knew it. She hoped Rad wouldn't be like that, staying single all his life and losing happiness because she couldn't give it to him. He had a kind heart, and he ought to have a good wife.

How Nanny Barton must love to come back and sleep in that quiet little room! She had slept in it herself once, the year that nobody but aunt Nancy had saved sweet potatoes for bedding out. She had walked the nine miles over there to get some, and aunt Nancy wouldn't let her leave until next day. Ishma shut her eyes, and again heard the loving old voice telling all about her girl, Nanny, who was so smart and was a real partner in a law firm in Knoxville. Ishma thought that if she could sleep in that room for a week she would have everything cleared up in her mind and would know what to do. If she could go there now aunt Nancy might let her stay right on until she was sick. Maybe after she was sick too, for there would be twenty-one dollars to pay her through the nine or ten days when she couldn't be up helping with the work. Aunt Nancy was old and lame and lonesome. Uncle Bill was blind, and his mind had gone weak. She'd be glad to have somebody. Yes, that was what she would do — right away ! Ask aunt Nancy to keep her until she could leave the mountains.

Laviny whisked by her with some dishwater to be thrown out. She thought that would make Ishma stir, but Ishma didn't care now if the yard swam in dishwater. As Laviny passed back, mumbling noisily, she couldn't help saying to her, "I wonder how aunt Nancy Barton is getting along."

"Purty well, I reckon, up in Heaven," came the quick answer. "You're losin' yer mind, Ishmalee. Don't you know she died over a year ago, an' her girl come in an' took uncle Bill away ? Lem Weaver 's got the place now. It must smell sweet with all his gang in it !"

Laviny went in, leaving Ishma motionless on the chair, trying to remember. Yes, it was while she was sick, just after the twins went, that aunt Nancy had died. The twins ! Again they were in her lap, beating the air with their tiny fists, their sinless bodies stiffened in convulsive accusation. The twins ! She mustn't think of them now, when her mind should be kept easy and free, as she could have kept it in Nanny Barton's vanished room. But there were other places. She must think of one where she could go. She could work for six weeks if she went right off. Maybe she could work up to her time. That would give her two months. She'd save her money — she couldn't go till Jed paid — she wished she could go tonight. Her feet would feel good on the earth — just walking off. She'd get a place — she couldn't stand Bainie any longer — Jim had to take his heel off Britt — Round and round spun her mind. She didn't hear Britt until he was at her side, looking down upon her; close to her face with his eyes deep and dark and soft. Why did he have to look like that when she was trying to get away ?

"That's right, honey," he was saying. "Get you a good rest."

Rest ! She hardened at that. "What you back for, Britt ?"

He pulled up a broken chair and sat down by her. "I got to thinkin'. I felt mean, leavin' you here so low-thoughted without tellin' you what I's plannin'."

"Guess that could have waited, Britt, and made no trouble."

"You heard what Si said about that Knoxville company huntin' up mountain singers ? They sent a man down to Carson, an' he heard me play that time I was there seein' about the taxes. He said if I'd come to Knoxville they'd shore give me a chance. Julie was there that day, an' we played together for him. He said for us both to come. An' that's what I was plannin' to do with the haystack money. Part of it, I mean. I wouldn't take it all."

Ishma sat up, not suddenly, but slowly, as if ages lay on her shoulders. What could she do with this boy ? How could she ever get anywhere ? Britt didn't notice that her voice was painstakingly even, dangerously natural. "You and Julie. That's what you were meaning to do with the haystack money."

" 'Course Julie 'd pay her own way. And we'd have plenty to come back on."

"It would be a fine trip for you — and Julie." The iron-like steadiness of her voice was still unfelt by Britt, and he went on innocently. "Yes, but I'm thinkin' about the money we'll make, not the trip."

"And this is what you've come back to tell me ?"

"It's not half. I want you to know what I'm goin' to do with the money I'll get out of it. There won't be a fortune, but it'll be enough, from the way that man talked. You've said many a time that two or three hundred dollars would put us where we could lift ourselves out. We'll have our little house, and grass the ridges for cattle. Mother'll be fair. I'll set a dynamo in Moonfeather Falls an' we'll have electric lights. You can make a dynamo do all your work, honey — cookin', washin' an' ever'thing. It'll be as easy as livin' in a city, an' we'll have the mountains too. It'll be great, Ish-my-own, an' all I need is some o' that haystack money."

"You haven't got any haystack money, and you are not going to have any. If you get to Knoxville, I reckon Julie will have to pay your way. She'll be glad to do it. She won't mind talk if you're the cause of it."

He began to feel something strange about her. "Why, Ishma — "

She got out of the chair and stood before him. "I want to tell you, Britt, that the next time you come so far to chirk me up, telling me something you're going to do, don't come till you've

144

done it. That's the way I'm going to do with you. You'll find out when it's done."

What, he thought, had happened to Ishma's voice? How much more was going to happen? He wished to God that that baby was here.

"You're not plannin' anything yourself, are you—Ish-my-own?" He stumbled over the pet name. How could he call this strange woman that? Her superb head was carried high; her straight shoulders had thrown off every weight and were free in beauty. Was his head swimming, or was the dusk actually piling up around her like waters that bore her up and away from him?

"If I'm planning anything, Britt, you'll hear about it in good time. You only need to know now that the hay money is mine. You will tell Jed to bring it to me, just as you promised."

"I—I thought I'd ease your mind a bit, Ishma."

"You have. You've eased it mightily. And you'd better get on up the hill."

His lips were twisted in the curve of pain that seems almost comical on a face that is rarely without a smile. Ishma saw it; and there were days to come when she would be able to see nothing else; but now she held herself steadily while he turned away and left her. Then she laid herself down, trembling till the big chair shook.

Laviny came out of the kitchen carrying a lantern, rusty and smoke-blackened, and seating herself began to clean it. When she spoke to Ishma, her voice was well spiced with sarcasm.

"Ishmalee, seein' you've rested a good bit, maybe you could make out to bring that jar o' milk from the spring-house that I want to pour inter the churn tonight."

Ishma rose silently and went off toward the spring. Laviny watched her until she became a part of the dusk. "She's walkin' mighty heavy," the mother reflected. "I'd hate to be misjedgin' her."

Bainie, in the middle-room door, eyed her mother at her task and sniffed aggravatingly. "What you doin', mommie?"

"Cleanin' up after Jim." Laviny threw the words at her as if she were throwing sharp pebbles.

"I don't reckon Britt ever went 'possum huntin'."

"If he took the lantern he made out to clean it when he got back. That's Britt. But it ain't Jim."

"You goin' to hang it out tonight ?"

"An' what if I am ?"

"Steve 's so big he could hep hissef up if he fell down."

"Shet up, er I'll send more'n words at ye !"

Julie came to the door and stood by Bainie. "Aunt Laviny, we're goin' up the hill back o' the barn, thinkin' maybe we can see the fire risin'. You come along too."

Laviny got up, saying she might as well. Her job was done, as much of it as *could* be done. They put off and the house was left in silence. Only the sleeping children were within.

Ishma was sitting on the rock wall of the spring looking down at the water. It was black in the twilight, but she knew it was crystal clear. Perhaps that was the way with things around her. They looked black, but maybe they weren't.

It was always this way with Ishma. Whenever she got out of the house and sat alone, her mood, after the first few breaths of release, became self-accusing. She had the sky, the woods, the winds, the stars; all so clean and mighty. How could she let anything that happened in a little house bother her ? She ought to bring it help — be to the house what the sky and woods were to her. Yes, that was the way she ought to stand in life. Not forget that the winds and the stars were behind her — that she could lean against their clean strength. Youth and health ! She and Britt possessed both. How could a few little debts matter ? They would soon sweep them aside and forget them. Her anger was gone. She was sorry for Julie. But of course Britt couldn't have that money. That was hers.

Why, she believed she was hungry. She'd forgotten to eat any supper. A tin cup hung on a nail in the spring-house door. She filled it with milk, and as she drank she heard a whistle on the lower trail. Steve was getting in. Big old Steve, like his father, with jolly words for everybody, and never a dollar ahead.

He had come up the trail whistling, but when he saw no light and felt the silence, he advanced cautiously. Here was his opportunity. He crossed the porch to the ladder-like steps nailed to the wall, and climbed to the loft. Up there, under the shattering roof, smelling of rot and moss, he had his sleeping bunk and his few clothes. Hastily he began stuffing his things into an old kit. When Ishma, her feet in sneakers, and stepping lightly as always, entered the kitchen with the jar of cream, he didn't hear her. He was over the big room, absorbed and hurried. Ishma, finding the house silent, supposed that he had passed it and gone on up the hill. Of course he had heard all about the fire. She went back to the big chair and again laid herself down. It was good to have the place to herself. Her mother must have gone with Bainie and Julie up the hill. They had slipped away from her, afraid she might go. That was fine ! All she wanted was a chance to get up to the fire by herself. But she'd rest a few minutes before she started. She'd go, and Britt would forgive her when he found it hadn't hurt her at all. And that nonsense about markin' the baby — she knew there was nothing to that.

She had thought she would enjoy the silent house, relieved of its assertive human presences. But too quickly it began to oppress her with its own claims to dirt and disorder. She forgot the crystal water and clean-swept skies, and thought of the bones which she had heard Jim's dog crunching under her bed the night before. She knew the floors had two days' litter on them. All of the quilts needed washing. She wished she could have two sheets on her bed. Bainie quarrelled because she used *one*. Bainie and Jim slept between the quilts. Every pillow case was worn out. She had to put her pillow under the sheet. What would the doctor think ? She couldn't be sick in that room again. She couldn't have Bainie bringing her soppy messes, whining at every step. She couldn't. She would never breathe again if she had to stay in that room. Jed said he would bring the money and the wagons in three days. Could she wait three days ?

She began to feel sick. It was that sour mud in the yard. She'd get up and go on to the fire. But she was strangely heavy, and lay still. There was a noise in the loft. She listened. Steve must be up there. She wanted to call out, but that would be an effort too. When he came down with a kit-bag in his hand,

147

he started off almost on a run, without seeing her. She knew what it meant. Steve was leaving. He was going away.

"Steve! Steve!" she shouted. Forgetting all heaviness, she was up and running after him. "Steve, you're leavin' out!"

He stopped, and waited until she came up. "What if I am? Whad I stay here for? You reckon my brain's all bug-juice? Whad I stay for?"

Ishma felt stunned. "Nothing," she replied.

"You got it right. Nothin'."

"Where'll you go, Steve?"

"It'll be the navy this time, I reckon."

"Oh, Steve, you'll never come back!"

"You needn't keer. I'm no good here to anybody. A feller kain't git along here at all without a little money to stock up with an' set him right. He'll stand in his tracks till the wind blows him down. If a man's got his land paid for, an' stock to work it, an' machinery, an' the right seed to put in the ground, an' 's able to hire help in a pinch, an' there's market for his stuff without givin' it all to the railroad, or the man at the other end, I reckon he can get along in the mountains. But when he's got nothin' but his two bare hands, he kain't swing it. Not nowadays."

"You're going to leave *us* here."

"Well, I kain't carry you all along with me, can I? An' I tell you, Ish, it's no bed o' roses I'm going to. It's a slave's life, but this is a dog's, an' a slave, after all, is human, an' can look out an' see something. But it ain't no cinch. I want a home same as anybody else. I'd stay here an' marry that darned little Julie, only me an' my kids couldn't eat rocks. 'By, Ish!"

She was clinging to him, and he wouldn't push her off. "Take me with you, Steve," she was crying. "Take me with you!"

"Lord, girl, whad I do with you?"

"I'll work, Steve."

"You ain't able now, Ish."

"I'll work right on. I'll not miss more'n two weeks. You don't know how I'll work. You can get me a place."

"Nobody wants a woman in your fix, Ish. An' I won't have a cent to pay for you when you're down. It'll take me a while to

148

save up something. I'm strapped now. Britt's all right, Ish. You've got a good man. Wish I's half as good. You stand by Britt."

She was still holding to him. Her hands wouldn't loosen. "I'm going with you, Steve. I've got to get off this mountain."

"Now you listen to me, Ish. A woman 's a woman. She's bound to carry the baggage in this life. They's no gittin' out of it for her. A man can walk off any time, but a woman kain't. God, or Nature, or something we kain't buck against, has fixed it that way. You make up your mind it's all right. That's all you can do right now. Goodbye, old sis. I've got to beat it 'fore mom comes along. You tell her I'll send her ever' cent I can spare. An' I won't fergit *you* either."

He pushed her from him then, and ran. She watched until she could see his tall figure no longer. Her gallant shoulders were slumped as she turned back to the house. Her head had forgotten utterly its deer-like poise. She was aching from head to foot, as if she had been thrown back from a stone wall against which she had violently flung her whole body. But her mind hurt most. Her thoughts seemed to be like fine stabbing needles that couldn't make their way out anywhere.

She was asking so little of life, she thought. That was her great accusation. So little of life; when, in fact, she was asking for more than life has ever given to anyone; an understanding of itself.

In her early years Ishma had rested sanely on her love of beauty in nature, and her unthinking union with it. She had moved largely and unconfined in that roominess of personal being. A leaf in the dawn, glittering on its twig, belonged to her as much as her shaken, clinging curls. A glance upward at an amiable, drifting cloud could ease a growing irritation within her, and sometimes her sense of grace would not abandon her for a whole day. A storm on Cloudy Knob would leave her feeling that she had taken a breath as deep as her being. Wind, curving about a ridge of silver poplars, could sweep life clean.

With adolescence, beauty was not enough. Nature made her lonely, hungry, impatient. An inquisitive denial of sensuous adequacy became her torture. Then Britt had entered, overwhelming, undeniable, restoring. Being was again complete. For how long? Surely their love had not vanished; it had strangely deepened; but where was its joy, its fullness, its soothing finality? She could still surge and grow dizzy with the thought of those first months together; but memory was not life. Life was again barren. It was a stripped, stark question. It hurt all the more because of Britt and Ned and the little new soul on its way into the barrenness, where its cry would never be answered.

Ishma didn't know that, to the mind born for questing, somewhere on its burning road, love and beauty must become hardly more than little nests for the comfort of the senses. Unaware of her high demands, she mistook the source of her suffering. Clean sheets and a sweet-smelling door might help but would never heal her mind.

She stumbled toward the house, and halted near it, despairingly turning her eyes to the sky. There, in the north, was a quivering, growing light. Thought of the fire seized her. She would go to the ridge. No one would be on Lame Goat Knob. From there she could look down on that burning glory. It could hurt no one. It could only help.

She heard someone opening the back door of the kitchen, and moved softly to the west end of the house. There she waited until her mother passed through to the front, then she started up the hill.

Laviny came out on the porch talking. "Ishmalee, them crazy gals went on to the fire. Where you at anyhow?" She went to the end of the porch and called her daughter, who was fifty yards up the hill, panting and pressing her heart.

"She's cruisin' aroun', I reckon," concluded Laviny, "an' I hope it will do the pore thing a little good. I'll go to bed soon as I've hung the lantern. Steve's shore to git in tonight, an' no moon to hep him." He would need no help, she knew; but the lantern was her way of telling him he was welcome in spite of her bitter tongue. "Bainie can sniff till her nose is hot," she said, as she lit and hung it to the corner post nearest the down trail, "but I've got a right to hang out a light fer the only boy-child I've got that the Lord let live."

It was three hours later when Ishma came around the house

from the upper yard, struggled up the steps, and fell down on the porch. Laviny, hearing a noise, came out, her head wrapped in a large handkerchief. She looked about, and by the help of the lantern discovered Ishma.

"I thought I heard ye," she said, crossing to her in a small fury. "Whad you mean, makin' me lose sleep like this ? You've 'bout killed yersef, an' t'other one too, I reckon."

"I'm all right," Ishma faintly assured her.

"You look it l Where you been ? You ain't been to the fire ?"

"No."

"I knowed you had more sense than to go."

"I couldn't get there. My breath kept giving out. I nearly choked more'n once."

"Thank the Lord l I'd laid out to give you a good combin' down, but looks like you've had enough. You git to bed now."

"I'll stay out here awhile. I want all the air I can get. My breath 's comin' hard."

"Kain't I git something to hep ye ?"

"No, go to bed, mommie."

"Well, I got to have my rest, an' they's no danger you slippin' off agin. You can please yersef 'bout layin' out here. But you'd better git on the chair."

Laviny went back to bed. "She'll lay still," she told herself, as she dropped to sleep. "No need to tie a cow with a broken leg."

Ishma reached the chair, and after lying still a few minutes she was breathing naturally. "My way is down the mountain, not up," she said. And she, too, went to sleep. It was sometime after midnight when she was awakened by footsteps nearing the cabin in the rear. That might be Britt coming down. No, it wasn't his step. Thinking she would ask about the fire, she went to the end of the porch, where she sat down, leaning against the corner post, with the lantern above her head. Beyond its rays the night was black. She had only a moment to wait before a man came into the faint circle of light, and she saw that it was Rad. He stopped when he saw her, and spoke her name. When she didn't answer, he softly repeated it.

"Yes, it's me, Rad."

His feet felt like stone, but he couldn't stand there without saying something. "I'm goin' down. They've got enough up there without me. We got the fire purty well shut off."

"Are the haystacks well out of danger, Rad ?"

"They are now. But it looked fer a while like they'd have to go. We all laid ourselves out to save 'em. What you settin' up for ?"

"Resting a little, out here by myself, and waiting for Britt. I like to sit in the night by myself sometimes."

"If you like it black you've got what you want tonight."

He came closer to her, and the look on his face made her say, "You go on, Rad."

"Yes, I'm goin'. Goin' furder 'n you think, Ishma. I'm leavin' out."

Oh, men could always go ! "Where to, Rad ?" Her cool voice had sharpened a little.

"Anywhere is better'n here if I kain't have you, Ish. I've been savin' a long time, to have something to go out on. Ever' since you got married. I made up my mind then I'd leave out. I'll never quit thinkin' about you till I git where I kain't see you."

"You don't see much of me, Rad. Not enough to bother you, I'd say."

"But I know you're over here, only three coves from my place, an' it's all I can do every day o' my life to keep from tearin' across where I can say a word to you."

"You know better than to talk to me like that. I know better than to listen too. You go on, Rad. And I hope you'll like it where you're going."

"I'm all ready to leave at daylight. I'm takin' Bud Wells' car over to him. He's in Waynesville, an' left his car over here at his daddy's. I've got it waitin' for me down at the turnin' place below Si's. My suit-case an' all in it."

"Where you going from Waynesville ?"

"Well, the world is big. I'll find some place I like. I'll take the train at Waynesville, an' set out. My God, if you's goin' too, Ishma !" Rad looked as if he were staggering backwards as he said it, but there was a crude glory in his face.

152

"You hush that, Rad," said Ishma, like a smothered storm.

"I kain't. I've held in for four year. You might let a man bust loose once in that time. It won't hurt you, Ish. There's been days when I've dropped the plough-handles an' turned my horse loose, an' got halfway over here 'fore I come to an' turned back. An' knowin' you's so troubled youself only made it worse."

"You've got nothing to do with my troubles."

"But how can I help it hurtin' me to see you so disappointed-like—"

"I'm not ! Not with Britt, I mean. If that's what *you* meant."

"He don't git for'd at all, an' you're feelin' it. If I could hep you I wouldn't go, but I kain't hep you, an' I'm goin'."

"And leave Lizzie Welch ?"

"I wouldn't marry Lizzie noway. If ever I marry I've got to go fur enough to forget you first."

"Well, go."

"You don't mean to be hard, Ish. You're just feelin' bad."

"What do you know about my feelings ?"

"I know you're miserable."

Ishma stepped into the yard. "But that mustn't bother you, Rad."

"There's a big, happy world out yonder, Ishma. Don't you ever think about it ?"

She was standing with her back to the balsam bush, and her hands were spread out toward the invisible valley.

"Yes, I think about it."

She knew she had to have it—that world. It might not be happy, but she had to go and see. In three days she would have Jed's money, and she could take the first step. Somewhere men must see clearly. Somewhere life held out an answer.

"Anybody can see what you're comin' to here, Ishma. It gets harder ever' year, an' you know it. You're not foolin' yerself. I've sold my horse, an' my yearlin's an' my bees; everything except my land and timber. I'll find work where I'm goin'. There's work out there for any man that wants it. I put four hundred dollars in the Carson bank last Friday. I'll show you my bank-book."

Ishma had never seen a bank-book. Rad held it carefully under the lantern. She looked at it, but didn't touch the wondersome leaves.

"You see the figgers. Four hundred dollars."

"You can go a long way with that, Rad. You can go far."

"It's enough for you too, Ish! I can take you too!" He was frightened again, and the words hurried out tumblingly.

"Don't, Rad! If I want to go away, I've got money of my own. I can leave if I want to. Now you go on from here."

"You've got money? You goin' away, Ish?"

"Maybe I am, and maybe I'm not. Anyway it's nothing to you."

"You kain't have much money, Ishma. Not near enough. A little egg-money maybe. You couldn't get along by yourself. Not now you couldn't. If you'll let me help you, I'll take Ned along with us, an' I'll give him a big chance when he grows up."

"Take Ned? I want you to know that if ever I go away from Britt I'll go without stealing from him. Ned is his as much as mine. I'd be fair."

"Ishma —"

She began to cry silently. What was the matter with her? Why didn't the man go?

"You leave me by myself. Can't I never be by myself?"

They heard steps on the trail above them. She couldn't let anybody find her with Rad. It would make talk. Bad talk. She stepped into the darkness behind the balsam bush. Rad, knowing what she meant, sat on the porch under the lantern, and was scanning his bank-book when Alec Craig came down.

"Hello, Rad? What you doin'?"

"Thought I'd rest a spell an' figger on something. Are you all through up there?"

"Jest about. But we got into it bad after you left. It's quiet now, an' I told my old woman I'd be back soon as I could leave the fire. They'll all be down d'reckly, lessn it's old Britt."

"What about Britt? He ain't hurt, is he?"

"Not what you'd call hurt. He's settin' up there on the ridge like a stone man."

"What's happened to him ?"

"Haystacks all burnt. What's that jumped behind that balsam ?"

"A cat run from under the floor. There it goes now."

"I kain't see good at night. Yes, sir, his hay 's all burnt. Not a straw left. An' he's jest settin' there. I thought there was a man in Britt, but he acts like a dead un."

"Couldn't you get the fire shet off ?"

"I say ! A big, dry pine, hangin' with bark, caught afire close to the field, an' when it got to burnin' high it fell lam over the fence. After the stubble an' trash got to blazin' nothin' could a stopped it lessn a rainspout busted on it. You comin' out now ?"

"Not down the trail. It's nigher for me across the woods."

"Well, look out for snakes. The fire 's got 'em runnin'."

When the dark had disposed of him, Ishma came from behind the balsam. The lantern's light was on her face.

"Lordy, Ish ! You're as white as a skinned locust. You ain't feelin' that bad about the hay, are you ?"

"Don't talk, Rad. Please don't talk." She stumbled forward and sat down on the steps, her hands covering her face. Rad stood by her, dumb and afraid to move. It was minutes, perhaps ten, before she made sound or motion. When she rose she seemed to stand tall, and reached her arms toward the unseen valley and beyond.

"It's all there," she whispered. There were walls about her. But walls had gates.

Rad, at her shoulder, began talking kindly. "What is there, Ish ?" She didn't hear him. Again her arms were flung out.

"All there !"

"What, Ishma ?"

"Everything."

"I'll give you everything you want — out yonder — if you'll go."

She turned to him, though she didn't see him. The wall has a gate. Here was a way to open it. At that moment Rad was hardly a human being to her. He was a friendly force who would help her turn the lock and let her pass out. She had forgotten her own body; and if she could have remembered it, she would have held insignificant anything that could be done to it. The side of her face toward the lantern shone as if light were quivering through the skin. Her heart was transparent, winged.

"I'll go, Rad," she said.

"With *me*?"

"Yes."

"You mean it? When?"

"Now, we can't go fast enough."

She was strong and sure. It was the man who was white and trembling.

"I'll be good to you — an' to the baby that's comin'."

She didn't know what he said. She didn't know that Britt was on the ridge, engulfed in woe. She began walking down the road. Her feet were light, her shoulders high.

"Fast, Rad, fast!" she said, walking before him.

CHAPTER VI

EPISODE

"Howdy, Britt !"

"Howdy, uncle Hewy !"

"Who's conductin' the sarvices today ?   Old Harney, er young Siler ?"

"It's Jim Siler."

"Better come off the fire-coals, Britt."

"I'm comfortable enough, uncle Hewy."

"You talk like a man what's got a snake by the tail an's snappin' its head off."

Britt made no answer, and uncle Hewy cocked his ear toward the meeting-house door. From behind it came an undulating rumble. "Yeah," he said, "it's Siler. He's prayin' now. I might as well set down. Reckon this heah bench ain't yo' private property, Britt."

The bench was not far from the steps in front of the Ivy Fork meeting-house. The old man took a seat by Britt, enjoying his scowl of unwelcome.

"Makes Siler mad ef you go in while he's prayin'. I'll wait till they start the hymns. Takes him forever an' the next day to git in all his big words in that prayer. Heah that ? He's jest got to s'licitood now, an' that means he ain't more'n half done."

It was a beautiful third Sunday; the first preachin' day since Ishma's flight. The ugly little meeting-house that had replaced the pioneer structure of logs, was built of rough, unpainted lumber, and stood retreatingly in the edge of the woods. Three wagon roads that led up to it from three winding gaps in the hills, were quickly lost in the choking green of the woods. Not far away Ivy Creek subdued its tumbling arrogance under a smothering screen of kalmia and rhododendron. A bit of flat land in the rear of the house had been cleared and was used as a burial ground. Back of that, Cedarcliff mountain rolled up and away to a snow-blue sky that held not a cloud. Ivy Creek settlement would have perfect weather for the most notable day in its history.

For the first time since he had become an ordained servant of the Lord, James Siler had before him a full congregation; an audience that in numbers at least was worthy of his talents. His pride rose toweringly to meet the honor. But it was not merely a packed house that he had before him. Not an eye in the assembly was too old or too faded to put on an extra gleam, and the dramatic throb in the air ought to have made the slight building tremble on its pins. Siler knew what was expected of him. Verily his people should not find him wanting.

He had been an Ivy Creek boy with advantages. His parents had sent him to Carson High School, and afterwards he had worked his way through a course of Biblical study at a small sectarian college where the higher criticism was touched gingerly, and only with the aim of making it bow humbly to traditional belief and superstition. Mountain lads who were strong enough to break out of the coves and seek the highway, were usually of a mind to assimilate truth wherever and however it was uncovered to them. If they found their way to Chapel Hill they did not stand debating by the stream of modernity crackling through the walls of the old University. They plunged in, and without pain cleansed themselves of the mental barnacles fastened upon them by an ebbing ancestral tide. Sometimes circumstances forced them into a college of more modesty and retirement, where only limited thinking was acceptable. Here they succeeded in ruffling the pools of acquiescence around them, and made their final exit noisily enough but trailing no honors.

Siler was an exception to these forthgoing minds. His narrow head rose ambitiously at the top, giving him the preacher's forehead without the thinker's breadth. Having chosen his college for its rigid orthodoxy, he went to it as a suckling to its dug. His course ended, he again proved himself the exception by returning to his father's farm, contented to divide third Sunday honors with uncle Ash Harney who had served forty years in the Ivy Creek pulpit. His manner of gathering up the loose, religious ends in the community, so contrary to the leave-alone policy of uncle Ash, had not met with favor. Sam Merlin said right out loud, "A long nose is easy burnt; he'd better not come sniffin' round my hearth." But everybody admitted that the young preacher was grand when it came to handing out the old-time religion in the meeting-house where it belonged. He sure would hit out hard and heavy this day.

The people had begun to gather early. Britt took his seat outside after everybody was supposed to be within; but stragglers were still hurrrying up. They stared at him in surprise, and spoke uneasily as they moved up the steps. "Ef you had to come," their eyes said, "why'n't you go in an' take a back seat where you'd orter be ?" Only uncle Hewy paused, finding in Britt's moody watchfulness a challenge. He had to get at what the boy was after. Hewy had a head-piece, he had.

Uncle Hewy Jones was little, old, and dried to the bone. He walked between two canes, but was chiefly upheld by his waspish temper. When he spoke, his voice crackled uncertainly, without affecting his determination to be heard. As he talked to Britt, there was a crowing note in his tone which made that young man want to punch him with the heavy stick that lay across his knees.

"I thought ol' Ash would have his tongue in this pan o' 'lasses, but I reckon Siler headed him off. What *you* reckon, Britt ?"

"I'm glad it's Siler." Britt didn't look up, but lifted his stick from his knees and placed it beside him.

"That tack-head ? Ef he had the brains he thinks he has, you couldn't git 'em inter a sixty gallon vinegar barrel. What you glad it's Siler fer ?"

"You stay round an' maybe you'll find out."

Uncle Hewy perked his head like a jay-bird and looked Britt up and down and all over. Under the inspection, Britt's hazel eyes deepened to a fiery dusk. "What you here for anyhow ?" he demanded of Hewy. "You ain't been to church in three years."

"What's ever'body here for ? They're here to vote, an' my vote 's as good as anybody's, ef they do call me a half infidel ! Ain't they churchin' Ishmer today ? Ain't they readin' her out ? **An'** I'm here to vote like a man, I am !"

"There's enough here without you crawlin' out o' yer coffin to —"

"My coffin !" shrieked Hewy. "Young feller, ef there'd been as much to you as there is to me right now, Ishmer 'd be puttin' on yer pone bread as smilin' as the fust week you's married. A man that kain't hold a woman, ain't a man. He's a piece. A sorry piece too. You hear it, Bud Green !" he laughed at a young man who was ambling toward them from the middle of the three roads. "I kep' ever' wife I had to her dyin' day, an' saw her buried right, I did !"

Bud took a seat by uncle Hewy and fell politely into the conversation. "How many wives you had, uncle Hewey ?"

"Eh ? How many ? Four. Four I had, an' I knew what to say to 'em. They'd let you know who wuz the man ef they's here today. There wuz Mattie Ann, who fell off a ladder the fust year an' died right off. A bit lazy, but I didn't let it hurt her. I saw she got about. An' Susan, she had yaller hair an' wuz right under my thumb. An' there wuz Emmy — Emmy — " he struggled with memory and triumphed — "Emmy *Jane !* She never put her foot out o' the house ef I jest lifted my little finger agin it. All fine women, with minds o' their own, an' I managed 'em. I knowed how."

"Ain't you fergettin' aunt Mary Kate, uncle Hewey ?"

"Mary Kate ? Say — there wuz Mary Kate. A good woman too. Put two ruffles on my shirts long as she lived. A good woman, Mary Kate. Buried her up on Larky 'stead o' down here. That's why I fergot her." He turned on Britt. "Crawlin' out o' my coffin, eh ? An' you couldn't keep *one.*"

"You might 'a' stayed at home an' let my wife alone. There's enough against her with no help from you."

"Agin her, man ? I want you to know I'm votin' fer Ishmer. I'm proud o' Ishmer. You ain't nothin' er you could 'a' managed her. When I got out o' bed this mornin', I said I'd come here an' stand fer Ishmer agin the whole congregation. I've got a mind yit, not a doty old piece like most of 'em 's got. I'll show 'em ! I've allers said a man 'at couldn't handle a woman wuz sarved

160

jest right when she walked off. You're big to look at, Britt, but you're purty small inside, an' I'm votin' fer Ishmer."

"He's through prayin'," said Bud, and rose to open the door and sidle into the house. As the door cracked open the preacher's voice rolled out distinctly, and Britt's face grew blacker.

"Listen at him !" said Hewey. "Takin' his text from the Old Testament. Goin' back thousands o' years to pick up a stone to throw at a woman. Goin' way back past Jesus, that smarty is — ridin' right over him !"

Then a new interest for Hewey came into the scene. A man of middle age, imitating the brisk step of youth, approached on the upper road. He was well dressed in clothes of modern cut.

"They're shore getherin'," said Hewey. "There's Hallet Ramsey, come on the number nineteen from Laneyville, I bet, an' walked up from Sam's sidin'. You're late, Ramsey," he creaked in reproof as the man joined them.

"Yes, it was hard for me to get in home today. I'm tied up in a big lumber deal in Laneyville."

"You hain't been home fer a good stretch o' time, hev you ?" The crowing note was again evident in Hewey's voice. He had something on Ramsey, without a doubt.

"I've been terribly busy. But it was my duty to come today. It is everybody's duty to be on hand in a time like this. I'm with you, Hensley, and I want you to know it."

He held out his hand, but it was not taken. Britt seemed engaged in shifting his stick back again to his knees.

"I understand," said Ramsey, much too superior to take offense. "Of course you are pretty sore. But the community will stand by you. I don't go too far, I hope, when I say that the community would stand by you if you took your gun, and gave the erring couple a good lesson. There are some who would call it nothing but your Christian duty. But I won't go as far as that. I am not presuming to advise you. I speak merely as a man who has the common good at heart. Morals must be preserved. Fail there, and civilization fails."

He paused for an instant of self-admiration before he repeated, "Yes, it is everybody's Christian duty to be here today. My wife and girls are inside, I suppose ?"

"Don't know as to yer wife," said Hewey, "but yer twins orter be. They rampaged past me on the road, cacklin' like orfant ducks. You'd better stay closter home, Ramsey. Them gals o' yorn need a daddy over 'em."

"You little wasp ! I can take care of my own family, Hewey Jones."

"Yes," cried Hewey, joyous in conflict, "an' that woman up on Brush Creek throwed in !"

Ramsey looked toward the church. "Shut up, you—" Then he realized that dignity lay in keeping cool. "You're old, Hewey Jones, and I'm not going to quarrel with you. You've done your duty in coming here to uphold the morals of the community—"

"Morals be shot ! I'm votin' fer Ishmer !"

"You old dog !"

"Who's the old dog, Hallet Ramsey ? You reckon I don't know about yore doin's on Brush Creek ? You reckon ever'body don't know it ? 'Tain't business that keeps you layin' up there away from home nine-tenths o' yer time. It's a black-eyed woman 'at's piecin' her apern strings right now 'cause o' you !"

"You look out, Hewey Jones ! You're an old man, but you can't talk to me like that !"

"Old ? How do you know I'm old ? You ain't been in this kentry more'n thirty year. Come down to steal the timber off'n our hills, you did. An' you pertend you're a Southerner. I dare you to say cotton ! I dare you to say cotton-*seed* !"

Hewey, between his canes, was jumping up and down on his tip-toes. His voice ended in a raging squeak as he craned his head to the highest possible stretch. Ramsey knocked the little straw hat off his head, called him an old fool, and went into the meeting-house. Again the preacher's voice rolled out in malediction as the door was opened, and subsided indistinctly with its closing. Unhampered by his indignation, Hewey took a large, red handkerchief from the bosom of his ancient ruffled shirt, and brushed his hat carefully. He then perched it on the top of his head, climbed the steps, and opened the door. A flood of words rushed over him. "—shameless, indulgent, defying the pure air of our hallowed hills—I call on you, my dear fellow-

162

Christians, to purge this stain from the sacred leaves of our church-book — to rise to the high call of duty — "

It was too much for uncle Hewey. He slammed the door fast and shook his fist at it. "Fool, am I ? An old fool ? You're all fools ! Take adultery out o' yore church an' it won't have legs to stand on ! I'll tell 'em !" He threw open the door and slammed it again with himself on the inside. Britt smiled with his lips, because they curved so easily, but his eyes were still sombre as he lifted them to see two girls near the steps. They were Julie Webb and Norie Ball. Norie was not contented with saying "Howdy, Britt !" as she went up the steps. "Law," she exclaimed, "how things do turn about ! Right here's where we stood that third Sunday after you's married, wishin' you an' Ishma joy !"

"Shet up, Norie," commanded Julie, who was passing Britt very slowly. They had not spoken to each other, but Julie said softly as she lingered, "You lonesome, Britt ?"

"Awful lonesome, Julie."

"You want me an' Norie to stay out here with you ?"

"Not lessn you just want to."

"I do want to."

"Well, I don't !" called Norie from the steps. And turning, she opened the door and went in.

"You might as well go 'long, Julie. I'm just as lonesome in company as I am by myself."

This was confession, not disparagement, and Julie whispered, "I'm sorry for you, Britt."

"Ay, ever'body's sorry. They don't know anything about it."

"I'm sorry different from the others. I liked Ishma a heap."

Britt became eager. "What for, Julie ?"

"I don't know. I just had to like her."

"So did I," said Britt, disappointedly, as if Julie had denied him a revelation. He had so often asked himself, why did he have to love Ishma ?

"But you quarrelled sometimes, didn't you ?" Julie reminded him.

"Not much, Julie. An' when folks quarrel it ain't always each other that they're mad at. I'll tell you how I feel, Julie. I'd ruther have Ishma livin' with Rad than have all the world to myself an' her not in it."

Julie's face became dreamy. "That's the way it is — that's the way it is," she said, swaying a little.

"What do you know about it ?"

"Maybe as much as you do," she answered, with spirit. Britt looked into her eyes, which were full of a sad defiance.

"Julie — Julie — you don't — you can't feel that way about *me* ?"

She began to cry, and turned to go up the steps. He followed her. Half way up to the door she stopped and looked down on him. He took hold of her skirt comfortingly.

"Ain't it a mess, Julie ?"

"No, it ain't ! I'd ruther it 'ud be this way than not be."

"Well, so would I." His mind was again on Ishma. "So would I. But I hate it for you, Julie."

"You needn't. You needn't hate it at all. Britt, when are we goin' to practice on that piece ? You ain't give up makin' that phonograph record, have you ?"

"I don't know what I'm going to do, Julie. I'll get through here first."

"Here ? What you got to do here ?"

"I'm not sayin'. You better go in, Julie. Folks 'll start talkin',"

She started, but couldn't quite go. "Britt, I want to ast you something else. When aunt Laviny gets her spells on, an' kain't look after Ned, you send him down to me an' mother. Bainie's got more'n enough with her own."

"Did aunt Cyn say I could ?"

"She won't keer. Will you, Britt ?"   ..

"Well, maybe. But if I go away I'll take him."

"Don't you do that, Britt. Don't go away. A man kain't get along with a little un."

"My daddy got along with me. An' maybe I'll go. Julie, you know ever'body here's down on me 'cause I don't go gunnin' for Rad Bailey. They come mouthin' around sayin' they're sorry, but what they want to say is, 'Why'n hell don't you get him ?' You know that's so, Julie."

"I reckon it is, Britt."

"The whole country 's ashamed o' me."

"It's mighty nigh that bad shore. But you don't know where Rad 's gone."

"I could find him. But if I lay Rad cold, where'll Ishma be ?"

"She'd come back maybe."

"What would I want with her here if she wasn't wanting it ?"

"She got so she didn't help you much, Britt."

"That's nothin' to do with it. There's bigger things than the day's work."

Julie was opening the door. She had seen two young men, Nat Wills and Jaby Pace, coming up from the woods, and she knew Britt didn't want to "start talk." Dropping him a wistful look, she went in. Jaby and Nat halted, looked at Britt, and nudged each other. The nudging was repeated several times.

"You watch me, Nat," said Jaby. He sauntered up to Britt. "Where's yer gun, Britt ? Fergot it, did ye ? Mebbe you left it by Rad Bailey's cold body ? I hearn you wuz goin' to give him a lead supper 'twixt here an' old age."

"If I had a gun I wouldn't waste lead on a thing like you." Britt got up and lifted his stick. "This is good enough for a hound dog. You get in there, if you're goin'."

"Just what I was meanin' to do, ol' feller," said Jaby, squirming away from Britt's stick and hurrying up the steps with Nat following him. "That stick o' yourn ain't pushin' me."

The boys disappeared behind the door, and by the time Britt had quieted down on the bench, Jane Febber came out. She saw Britt, and immediately seated herself by him, her plump, red face beaming intelligence and good will.

"You mustn't take it that I'm not sorry for you, Britt," she began, "but I couldn't vote against Ishma. They're votin' now, an' that's why I've come out."

"Thankye, Mis' Febber."

"Thank me ? Ain't you against her ?"

"I'm not sayin'."

She gave him a look of understanding. "You come home with me, Britt. Don't you mind the way folks are talkin'. I put a chicken in the pot 'fore I left home, an' Ben an' Lizzie are there today."

"Thank ye, but I'm goin' to take off soon as I'm through here. I made up my mind about a minute ago."

"Take off? You goin' into the mountains?"

"Fer a spell."

"Now, Britt, that stuff 'll pizen you. They're makin' drink now that 'ud kill a billygoat. You stay off it. Don't you go takin' to the woods like a wild hog."

Britt dropped his head, miserable beyond speech. Within the house the congregation began to sing "Old Time Religion."

"Listen to that Sue Rhodes singin' off key," said Mrs. Febber cheerily, but Britt could not smile. "There — that's the benediction. They're through now, an' I reckon they all feel better, havin' sent Ishma to burnin' hell. Just betwixt ourselves, Britt, she's better 'n more 'n one woman in there that voted big — an' I guess about *all* of the men."

"Thank ye, Mis' Febber," mumbled Britt. He was clutching his stick tightly, and the blood was rushing in and out of his cheeks as if he were panting. The door stood open. The people were rumbling and flowing out. Old Samuel Wayne and his wife were the first down the steps. Samuel was chuckling.

"Good work, Elminy! That'll teach the youngsters something. When I heard Siler throwin' them burnin' coals around, I was thankful I'd never had a leanin' to wildness myself. I shore never did."

"No more did I, Sam'l."

"No more did you? I say you didn't! No more did you? That's mighty free talk, Mary Elminy. No more did you? Whad you mean by that?"

They minced aside, bickering, and others pushed through the knot inside the door and streamed down the steps. The men gave Britt only a glance and a hurried greeting, but the women looked more lingeringly. Was he not young, handsome, and no doubt soon to be divorced?

Britt rose and stood near the steps, a little to one side. Three or four chattering girls surrounded him.

"Let's go to the spring, Britt."

"No, thank ye, Kitty."

"What you waitin' fer?"

166

"Maybe you'll see."

Mrs. Ramsey passed with the twins, and was voluble. "Don't hang your head, Britt. You've got friends left, and what you've lost is well lost. Don't you want to come home with us? Mr. Ramsey may have some good advice for you."

"Not now, Mis' Ramsey."

"Do come Britt!" urged a twin. "You're not thinkin' of Ishma now, are you?"

"Maybe I'm not."

"She's not thinkin' of you anyway."

"Maybe she ain't."

"Come, girls, come!" said Hallet Ramsey, as became a father on duty.

"We're goin' to have a candy-breakin' Thursday night," persisted the other twin. "You come, Britt."

"Sally, you hear me!" called Ramsey. He got them started, but their eyes kept trailing back.

"It's his hair," said Sally. "I b'lieve it would shine in the dark."

"It's his eyes for me," said Janie. "About the time you know they're hazel they turn out to be brown."

"Black, you mean."

"No, I don't."

"Well, I do! I saw him lookin' at the preacher when he came out the door, an' they's black."

Siler was still on the steps, smiling, and shaking outstretched hands. He had done his job well. He knew it, and they knew it.

Down below him a half-grown boy began to wipe his cheek vigorously. "Aunt Min, you gether that up," he said, as he wiped.

"What's the matter, Stan?" asked aunt Min.

"If you're goin' to shoot ambeer, you gether it up fust."

Aunt Min laughed with the crowd. "Shore, Stan. Didn't know I wuz scatterin'. Here, Britt, you try this." She offered him some tobacco. "Take it, boy. It's yore brand — spit er die." Again the crowd laughed, but she got no smile from Britt. "What you so way down about? You ought to've come in an heard the preacher layin' Ish out. My, he piled it on! That would 'a' brought ye out o' the sulks, Britt. My gizzard 's curlin' yit."

"He shore talked straight," another voice asserted. "I never hearn abody pitched into like that. But we kain't say it weren't due her."

"Who's the preacher goin' home with ?"

"Granny Tims. She's got him."

"I be bound fer her. She's swingin' right onto him. They'll roast Ish again when she gits him home. They won't know whether they're eatin' chicken or fat-back."

"Thank you, my good friends," Siler was saying, "but I'll go with sister Tims today." Then he moved down to Britt. "Here is the boy. Your hand, my son. You needn't have been ashamed to come in. It was an honest shame. Cheer up, my lad. Give me your hand."

The hand of the church remained untouched for an embarrassing moment before it was withdrawn. "Come, come," said Siler, "you'll get over this. We all have our troubles, and yours we have tried to relieve. The erring one has been cast out. We have administered justice in the name of the Lord."

Britt turned a look on Siler that ought to have enlightened him. It didn't, though the crowd saw and thrilled. "Take off your coat," he advised the preacher.

"My brother — "

"Take off your coat !"

"My coat, boy ? What do you mean ?"

Alec Craig pushed up to Siler. "He's goin' to fight. You'd better come away."

"Fight ? What ? You misunderstand !" But Britt called out, "Fight is what it is ! Get ready !"

"This is sacred ground."

"All right, come off it ! Plenty room in the road."

"I do not fight," said Siler, armored in dignity.

"Then I'll have to use my stick on you," said Britt. "I thought maybe I would."

"My young friend — "

"I'm no friend o' yorn, ner of any man that talks about my wife."

"Your wife, boy ?"

" 'Course, my wife ! Didn't I take her for better or worse ?
An' this looks like worse to me. Didn't I swear to honor and
protect her, an' ain't she needin' it today, with yore big mouth
goin' like a blow-hole ?"

"But she's left you ! She's gone with — "

"Shut up ! What's that got to do with what I swore ?"

"The boy has gone mad. Trouble has — "

"All right, I'm mad !" He slapped Siler's face. The crowd
tingled and held breath. Would the preacher — or wouldn't he?
Siler threw off his coat. He would ! The crowd breathed again.

"Fine !" cried Britt, and slapped Siler's other cheek. A hoarse,
happy roar went up from the faithful.

Siler was taller than Britt, a pinch or two heavier, and fully
as angry. As a working partner on his father's farm, with his
student days definitely closed, he kept muscles and sinew in strong
play. They could leap into action quite as readily as Britt's.
Also, like most highlanders, he came from valiant stock. When
he shot back after Britt's second slap, his blow carried more than
the weight of his own rage. It was augmented by a compulsion,
quite incalculable and surprising to himself, direct from his fighting forbears.

Si Welch, devoted to drama wherever it showed itself, saw a
chance for a real spectacle and began to shout for a ring. "A
ring ! A ring ! An' this has got to be refereed !"

Sam Merlin took him by the arm and jerked him into conference. "You goin' to spile the biggest show we'll ever git a chance
at ? The preacher 'll freeze up soon as we begin to talk about
fightin' by rules. He'll turn the Scripter on us. We can have
Scripter any time, steady as pone-bread, but this thing ain't fer
but onct. It's got to be kep' hot. Let 'em jump at it foot an'
fist, pound an' poker, maul an' squeeze, an' we'll see blood a-
flyin' purty. Turn on the reg'lations an' you might as well turn
on a crick full o' ice-water. Siler 'll walk right out on us. We
won't see a thing but Britt follerin' him with that club an' the
sheriff draggin' the boy to jail."

Si saw the point quickly and gave over formalities. The scene
already deserved rapt attention. Britt had received that first

blow on his shoulder, and reeled. Half-way to the ground, he had brought himself erect again by the sheer power of rage, but was forced to dodge quickly to escape another slug from Siler. The preacher meant to fight hard. Britt was going to get what he had hoped for — a fight that he would have to back up with every drop of his blood. Siler's first blow had left him in no doubt that he would have to take a terrific mauling. But he would have the imponderous, male joy of hitting back, with interest mightily compounded. That is, he would if he could keep his foothold and his consciousness. That he might lose both was intimated in the third thrust from the preacher, now quite unclerically rampant. His arm was long, and he rammed it forward with the lunge of annihilation. There wasn't time for Britt to jump back. He slued his body without moving his feet, and the slugging fist barely grazed his stooped left shoulder. There was a shout and a groan from the crowd — the shout for Britt's agility, the groan for his failure to "stand to it." His movement, unplanned and instinctive, was supreme tactics. Siler, jabbing the wind, almost fell forward, and before he was steady on foot Britt had moved a step back, just enough for his arm to shoot up and out and fall on Siler's chin with a force that ought to have buried that feature in his neck, and did nearly break Britt's knuckles. Siler went back, sprangling on the air like a mashed spider, but he didn't fall, and Britt leapt in, closing both arms around the preacher's waist. He would throw him, and if he didn't cry "quits" he would pound him until he ate dirt. He wanted to make his big mouth so sore he would have to keep it shut for a week. But it was too early in the fight for Siler to be thrown. He wrestled free with strength to spare. Britt danced off and glared for a minute. If he could only hit that mouth! He went in, but his blow merely glanced the preacher's nose, and his nose being his proud and sensitive member, and his forbears still on the job, he went squarely with his right for the centre of Britt's face. Britt saved his nose, but his left cheek took a stinging thud, the back of his neck cricked, and he went down hard — the first flat fall of the encounter. Siler drew back and paused triumphantly; a little too long. Though Britt had a hundred bells clanging in his head, he sprang on the gloating Siler, as if the ground itself were plunging upward. They clinched and reeled, but the preacher rose tall, and it was Britt who was pushed earthward. If they fell he would be underneath, in a fine position for the pounding he had intended to give his opponent. Something had to be done before he touched the ground. Suddenly releasing Siler's waist, he shot his arms straight up and brought them down again, tightening them around the preacher's arms and body. When they struck earth, though Britt was underneath, he had Siler's arms bradded to his sides and there could be no pounding. He could hold him there all day, but he knew that a deadlock would not be permitted to last more than a few minutes. Siler would be pulled off and accorded the victory. If only he could roll over and put his enemy under him! He strained with all his might, but Siler strained too, pressing Britt's body into the earth. His shoulders dug into Britt's chest, his knees dug into Britt's thighs. There was a continued pause. The locked combatants were as still as the stone face of Cedarcliff indifferent above them. And the crowd waited, heavily silent.

"We'll give 'em five minutes," whispered Alec Craig.

"Ten!" said Si, unwilling to lose his drama. "Something 'll happen. The preacher 'll break, er Britt 'll bust. Give 'em a chance."

Britt knew, as well as everyone present, that if the preacher got his arms loose it would be all over for the man under him. He would have to surrender or take a pounding that would drive him out of the county. He'd never lift his head in Wimble again. And if he kept Siler's arms prisoned and didn't break the deadlock he would lose anyway with the other man on top. Damn Wimble, and everybody in it! It was Ishma he had to think about. This was *her* fight.

Sweat streamed from him. It felt like blood on his skin. Blood with red pepper in it. He strained till his eyes were like hot coals, ready to flame in his head. Looking up with burning vision he saw her. Only her head above him in the cool, blue air. He saw right into her eyes. She was looking as she had looked that time after the twins were born and he lay helpless in the other bed. "We'll fight through, Britt." He strained

171

again, his veins at a bursting stretch, and slowly, an eighth of an inch, a quarter, a full inch, two inches, he began to turn their two bodies as one.

The cheering during the early part of the fight had been divided, rather more for Siler than for Britt. The preacher had drawn sudden loyalty to himself by his very human response to the call of the flesh, while Britt suffered from the fact that he had not shone brightly in recent neighborhood annals. But, after all, no one held a grudge against him, which could not be said of Siler. More than a few were nursing resentment against his "long nose." Support had gathered for Britt. Who said he was a coward ? Who said he would eat mud out of any man's tracks ? His daddy had been a preacher too. The best one that had ever clucked a mule up Rattler trail. And his mother had been a Wimble girl. Why, Britt was their own boy ! As they saw him slowly break the deadlock they distilled a noise that began low and rumbling, then tore the sky when he was finally on top with his opponent's shoulder blades taking their turn in trenching the ground.

Britt was praying that Siler would prove stubborn and not cry quits. This, by mountain law, would give him the right to pound his opponent, provided he could get a hand loose for the pommelling. And he hadn't landed on that big mouth yet. What ecstasy to come down on it blow after blow until Siler could barely mumble " 'Nuff !" But he didn't dare loosen his hold. He must get his knees on the man's chest, if possible, before he freed his own right arm for destructive use, and that was difficult to do while keeping his opponent's arms pinioned. He began wriggling his knees upward, and the victim, feeling a slight release on his thighs, kicked enormously skyward. Britt's hold was shaken in his plunge toward Siler's head, and in an instant four arms and legs were engaged in blind assault, like a windmill disintegrating in storm.

The crowd roared for Britt. Britt who was making the preacher fight. On Sunday ! Right before the meeting-house ! The joy of forbidden indulgence rocked their bodies and gave unbridled force to their cries. God's law and man's was broken, and the preacher was doing it. They were watching it crack —

172

that mighty law. And the earth held. They howled, they clapped, they stamped, they rocked, while the combatants battled, rose, fell, rolled, and rose again, so equally matched that the watchers began to fear the struggle would end in a draw. It was too good a fight for that. They must have a victory, something that could be celebrated, talked about, thrilled over, and preserved, with personal additions, in their county's history. It must be a victory even if they had to give it to the preacher. And just then it was looking dark for Britt.

Siler again had him pinned to the earth, with an advantage that he had not held before. His right arm was free, while both of Britt's arms were crushed to his chest.

"I'll give you two minutes to say you've had enough," said Siler. Two minutes passed. The long right arm went up. "The Lord loveth whom he chasteneth," righteously gloated the preacher, his voice ringing with victory. Britt shut his eyes as if fainting, and gave up all resistance. Siler's fist hung in the air for a second. A second was all that Britt needed. With a wild surge his own right was free and around Siler's neck. Again they were madly rolling.

While they were locked and tumbling, Britt's shirt had an adventure with a broken root tightly fastened in earth. The next moment he was naked to the waist, and the shirt was a muddy strip on the ground. Aunt Peggy Ledbetter retrieved it with a long stick. That shirt, washed and purposely unmended, would repose in her lock-chest for the rest of her life, except when taken out by request for proud exhibition. The crowd did not follow aunt Peggy's provident motions. It had good other use for its eyes.

Siler, as to clothes, was faring worse than Britt. A jagged stump had made a hole in his trousers, and in one of their inextricable struggles, Britt's foot became entangled in the hole. After that, Siler's right trouser leg flew in the wind, split from hem to waist-band.

The conflict was turning crimson. The preacher's nose was awry and streaming blood. Britt's lower lip was laid open. His naked, pink chest, and Siler's white shirt and "slips," were tragically streaked and spotted. Some of the women were growing

173

pale of face, but their eyes lost no glow. Sam Merlin called out a bet — a hundred pound shote on Britt — and Si Welch took him up with a bull yearling. He wasn't particularly for Siler, and he rather felt that he would lose the yearling, but he couldn't pass up an opportunity to set his name in deathless chronicle. The story of this day would be told as long as a fireside remained in the mountains.

Andy Weaver, who had driven his family in a wagon from Silver Creek, had left his team coupled for the home road when the fight began. The shouting startled his mules, but when they dashed wildly away towards Ivy Creek nobody looked more than once in their direction. Marth Weaver pulled her husband by the arm and told him to go after the mules. "You go yersef," answered Andy, with eyes glued on the conflict. "This ain't no place fer a woman." But Marth refused to desert him.

The two men were gasping in an unending battle. For the moment they were apart, eyeing each other with no thought of surrender. They both needed breath. Britt could still make vicious use of his left arm, but a crippled shoulder made him want to howl with pain if he tried to strike out with his right. Siler stood as if a breath would blow him over. Britt had met his rock-like resistance often enough not to be deceived; but it was time for a finish. He threw himself bodily on the preacher, who came alive and hooped him in iron. Britt raged, his arms fastened, his shoulder speared with pain. He threw back his head as far as he could and brought it forward murderously against Siler's cheek-bone. Being a sharp cheek-bone, the bruised skin gave way over it, and the ragged, bleeding splotch on his paper-white face relieved his ghastliness with a brigand touch. Britt saw black, and wondered if a man could live with a cracked skull.

Siler's grip held. Again they fell, rolled, and fought all over the ground, blindly arriving at the graveyard in the rear of the meeting-house. Invasion of holy ground was complete.

"Better stop it," said Alec Craig, at last. "They're hog-bloody, an' won't quit till the breath 's out of 'em."

"Stop 'em yerself," said Sam Merlin, the only one to reply. "I ain't mixin'."

"Oh, Lordy," cried Sue Rhodes, "they've broke down a tomb-stone !"

"Run see whose is it !" said another, more curious than coura-geous.

"It's Granny Whitt's," Alec's wife informed them. "Wouldn't she be mad if she knowed it ?"

Beyond the tumbled tomb-stone, Britt's left arm was knocking Siler down as fast as he could rise to his trembling feet. "Britt's makin' bloody butter out of him. We'll have to call the boy off er get a new preacher," said Alec.

Then Siler was lying still, making no move to get up. Alec announced the end. As he went to the relief of the prostrate church, a last shout rose to heaven for Britt. A woman ventured regretfully, "Ain't it a pity Ishmer couldn't see it ?" And in all the hearts that had so recently denied her fellowship there was no stir of dissent.

While Alec was heading the rescue, Si Welch called two or three men apart. Si was the best ballit-maker of which the county could boast, and the men whom he had singled out were good seconds. By the time the preacher was gently picked up and set in uncle Samuel Wayne's buggy to be taken home, the ballit-makers had put something together that would do to begin with.

Britt was looking about him with imperfect vision. One eye was fast shut and the other a bloody red. His lips were enor-mous bulbs. His right shoulder was disjointed. His arms and naked chest were acquiring great spots of smudgy green. Both ankles felt as if they were broken, but he began to escape, push-ing his way through the crowd, determined not to go off limp-ing. His mind was strangely bright. Things had cleared up; he couldn't understand why, but they surely had. He wouldn't "take off" now. He'd let drink and the woods alone. He'd stay with Ned and Laviny on Cloudy Knob, pushing things through, and some day —

"No, sir !" shouted Si, detecting his outward movement. "Hist him onto that big stump, fellers !"

Britt was lifted up. Sore pains kept him from resistance. "Easy boys," he said, managing to move his swollen lips and flash his white, miraculously salvaged teeth in a grin. "A feller's sort o' raw with the hide off." They set him on the stump, and a circle was formed around him.

"I'll sing the first verse an' the chorus," directed Si, "then ever'body march an' sing after me. Don't nobody stand back now. Pay 'tention to the words an' you'll get 'em right. We'll sing it to 'Lovin' Babe.' Ever'body knows that tune. Whoever wants to, can be makin' up words to it. We've got four verses an' the chorus."

There was little music in Si's voice, but vigor reinforced melody as he threw the words of his ballit up and against Cedarcliff mountain.

> 'Twas on the forks of Ivy, boys,
>   A Sunday fine in May,
> Our preacher threw his long coat off,
>   A fighting man is he!
>
> Then come, my dear, an' come, my dear!
> Come give me yore right hand!
> For I have seen the purtiest fight
> Was ever fought in the land.
> Ay, come, my dear, come to me now!
> Give yore right hand to me,
> I'll sing ye 'bout the purtiest sight
> These eyes did ever see!

The march began, with Si leading, and the song filled the three-pronged valley. Britt tried to climb down and escape, but they caught him by his burning ankles and held him on his pinnacle of torture. Si began to throw out the second verse.

> A fighting man is he, my boys,
>   But there's a better yet;
> The man who made the preacher fight
>   Is Wimble County Britt!

Again the men sang, and the ground shook with the chorus that now was firmly captured. When the pause came, Si was ready.

We'll sing him high, we'll sing him low,
An' we'll not stop fer night.
We'll sing him till the chickens crow,
Who made the preacher fight.

Si was in such a tilt that he pitched into the next stanza without waiting for the chorus.

The preacher 's lost his breeches, sirs,
An' Britt he's lost his shirt.
They soak in blood, they pound the mud,
But never they'll bite the dirt!

After this stanza the chorus was sung by the men with no help from Si. He was deep in thought, silently bourgeoning thought. All ballits ought to end with a lady. A ballit wouldn't do at all if it didn't end with a lady. It might be a man's ballit to begin with, and all along the middle, but when it got to the end the woman had to be there. Si looked up, noting that the men were silent, waiting for him.

"Now," he said, "I want ever'body here to make up lines fer this ballit, an' git 'em to me by next Sat'day night. We'll meet at my house. But howsomever long it is, it's goin' to end thisaway."

He gave them his final triumph.

An' Ishmer she was cryin' that night,
Cryin' to Rad Bailee,
I wish I's home with my ol' true boy,
A sittin' on his knee.

A shameless tear started from one woman's eye. Another, in a voice that timidity softened, asked venturously, "You reckon she'll ever come back?"

"Ef she does," said Mandy Welch, with good courage, "maybe she'll be welcome."

CHAPTER VII

IsHMA lived numbly, and almost mute, until her child was born. Rad had taken her to Winbury, a town of many mills in the mildly billowing Piedmont region between mountains and lowland. They rented one room of a little dwelling on the drabbled fringe of the town. The scattered cottages around it were old and shabby, but this one of their choice had been built only three years before by the carpenter owner, Pace Unthank. It possessed such luxuries as water, lights and sewerage, to which Rad, with pride and frequency, called Ishma's attention. Its four rooms were tiny, yet larger than in the houses thereabout, and a bath-room on the back porch gave it distinction above its neighbors. There was a small front yard, and a larger one in the rear that ended in a strip of ground which could be used, but wasn't, for a kitchen garden. A path ran through it between two rows of raspberry bushes. Along one side, marking its boundary, was a discouraged hedge of mock-orange. The remainder of the ground was covered with muddy litter.

Rad had been only a few days in the house when he discovered that the owner was on the point of losing it to a Building and Loan Company. After a cautious fingering of his cash, he decided that he could meet the overdue payment and cover the price of the lot. Unthank's equity, aside from the lot, amounted to seven hundred dollars, and this would be clear gain for Rad. The owner felt himself lucky to save the price of the lot and pressed the trade to a close. Rad assumed payments equal to nine hundred dollars. He thought he could meet this later by the sale of his timber and perhaps his land.

Unthank was glad to remain in the house and pay rent for

his family's share of it. They had one bedroom, the run of the kitchen, and a cot in the living-room for their oldest child, Leta. The small rental, and ten dollars in Rad's pocket, had to keep him and Ishma going until he could find work.

Pace Unthank was a good workman badly handicapped by a sick wife. Her invalidism was due to rapid child-bearing, and the husband, generous enough to admit his responsibility, put up complaisantly with slovenly cooking and a brazenly untidy house. Ishma silently busied herself with setting the place in order, and after a few days the two families were taking their meals together. The cooking was done by Ishma, and Rad kept the household accounts. This relief revealed Unthank as a jolly person with an appreciative sense of favors.

"Mis' Bailey," he said, "I'm losin' a wrinkle a day. You're not much fer talkin', but what you do more'n makes up for what you don't say."

Ishma rarely spoke, but she never paused in doing. When Unthank told her that she worked as if she were afraid to stop, he didn't guess how true the words were. Rad vainly urged her to go out with him. "You've come to see, an' you ought to see. This is a great town. It's what you wanted, ain't it ?"

"I'll see it after a bit, Rad. Let me wait a bit."

"Suit yerself. You'll feel different when the baby gets here."

But Ishma knew that the expected baby was not keeping her at home. She was afraid to become conscious of the world about her; afraid to lift knowing eyes in that glittering region which lay a few streets away from the little cottage. Was it great ? Was it fine ? Was it glorious ? Whatever its value, she knew it could not be worth the price she had paid; the price which she never would get through paying.

The daily shock of finding Rad at her side did not grow faint and usual. Every morning she would lie still, trying to think that Britt would be calling her in a few minutes. Then Rad's husky, unmusical voice would begin a half whisper, "Lord, girl, I ain't fit for luck like this ! You goin' to be satisfied, Ishma ?" Without opening her eyes she would manage to make him hear. "Yes, Rad, I'm going to be." Sometimes she would change it to "I've got to be." But when Rad was out of the room, starting the fire in the kitchen stove, she would stiffen like a dead person, and tell herself in one of her grandmother's phrases, "I'll unbe it ! *I'll unbe it !*"

Pace helped Rad get work. He could do rough building, and one night Unthank told him that the boss said he could come on the job next morning. "Don't rattle the bell about not knowing much," advised Pace. "You'll be my buddy, an' you'll learn quick. Anybody can put on sidin', an' that's what I'm doin' this week. You needn't tell 'em you kain't build a court-house. I know more'n that boss anyhow. You've got to join the union, an' that's forty dollars, but you don't have to pay it all down, an' I'll get it fixed for you. You're in luck, Bailey, with work so mighty slack."

Rad knew he was in luck, and did his shrewd best. "Anything to keep out of the mills," said Unthank. "If they get you once, you never pull loose, an' it ain't no life."

The carpenter's contempt for the mills had colonial roots. His progenitors were Quakers, of the land-holding variety. Grants from George III had been in the family. Later generations, finding religion and slave-holding at odds in their blood, subsided into unprofitable neutrality. During the starvation years after the Civil War, most of the family acres slipped from Unthank control, and Pace belonged to the landless generation. But traditions were in him. He had gladly given up life as a tenant on the lands of his ancestors, but he didn't join with those who were desperately flocking to the mills. He had persisted in making a respectable carpenter of himself.

"You needn't feel so set-up," said an ex-farmer who had become a mill-worker. "If the mills hadn't come into the country you wouldn't have anything to build. You owe 'em your living. It's all the same."

"I reckon eight hours an' twelve ain't all the same," Pace answered. "You folks kain't even organize, you're so dog-gone bossed. An' they's some difference, ain't they, in seventy cents an' hour an' twenty-five ? We don't lick anybody's hand fer a little two-bit piece."

Rad heard this and took thought.

ONE DAY, when the dusk was gathering, Ishma stood in the doorway of her home. For nearly a month she had been the most efficient member of the combined household, but she had never stepped beyond the doorway. Towards dark she liked to stand there for a deep breath, watching the people indistinctly passing, and wondering if any of them were from the mountains. On this evening she saw a man stop and enter the yard. She had only a dusky glimpse of him, enough to see that he was a stranger, before she turned and fled through the living-room into the kitchen. Pace was at home, and looking out she saw the cause of her flight.

"Don't run, Ishma," he called. "It's nobody but Derry. He's a doctor too, an' you'd better get acquainted. He always looks after Genie."

But Ishma did not come back. Sitting by the little cook-stove, she heard, perforce, the conversation beyond the thin wall. When the stranger's voice fell on her ear she gave a start and her body continued to tremble. It was not the voice of Britt, but it had the same merry note and melodious low pitch.

"Hello, Genie!" she heard the man say. "You alive yet? Guess you didn't take that poison I left the last time I was here."

"Ever' drop," returned Genie. "There's the empty bottle in the winder. An' I've got to have some more."

"Nix, Genie. No more of that."

"But I've got to have something, Derry."

"You're right you have. And I'm going to give it to you. Here, you kids, jump out o' here. The first one out the door gets this dime."

He tossed a dime into the yard and the little boys scuttled for it. "No, Genie, no more drugs. What you need is information. This is for you too, Pace, and if you don't do as I tell you, Genie will be dead in six months, or in Morganton."

Ishma felt her heart pound. Morganton! That was where they sent insane people. She listened to the voice for five minutes more, then stopped her ears with her fingers. She was gasping and horribly disgusted. The man wasn't decent! How could he? with that clear, clean voice? A few minutes later she could distinguish Genie's tones and lowered her hands. But the man began talking again, answering a protest of Genie's.

"So you think God would like to see your children motherless, eh ? Would enjoy it so much that he would bring it about by adding another orphan to the lot, eh ? Well, my God isn't that sort of a fiend. You do as I tell you, and in another year you'll be able to be a mother to the children you've already brought here. Believe me, that will please God a lot better than to have them crying around your coffin. Goodbye !"

"Wait, Derry, and have some supper," said Pace.

"One of Genie's suppers ? No, thanks."

"We've got a cook now. Rad Bailey's livin' here, an' his wife handles the kitchen. Everything else too, mighty nigh."

"I thought the house had undergone a glad sea-change. Your cook, I suppose, is that goddess of the dusk that I saw in the doorway. Just from the mountains, I'll bet !"

"Ishma ? That's her."

"Ishma." Derry was reflecting. "Think I'll stay to supper."

"Good boy !" said Pace, and went into the kitchen. But Ishma was not there, nor in her bedroom. From the back door he saw a dim, gliding figure merge with the dark, and he returned to tell Derry that Ishma had disappeared. "Gone to the neighbors, I reckon, though she's never done that before. She's expectin', you know, an' sort o' shy of strangers."

"Expecting ! Just the usual bed-made then. She didn't look it. All right, Pace, I'll not take a chance on supper. You two do as I tell you. I'm not coming 'round here any more to patch up a dead woman. So long !"

"Stayin' at the Pott's House ?"

"No, the Immington this time."

"My, you gone swell, Derry ?"

"Not so's you could tell it," said Derry, from the yard. "Meeting an old college egg there. He'll square the desk."

A merry chuckle came from the street, and Derry was out of hearing.

Ishma had left the house, bearing tumult within her. Not since her departure from Cloudy Knob had she let her feelings plough their way to the surface. Now, suddenly, a voice too much like

Britt's had broken through her guard and she was only an uncontrollable channel for agony. She must stop it, conceal it at any cost! If she could get to the woods! Surely there must be woodland somewhere not too far away. She would find it if she kept walking, walking, walking! But she took the wrong turn, and instead of passing between straggling, thinning, and ever more dingy houses, she was on a main artery going to the throbbing heart of the town. She didn't notice the gradual change in the appearance of the street. Clamor within was too great. It was the first time she had been alone since leaving Cloudy Knob. Throughout the days the tiny house had been full of children and the invalid Genie. At night there was Rad. Whenever he came up the steps and looked in at the door, it seemed to her that his presence enveloped the earth. There was no roof, no ground, no sky — just Rad between her and every thought and glimpse of life. So she didn't think, she didn't see. He was kind too. The pretty dress she had on was a gift from him. He had gone to one of the big chain stores on a Saturday night after his first pay day and selected the dress himself.

"We can begin to spend now," he said, "an' you got to have a dress before I buy a shirt."

It was a washable print, $4.98, with ruffles, and "gethers" that could be let out. Rad had seen to that. "When you don't need it big, you can make it little again," said canny Rad. Ishma, if she had not been beyond tears, could have wept over his providence.

She walked forward, seeing nothing at all, from crown to toe a surge of rebellion, warring with herself. Why had she done it? How could she? A mad woman, of course. She would walk the night out, and tomorrow she would be found and sent to some place where mad women were kept. Why hadn't Britt followed her? He ought to have known that she was mad. He ought to have followed her and driven her back. He didn't have a dollar, but he could have tramped and begged his way to save her. She was his wife! His wife — and what had she done? The picture turned black, and her mind became a whirlpool.

Derry Unthank, walking behind her, recognized the figure of the woman he had seen in the doorway, and admired the calm length of her outline, the vital grace of her stride. No suggestion of heaviness or uncertainty. A different sort from the helpless, undetermined Genie. This one — what was that name ? — Ishma — she would keep a man in his place, pick her own way and time. She would make her great gift to the race consciously, knowing its value. He wished he could see her face, and hastened his step to pass her, giving a quick look at her profile. What he saw made him hurry on. The disillusionment was almost a pain. A walking stone. As passionless as dead. She could warm herself by a Greek marble. But perhaps a glimpse wasn't fair to her. It might be that the dusk had drunk all life from her face. He would stop under the next street light and see. They were passing a cemetery, high-walled, that the town had callously encircled. Stepping close to the wall half-buried in vines, he waited until the light fell on Ishma's wide-open eyes. Two streams gushed from their hot depths and ran unbrokenly down her cheeks. He needn't have pressed to the wall. She wouldn't have seen him had he walked beside her. He let her pass, barely crushing the impulse to seize her by the shoulders and cry, "For God's sake !" She went on, with that calm, even stride contradicting her burning eyes and the hot streams on her cheeks. Derry watched her until she passed under the great magnolias on Carolina Avenue. "Like Tragedy going home," he thought, as the heavy shadows concealed her. Then he took a cross street that would bring him to the Immington Arms.

Ishma came out of the shadows into waves of light. She was on the public square in the centre of the town. It was Saturday night, the festal night of the week, and the radiance of it swept obliteratingly through her. Winbury was almost a city, and she had never walked in one before. Light, light, light, roads of light everywhere ! She stood silent, thrilled with something like the joy that she had felt when, as a child, she had stood on Dancer ridge and watched the historic fire that burnt over Silver Valley. But this was beneficent fire, lighting the ways of men. She was near a great building with huge columns. Before it a temporary platform had been erected. There were men and women sitting on the platform, and down below, floating around it, on the pavement, and in the street, was a crowd of jostling, laughing people. A nationally known speaker had arrived in the town, and the people had gathered to hear his words of wisdom. Ishma could hear his voice rolling out through a megaphone with words of praise for the great country of America and congratulations for the lucky people — themselves ! — who belonged to it. She crossed the street and looked back at the building. Its entire front was illuminated, and above the heads of men and women on the platform with the speaker, she read the large letters telling her that it was FADIN COUNTY COURT HOUSE. What a wonderful building ! The lighted dome seemed to reach the sky and make the stars dim above it.

"Walk in, lady ! Walk into fairy-land !" She turned towards the voice and saw that she was standing in the shining entrance of a shop where people were going in and out. Through the glass doors and windows she saw counters and tables and seats, flowers and decorations and lights, with people buying, selling and eating. There were little dishes and big dishes, glasses and straws, and clean-faced boys in aprons behind the counters and serving at the tables.

The man who had addressed her wore a sarcastic grin, but Ishma didn't note the sarcasm. He was lean and hungry, with uncombed hair, muddy shoes, and ragged overalls. She had been accustomed all her life to seeing men look like that. So she smiled back and said, "That's what it is — fairy-land. You going in ?"

"Not tonight, I reckon," he answered sheepishly, and moved on up the street. She was sorry, for she would have liked to step into that charmed light within, and she was too shy to enter alone. There was no trace left in her of tragedy or tears. With every sense awakened and magnified, she moved on, up the road of wonder and delight, pausing by festal doors and windows as if held on enchanted feet. Over one entrance there was a bright sign reading "FIVE CENTS TO FIVE DOLLARS," and in the window were beautiful frocks for women, some arrayed on wax figures, while others swung daintily from mere hangers. They were all marked $4.98, and some of them were of silk ! The ruffles, the drapes, the colors, held her in a happy daze. Suddenly, at the back of the window, she beheld a familiar dress. It was like her own. Exactly. Rad had chosen well.

It was as pretty as any of the others. On a wax figure too, and such a nice one! It was almost real. So calm and kind looking, and the eyes large and eager and deep. She wished the figure were alive. Surely she would go in and speak to it, for that was what it seemed to be waiting for — someone to speak to. She turned away with regret, and as she turned she saw the figure move its straight, broad shoulders and start out of the window. Startled, she threw up her hand. So did the figure. Then she saw that she was looking into a mirror that lined the back of the window, and the figure was her own reflection. Can I be that nice? she thought, and looked again, to make sure. Why, one could hardly tell that she was heavy! It was her strong shoulders and hips, she reckoned, that made her load seem light and kept her body straight. But she didn't want to get back to herself, and in an effort to re-enter her world of enchantment she went into the store. Beads — beads — beads — all colors and sizes and shapes and lengths. She could bury her soul in them — just beads. But she moved on. Handkerchiefs — how dainty! Tiny ones of silk with little flowers on them, and thin ones, colored like rose leaves and forget-me-nots and lilacs. Hundreds of them, prettier and prettier. On she went, up and down the aisles — hairpins, combs, belts, candies, candies! Toys — oh, if Ned could see them! A pain started at her heart and ran down her side. "Are you sick?" asked one of the fairy girls at the counter — one with very pink cheeks and a white nose. "No, no!" Ishma murmured, and hurried on to a counter radiant with scarves — only 98¢.

When she came out of the store she was ready to go home. She had not eaten since breakfast, and her knees were shaking. Perhaps Rad was looking for her. It wasn't fair for her to treat him this way. He had done his part fully and kindly. She oughtn't to make it hard for him just because it was so hard for her. She must be fair. The few hours she had been away had eased the friction of body and spirit. Nothing was unbearable any more. She didn't know how to turn towards home, but she knew the street and number of the house, and a policeman could tell her how to find it.

She looked about for a policeman. There was a wonderful individual in cap and uniform standing before a revolving door under a great portico. She went up the steps toward him, and again a sharp pain seized her. When she put her question the magnificent door-man replied, "I don't know, ma'am. You'll have to ask a policeman." She looked in at a big room filled with men winding about in every direction and going nowhere. At one side was another big room where men and women sat at little tables, eating and drinking. What long legs and necks and backs! thought Ishma as she looked at the women with bits of silk draped around their middle. Oh, she must get home! Her eyes swept a circle, but no policeman. She would have to sit on the steps and rest a little. His Magnificence must have read her intention, for he said in her ear, "This is the Immington Arms, lady." That ought to have got her started, but the stubborn thing stood still, and he added severely, "You'd better move on." She looked appealingly through the plate glass into the room where the women sat. One of them looked steadily at her, then made a remark to her companions, two men, who turned and looked at Ishma.

One of the men leapt to his feet, said something to the other two, and hurried out. "Call a taxi!" was his stern order to his amazed Magnificence, who immediately obeyed. "I'm Derry Unthank," the man said to Ishma, "cousin to Pace, you know. Yes, sit right down on the steps till I can put you in a taxi. No, you needn't say a word. It's all right. You'll be home in a few minutes."

She shut her eyes and listened to the voice that held a merry, flexible note, like the voice of Britt. "A twinkle," she had always called it. Derry put her into the taxi and got in beside her.

"Yes, I'm going too. Don't talk, just be still, perfectly still." She closed her eyes again and rested until the taxi stopped before the little house. They got her to bed and sent for Grandma Huffmore. The children, except the smallest, were hustled to a neighbor's. They were used to that. Derry sat in the shoe-box of a kitchen and cursed himself for not having taken her to a hospital. Too late to move her now. He cursed himself again for not having stopped her when he passed her in the street. All those hours on her feet, and all that mental stress borne alone!

187

Every fifteen minutes he went into the room. Grandma certainly knew her babies. He and Grandma Huff were old accomplices. About daylight the child was born, a small-boned, perfectly formed little girl.

"It won't trouble her long," whispered Grandma to Genie, who was wrapping the baby in pieces of a torn sheet while Grandma dug into a box to find the few little things that Ishma had prepared. "I never knowed an eight months baby to live a year."

"Who's going to take care of your wife?" asked Derry of Rad, who looked up helplessly. "Grandma can take care of the baby for a day or two, but you must have somebody for a couple of weeks, strong enough to keep your wife from jumping about."

"I reckon the neighbors 'll come in," said Rad, as he would have said back in Grape Vine Cove.

"What neighbors? Every woman around here works in the mills, if she can keep on her feet. But you might get one to stay out awhile if you pay her the same wages."

Rad winced, and rallied generously. "I'll pay it, if I can get her."

That was how Ishma and Mildred Ross became friends. Mildred was glad to come out of the mill for two weeks and play nurse. "But I don't dare let the boss know it," she said. "I let him think I was ailing and just had to have a little rest. Which is about the truth. It's a rest to be over here with you, Mis' Bailey."

"Please call me Ishma," said her patient, looking into Mildred's intelligent blue eyes and knowing she was going to like her very much.

Mildred didn't stay at night, because she had three children at home and their father was on the night-shift. During the day the two oldest were in school and the youngest was cared for at a nursery provided by the owner of the mill where the mother worked.

"Gracious, it's good to get out of that spinnin' room for a while," said Mildred happily. "I'll learn how to breathe again before I go back to that steam."

Derry left Winbury as soon as Mildred was installed and had received his instructions. He was still growling to himself for not having taken Ishma to a hospital. "That thimble of a bed-room with the sun burning the walls, and every sound slashing at her ! What kind of nerves will she have when she gets up ?"

For ten years he had given help to the wives of the workers in the mill section of Winbury — Spindle Hill, they called that part of the town, which was so flat that every summer rain filled it with puddles and mosquitoes. He had often been concerned about the women, but it was easy to forget. This time it was different. He had trouble in putting Ishma out of his mind as he travelled back to his Yancey County farm. The tall woman with grey eyes that seemed to breathe as they questioned the uni-verse, cramped in that hot little room, on that bumpy bed, with thin, ragged sheets, and no silence, no peace around her. And she needed silence as one needs food; needed peace as the lungs need air.

Derry didn't go often to Winbury now. He was only thirty-five and strong as steel, but he said it used him up. He had found other ways of being useful to humanity without wasting himself. What those ways were, Winbury had not found out.

He belonged to the only successful branch of the Unthank family. His father had owned a thousand acres of land up near the Virginia line — land that produced fine burley tobacco. This father had worked with his own hands, as hard as any of his hired help. Whenever he sold his crop he laid half of the profit by for the education of his three sons. They should have what he and mother had missed. The other half was put into mill stock. The two older boys, considerably older than Derry, went west, entered railroad service, and moved steadily up the official ladder. Their share of the mountain land and the few thousands of mill stock, they lightly tossed to Derry after he had returned from Harvard to be a mountain doctor. "The kid will never get on at that," they said. "He can have our chicken-feed." As a doctor, Derry had given of his strength and time plentifully, and he had managed to save his land and mill stock. The land sup-ported him, and the income from the stock went into those "other useful ways" that he had found for serving mankind. He was about as happy as a man could be, troubled with the old incurable urge to remould the world a little nearer his heart's desire. By the time he reached his farm he was whistling "Cindy," and told Aunt Binnie, who kept house for him, to get out his fishing "cooterments." Ishma was forgotten.

Down in Winbury Rad was looking after Ishma and the baby at night. She would lie for hours in pain and motionless rather than disturb him. When the baby cried, she tried to move herself noiselessly and take it up, but invariably Rad would awaken and she would be scolded softly for not calling him.

"You needn't be skeered I'll drop her. I helped mommie take keer o' three younguns 'fore I was twelve years old."

"I'm not afraid, but you need your sleep, Rad."

"Shucks! I like to be awake when you are." He would look at her until her heart turned ice-cold while her lips struggled with a smile.

Sometimes he insisted on leaving the light burning, or pretended to forget it. He liked to lie with his eyes almost shut, watching her face, and her dark, short hair curling against the pillow. Maybe, he thought, she will talk a little. But she seemed to go instantly to sleep, and after a few minutes he would reach out disappointedly and turn off the light. Then her eyes would fly open and stare into the dark as if her brain were pushing at her eyeballs. Rad was too good to her, she thought. Why didn't he grumble and complain, and make it easy for her to hate him? She had waited and watched to see him show harshness, or at least indifference, to the baby, but even Pace had noticed how kind he was.

"Don't be a fool over nothin' but a girl, Rad," said Pace. "Save a little heart for the boys that'll come along. What you goin' to call her? Ishma, after her mother, I reckon."

"No," said Rad decidedly. "They ain't but one person for that name." He looked toward the bed. "We might call her Laviny, for yer mother, Ishma."

"I never liked that name," she answered. "Mommie don't like it either."

"Well, my mother had a pretty name — Vennie. How'll that do?"

"She's so little. I believe it would suit her, Rad." She didn't look at him, and a dark flush spread over her face. "Your mother was a fine, good woman, I've always heard."

"You heard right. You couldn't best her yerself, Ish, old gal. And that's sayin' something. It's Vennie then, ain't it?"

"If you are willing, Rad."

"It'll pleasure me a lot. Little Vennie!" he said, patting the warm, tiny bundle.

Ishma had turned to the wall, feeling very sick. It would clean the air, she felt, if Rad would say he'd be damned if Britt Hensley's youngun was goin' to be named for his mother, or something like that. And the worst of it was that Rad wasn't acting a part. He meant it. He was going to be so good to her that her heart would not let her be unfair. She could never leave him. He had gone from the room and she heard him in the yard working on an ice-box because she couldn't bear the water they had to drink in Winbury, it was so warm. Every time she fell asleep she dreamed of the cold water gushing from the spring under the three birches on Cloudy Knob. She would dip it up with her hands, and just as her lips touched it she would awaken, parched and aching with thirst. Mildred would hand her a drink, and after one sip she would put the glass down. "I can't swallow it. I can't."

Finally Mildred told Rad, and he decided to make an ice-box. He couldn't buy one, for all of his money was gone. He had only his daily wages which barely met their increased expenses, and he was dead set against buying on the installment plan. " 'Stallment, that's what it is," he said. "You never get a step furder if you mess with it." The boss gave him what was left of some narrow oak flooring, and a dollar induced a junk dealer to part with enough new lining for the box. He worked on it at night, in the yard by the light of a lantern, so as not to disturb the family trying to sleep, and three night's work until eleven o'clock finished it. When it was finished with a perfect lid, and enamelled within and varnished without, it was, according to Genie, the best-looking piece in the house. Rad had put in a compartment for water, and a faucet. "That beats the store 'frigerators," said Pace, proudly. "Room for everything. We can let Grandma

Huff keep her butter in it. She's always complainin' about her butter meltin'."

When the ice was put in, and Ishma had her first cold drink from the box, Rad stood watching her with eager eyes. "It's fine, Rad," she said gently, wanting to cry out.

"Better'n that sloppy icecream I brought you, ain't it ?"

"The icecream was good, but this is too. I'll not want anything more. You needn't do anything more for me, Rad. I've got everything now. And I'm getting up tomorrow. Mildred can go back to her work."

"Mildred's goin' to stay another week, whether you get up or not," announced Rad. And Mildred stayed.

Ishma learned a great deal about mill work from Mildred, and made up her mind to go into the spinning room with her.

"It's easier in the spooling room," Mildred said, "because it's not kept so hot, but the places there are all taken."

"I'm strong now," said Ishma. "I can stand the heat."

Then Mildred had to tell her that Vennie would be an obstacle. "You see, she's not a bottle baby, so she can't stay in the nursery. They wouldn't let you come out to her except at twelve when you could take time off from your dinner, and she'd starve that way. She's a nervous little thing, and is goin' to be somebody's job."

That was true. After Mildred left, and the weeks passed, Ishma was in no doubt about it. Vennie was somebody's job — and that somebody was herself. If a strong light fell upon her, she would wince with pain. If a door slammed, or the children shouted, she would scream as if she had been struck. Her little face that had been so round at first, began to look sharp and starved, though Ishma's breast was bountiful. If anyone except her mother took her up she would shake with fear and be in such misery that it came to be a law of the house that no one should touch her. When she was four months old, Derry dropped by to look her over. The eyes he raised to Ishma's expectant face were full of pity.

"Oh, she'll live all right, and will grow out of this. But it means ball and chain for you. Make up your mind to that."

192

"Kain't we get her hardened some way ?" asked Rad, in a sore voice.

"You can try it, and work up a fine case of St. Vitus' Dance. No, you'll have to ease her along and give her a life absolutely without friction until she is four or five years old."

"I want to go to work," said Ishma.

"In the mills ?"

"Yes."

"You reconcile me to the baby. If she keeps you out of the mills, she has earned her place in the sun. And you needn't look at me as if I'd got your planet by the tail and was dragging it away from you."

"It suits me, her not goin' to work," declared Rad. "I can make a livin', an' I'd ruther have her at home."

"So would I," said Derry, in a tone that he hoped was quite professional, and began giving Ishma revised instructions for the care of Vennie. When he had finished, he turned to Pace. "You must get out of the house, old boy, with your gang of youngsters. The child must have peace, first, last and always."

Pace said he'd been expecting that order and he thought he could manage it. He knew he had a rowdy crowd. All of his children were boys except Leta, who was fourteen and in High School. Having no mind for scholarship, but considerable pride, her struggle to keep her grade took up nearly all of her time out of school. Her only function in the house seemed to be an effort to secure impossible quiet by screaming at the boys or driving them into the street.

"How's Genie coming along ?" asked Derry.

"Up-gradin' fast. You see —" Pace stopped, embarrassed.

"I see," commended Derry. "Well, Genie can cook a meal occasionally now. You get out and let Ishma and the baby have the house."

"I s'pose you'll let Rad stay," Pace chuckled.

"On probation," Derry answered, with no humor at all. Rad looked puzzled, but Ishma's face was swept by a flush, and Genie gave her a wink that she hated.

The wink was reminiscent. They had been talking together,

those two. One morning, a few days before Derry's visit, Ishma had remained in bed, and let Genie get the breakfast. After the men were gone, Genie went into Ishma's room, walking softly and shutting the door carefully. She had learned that it was wisdom to defer to Vennie's preference. Ishma was weeping silently and the child was feeding.

"Goodness, Ishma! Don't you know better than that? A mother's tears will poison her milk. Ain't you never heard that?"

Ishma dried her eyes. "I want to ask you something, Genie, and don't you get mad at me, because it may mean whether I'm going to live or die."

"My goodness! Of course you can ask me!"

"Are you and Pace living like Derry Unthank told you to?"

Fire came into Genie's eyes. "Yes, we are! Don't you see I'm getting strong again? And why? 'Cause I'm not havin' to worry about another baby comin', that's why. If you can make sin out o' that, go ahead."

"I don't care whether it's sin or not. I want to know what he told you."

"Oh!" Genie's face became eager and sympathetic. She told. Ishma kept silent. "I'll get Pace to talk to Rad," ventured Genie, softly.

"Yes. But I must talk to him first."

The following night, when Vennie cried and Ishma had soothed her, Rad started to turn the light off, but Ishma stopped him. "Let it burn a little, Rad."

She knew that it gave him pleasure to watch her. He began to talk happily. "Vennie's a lot of trouble, Ish, but she'll grow out of it. You'll have better luck with the next one."

That was very bold for Rad, but looking at Ishma made him heady. She caught her breath and began to whisper, "You want children, Rad?"

"Gee, lady, I reckon I do!"

"Wouldn't it be better if — they didn't come till you get the home paid for?"

"I'm not worryin'. My timber 'll take keer o' the place."

She was very still, and he began to feel that something was

wrong. Finally he said, "You worryin' about kids? You needn't think we're goin' to turn 'em out like Genie an' Pace. I'll give you time."

"You're good, Rad — but I was thinking — "

"Let's have it, Ish."

"I'd rather we'd be married proper before we had any."

"So'd I, sure I would, but you ain't got no divorce." He might have added that she couldn't get one, but he remembered not to. She had no answer, and a moment later he said that maybe Britt would make a move on his own.

She seized the lifeline. "Yes, of course he will! He knows I don't want to live like this."

"You're mighty sure he'd do you a favor, but what about me? He's not studyin' to get the rocks out o' my road."

"He never came down here to bother you anyhow. Let's wait, Rad, and see what Britt does."

"I s'pose he'll want to get married hissef 'fore long."

Ishma was on fire with denial, but she made no sound, and Rad went on, "He'll get a divorce for his own reasons, not for ours. He's that much of a man, I reckon."

Rad had considerable contempt for Britt because he had been unable to get on in life. He had let a fine woman like Ishma work hard and suffer, and do without a home of her own. Rad was glad enough that Britt had made no trouble for him, but that, too, added a little to the contempt in his tone. Ishma felt it, and became strong and defensive for Britt's sake. *"He* would know," she said, "how I'd feel about having children with no right to call their own father daddy."

"You shore he's studyin' about yore feelin's?"

"He couldn't help but know, Rad. He always knew how I felt. He'd know about this."

"Is it worryin' you a whole lot, Ishma?"

"I'm thinking about it every minute I breathe."

"You'd be satisfied if you didn't have to worry about that?"

"I'd be a lot better satisfied than I am now."

"Well, it's something for me to think about. You go to sleep now." He put out the light. After a minute, Ishma spoke. "Rad, are you asleep?"

"Gettin' there." He imitated a doze, though his head was on fire and his breast aching.

"It's just that I don't want to feel any wickeder than I am. That's bad enough."

"All right, honey. Let's go to sleep."

She said no more, feeling that he was ready for Pace.

And that was why Genie had winked. After Derry left the house, and the women had gone into the kitchen, Rad began to look angry.

"Whad he mean? I'm on probation?"

"Guess he thinks Ishma has got her hands full for a while."

"Without any more kids in her lap? Is that it?"

"Maybe. For a while. Lord, I don't know what she'd do with another'n like Vennie!"

"There won't be any more like *her*." Britt's youngun, he thought, and bit his tongue in time.

"Can't be sure. Best way is to wait till Vennie gets off her hands. She's shore enough tied down."

"A man's got to have his rights."

"Yes. I had my rights, and see what happened. I lost my house, I nearly lost my wife, and if you hadn't come along with a little cash my family would have been in the street. If that's where havin' your rights brings you, I'd rather do without 'em." He looked toward the kitchen, knowing the women were on the other side of the wall. "Let's take a walk," he said. Rad, sullen and flushed, followed him out. Ishma and Genie had listened, still as mice, to the conversation. They knew what Pace had to say to Rad.

As the months passed, Ishma's strength came surging back to her. Little Vennie's thin, tugging hands were a constant test of patience. Her tiny body retained the perfection of an exquisitely made doll, but as the diseased nerves became assertive, the round face shrunk pathetically, and the sleek, lovable hair, dark and curling like her mother's, was succeeded by a meagre crop of tow. "Just like I was when I's a youngster," said Rad, accepting the change cheerfully. But Ishma felt that fate had struck once more. "Just a little scrub of a kid," she told herself. "That's all I'm living for." She pressed the small head to her

196

bosom, and loved it dearly, but she didn't let her affection deceive her. And she was honest enough to take full blame for Vennie's disaster. "If I'd have stayed satisfied on the mountain, she'd have been all right. She wouldn't have had any nerves." But only to her midnight self did she confess it.

The child's progress demanded unbroken routine. Ishma could not take her out, nor could she go herself and leave her behind. Vennie cried constantly when her eyes sought in vain for her mother. The restriction was more of a trial to Rad than to Ishma. He had looked forward to taking her to the movies, to church, to showing her around. He was no longer afraid of meeting someone from the mountains. There were highland families in Spindle Hill, but none from his own county. Bert and Cindy Wiggins were in Winbury, but they were on the opposite side of the town, working in the Sherwin mill, at least five miles from Spindle Hill. They were too clannish anyway to get folks from their own home into trouble. They'd never talk against the mountains to any low-country "lint-heads." Rad was picking up friends among a different sort, grocers, carpenters, truckmen, and so forth, and he wanted to go out with his wife as they did with theirs. He wanted them to see that he had something to be proud of. None of their women could hold a candle to his, he knew very well, yet they might be thinking he was ashamed of her, leaving her at home all the time. Rad had begun to brush up his speech too, and tried to talk more like Ishma. He never laughed at her now for being "proper."

"You've got to get out some, Ish. You ain't seen this town but once — that night — "

"Don't talk about that night, Rad. If I hadn't gone crazy that night, Vennie wouldn't have come here too soon. I'm going to pay for it if it takes all of my life. I don't want to go anywhere."

"Well, I do. And I want you with me."

"I've heard there's park, with a lot of woods, around here somewhere. I'll fix up a picnic dinner Sunday, and we'll go. We'll stay all day."

"I was brought up in the woods an' I've had enough of 'em. It's too cold now anyway."

They didn't go, but Ishma carried the baby out to the near-by fields as often as she could. They were very unattractive, full of weeds and mud, but here and there were little dry mounds where she could put the camp-stool that she took with her. Holding Vennie on her lap, she would sit reading for an hour or two. There was no library in Spindle Hill, but Rad brought her books from the one up in the big town. She didn't care much for them, but reading was good practice. Once in a while Mildred, who had gone to school up to second year High, found time to go to the library on Saturday and select something that they both enjoyed. But Ishma found no relief from her incessant inner questionings. There were many mild winter days when she sought the fields, but she always returned in time to fix an attractive supper for Rad. He did the marketing, from a careful list which she gave him. With access to groceries, and a not altogether barren pocket-book, her talent for cooking flourished, and Rad's lunches were the envy of his fellow workmen. He had worried about the cost until he found that his good meals did not mean bigger bills. Ishma knew how to stretch a penny, and all that first long, hot summer the ice-box was her magical ally. All in all, Rad was contented but for one grievance. Ishma couldn't go out with him.

When nearly a year had passed, and the warm Spring weather came to stay, Derry happened along and was again consulted about Vennie. She was improving. He was sorry he couldn't advise a hard spanking and a disciplinary separation from her mother. If he did that, Vennie would certainly avenge the punishment in some disastrous way. She might cry herself to death, or throw a fit which would mean permanent injury. Go softly, and let her grow, was all that he could say. But he looked at Ishma and knew the pain of her inward chafing. A war-horse pulling a toy sled. Good job if the kid would croak !

After Pace and Genie moved out, Ishma had found relaxation in keeping the house neat. She trained Vennie to sit quietly on the floor and play with her toys while she groomed and rubbed and polished everything on the place, always taking care to be where the child's lifted eyes could find her. Rad bought a living-

198

room suite at a cash bargain, and she kept it perfect in the dust-laden air. One day her polishing rag swiped a wet spot on the shining wood, then another and another, and she discovered that she was dropping tears. This wouldn't do. She'd have to get out. Get to work that *meant* something. And a door opened for her so quietly that she hardly knew when it happened.

Grandma Huffmore was taken ill, and Ishma, with Vennie pressed close, went to see her, choosing an hour when she knew there would be no children in the house to start friction. Grandma's widowed daughter, over fifty, was working in a mill. Her grand-daughter, thirty, also was in a mill, with her children in school and a nursery, except a little boy of five who was Grandma's nurse. Ishma, as soon as she entered, sent him out to play, and put Vennie on the floor. She took away the cold corn-bread and forlorn piece of bacon on the chair by the bedside, and replaced the untempting morsels with toasted rolls, buttered and delicately spread with honey. She had brought with her a little pitcher of milk, cold and sweet from her unfailing box, and this was poured into a glass which she first washed and rubbed till it sparkled. All the time Vennie was watching her with eyes as interested as Grandma's, forgetting to turn to her cotton-wool sheep and rubber rabbit.

"I was thinkin'," said Grandma, "that I'd leave that cold stuff for my supper. No use eaten' when you don't want nothin', an' things are gittin' scarce on the shelf, with me not goin' out to work."

"I'll put it up, Grandma," Ishma reassured her. "No use wasting food when there's a lot of children around." She went into the kitchen with the stuff, leaving the door open so that Vennie's eyes could follow her. When she returned, grandma's attention to the rolls and milk could be described as "gobbling."

"I never thought I'd enjoy eatin' again," she declared as she finished. "That milk makes me think of the old spring-house on the farm when I was a girl. I've had to quit coffee, an' that coky stuff is so meller it makes me sick. No bite to it at all."

Ishma went every day to grandma's until her patient could get out of bed and had begun to think about taking a "case." "I'll be in time fer Ben Whitt's wife after all," she said. "An' we're hurtin' fer money. You paid me when you's sick, Ishma, an' the first cash I git my hands on will be yorn."

"You'll not give me a thing," Ishma declared. "It's worth the little I've done just to find out I can take Vennie around a bit."

Grandma was reflecting. "That makes me think, Ishma, maybe you'd go an' help Annie Weaver out. She's broke her ankle, an' has to lay there with nobody to hand her a fresh drink from six in the mornin' till six at night, 'cept 'tween eleven an' twelve when Jim runs home from the mill an' back again. His mill is so fur away he has to eat his bite while he's runnin'. It's a pore way to spend his restin' hour anyhow."

"I'll go," said Ishma, "if there are no children to bother Vennie. I wouldn't do anything to give her a set-back."

"Not a kid in the house. Annie birthed twins that died, an' got so tore up she kain't have any more."

Ishma went to help the Weavers, and after Annie's recovery, she passed on to Mame Wallace. Mame had small children, but the married daughter, oldest of Mame's ten, agreed to keep them out of the way with her own. She could do that and "dress-make" too. They couldn't be left in a nursery because the mother didn't work in the mills.

Mame had pellagra. She was an advanced "case." Having to choose between going on the county and dying at home, she chose home and the further starvation the choice entailed.

It was during this period that Rad's wages didn't seem to stretch as far as formerly. Ishma never spent his money without telling him, but at times when she had to confess to buying special food for Mame, she saw his face darken, and yearned with new desperation for money of her own. Would she never be able to work like other women? Vennie's improvement in health and temper gave her courage. One day she ventured to leave the child at a mill nursery. It was against the rules, for the nursery was for working mill mothers only, but the supervisor had come to know and appreciate Ishma, and agreed with her on a trial. The mother had not been three minutes away from the building before an attendant came flying after her. Vennie was lying dead-white and scarcely breathing. She was resuscitated and comforted, but it was a week or more before she regained her lost vantage. She did not cry as formerly, but she was in a pitiful state of subdued fright, and not for one minute would she let go of her mother's hand or skirt.

"We had a child like that once before," said the supervisor to Ishma. "The mother *had* to work, and the child died. You thank the Lord you can stay with yours."

Ishma tried to be thankful, but made poor work of it. Vennie regained her shell-pink color, and seemed to forget her fright; but Ishma resolved to make no more experiments, and kept strictly to Derry's programme thereafter. She was still nursing Mame when Derry re-appeared in Spindle Hill. He wanted to get a squint at Vennie, he said, and he was pleased with her looks. Her cheeks were rounder, her hair was turning dark and resuming its curl, and there was a flash of healthy independence in her eye.

"You are doing it, Mistress Bailey," he said, thrilling her with hope. Then he turned to Mame, for they were talking at her bedside. "Just starved yourself into bed, eh, Mrs. Wallace ? Forgot what I told you two years ago ?"

"Don't be hard on me, doctor. There's so many of us."

"And of course when the biscuits won't go round, mother will hunt up that piece of day-before-yesterday's cornbread and be perfectly satisfied with it."

"I got so I'd ruther have it. I'd just ruther have it, doctor. I got used to it because brother Jim always sent me a bushel o' meal from his farm ever' two or three months. I don't know how we'd got through without that. I'd always bake a big pone for supper an' give the children milk with it."

"That was fine, but mother didn't take any milk, and there was always enough of the pone left over for her to nibble a bit for breakfast and dinner next day."

"I liked it, Doc. An' Mis' Emery let me go over to her house ever' day an' get some cold water out of her 'frigerator to drink with it. That made it good. She kept a bottle o' water just for me, knowin' I liked it with my bread. It was better 'n milk that got as warm as dishwater in the coolest place I could find."

"So between brother Jim and Mrs. Emery you've been fixed up fine."

"It ain't too late, is it, Doc ? The least 'uns 'll need me bad."

He turned from the appeal in her eyes and met the same tragic question in Ishma's.

"I'm beginnin' to eat now," Mame struggled to say, trying to fill the silence that settled fearfully upon her. "Ishma brings me things. I try 'em all. I took three big swallers o' milk this mornin', an' didn't mind it a bit. I got it down, didn't I, Ishma ?"

Ishma choked a little before she answered, "Yes, you did, and I believe you could take a sip more now, and show Doctor Derry."

Mame's pathetic triumph collapsed. Her face twisted with aversion, and Ishma hurried to say, "But maybe we'd better wait a little. It hasn't been three hours yet."

"You ain't told me if it's too late, Doc," Mame whispered.

"Who's talking about too late ? You know you're not a quitter, Mary Wallace." A wave of light passed visibly over her face. "Mommie called me Mary," she said.

Out in the street Derry's voice became ferocious, yet strangely not unpleasant. It sank into intense bass notes just as Britt's did when he was angry.

"Too late ! Yes, too damned late ! Thirty-five years too late. Mame Wallace went into the mills when she was eleven years old."

Ishma wasn't thinking of Mame. If she couldn't get used to this thing in Derry's voice she would have to stop seeing him. She could go on with life only when she forgot about Britt. They walked a block before she pulled herself back from Cloudy Knob to the dirty street in Spindle Hill. The sidewalk was broken, and there had been a recent shower.

"What puddles !" Derry drew her from the mudhole where her feet had blindly splashed. He was still talking, but not ferociously. The world was accepted again, though protestingly.

"I don't know why they stand for it. They're not a foreign race in a strange land, like so many of the workers in the North. Up there, with all the timidity and bewilderment that comes from being far from their own base, they put up a big fight now and then. But here, right in the land of their fathers, they go to the shambles as if they belonged to the butcher."

"Maybe they're like Mame — starved too long. I've heard Grandma Huff tell what it was like before the mills came."

"Yes, I know all that, but if blood means anything it ought to outlast two or three generations of lean years. I'm tired of that old excuse, the Civil War and the desert of time that followed."

"But most of the strong men were killed, Grandma says. Her father was in a regiment that set out the last year of the war, and there wasn't a man in it between the ages of sixteen and fifty. And after the war it was the old men and women and children who had to work the farms. The horses were gone, and the cattle were dead, mostly, and there was nothing to fertilize the fields with. If they got them ploughed they were lucky. And there was no money at all. Just none at all. So you see how they felt when the mills came."

"You've been picking up an education, haven't you?"

Ishma was hurt by his amused tone, but she persisted with her history. "Grandma said that she was thankful to put her two little boys to work for thirty cents a week. When there's no money at all, sixty cents will go far."

"Yes, forty years ago sixty cents would buy a pound of coffee, five pounds of lard, ten pounds of salt, three of brown sugar, and leave the brawny toilers five cents for clothes and other luxuries. It would go far, Ishma, and they had to work only thirteen or fourteen hours a day. A twelve-hour day came sometimes, and gave the lads quite a rest. We've improved since those days. Twelve hours is the usual thing now."

"You are making fun of me, and I'm puzzled enough."

"You are doing fine. In another six months you'll be ready for a look-in on Karl Marx."

"Marx?"

"A gentleman that I hope to introduce to you some day, in mild installments."

"But why installments?"

"How could we do anything in any other way in Spindle Hill? Isn't this the era and centre of the installment plan? The very time and place?"

"But a man can't be introduced in little bits."

"This one can. His body was removed from earthly vision some years ago. He is represented solely by his mind, and that must be taken in judicious nibbles."

"O, you mean books !"

She was so eager that he felt shamed. If she had had *his* chance !

"I've been wanting to ask you to help me get the right kind of books. I don't like novels. They only *talk* about life. I want something that explains it."

Derry caught his breath. "You're not asking much."

She didn't get his double meaning, and thanked him so honestly that he wanted to kick his own shins. Already he was wondering what he would select for a start. Something meaty, but mild. George's *Progress and Poverty,* perhaps. No, an easy accounting of the planet. Then a history of Man, neat and spicy; he knew plenty of them. "I'll fix you up, Ishma," he said, as they reached the corner where they were to separate. She threw him a radiant look, and hurried home to cook Rad's supper. Dropping Vennie from her hip, she made a fire, looking anxiously at the clock. It was becoming difficult for her to keep the house immaculate, look after Rad's clothes and meals, and give her patients all the time they needed. She had others now besides Mame. But she thrived on difficulties and wanted no rest. Rad was becoming critical. He would go spying through the house, looking into corners and cupboards for dust and disorder which he never found. Sometimes he would pull his clothes out of the drawers, or the closet, and look them over for slight rips and missing buttons. All was perfection. Ishma was fulfilling her bargain.

She was never away from home when he was there. Her evenings and Sundays belonged to him. He had not the least ground for complaint, yet he wanted to scold and swear and command her to stay at home. He didn't want her to go about making a servant of herself for mill-folks who were not half as good as she was. She ought to keep her head up and go with her equals, as he was doing.

Derry left Winbury the day after his talk with Ishma about

books, and a few days later she received several volumes from his own library. She tried reading them aloud to Rad, but he soon begged off. That stuff made him sleepy. He liked reading when there was something to it — movie magazines, *True Tales,* and mystery novels. "Read something a feller can keep awake on, Ish, if you've *got* to read." And rather than return to his choice of reading matter, she would sit and talk, which he liked much better. But there were nights when he would go to a meeting of his union; also he was beginning to attend church occasionally; and sometimes he would stroll through town with a friend, or drop in at a movie. These hours of release she kept for Derry's books.

It was two months before Derry Unthank came again, and joined her in an effort to pull Abe Creech through pneumonia. Sarah Creech was on her knees to them, dazed by the fear of being left a widow with seven children and not one of them big enough to go to the mills.

Ishma and Derry were on the street together, feeling the relief of out-doors after the high tension at a doubtful bedside. A woman walking rapidly came up behind them. It was Kansie Bennett, tripping along with every fibre straining its best. Her body was tiny, and she had eyes like miniature torches. Two years before, she had come from the mountains with her husband and six children. Another child would be due in about two months, but she went every day to the Greybank mill, and was now rushing home to get the family supper.

"O, Mis' Bailey," she began, slackening her running pace, "you're not goin' to fergit what you promised. I've been tellin' May she'll not have to stop school. Looks like it'll kill me if she has to come out an' lose her grade."

"Don't you worry, Kansie. That promise will be kept."

"I'm countin' on it. It shore helps to keep me goin'."

She ran on, and Ishma began to tell Derry about May Bennett. "Sticks to school, and doesn't even know she's lovely. If she loses her grade, she'll give up and take to the mills, as her older sister did, and her mother is crazy to have her finish High School. She gets in a fever about it. And between me and Grandma

Huff we're going to manage things so May won't have to come out when her mother is sick. We can do the housework for the family, and look after Kansie, for a month anyway."

"I know her husband," said Derry. "Alf Bennett. Undersized, like his wife. Mountain folks, but French stock. Alf has energy in every atom. Strained his heart at lumbering. Millwork is better for him, but he's likely to kill himself on the job. Plenty of spirit. Bet he could carry a gun. I'd like to see more of the hill folks coming in. They'll pep up these dubs down here. Do you see that old fellow doddering along yonder? Know who he is?"

"I've seen him around, but I've never asked about him."

"That's Grandma Huff's boy. One of 'em that began work at five cents a day. Forty years in the mills. Looks about eighty, but he's only fifty. The other one is dead."

"Grandma never told me he was her boy."

"She wouldn't. He's not much more than a beggar. Lives on what he can pick up Saturdays around the Square, and sometimes the sweepers let him putter about and rake out trash for them. Forty years! Twelve hours a day! Ought to be rich, oughtn't he? You know the Huffmores were aristocrats once. Get Grandma to tell you about old John Huffmore. He refused to let his children work in the mills. Kept 'em at home starving and wearing rags. They almost became clay-eaters, and he wouldn't give in for 'em to become 'mill-hands.' Finally he knew something had to be done if they lived at all, so he went to the Yadkin river and drowned himself. Next Monday three of his children reported for work at the nearest mill. This question of blood has strange ways of working out. Old John could have gone in for whiskey, but he had religious scruples. Whiskey saved a lot of the old-timers through here. A little corn would go far, as you said about the sixty cents, if it was turned into whiskey. We probably owe our escape from extinction to whiskey and the mills. Praise the Lord, O ye faithful!"

They were passing one of the mill nurseries, and Ishma's feet lingered. She could see the children in a big room playing, and the white-clad "mother" walking among them. Vennie, close in her arms, lifted her small head and looked too. It was the same place where she had been left for an eternal three minutes without her mother. As if fearing another desertion, she clung tightly to Ishma's neck.

"No, no, Vennie! Mother'll not leave you."

But Ishma looked longingly within. She loved Vennie, but she had so much love and strength left over. And she still believed that it was worth while to bring up children in Spindle Hill. As she moved away slowly she seemed to be leaving herself behind in the white frame building, making the children happy, helping the world get on.

"I could take care of fifty as easy as I could care for one," she said to herself rather than to her companion.

"You certainly could," he agreed. "But don't worry. Your time will come."

It came much sooner than he dreamed, and in a way he had not foreseen.

CHAPTER VIII

THE winter that followed Ishma's busy summer added "flu" to
the indignities that winter always heaped upon the inhabitants of
Spindle Hill. With all of her efforts, she could not do enough
to relieve her heart. Rad was cherishing a feeling of neglect,
though Vennie had begun to show an affection for him which
was gratifying. He was quite proud one evening when she sat
on his knee and begged him to kiss her woolen sheep that Ishma
washed to daily whiteness. He had never, or very rarely, thought
of the child as Britt's. She was Ishma's and Ishma was his.
That is, she would be if those meddling mill people would let
her alone. Lately there were days when he felt that she belonged
to everybody except himself. She tried to be at home when he
was there, but her talk was all of the neighbors, of the sick, of
the schools, of the hopes of this one, the despair of another —
anything, anybody, except himself, Rad Bailey, who had saved
her from the misery of Cloudy Knob, and given her a house with
four rooms, and a toilet on the back porch. He was going to
give her a good name too — make her as respectable as anybody
that walked — just as soon as old Britt come to himself and got a
divorce. Lord, what if he didn't mean to get one ? What if he's
settin' up there waitin' fer Ish to come back ? Shorely to God,
he wasn't that big a fool !

But hadn't he himself waited four years for Ishma, when she
was another man's, and childin' the third time ? Talk about
fools, he needn't go any furder than himself. No danger of her
going back. He could cut out that worry. She could have it
easy now, if she'd let herself, and her home was like a picture.
He looked at the pretty curtains — she washed them too much,
they'd give out soon, he's afeard — and the living-room set —

how did she keep the dust off it, an' the street not paved ? And there was the spankin' fine kitchen range that he'd bought her — she'd shore made good use of that — and something last and best, a set of porch furniture, where, on Sunday afternoons, he and Ishma and Vennie could sit together in sight of all the envious passers-by. Ishma would read to him then, or talk. She'd got to be a first class talker, he allowed, and knew a lot of nice, easy words. He'd ruther sit with her than be hangin' round with the boys.

He was goin' to have two or three kids sometime, but there wasn't any hurry. Ishma wasn't twenty-five yet. That was a good idea of hers, to get ahead first. Kids cost something down here. If you wanted to feed well an' wear good clo's, an' be comfortable all round, you had to go careful. He'd save up, an' if old Britt didn't get a divorce he'd have kids anyway. But he was takin' up with the church now, an' what if folks found out ? He couldn't risk bein' made a show of. Some people wouldn't keer, but he reckoned he had the right kind o' pride. Yes, he'd better be careful. Ishma was right. She always was right, when he thought it over. She'd stopped giving away his wages. He hadn't had to call her down for that in a long time. He'd got rid of his mountain timber, and the home was all paid for. Now they could begin to save — for the kids. If only old Britt —

Jobs were getting scarce. He'd have to look out, if he kept at work. And that was what he meant to do. Hard times couldn't slip up on *him !* He wasn't a man to forget his family. But Ishma ought to go round with him more, now that Vennie was gettin' human an' lettin' him take holt of her. He could carry her up the street, and it wouldn't hurt her if they took her to the Square on Saturday nights where they could get with *his* kind o' folks. They'd taken Ven once and it didn't hurt her at all. But Ishma didn't care for it. Said it was all gold the first time she saw it, and all brass the next.

It was too cold to go pleasurin' outside, and she didn't care for the movies. That was all right in principle. A bad habit, an' cost money. But they ought to go once in a while. She didn't care for anything but runnin' around an' waitin' on mill-trash. There were plenty o' nice fam'lies she could take up with. Sid Brinn was a grocer, an' after him to put his letter in the church. An' there were carpenters an' truckmen, an' some o' the store-keepers — all sorts o' good families. Ishma was gettin' to be awful nice lookin'. He wished he could take her with him to the mountains next time. He'd have to see about that boundary line. Awful bother going back, an' would take money. He'd find out from Bert Wiggins if Britt had got back from Knoxville. Just as well to go when he wasn't around. He wondered why Ish had never run across the Wiggins family, and he hoped she wouldn't, though the Wiginses were shut-mouth folks. They'd stand by people from their own county. He wasn't afraid they'd let it out that Ishma wasn't his wife in a reg'lar way. But he was glad they were on the other side of Winbury. He had met Cindy one day and she told him she was coming to see Ishma the first off-day she had. Lord, he hoped she wouldn't ! It might get Ish stirred up.

Rad glanced at the clock, his mother's clock, which he had brought down from the mountains when he went back to sell his timber. It was past time for Ishma to come home. He would start a fire in the cookstove.

A few minutes later when Ishma entered with Vennie throned as usual on her arm, Cindy Wiggins and Genie Unthank walked in with her. They were all talking in the friendliest fashion, with no suggestion of a secret burdening the air. Cindy, who had known Ishma from childhood, addressed her punctiliously as Mrs. Bailey, because of Genie's presence. Rad came from the kitchen to exhibit ownership and hospitality.

"I was tellin' Bert last night," said Cindy, "that I jest had to get over to see Mis' Bailey, but this was a bad day fer it. My Elbert — the baby, you know, Mis' Bailey — he's ten now — was sick an' I got the boss to let me come into town an' see a doctor about him. Our mill doctor ain't good fer shucks. The boss didn't want me to come, but we're puttin' in five full hands, an' he give in when he saw I was set on havin' a doctor fer my kid that he'd be willin' to have fer hisn. That mill doctor don't tend to *his* fam'ly, an' I knowed it. But I've got to hurry back. They'll all be comin' in to supper 'fore I get home."

"You'll have four grown men coming in hungry. They must keep you busy, Cindy," said Ishma.

"My, I wish they *would* get hungry. They've ever' one lost their taste fer eatin' since we come down here, an' I kain't get nothin' fixed to suit 'em. The three boys are all doin' night work, an' they don't keep peart at it. My, you've got a cute place here, an' it's fine Rad owns it. He always was a great one fer havin' his own things."

A queer look passed over Cindy's kind, broad face. She was thinking, and Ishma knew she was thinking, of the one time when Rad broke his rule and took something not his own.

"You must be tickled to see an old neighbor, Ishma," said Genie. "Ishma and Rad are fine folks, Mis' Wiggins. Me an' my husband took to 'em right off. We think they're plenty good."

"You're thinkin' right," Cindy answered. They talked on for a few minutes, then Cindy had to leave.

"I ortent a took time to come," she said.

But Rad had to show her the place. She couldn't go till she had looked at the climbing rose, the bed of pinks, and the hen and chickens cooped in the back yard. In the front there was a swaggering bunch of March bells, a bed of dahlias, and two little maple trees. Nothing was in bloom, but Cindy said she knew how pretty it would all be in the Spring.

"I ain't got a flower," she lamented. "The mill house we live in is so bad we're goin' to move the first chance, so I'm not puttin' out anything. They've promised us a better place, 'cause we're givin' 'em five hands, an' not fussin' about takin' night work fer the boys. Bert 's in the card-room, but I'm spinnin', an' the heat has got me weakened down. You know how strong I was, Mis' Bailey."

"The strongest woman in Wimble County, everybody said."

"I ain't that now. This doctor I saw today about Elbert says I've got low blood pressure. There's times I couldn't say 'sooey' if a hog had me down. You come to see me, Mis' Bailey, you an' Mis' Unthank."

"I'm coming right away," Ishma replied. "I want to ask you about everybody up there. I suppose you hear regular."

"I see most ever'body that comes from our county. They come right to Bert the first thing."

When Cindy and Genie were gone, Rad felt constrained to give Ishma a little advice. "It won't do to begin runnin' to the Wigginses. You'll meet somebody over there you won't want to see, an' first thing you know the talk 'll be flyin'."

Ishma knew her mind. "I'm not afraid of what they'll say, and I'm going to Cindy's tomorrow."

Rad went with her, and carried Vennie. They took a street-car across Winbury. It was the first hour after supper, and they found Bert and Cindy sitting on their back porch. From the front of the house they could see only the drab street and the funnels of the mill which was the scene of their daily, breathless labor. But from the rear they could look on a horizon of rising hills, with King's mountain in the distance, doubling like a fist, as if for another historic blow. So they sat at the back of the house and pretended to ignore the smell of sewerage issuing from the cubby at the end of the porch. It wasn't many minutes after the arrival of their visitors until Ishma and Cindy left the porch to the men and were in confidential possession of the living-room.

"I'm not one fer blamin' or excusin', Ishma," said Cindy. "What you've done, you've done, an' it's yore business. I'll take keer o' yer good name down here as fur as I can, but I kain't promise for ever'body else. Tim Wheeler was here last week, an' he said you an' Rad ort to be took up. He was fer puttin' the law on you. But you know that was jest Tim's talk."

"Did he tell you about the folks — up there?" asked Ishma, faintly.

"He's married Julie Webb, you know."

Ishma clung to a chair. "Married! Britt — "

"I'm talkin' about Tim."

The blood came back to Ishma's lips. Her smile made the tears start in Cindy's eyes.

"I've never heard a thing that happened since I left, Cindy."

"Your mommie took on awful. She'll never git over it, Ishma. It's made her hard as rock. You an' Steve leavin' out the same night near about killed her. But the folks up there have got through talkin'. I reckon they wouldn't bother you if you'd go back. After Britt had that fight with the preacher —"

"What about?"

"Why, about you. They churched you the very next third Sunday. The preacher, Jim Siler, went for you awful. An' Britt laid fer him as he come out the meetin'-house. I'm jest tellin' you like it's been told to me. When they picked Siler up, he looked like he'd been hauled out of a barrel o' red paint, he was so bloody."

"Rad went back to sell his timber, but he's never told me a thing."

"Well, ever'body was fur Britt after that, though looks like it ort to be t'other way. Britt's not settin' up to any woman either, though they's talk about his goin' to get a divorce. You ain't had no papers yit?"

"No. You'll git 'em, from what Tim said. He had it from yer mommie. Tim an' Julie live right close to her now, in uncle Zeke's house. Aunt Laviny was goin' on one day like a crazy person 'bout you livin' in sin, an' Britt told her you wouldn't be doin' that much longer. He was gettin' a divorce, he said, so you could be married proper, ef you wanted to be."

"If I wanted to be?"

"Yes, that's what Tim said Britt told her — jest like that. Tim says they're makin' a man out o' little Ned. He's beggin' to start to school now an' him only five. Britt made a little money out o' them records him an' Julie fixed up in Knoxville. But they say it's all spent. I reckon they wasn't much. He put ever' bit of it into yer mommie's place, Tim said. Jest dropped it, I reckon. You know he wasn't ever much fer managin'."

Ishma stood up, surprised to find that she could hold herself steady on her feet. She couldn't listen any longer. She felt that she must set off running. She must run all the way to Cloudy Knob. She thought if she opened her mouth it would be to utter a wild cry. Yet she heard herself saying, "We'll have to be going," with no emotion at all. And she added gently, "You'd better stop work for a while, Cindy. Give yourself a chance."

"Stop work?" cried Cindy, amazed. "Why, I'm payin' on a sewin'-machine, a 'frigerator, an' a bed-room set! I've wanted a sewin'-machine since I was twelve years old, an' I'm gettin' it now. An' I had to have a 'frigerator. A mountain person can't drink the water down here in the summer time without coolin' it off. Can't do it an' live. I had to have a bed too. Up in the mountains it didn't make any difference if I slept on a pallet, I could *sleep*. But down here I come out o' the mill feelin' like a squeezed dish-rag, an' if I don't get my sleep I'm done fer. I had to have a bed I could rest on. Then I had to buy two more fer the boys. I couldn't take the best, an' leave my younguns to the cobs. They work as hard as I do. Well, I'd better not say that. You know I'm paid 'cordin' to what I git done, an' I never could stand fer anybody to go ahead o' me, not even my own blood. Here's my pay slip I got today."

Proudly she took a slip of paper from her pocket. It stated that she had earned fourteen dollars.

"That's for only sixty-five hours. We don't work Saturdays after one o'clock. Bert can't beat that. I've made as much as fifteen, an' one week it was fifteen-fifty." Her voice sank and trembled with importance. She who hardly had handled that much in a year up in the mountains earned it herself in one week.

"Bert an' the boys want to buy a car soon as I git the house-things paid fer. But that sort o' skeers me. Looks like though, with only six in fam'ly an' five workin', we might do it. Then we can drive back to the mountains on a Saturday night an' come back Sunday night, an' won't miss a day out o' the mill. It'll be worth it to drive up there an' git a good drink o' water. But I like to live here, if I *can* live."

Her voice seemed to catch pitifully at something that she wouldn't let herself believe. "But you *can't* live," Ishma was thinking, while she gazed at this changed Cindy, with heavy lines in her face, sagging shoulders, and slow feet, all unlike her mountain self.

"I'm goin' to hold out if there's any way. It beats livin' in that holler under Cloudy Knob. I can always get out of a Sunday, if I don't feel too used up. An' ain't it a grand town ?"

"I'm glad you like it, Cindy." Ishma was hurrying out. "I must get Vennie home. I don't often keep her up this late."

214

"You'll raise her, Ishma," said Cindy, kindly. "She's a peart child."

For weeks thereafter, Ishma was careful to reach home before Rad, and visit their mail-box on the paved highway. One day she took out a large envelope which contained her summons in the case of Britton Hensley vs Ishma Hensley. She was to appear at such and such to answer such and such. When she returned to the house she burnt the envelope and its contents in the kitchen stove. She would say nothing to Rad about the summons. And she told herself over and over, "Britt is doing it for me. Just for me."

One day she asked Rad why he hadn't told her about Britt's fight with Siler. He looked hurt and superior. "You reckon I's goin' to tell you they'd read you out o' the church ?" he finally replied. But she knew that was not the reason that he had been secretive.

Not long afterward she noticed him casting a look of deep disapproval at Vennie. "What's the matter with her ?" she asked him, almost sharply.

"Can't you see for yourself ? The brat is beginnin' to look like old Britt."

"No ! It's not so !"

Just then Vennie made her monkey toy squeal, and throwing back her head she laughed in Britt's very manner.

"Oh, God !" said Ishma, sitting down, her head and heart swimming.

"Didn't I tell you ? But don't take it hard, Ish. Little old Ven is all right. Come here, Ven. Come to daddy Rad."

The child went to him obediently, and he took her on his knee. But Ishma felt that the ground was rocking under her feet.

The winter that had set in harsh and hard, made busy days for her, and it was good to have no time for herself. First there was Kansie Bennett. Derry came down from his farm to help her through, but he stayed only a few days. Grandma Huff gave out the first week, and all of the burden fell on Ishma. The care of Kansie's house and children, made it difficult to give

Rad and her own home, with ever exacting Vennie, a just share of her time and labor. Two months passed, and Kansie was still in bed, making frequent announcements that she would be up and back in the mill in a few days. But Derry had told Ishma that Kansie must stay out of the mill for a year if she wished to live, and she did have a strangely tenacious desire to prolong her drab life. "I've got to stay with the kids till they're big enough to kick out fer thersevs," she said. She got up and began to care for the house and the children, but no strength came for the mill. It seemed that May would have to come out of school after all. Alf could not make enough to keep the family in food and clothes. No man in Spindle Hill could support his family on his own wages alone. A mill-hand wasn't expected to do that. It was such a commonplace that no one thought of it as unreasonable that a man could not make enough by twelve hours of daily labor to feed and clothe his young family. A commonplace upheld by the church and defended by the law. If a worker came out of his daze between law and church, and questioned it, he was a "bad influence."

Alf's boss told him that unless he could provide another workhand he would have to give up his house. Ishma set out to find someone who would be willing to crowd in with the Bennett's as a boarder, and discovered a doff-boy, seventeen years old, who had no home. He would be glad to sleep in a bed with Kansie's three little boys, and take his chance at her table, for four dollars a week. The usual rate was five, and he'd like to save that extra dollar. Sometimes his pay-check called for less than seven dollars for six days' work.

The house problem settled, it was easier to tell Kansie of Derry's decree. "Lucky she's a bottle baby," said Kansie one day, as she fed her youngest. "I can leave her in the nursery right off." And Ishma told her that it would be a year before she could go back to the mill.

"But May!" cried the mother. "She's got to finish! She can't come out of school!" Her voice was full of agony. May might have been about to fall over a precipice. The voice dropped to a defeated whisper. "Kain't I have *one* to get through?"

Ishma thought it might be managed. Alf could keep them

in food, but what about clothes ? Could the family go without anything new until summer time ? They would try it anyhow. Except May. She couldn't stay in school without money for books and clothes. And she must stay. That was what all the pother and bother was about.

Ishma went to the pastor of a church — one of the churches provided for the mill people. Half of the pastor's salary was paid by a benevolent mill-owner. The other half was collected from the workers who attended the church, and usually fell far below the promised amount. The pastor couldn't be blamed for feeling a little acid and critical.

"Do the Bennetts attend church ?"

"No. They usually do their washing on Sunday. The man helps his wife that day."

The pastor's blue eyes grew icy. "That's bad. Surely they could manage better than that."

"I don't see how," she said simply, with her grey eyes levelled at him.

The pastor coughed. "There is a fund — but I will inquire further as to the character and needs of the family. Then I will send for you."

He did inquire further — of the mill-owner who contributed so generously to his salary. It was a small matter to approach so big a man about, but he never quailed before duty.

The big man asked how many members of the family were at work. Only one ? And he had a weak heart ? Not much of a contribution to the mill force. And a large family of small children ? Small. Well, it seemed to him that a family of that description ought to get out on a farm and not become a charge on county or church. That would be his advice. Tell the man to take one of the little tenant farms roundabout, until the children became old enough for service. Lead them in the way of self-respect, not pauperization. He advised that as a Christian, which he hoped he was, and as a citizen of their good little town. The pastor thanked him fervently, as a Christian and a citizen, for giving his time to a really small matter, and took his leave.

He never sent for Ishma.

She went to the county relief, asking for clothing for May, and was told that they did not help children of fourteen who were able to work.

"But this is an unusual child."

"That's fine! She will be able to take care of herself."

Ishma went home. She was a little late getting in, and Rad had been to the mail-box. He held up a letter as she came into the house.

"Want me to open it?" She had seen the Yancey county post-mark, and said, "Yes, Rad."

"There you are! From Derry Unthank — and a check for one of your ten thousand cases, I reckon."

Ishma took the letter. Derry said that he was stealing the money he was sending her, but it wouldn't get him into trouble, and she needn't be afraid to use it. He had meant to help May all the time, but he had wanted Ishma to go a little further with her own education first. He was more interested in hers than in May's.

"Put on supper," said Rad, "an' I'll look after it while you fly to Alf Bennett's. You look like an airplane would be too slow for you."

"Thank you, old boy," she said, looking so happy that he had to pull her to him and squeeze her shoulders as he kissed her.

"Soon as I get a better job, Ish, I'm not goin' to be so close-fisted with you." But she knew he would.

The weather grew bitter. It was not so cold as in the mountains, but it was clammy and dragged one down. The "flu" became rampant, and deaths were frequent. When Spring brought relief, it seemed to bring only more weariness to Ishma. Mind and body, but most of all her heart, were weary. Pace had died, and Genie, the proud carpenter's wife, was in the mills, trying to support her three little boys and keep Leta in High School. Her youngest boy was dead. And Mildred's husband was dead. Cindy was still in bed from her second wrestle with pneumonia, and she had lost her sewing-machine. Her Elbert was staying out of school to do the housework and keep his mother in bed. Her oldest son, a night-worker for three years, had become tubercular, and was back in the mountains with his uncle, Jack Wiggins, who wouldn't do him any good, Cindy thought. It was a hopelessly sad household, but it was no exception. There was bitterness and want under almost every roof. The mill-owners were adopting a process of management called "rationalization." It meant fewer workers and greater production. A "drive to the limit." The workers called it the "speed up" and "stretch out." "We'll thin out the no-goods," said the bosses. And the "hands" began to fall by the way. Alf Bennett was among the first to go, and Kansie returned to the spinning-room six months short of the year Derry had prescribed for rest. May came out of school to work at her mother's side, and Alf, with his weak heart, did the housework and cared for the small children.

Ishma had troubles of her own. A letter had come from Britt, brief and direct. "Dear Ishma, I've got a divorce. You and Rad can marry proper if you want to. Britt."

Rad knew nothing of the letter, and she was dreading the time when someone would tell him of Britt's divorce. She had no purpose. Life was merely hustling her along, with Vennie in her arms. But she knew she was going back to Cloudy Knob. In another year she could take Vennie safely on the long trip. She couldn't ask Rad for the money, but she could start afoot, and kind people would pick up her and the child. She would get there, and see what would happen. She didn't think any farther along than that.

One day after the warm weather came, she felt that she would choke to death in the house. She looked at the hot kitchen stove that Rad was so proud of, and thought of the meals she had cooked with no stove at all. Red-white oak-wood coals under a hearth oven with a pone in it. A pot of vegetables swinging over the fire, and milk from the spring-house. Clouds on the mountains to be looked at, instead of an overstuffed sofa. Up there where it made no difference what you had in the house. The neighbors wouldn't slant their eyes at you and make you hang your head.

She rose from her chair, took up Vennie, covered her little, curly head with a sun-bonnet made specially for her protection, and started off to find a cool spot in the woods. She had heard of the public park, but never had been there. Today she would find it. She had promised to see Nancy Barnes, but she could stop on her way for that. She wouldn't stay — not if Nancy were dying. Wasn't she herself dying ? She didn't know what was the matter with Nancy, but had received the summons to come at once, and that usually meant disaster of some kind.

Nancy wasn't sick. She was physically very fit, and mentally raging. Ishma reached the house, which was a double one with two front rooms, each with its own door opening on the porch. Both doors were closed, and on one of them a piece of white cardboard was tacked, which bore the words:

> be quite
> nite hans

meaning that night workers were trying to sleep within and were appealing for quiet. From behind the door of the other room came the sounds of a hub-bub that proved the futility of the appeal. Ishma would not risk taking Vennie into the house, and sat down to wait on the steps. In about five minutes the door that shielded the commotion was opened, and a little woman slipped out of the room, closing the door quickly behind her. Ishma recognized Ella Ramsey, Nancy's mother. She saw Ishma, and with evident pleasure crossed the porch and sat down by her, greeting her with blue eyes that were unafraid and twinkling with eagerness.

She was that blest sort of person whose humor can defy every tragedy — who can go on sparkling into the second century if they have the tenth part of a chance. Ella Ramsey had not had the hundredth part of a chance, but at fifty-five she was still twinkling, and sweet as the core of life. She had on a well-washed print dress, brief as a girl's, with little ruffles on the short sleeves and around the low neck. The tiny flower of the print was the color of her eyes.

"I didn't go to work today," she said, slipping softly up beside Ishma. "Nancy got so upset."

"What is it all about, Mrs. Ramsey ?"

"I'll tell you in a minute. I've got something important to talk about first. Been wanting to see you for the last week or two, Ishma. Have you heard anything about the new union ?"

"Well, a little."

Ella over-rode the reticence of Ishma's answer. "I'm all for it. Fact is, I ain't had such a present in a long time as that new union." Her chuckle was like the tip end of a jolly song. "This is another sort from the old United. When that went back on us after we'd won the big strike in '21, and the leaders sold us to the big bosses and ran away with our money, it near took my life. I'd talked an' walked an' fought for the United. And I was sold out before I begun. But this new one, the National, it's got me back to the faith."

"I've heard it's getting a lot of members."

"Not half fast enough. If this speed-up goes on, a lot of us will be knocked out before we get enough members to call a strike. The workers are all skeered. I never saw such a trembly lot. And what I want of you, Ishma, is to do some scoutin' for us. Help us bring 'em in."

"How can I ? I'm not in the union. I don't know *anything.*"

Mrs. Ramsey's hand went up gracefully in protest. "That's just why you can help. Ever'body likes you. Ever'body knows you ain't out for anything but good. In some o' these houses — I'll give you a list all made out — they're so skeered they'll lose their jobs that they turn blue-white if you say 'union' to 'em. If I was to walk in on some of 'em they'd run out at the back door."

The chuckle came again, and the clear, pink skin was screwed into wrinkles around the glowing blue eyes. "But you could go in. They know you've got nothin' in it, an' you're the one they'll listen to. Your name has gone fur around here, Ishma. Ever' door will say 'come in' to you."

"But I wouldn't know what to say !"

"You will after I've told you. I want you to ease along an' open the way, an' keep 'em from bein' mad an' skeered. You are to let 'em know that this is an *honest* union, run by ourselves. Lord, I can't blame 'em for bein' mad when I think of what the United did to us. I was in Concord that summer, right in the front row, talkin' union till my tongue was near split. Funny things happened too. That was my cousin that bit the policeman. You've heard that story, hain't you ?"

Ishma hadn't heard. "It's been printed lots o' times, in the papers. My cousin, Jane Sawyer, had a full, double set of false teeth, good as if they growed in her mouth. A policeman was twistin' her arm an' she bit hisn to the bone. When they had the trial he was there with his arm swelled up, an' he scuffed his eyes at Jane, an' says, 'Yes, that's the woman who bit me !' Jane threw back her head, an' there wasn't a tooth in her mouth. 'This is what I've got to bite with, Judge,' she says, an' ever'body roared. The Judge laffed too, an' the policeman got so red I thought he'd start blazin'. The Judge told him to go 'long home an' think up something else. Yes, funny things happened. I heard something yesterday that made me laff down to my toes. You know the old Frenston mill has got a boss, Cripp Ritter, that thinks he's the only man up on hind legs. All the rest of us are still grabblin' along on all-fours. He got a whiff of the new union an' called in his head man. 'Jim' he says — it was Jim Hogan — 'you snoop around and find out if we've got any fleas an' rabbits in this mill that belong to that new union.' So Jim snooped an' got all the names. Next day old Fly-in-the-soup called Jim into the office. 'Got them names ?' he says. 'Shore !' says Jim, an' stuck out his list. 'I don't want to look at it,' the old hog-in-the-dough-pan says. 'You just send 'em in here. Send 'em right now. A minute 's too long for lice like that to stay around me !' An' Jim says, 'Go pull yer switch-board then, they're all in it but three.' And that was so, Ishma. The Frenston works five hundred men, and Jim had the names o' four hundred and ninety-seven."

"What did the boss do ?"

"Couldn't do nothin'. He jumped up like he meant to see if God was at home, an' shouts to Jim, 'You git out o' here !' So Jim went back to work, an' the boss ain't opened his mouth to him since."

Ishma laughed with Ella Ramsey. "You don't need me at all," she said, "if they're coming in like that."

Mrs. Ramsey's face subdued all its twinkles. "That's the way we *want* 'em to come in. The Frenston shows how. There's twenty-five mills around here where the ground ain't hardly scratched. An' we want quick work. That boss, Ritter, is keepin' quiet only on one side of his face. He went to the owners an' they've called a meeting. They'll hatch something, an' whatever it is will be mighty rotten for *us*."

"What do you think it will be ?"

"My son Rob is tryin' to find out what they're cookin' up. He'll get it out of Abe Williams, maybe. Abe is a big furniture man, but once he was a little neighbor boy of ours an' him an' Rob were close as twins. Rob had to go to the mills, but Abe had an uncle who set him up in a little business, an' now look at him ! He goes to all the swell eats where they talk about how to get the best of us an' keep us down. But he's never got above Rob yit, an' when the doctors told Rob that he'd have to come out o' the mills er be brought out feet first, Abe give him a job truck-drivin'. I'm expectin' him to bring his truck by here any minute. That's what I come out o' the house fer when I saw you settin' here. I was glad to see you too. When Nancy sent that word to you yesterday, I says to myself there's my chance to get the best recruiter in Spindle Hill. An' I've got you, ain't I, honey ?"

"If I only knew enough," protested Ishma.

"You can learn mighty fast. It's like I've been tellin' you, we need somebody they ain't afraid of an' will believe in. That's you, Ishma. When I was castin' around for helpers, you was the first one I thought of. Soon as you get a door edged open, so it won't shut on us, one o' the union workers 'll be right there. We're workin' a lot o' places already, but we've got to get into *every* house." She lifted her head, listening. "I hear Rob right now."

There was no truck in sight, but very soon one drove around the corner. Mrs. Ramsey's ears were as quick and definite as her tongue.

Rob would have been tall if his shoulders were not so round and stooped. He was fat too, but of a sickly color horribly suggestive of pernicious anæmia. Ishma knew nothing of anæmia, but felt that Rob was out of health someway, for all his bigness.

"We're talkin' union," said his mother.

Rob turned suspicious eyes on Ishma. "Which un you out fer ?"

"The National, o' course," said Ella.

"You better be keerful, mother."

"I know who I'm talkin' to."

"That old United got off with three dollars o' mine. I had that much in the fund when the sekertry lit a rag."

"We can forget that now, Rob. Has Abe said anything yet ?"

"He's said a little that meant a whole lot." His eyes were still searching Ishma's face.

"She's all right, I tell you. Whad Abe say ?"

"They've had their meetin', the owners have. One of 'em got up an' proposed a shut-down an' starve-out. 'We'll git there first,' he said. 'Six weeks livin' on air an' water, an' they'll come back on their bellies fer half wages.' "

"I knew that would be it," said Ella.

"They said they wouldn't wait fer the workers to strike. That glues 'em together an' makes 'em harder to handle fer all time, they says."

"An' that's why *we* want it." Already she was meditating, planning, gathering her forces.

"Here's yer ginger ale, mother. Just off the ice." He handed her a bottle. "I've got to run." He went down the steps, and the truck was soon out of sight.

"He's my oldest," said Ella, her eyes softening, "and he always was a good boy. Went in as doff-boy at eleven, an' come out at thirty-five. He's sort o' suspicious though. When he was about twelve, the boss got mad one day an' said Rob was shirkin'. Said he'd teach him a lesson. An' he hung Rob out the window, tied to a rope, in the blazin' July sun for three hours. The brick wall was so hot he'd keep pushin' away from it to keep from burnin'. Rob's always been sort o' suspicious of the whole human race ever since. He wasn't shirkin' either. He was sleepy. They'd kept him on for a day an' night finishin' up a job o' thread that was due on the market. He's been holdin' that agin the bosses for twenty-five years, an' it ain't done him no good in-side."

"He ought to hold it against them !" said Ishma burningly.

"Well, I've tried to raise all my children to be God-fearin' an' forgivin'. There was eleven of 'em; one ever' two year long as Ramsey lived. We were farmers to begin with, an' we had enough to eat, but nothin' else. I made a good garden, an' I'd can stuff all night 'fore I'd let it go to waste. But there's more to life than a belly, an' we had to go to the mills for money. Ever' two years we'd move back to a farm, on account of a new baby comin'. Ramsey's wages in the mills wasn't enough to keep us when I wasn't workin', but on a farm we could live whether there was any money or not. We could keep the children alive and well. Ramsey was a good farmer, and I was a good helper, so we could always find a place. But as I's tellin' you, there's more hungers than the one gnawin' yer stomach, an' we'd get back to the mills soon as we could, thinkin' ever' time maybe we could lay up a little money. The mill boss would give us a house soon as we got back, 'cause we's two good workers."

"I've tried farming too," said Ishma, "and I hope it's easier in the mills."

"Well, it ain't. We tried to live right an' go to church, but we were too beat out. It's easier to be God-fearin' on a farm than in the mills. I got too tired to pray. That was the way I felt at night when I'd come out o' the sweat. I raised my boys an' girls right though. They weren't these cheek-paintin', rip-roarin' kind. That's what I tell Nancy about her girl, Em. She's let her just raise herself. That's what all this trouble is about now."

"What *is* the trouble, Mrs. Ramsey?" Ishma asked, thinking that she must hurry out of this if she was to get to the park.

"Why, Em, Nancy's oldest girl, ain't but fifteen, an' she had to go an' buy a dress on 'stallments just as soon as she began to draw wages. You know some o' these youngsters that have to go to work so early, get all their brains crowded out, looks like, with the work an' long hours, an' soon as they get a little pay in their hand there's a 'stallment man waitin' fer 'em. Standin' right at the mill door sometimes, to begin his little song soon as they come out. He tells 'em how easy it is to have what they want, even if they haven't got more'n a dollar to pay down. I know some girls that are payin' fer dresses they've done wore out. Em bought her dress from that little, dark-lookin', swell-lipped feller in Bee Street, Mincy, they call him, an' she couldn't pay fer it. She lost two weeks with the flu, an' when she went back she was weak an' shaky, an' couldn't hold down enough frames to make much. She let a lot of work get tangled up, an' I couldn't blame the boss fer holdin' out on her. She told Mincy she'd pay as soon as she could, an' he said that was jake with him, and wouldn't she go fer a ride some purty night when it wasn't too cold. Em didn't tell her mother. She slipped off an' went fer the ride. She didn't want him to git mad, she said. When they were goin' through a dark place in the woods, Mincy said, 'Here's where we stop.' 'What fer?' says Em. 'You know, baby. Jump out,' says Mincy. An' Em set there gettin' mad. She's a big girl fer her age, an' she's tough like me, an' when he tried to pull her out o' the car they had a right peart fight. He finally got Em pulled out, but he couldn't get the best of her. He got her dress off though, right over her head, an' jumped into the car with it. 'I'm takin' what belongs to me,' he called back to her, drivin' off. 'Hope you'll have a nice walk.' An' Em was left there in nearly nothin'. Just a little brasser that the girls wear nowadays, an' knickers. Half her skin was takin' the air. She walked on to the nearest house, an' a woman let her have a big apron to cover herself with. Em's cloak was in Mincy's car. She walked all the way home 'cause she was ashamed to ask for a ride, an' maybe was skeered too. Nancy's been cryin' an' tearin' around ever' since. Says her girl 's ruined, but me an' Em are takin' it fine. I told Em she'd got her lesson early enough fer it to do her some good, an' she said that's right, grandma, I have. The men folks wanted to go after Mincy with tar an' feathers, but I made 'em shet up on that. Where'd that sort of a thing get us? The way to fix Mincy is to get word around that nobody is to buy anything from him any more. That'll soon run him out. An' that's what they're goin' to do. Em scratched him up purty bad anyway. She says he'd never have got that dress off her if the flu hadn't done her up first. Em is sort o' like me, a fighter. When her mother says 'Ain't you ashamed to show yer face?' she says, 'It looks a lot better than Mincy's. If they's anything wrong with it, the lookin'-glass ain't told me.' An' she's gone back to work today. I've been thinkin' that maybe if the youngsters don't pray as much as we used to, they've got more spirit. An' that's what we're needin' now. Needin' it bad."

She stopped for a moment to listen. "Nancy's quiet now. This is her first quiet spell today. Maybe she's wore out an' gone to sleep."

"I'd better not go in then," said Ishma, getting up and taking Vennie in her arms.

"When 'll we finish our talk, Ishma?" the blue eyes besought her.

"Couldn't you come around to my house tonight ?"

"Now looky here, honey, I know you're all right, but I'm not sure o' Rad. You'll excuse me, Ishma, but nobody 's sure of Rad. You've showed what you are, clear as sun, but it's sort o' mistin' around him. Us mill folks don't know much more about him than we did the first day he come here."

"I couldn't work for you without telling him."

"Then you won't work fer us at all. An' you're givin' up a big chance. What you been doin' is just patchin' around, an' you'll soon find it out. This 'll be main business. You'll be where what you do counts. An' it's a shame fer a woman like you not to count."

Ella's words seemed to twist around Ishma's buried desire and bring it to light. Of all things, what she wanted most was to count, to be part of something real, as everlasting, at least, as humanity.

"I'll come back tomorrow to see you. I'd like to help, but I've got everything to learn."

"You come. I'll be lookin' for you." As she turned toward her daughter's door, her face lost part of its light. Personal matters were small matters to Ella Ramsey, unless they were related to her consuming purpose — a livable wage and endurable hours for the workers. This new union had given her a hope of something more. A day might come when the workers would own the factories they worked in. It was almost too great a hope to be carried in the heart. She would tell Ishma about it tomorrow. She mustn't unload on her too fast. There was a woman that she must set to work in the right way. She was valuable. Ella would have felt a sharp thrust of loss had she known that it would be six months before she and Ishma met again.

The year was still at Spring, but it was a warm day for walking. Ishma inquired of a passer-by and was told that the park lay "right nigh, about three blocks east." That was news. She had thought there was a long walk between her and her goal. In a few minutes she caught sight of much greenery, tall trees with leaves cool against the sky, dark shadows and lanes of green lower down, and spots of color, some brilliant, others gentle. It was all enclosed in a high picket fence, and she made her way to the wide gate. Vennie began to clap her small hands. She had caught sight of a fountain rising from a green, open space on the other side of the fence, and demanded to be put down so that she could run to it.

"Wait, lamb. We must go through the gate."

Within the park, a little to the left of the gate, was a small rock cottage half covered with vines. The gate was locked, and she stood by it wondering where she could find the right place to get in. A man came out of the cottage.

"You got a pass, Miss ?" he asked.

"Why, no."

"Then you can't come in."

Ishma was perplexed. "But I thought the city park was free for everybody."

The man laughed. "You're right about that. It's free, but this one ain't. This belongs to Beverly Grant. You've heard about him, hain't you ?"

"Yes. He owns some of the mills."

"About five, if I can count c'rect. If you're a friend o' his, you may walk right in."

"You know I'm not," said Ishma, unsmiling, and thinking of Vennie's disappointment. The child was tugging at the gate, getting ready for an imperious cry.

"You'll find the free park about two miles furder on, an' when you see it you'll know why it's free."

Ishma pulled the screaming child from the gate. "I want fowers, I want fowers," she was crying.

"Here now, I'll get her a flower. Guess I can steal one for a purty little gal."

A big magnolia tree sheltered the gate. It was early for the bloom, but he reached up and found a wonderful half-open flower which he plucked and passed to Vennie through the pickets. Ishma flushed. A stolen flower for her child! The man saw her rebellion. "Now, now," he said, with his first genuine smile, "it won't hurt either of us for the little gal to have it." Slowly she returned his smile, and moved off with the pacified Vennie. Two miles further to go, and the sun was merciless. Vennie refused to walk, and the hot little body grew heavy on Ishma's hip.

The villages that made up the outskirts of Winbury extended from the town like the outspread fingers from a palm. Between the fingers lay wide strips of weedy land, owned by some speculator waiting for another mill to push up prices. Flat, unsightly covered with briars, and here and there a stench rising to reveal the weed-hidden presence of stagnant water, the sun beat down upon it as if the land itself had sinned and was receiving punishment. Ishma followed the highway across two of these repellent wastes. Between them straggled a long strip of mill houses, looking almost deserted, because the tenants — husbands, wives, and children — were at work. Now and then a bent figure, with a face like wrinkled putty, could be seen shambling after chickens or weeding a mite of a garden. The great game of wage-earning had got beyond them.

Ishma's feet were burning on the asphalt, but there were no shady retreats by the way. She had to keep on. It was no wonder she had heard so little of the city's free play-ground. A sandy road branched off from the highway, and she saw a sign indicating that she must take it. Another stretch of shadeless land and hot earth, then another sign in large letters — PUBLIC PARK — told her she was near her holy ground. There was no special entrance. The road, not so sandy here, simply continued into a grove of scrub oaks, small and scattered. No flowers, no shrubs, no fountains. She went on into the thin woods with their few stunted trees. Disappointment made her heart and her feet heavy, but Vennie did not want to stop or rest. She wanted more "fowers."

Ishma walked on achingly. A murmur which she recognized fell on her ears. Oh, it was true! There was water somewhere, tumbling over rocks. It was easy to walk fast then, and very soon she came to the stream. It was only a few feet from the road in one place, where the water swerved and curved back, as if it had intended to cross the road then turned again. The stream, where it curved, was wide and shallow. She sat on the bank, pulled off her shoes, and dipped her feet in the water. Then she took off Vennie's shoes and let her splash ecstatically.

The brook came from higher land, and just above them there was a little fall of water, shining and singing. Vennie, playing in the shallows, was so amused that Ishma thought she could be left to herself for a few moments. There was a small but gracious beech-tree on the bank. She drew her feet out of the water and went to the shade of the tree, her bare feet grateful for the cool moss under it. Now she could rest and think. For a long time she had been wanting to get away somewhere and think. At least she told herself so. But instead of putting her mind to work, she released it utterly from thought, threw herself on the ground, her face pressed against it, and began to cry as if she were made of tears. There was no barrier in mind, soul or body against that flood. She cried like an unspent storm; like a storm that would never be spent. Vennie ran over to her, and for the first time Ishma could not feel the little hands that tugged at her flesh. The child gave up her fumbling and sat silently, looking at this strange mother. At last she uttered a scream that brought Ishma, startled, to her feet. When she saw that Vennie was safe beside her, she sat down again.

The fright had assuaged the torrent. Her body shook, and the physical pain in her breast was unbearable, but her cheeks were no longer washed with a burning flood. Slowly she came back to stolidity, though not to full awareness. She felt that she was with Britt, in the mountains where life was sweet. That passion of weeping had transported her to the hills of her longing. They were together by the Nantahala. She could feel his hands on her hair, his kisses on the back of her neck. Pretty soon he would say, "Come on, big girl, let's jump in !" They would go to the river bank, and — Vennie was falling into the water — she would be drowned !

Ishma sprang to the rescue of Vennie, who was merely paddling in the shallow stream, not the least endangered. She sank back again on the moss, and tried to recapture her reason. If she let herself go like this, what would become of Vennie? But what did Vennie matter? Was her life to be forever bound up in a child's? Was her horizon always to be Vennie's horizon? Was she never to reach the world? She could forget Britt, perhaps — she could believe in herself again, if she could touch life where it was real, as real as she used to feel it in her dreams. That night when she had walked down the mountain, it was towards something. She had not been thinking of Rad then; she hardly knew that he was walking beside her; she only knew that she was going out, and that her dream was bright. Then she had come to the little house and Vennie.

She thought of a time when, as a girl of ten years, she had gone for a long climb up a mountain trying to reach a grey spur from which she knew she could see the far world. She remembered the hot, eager blood that was in her as she scrambled up over rocks and squeezed through thickets. Near her goal, she found herself between a cliff and a jutting boulder. Climbing up between them, she sat down with her eyes shut. She hadn't looked back for the last mile of her climb, saving her emotion for what she should see from the top. Safely on her ledge, she turned and opened her eyes. There in front of her, growing out of the cliff, was a stunted loblolly. Its roots bored into the crevices below, but its bushy little top reached up until she couldn't see over it. Wedged in between boulder and cliff, she could go no higher. She could do nothing but look into the branches of that poor little pine that hid the far valleys, the sunlit peaks, the long, dreamy ridges, and the pale path of rivers. Later she scrambled down to a lower ledge and her eyes found what they had sought, but ecstasy could not be re-born.

Now she felt that she had again come a long, hard way, and before her, filling her road, was a little stunted child, doomed from her birth to insignificance. She had heard people say that they were fulfilled in their children, but for her the mother's sacrificial gesture could have no meaning. She would never find the slightest sense of self-completion in Vennie. Her intelligence was too steady on the job for such an illusion. With Ned it might have been different. That was part of her punishment. The exchange was just. Ned for Vennie.

Lately a new torture had stolen upon her. The child, in spite of her likeness to an animate doll, and her hair that had grown dark and sleek again, was revealing little ways and movements that were merciless reminders of Britt. She would have to bear those stabs through life. And how could she? It wasn't possible.

Gradually her mind ceased to whirl and her blood grew cool. The beech-tree shadows, the clear water steadily singing, the feeling of green life about her, had their elemental effect. Nature, whose child she was, took her back. The breast offered her was thin and unbounteous, but it served. In her mountain days the earth that had given her bread had done more than feed body and spirit. It had made her part of itself. Fields, woods, cliffs, peaks, unbaffled waters and far horizons, were not merely her background. She was of them, and would always be. Their essence was with her like a spatial self wherever she went. It was this that once had made Derry Unthank ask her if it didn't hurt her to go into little houses. "You can't possibly get all of yourself inside, Ishma." She had laughed and asked, "What do I leave out?" "Why," he had said, "a mountain or two, some miles of deepwood, and at least one waterfall."

Her face found its color again as she looked back on her child self, with wet face and tumbling hair, helping the rain and wind wash the hills clean and tangle the tree-tops together. In Winbury rain meant shut windows and strangulation. The wind was only a disturber of dust and temper. Something to flee from, not run with. And the people were so helpless. They had their jobs. Outside of that, what did they do? They didn't even bury their dead. That was another's job — someone was paid to do it. Every man, at some time or other, ought to know what it was to dig a grave for a fellow-man and lay him in it. Every woman ought to know how to tenderly handle the dead, and care for a new-born child.

The soft purr of a car coming over the sandy road made her leap up and look for Vennie. There she was, in the middle of the road, making little towers of sand and slapping them over. Just around the sharp curve the car was honking. For a second

232

Ishma was a frozen fear, then she dashed to the child, so swiftly that her feet did not feel the ground. But the car won.

They were carefully picked up by the big, middle-aged chauffeur and the white-lipped woman who had sat in the car, and taken to a hospital. Vennie was unmangled, but dead. She had been tossed aside, and the quick fall had broken her thin, little neck. Ishma was unconscious. There was a broken ankle and arm, and perhaps further injuries. She lay on the white bed for a day and night without opening her eyes. The wound in the temple, made by the sharp edge of a rock, was cleansed and dressed, but the nurse did not bind up the beautiful head. Her face held the contours of remote bliss, and it was strange how great a sense of life the motionless figure gave out.

The doctors and hospital staff were puzzled as to where Ishma "belonged." "She's not a mill-woman," said one. "Anyone can see that, without looking at her hands." But she was cheaply dressed. Evidently poor. "The child's clothes are pretty," said a nurse. "And hand-made, to the last stitch."

The doctor in charge thought again. "Put her in a private room until we get information. There are three vacant anyway."

Ishma returned to life, not moaning over Vennie, but crying for Britt. Her outer self had been rent and her heart could not be hidden. She was past caring. But when the nurse asked softly, "Who is Britt?" fear came back, and she lay silent. By and by she began to remember what had happened, and terror came into her eyes. She wanted to ask about Vennie, but was afraid. The nurse understood.

"Be quiet now," she said, "and we'll tell you everything soon. There's nothing to worry about."

Vennie was safe then, and she could go to sleep. She would never get enough sleep, she thought, as her eyes closed. A few minutes later the head-nurse came in.

"Why didn't you find out her name?" she asked in disapproval.

"I thought questioning would excite her," explained the attendant nurse.

"Always get information the first moment possible. She's in

a private room, and may not have a penny to pay for it. Mrs. Beverly Grant says that she will not be responsible to the hospital. It might be interpreted as an admission of guilt, if a suit should be brought. And it was a plain case of carelessness on the mother's part."

"Must I waken her ?" asked the nurse, willing, but not eager, to placate her superior.

"Yes." But as she said it she looked closely at the patient. A serene power seemed to emanate from the sleeping form, mocking the authority of a head-nurse. "No, let her sleep," she said, and went out, leaving the attendant surprised but grateful. She was going to love this new patient.

Ishma slept for three hours, and awoke with sane eyes that hurried to ask questions.

"Shall we send for Britt ?" parried the nurse.

"No, no ! Send for Rad. He will take me home." She gave the address and the nurse went out with it. When she returned she told Ishma very gently of Vennie's death. Ishma closed her eyes, her face bloodless. The nurse bent to hear her talking incoherently. "Killed her — one minute — two years — then killed her — all gone in one minute — two years — " The murmuring continued until Ishma again lost consciousness.

Within an hour Rad was by her bed. When Ishma had not returned home, Rad became devoured by a single fear. She had left him. She had run away. He sat helpless, seeking no other explanation. There was no other. He sat up all night, waiting for a footstep that he *knew* he would never hear again. He ought to have known she would do that. He ought to have been prepared for it. But he wasn't. And it knocked him clean out.

The next day, he picked himself up and went to work, saying nothing of his loss, and announcing that he had been sick, a deception well supported by his looks. The second day he couldn't go to work. Something *might* have happened to her. She wouldn't have gone without a word. She would have left a letter — something to relieve him — a kind letter, like herself. He had been insane to think anything else. Something had happened. He must go to the police. But what was the use ? She was dead. He tried to stand up, and his shaking legs reminded

234

him that he had eaten nothing for two days. But he couldn't eat now. He must get to the police. When he opened the door there was a messenger coming up the porch steps. He learned that his wife had been injured and was in the Harrowden Hospital.

"Thank God!" cried Rad, while the messenger stared. Strength rushed back to him, and in half an hour he was sitting by Ishma, smoothing one of her hands and holding it to his cheek.

"Why, Rad!" she said, opening her eyes. A quiet glow of trust came over her face, and a rush of joy went through him.

"You must go now," said the nurse. He rubbed Ishma's hand once more across his cheek, and laid it down. "I'll be back soon, Ish," he said, and went out. He had wanted to call her all kinds of pet names, but words of endearment did not drop easily from Rad's tongue.

He had been told of Vennie's death, and knew that he was expected in the office of the hospital. The body had been embalmed and was held awaiting information. The hospital management had taken a risk on the expense. The amount was a blow to Rad. Didn't he have anything put by for a rainy day, the staff representative wanted to know?

"Not a dollar ahead."

"That's bad. A man ought to save a few cents out of every dollar. Anything might happen. What do you own? Nothing, I suppose."

"I own my home."

"Clear?" asked the staff, hardly believing in the good luck.

"All clear," said Rad proudly.

"Beg your pardon for impeaching your management," beamed the staff. "That makes everything all right. A little mortgage will do it. We can arrange that right away. What is your home worth?"

"Twenty-five hundred."

"Splendid! You can get a thousand on it easily."

Rad was dazed. "It can't take that much," he stuttered.

"Man, your wife has been saved alive. Don't you think she's worth it?"

"She's worth a million, if a man had it. But we've got to live. I'll get her out o' here and take care of her myself. My mother broke her leg once, and never went to a hospital, and never had a doctor. And she got straight as ever, without paying out more than five dollars to a bone-setter. A thousand dollars!" He rose up. "My wife's goin' out o' here quick, if I have to carry her myself."

"Sit down, and let's be reasonable," said the staff. "I didn't say the cost would be a thousand dollars. I said you could get that much on your house."

"Well, let's have it," said Rad, sitting down. "What do you figger it up to?"

The bill for embalming was submitted. To this was added the cost of room with board for Ishma one week in advance, a private day nurse, a private night nurse, medical supplies and incidentals.

"Only one hundred and seventy-five dollars, you see," murmured the staff. "Of course that doesn't include the bills for the surgeon and doctor. And the baby has to be buried. If I were you I would get five hundred dollars from a Loan Company, and you can put on more if needed. Very likely five hundred will be enough. If there are no complications, Mrs. Bailey can be moved in a few weeks."

"It will be sooner than that," said Rad, grasping his hat and getting up.

"When may we expect you with the money?" smiled his inquisitor.

"When I get it, and I don't know how soon that will be."

"Of course," said the staff, regretfully, "it would be very dangerous at this point to move Mrs. Bailey into the public ward. But it could be done, if you are willing to risk her life."

"Don't you touch her!" Rad shouted. "I'll come back with yer derned money!" He went out, and "Scott-a-mighty!" said the staff, his handkerchief to his forehead. He knew that it would take thirty days to secure a loan from a regular company, but a man like that had to be prodded.

In the hall, Ishma's nurse was waiting for Rad. "The baby is very beautiful," she said. "I'll take you to her." He followed the nurse, and found Vennie on a stretcher, very beautiful indeed.

"Mrs. Bailey wants to see her," said the nurse, "and the doctor has given permission. He says she will be more quiet afterwards."

The nurse picked up the hard, flat cushion, and the little body lying on it. Rad followed her, dumb and aching, forgetting that he had been forty-eight hours without food.

"She looks like a lovely doll," said the nurse, as she stooped and held her burden by the bed.

"Yes. A lovely doll," thought Ishma, without tears, looking calmly on the little chiselled face with dark curls, like her own, falling about it. Aloud she said, "I want Britt to see her. We'll send her back to the mountains, Rad. We'll bury her up there with mother's babies and the twins."

The nurse slipped out with the body, leaving them to make their plans.

"But you couldn't go with her, Ishma."

"You could, Rad. You could go."

"Take her to Britt?"

"Yes. She's his. And he's never seen her. I don't want her to be buried and her father never see her."

"You're a strange woman, Ishma. Don't you know that I can't take her to Britt?"

"Why not?" she asked. Then she saw that he couldn't. "Maybe you're right. But we can get Bert and Cindy to take her. Martha Emery will lend them her car. I know she will. And it won't cost a thing to send her except to buy the gasoline and pay Bert as much as he would make at home. Cindy is not able to work now, and she'll be glad to have the trip. Her boy is sick up there. She'll love to do it for me and Vennie anyway. You know, Rad, it would cost a lot to bury her down here. They could drive through in one day if they started early, and the next day they could put her in the graveyard. It won't cost a thing up there."

She hammered on the cost in that ridiculous way, and held back her tears. She must made Rad see how easy it would be. And at last he saw.

"We'll do it, Ishma. I'll go right now and ask Bert. It's lunch time at the mill."

Her clinging hand told him how grateful she was. "You're so pale, Rad. Are you eating like you ought?"

Recalling his fast, he almost collapsed. "No," she said, "you're not. That good cafeteria is right in the block next the mill. You get you something to eat there before you see Bert. Take care of yourself, Rad. We mustn't both fall down at the same time, you know."

Her protective voice made him whimper, "I'm needin' you, Ish, I'm needin' you."

At four o' clock the next morning, little Vennie began her journey to the mountains. Ishma lay silent, thinking of the tiny body getting nearer and nearer the hills.

"I couldn't bear to leave her down here by herself," she said. Then she pressed her heart hard with both hands. What did she mean by that? Was she telling herself that she was going too? The lowlands could hold her no longer? She, too, was going back to the hills?

She knew that she was to live. The doctors had assured her of that. But where? Cindy and Bert would find out about Britt's divorce, and as soon as they came back Rad would know it too. Then she must marry him, and that would be the end of life. But to leave him would be intolerably dishonest. Leaving Britt was different. There had been no bargain. They had loved, and married because they loved. When she left him, they suffered equally. But Rad had given her all he possessed. He had been a good father to Vennie. He had heaped obligations upon her. Her heart grew tender as she thought of his generosity to her child. She had made a bargain with Rad. He had been faithful in fulfillment. She too must be honest. If that meant marrying him— Oh, but something might happen! Maybe the doctors were wrong. She might die after all.

She'd think it all out tomorrow. Rad looked so thin and starved. He'd take it hard if she died. He'd take it harder if she didn't marry him. She'd decide tomorrow. The dope they were giving her made her so drowsy. She couldn't think. She wondered what Britt would do when he saw Vennie. Would he stand and look, or would he touch her, and cry a little. She remembered the tiny hands. ' He would have to kiss them — he couldn't help it ! She would be sent back too, if she died. Perhaps that would be the only way for her. Oh, Britt, here are my hands too !

So drowsy. Tomorrow —

CHAPTER IX

ISHMA, on her hospital bed, as indifferent to social distinctions as her birthland hills, was making friends. Her calm acceptance of them seemed regal to Mrs. Beverly Grant, pleasing her like a fine form of flattery.

The hospital owed its foundation to the Grants. When Beverly had built his modern home, and surrounded it with ambitious landscaping, he had given the old Grant mansion, with its rambling grounds, to the town of Winbury, for the hospital whose absence was threatening municipal decency. The donated acres were near enough to Grantwood to add to the serenity of Beverly's view with no pathological obtrusion, and no additional taxes. His wife, Virginia, maintained a hovering interest in the institution, keeping the Grant generosity genteelly alive. But she had made it clear to the hospital officials that her concern for the patient, Bailey, was purely human, quite unrelated to the fact that she had been sitting in her car when the woman precipitated herself before it.

The police had refused to accept Beverly as her representative. They had, in fact, obliged the mistress of Grantwood to appear in person at headquarters. But they had been very nice to her, in spite of having given her innocent chauffeur a painful half hour. It was all over apparently. Nevertheless there lingered with her the fear that the husband of the injured woman might be moved to make trouble. She might be forced into court. To an unprincipled lawyer, nothing was sacred. The assumption of responsibility in any form could be used against her. Beverly had laughed at her fear, but big old Beverly was such a child in everything that wasn't textiles. It was up to herself to protect her sensitive nerves against humiliation and attack. That visit to police headquarters had shaken her faith in such safeguards

240

as money and position. So she had begun to visit Ishma, beaming upon her with pleasant warmth, all criticism prudently drained from her smile. And, like other admirable people, she enjoyed her own magnanimity. Hadn't the creature been criminally careless, as Beverly said ?

Then she found herself liking Ishma. Her interest, even her admiration, was caught by something undefined and impersonally large when she was with her. It became less difficult to cancel engagements and go to the hospital at the instigation of Billie Joe, her twelve year old daughter, whose friendship for the "mountain lady" had rapidly become an inconvenient enthusiasm. Beverly himself was hitched to Billie Joe's chariot. One day when she had called at her father's office, she induced him to drive by the hospital on their way home. He was much older than his wife, but handsome in his affable fifties. Ishma liked him, and felt serene in his presence.

The night after his call, he said to Virginia, as he turned the second page of a book, "We can't let a woman like that suffer."

Like that meant Ishma, of course. Well, it was the best way to describe her, thought Virginia. She recalled trying to tell Sayles Norburn what Ishma was like, and what she had wanted to do to him when he replied, "Ah, I can see her. Mother Eve in a pale blue kimono. Or is it sea-green, for her eyes ? Did you put her in sea-green, Virginia ? I like your picture, but don't ask me to go in person for a view."

Beverly was politely waiting. "You needn't worry about her suffering," she assured him. "I've found out that her husband is an excellent carpenter, and always has a job. He owns property too. You've told me a thousand times not to help those who can help themselves. It destroys initiative and effaces ambition."

"Quite right," approved Beverly.

"And you know you've cut down my allowance for charities one half for next year."

"Yes. The mills are not going to make it." He turned a third page. "But when she gets out, you might take her to the beach with Billie Joe. Bee Jay likes those mountain stories she tells, and she 'd be a more interesting companion than Minnie."

And only the day before, Beverly had asked her if she didn't think she was letting Bee Jay see too much of that woman.

"We'll wait a bit," she cautioned, though she had previously decided to annex Ishma to her sea-shore party. "She has just begun to walk a little."

"She'd get along faster if she were out of that box of a room. Can't see anything but the back yard. Why don't you put her in that corner room of the old mansion wing? There's a verandah, and a fine view of Grantwood Park. Isn't it vacant?"

"It usually is, and for a good reason. It's so expensive. We can't expect her husband to pay for an actual luxury, and *we* are not going to do it."

"All right, my dear." He settled himself for half an hour of serious reading. That collection of articles from the *Manufacturer's Record* was rather good.

A day or two later, when Virginia and Billie Joe went to the hospital, they met Rad in the hall. Billie Joe, who knew him, introduced him to her mother. He told them they would find Ishma in the women's ward. She had been moved that morning.

"But it smells so, Blessed! I've been there. Ugh! it smells! I had to run out."

Virginia frowned. "She'll have to be put back into her room."

"I reckon she likes it where she is," said Rad. "And it's a lot cheaper. I've got to think about that."

He had been greatly relieved when Ishma asked to be taken to the ward, and had promptly gone to the office to make her request a demand. He had never told her how much the room and nurses were costing him, and her imagination never reached the awful amount, but she knew that the ward would be cheaper. What to her seemed more vital, in the ward she would see other patients and talk to them. She might get so interested that she could stop thinking about what she was going to do when she got up.

Rad had said nothing of Britt's divorce, but there was a look in his eyes, a sort of quiet triumph, that told her he knew. As she thought of it, a heavy weight seemed to be pressing down her limbs until she couldn't move. She felt that she would have to lie there indefinitely unless she could set her mind on destinies not her own. Twice only she had forced herself to rise and walk

242

across the room, though it had been over a week since Dr. Benn had told her to make the effort. In her strong body the fractured thigh had healed with a swiftness that amazed the nurses and made the doctors look wisely at the ceiling. But healing had brought no desire to move, to act. Once before, in that other, long ago life in the mountains, she had been as obstinately inert. That was when she was ill after the death of the twins. She remembered the voice that had given her courage, the voice that had seemed to drift whisperingly about her, taking away all regret. Now there was no whisper on the air to help her rise. She had lived outwardly and barrenly too long. That was it. A body empty of spirit held no invitation for the voices of celestial reserve.

Vennie's death no longer troubled her. There was no painful stir of conscience as she thought of it. Dear little Vennie had been consuming out of all proportion to her significance; and now she was laid away with all insignificant things. But her disappearance was of infinite consequence. Life was before Ishma again. She was face to face with a decision that she had no power to make. Her heart, her blood in every channel, was pushing her to Britt. Her sense of justice urged her not to forsake Rad. And another feeling that had its roots in the desire to approve of herself bade her to abide by what she had done. She couldn't be this and that and back again! Mind, if not life, must have a stable course. She wanted to believe in the integrity of her mind; wanted ardently to believe in it, as most people do whose great decisions are made by a sudden release of emotional power, with the mind utterly off guard.

That first day in the ward did make her forget. It left her too exhausted to think at all. Two patients had been brought in, successively, from the operating room, and all windows were kept closed while they were recovering from the anæsthetic. Ishma felt that she would be glad to die in exchange for one breath of pure air. She sickened until a nurse, rushing by, stopped to put a wet towel on her face. Everybody was busy. The nurses did not walk, they ran. A child on the bed nearest Ishma cried vainly for attention. Ishma tried to rise and go to her, but fell back, weak with nausea, on her bed.

"Jane!" she called, as soon as she could speak. It was Mildred Ross's little girl, her youngest. Ishma stopped a nurse, and some cloths were removed from under the child. She recognized Ishma, but with the apathy of the dying. By and by Mildred came in, and the two friends talked. Mildred's eyes were dry. She had no time to weep.

"You can shed my tears for me, Ishma. You have time, lying here. I've got to run back to the mill."

Virginia, out in the hall, was talking to Rad; adroitly sounding him out. The result was relief from her secret fear. This ineffectual person, eager to save money by putting his wife in a ward, and pathetically bluffing about it, would make no trouble for her.

"She wanted to go in the ward," he said. "And I've got to keep her from fretting about Ven. I don't want her to get to studyin' about it's bein' her fault the baby got killed. She'll have plenty to think about in the ward."

"Certainly we must keep her mind easy," Virginia agreed. "But I think it is a mistake to take her out of the private room. In fact, I was thinking of having her put into a better one, the big room on the third floor corner, with six windows and a verandah."

Rad suddenly looked ugly and stubborn.

"I've paid the last dollar I'm goin' to pay for a private room," he said. Virginia told him, judiciously, that she would pay the difference between the new room and the old one.

"I'll pay fer the ward, an' nothin' else," said Rad.

Billie Joe drew her mother away. "Where are we going, my own?" asked Virginia.

"To the office, of course. We've got to get her out of there."

And Billie Joe's positiveness did exactly that. Miss Aimes, the supervisor, had been having trouble with Rad. The hospital bills were paid up so far, but he was resisting further charges, and Dr. Benn and Dr. Maddux had not received a penny. When Mrs. Grant proposed paying for a private room for Ishma, the supervisor picked up heart. Perhaps her benevolence would extend as far as the doctors. Miss Aimes was almost engaged to Dr. Maddux. It would be more than a pleasure to tell him that Mrs.

Grant's interest in the patient had finally reached her pocket.

But she was insisting on having the large and beautiful "convalescent" room at the price of a small one.

"It might as well be used occasionally," said Virginia sweetly. And with still more sweetness she added, "I don't think you've had anyone in it since I had it re-finished in canary and blue," a reminder which the supervisor heeded. Of course it could be arranged.

Ishma was hardly conscious of the change when it was made. She agreed to it because Billie Joe was so eager, and it didn't seem kind to refuse Mrs. Grant's help. Even though she had been innocently connected with the accident, she must want to do something about it, with all the money she had. Ishma knew that was the way she would feel if she were in Mrs. Grant's place. She couldn't think any farther than that, because she was so weak and incapable at the end of her day in the ward.

All night, after her removal, she dreamed of wailing children and weary, hopeless mothers, and felt smothered by hospital odors. But opening her eyes the next morning in the lovely room, she gave a gasp of joy and fell back into sleep that was deep and restful. When she awoke again, a nurse was there to wheel her out on the verandah and bring her breakfast, a very special breakfast planned and ordered by Billie Joe.

Since she had been in the hospital the regular appearance of her meals had seemed magical to her. She who had broken land, dropped the seed, hoed, gathered, and hauled in; had gone to mill, carrying the meal home on her shoulder; had cut the wood and made the fire that cooked it, before she could eat her bread, had only to put out her hand and draw to herself full sustenance for her body. The day before, in the ward, she had been unable to eat. For the first time, her miracle tray, as she called it, had been rejected. But that morning, in the pure air of the sunlit verandah, she thrilled again with the magic restored. Her breakfast finished, she leaned back in the pillows of her wheel chair and detached herself from every burden, trying to understand what a life of perfect material comfort would mean. Something great surely. It would be like standing poised on the tip of a mountain, ready for flight to any horizon.

She was going to think things out up here. But she wouldn't begin that minute. She would sip a little at her fount of perfection.

It was a meagre sip. The nurse was standing by her, talking. She was a new nurse, Miss Lester, instead of Ishma's former one, who had been so comfortably tactful and affectionate. Miss Lester was artifically cheerful, talky, and impressed by serving the "best room." Mrs. Bailey was not to be bothered by visitors that day, she was saying. Only Mrs. Grant's daughter in the afternoon. Tomorrow, late, Mrs. Grant would come, and perhaps make tea. Today she was to have complete rest. Only a little exercise, walking about in the room and hall. She was by no means to try the stairs. "And I shall be coming in to take your temperature and give you your bath. And the drops." Those inessential, hourly disturbers! So that was the morning, thought Ishma. Well, she would have the afternoon. But the walking tired her, she kept it up too resolutely, and after the luncheon tray had appeared and gone, she fell asleep. It was hours into the afternoon when she awoke refreshed and the world made new. Her wheel chair was on the porch, and she walked steadily out to it.

A moment later, Billie Joe was there, settled at her side, eager for stories, *real* stories. Wouldn't Ishma finish telling her about the time she got lost on Bear Mountain, and kindled a fire with punk, and waited for the stars to come out so she could see the one that she knew would be shining over her home, and she went without any trail, through thickets and panthers —

Yes, Ishma would tell her. They talked until the sun was setting. The nurse came in with the tray, and Billie Joe was leaving the room when May Bennett came in. The girls gazed at each other, and Ishma introduced them. They were both pretty, but May had grown tall, and looked anxious and tired. Plump Billie Joe seemed winged with health. She hurried away, and Ishma had May sit down. Her eyes encountered the tray and could not leave it while she talked.

"Mother said she had to know how you were gettin' on, and I told her I'd come straight here from the mill."

"You haven't had supper then, and it's lucky for me you've

246

come. I can't eat a bite. I've simply stuffed myself today. But if I don't eat, the nurse will bother me with questions. So you do my part for me tonight, honey."

But May could only nibble at the food. Her stomach was too unused to full meals and soon oppressed her. They didn't try to talk of the school she had lost, of Kansie's having to go back to the mill, of the father losing out in the "speed-up," though both were thinking of just those things. May soon stood up, saying she must hurry home, and help her father get supper. "Mother just drops when she gets in, and the baby is sick. They'll all be glad to hear you're gettin' on well."

Just bare words, bare facts, and she was gone. Ishma reflected that she had spoken no word of encouragement to the baffled child. What could she say to a girl who felt that her life had been taken from her ? She wished that she could have prattled a little, like other people. Could have told May that all was for the best, if we only knew, and that no life could be so drab that radiance could not enter it from somewhere. That would have been a lie, and she had never been able to utter even polite and helpful lies. Feeling very tired again she laid down on the bed, still with her lovely wrapper about her. Virginia had been lavish with bed-room apparel.

Then Rad came. Ishma had left the light on and he entered the big room unguided. He had a new job and felt that he must take care of it, so he usually came at night when he was tired and sleepy. The room was strange. He crossed the wide floor uncertainly and sat down with relief when he reached the bed-side. Ishma in her silken ruffles and folds seemed strange too. Queer that she looked so much at home. She mustn't get to liking this sort of thing, so she wouldn't be satisfied with their little house. He'd get her back the first day he could. The doctors didn't give him any satisfaction about her. All they did was to pester him for money. He wasn't going to put a second mortgage on his place, not if they never got a cent. He'd told them that, flat out. They'd have to wait till he could save it. Maybe Mrs. Grant would pay something, since she'd taken this new streak about Ish. If she wanted to, he was going to be agreeable about it. He'd help if he's in her place.

Ishma asked him about her mill friends, but he didn't know much. He was a carpenter, was Rad. He knew that Genie was about to go under. Looked thin as a match, and wasn't makin' as much as the family could eat. The speed-up had got so bad she could hardly hold on. Cindy Wiggins was goin' to die, he reckoned. Hadn't seen any of the Bennetts, but guessed it was bad enough with 'em. Folks oughtn't to have a houseful of children with nothin' to take care of 'em on.

Ishma smiled at Rad's progress in practical philosophy, but the smile died suddenly when he said, "*We* can have kids now, Ish. Old Britt has got his divorce. They must 'a' sent you the papers, but I reckon you had yer own reasons fer not lettin' on. We'll be married soon as you come home."

Her mind spun about for an answer.

"We'll have to go away to be married. To Charlotte — or Spartanburg — or somewhere, so nobody 'll know. You wouldn't like it if people here where we have to live found out about us."

"You think of ever'thing, Ish. 'Course that's the way we'll do it. You've got a head for both of us. I'm nothin' without you. I don't feel more'n half alive, with you out o' the house."

He wanted to kiss her, to hold her tight, and feel her soft curls under his chin, but he was too shy in that amazing, big room, and she was looking so white and tired, it might bother her.

"You want to go to sleep?" he asked.

"I believe I do, Rad."

"Well, I'll get along." He looked at her again, and she seemed to sink in her pillows, so he touched her hand almost as if by accident and went out, his mind fumbling as usual until he found himself outside the great front door. There he stopped and swore. "She's got to come back home. I've got to have her."

Ishma slept little that night, thinking of Rad, and what she must do. She couldn't marry him. She couldn't go back to him. But how was she to respect herself if she didn't? How could she use him just as long as he was necessary to her and her child, and then cast him off? She must be free. She must work for herself. She must save money. And deep within her, like an inward falling manna, a hope fed her hungry heart, the hope of going back to Cloudy Knob. She didn't know what she

248

would do when she got there, she never tried to picture what might happen, she only thought of going.

But there was much for her to learn in the life down here — why did people have to struggle and starve in a world God had given them ? — that new union — and Ella Ramsey — there was something there she must know. If Derry would only talk to her without joking. He didn't have any doubts about anything, and he always seemed just ready to clear things up for her, only he didn't. If he knew how the world, and man, was made, and what had happened to them all along, he ought to know what was the matter with them now. Maybe he couldn't talk much to her until she had read more and knew more herself.

She loved her mill friends, and wanted to help them if she could. She thought of Genie and her famishing children — of May, half-starved, and all the little Bennetts — of Mildred Ross and the tears she had no time to shed. About daylight she fell asleep. The night nurse, who had been in the room every hour or so and had observed her restlessness, left a note for Miss Lester, advising her not to wake the patient for her breakfast. When Ishma opened her eyes it was nearly noon, and she was so hungry that she ate all of the food that was brought her. Fed and refreshed, she ought to have been ready to examine her own problem. But it was to be a busy afternoon. Billie Joe was coming early, for this was Saturday. Derry was visiting in the hospital, the nurse said, and she knew he would be up to see her. He had come down from his farm when he heard of her injury, and had remained in Winbury "snooping around." Mrs. Grant and her husband were coming later in the afternoon, and might bring a friend. Ishma hoped it wouldn't be that writer, Mrs. Owenby, who had come with Virginia once before. There would be no time to think things out. She was reprieved for a few hours, and she would try to enjoy them. The Grants were such kind people. She admired them, and she loved Billie Joe. Tonight, after they were gone, she would sit on the balcony and make up her mind, if she had to sit there till morning. She believed she was strong enough to leave the hospital, but how could she move until she knew which way to go ?

Derry came earliest, for a few moments. "So here you are,"

he said, entering the big room, softly bright in canary and blue, with the sunlight kindly subdued. "Here you are, qualifying for *Rampole's Island*. Your eyes are big and mountainy, but already I detect a possessive gleam in them. For God's sake, don't get the acquisitive squint."

"*Rampole's Island?*" she queried, going for the words that most interested her, as she always did after one of his rambling speeches.

"That's Well's new book."

"And I'm to read it when qualified?"

"I meant qualified to live on the island."

"Can't I do both?"

"Not happily. Anyone who qualifies for reading the book is miserable on the island. Anyone contented on the island would burn the book."

"But which do you want me to do?"

"That's something you'll choose for yourself—when you're through with school."

"When will that be? I've begun to think I'll never get through."

"You will! But there'll always be post-graduate work, of course. You'll be in a big class though, and have lots of friends, if you can find them. They're horribly scattered—France, Bulgaria, China, Hungary, Russia, the Andes—horribly scattered. You'll have to get about to find them."

"I'm going to get about."

She said it serenely, definitely, as she had never said it before; luxury in her veins making anything possible.

"Ho, the leaven works quickly. She's in a beautiful world, and she'll do as she likes, she will."

Ishma's face was burnt over with a blush.

"It's not that sort of getting about, dearish." The pet name softened the criticism. "You'll go barefoot with a wound in your side, if you find the friends I mean."

"You wear pretty nice shoes," she rallied.

"I'm only a half and half. You'll be the whole thing." His voice was yearning, the humor all out of it. She could feel him watching her, down the years.

250

"Don't, doctor Unthank. Don't! I've too much to learn. I'll never get ready."

"Ready for what, my dear?" It was Virginia Grant, entering unannounced, by right of proprietorship. With her was Billie Joe and Sayles Norburn. "Ready for what? Tell us. Then I'll introduce Sayles."

A glance from Derry told Ishma how close they were in sympathy. His eyes said that it was impossible to explain to Virginia. He began to chaff her. They were old friends. Old enough to have an occasionally bitter set-to. She had told him once that she didn't know why she tolerated him, and he had smilingly replied that her tolerance under such difficulties certainly showed that she was very fond of him.

Ishma answered Sayles' greeting, and caught at Derry's words. He must go to the ward, he was saying. A doubtful case. One of Ishma's little friends.

"Jane?" she asked.

"Yes. Little Jane."

She half rose from the big chair which Virginia had packed with pillows. "I wish I could go with you."

"You've been missed, Ishma." He went out, saying that he would come back later for Virginia's tea.

"Derry has no tact," Virginia criticized. "But he seems to get on with everybody. You must forget little Jane, and all the sick and miserable, Ishma. This is to be a happy afternoon. I'm going now, for half an hour, with a committee that's inspecting the hospital, and I'm taking Sayles."

"Ask me!" said Sayles.

"You are going, I said. Billie Joe thinks she hasn't seen Ishma if she doesn't have her to herself for a few minutes. And I don't intend to let my invalid get tired."

She went, taking the reluctant Sayles.

Ishma was silent, wondering what Derry Unthank had seen when he was looking at her down the years. Billie Joe was silent too, for a moment. To the child, Ishma's life seemed to have been a constant adventure, more exciting than she found in her books. Think of going barefooted and playing in the rain, not for a funny stunt, but just living like that! And there was the pet coon which Ishma had caught the night she went hunting with Julie Webb and the boys. While they were off getting their 'possum, she got a beautiful black coon that had its foot fastened under a rock. And those cave houses on Bear Knob —and the eagle that carried off her cat— Oh, just more and more stories. She'd hear them all when they got to the seashore. Ishma didn't know she was going, but Blessed had told Billie Joe. Daddy and Blessed didn't know any real stories. They had to get them out of books. Nothing had ever happened to *them*.

But today Billie Joe was silent, and Ishma looked up. "You're thinking, Billie Joe."

"Just wondering. Wondering whether I'll grow up tall and beautiful like May Bennett, or just pretty."

"You are beautiful now, Billie Joe. You don't have to wait. You are as lovely as May. Perhaps lovelier. May is so thin. She doesn't get enough to eat."

Billie Joe was speechless. She had read of people, in stories, who got very hungry, but she had never met one.

"Why don't she eat ?" she finally asked.

"The family haven't enough money to buy food."

"Let them go to work then," said Billie Joe, indignantly.

"They do work. May's mother goes to work, and she has a little baby. May works too."

"And they can't make enough ?"

"Not nearly enough. I'll tell you about May." Billie Joe listened, and Ishma told her of May's effort and defeat.

"Where does she work ?" asked the child, her mind still in chaotic struggle. Here was a mill girl who cried to go to school. And she had thought they were all ignorant because they wanted to be. Ishma told her that May worked in the Sherwin mill.

"That's one of father's mills." A further silence, and then, "I'd be glad if I could stop school. But I'm sorry if May wanted to go and couldn't."

"Who wanted to go where, little Miss Intensity ?" asked Beverly Grant, coming up in time to hear his daughter's remark, and taking the seat to which Ishma gestured as casually as Virginia could have done. "Let's have it, Bee Jay."

She immediately possessed him of May's story, with emotional embellishments. The finale came with, "And she works in your mill, father."

"Well, well! How fortunate that I have work for her, since she needs it so much!"

Billie Joe looked disappointed, and Ishma felt that something was sour in Beverly's good humor. But there was no time to make sure, for Virginia was there, with Sayles Norburn and Derry Unthank.

She wanted to ask about Jane, but Virginia was being very sprightly at the moment, making tart little digs at Derry. Sayles took a seat close to Ishma's chair and began to talk. "Eyes like the sea, of course, but in a grey mood, or green? Virginia couldn't tell me, and I can't sleep again till I know." His voice was low, and Virginia's banter rather high, but Unthank heard.

"I'll tell you, Sayles. If she's very happy, or thinking faster than the other fellow, they're sea-green. If she's sad, or thinking deep, from the centre of the earth, they're grey."

"I envy you your opportunities, doctor. You make me wish I had chosen a medical course."

Derry's look implied that Sayles would speedily need medical attention if he could have his way about it. Virginia, concerned for the amenities, became genuinely sweet. "If Derry is right, we shall all try to keep Ishma's eyes sea-green for this afternoon. And Sayles must not forget that personalities don't make polite conversation."

"Sayles has a splendid forgettery," said Beverly. "He couldn't remember the conference last night."

Sayles felt a little hostile. Couldn't they let him enjoy himself? This bum Southern town offered few amusements.

"What's the good, my going to your conference, Beverly? You won't listen to me. And I've got the right idea. You can't cut off a mountain at a blow."

There was a ripple of laughter from Ishma, very low, but it filled the room musically.

"Now what have I done to *you*?" asked Sayles.

"You made me think of an old rhyme of my father's. Mountain folks like to put old sayings into rhyme, and I think he knew them all."

They waited, but she was silent. "Don't you know you've a penalty to pay for laughing at me ?" said Sayles. "You have to repeat the rhyme."

"I don't mind at all. It goes like this:

> *I dug at a mountain like hell afire,*
> *And all I did was wheeze,*
> *Till I chawed my 'backer and leaned on my spade,*
> *And tuck it off by degrees.*

"There !" said Sayles. "That's what I mean, Beverly. This protuberance, this mountain, this huge textile problem, you fellows want to lop it off at a blow, with a universal lock-out, or starve-out, and all you'll get will be a wheeze. It'll stand up bigger than ever. Now a dent here, a dent there, is my way, till we have a dead ring around it. Pick out the obstreperous bunches, and get their belts tightened till they can't think about anything but their stomachs, and the mills will run as usual. The other way, you won't get production, and you *may* get a man-sized rebellion."

"We've never expected any help from you, Sayles," said Beverly, with the cut of mild dismissal.

"Here's tea," said Virginia, in a tone that was like a soft pull at Beverly's sleeve. Fortunately, this impractical partner came down from New York only twice a year.

"That's right, Virginia," said Derry, carelessly audible. "There isn't room in your tea-cups for Sayles' mountain."

"Beverly's mountain," corrected Sayles.

"He shan't bring it here. The only mountains I'll tolerate with my tea are Ishma's. They cast shadows of peace, not enmity. But it's the sea I want to think about now. I've decided that Ishma will be well enough in a week or so to go with us."

"Oh ! The sea !" whispered Ishma, staring into greatness.

"I'm going too. You asked me, didn't you, Virginia ?" from Sayles.

"I did, and you said 'Not on your life !' "

254

"You mistook my words, Virginia. I wouldn't miss seeing lady Ish to the sea-shore for anything on Deauville beach. Lady Ish and her wild sea-wish !"

Ishma drew her eyes from the sea. "I can't go. Don't make. me want it. My heart is like my father's. It gets uncomfortably hot when I want things I can't have."

"That's not a peculiarity, lady Ish." His quick glance swept her long, pliant figure. "So you are like your father ?"

"Not so much as I wish I were. I haven't got his humor. He liked to laugh at himself, and I don't. He made funny songs about himself. I couldn't do that at all. There was one about his heart that would never grow cold. He wasn't afraid of going to hell because the devil had fire enough and wouldn't want to make his place any hotter." She said it gravely, not knowing how incredibly cool and sweet she was looking against her high pillows.

"But the song, the song !" said Sayles.

"I remember only one verse. I couldn't forget that part because I read the Bible so much to my grandmother, and I was terribly afraid that my father would 'rip and tear' his way to hell, as my mother sometimes told him. He would always sing it to her then.

> O, when I die, just wash the slate;
>   Of hell I have no fear;
> The devil will shout and slam the gate,
>   Don't bring that red coal here !

"And the red coal was his heart," cried Billie Joe, clapping her hands and ignoring her mother's shocked eye.

"Your father had courage," said Beverly.

"And a gay spirit," said Sayles.

"I wish I could have known him," he appended, flattering the idol in her heart, and feeling a magic in himself as her eyes deepened.

"I must get down to the ward," said Derry, unnecessarily loud. "It's Jane ?"

"Yes. We'll have to let her go, dearish."

"Oh !"

"What's the matter with her ?" asked Virginia, indifferently interested.

"Neglect."

"These mill mothers !"

"Mildred Ross is a good mother," defended Ishma. "Derry means that she *had* to work, and the child *had* to be neglected."

"You and Derry seem to have a technic that I don't understand."

"It wasn't the mother's fault, Virginia. Dysentery from poor food, when Mildred would have liked to give her the best. No shade around the house — just an oven in the sun — and certainly not what Mildred would have *selected* for her children. She'd prefer *that* for them." He waved toward the trembling greenery of Grantwood Park.

"Where's the father ?" asked Virginia, still virtuous. "Another case of desertion, I suppose."

"No, my dear. The Lord took him, as he is going to take little Jane."

"No, no !" murmured Ishma.

"Why, dearish, you are not questioning the way of the Lord ?"

"You stop that, Derry !" Virginia commanded. "I'll not have it before Billie Joe."

"Has God done wrong ?" asked Billie Joe, with terribly wide eyes.

"My darling !" supplicated Mrs. Grant.

The appeal aroused her daughter's resistance. "He kept May out of school. Made her work for father. How much does she make for you, daddy ?"

"I rather think, Bee Jay, that she is working to earn food and clothes, and not specially for me. There are times when we run our mills at a loss just to give people work and help them live. Hand that back to uncle Derry when he begins to talk to you about his little Mays and Janes."

"He's not going to talk any more," asserted Virginia, her lips thin and her eyes cold. "You simply can't scatter your wild opinions in my family, Derry. I shall protect my child."

"Sure, you will ! And while you are protecting her against

the advance of knowledge, why not insulate her against earth-quakes, tidal waves, and old age ?"

"You make it possible for me to say goodbye with pleasure, Dr. Unthank."

"You'll come back, Derry," said Beverly, with grace.

"He will not !" was Virginia's fiat.

"He'll have to stand with us. He's one of us so far as his bank account is concerned. Blest be the dividend that binds, eh, old boy ?"

"So long as there *are* dividends, I want mine in full. I'm making good use of them."

"That's what all of us think. You see the question muddled through your sympathies, Derry. You mix too much with the hopeless. I hear you 've been talking for this new textile union — the National."

"Yes. I'm making a speech tonight to the Grant-Norburn employees. You are all invited."

"Confound you ! I'd hate to see you in jail, old chap."

"You won't mind it in a few more weeks. You'll try to put me there."

As soon as he was gone, Virginia became feminine. The scene hadn't happened. "You men must go now, and, Beverly, take Billie Joe home. I mustn't let Ishma get tired, and we have to talk over clothes for the seashore."

"I go if I must," said Sayles. "But I'm promising myself to help lady Ish watch the sun die tomorrow."

He was careful to make his smile grave, and a little aloof, but she smiled back without asking him to return.

"It has been a rough party for a convalescent," said Beverly, as he passed her, going out with Sayles.

"No ! It has done me good," meaning something very different from Beverly's suave concern. She felt eager, on the edge of revelation. Sayles would tighten their belts, would he ? And Beverly — what would *he* do ?

When the men were on the stairs Virginia became active.

"I've got a dress for you, Ishma. Do you think you can walk into the room and try it on ?"

Ishma said she was strong enough, that she never felt better, but Mrs. Grant ought not to buy her any more clothes. The lovely wrappers and things were enough until she went home, and then she would be at work. Virginia ignored the reference to work, and went on talking.

"You'll need quite a number of things for the seashore, and I must begin to fit you out. I found this yesterday, and I hope you will like it. It's only a sport suit, beige and green."

She had it out of its box and was holding it up. "Are you sure you are not too tired to put it on? I'm anxious about the fit. There was so much gabbling here it set bells ringing in my head. It will be more quiet now, since we're not going to see Derry again."

Ishma put on the dress, a little awkwardly.

"I ought to have called the nurse to help you, but she says that the least help suits you best. There! It looks exactly as I thought it would. That shade of green is just right with your clear skin and dark hair. And you carry it like a model. No, I don't mean that. You wear it as if you had never worn anything but perfect clothes."

She noticed that Ishma was not speaking. "Don't you like it, my dear?"

"Yes, it is lovely. Please excuse me. I was thinking."

"You can't think about anything more important than clothes, you will find out, Ishma. I went to three shops before I saw the dress I was looking for. You can't wear just anything. You're not that type."

"But I shall have to wear just anything. Whatever I can get. I shall not earn enough for dresses like this."

She was afraid that Mrs. Grant would be hurt. Her words sounded ungrateful to her own ears. But Virginia was pleased.

"That's the way I like to have you talk, Ishma. So many people that I have tried to help just took me for granted, and pretty soon were expecting me to help them as if it were my duty. It's so easy to spoil people. But I could never spoil you. That's why I've decided to take you to the seashore and give you the treat of your life. It won't hurt you. You'd be surprised to know what that dress cost, but I spent the money with pleasure."

258

Ishma was strangely unresponsive. Her thoughts were tumbling around so many things and people. Poor staggering Genie — young Bert Wiggins, off in the mountains, dying with tuberculosis because Grant-Norburn couldn't afford air-cleansing devices in their mills — little Jane — lock-out — union — why wouldn't Derry sit down and talk to her until everything was clear? Her eagerness, her poised expectation, was gone. If she could get away — back to the mountains, with peace — and Britt! And oh, perhaps she could! What was making it impossible but herself?

Her thoughts returned to Virginia when she realized that the topic was no longer dress. It was Rad.

"I think I'm right in telling you, Ishma. Perhaps you can influence him. He has flatly refused to pay Doctor Benn and Doctor Maddux."

"But he *will* pay them, Mrs. Grant. He only needs time. Rad is honest. And I will help just as soon as I can."

"That isn't the point. He could pay now if he would. He has only to put a second mortgage on his house — "

"A second mortgage?"

"Certainly. The first was for five hundred only. It will bear that much more. The supervisor spoke to me about it today, and then I had a talk with Dr. Maddux."

Ishma sat down in the new dress.

"Perfect! It looks as well on you when you sit as when you stand! The lines fall just right. One must always consider that in buying clothes."

"Rad mortgaged his home for me?"

"Didn't you know? It was the only decent thing for him to do, Ishma."

The little home mortgaged! She knew how that must have hurt Rad. Why, it hurt *her*.

"Dr. Benn feels the same as Dr. Maddux," continued Virginia, unaware of Ishma's emotion. "We have decided that he should be made to pay. When you help people who are able to help themselves, you do them an injury. That's the first law we learn in distributing charity."

"Rad wouldn't want charity."

"He doesn't want to pay. And that looks as if he wanted somebody else to pay for him. Or wants the doctors to give him the debt. And they are overworked and underpaid already. I don't see how they keep up their homes and their cars. Let me see you walk across the room, Ishma, if you are not too tired."

With thunder in her ears, Ishma rose obediently and walked across the room.

"I don't understand it," Virginia commended. "Your walk is perfection. And you don't even know what eurythmics are."

"Perhaps it's because I was always strong enough for my job. Women and children who have to hoe and grub are often too frail for the work, and they grow bent and strained looking. I could always stand straight under anything. I could pick up a number ten plough and carry it up hill." She looked down at her dress and laughed. "I wore overalls then."

Something imperial in Ishma's laugh made Virginia Grant look wistful and a little troubled. Could she actually "help" this splendid creature ? It wouldn't be by hanging bits of cloth on her, and inviting her to be a playmate for her child. For an instant she glimpsed a bit of another road, but it was bewildering, almost fantastic, and she turned away. Yet there was the hint of a quaver in her voice as she said, "I'm not sure whether I'm doing you harm or good, Ishma."

"Good, Mrs. Grant. It has all been a great help. Derry Unthank was right. I needed education."

Virginia smiled again. "Derry is right about some things, I admit, though very wrong — unbalanced, I may say — about others. That book on the table, I saw him leave it as he went out. *Rampole's Island*. A disgusting thing. I read it half through. I never knew a normal person that could finish it. And you are absolutely normal, Ishma. Don't ever think you are not, and try to run this way and that because Derry Unthank says so. You are genuine. That's why people like you at first sight. They recognize something real. Life gets a touch of value, and it cheers them. Here I am loitering around you, when I ought this minute to be dressing for Mrs. Thwaite's dinner. I'm taking Sayles, to keep him away from Beverly. I hope he'll be going back North soon, or to Paris, where he belongs. The only way he can help us is to do as Beverly tells him and be satisfied with drawing his money. I must go now, my dear. And you don't mind what I said about your husband?"

"I'm very glad you told me, Mrs. Grant."

"I wouldn't mind paying the whole bill as you know. It isn't that at all. I shall spend much more on you than all he owes before we are back from the beach. It's just that I think he ought to be made to pay as far as he can. He's the sort of person that it would be easy to pauperize by too much help, and that would be very unpleasant for you."

Would she never go, thought Ishma? She was having hard work to appear undisturbed. It had become impossible to speak. She could only smile, and she couldn't do that much longer. But with a few more observations on life as she knew it, Virginia left. Ishma stumbled back to the porch. There wasn't air enough in the big room. Her lungs, her chest, seemed to be straining and swelling, pressing up, filling her throat, pushing her down. She sank to a chair, wanting nothing in the world but water.

Miss Lester came in with her supper.

"Here we are! And there's a special fruit salad. You'll like your supper, Mrs. Bailey. Oh, what has happened?"

"Water!" was all that Ishma could say, and the nurse quickly held a glass to her lips. Ishma sipped, managed to swallow, and the great lump began to leave her throat.

"I was strangled. I don't know . . . all right now."

Miss Lester didn't want to leave. Ishma forced a smile and got her out of the room. Strange that a nurse, of all people, couldn't know when she was wanted. The trivial irritation helped her, filling the moment. In a little while her physical distress was over, except that the sight of the tray sickened her.

She knew what she was going to do. She had known from the moment that Mrs. Grant told her about the mortgage.

The sun was down, and the sky above and beyond the park trees was shimmering tenderly. She had thought of how she would sit there after sunset, in the soft glow, waiting for the softer twilight, with the world removed, dispassionately deciding her fate. And suddenly there was nothing to be decided. She turned her back on the etched trees and the pink-gold sky. That was only a picture.

Pressing her entire weight on the ankle that had been broken, she felt no discomfort. There was a slight pain up where the thigh had been fractured, but that was nothing. She was strong, ready for work. Another idle moment would be intolerable, piling up her dishonesty.

She couldn't wait and go through with explanations to Virginia. A note would do, as nice as she could write. Amazed and ashamed, she found herself instantly through with the Grants.

"But I shall have to wear this dress," she said to herself. Her own clothes, badly torn by the accident, had been discarded. Her old shoes were gone too. She'd have to wear the thin slippers that she had on. Sitting down, she began to write her note to the Grant family, asking them to forgive her for leaving without saying goodbye. "I must go home and get to work. It would be wrong for me to stay here longer, now that I am feeling so well. So many, many thanks to you all! Mrs. Grant, I am wearing the dress because I have no other with me. I will send you the money for it just as soon as I can save it. Please let me know how much it cost. I wish I could repay you for your kindness, but that would mean a need on your part that I hope you will never know." She signed herself, "Your grateful Ishma," and rising, started to ring for the nurse, when she noticed the laden supper tray. Her nausea was all gone. She sat down and ate every bite of the meal. Already she was feeling the vigor that comes from knowing certainly what to do. Her reluctant body was no longer a barrier. Her mind had begun to race again.

She smiled as she got up and rang her bell. "I'm on my way," she said. The nurse came immediately, and was delighted to see that the supper had disappeared.

"You are feeling better, Mrs. Bailey?"

"Much better. Quite well, in fact. Please show me the way to the office. I want to see the Supervisor."

"She will come up here. You can't go down, you know."

"But I can, Miss Lester." She moved out of the room. "I suppose these stairs are the first thing."

The nurse caught her by the arm. "Dr. Benn said —"

"Yes, I know," said Ishma, firmly detaching herself. "But I am well now, and responsible for myself." She began to go down the stairs, and managed not to let a few twinges in her thigh be reflected in her face. The nurse followed, beseeching. This might cause her demotion. Ishma thought of that.

"I shall tell the Supervisor that you couldn't hold me in the room," she said, smiling. "I really am stronger than you."

Miss Lester decided to get to the office as quickly as possible, where help awaited. She knew that Miss Aimes was in. It would be luck if Dr. Maddux was there too. But it was only Dr. Rolfe, a new interne. Miss Aimes rose on her dignity, trying to achieve height before the towering Ishma, who calmly announced that she was leaving the hospital. She knew there were unpaid bills, but the sooner she could get to work the sooner they would be settled. Miss Aimes could understand that. And she wished to thank everybody.

"Get Dr. Benn on the 'phone," commanded Miss Aimes. Tell him to come at once. Quite important." The office girl took up the 'phone. "Of course, Mrs. Bailey, you will await his arrival."

"No," said Ishma. "It isn't at all necessary for me to see him. Please assure him for me that he will be paid."

"But you can't go out of the hospital until he discharges you."

"Why, I am able to walk, Miss Aimes, as you see. I've just made two flights of stairs without the least trouble. Goodbye, and thanks, to you all."

She went out, regally and forever. Miss Aimes tried to call after her, but anger choked her. Miss Lester trembled, fearing that anger. The office girl was looking admiringly at Ishma's disappearing back, and the new interne had shifted his position so that Miss Aimes could not see his unsuppressed smile.

Ishma walked rapidly through the grounds toward the streetcar line, and had only a moment to wait before the car came which she boarded. There was no one on it except a woman with a poverty-lined face and a wizened little boy. A wave of friendliness flooded Ishma. These were her kin. She didn't know the nearest point to her street, but the conductor did, and assured her he would not forget to put her off at the right corner. When she smiled as she thanked him, he smirked happily, and said, "We don't get the ladies for a ride nowadays unless their cars are in the shop." This made Ishma remember her dress, and she gave a low laugh. At last she was a lady!

Off the car, and nearing the house, she began to think of Rad. She hadn't thought of him at all for the last hour, yet what she was doing was for his sake. No, it was for herself. Her mind, her peace, her self-respect. She wouldn't put it on Rad. But her step grew slow, and a faintness slewed numbly around her heart. Would he be at home? And what was she going to say to him? Perhaps she ought to have given herself another day at the hospital and put her thoughts in order. But another day would have been as barren as the preceding one. It might have left her even more confused. She might have weakened and tried to find reasons for not coming back to Rad. In that first hot wave of light after Virginia's disclosure, she had seen the way clearly, and she must keep on it.

There was a light in the house. As she entered the yard she could see Rad sitting at the little table in the front room. Both elbows were on the table and his chin was resting on his crossed wrists. She could see his supported face. He looked like a faded, desolate little boy. She noticed that he had let his hair get long, and his blue work-shirt was worn in holes on the shoulders.

Suddenly he sat up and brought his fist down hard on the table. She hurried into the house. Rad stared, then jumped toward her.

"Lord, it's you, Ish! Old gal, it's you!"

He grabbed her and pulled her to his lap. She smoothed his hair and said he must go to the barber's.

"Little old two-bit pieces ain't so plenty, Ish."

She got off his lap and pulled her chair close to his. "I know all about it, Rad. Mrs. Grant told me today."

"She's not goin' to help any?"

"No. But I am. I'm going to work right away. I'll pay off the debts. Every dollar of them. I can work now."

They both thought of Vennie, and were uncomfortably silent. Yes, Ishma could work now. "You can't stand the mills, Ish. They're drivin' the hands awful. Genie 's been tellin' me."

"How is Genie?"

"Next to dead. I saw her today. She can't hold more'n four frames, but they let her keep at work and make a little, 'count o' Derry havin' a talk with the boss. Genie said Derry was sendin' the boys up to his farm to get fat. She an' the girl are stayin' in a room at Grandma Huff's, but they'll have to leave, 'cause Grandma's got to have pay fer her room."

A flash from somewhere lit Ishma's way a few steps ahead. "I'll tell you what, Rad, we'll let Genie and Leta stay with us. Genie can keep house for her room and board. That 'll give me a chance to work harder and make more."

"Genie can't cook."

"She can learn. I'll make her. And she'll get strong if she quits the mill. She'll keep the house nice."

"It shore needs somebody."

"I see it does. I'd better stay at home tomorrow and get everything shining again. Then we'll have Genie keep it that way."

Rad still looked doubtful. "You're a great one if you can make a housekeeper out of Genie."

"We'll try it anyhow. I've a good mind to begin cleaning up tonight."

She went to a closet and took out an old dress. "You go off to bed, Rad, and I'll do a lot of work. I'll sleep right here on the sofa when I get tired, and not wake you up."

She tried to speak casually and not look at Rad. But he seemed to swell and fill the room. It was a full minute before he spoke, and she filled the silence with movements in the closet.

"Ishma, come out here," he said. She came out, her face an innocent inquiry.

"You look mighty fine in that dress. *She* gave it to you, I reckon."

"Yes, but I'm going to pay for it when I get work."

"You look fine in it. But I'd ruther see you in yer night-gown.

265

That 'ud look good to me. You got the one Genie made fer
you, with little ribbons on it ?"

"Yes," she answered, with her lips, her voice stricken.

"Put it on then. Let them old clo's alone. You're not goin'
to clean house tonight. I declare, Ish, I feel like we'd just got
married. It won't be long, nuther. Whad you say, maybe I can
borrow a car an' we can run up to Spartanburg an' back tomorr'
night. I've got three dollars."

"That wouldn't more than pay for gas and oil, Rad. And we'd
have to buy a license and pay the preacher. I've been thinking,
suppose we wait till — till we're out of debt — "

"Good Lord !"

"I don't mean the mortgage, but the doctors. The mortgage,
we'll just have to pay interest on that for a while — two or three
years, maybe. But I'll clear it off. You give me time, Rad."

She went over to him, softly eager. "You know, Rad, how
hard it was for us with little Vennie. Expense always, and no
good times. We don't want that to happen again."

"It wouldn't !"

"There's always a risk. I'm free now, and I can help you.
Let me stay free, Rad, and not risk getting tied up till you're sure
out of the woods. I'd be miserable all my life if you had to stay
in debt on my account. You'd always be dragging along, and
I'd feel it was my fault."

Rad loathed debt. He felt weary and frightened under it.
Ishma's argument was telling. But pshaw, there was no risk.
They'd pull out.

"I mustn't get where I can't help you," Ishma was repeating,
louder now and more determined. "I've never been free before.
Let me be free, Rad. Just free to work and help you."

Suddenly he was white with anger and fear. "You're quittin'
me, Ish ! You're quittin' me !"

She put her arms about his shoulders, and he caught her in a
terrible grip. "It ain't fair ! It ain't fair fer you to quit me !
Ain't I done enough ? Ain't I done ever'thing I promised ?
Ain't I more'n done it ?"

Choked in his embrace, she tried to speak soothingly, and after
a few minutes he listened.

266

"I'm honest, Rad. You've got to believe that. I'll not quit you so long as you need me and want me with you. But I don't want to tie up, and have children, and get helpless again, when there's so much to do. It's the first time in my life that I've had a chance. You won't take it away from me, will you?"

He fell back on his old answer. "You're a strange woman, Ish."

"I'm not strange. I just want my chance. It's been so long coming. I want it now most of all for your sake, Rad. You know I could walk off if I wanted to, but I'm not going to do that. I'm not thinking about that at all."

Again he was looking like a little boy, now whipped and sullen. "How long you want to wait 'fore we're married, Ish?"

"Till the doctors are paid. It won't take so awful long to save up two hundred dollars. And I'll stay right here with you."

"Like we did before you got hurt?"

She was calling up her strength to say "No," when they heard feet on the porch, then a heavy knock. Ishma opened the door and faced Bert Wiggins. He was astonished to see Ishma, and began to talk with jerky, dry sobs between his words. He thought Cindy was dying. She was in a heavy sleep, and wouldn't wake up. She'd opened her eyes once in two days, an' then she didn't know him. The doctor had said he couldn't do anything more. Never had done anything anyway. He had come for Rad, but if Ishma would go— He dropped back and stood on the porch. Rad called to him to come in, but he never moved.

Ishma gathered up a work-dress and apron, and stooped down to put on some old shoes. "You can't help Cindy, Rad. You go to bed and get ready for work tomorrow. When I come back I'll bring Genie with me. You'll have a pretty little home even if your old lady is going to work." She went to him, kissed his cheek, and rubbed his hair. "And you get this patch o' sagebrush trimmed up."

"You bet!" he said, with a smile. Then he remembered Bert and went out to him. "I'll go too, old man, if I can do anything."

"Ishma 'll be enough tonight. I'll want you worse if Cindy don't pull through."

They went away, and Rad was again alone. But he was not desolate. He wasn't losing Ish. He shore had been scared for a minute. But she was going to stand by him. And after all she might be right. She generally was. They'd be comfortable enough for a year or two, and there was plenty of time. He wasn't losing her.

As he went to bed he felt that life wasn't treating him scaly as it was treating old Bert. Poor fellow, about to lose his mate! Ishma was strange in some ways, but she was his, and she'd come around to getting married. She'd be a fool not to, and Ish was no fool. She was square. She was going to help pay out. Maybe work would steady up and he could save more too. That debt wouldn't bother them. They'd soon wipe it off, with no new expenses coming on. Kids cost a lot down here. Just as well to wait, like Ish said. And he had *her* anyhow. She's worth a dozen kids. He recalled that first day in the hospital when she had looked so hurt and white. Well, that was over.

Rad was almost happy as he fell asleep.

CHAPTER X

MILL BAT

CINDY roused from her stupor, but did not open her eyes. She was back "on the cobs," her easy bed having followed her sewing-machine and refrigerator on the well-worn return path to the installment house. In a feeble quaver she babbled, not of green fields, but of "the spring by the poplars — a drink, Bert, a drink — in the old gourd — right off the lizard's back" — Then she died, and the broken family wobbled bewildered on the road of adjustment.

Rad, in need of money himself, came to help Bert, using his good credit to obtain a cheap casket and other bare essentials. Ishma saw again that he could be gentle and generous. Watching Cindy die had brought her back to the old homely philosophy that had served man since he began to trudge on two feet; nothing mattered along the short lane of life except to add what cheer one could fo the way. With bodies open to wounds, with minds littered with delusions and pricked to their sane core with disappointments, men and women pushed and struggled along. If she, a mere unit in that countless number, had anything in her that could help, she would let it flow. She would withhold nothing. Secret yearnings and aversions alike could go unfed. Ambition, the burning intellect, the vain reachings out, what meaning could they have if they did not in some way add to human happiness? This was what she asked herself, standing by Cindy's coffin. The wrinkles were gone from the blue, pinched face. Cindy was lapped in peace. But this was what life should have given. Death ought not to be an escape. She, at least, would do what she could for life. Favors, sweetness, comfort — she would put all she had into it.

She would go back to Rad with open heart and hands. She wouldn't fail with him as she had with Britt. She had had the great chance of her life with Britt. The chance to give and help.

And how feebly she had broken down before it! She wouldn't fail again. She would marry Rad as soon as they were out of debt, and bear him children. In the meantime she would keep him contented. That would not be so difficult now, with life accepted and her mind no longer exploring ways of release.

When she went home, after three days in Cindy's forlorn household, she took Genie and Leta with her. At once she began teaching Genie how to keep the house spotless, how to bargain at the M & N, how to put good food on the table. But Genie gave little promise as a pupil in domestic engineering. Leta was working as a spooler in the big Greybank mill. She was pale, tired, discontented; as unhappy at work as she had been in school.

Ishma kept very busy during the day, training Genie, renewing contacts with her mill friends, and getting all in order for her new scheme of life. She would soon be a factory worker. At night, in the big bed with Rad, she wore the gown flecked with ribbon and bits of lace. Genie was put to making another. Rad was very happy. There was a quietness about Ishma that awed him a little, but she had never seemed so sweet and manageable.

And she was not suffering. She felt wrapped in a great spiritual charity that absorbed all consideration for her body. This new, external self could not be hurt. Fortunately something happened to annul her own deadening mental grip and bring her body back to life. This was merely the adventure of going to work. She surged again with restless longing and hope. Self was resurrected with all of its sensitive endurance and questioning pain.

It began the moment she passed through the door of a mill. There was thrill for her in the roll and swell of the machinery. The all-enveloping noise was like a vast chant coming into a life empty and soundless. She soon began to detect rhythms in it; dips and bursts, pleadings, remonstrance, approval. She listened with wonder and respect even when it was vicious and goading. This was between the long hour between five and six when her fingers failed in the delicate cleansing of whirling spools and the joining of broken threads; when her feet seemed nailed to the floor and the alley stretched out for miles as she tried to go up and down, up and down, between the frames.

She had gone with Leta to the Greybank, and Stark Branner, the boss, had offered her the spinning-room or nothing. Take it or leave it! Having learned from Mildred and Cindy something of the dispiriting and never alleviated heat of the spinning-room, she had smiled and said that she preferred nothing. There were dozens of mills around Winbury, she thought, and was walking out of the office when Branner stopped her. She had told him that she had never worked in a mill, and he had supposed she would accept any place given her. Beginners always did. They had to. When he saw her turn away with no sign of disappointment, he felt that he must not let such good working material pass to another mill. She looked as if she would hold out for ten years at least, under the stiffest speed-up, before they would have to scrap her. After she'd been broken in she would be a good pace-maker, and that's what they needed now to get the workers settled down in this new "rationalized" system. Pace-makers. He couldn't let such a prospect go. Strong, outdoor women were hard to get hold of. Usually they came to the mills half worn-out, then blamed the system with their collapse.

"Wait a minute," he said. "I'll change you off with a spooler." He looked at the pale, negative Leta. "No use to save her," he thought. "She'll dwindle out in a few months anyway." Aloud he said cheerily to the girl. "We'll put you in the spinning-room and Mrs. Bailey can go into your alley."

"That won't suit me," said Ishma quickly. "Leta is not as strong as I am."

Here was an independent spirit, thought Branner, the kind they didn't want, from one point of view — but from another — Ishma was giving him a parting smile. It would be something to break that woman — or to please her — he wasn't sure which — but he wouldn't let her go.

"The fact is, Mrs. Bailey, this Unthank girl isn't worth much to us as a spooler, and sometimes a poor spooler makes a good spinner. Instead of firing her, we want to try her out in the spinning-room. Somebody will have to take her place as a spooler, and it might as well be you if you want to try it."

Leta had turned yet whiter at the prospect of being fired. She knew she was a poor worker, her pay envelope never held more than a call for five dollars for a week's work, but she had tried hard, had accepted night work without a murmur, and struggled through eleven long hours five nights a week, without an hour's absence to her debit. She had done her best, but with nervous haste and little strength, she tangled her work and wasted good cotton thread. The noise drove her mad, and the heat even in the more endurable spooling-room kept her wilted. But to lose her job! How would she live? Derry had all the boys, and she would die before she would ask him to take her too.

Ishma looked at the girl's quivering lips, and took her hand. "We'll find another place, honey," she said.

What an exasperating woman, thought the boss. But he had to have her.

"All right, I'll try her where she is for another week or two. And you may start in the spooling-room this morning." He wouldn't suggest night-work to *her*. If she started to walk out again, she'd be gone. "You needn't expect to catch on to the work right off, and by the time you are makin' Reece-Durkin rich with your labor, somebody else will have dropped out and we'll have you ready for the place. They're droppin' right along," he added warningly. "All the loafers an' weak-knees."

Ishma found the work hard, in spite of the exaltation and the thrill. At the end of her first week, her pay envelope contained a voucher for only two dollars. Her hands were large for delicate, swift movements. But they were poised and sure, and her pay went up to six dollars the second week. After that she rapidly gained control of her work. At the end of two months she was drawing twelve dollars a week. A third month brought the amount up to fourteen, as much as the fastest worker on the floor was making. The boss frequently passed through her alley, with a lingering and approving eye. "You'll get up to seventeen dollars in six months," he encouraged her. "That'll make some o' these whiners an' slackers shut their mouths." Which made Ishma understand why she was getting bitter looks from some of the workers. What a strange system, she thought, where to do your best meant hurting your neighbors!

As her hands became more easily skilful, the machines became more sensitive and alive. They could kill, but they could create.

That was their first, great function. When she came in to them she felt that she must greet them good-morning, and start the day comradely with the secret force producing so endlessly and enormously for the markets of men. When she left them she caught herself nodding back as she went out the door. She understood how the mill "got you," how the workers could say so pathetically, "I'd like the life, if a feller could live." If they could live! That was all they seemed to be asking for. She heard little talk of the union during her first days in the mill. To her, all of them, men, women and children, seemed to be in a set strain to hold their jobs. The old days when a "hand" could rest or take it easy for about ten minutes out of every hour, were a fading memory.

"We'll have to ask leave to git a drink o' water purty soon," said Keet Slade, the jester of the spooling-room. A big laugh answered him from the workers collected outside the door, eating their lunch out of paper bags and tin boxes. During work time they were in the habit of reviving themselves with a drink of water about every two hours. Tampering with this privilege would be an insult so unthinkable that it was matter for laughter. A few days later the sub-boss came in and the machinery was halted long enough for him to inform them that they could go to the water-faucet only with the permission of the supervisor in the room, and no one could get that permission more than twice a day. A notice confirming this announcement was tacked on the wall by the big entrance door, and the sub-boss departed hastily. For the rest of the day there was silence among the workers. Nobody looked up to smile or shout a word at another. There was no laughter or joking outside the big door at lunch time. When they left the mill at night, shoulders were humped, faces were sullen.

Next day, in the big room, under the roar of the machinery, Ishma felt a human silence weaving all the workers into a tense, compact body. Suddenly in a far corner there was stir and commotion. Looking across the distance, she saw Ella Ramsey, voluble and twinkling, confronting a very red-faced boss. She recognized Branner in a state of swollen indignation. Ishma saw him take Ella by the shoulders, whirl her around, and begin to push her out. To get to the entrance he had to proceed across the room and down, passing near Ishma's alley.

"Look out! You've torn my pocket!" Ella cried out, and from that pocket apparently there streamed a lot of cards and bits of paper that were scattered over the floor like leaves in the wind, and were eagerly gathered up by the workers. One floated to Ishma's feet. It was a form of application for membership in the union. She picked up another bit — a stiff little card on which was written, "Go to the speaking tonight by the railroad tracks back of Brinn street and feed your brains."

Ella seemed to have a dozen pockets, all torn, and all emptying themselves as the boss shook her and proceeded doorward. As they neared the entrance, she began to fear a kick in the rear. It would never do to go out ignominiously. She knew the value of a triumphant exit. Unexpectedly she became passive in her captor's hands. As he had been pushing her along against all of her resistant force, they both plunged headlong for a few steps, and before he could regain his balance, Ella had twisted herself around and faced him. When he grabbed her again they were near the door and his back was turned to the room, while Ella faced the workers. He was unable to hold her still, and she danced from side to side in front of him, her glance darting over the room.

"Look at my partner, folks!" she cried above the whirr, loud enough for those near the door to hear and become carriers of her words. "I didn't pick him, but I'm trainin' him! He ain't ever been to dancin' school!"

He shoved her backwards out of the door, her face still beaming on the roomful of workers. As they had their last glimpse of her she was shouting "Down with slavery! Liberty or death!" Branner followed, nigh to bursting, and the great door closed.

"'Rah fer Eller!" shouted a voice, and instantly a hundred voices were shouting "'Rah for Eller!" When they ceased, again over the room a big voice bellowed, "'Rah for the union!" Silence, except for the whirr of the machines. Then fear seemed to leave every heart, and the shout that went up was one Ishma never forgot. She looked about her. Cheeks were burning, eyes were on fire. She could scarcely recognize her pale, stolid companions of a quarter of an hour before.

That night she didn't want to go home. She would have liked to go into a little restaurant called "The Roast Pig" for her supper. The man who kept it was a mountaineer, born in her own county, but he had been a miner in Kentucky and Virginia before coming to Winbury and setting up his little eating-shop. A union leader, Amos Freer, from Boston, took his meals there. She had seen him several times, at a table by the window, with young workers about him. She wanted to sit at the next table and hear bits of their talk. But Genie had been giving Rad very poor suppers lately, so she bought him something special and hurried home.

Leta was there. Ishma glanced at her white face and asked her if she felt well enough to go to work that night.

"I'm not going back," said Leta.

"She sure ain't," Genie cut in. "What you s'pose that spinnin' boss did to her?"

"She's not in the spinning-room, Genie."

"Yes, I am," Leta told her. "I've been there a month. I didn't tell you they'd put me there because I was afraid you'd give up your place and maybe you couldn't get another. They make it hard for a hand that flies up and leaves. And there's so many new hands comin' in from Georgia. It's awful hard in the spinnin'-room, and just as I had learnt good and begun to draw pay, the boss put me in a room with the new frames. They're a lot harder to work, and I couldn't make hardly anything. Just look at my finger ends — they're worn to the blood — an' I've got blisters all over the inside of my hands."

"Did he fire you, Leta?"

"No, but it's the same thing, I reckon. Last night when I got to the mill I told the boss I didn't want to go into the room where the new frames were. I said I was going back to the old frames; and he took hold of my shoulders and shoved me into the other room. I was so mad I walked out as soon as he turned me loose. So I'm out of a job, but what's the use workin' if I don't make anything? And my hands are so sore."

Leta began to sob, and Genie told her to shut up while she said something. She then told Ishma that the supervisor of one of the mill nurseries had said she could have a place helping to take care of the babies. The pay wasn't much, but it would be more than Leta was earning. And she wanted to know why Leta couldn't do the housework and cooking, and let her go to the nursery.

Ishma had known for some time that Genie would have to be replaced, but she felt that to exchange her for Leta would make matters worse. She gained time by proposing to wait for Rad. They would talk it over with him. When Rad came in, he surprised Ishma by immediate approval of the plan. "Leet is smart an' she's young," he said. "She'll learn. Won't you, Leet?"

Leta's pale face grew pink and eager. "I'll try my best," she said. She loathed the mills as she had loathed school. All she had ever wanted was to be mistress of a little home, but this was her own secret, guarded with bashful shame even from her mother. She thought she couldn't have a home without a husband, and she was too timid to go out and hunt her man. Here, without that impossible effort, she was attaining her heart's desire. Her thin shoulders expanded energetically, and her head took a tilt upward.

"What's for supper?" asked Rad, with no hope in the question, and a critical eye on Genie.

"I haven't started it," she answered, "except I built a fire an' the stove's hot. Leta's been so blubbery I couldn't think of supper."

"Come, Leta," said Ishma, "we'll soon have something ready."

Leta followed her joyfully, and in half an hour they had creamed eggs, flavored with cheese, in a bowl full of yellow sauce, hot sally lunn with butter, a chop and coffee for Rad, and a glass of milk for each of the women. Leta wanted to put a table cover over the oilcloth, but Genie said there wasn't any clean.

"There'll be clean ones from now on," crowed Leta, and Rad laughed, twitching a string of her straight hair.

"Get that long face fattened out, an' you'll be cute," said Rad.

Thus Leta was established, and amazed them all by her deftness and aptitude. As the weeks passed, Ishma, delighted and relieved, could give herself with less reserve to the one thing that now interested her, the union. Every week half of her money was laid in Rad's hand to be taken to Dr. Benn and Dr. Maddux. The other half was her own, and she found that even that fortune did not cover her needs. Books, papers, an occasional supper at "The Roast Pig," union dues and assessments, were now among her items of expense, as necessary as print dresses, shoes, stockings, and the two articles of underwear still permitted to women. She never on any occasion wore a hat.

She had joined the union three days after Ella Ramsey's dramatic appearance at the mill. A few evenings of work at Ella's side had cleared up for her the difference between the old union and the new. The United Textile Workers Union had a long record of compromise and sell-outs behind it. Through tragedy and despair the workers had learned that it could not be trusted to hold their rights for them after they had been desperately won. This was being demonstrated for them at that very time in Elizabethton, Tennessee, where mountain men, women, boys and girls, had fought and won a living wage and recognition of their union, only to have all they had achieved set aside in "conciliatory" conferences over their heads.

The new Union, the National Textile Workers, had not existed long enough to have a record behind it. Though it had done nothing to cause distrust, it had yet to win the confidence of the workers. All depended upon the faith which the leaders could inspire. "Will they stick to us?" was the invariable question that met Ishma when out to get new members. By this time she knew those leaders — their history, their unlimited self-sacrifice, their readiness to risk their lives in the workers' cause. They were not living in hotels or comfortable boarding-houses — not wearing immaculate clothes in which to appear at conferences with the owners and bosses. They were sharing the hard beds and poor food of the "mill-hands," and dressing hardly one degree better. They were of a sworn brotherhood; sworn to serve to the gates of death, or through them, their ideal of a just world. Ishma's loyalty leapt to them like a stream that had broken through a long obstructive barrier.

"Yes, they would stick!" "No, they were not outsiders, any

more than Jesus was an outsider in Galilee, or Paul on Mars hill."

"But folks say they don't believe the Bible."

"Well, there is one part of it they believe anyway; the part that says one man shall not sow and another reap, one man shall not work and another eat up his harvest; the rich shall not add house to house and acre to acre, while the workers are without roof or land."

Ishma knew her people, and Ella Ramsey was right. She made a good recruiter. Gradually, as Leta was able to give her more relief, she spent more of her evenings away from home, and found it increasingly difficult to appear there at Rad's bed-time.

"It's all right, old gal," he said one night when she came in a little after nine, "you runnin' around to tuck in the sore an' lazy, but you've got to show up fer sleepin'." He didn't know that she had exchanged her old diversion of looking after the sick and needy for something far more exhilarating, something that had in it both hope and promise.

"You can't miss me much, Rad. All I do when I'm here is to stick my nose in a book, while you and Genie and Leta play flinch."

"Well, I look up once in a while, an' I don't get tired seein' you settin' around. I tried to read that stuff myself 'fore you come in," he added, eyeing a book on the sofa, "but I couldn't see any sense in it. One o' Derry's, I reckon."

She picked up the book as if to shelter it. "Yes, *Woman,* by Bebel. He was a German."

"Guess that's why I couldn't understand it. Say, Ish, there's a movie on tomorrow night that I want to see. Tom Mix in the best ridin' show ever put out. We'll go."

To give up her time was like giving up more than rubies, but she agreed cheerfully. Rad had gone into the bed-room and was hastily taking off his work-clothes, getting ready for sleep. She followed him, and very slowly began to undress. She had got into the habit of lingering over bed-time preparations, and remembering to do this or that neglected "turn." Tonight she put on a kimono over her gown and went out to the back yard to set a tub for the rain which she knew wouldn't come. She wanted rain-water for washing her hair, she said. Out in the yard she looked up at her old friends, the stars, for strength to go back into the room. They put her in her place. Agony that filled to the brim one entire human life seemed a small matter when she thought of the worlds out there. And her life held much besides agony — much that should make her happy. She had health, work, home, friends — a good man — Oh, if he would beat her and let her get away ! If he would cut her to the bone ! Again the hot thoughts were tumbling through her brain. The stars couldn't help. All their unfeeling magnitude meant less than one drop of warm, aching blood. Slowly she turned, climbed the kitchen steps, rearranged the cook vessels that Leta had set in perfect order, and went into the bedroom. The door was partly open. She slipped through, hoping that Rad would be asleep. His eyes were shut, and he was breathing with the regularity of deep slumber. Noiselessly she lay down beside him and became motionless. Then she felt his arm steal around her waist, and heard his happy chuckle.

The next day Ishma had not been at work more than ten minutes when she became conscious of a whispering wave going over the spooling-room. It had rolled in from the spinners, who had it from the carders, and the doff-boys helped it along. A beloved union official from Boston would be on the speakin' ground that night, and would be sure to make a speech. He had been down in South Carolina where a strike without leadership was in progress. The speed-up, long hours, and starvation, had brought a sudden outburst of rebellion. The official had been sent down to organize an effective union, but the workers were inexperienced in protest, and were still naïvely hoping to arouse the sleeping benevolence of their employers to the point of permitting them to live. They had rejected the offer of advice and aid, and with solemn politeness had escorted the official out of the town. He was now on his way back North, and would stop over for two hours in Winbury. It would be a great night. All day Ishma tried to make up her mind to break her promise to Rad.

She had begun to consider herself an intelligent person, yet she would suffer unspeakable boredom and lose a great hour in her life because she was too feeble-minded to hurt Rad's feelings.

She hoped to get off early to the picture, and in that case they might be back in time for her to rush to the meeting and hear a little of the speaking. She could let Rad think that she was going to Mildred's, which would be true, for she intended to go home with Mildred and spend the night there. She had done that once before, on a night when she had found it impossible to enter the little bed-room. Mildred always had a conveniently sick child.

She cleaned her machine and quit work half an hour before the usual time. When she worked fast and got ahead of the stock, the boss would say nothing if she walked out a little before six o'clock. She hoped Rad would be at home so they could have early supper. In her haste, she cornered across a vacant lot and approached the house by the back way, through a narrow lane between two neighbors' gardens. As she stepped on Rad's ground a bunch of tall privet helped to conceal her approach. Then came a row of nearly leafless mock-oranges, and through them she could see Rad and Leta sitting on the kitchen steps. On Leta's knees was a plate, and in her hand was a large piece of lemon pie — Rad's favorite — which she was holding up for him to bite.

"Gosh, Leet! You can cook as good as Ish!"

"Better!" said Leta, with a toss of her head.

She had "fattened out," as Rad had predicted, and was pink and pretty. She also looked mature, not the frail innocent of a few months past, so quickly sometimes does getting what one wants make padded muscles and rounded curves. Ishma, who had thought of her as a child, was suddenly enlightened. She stood behind the mock-oranges, re-ordering her disarranged thoughts, until the pie was finished.

"That's all," said Leta.

"No, 'tain't," Rad protested, grabbing and kissing her.

He needn't have grabbed, thought Ishma. Leta was ready for it. Then she turned back down the path, out through the lane, and came up to the front door, making an unsubdued entrance. Rad came in from the kitchen.

"Glad you got home soon, Ish. We'll go to the seven o'clock show."

280

"I've been wondering, Rad, old boy, if you wouldn't take Leta tonight and let me stay with Mildred."

"Mildred ! Her brats are always sick !"

"Leta would enjoy going."

"We can take her with us."

"I could go tomorrow night."

"This picture ain't on but one night. But all right, if you don't *want* to go. I ain't makin' you."

She saw that he was only trying to look sullen. He was pleased. The rush of deliverance carried her to him. Her beautiful mouth, big, friendly, pitying, found his cheek and pressed it.

"You're good to me, Rad," she said. Then he was clinging to her. His voice shook a little as he whispered, "You come too, Ish !" Her endearments always melted him and made him painfully love-sick. She must remember that hereafter. She must not put herself for one moment between him and Leta.

Her plan had been born the instant of their kiss on the steps. The skies had opened. Rad in love with someone else ! Or at least beginning to be. Her feet would hardly stay on the floor. She must get out quickly, or her happiness would spoil everything. Rad falling in love ! She had never thought of that possibility. It was such an easy door out. Perhaps that was why she had never thought of it. But she must be careful and not startle him. His interest in Leta must be fed gently, until it became stronger than his will or caution.

"I'll not wait for supper," she said, turning through the door. "You and Leta laugh a lot for me."

She was gone, not looking back, because she knew Rad's eyes would be wistful.

It was early March, and the dusk was heavy at seven-thirty after a gloomy day. Ishma found her way to a back lot between the railroad tracks and the rear of some shabby little buildings that fronted on Brinn street, the main street of Spindle Hill. The train bringing the speaker would not arrive until eight o' clock, and the workers had not begun to assemble. She sat down on a pile of outcast telephone poles, and looked into the darkness until she could distinguish the railroad embankment that acted as a

281

sort of sounding board for the voices of the speakers. Before the embankment was a small platform made of scaffolding discarded by carpenters after repairing one of the shabby buildings fronting on Brinn. On this exiguous stage the speakers and their helpers were to stand.

Ishma was glad of the night and the loneliness. They helped her to calm herself, to weld herself again into an entity. The sudden vision of freedom had struck her with shattering force. She felt a thousand times divided; centrally void, with shreds and ribbons of self flying with thirsty joy into the universe. The night gathered her in, pressed her together with cool, lingering vapor like attending hands. And the silence helped. The hollow hush in the little bowl of earth beside the railroad tracks spread for her over the world, annulling all the noisy mistakes and trumpetings of creation. She drew back on her throne of telephone poles, witness for Life, waiting another venture.

Sooner than she wished, little groups began to appear, softly materializing from no apparent source, and scarcely distinguishable in the light of lanterns swung fitfully about. Conversation on the most casual subjects was more or less guarded, giving a cautious eagerness to the trivial word. More and more the workers gathered in, until the groups merged around the speaker's stand and stretched back to Ishma's perch on the pile of poles. Two or three exhausted women dropped down near her, followed by others until there was room for no more. One woman had three children with her.

"I didn't have a soul to leave 'em with," she said, "an' I couldn't stay away. I thought the best thing I could do for 'em was to come out an' learn how I was goin' to feed 'em since the flu got Jim, if there's anybody smart enough to tell me."

"You workin', ain't you, Sue ?" asked a voice out of the dark.

"Makin' 'leven dollars a week, an' they give me house rent."

"God bless 'em !" said the ironical voice.

Another woman was plaintive. "That nurse that's goin' round says I've got to have a quart o' milk a day for ever' child, an' they's five of 'em at seventeen cents a quart. You can count it up."

"There's Dan Ogler with the big lantern fer the speakers."

"I hope the tall feller 'll hold it up tonight, so we can see 'em good."

Suddenly there was no more talking. Three men were seen mounting the little platform, with the aid of a small dry-goods box. Two women were helped up. Then a tiny creature was lifted bodily from the ground to the platform.

"That's Eva Blaine," whispered the woman next to Ishma. "She come to my house, an' I run out the back door. But she went around an' stopped me, an' I never heard a body talk so much good sense as she did. That's why I come tonight."

The six stood on the platform waiting for the seventh to take his place beside them. The seventh was the speaker from Boston. When he was up, Dan Ogler held the big gasoline lantern so that for a moment it illuminated all on the stand. A rumble of satisfaction came from the crowd. The speaker was no smart Alec, he was a nice, easy lookin' good sort of a man. Old enough to know something. His hair was slightly grey, and the ascetic mould of his face was broken by a smile older than his years.

"He looks like he didn't have no more to eat than we're gittin'," said a voice near Ishma.

"Shet up! Fred's introducin' him!"

Fred Beckton was saying that their comrade from the North had to leave by a ten-o'clock train, so he would take time merely to speak his name. This he did, in a voice that rang proudly out to Brinn street, challenging any policeman's cocked ear. The one on the beat happened to be fat, old Azbury Huff, troubled with corns, who muttered "Give 'em rope! Give 'em rope!" and jerkily waddled on.

Everybody was leaning forward as the comrade from the North began. For several minutes he talked to them of familiar things; their struggles, their hardships, their fight for the union. Then he paused, and looking at them with a smile that seemed to come slowly from the back of his brain, he said: "Now I am going to talk to you of something that every worker should know. Something that has been used to scare you and make you feel like children in the dark stumbling toward a deadly foe. I hope I can take away that fear; that I can convince you this thing is no monster in wait to destroy you the moment you set out to gain for

283

yourselves and your children a better life here and now. I am going to speak to you of communism."

A gasp went over the audience; a gasp of dazzled relief. The bogey that had been haunting their days and nights was to be dragged out and exposed for whatever it was.

"Who has set up this monster to keep you afraid ? Who but those who want to keep you in chains ? The bosses. You read of it in their newspapers, and hear of it from every mouth they can hire to lie for them or spew ignorance. I hope I can speak so clearly that after tonight when someone, with shudders of horror, tells you that a certain leader of yours is a communist, you will be able to answer, with no shudder at all, 'And who but a communist *should* lead the workers ?' You will know that honor, that compassion, that wisdom, are not denied a man because he is a communist. Who has a greater claim to honor than one who leads a fight against a system that is making honor among men more impossible with every day that it totters on its rotten base ? Who can have greater pity than one who would lead men forever out of the need of pity ? Who is more wise than the man who knows when a change in the world is due and sets forth to make that change before delay has wrecked mankind ? Who but such men should be our leaders ? They are worthy of trust as deep as the people of old gave to Isaiah with his words of fire."

Another, slighter gasp went over the audience. He didn't sound like he was going to knock the Bible anyhow.

Ishma looked at the faces where here and there she could see them, pallid and straining, in the dim light of the lanterns. She knew the yearning and thirst that was on them, stirring through the lines and scars of an ever losing battle. Faces like these had hid in the catacombs, bearing a light that no darkness could put out. That hunted light had encircled thrones. Faces like these had whitened in the dungeons of serfdom, while bleeding fingers dug away the foundations of feudalism. That bleeding strength had overturned kingdoms. Was this starved, feeble handful part of an unconquerable host ? Would they win again, and the mountain in their path be levelled ? Or would they fall and rot, more fertilizer for its rank, material blooming ?

284

"Some of you here," said the comrade, "perhaps all of you here, need go no farther back than your great-grand-parents to find pioneers facing a wilderness. When your forefathers made their first trails through this land, they travelled in groups, bound together against forest enemies. I have read of some of those groups; the Walkers, the Coopers, the Silers, the Wilsons, the De-Harts. All brave men, but not one of them thought of taking his wife and children on the trail and beating a path for them only. Every man was as much the protector of every other man's wife and child as of his own. When they settled along the rivers, or in the upland valleys, they helped one another to dig wells, to build fences, to hew logs, to build houses and barns. No man made his family comfortable leaving another's family shelterless.

"Today we have greater need to band together than our forefathers knew. We are living in a wilderness more bewildering, more threatening than theirs. An industrial wilderness that will subdue mankind, if we workers do not unite in our million-powered strength to conquer it. There is but one road of survival for the human race. It must come out of the competitive jungle where it is swamped, and where nine-tenths of mankind are fighting for breath. It must find the firm and fertile ground of co-operation — of working together. There the house of life must be built if it is to stand. And it is we, the workers of the world, who must lead the way out, who must find that ground, who must build that house."

It seemed to Ishma that the head of every person there rose a nick upward. Were they, the dumb, the scorned, the forgotten of civilization, called to come and be of the vanguard? They waited through another pause, eager as burnt fields scenting rain.

"But how shall we set about it? What have we to aid us? What have we against us? Let us look over the world and see. Let us take stock. Let us look into our birthrights. First, we have our earth, the home of humanity, the land that feeds us, that gives us our material and our foundations. Earth with her gifts, her oil, coal, rubber, minerals, her forests, her waters, and the air above her, where ships now ply and our words vibrate.

"Second, we have our machinery, our implements — as necessary to us as earth itself if we are to be more than naked wanderers. The tools, the inventions, born of our needs and aspirations, our skill, our ingenuity, our genius — these are our racial triumphs and heritage. No man, nor group of men, has the shadow of a right to deprive us of our share in them.

"Third, we have our great systems of transportation — railroads, ships, motors of every sort and kind — for bringing what we have made to the doors of those who need it. Our children want shoes. They will come, let us say from Lynn. We need flour for our morning biscuits. Kansas — Manitoba — will send it to us. Our right to transporting power, to banish hunger and need, is as justly ours as the right to produce, the right to inhabit the planet on which we were born.

"So rich as all this, we ought to walk proudly on our earth. What has happened that we — well, that we don't ?"

The lantern light revealed a smile that invaded the audience, releasing for a moment the tension of every face.

"What happened to disinherit us began very far back in human history. We cannot retrace that path tonight. We can only look at where we are today. I need not tell you that the millions and millions of workers bound hand and foot to factories and fields, are no shareholders in the earth and its riches. We grow all the food of man, but how many who slave in the grainfields can write their title to an acre of soil ? Read the statistics which the capitalist governments compile for their service, and you will see. It is the same with machinery. We produce the world's goods, but we own no factories. We have no voice in distribution, though a wheel could not be turned, nor a cargo reach its destination without our power. If we owned the powers of transport, no worker's child the earth around would go hungry while Louisiana poured cane-syrup to her bayous and the wheat of Kansas farmers grew old in storage. You see what has happened. Our birthrights as members of the human society are gone. Communism will restore these rights. The workers of the earth, wherever they toil, under roof or open sky, in every country of the globe, should and shall own the industries of the world and administer them. That is communism.

"Does it frighten you, my fellow-workers ? Does it fill you

286

with terror to think that instead of a few men owning the world and letting us run it for their profit, we shall own it and run it for the good of all who live ?

"Let no one make you believe that we need the help of the bosses. The mechanism by which commodities are created and exchanged is so intricate and subtle that to bungle it in one hemisphere means dislocation in another. It is our hands, our intelligence, our labor, that keeps this vast and delicate body at work. There is no broken thread of industry that we can not follow up and make good, no smallest, hidden wheel that we can not find and adjust. Our labor disasters are not due to our ignorance or lack of skill. They are due to the greed and negligence of owners who wish to fill their pockets at the risk of human life. While I am speaking these words, twenty-four comrade-workers are smothering and roasting to death in a Pennsylvania mine, because that mine did not have proper devices to make it safe. And will the owner go to the electric chair for his murders ? He will not. He is in the United States Senate, and he will stay there until we put him out by putting an end to capitalism and its crimes. Three days ago a ship went down in mid-sea, taking with it one hundred and thirty-nine lives, because the owners of that ship wanted the profits from one more trip before junking it. To go through half the list of such crimes would keep me standing here until daylight. I will mention only one more to show you what it means for our industries to be owned by private groups, or by governments controlled by private groups. I will take for this illustration the industry of communication. With its telephones, radios, wires and wireless, communication has become one of the great industries of the world. Perhaps it is now the most important, since over its highways of information any lie can be driven into the hearts of the people. In 1911 the world was in the shadow of war. The militarists of Germany, the chauvinists of France, the industrialists of England, the Czarists and bureaucrats of Russia, all felt the need of war. German and French militarists knew they would have to strike soon, or yield to the increasing power of the workers. Autocracy in Russia was shaken by the desperate surge of the people. In England the Lancashire looms that once had paid five hundred per cent profit were beginning to run below cost. Colonies and markets had to be won or profits would be gone forever. A war would be timely and welcome to all except the workers who were to fight it. France and Germany were on the edge of battle. Each nation was enveloped in a blur of lies. But the workers began to clear away the blur. Messages flew back and forth. The workers of Germany and the workers of France bared the truth to each other and declared against war. The great cataclysm was postponed.

In 1914, in the first days of impending war, the governments took care to sever all communication between France and Germany. No word could pass except through those in power. We know what that word was. Berlin was marching on Paris, Paris was marching on Berlin! Denied any way of getting at the truth, cannonaded with lies by the press of both nations, the workers were thrown into panic, unreason, stampede. Four years later the bodies of ten million young men were rotting in the soil of Europe. If the people had owned and controlled their channels of communication, that could not have happened.

"You may have heard of a famous remark by Jay Gould, that the capitalists have nothing to fear so long as they can get one half of the working people to fight the other half. They will not be able to fool us much longer. We are going to have our own press, our own wires, our own instruments and channels of communication. Then let them put over a war if they can. Instead of getting their war, they'll get what they gave those who opposed them in 1914 — the hoosegow."

He paused, and a raw-boned mountain mother with two scrawny boys in her lap began to applaud. The children put up their thin hands and clapped with her. In a few seconds every one present was clapping and shouting. A through freight tore along the tracks behind them and they clapped above its thunder. When silence came the speaker began again, his face a white gleam, and his voice sharp and swift.

"Under communism there will be no wars. Who will make war for markets when goods are produced for use only and never for profit ? Under communism there will be no poverty. *No poverty !* Can you imagine how that will change the world we live in ? If the devil were asked to choose one instrument, and

288

only one, for making earth a hell, he would choose poverty. There is no crime that men have not committed in an effort to escape it; no crime that they will not continue to commit so long as it is with us. Only communism will drive it from our world. Our children will be set free. The inhuman evil of child labor will vanish with the thing that spawns it, poverty. The two million children in the mines and factories of this one land will come out into the sun. There will be no old people living in terror of want or of charity. White hairs shall be more than honorable; they shall receive honor. To be always poor is like living in a continual frost. At last the ice gets to the marrow, so that a man scarcely knows when he exchanges it for the indifferent chill of death. Communism will be nurture and warmth in his veins. There will be no millions of men with empty stomachs and blistered feet pleading for work. The breadline, that peculiar and amazing institution of these times, will be no more. No matter how glittering the front that capitalism may flaunt, at the end of its proud parade it wags the tail of a breadline. If it were to go on review before the God whom it claims to worship, I wonder what it would do with that tail. The capitalists could not assure God that the breadline was his responsibility. They have had charge of things too long for that.

"At your head-quarters there is a photograph of a letter written by a mill-owner to his manager. The owner lives on a great estate in the North, and his mill is the largest in your county. That letter ought to be copied and framed and hung in every shack where a worker breathes. I do not say lives, for life means an abundance that we have yet to taste. That letter ought to be kept before your eyes as constant proof that man and not God is the author of your poverty. In that letter the owner congratulates his manager on the skill with which he has established the system which you call the 'stretch-out.' He congratulates him because he has speeded up the work so as to double the output, and has lowered the annual payroll by five hundred thousand dollars. Five hundred thousand dollars taken from your wages in one mill, though you were giving double work in return ! You made it and he took it.

"What will become of that five hundred thousand dollars ? It will go to add to the luxuries, or the lauded philanthropies of that man's family, or it may go to set up another mill where more workers will use up their lives to make more money for him. And there are some people ignorant enough and insolent enough to ask us what we would do without the rich man's capital. We, in slavery, in disease, in daily fear of losing our jobs, fear of hearing our children cry for bread, we know what to do. We ourselves shall use the capital we produce, to build our own factories, to provide our own machines, instead of making a gift of it to a drinker of blood and eater of children's flesh. We shall take human life out of the hands of men who know nothing better to do with it than crush it and waste it. We are gathering our strength to end the slaughter. We are gathering it here now in this new union; in the fight we are making in this town against the horrors and drawn-out murders of the 'speed-up.' We shall learn right here what organization means; its power to us as workers. And we shall need every fraction of that power. The work before us is not easy. We are going to have a hard time keeping what we make and getting back what we already have given away.

"I have told you that communism is not a beast waiting in the dark to devour us and our children. It is a great mother calling us to peace and plenty. But there *is* a beast between us and those arms of safety. All the established might of capitalist society and government will be turned against us. We shall meet the venom of lawyers and juries, of judges and false witnesses. Men called 'men of God' will shout against us from their pulpits. All the machinery for keeping our minds and bodies in slavery will be fiercely set to work. If we are beaten and tortured now, when we merely ask for a shorter day or protest against a wage-cut, what will they not want to do to us when we ask for all that is ours ?

"The blood of the brave has fed and watered every great change by which man has moved forward; and the change that is surely coming is the greatest of all in the long up-hill climb of humanity. It will call for blood as the sea calls for its rivers. But we shall win, fellow-workers. We shall win as our brothers in Russia have won; as they are winning now in China, in spite of the gunboats and bombing-planes and gold of Britain and America. We shall possess this earth which is soaked ages deep with our sweat and our blood. We shall not cease asking and taking and fighting so long as there is one child in the world whimpering vainly for bread; one child shivering sleepless in the winter's cold; one child lifting its eyes for true knowledge and receiving a lie. We shall clear this jungle; we shall cleanse these shambles; and leave for our children a land of peace and fair meadows. To die in such a cause, as some of us must, is to die triumphant."

Some of the women had risen, their weariness forgotten, and pressed softly nearer the speaker's stand. In the vacant place by Ishma a man sat down. She didn't look around, but when a hand stole over and took her own, she knew it was the hand of Derry Unthank and returned its greeting pressure.

When the last word was spoken by the comrade from the North, a local speaker rose, hesitating for words in the charged silence. Derry whispered "Come!" and drew Ishma back into the shadows away from the gathering. "Let's walk to the bridge," he said, and spoke no more until they were in the street.

CHAPTER XI

UNFETTERED

"A PITY there has to be more talk tonight," said Unthank, slower of step. "If they could go home and sleep on it, this thing would be simple and clear by morning. They wouldn't go to work tomorrow all fuddled up."

Ishma said nothing for some distance, afraid that he would find her fuddled too. When she began to talk, he didn't like the timidity in her voice. "But how can they help getting mixed up ? It's too wonderful, this new world that we can get for ourselves. I can't believe *all* the time. And when I do, it makes me dizzy. Sometimes it seems to be right here, all about me, in spite of what my eyes are shouting to me. When I see it like that, I feel little wings fanning all over my body, and I've no use for the ground. But the world as it *is* pushes so hard, the new one is soon covered up again."

They had reached the bridge, and were standing by the railing. Unthank was looking out, above the horizon, as if reading something there. She knew he wasn't thinking of her and her small confusions. He didn't talk to her enough. It wasn't, she had discovered, that she was uninteresting. She knew that he talked patiently, by the hour, to the most ignorant men in the mills. A high riding moon sculptured his profile in palest gold against a thin, blue atmosphere. His dark hair, rippling like water, looked so deep that she felt she could put out her hands and swim in it.

Feeling alone and tired, she turned from him and looked down at the white foam on the river, too far below them to seem turbulent and vicious. Yes, men would find their freedom, but how they would have to struggle for it ! She couldn't keep her thoughts from drifting back to the mountains and their unquestioning slumber. Back there, "mass-production" and "mass-

292

consumption" would fall like words from a foreign tongue. Imagine Britt as "mass-conscious" ! Her Britt.

"My people," she quoted softly, "shall abide in peaceful habitations, and in safe dwellings, and in quiet resting places."

Then Unthank looked at her. In her face was a light not borrowed from the moon. As she turned to him he could see the willow-green flecks in her eyes slipping up to their dark centre. Tiny wood-birds creeping to a forest pool. But that did not make him gentle.

"When ? Where ?" he asked, each word like a sharpened knife. She saw that he was suffering. It wasn't peace that he had read on the sky. "Where, Ishma ? In houses like Beverly's, where people live between two millstones, clamped by two fears —fear of the bigger competitors above them and the squirming workers below ? Or in the mill villages where men and women barely survive exhaustion ? Or is it on the farms, where they must work until they are half brutes and surrender to semi-existence ? Was it possible where you lived ? Was it quiet ? Was it peaceful ?"

"It seems so now. But I didn't know it then."

There was retreat in her voice, and yearning for the silent hill-tops. He saw her surrendering, running away.

"Ishma, let me tell you how old your thought is. Centuries before Christ the Chinese were trying to solve the problem of economic adjustment. They couldn't shift the burdens from the backs of human beings to machines, for the magic tools then existed only in the imagination of dreamers, like Aristotle. And when it is a question of my back or the other fellow's, it is always the other fellow's. Injustice seemed to be a condition of civilization. Philosophers, who knew courts and palaces and high places, were overcome with hopelessness and fled from society. That was their protest. They sought a hidden life on the farms, as laborers earning food and drink. 'The world is a seething torrent,' they said. 'There is no hope for it. Let us dig, and plant, and die in peace.' They were justified. The ideal of industrial unity had not been born. The medium for its birth was not in existence. All they could do was to protest with their lives against injustice and corruption. We are not so justified. We have the ideal, and the means to realize it. The ages have not passed in vain. With our bodies in the twentieth century, we don't want to clothe our minds with the habits of three thousand years ago, even the best of those habits. We are going to stay in the fight because it is a fight that can be won. Don't run away Ishma, because if you do you will find that you have to return. And three thousand years is a long way to travel, there and back."

Ishma leaned on the bridge railing, feeling chained to it. Of course she would have to stay in the fight. She would never see Spring on the hill-tops again. Unthank had wanted to bring eagerness and hope to her face, and was shocked by the despair he saw there. Looking at her troubled mouth, he was startled to find that he wanted to kiss it. "That's all for tonight," he said, hiding his discovery in a low ring of laughter. "We'll go home."

As they walked back he became self-accusing, remembering that she had been on her feet all day in the mill, and he had brought her on this long walk.

"I wish I could pension you, dearish, and have you work for me instead of Reece-Durkin. I need you awfully. Five new pellagra developments. Do you *have* to work in the mills ?"

"Yes. For a year at least. After that maybe I can help you, if you still want me. I'd be happier if I could use my time for families too poor and sick to pay for help."

"You love people, don't you ?"

"I believe I do, but I'm not always sure."

To his intense surprise he found himself saying, "Ishma, could you love *me?*" He, Derry Unthank, dedicated to the lonely road, asked that of a woman. He needn't have been alarmed. Ishma's hesitation soon became words.

"No. I love my husband. But it would be easy to worship you."

"Worship ! For Pete's sake, why ?"

"Because, more than anybody I know, or ever knew, you are trying to do what God ought to do. And I wish I knew how to help."

He saw the tears in her eyes. "Ishma, you are the great

Earth-mother. How do you happen to be in love with a mere husband?"

"I don't know. It just is."

"Rad's a decent sort, but you are so much more than that. I can't see how it happened."

She felt that her heart opened and looked out of her body. She couldn't hide it, and it didn't matter.

"I'm not married to Rad. My husband is back in the mountains."

Unthank didn't look toward her. He knew it would be several minutes before he could speak naturally or easily, and for that reason he kept silent. It would be cruel not to speak with a large, careless understanding. At last he looked, ready to smile, and said, "You love him, and you left him?"

"Life was hard up there. I *thought* it was. It was hard for him too. He had a heart like a song, and I was not helping keep it sweet. Perhaps I'm a racial product too. Material things have become a part of human beings, and I was aching for my share. Away off, up there, I felt loss like wounds. I didn't know. I had to come and see. And Rad was a way."

She tortured herself with the bare, sordid statement. But because he was silent she became defensive. "I tell you the life *was* hard!"

"Don't, Ishma! I know all about it. My own mother — it killed her — and her life was easier than her neighbors' lives."

"You wouldn't want me to work for you now."

"I wish you could begin tomorrow."

She leapt with resurrection. Derry Unthank knew the worst of her, and he was still her friend.

"I'll stay in the mills," she said, "until the doctor bills are paid. It's not fair to go off leaving Rad with a big debt and the house mortgaged on my account."

"I thought Beverly paid those bills."

"No. Rad owned his home, and Mr. Grant thought — they all thought that he ought to pay."

"I see. Thrift penalized as usual. No wonder it's scarce. Ishma, I'll see those doctors. And I'll see Beverly. You'll not have to pay another dollar."

"Yes, I will. They know I'm working it out. They think it is right. And I reckon it is, if anything is right."

"We know that nothing is right, but everything is going to be. That is our creed, Ishma. It will be well with the world some day, because we know that all is wrong with it now. That being the case, let's go by the Roast Pig and hear the committee on perfection devise ways and means. They'll be sitting up all night, talking, talking, talking, like real Russians."

They went by the Roast Pig, and Ishma, bright and fevered, listened until daylight, as if the murmur of those asseverating voices were the waters of life to her.

About a week later, she received a letter from Beverly Grant. Enclosed she found receipts for full payment of bills, signed by Doctors Benn and Maddux, and Rad's deed of trust to the Winbury Mortgage and Loan Company, duly cancelled by the Clerk of Court. Beverly wished her well, and hoped that her life in the future would be free from accidents.

Leta had run up to the mail-box and brought back the letter, commenting on its size and fatness before going into the kitchen which was now her unmolested province. Ishma sat so still with the letter in her lap that Rad asked her which of her pets was in trouble this time. She handed him the letter, not seeing him, staring steadily through the wall. Rad's reaction was as violent as Ishma's had been calm. He gave a whoop, and called Leta from the kitchen to hear him read it a second time.

"You can get yer radio now, Leet! Ish won't have to put in half her money on the doctor rogues."

"That'll be fine," said Leta, with small enthusiasm, and returned to her kitchen. Ishma came to life and followed her. She made several efforts to speak before her voice gave out a sound. Going to the faucet she filled a glass with water and drank it slowly.

"Leta," she began, when at last she could speak steadily, "you seem to be getting on so well with the housework and cooking, I think I'll go to Mildred's for a week or two, and help her with the children at night. She's about dead on her feet."

"Go, if you want to. I can manage." Leta turned her head

away as she spoke, but too late to conceal the sudden gleam in her eyes.

"I'll not tell Rad, Leta. He would try to argue me out of it. But when I don't come home tomorrow night, you tell him that I asked you to let him know where I was."

She spoke with lowered voice, careful of Rad in the living-room.

"I know you'll be good to him, and try to keep him from missing me. You know what he likes to eat. I can't tell you anything about that."

"You sure can't !"

"He's a little set in his ways, but when you know what they are it's easy enough to please him. I showed you how to fix the bed. And when you dust the mantel don't forget to put his pipe back in the same spot. And don't wind the clock. He always wants to do that."

"I'll keep him smilin' if there's any chance. You can stay as long as you want to."

"I'll be around in a week to see how you are getting along."

"You needn't be afraid I can't manage," said Leta, impatiently. Couldn't anybody see that she didn't need a boss over her ?

Ishma went back to the sitting-room where Rad was still mulling over the letter. His excitement had died down and he was quietly sucking in the full meaning of the good news. He felt Ishma's gaze upon him, and had no intimation that its warmth came from the kindliness of eyes that were saying goodbye. She could admit that, in an ordinary way, he was good to look at. He was keeping his hair well cut and smoothed, his shoulders were youthfully lifted, and he seemed to carry with him an air of subtle adventure. Leta, of course. He wasn't handsome like Britt with copper curls and fire-brown eyes, nor interesting like Derry with his pale face and black hair undulating from a high forehead. But he was a man whom a girl with intense domestic longings could find it easy to pet and amuse. Ishma could forgive Leta's intention to displace her. It was only the thoughtless cruelty of youth bent on getting what it wanted. Leta could fulfill her talent only as mistress of a home, and her Biblical momentum toward her goal ought to be commended. Ishma so

297

sincerely wished her happiness that she had an impulse to tell her there was no legal obstruction to her marriage with Rad. But if she did that, Leta might push him along too hastily. She knew that the old worship of herself was still in him. The look in his eyes as he lifted them from the letter, made her heart sink. She was still part and parcel of his life. But he desired Leta, more or less. Did he intend to play with the child ? To take advantage of her evident willingness to cuddle about him ? Would he refuse to marry her ? If that were true, how could she abandon Leta ? Genie was useless. Leta would drive her chariot of desire through any protest of her mother's.

The maternal spirit that was so strong in Ishma, leapt awake. Must she stay on guard a little longer ? But she couldn't stay. Not for one night, when it was possible to go.

Rad dropped the big letter. "Want to frame it, Ish ?" He was in fine humor and didn't notice that she made no reply. "It would 'a' been decenter of old Grant to have come across at first, that's all I've got to say to *him*. If he's expectin' 'much obliged' from me, he's not goin' to get it."

"I'll have to write him, Rad."

"That's your own business, but leave me out of it. I can forget the whole thing now, an' that's what I'm goin' to do."

He sat down. Ishma looked toward her hat. Rad wanted to know if she was going anywhere. If she was, he'd go along too. "We ought to celebrate, seems to me."

"It's — it's mill-folks, Rad. You wouldn't care about going."

"Oh, well ! How's your union comin' on ?"

He meant to be pleasant, but his tone was patronizing. He belonged to a carpenter's union, which was all right and proper, but a union of mill hands was a presumption, if no worse. They ought to take what they could get and be glad of it. Ish was a mill-worker, of course, but she was a wonder all by herself. She didn't rate with that trash. He didn't approve of her joining the union, but he could be good-natured about it, so he asked her how it was comin' on, just to show her.

"About as well as yours, Rad."

"Don't get mad now. You're tetchy lately. Workin' too hard. We'll fix that. You're goin' to quit the mills now. I can take care of you. And you been losin' too much sleep over at Mildred's. I'd ruther hire a nurse for the brats."

Already his pockets were full. Ishma was wondering if she could manage a quarrel. But that might heat, rather than cool his devotion.

"It's good to lose sleep in a good cause. It helps more than resting quiet sometimes."

"What you mean ?" His voice went down. Leta would be listening. "If you're hintin' about — what we know — I'm ready to go to the preacher's right now."

"Well, I'm not !" She had not intended to be so abrupt, but the truth had leapt from her.

"An' you ain't ever goin' to be, I'm thinkin'. You can't talk debts any more. What else you got to put up ?"

"There *is* something else, Rad," she said gently. "I've noticed something about you that makes me afraid to marry you."

"Afraid ?" This was so new that it made him gasp.

"It's so, Rad. You like for people to think well of you, you'd like to be a church member up on Laird street, and pass the plate or something. You look well in a Sunday get-up. You look like a tax-payer — a man whose vote counts. And you want to associate with your own kind — with grocers, plumbers, carpenters, and that sort. I'm all for the mill-folks, and I'll always be. You can't change me, Rad. And you'll not get far on your road with me for a wife. You — "

"For God's sake, don't talk so loud ! An' talk sense !"

"I'd better go help Leta," she said, getting out quickly and leaving her barbs well planted. She had spoken Rad's own thoughts, but he had to get acquainted with them. He looked after her. No use to follow. They couldn't talk before Leta. He would go into the yard and blow off.

Ishma had decided to warn Leta about being too free with Rad. She couldn't stay on guard. Whatever happened, she knew that she would never enter Rad's bed-room again. She must go.

"Leta, what do you think about my getting Grandma Huff to stay with you while I am gone ?"

"I think you're crazy !"

"Grandma has a sharp eye and a quick tongue. Folks wouldn't

have anything to say about my leaving you here with Rad if she was around. They'd say nothing could get by *her*. You're so young, Leta. I don't want any harm to come to you from people's bad thoughts."

Leta turned on her, white and hard.

"It ain't no worse for me to be here with Rad than for you to be !"

"What in the world —" Ishma paused, amazed, at Leta's fierceness.

"I can't stand it much longer. You know he likes me best. And you're not married to him. He'd marry me this very night if you's gone!"

"Leta ! Who told you ?"

"I heard all about it over at Cindy's, 'fore she died. Her boy, Martin, sat up with me one night in the kitchen, and he told me all about you. I've never breathed it. I swore to him I wouldn't. You can get by with anything looks like, an' folks'll take up for you. Martin said he wouldn't do you harm for anything in the world, but he was tellin' me the truth. I've never told it, not even to mother. I've done you a big favor keepin' it to myself. I'm honest more ways than one."

Ishma's anger was mixed with deep disgust. She opened the door to the living-room to see if Rad had heard, and saw that he was still in the yard. He was near the gate, moving about slowly, apparently seeing nothing and thinking hard.

"He might have heard you, Leta."

"I wish he had ! It's time the thing was settled. He ought to choose between us."

Ishma smiled. "Shall I call him in and ask him to do that ?"

Leta began a wild weeping, and surrendered. "No. You know he would take you. But you don't want him. You know you don't. He likes me till you come around, then he forgets I'm alive. And you know you don't want him. It wouldn't hurt you to give him up, but it would kill me. And he ought to marry me now, after I — I — "

Her face, a bright red, and her eyes filled with a hurrying, reckless shame, astounded Ishma with the truth.

300

"You mean that you — already — "

"Yes. That night you stayed out."

The vicious cut was not noticed by Ishma. She was asking herself how soon she could get away. Would it be an hour — a minute ?

"Leta, I would like to walk out right now and never come back — never see you or Rad again. But do you think that he would marry you if I did ?"

"If you'll tell him you're going, and make him believe it, I know he'll marry me."

"Very well." She opened the door and called to Rad, who came in slowly.

"What's the matter with you women ? I'm hungry. Can't the two of you get supper ? You ain't been quarrellin' ?"

"No. We've come to an understanding, Rad. Leta will make you the kind of a wife you need."

"What ?"

"Just what you need, Rad. You will be proud of her. More and more I am going to be what you dislike. I'm going to stand with the mill people through everything, and that may put me where you'll be ashamed to own me. Leta won't make any trouble for you."

"She knows ?"

"Yes. Surely you didn't think she would go as far as she did with a man that she knew couldn't marry her !"

Rad's mouth fell open. "Go as far — " He stammered, and turned as if he meant to fly.

"Wait ! Let's have it out, Rad. You can't expect me to stay with you now, when I know about you and Leta. I've felt for a long time that I'd be doing you wrong to let you marry me. You wouldn't be happy. You don't quite know it, but you're tired of me, Rad."

"It's a lie ! I'd ruther look at you an' have you around than the purtiest girl in the world ! You're a lot more than looks, Ish. You've always been, you'll always be !"

Leta's face was bloodless. She gazed at Rad with a terrible fear in her eyes. Ishma could have wept over her. She went to Rad, and started to lay her arm about his shoulders, but checked her gesture. She wanted to plead for Leta, not for herself.

"I'm going, Rad. Promise me that you will marry Leta. If you don't promise, you won't keep me anyway, and you're not likely to see me again. Promise, and we'll always be friends."

"What'll folks say about you?" he asked between scowls and sobs.

"I'm not afraid. I have my job, and I have friends who will stand by me. I'm not the coward I once was."

"You've never been a coward — you've been the best — oh, Ish, you don't mean it!"

"You'll be happy with Leta. You know I can't stay here after what has happened."

Rad raged at Leta. "Whad you let it out for? Ain't you ashamed o' nothin'?"

"Listen, Rad. You are twelve years older than Leta. *You* are to blame, not that child. If you marry her, I can respect you again."

She opened a closet and began gathering up a few things which she put into a small bag.

"I'm going to Mildred's," she said, putting on her hat. "You'll find me there if you need me. You get the license, Rad, and I'll meet you and Leta tomorrow night at eight o'clock. We'll go to preacher Stiles —"

She stopped. She couldn't expose their lives like that. Rad was breaking out again.

"What'll folks think about *me*? You mayn't keer about yerself, but I've got something I'm not for throwin' away — a good rep in this town! What'll they think o' me? Turnin' you out, an' takin' up with a kid! An' Sid Brinn wants me to join the church. I'm promised. *You* don't keer, but I do. When folks find out how we been livin', what'll they think o' *me*?"

Ishma put her bag down and seated herself. She didn't intend to disgrace Rad. Here was a problem.

"Let's think it out. There's a way, I'm sure. Get the supper on the table, Leta. Rad's hungry. Your mother must have stopped somewhere."

302

"I won't eat a bite, Ish, unless you eat too," said Rad.

"All right, I will."

They had supper, and Ishma talked and smiled so happily that Rad, in amazement, ate a full meal.

"You'll have a fine cook in your house, Rad," she said, while her mind was racing in a strong undercurrent to save his good name.

"I believe I've got it. We'll get on the bus tomorrow and go to Charlotte. Leta's name is Mary Aleta, and yours is William Radburn. We'll get the license for William R. Bailey and Mary A. Unthank. You can be married right there in the Clerk's office. We'll take Genie for one witness, I'll be another, and somebody in the office can be the third one. We'll come back, and I'll leave your bed and board, Rad. I'll let folks know that I've left you and that I don't intend to go back. They can think we've quarrelled about the union, or anything they please. We needn't have any mean talk, and I'll take the blame for leaving you. Folks will be sorry for you, and say you ought to have a divorce. You can talk around about getting one, and after a while you and Leta can take another trip to Charlotte and come back married. Nobody will say anything. You can join the church too, Rad, and that will help some. It'll be easy enough."

"Why can't we wait then? Why do we have to get married tomorrow?"

"Because I'm not going to stay here after what you've done, and I'm not going to leave Leta with you until I know you are married. So that's settled. I'm going to a meeting now, but I'll be back tonight, and we'll start early tomorrow. Don't wait up. I may be late, and I'll sleep on the sofa."

She glanced at Leta as she went out, and saw that she was flushed, happy, seductive. Rad was not looking up, but he would be consoled.

Ishma's plan was carried through the next day. Leta was grateful, and surprisingly timid. Rad was sulky, uncertain, and half happy. Ishma kept herself calm and practical. But as soon as the ceremony was over, relief and triumph surged through her insupportably. She had to get away by herself.

"Genie, you go along with Leta and Rad. There's somebody I

303

want to see in Charlotte — one of our organizers — and I'll take a later bus."

Before they could question her, she was gone. Gone to walk in the air of liberty, and faint under the breathless sweep of it. Before she was a block away, she had fallen to the sidewalk, from sheer, trembling joy. Her heart seemed to stop beating, her knees would not support her.

A taxi-driver and his elderly passenger picked her up and rushed her to a hospital. By the time they reached the door, Ishma was smilingly alive, and refused to go in.

"I'm so much obliged," she said, and opened her purse. But compensation was refused. Such radiant life after so complete a swoon, made both driver and his fare wonder. The taxi man seemed to mix her up with something celestial. "Where could she 'a' dropped from ?" he asked his gentleman, who also seemed to be meditating on miracles as they drove away from her smile and the tremblingly conquering wave of her hand.

CHAPTER XII

EXTERNALLY the next three months were never very clear to Ishma. Afterwards, striving to give them coherence, she could picture only a staccato of events vivid against a vague, unreal flow. But within herself there was light, there was surety.

She forgot Rad. Several times he tried to see her, so Mildred said, and she put her mind on him with effort, not successful enough to give her a disturbing pang. She was free! Every day she went to the mill and walked up and down in her alley from six to six, with an hour at noon spent on her feet as she talked "union." Communication was cautious and disguised under the big roof, but it was understood. She learned how to talk to a worker's back and shoulders, making apparently casual words carry a hot stream of meaning. She ate her lunch drifting and talking. Aching feet did not matter. She was free!

Mildred was glad to share her home with Ishma. Her children were frail, and never missed any of the diseases that were always threading their devitalizing course through the half-fed mill-towns. In slow file they went through the irritant fire of measles and the raspings of "black-face whooping-cough." A threat of small-pox shadowed the air for a time. But the shadow passed. Mildred and Ishma breathed again. Spindle Hill, absorbed to the last gasp in getting a living, could not indulge in the panic that precipitates an epidemic. Ishma looked in the mirror at her weary eyelids and smiled. Weariness meant nothing to youth and the hope that was hers. That greater part of herself, meant to march with the racial entity, was out of its prison. Her body might grow cold and rot with death, but here was something of herself that would go as far as mankind. She ceased to confuse her liberation with escape from Rad, and drank of freedom at its timeless source.

Weary days, and nights of too brief sleep, left her joy untouched. She was upheld by that supreme ecstasy, the conscious-ness of transmuting daily life into an ideal. She was part of the creative gesture, building a brighter world; a world so near that she could stretch her hands over the border and feel them tingling with its sun. The dry bread that she ate at Mildred's table was sweet with life to come. The tri-weekly pot of beans, the ever recurrent potatoes — boiled in their jackets so that nothing should be lost, and eaten without butter — became an endurable prelude to the feast from which none would be turned away.

In spare wedges and slices of time she continued her studies. Derry Unthank supplied books with the zeal of a teacher who has found the beloved disciple. He had led her over the long outline of man's story; the struggle in the dawn; the serf ages; the capture of the world by commerce: the final intrenchment of capitalism behind industrial machinery and the guns of an army. She was now studying, in bloody segments, the emergence of labor. The failures, the tramplings to death, the shortened lives of whole generations of toilers, did not terrify her or weaken her faith. With a mental eye that covered the long trail of desperation and courage, she saw the constant resurge of mass-power to greater meaning and circumference. Workers could not forever feed their lives to society without transforming it to their own blood and bone.

Ishma laughed when she thought of the illustrated history that had been such thrilling food in her childhood. A painted curtain that had never risen on the play. How small seemed that world which she had set out to find at the heels of Rad Bailey! She had fumbled at a narrow gate and it had opened wide as the footprints of man.

"What's to become of us, Ishma?" asked Job Waygood. "I hearn today, over in Kannapolis, they've got a new machine where they can put one man to 'tendin' a hundred and eighteen looms. I mind me when a man who could 'tend thirty-six was the pride o' the county. Most of us couldn't do more than fifteen or twenty. A hundred and eighteen! What's to become of us? Reckon we'd better go in fer smashin' the machinery?"

"You don't want to smash human progress, Job, and you couldn't if you wanted to."

306

"We don't want to starve nuther, but that's what it's comin' to, looks like. There's more'n me ready fer smashin'."

"You'd only smash yourselves. That's what happened to the weavers in England over a hundred years ago. We don't want to repeat mistakes, Job."

She told him the agonizing story of the English and Scotch weavers.

"But what are we goin' to do, Ishma ?"

"Just what we're doing now — organize. We're going to get together till there's not a working man left out, white, black, yellow or brown, the world over. When a new machine is put in, we'll not merely install it and run it. We'll own it. That machine, instead of making profits for one family up in Pawtucket, will shorten the working day for a hundred families in North Carolina, and do it without cutting down their bread supply. You'll have time to play a game of horse-shoes after work, maybe."

Job, whose outlet for adventure lay in playing horse-shoes, had been known to instigate games on Sunday for lack of daylight through the week.

"Own it !" he said, grinning. "Shucks ! I'll be dead a hundred years 'fore that." His grin faded. "I'm a union man. What good is it doing me ?"

Ishma looked at his shoes, with toes in a hard, turned-up wrinkle, and the heels worn off. She knew how uncomfortable it must be to walk for hours on a hot floor in such shoes. She looked at his thin attempt to hide his nakedness, and recalled Derry's remark that "The idiotic mill-owners could increase their market right at home by making it possible for the worker to wear two shirts a week instead of one shirt for two weeks." Not only was Job's clothing thin. The attempt of nature to cover his bones was successful by a narrow squeak. But there was an undefeated gleam in his eyes, and Ishma answered the gleam instead of his question.

"Let's not think of what a little piece of a union like ours can not do, but what a union that covers the earth *can* do. If all the little pieces said 'it's no use,' we'd go on slaving to the end of time. It's no good for the workers in the North to have unions so long as the mill men can come down here and find slaves that will go on producing for them. It's no good for the workers of America to have unions so long as Germany, England, and other big nations can keep their workers in slavery and produce goods at less cost than we do. If we are pushed to the wall in spite of our union, it isn't because the union is wrong but because it isn't big enough. It's because it doesn't cover the earth. We'll do what we can to make it big enough, instead of punching holes in it. And here's a new leaflet that will pep you up, Job."

He took the leaflet, grinning again. "I ain't skeered except when I begin to think about my fam'ly. If we do win out in God's time, Ishma, an' life gits easy fer ever'body, won't the big fam'lies eat up the earth? Won't there be too many of us? I've hearn that."

"You've been listening to Beckwith."

Job flushed. "He's a college perfessor."

"Yes. And we've found out who's paying him to mix around here. The Greybank mill."

"You shore o' that?"

"It's absolute fact, Job."

"Doggone his doggoned skin! He set around my house fer two hours last night."

"When you listened to him, you were listening to the clink of Greybank money."

"The doggoned snooper!"

"He had a lot to say, I reckon."

"He shore did."

"And today you are talking about smashing with your hands instead of fighting with your brains, and you're asking what's the use of a union. I thought you had a better nose than that, Job. You ought to have smelt the Greybank in that fellow."

"He sounded like he knowed something. An' when he said we'd always had wars an' always would, an' we'd always had spells o' hard times, an' always would, an' if life got too easy there'd be so many of us we'd eat up the earth like the locusts in Kansas, I couldn't think o' how to dispute it. It sounded sort o' like it might be thataway."

"He's right about the wars and the hard times so long as we

have to make profits for the family up in Pawtucket before we can spend a dollar for ourselves. But we know that's not going to last, Job. We're going to quit that foolishness. And about our overrunning the earth, we could make this little State of North Carolina support everybody in America if we had to. It will be a long time before the earth is used up. Our own country could take care of every human being now alive. Think how much that would leave for the people to come? In Africa there are the Congo lands, with hardly anybody in them, and water-power that would cover Niagara a dozen times — all waiting for people to be born. And there's the valley of the Amazon, as big as the United States, waiting for the engineer and the farmer. Only there won't be any farmers. There'll be giant farming industries, tilling earth with machinery, and sending food in airships to any place where men want it. It will be a long time before we need to worry about using up the earth. You've heard of the great deserts. They'll be turned into grain-fields, with water from miles and miles away. Why, Job, if we come to it, we can use Greenland and the lands around the South Pole. We can cover acres and acres with glass and warm them with electricity, if ever we need them!"

"Gee!" said Job, his widened eyes and mouth making her information flow with a rush.

"We'll hitch up the Gulf Stream, and make it warm any part of the world. If we begin to feel hungry because there are so many of us, we'll think up a new way to get food. But it will be a thousand years before we have to study about that, and by that time we'll know how to have just the children we want, and not one over. We won't have five and save three. We're learning that now, and we'll know a lot more about it by the time supplies run short. We'll have the kind we want too, and not have to sift a hundred to get one we're proud of."

She fingered another leaflet in her blouse pocket, but she didn't give it to Job. His eyes were on the ground and his face was too red.

"I hope the perfessor will come around again. I b'lieve I could give him some back-talk now."

"Fine, Job! See you at the meeting tonight."

But not all of her interviews were successful. A worker could be incurably patient, or incurably suspicious. Behind both patience and suspicion was the wild fear of losing a job; the fear that gave panic or numbness to the blood. The wolf was nearer than the door. It sniffed no longer above the cradle. Its tooth was in the father's flesh.

The mill workers were getting used to the thought that a strike must certainly come within a few months, when suddenly it was there. Five men in the Greybank were spotted as members of the union and dismissed. The following morning, just before daylight, the night-shift walked out, and knotted expectantly at the gate, waiting for the day-shift. There was no shouting and little talking, but a good deal of rubbing together of arms and shoulders in the unfriendly half-light. The primitive speech of touch was more reassuring than words. They had struck for self-preservation, which united them back to roots deeper than any later acquirements of civilization, such as putting on language. When the day-shift came up and learned what had happened, more than half of them refused to enter the mill. Only about three hundred of the two thousand Greybank "hands" were finally inside. Not more than a third of the seventeen hundred strikers were members of the union, but they trooped together to a vacant lot back of the union head-quarters and listened to their leader, Amos Freer. Amos knew what to do. He had begun his training for leadership as a boy in the noted Lawrence strike, and he was still warm from victorious service in the long drawn-out textile strike at New Bedford. The National Textile Workers Union had sent him to Winbury as an organizer. For three months he had been living in Spindle Hill, getting acquainted and measuring up his material. He knew whom to place on committees, and within a few hours an eager management was at work. That afternoon Amos led the picket line. Ishma watched him with wide, drinking eyes, as he spoke in low, assuring tones, dispatching this man or that woman, this boy or that girl, to lines of duty. She felt left out, unnoticed. But before night-fall he sent for her.

"There are two places where I'd like to put you, Mrs. Bailey, but naturally you can occupy but one. The first is inside the mill — "

"Inside."

"Yes. Among the scab-workers. The bosses will bring in help from Georgia and South Carolina as fast as they can get it. And they'll induce workers to come from other mills by a temporary increase in wages. I'd like to have you inside to take care of them, and get accurate reports for us."

Ishma's high ardor went stale. To scab! To spy! Even for the cause, could she do that? Amos Freer read her heart as easily as he read her face.

"I didn't think you'd like it. But you'd be fine in there. You give men and women faith, and they need it. Courage breeds courage, and you've plenty of that."

"What was the other work?" she asked feebly.

"Visiting the homes and looking specially after the children."

"I'll take that!"

"You'll take it?" He seemed amused. "You've a big lesson in discipline to learn, Mrs. Bailey. You'll go where you are sent." His smile spread until her startled face reflected it. "But I'm going to send you to the children. Eva Blaine will give you instructions."

He held out his hand, and she didn't know how hard she pressed it. But Amos knew. He was used to being a refuge, a safe shore for impulsive tides.

Eva Blaine was one of the group who had come into the community with Freer as aids and speakers in the work of organization. Her small body was packed with efficiency. Tucking her arm into Ishma's, though she had to reach up to do it, they went into immediate session.

Within three days Ishma could have supplied any demanded report concerning the children whose welfare was involved in the strike. When fearful mothers asked tremblingly if they could be sure of food for the children, she would fill them with an almost blithe confidence. Not only the children, but parents would be fed. They wouldn't have too much, perhaps not always enough, but they could count on getting as much as they had been able to buy while they worked. Not a family in the mill lived on full rations every day that came. They couldn't all have milk, for instance, but the children and the sick could have it. There might be no meat, except a bit of salt pork for seasoning, but there would be bread, potatoes, beans and onions; perhaps sugar. Committees were going among the farmers and getting donations of vegetables, meal and molasses. Many of the small business men of Winbury were contributing. The small business man knew where his trade came from, and he meant to keep, if he could, the good-will of the mill-workers through the passing storm. Also, as Ishma could tell them, they would have help from the International Workers Relief, whose agents had appeared on the ground as by magic. But of course it would take a great deal to feed two thousand men and women, and an apparently innumerable troop of children, three times a day. Meals might be cut down to two for grownups, she told the anxious mothers, but children would not be stinted.

"I could live on one potato a day an' never miss the picket line," said Grandma Swithin, fifty years old, and eyes in a fiery dance. She was the first to be bayonetted. But that was later, when the strike was three weeks old.

Ishma very soon knew every sick and feeble child in the strikers' homes, and their special need. She knew those who were in school, and those who were out, and for what reason; those who had proper adult care, and those who had little or none; and many other things. Amos Freer summoned her for a talk, and when they were through he gave her one of his famous composite smiles, too sad for cynicism, too cynical for tears.

"Let their talents alone, Mrs. Bailey. Don't thrust any little geniuses upon us. We'll be lucky if we can put food in their mouths."

Ishma met his smile sternly. "Mr. Freer, every child in Russia gets a free musical education if he wants it."

Amos broke into laughter. "You jump too fast, comrade. We haven't got to Russia. This is only a tiny corner of a great capitalist nation, and we are in an acute struggle for bread. Bread — bread — bread! Don't forget that. And let me mention that you look a bit thin yourself. Are you getting your share of food ?"

"More than I need. I'm helping at the Roast Pig, so I sha'n't have to draw on the relief. I get plenty, but it's sweltery in that kitchen."

"How have you had time to cook and get up all this information ?"

"I help only in the middle of the day, and about two hours at night. It's true, what I'm telling you. There are about forty children that ought to be sent out to the country somewhere — on the farms, or up in the mountains — "

"Don't jump so fast, daughter."

"They'll die down here."

"Bread — bread — bread. We'll not let them die of starvation at least."

"The W. I. R. — "

"Yes. Remember that the 'I' stands for International. What does that mean ? Relief jobs in every country of the world. Ten thousand strikers in Germany, five thousand in Jugo-Slavia, twenty-five thousand in Massachusetts, fifteen thousand in California, millions the world over. They'll do what they can for us, but they can't do everything. Aside from the help of a few generous liberals, their funds are made up of pennies and dimes from the workers who haven't lost their jobs today but may lose them tomorrow. We can't expect them to give our children a change of climate. They'll help get us bread, and they'll help get us tents when the strikers are thrown out of their homes — "

"Thrown out ? Do you mean they'll be thrown out ?"

She knew from hearsay, and from her reading, that this usually happened, but she was aghast before the imminent fact.

"Just as soon as the enemy becomes convinced that we can't be bought off, and that we're not to be scared away by bayonets, we'll be put to every expense that can be forced upon us. They know now that we can't be scared."

"The bayonets look awful, but the troops are rather nice," said Ishma, recovering a smile, and remembering that she was due on the picket line. "They don't hurt anybody, just drive us along.

They laughed yesterday when Grandma Swithin told them that if they were her boys they wouldn't be too big for her to spank."

When she left Amos, his blue eyes followed her for a moment. She was good material. He was only thirty, and unmarried, but there was nothing greedy in his pursuing gaze. For him, women rated according to their value to his cause. If he had a special tenderness, it was for little children. They clung to him and chattered as to an equal. One night, on the speaker's stand, when he had not been billed to speak, he announced, "I've got to say a few words, because a little chap here has just told me that he came to hear *me.*" His only quarrel since taking charge of the strike had been with a father who was punishing his child with more severity than the slight occasion called for. Freer ordered him to stop, and the man turned on him.

"I'll do as I please with what's mine ! And what are you goin' to do about it ?"

"He's not yours," said Amos. "He belongs to humanity. And if you please to abuse him, I'll please to have you arrested."

"Kain't no dern furriner talk to me like that," said the man, advancing. A woman took him by the arm. "Freer ain't no furriner. He's got blue eyes, an' skin like a baby. He's got light hair. It's mighty nigh red. He ain't no furriner. You can look at him an' see he ain't."

The quarrel was adjusted, but an echo of it got to the Winbury *Comet* and reverberated through the country as a disgraceful scrimmage. It was an example of the lawlessness advocated by Freer and the degenerates associated with him. Perhaps the law-abiding citizens would not have to clean out the nest of vipers after all. They'd bite themselves and die of their own poison.

Ishma had doubted her eyes on first reading the columns of vituperation that glared from the *Comet*.

"But it's lying," she said to Ella Ramsey, holding up the incredible sheet. "They call Amos Freer an outlaw — 'a ruthless brute, leading the ignorant and harmless into strife and murder.' They're saying that of Amos Freer !"

" 'Course they are," said Ella, undisturbed. She had lived through the Concord strike of 1921.

"But look ! Here's a letter that the same as says he ought to be lynched. 'If the law will not act, people who love their homes and children, should take the punishment of this scoundrel into their own hands. We are not advocates of lynching, but brutes less guilty than this man have swung at midnight in our home-loving county.' Oh, they'll kill him !"

"They'll be put to some trouble first. He's sleepin' with four boys on guard, an' their guns handy."

"Look at all the names signed to that letter ! And one is the Reverend James Mullen. A preacher ! A Christian !"

"Yeah, but remember who pays his salary. 'Tain't us mill folks. We only make the money that pays him."

The strike had moved along a customary course. On the second day troops had been summoned to combat disorder that was practically non-existent. Five companies of militia had appeared, and with fixed bayonets stopped the march of men, women and children around the mill. There was no rioting, no assault; but more or less pushing, tugging and bickering. Behind the doors of the textile lords there was disappointment. They couldn't jail leaders without some justification for arrests. Police and militia were in the field. Why didn't something happen ? Something *must* happen. The obedient press yelped, loud and long, but no yelp in return came from the people. Was the mob spirit dead ? Had the rabble begun to think ? Was there no heat left in the veins of kukluxery ?

The noisy *Comet* became noisier, and the farmers and the rabble did not rise to its call. Strangely, unreasonably, popular sympathy seemed to be with the strikers. The "race issue" was dragged out. Never had this failed the forces of disruption. But now no fires could be kindled by shouting "nigger lover," and "Would you want your sister to marry a black man ?" Nobody seemed to have a sister in danger of being led to the altar by a person whose color was that of Hannibal, Toussaint L'Overture, Kahma, and the wise Mdombe, of the Balataleles. The fires would not kindle. They sputtered a little here and there, and died to cold ashes. A new and unheard of leaven seemed to be at work. Negroes were admitted to strikers' meetings; they were accepted as members of the union — that infernal new kind of union they could neither bribe nor "stomp" the life out of.

315

To aid the hesitant militia, and give more power to the "stomping" process, the committee of one hundred was organized among the scabs, foremen and superintendents. Backing the committee were politicians, attorneys in the pay of mill owners, business men, preachers and other representatives of law and order. Now something would happen!

Ishma awoke one morning to find Mildred sitting by her cot, waiting to relate the tale of the night. Over a hundred masked men had broken the union headquarters into splinters, and raided the relief store. All of the food had been thrown out, trampled and befouled. Packages had been torn open, sacks of flour ripped up, cans of milk beaten in with hammers, and beans, lard, syrup, mixed with mud and water. Nothing was left. The "rather nice" militia had slept quietly not two blocks away, safeguarding with polite inattention, law and order as the bosses saw it. Two police badges, a black-jack, and tools identified as belonging to the Greybank mill, were found among the ruins of the headquarters.

"There'll be nothing to eat today," said Mildred, weeping for her children.

They went without dinner, but by night-fall the country had responded and food was coming in. The attempt of "law and order" to "stomp" out rebellion and save civilization by splintering a few boards and defiling a car-load of food, had failed. Sympathy for the strikers rose, spread, and found its way to the far corners of the State. The bosses did not see it or feel it. They pushed on with the fight. Three of the military companies were withdrawn and their places taken by special deputies; men of no wisdom and little mercy.

The days flowed by in an ugly dream for Ishma. With unbelieving eyes she saw women prodded in the back, their arms cruelly twisted, children with bleeding legs, Grandma Swithin with a two-inch cut on her shoulder, harmless pedestrians scattering into yards and climbing banks for safety. She saw a woman of nearly sixty years beaten over the head until her eyes were closed and blackened, a woman who was not even a picket-line offender. A boy was stuck so deep that he was rushed to a hospital instead of jail. Later came rumors of blood-poisoning.

316

Leaders of the line were daily seized, thrown into cars and carried to prison, where they were denied water and tortured with vile fumes. They were bailed out as soon as possible, but it was difficult to get enough money for all who were imprisoned. The International Labor Defense was helping valiantly, rapidly exhausting its funds and trenching drastically on its sources of supply.

Ishma never led the line. She with her two adjutants, Mildred and Em Wallace, had no time for days and nights in jail.

When the deputies had come into the field with their guns, Amos had difficulty in persuading the mountain men to peace. They hunched their shoulders, grinned, and announced that they had guns o' their own, an' it was time to git 'em out.

"We've always been free-blooded," they said, "from time back."

"Yes, your forefathers went into the mountains to get rid of bosses," Amos admitted, "but you've come back to the bosses' country."

" 'Tain't fair fer all the guns to be on one side."

"No. Fairness is not the question. What could your few guns do against the army of the United States ?"

"These men ain't in the army."

"But the army is back of them. Try a shot at them, and you'll find out."

"I've got a boy in that army," said Tod Whisenhunt, struck by a thought. "Next time he comes home on leave, I'll have something to tell him."

"That's what we want," said Amos. "Fathers who know enough to tell their boys something when they come home. I'll bet you, Tod, that up in the mountains you were a bit proud when Jim came back in uniform, and you let him do the talking."

Tod's grin was sour. "Don't ask me what I think o' that uniform now. I'd like to git holt o' Jim's an' make a skunk bed out of it."

There were younger men of the lowlands who stood with the mountaineers for guns. They were of a generation not overshadowed, as their parents were, by the thought of what the mill barons had done for the "poor white." They read in the papers of the occasional visits of northern magnates to their hold-

317

ings in Winbury, their compliments to the enterprising little city, their pleasure in being connected with the forward looking element of the great, new South, and their regret that pressing interests must limit their stay to the few hours snatched on the way to Palm Beach, etc. They looked, this younger generation, at the rising mansions of their own barons; their estates with rolling acres of cool woodlands, and stretches of golf green; their automobiles purring along the highways with the dignity of the best models; their snappy roadsters making a gay, transient blur to the eye, and leaving a whiff of contempt not so transient. They looked at these things, and began to think of what they, the trash, the cattle, the despised millhands, had done for the barons. "We whipped the British at King's Mountain," they said, straightening their thin shoulders. "Reckon a little o' this country belongs to us."

"That's right, buddies," said the mountain men. "Don't let nobody run over you as long as you can crook yer arm 'round a gun."

It was some time before Amos could make them see that it was better *tactics* to go unarmed. They finally surrendered to that word, and no weapon was carried on the picket line. This did not mean that the strikers were passive. The women, in particular, resisted arrest. When Anna Jenkins objected to being pushed roughly along by a soldier, and he ignored her objection, she struck him over the head with a stick, and rebelled so vigorously that three brother soldiers were called up to help take her to jail. Anna was the mother of four children, the oldest only five years of age. The youngest had been but two months in this great land of opportunity for all. The mother's last pay envelope had contained four dollars for three night's work of eleven hours each, and this probably was bearing on her mind when her stick fell so heavily. Certainly it was not well-fed muscle that gave it heft. Anna explained her stubbornness about going to jail by saying that "her baby needed her breast." It took one hundred dollars of the strikers' funds to return this mother to her children.

More and more unreal became the life that flowed around Ishma. But there were days that wrote on her soul with fiery realism, and for months came back in her dreams.

318

When the Mill Company began to put families out of their houses, those most active in the strike were chosen for eviction, as a lesson to the more faint-hearted. This failed to intimidate, and the Company went at it more heartily with mass evictions. Fifty families were thrown out in one day. The houses of sympathizers were soon overflowing, and could hold no more. Families, with their belongings, were huddled in alleys, in yards, by the street side, taking rain and sun, light and darkness with the stolidity of the stunned, or the courage of the defiant. A few were in tears, and a few looked about them like incredulous children. Had this thing come on them? their eyes seemed to appeal. The union had promised tents, and no tents were forthcoming. The deputies strutted about, smelling vilely of whiskey, telling the huddled women that's what they got for believing goddamned foreigners, red Russians, and people who didn't believe in no god.

"You listen here," said Ella Ramsey, whose family was among the first to be put out. "Down in South Carolina, at Ware Shoals, the strikers wouldn't have anything to do with outside leaders — told 'em to go away an' they'd make their own fight an' their own peace. They knew the boss had a heart an' they'd get to it. They went on the picket line carryin' Bibles an' singin' hymns. An' what happened to 'em? They're beat an' scattered an' their homes gone, starvin' in this hole an' that. Their fight 's clean lost, same as if they hadn't been carryin' Bibles an' singin' hymns. If you was carryin' a Bible, an' a thug twisted yer arm, or struck you with a black-jack, it would hurt just as bad as if you'd left yer Bible at home. It would hurt worse, 'cause you'd been a fool in the bargain, an' that would make you feel like you wanted to wallop anything you could hit. Now we're goin' to stick to our leaders. You hear that? Amos Freer is a different stripe to them black-headed thieves that took our money in nineteen and twenty-one an' run with it. He'll stick to us as long as we stick to the strike. Here, you women!" she called to all within hearing, "let's sing 'Solidarity' fer these nice fellers. If they're goin' to hang around, smellin' so sweet, we've got to entertain 'em."

The women crowded up, and all who could sing poured the

319

strong words of their favorite song into the ears of the deputies. Those who couldn't sing were even more effective in the attempt.

In some of the houses there were sick children, but the Company doctor was there to testify that they could be carried out safely, and evictions were not halted for so slight a circumstance.

Thelma Rowe was expecting a baby. Seven months before, when her husband died, she had gone to work. Nine dollars a week had to provide for herself and three children. She didn't join the union. She was afraid. That nine dollars had to come or the children would starve. The union might help for a while, but if the strikers didn't win, where would she be then? On the blacklist, and nobody would give her work. She had to stay with the Company. But her loyalty didn't save her. When she grew too heavy to work, the Company wanted the house. Hadn't they been exceptionally kind already? Letting her occupy the place when it was their rule that every house should hold at least two able-bodied workers? The welfare department sent a representative to her. She was told that her fare would be paid to her sister's, in South Carolina.

"No," said Thelma. "My sister's got it as hard as I have. They're strikin' in Ware Shoals too."

What could be done with a person so obstinate, except to repossess themselves of their own property? A Georgia family with three working members was ready to go into the building. Mills couldn't be run on sentiment. They had to make money or shut down. The Rowe woman was suspected of sympathy with the strikers anyway. This sympathy had to be stamped out or they would never get through with the job of cleaning up.

Thelma looked up at Ishma, her face dead-white, with red spots coming and going in it, and said, "I'm gettin' sick."

She was in a rocker, her household things piled about her. "Somebody find the legs to that stove 'fore they're clean gone." A neighbor got busy hunting the stove-legs. Ishma saw a dark, curly head poked from behind a wash-stand. Near her, a little girl was trying to get under some pillows that lay on the ground, their ticking bare and dirty. A two-year old was playing with a broken sugar bowl. "It was my mother's sugar bowl," said Thelma, a big tear falling. "But it don't matter now. I told

320

that Company doctor I was gettin' sick, an' they mustn't put me out. An' he said, 'No, Mis' Rowe, you don't play no tricks on me. You'll go a week yet.' An' here I'm like you see."

"Ay," said a neighbor, "these are awful times, but maybe they could be worse. Miss Blaine says we're not havin' it so hard as she's seen it in places up North. She says for us to keep in heart, an' that's what you got to do, Thelma. She told me about two women in a strike up North who were big like you, an' they went on the picket line, thinkin' the police would be too 'shamed to hurt 'em. But they got beat up so bad their babies were born an' they nearly died. No danger o' that happenin' to you. The deppities won't lay hands on you."

"But you see where I am. I'm terrible sick. I wanted to hit that Company doctor over the head when he told me I'd go a week." The pink spots went suddenly from her face, leaving it all over white, like dough. "Oh, Lord, I ain't needin' this punishment!" she groaned, as soon as she could speak. "But I reckon it's like you say. I ain't got it as bad as some."

Ishma went up to the deputy who was guarding the house. "You'll have to let me bring a mattress back into the house, and I want you to help me put Mrs. Rowe on it."

"Kain't do it, ma'am. There's another fam'ly comin' in here. I'm expectin' 'em ever' minute. You'll have to call the hawspital."

"The hospital won't take her. They're always full when we ask them to take a case. And she can't be moved now. You'll have to let her in."

She began to drag a mattress towards the steps. The man pushed ahead of her and locked the door. "Got my orders, ma'am."

Ishma looked at him as if he were a new kind of animal. "Well, perhaps you *didn't* have a mother."

She laid the mattress on the ground, placed three chairs between it and the street, and hung quilts over the chairs. A woman was sent for a kettle of water, while she righted a small oil stove and lit it. Farther down the street two evicted women were sitting among their scrambled possessions. Ishma's call brought them to her help. They got Thelma onto the mattress.

"She ain't union," said one of the women, not ungently.

"She will be after this," said Ishma. Thelma's eyes rolled toward her with assent. "If I live," she gasped.

Suddenly the deputy turned the lock and flung the door of the house open. His cheeks were fiery red. He was a young man, only twenty-two or three. "Bring her in !" he called.

Ishma gave him a look reinstating him as a human being. "You help us," she said.

He came down and took one end of the mattress. Ishma lifted the other end, and the women helped, one at each side. They got Thelma up the steps and into the house.

"Go and 'phone the chief of police to send a doctor here," said Ishma to the man.

"Might as well. Hell, I've already lost my job. An' I'll say I needed it."

"No, son. No man needs this sort of a job."

"I'll 'phone," he said, starting off. "But you'll not get a doctor sent out here."

Ishma knew she wouldn't, but she must try. The Company doctor, of course, was too busy certifying cases for eviction. And Derry Unthank had gone up to his farm for two days of escape after a week without rest.

She could do no more for Thelma, and leaving the women to watch by her, she hurried down the street to Sue Shelton. Sue sat in the yard, on top of her cook-stove, clutching her Bible and the family album. Her eyes stared at nothing and at everything.

"She's been like that ever' sence they threw her out," explained a neighbor. "I tried to git her to come into my house, though I've got nineteen sleepin' there now o' nights. But she wouldn't."

Ishma tried to tell Sue that she would be taken care of. They would find a place for her children and her things. Nothing would be lost. But Sue only stared, and muttered something about the righteous begging bread. Ishma took up the youngest child and laid it in the mother's lap. She looked at it in horror, and would have let it drop if Ishma hadn't caught it. "They hain't buried it !" cried the mother. "It's dead, an' they hain't buried it !"

Ishma could do nothing for her. She sent the children to headquarters, in care of a neighbor, and, with trembling knees, went on her way. A feeling of nauseating futility had taken possession of her brain.

The day was nearing twilight. She felt that she must get away somewhere for an hour or two, and started on the road leading to the bridge where she had walked with Derry Unthank. She hoped that Derry would stay at the farm until he had regained his energy, but how he was needed! If she could have had him that day to rely upon she wouldn't feel so weak and shaky now. She had only her strength to give. Derry had so much besides that. Education, training, fine skill, money. She knew that the dividends from his mill-stock went to the support of a printing machine up in Pittsburgh, pouring out leaflets of information for the workers. If he took their money, he said, he'd give it back in the food of freedom. He'd feel like a thief if he used it any other way. That was why he had called it stealing when he had given her the money for May. And he had been right. The money had counted for nothing against what they fought — conditions that were forcing May, and a hundred thousand Mays, out of school.

After so bitter a day, it was heartening to think of Unthank, his energy, his talents, his labors, his sympathy that was so much deeper than it seemed. He was still nebulously in her mind when she passed a drugstore and, glancing in, she saw him. He was looking well, actually jolly. A soda-clerk was giving him a drink, and they were both laughing. And Thelma Rowe and Sue Shelton in half a mile of them! She stood there, her eyes accusing, until Unthank came out.

"Hello! hello! My way is yours," he greeted, taking her arm and almost propelling her up the street.

"I'm glad you're feeling better," she said precisely.

"Indeed? You look as if you'd consign me cheerfully to a torture chamber. But let's find a seat. Yonder 's an oak tree and a bench." He guided her to it, and she sat down, surprised at the relief it gave her.

"The farm cure is great. It's time I sent you up there for a week — "

"Oh, that's impossible now!" She poured out the story of the day, and was resentful because he remained so vigorously unshaken. She herself was near to thinking treason. Were they taking the right way? What if the fight could be won only by spirit, an outpour of spirit the world over? Spirit that knew no impossibility. If the workers were as starved and exhausted in other places as they were in Winbury—

Unthank had plunged into sparkling prophecy. The submerged millions were nearing their day. Mass-consciousness was becoming the mood of the economic world—

She interrupted with a blunt cry. "Don't you recognize spirit at all? Maybe that will open the way for justice, instead of justice coming first."

He shot her a keen look that slowly became gentle. "You *are* tired," he said, with a patience that comforted. But his next words angered her. "Ready to throw the whole problem into the lap of any god that's sitting handy, aren't you?"

He took a bill-fold from his pocket. "I've got something to read to you, Ishma." She was impatient at the thought of reading anything, with the world bleeding all about them, but she quietly watched him open a folded paper, the torn page of a book.

"Up home this time, I overhauled my father's little library. It was a good way to forget Winbury. I poked into some of his Swedenborg books. My father was a bit of a mystic, like your grandmother. We've both got it in our blood, and it doesn't make things easier for us." He tapped the paper. "I found this passage, and tore it out just to read to you. It's about the antediluvians and how they brought the flood on themselves. The 'flood' wasn't water. It was consuming self-love and glory."

He began to read. The daylight was still strong enough to reveal familiar words. " *These people* [says the old chap] *were of such a genius that they were imbued with direful and abominable persuasions concerning all things that occurred to them or came into their thought. They would not go back on them one whit, because they were possessed of an enormous self-love and supposed themselves to be as gods and whatever they thought was Right. This persuasion, when it took possession of a man, was like a glue, catching in its embrace all of truth and good that was in him, with the result that truth and good could no longer be stored in his mind, and that which had been stored became of no*

324

use and could not increase itself, for it grows only by use. Therefore when these people arrived at the summit of such persuasions, they were suffocated by an inundation not unlike a flood. This enormous idea of self was so deadly and asphyxiating that after death, when they reached the land of spirits, they were not permitted to be with any other spirits, for they took away from them all power of thought by injecting into them their fearfully determined persuasions."

"There!" flourished Derry. Ishma put her hand to her throat. "Yes," he said, "it's enough to choke a body just to think about them. And that same disastrous persuasion is usurping the minds of men today. You say that spirit will overcome it — "

"I do not. I asked you if it might not be a way."

"Well, if you don't say it, there are plenty who do. There's a cult now whose members claim that if enough of us stand off and sing the song of Isaiah,

> *And the earth shall be full*
> *Of the knowledge of the Lord,*
> *As the waters cover the sea,*

power will fall from the hands of the arrogant mighty much as the walls of Jericho fell when the rhythm was right for it."

"But I don't think — "

"Wait a minute. And stop trying to burn this cool twilight air by starting a fire in your cheeks. I know you haven't signed up with the cult. But your mind is tired enough to want to slip back nearly twenty centuries to the Golden Rule as a cure for industrial ills, forgetting that in the time of Christ an industrial world system didn't and couldn't exist. If everybody on earth today loved his neighbor as himself, and society as a whole stuck to the profit system, half the people would still be on sufferance, or on the charity of the noble other half. It's a matter to be adjusted by intelligence. Spirit cannot preside over a perverted, antediluvian mind. Give spirit all the play you can, but don't let your intelligence shirk. It might die and leave you. We fought hard enough, and long enough, to win our inner light — our new instrument of vision — this mind of ours. At first it didn't illumine the region very far around us. We could see the misery at our side and strive to relieve it. We could feel the blows that fell upon a friend. By and by we could see the enemy's point of view, and forgive those who hurt us. We saw, reaching out and around us, the soft hands of charity. We beheld the bright face of love. But the light grew as we used it. Not only could we see misery around us, we began to pierce to its cause. Before that time we had accepted sorrow and given it beauty. We made songs of shadows and suffering. Over ugliness and defeat, we threw the sheen of art, the pale holiness of resignation. We guarded our griefs jealously. We hugged them as from God. We went about our jails and almshouses with the shining stolidity of virtue. But intelligence has won. The new instrument has not failed us. We see full circle. We know causes. And what happens ? Our jails and almshouses are memorials to our shame. Our wars are the first and last word in imbecility. Our charitable hands grow loathsome, our griefs absurd, the bright face of love simpers inept. We have work ahead. We have to unclog the gate of evolution. We have to sweep out the clutter of unseeing ages. We have to release even spirit through the door of intelligence.

"Well, we begin, and right before us, blocking our way, are the antediluvians, the men with the deadly persuasion, the extinctive thought, the unlit mind. What shall we do ? Shall we, or they, lie down ? Shall we take away their power, as we know how to do, or shall we let the banked up ages of antediluvia roll over us ?"

"Are you fair to me ? I wasn't questioning our aim, but our method."

"There's only one method. Everything else has been tried. They've been preached to, sung to, and prayed to, and still they trample the generations down. Don't dream that they will become channels of spirit and give up their power. Spirit is a courteous thing; it enters only by invitation; never where gates are choked and barricaded against it."

"If you had been where I have been today, you would — "

"Sure, I know about that. I'd be in the trough of despond

326

too. Stalin, Hitler and Chiang Kai-shek would all look alike to me. You need just what I said; a week at the farm."

"You know I can't possibly —"

"A whole week. I needed only two days, but I'll give you a week."

"Why do you keep shutting me up ?"

"Because I don't want you to say things you'll be sorry for after the good night's rest you are going to have. I'll take your place on that Committee."

"I do so little. If I could do as much as you !"

"So little ? I'll tell you what I used to think of when I'd see you laboring with Vennie. An Amazon sentenced for life to pick up chips. But you're not picking up chips any more. You've got both hands under evolution, and you can swing your part of it. Believe that, because it's true. And now we've both said quite enough; I'm taking you home."

Ishma went to bed as soon as she reached Mildred's, and at once fell asleep. Derry Unthank had been exasperating, but assuring. She slept twelve hours, and rose with such strength that she laughed at the thought of a week on the farm. She didn't need an hour !

During those days of evictions she worked ceaselessly; up and down the streets, tramping with unbreaking faith the road of the "impossible." At the end of the week the tents arrived. Families could be sheltered. The union had leased a tract of vacant land beyond the railroad tracks, and here the strikers had thrown up a crude shack for use as head-quarters. Around this shack tents were speedily set up, and the evicted families moved into them. Thelma Rowe and Sue Shelton were not among them. Thelma was dead, and Sue was in an asylum. Their little children played around the tents, cared for by the women of the union.

As the tents went up, the spirit of the strikers rose in unity. They could hold out now until winter. What more could the bosses do to them ?

A great deal more, suspected Nat Thrum, from the Pittsburgh region, where he had seen a miner jumped on by special police

327

and beaten steadily for two hours. The beating was done by two men alternately resting each other in their exhausting work. The man's eyes were knocked out, his head broken, and his lungs trampled flat. When dead, the undertaker was charged to "fix him up human again." But his wife didn't know him when she was permitted to see him after the "fixing up." She laid her hand on his chest and it caved in flat. The man's crime had been two-fold. First, his name was Rakovsky: and second, he had appealed to the police in behalf of a young lad whom they were beating up. Mere death was too light a punishment for such insolence. It should be death by torture, and it was. The special police were tried, acquitted, and sent back to their jobs. Such finished practitioners must not be lost to the force.

With this instance fresh in mind, Nat looked uneasily on the Winbury situation in the hands of special police. A few others shared his fears. But the strike colony, on the whole, was cheerful and given to hope. The women lost their strained look, and began to smile frequently. Some of them were getting a rest for the first time in their lives, and at the same time were assured of two meals a day.

"If a hundred and eighty million Hindu peasants can live on one meal a day an' work in the fields," said Job Waygood, now unquestionably of the faith, "we ought to live on two when we're not workin', an' lay up fat fer hard times."

Amos helped the men organize a sports club. A young college woman, Frances Kayle, came down from New York and took charge of the children's classes and amusements. This released Ishma, and she was placed on the collecting committee. Amos thought she would get on well with the farmers, and food was now their greatest daily concern. Joe Wallace taught her to drive his old Ford, and she rattled it into the corners and byways of three counties.

Amos was right again. Everywhere Ishma was welcomed, even when nothing was given, or when gifts were made reluctantly.

"Yes, I'll send 'em some truck," said Jeb Windstaff, "an' I hope it'll stop their mouths."

Squire Hull, who owned a big old-fashioned farm, with three

tenant shacks on it, said he would send in a load "o' this an' that, an' they won't be no poison in it, though some folks, I won't say who, are comin' round here hintin' that it wouldn't be no sin to put in a haws-dose o' something an' make 'em so sick they wouldn't feel like runnin' Reece-Durkin's business. I'd hate for you to git holt of anything like that, Mis' Bailey." His grin was followed by an unsuccessful wink that involved his thick, white eyebrows and bald crown.

"I'll not be afraid to bite into anything you send us, Squire."

"You'd better be, young woman, if you go to botherin' my tenants. They ain't got a thing to spare. I'm puttin' in fer them."

"But I'd like to have a little talk with them, Squire."

"No, you don't! They're not makin' me a dollar now, with prices lower 'n the ground. I give 'em patchin' acres to make their victuals on, an' take only a third o' the main crop. An' that ain't enough to cover taxes this year."

"My goodness, Squire! You'll want to hear what I've got to say too! Come on, let's hunt up your tenants and all of us talk it out."

"It's ding foolishness," said the squire, "but if I go along I reckon I can keep you from doin' any harm."

He led the way, and they talked it out. When Ishma left, the Squire was both nodding and shaking his head, in a very muddled manner. But somewhere, in a corner of his mind, was the disturbing glimmer of a bright and not impossible dream.

The poorer farmers met her gladly, though in some cases she had to break down fear and suspicion. Mothers who had given sons and daughters to the mills, wiped their eyes on their aprons as they talked. "I always wanted Tom to go to college, an' larn to be a preacher," said one, "but when he come fourteen, looked like it was the mills er nothin'." "Jane wanted clo's," said another, "an' all me an' her daddy could do was to keep something to eat."

The women always asked Ishma to come back, and she always promised. "She's nice an' common," they'd say of her.

On the surface the strike seemed lost. The big Greybank mill was running day and night. Workers had been brought in to take the place of the strikers. The picket line was never permitted to get near the mill. Reece-Durkin announced that the strike was broken, and the *Comet* promulgated that the community had only one duty left; to get rid of the fomenting element still persisting in the defeated strike colony.

The strikers, however, knew a different story. Many of the new workers had joined the union. Within the mill the number of converts increased daily. It wouldn't be long until the leaders could call a second strike, which they believed would bring out the entire force. Strong in this belief, the strikers could endure the daily arrests, fines, and abuse. The *Comet* continued to cry, "How long will this godless crew be tolerated?" Ugly threats crept into the taunts of the special police. The water in the colony spring became undrinkable overnight. Talk of flogging and lynching could be heard if one stopped for ten minutes in Central Square and listened to remarks casually flung out.

There was an outbreak of strikes throughout the mill-towns of the State, and while this gave encouragement to the colony, it also meant a scarcity of supplies because of the greater drain on the resources of sympathizers. Daily it became more difficult to collect enough for the needs of the colony and build a reserve for the second strike which soon must be called; but the collectors travelled farther and constantly, and somehow managed to steadily increase their fund. The council planned the second strike with the greatest secrecy, knowing that exposure would invite swift and deadly measures. In the recent history of labor, more than one strike had been forestalled by kidnapping, torture and murder. The colony had no leaders that could be spared.

Drunken deputies were swaggering about the country, talking of going to head-quarters and cleaning up the goddamned mess. "It'll have to be done. What's the use o' puttin' it off?" The strikers, through their council, openly announced their intention to protect their new head-quarters. The destruction of the first had proved that they could expect no protection from the military or the police. Only one course was left them — to protect themselves. Seven young men were given arms and put on guard around the building. Ishma felt that she was living in the last moment before an explosion.

CHAPTER XIII

A NEW FRIEND

ONE SATURDAY afternoon Ishma went across the town into the Winbury that lay east of Central Square. This was where the farmers gathered, along with workers who had the afternoon off, and where peddlers and fakirs found a gullible clientele. She wanted to meet a farmer, Abraham Beasley, who had helped the strikers more than once, and might be willing to help again.

She didn't take the old Ford, feeling the need of a long walk. Perhaps she could banish mental weariness by giving her blood a race. Her feet fell lightly on the pavement. She half-shut her eyes, and imagined herself climbing a mountain — Blackspur, south-east of Cloudy Knob. She pulled up by cedars and laurel, and familiar jutting rocks to the top; and looked over Farmer's Square. Her face was glowing; tiny, moist pearls lay on her temples. She felt better. Mountain air. What a tonic!

The streets fringing the Square were full of people. She found herself searching anxious faces, and looking into eyes too crowded to admit her; crowded with the jumble of wants and needs.

"I've got to have new harness," said Clint Mason, "an' I'll have to mortgage my team to pay fer it. Next year, I reckon I'll lose the team." Clint was old. His eyes were full of harness; harness that was swathed in fear and streaked with horror of a mortgage.

"I've got a tractor," said Bill Penland, "but it's second-hand an' in the shop most of the time. Costs more'n a team would eat, an' don't give me no manure. You hold on to yer team, Mason. Me an' the woman brought in a truck load o' green stuff today, an' after peddlin' out an' payin' up, we ain't got enough left to buy her a new churn. She's been borrowin' Mandy's fer two weeks. We almost set up nights with them early tomatoes an' strawberries, an' we might better been asleep."

Ishma couldn't get into big, bony Bill's eyes at all. They were full of frosty nights, thin, worked to death woman, and a stubborn tractor sitting with all of its hot weight on his brain. No room for the new world there. Yet it must be there — down under — down under ! Her own eyes dropped for rest into the iridescence of a fountain shining from a patch of green in the centre of the Square. On the ground around the fountain there were banana skins and scraps of paper that had wrapped greasy sandwiches. She lifted her eyes back to the fountain, up through the glistening tops of magnolias, and on to the lovely, lazy clouds shifting to shapes that laughed at her and threw her back to the ground, the banana skins, the people.

A little bride passed, in cheap array, dingy and limp. She was clutching the groom's arm; her anchor now against all tides.

"Let's get the cups an' saucers, Ben."

"All right, Trudy. But there won't be enough left for the ice-cream."

"Oh, it's so hot, an' I'm so tired." She felt her anchor wobble. "But I reckon we ought to get the cups." The anchor steadied itself.

"Course we ought. Your mother never asked us to stay more'n a week, an' we've been there two." He looked at her with relenting tenderness. "I'd like to buy you the cream though, an' set at a table."

"I know you would, Ben. Let's go to the five-up-to-five-dollar place. They've got awful nice chiny there."

Ishma watched the young things go. Parents of the future, with a margin that wouldn't cover two dishes of ice-cream. She shuddered, wrapped in a sudden, icy breath. She was seeing herself on a winter hill burying her twins. Hastily she shut out the vision, and again began looking at the people about her.

Gradually she became possessed of a secret. Every sordid and ugly life had its hidden war in the service of a dream; its struggle behind drab matter-of-fact; its timidity and pride, fearing to be found out. That was the mystery she had so often seen in chilled, coffined faces. Dead lips drawn over life-long, unconfessed defeat; curved with the triumph of concealment; the dream safe from life's insolences and surprises. But suppose it could be released into life ? — into growth ? That bright, yearning germ,

332

which no heart was without ? What incalculable gain ! Every man at his best. That deep-hidden best that never had been permitted a single bloom under the bars and irons where he fought for sustenance. What streams of active beauty would flow into time ! Time, which is creation's reservoir.

Ishma looked through her desire with transforming eyes. She saw the world impending in tomorrow, and full of love for it, and adoration of it, she brought her eyes back to the world about her, eyes full of tenderness and madonna gifts. Even the darkest, and to her unknown, wards and corners of existence must feel the coming sun. Life, which she could only imagine in its bright wonder, pressed out the thin walls of the life that she knew, as the sea which she had never seen sometimes lay in her bursting heart.

She looked through her desire, and saw Farmers' Square shining as from the hands of the old Greeks, but there were no human chattels skulking behind the façades, or dragging their burning feet from the outlying gardens and plains; casting always their slave-shadow across the mind of genius and scholar. In the land where no one was driven, every soul could find beauty, every man could find his soul. No loneliness there, where every human being could walk thus undeserted.

Out over the land, miles and miles beyond the square, she saw towers arise and sturdy temples spread. Boys and girls entered the temples and looked out of the towers as easily as they would enter, or look out of, their own homes. They were all there. Not one was shut out because the crop had failed, big business had wrecked a little one, father had fallen sick, there were too many babies in the house, or brother had tasted of sin and the lawyer's fee was heavy. They were all there; with faces not marred by secretive struggle, not shadowed with envy, not blurred with despair, not emptied by folly. Intent with spirit, aspiringly bright, they were open and unashamed because life offered them no shame. And among them none was stronger or more beautiful than Edward Britton Hensley.

A woman rubbed against her. "Excuse me, please," said a cracked, timid voice. Ishma saw an old woman whose right hand clutched a basket of radishes and tomatoes. There was a little bunch of flowers on top. She might get a dime for the posy, so she had put it in. Ishma wanted to touch the knotty fingers that were tightened on the handle of the basket. She wanted to smooth them, and tell them they should make soft music and touch lovely things. She thought of her mother's hands, stringy and warped with a lifetime of hard work. Perhaps she would go home and tell her. Tell her that mankind had found a better way, without the sacrifice of heart's blood and beauty. But her mother would say, "Stars alive, Ishmalee! You've gone crazy at last. After all the prayin' I've done to keep you straight-headed!"

She thought of that rasping old voice, and longed to hear it, if only to hear herself reviled and cast out. An aching set up within her that had nothing to do with the new world. It told her once more that she was tied to the stern, begrudging earth with bonds of flesh that no dream could break. Britt held her. Britt was drawing her back. She would go to him with this new wonder in her heart and give it to him. She would go soon. She couldn't leave the work or friends now — but when the strike was won she would go.

If Derry were to die, she knew she would feel intellectually adrift, but only for a while. There was mental stir in her which more than hinted of a day when she would need no guide for her thinking and acting. If Derry were to die, the world would still be a place for work and hope and the blossoming rod of faith. But if Britt were to die, she would lose part of her body. She would be short of breath; she would move crippled and incomplete through the world.

The northern half of Farmers' Square was given over to trucks and vehicles showing every degree of age and abuse. The smarter, newer cars were parked in a narrow strip bordering the southern side. Among them Ishma recognized the car of Abraham Beasley and began to move in that direction.

She walked slowly along the way of transmutation, busily repairing life. Every step called for the rescuing thrust of imagination; every step was a test of faith. One little group coming towards her resolved into well-known figures. There could be no juggling here.

334

"Why, Kansie," she called, "did you walk all the way from the tents ?"

"Yes, but we come slow," replied Kansie Bennett, at the head of her little company. "I took my time. It ain't hurt me none." As she spoke, her blue lips told another story. "I've been restin' so much in the tent I thought it 'ud help me to get out. An' all the younguns was bent on comin'. May here, she got married today, and —"

"May ! Married !" Ishma looked at the embarrassed youth walking by May and recognized the doff boy whom she had secured as a boarder for Kansie so that she could keep her house. May didn't look happy. Her young, cool beauty had wilted; her eyes avoided Ishma's. No hope and eagerness in them now.

"Yes," said Kansie, "they got married, an' we thought we'd come over here an' look around, sort o' pleasurin' like. But I wish we'd left the younguns in the tents. They're wantin' ever'-thing they see. I like to never got 'em away from that place where they're throwin' balls at a rooster's head. If a boy wins he gets a jack-knife, an' if a girl wins she gets a dressed-up doll. It's a nickel a throw, an' there hain't been a nickel in the whole Bennett fam'ly for three weeks."

"I didn't want to throw," protested Sara, who was ten. "I wanted some chocolate drops."

She more than wanted the drops. She was perishing for them. Her thin, starved body was screaming for carbohydrates.

"How could May and Chick get married without a little money ?" asked Ishma.

"The preacher didn't charge anything. It was preacher Stiles, an' he sent out word some time back he'd marry any of the young folks fer nothin'. It might keep 'em from doin' worse. Abe Wilks lent Chick the money fer the license."

The younger children began tugging at their mother. "I reckon we'll move on around the Square," she said, "seein' it's all we can do. 'Tain't much of a weddin', and' I thought life was goin' to be different fer May, but —"

Tears began to tremble in Kansie's eyes. "Come on, mother," said May, with her first show of energy. "Goodbye, Mrs. Bailey." Her thin, declicate eyelids were unlifted. She wasn't going to

335

let Ishma read the story of her surrender. They parted, and a moment afterwards Ishma had come to a standstill before a group of men and boys who were crowding around a high truck with a canvas cover. On the canvas words were painted. "See the great What-is-it ! The wonder of the world. Animal with tail like a fox, webs like a duck, snout like a hog, and other surprises. To see is to believe ! Only ten cents."

A man standing in front of the truck kept repeating the painted legend, adding other alluring and suggestive phrases. Ishma pushed among the group. The man got before her. "No ladies, ma'am. This is for men only, and boys over sixteen."

A boy not more than twelve years old was thrusting up a dime. The man took it and pushed him along towards the truck, where another man stood ready to lift the canvas a few discreet inches. The man shoved the boy away after a moment's peep, and a bearded farmer, with eyes small and opaque, like the eyes in a scalded hog's head, took his place. His broad shoulders jerked and wriggled as he peered under the canvas. Ishma looked at the boy, and saw in his face the thrill of forbidden vulgarity overlaying youthful shame. He caught her eye and turned a flaming red, as he slipped behind two older boys who were waiting their turn for a peep. Ishma looked about her, and on every face she saw the same vulgar exposure. Here was something she couldn't transmute. Tears were burning in her heart. How could this thing have been done to man ? — her radiant man ? In the crowd she caught sight of Sid Brinn and before he could get his six feet three out of the way she was speaking to him.

"Why don't you church people stop this ?"

"It's for the town council to stop it, not us," he mumbled, trying to lose his big figure in the crowd.

Ishma felt a hand on her shoulder, and a twinkling voice was at her ear. "And so she goes

> *'the gauntlet way,*
> *Past flame and spear, enraptured driven*
> *To set drab tents of man fair on a ridge of heaven.'"*

"Derry, you must stop this," she said, turning to him. "You must go to the council."

336

"I have been. This is the fourth Saturday that this disgraceful truck has stood here. The mayor promised me it should disappear, but you see it doesn't. The man has a license for the show. He pays twenty dollars for each afternoon. So you see — "

"I see."

"Don't be dismal. I've just had a word with your Abraham Beasley. He said tell you he was ready for another contribution. You'll find him over there behind his car. Go, and get cheered up."

Derry left her, and once more she started on.

ABRAHAM BEASLEY wore the scars of civilization. Orphaned when two years old, he had grown up without schooling. At twelve he was doing a man's work. Farmers were glad to have him. A boy expected no pay except board and make-shift clothes. At twenty he had married and set out resolutely to win land and home. He had chosen a strong girl; she would have to stand up under hard work. He was careful too that she could read, write and figger. He had picked up a little education for himself, but she might have to supplement it at times.

They began their fight absolutely bare. At sixty-five Beasley owned a thousand acres of land, and was pointed out as an example of what industry and resolution could accomplish in the land of the free; a pillar of rock in the way of agitators and advocates of social change. Catch Abe Beasley listening to any talk about communal ownership of land ! Land that he had fought and scrambled and scratched for, that his children might inherit ! This was the general talk, and it had kept Ishma away from Beasley. But one day he had come up to her on a Winbury street and laid a ten-dollar bill in her hand. Later he had sent in a truck load of farm stuff. And now she was seeking him out. When he saw her coming, his forehead scowled, but his eyes welcomed her.

"Get into my car," he said. "We'll drive out to my place."

She got in, wondering why, and they were soon on the high road leading to the Beasley farm.

"I've got to be at home to meet a man who has never found

337

me behind time," said Beasley. "He's to be there at five o'clock, and it's four-forty now."

"But what do you want with me, Mr. Beasley ? It doesn't take a minute to hand over a ten-dollar bill, you know."

"Maybe you're not goin' to get any this time. How are things shapin' over at the colony ?"

"All right, I hope."

"Hope is good for the mind, but it don't fill the stomach. Don't you think you're all a purty crazy lot over there ? A handful o' hungry-bellies thinkin' they can make these United States come to their whistle !"

"They've got courage," she said pleasantly.

"Conceit, you mean ! It's hard to believe unless a man happened to see it for himself."

"Why do you help us if that's what you think ?"

"Because you're right." His teeth clamped down on the words, and his lips looked as if he would never open them again. Ishma was more astonished than when he had so unexpectedly approached her and given her money. She kept silent until he had turned into a rutty side road with black-jack and scrub oak on either hand, then spoke in surprise.

"This isn't the way to your farm, Mr. Beasley."

"No. It's the way to the lynchin' tree. But we're not goin' that far."

"Has anybody ever been lynched on that tree ?"

"Sure. The last time was twelve years ago. I held the rope. Aren't you afraid of me ?"

"Not a bit. I don't believe you would hold that rope now."

"No, I wouldn't. A man can change a lot in twelve years, if he uses his mind. There's a knoll out here we're goin' to the top of."

He turned into an opening in the sparse woods and the car ran bumpily along for a hundred yards.

"Now look !" he said, stopping the car.

There was no intervening woodland between them and the slope that rolled gently away to the gracious acres of a large farm.

"This is the only place I can come an' see everthing I own at one sweep of the eye."

338

"O, it's fine, Mr. Beasley. A lovely farm!"

"Yes, it looks purty easy an' peaceful. Well, we'll go down." He started the car, and in two or three minutes they were back in the high road. Five minutes more, and he drove into his own yard.

"You get acquainted with the women folks," he said, as Ishma stepped from the car, "while I see my man. Yonder he comes, on the dot."

Ishma watched the two men meet and start toward the barn. A woman came out of the house and stood at her side. She was tall and gaunt, but Ishma forgot her bony figure when she looked into her eyes. They were a clear, undimmed brown, with a gentle patience in them that knew no ending.

"Martha, one of my son's wives, is here," she said, "an' we've been washin' up the blankets. It's late in the year for that, but I've been terribly busy all Spring, an' my blankets are not goin' to be turned over to hired help so long as I've any hope o' gettin' to 'em myself. Though Abraham takes on like it's something new for me to work."

She was leading the way to the back of the house. "We've only got the last haf dozen to wring out. You set here on the porch an' we'll be through right now."

In a few minutes the job was done, and the three women were sitting in a gossips' half circle on the porch, though Mrs. Beasley sat a little uneasily, and very soon said that she'd have to be starting supper.

"We've not got many to cook for this year, but they know how to eat. There's only three hired men, and Jim's family is staying with us, an' George, my youngest son, has got two college boys visitin' him. That's all unless somebody drops in. We're dwindlin' out, looks like."

"You sit right still, ma," said the daughter-in-law. "It's my time to set the supper on, and I reckon I know how."

Mrs. Beasley looked doubtful as Martha went in, but she kept her seat beside Ishma, and her gentle talk flowed on. Ishma knew enough of farming and hard work to make a responsive listener, and she liked to hear the sweet, easy drawl of the older woman.

339

"The air 's a little dampish, ain't it ? There's been a rain not far off, over there in the west. I hope Tim Shelton's cotton didn't get too much of it. My, my !" Her face lit up, and the bright brown eyes were strangely bent on a cloud in the west.

Ishma had been looking with joy at the changing sky. That cloud was different from anything that she could remember. It lay in lines of color, like a rainbow, but it was curled like a snail-shell, and out where the snail's horns might have been was a fan-shaped sweep of violet much larger than the cloud itself. As they looked, the violet fan curved around the snail-like circumference, and the whole thing began to fade, like a vast, many-colored wheel retreating to its heavenly centre. Mrs. Beasley looked from the sky to Ishma's face.

"You think it was purty ?" she asked timidly.

"The loveliest thing that I ever saw !"

Mrs. Beasley's bosom got rid of an immense sigh. "Now what's the matter ?" thought Ishma, and she asked aloud, "Did you ever see anything like that before, Mrs. Beasley ?"

"Yes," said the older woman, suddenly decisive. "Forty-five years ago. The day me and Abraham got married. He was workin' for Jake Anderson that year, and I was helpin' Sally, Jake's wife. She was sickly. We got home from the preacher's just in time to start supper. Abraham left me at the gate while he went to put up the horse an' buggy. There'd been a shower in the west, just like today, and I saw that very cloud, but purtier, if there was any difference. I stood there lookin', though I knew Sally was thinkin' I ought to be gettin' to the kitchen. I'd seen her at the upstairs winder waitin' for me when we drove up. But I watched that cloud till it was all faded out and Abraham came back. I was ashamed to tell him what I'd been waitin' on. He was great for laffin', and I didn't want to be laffed at. So I asked him, in a hurry like, what had made him so long, just as if I'd been waitin' for him, and Sally put her head out and told him he'd better go drive the cows up before supper, 'cause it was goin' to be dark by the time Judy got it ready. My name is Judy. So Abraham went off, and I hurried into the kitchen. Seems to me I've been hurryin' ever since."

"And you never told him about that cloud ?"

"I never spoke about it in my life till I opened my mouth to you. But I thought about it many a time, partickly when I was in bed after a birthin'. I had time to remember then. I'm sixty-three years old, and that was the purtiest thing I ever saw, not excusin' this one today."

"I wish you had told Mr. Beasley. I don't believe he'd have laughed at you."

"I come nigh tellin' him that night after we went to bed. I was just gettin' my mouth sort o' fixed up for it, when he said that he reckoned sleepin' would be better for us than talkin'. He had to get up at four o' clock in the morning. And it's been four o' clock in the mornin' ever since. Maybe we could live easier now, though I'm not sure, with all the children and grand-children to be helped along. And I've got so used to workin', my hands wouldn't know how to be still."

The brown eyes had begun to glance uneasily toward the kitchen door, and the moment Abraham appeared she excused herself to Ishma and went in. Abraham sat down by Ishma, his eyes scowling after his vanishing wife.

"I don't know what I'm goin' to do to make her stop," he said. "She's had a forty-five year start, and it's hard to make her slow up."

"You might try slowing up yourself. Sit down on that old horse block in front of the house some day for two or three hours, and I'll bet she'll come and sit down by you."

"That's a good idy. Blamed if I don't try it! First day I get time. We've done all our talkin' standin' up. I courted her at Sally Anderson's wash-tub. It wouldn't surprise me a bit if she sat up in her coffin to see if they'd washed her feet proper. Look at that row o' blankets! Twenty-nine, Martha said. No, I won't look at 'em."

He squared his chair with his back to the yard. "I reckon you're waitin' for me to tell you why I think you're right. That's what I got you out here for. It come over me sudden when I saw you today that I wanted to talk. Guess you've heard that I'm a hard-workin' man."

"Everybody says so, Mr. Beasley."

"They don't know *a thing*. When Judy an' me got married

we worked two years for Jake Anderson, an' all we had at the end of it, more'n what we begun with, was a baby. We'd worked from four in the morning till near midnight, week days an' Sundays."

"Sundays too ?"

"Jake didn't call it work. It was 'look-over' day, he said. When I got through feedin' an' straightenin' up the barn, I had to curry the horses slick, wash the big carry-all, an' drive ever'body to church but Jake. He wouldn't go. It was his only chance to enjoy his home an' rest, he said. He'd lay around an' smoke till we got back. Then I'd go to the pastures, and around a three-mile fence lookin' to see no hogs had made root-holes under it. We didn't have stock-law in our county then. When I'd salted the cattle an' got back home, maybe I'd have time to take a nap in the barn 'fore supper. Judy was in the house cookin' an' cleanin' up an' waitin' on folks. Sally had lots o' company, bein' sickly."

"I know about work never ending," said Ishma, her mind rushing back to Cloudy Knob, "but I had my Sundays most of the time. They kept me up. I don't see how you got along without them."

"When I saw we wasn't gettin' a thing out of our work — it was like pourin' water in a craw-fish hole — I told Jake I'd stay with him if he'd let us move into a one-room shack standin' in an old field, an' I'd buy the ten acres around the shack if he'd let our work go on the pay till he was shore he had enough. He said he thought two years would about cover it if we'd both put in ever' day we's in health, an' make up fer any days we had to lay off fer sickness. He thought that the land was forever sucked out, but I knew I could feed it up in three years, an' make it crop-bearin'. Me an' Judy had been studyin' how."

Again Ishma was back in the hills with Britt, a twin on her arm, standing before the Wiggins' place. And they had given it up !

"But how could you *live* ?" she asked.

"I'd told Jake that while we were makin' his crop the first year, he'd have to throw in a half bushel o' meal, five pounds o' fat-back, an' a quart o' molasses, every Saturday night. He could do that an' not miss it, so he said all right. Judy's mother gave us a feather bed an' some old quilts, an' I fixed up a frame an' some slats. Her sister let us have a coffee-pot with a hole in an' I sawdered it with Jake's outfit. Sally gave us an iron tea-kettle an' skillet, an' let Judy scrub up some ol' tin cups an' bucket lids, so we were set up fer dishes. Judy made a bargain with Sally to go on helpin' her with the work on Sundays if Sally would start her off with a dozen hens. We didn't have anything to feed 'em on, but they scratched all over the ten acres, an' come up with enough eggs to trade in fer what we's bound to have. I put in Sunday 'lookin' over' fer Jake an' got enough barn-manure fer a good garden. So we made it through. But our life was just work. We hadn't been moved more'n two months till I said to Judy that I'd thought up a way to get on faster. She said if it meant more work she didn't know how we'd get it in, but she'd try anything. I said we'd ask Jake to let us clear up a swamp on the lower end of his place an' put the ground in for ourselves. Jake was willin', an' said he'd give us all the crop the first year, an' half of it the next if we'd get it in good fix. He thought most of it would be too wet, an' we couldn't put in more'n a third, but I dug ditches an' got it all in. That swamp land gave me my start in life."

Ishma, with tears ready to fall, was thinking of the winter that Britt had spent clearing the six-acre hill-side.

"But how did you get the time ? Where did it come from ?"

"Took it out o' sleepin' time. It never did take much sleep for me, but Judy complained sometimes about not gettin' enough. Jake had made us promise that we wouldn't take any time out on him fer the swamp, so we put in his ten hours, an' soon as we could get in from the fields I'd blow up the fire in the fire-place, Judy would slap on a hoe-cake an' a few slugs o' fat-back, an' by the time the coffee was boiled, we'd be ready to swallow our supper an' light out fer the swamp. I took a big box an' fixed it up on stilts to put the baby in, so the snakes couldn't get at him, an' if it was a dark night we'd set pine torches around an' work same as if it was daylight. We'd get a good stretch cleaned up ever' night, an' knock off at ten o' clock. It was February when we begun, an' we had to work fast. Jake was havin' us clean up all of his fields good an' proper, an' sometimes I thought it was too hard on Judy, with another baby on the way, but she didn't want to stop any more'n I did. What we sold that crop for bought us a horse an' cow, an' enough rye to seed my ten acres. After that all we had to do was to keep at work. In five years I'd bought all the swamp from Jake an' drained it. That cleared out the mosquitoes, an' we didn't have to bring up our children on quinine."

"And you got your thousand acres by work like that!"

"Hard work, an' a little good tradin'. I wanted to leave every one of my children a farm, and I've got enough to divide up into eight good passels. There was eleven children to begin with, but they've thinned down to eight. I never could see how Judy got time to bring 'em into the world. She never stopped except for a baby, an' right now it seems to me like we've never really got acquainted."

"You've provided for the children anyhow, even if you don't know the mother very well."

Abraham's chuckle was followed by a wave of gloom. "No, that's just what I haven't done. If they're kept out o' the poorhouse it won't be by me an' mother workin' our lives out. Not a blame one of 'em wants to farm, though two o' the married boys are helpin' me run mine now, an' their wives are countin' the days till me an' Judy die. Then they'll buy a town house which they'll mortgage an' lose in about three years. That's something to work forty-five years for, ain't it? We ought to feel good, me an' mother, rememberin' the nights we set up fightin' sprouts an' swamp snakes."

"But the other children? Can't ya count on any of them?"

"My oldest boy is a mill superintendent, and a good one, let the owners tell it. He drives the hands like cattle, an' turns out the goods. He's hard an' he's shrewd. He'll make it through life without any help from my land, but I'm not proud of him. The one I *am* proud of is my youngest boy, George, who wants to be a scientist. I'm puttin' him through college, an' he's got two or three more institutions picked out to go to afterwards. He'll never make any money. He's smart in his mind, but he ain't worth a fish-hook for business. I'd be proud to have him go on studyin' all his life, on the chance of his gettin' at something

344

that human beings need, if I wasn't afraid he'd starve or freeze to death some cold night after me an' mother are gone. A farm won't do him any good. My girls, all four of 'em, are married an' not livin' round here. I get letters from 'em now an' then, always hintin' for a loan, an' hopin' me an' ma are takin' care of our health. Their men 'll be glad enough to bite into my place an' sell the bite the first chance. They may be all right, but they ain't much more'n strangers to me. An' me an' mother — "

His voice dropped ruefully into memories. Ishma said nothing. She was thinking of how bitterly she had resented giving away a few years of her life, of how weak and small she had been compared with Judy Beasley.

"No," he said, picking up his monologue, "about the only satisfaction I get out of my possessions is when I look down on 'em from that knoll I took you to today. It looks mighty soft an' complete from up there. All finished off nice for my heirs. But when I come down to a close-up there's so many things jumpin' at me to be done I might as well try to sit down an' be comfortable in a bunch o' hedge-hogs. An', Lord, the old man is gettin' tired. That's why I'm wantin' mother to stop. She must be feelin' sort o' the same way.

"I don't blame my boys a bit for not wantin' to farm though. Here's one gang o' farm-doctors that's for years been sendin' out their demonstration trains an' bulletins an' college professors to tell us how to produce more an' work harder. If you're up against it, it's just laziness an' ignorance. Learn how, an' go to it, an' you'll be all right, they told us. And when our big crops had to be sold for less than they cost us, along comes another gang an' says the trouble with you farmers is you're producin' too much. Cut it down an' you'll be all right. We'd worked too hard and ruined ourselves. An' we pay 'em a big salary to ride around an' tell us that. It's a spectacle, ain't it? Now they're beginnin' to talk about a live-at-home cure. We farmers are to go back to the days of Adam, while the rest o' the world rolls along into the twenty-first century. It makes me tireder than ever I was after workin' sixteen hours a day to save a crop that wasn't goin' to pay me half wages. Strange how some

345

people, who think they're intelligent too, can go on believing they can team up the first age of man with the last and get anything out of it but tangle and trouble. We've got to pool our farms, our tools, our labor, same as in any modern industry. We've got to let go before we can get a holt. We've got to get out before we can get in."

"These beautiful acres — that you've given your life for — this farm with your blood in it — you'd give it all up?"

"Give it up? I wouldn't be givin' it up for *nothin'*. What did me an' mother work for? Wasn't it for just two things? To provide for old age, and to give our children a chance. An' ain't that what the new system will do? Only it will give us a guarantee on 'em, which we never had before. Haf the old people in the poor-houses worked themselves there. Me an' Judy happened to be lucky an' healthy, on top o' the work. I'll tell you, my gal, when I think how easy it would be for the world to begin living under that guarantee, I feel like I've been cheated out o' my whole life. Mother too. Give up this farm? Look what I'd get — for a piece of earth that my children are goin' to lose anyhow."

"It could be easy — the great change — but it won't be. If it comes while you live, it will be very hard for you. There 'll be a bitter time of fighting and privation and adjustment. So many people have spent their lives like you, in straining for possessions, and unlike you they will see and feel nothing but their loss, and struggle against it. They'll fight for their piece of earth, forgetting that they are exchanging it for a share in all that the earth can yield."

"Well," said Beasley, "I hope it will come in time for me to do a little fightin' on the right side. I've had to fight all my life. It would be a good way to end up."

He shut his mouth as if he were through with talk. Ishma was looking at him with shining eyes.

"And I thought you were one of our solid enemies, in our way like a stone mountain. How did you ever come to think like this?"

"I reckon I wasn't a fool to begin with — an' about ten years ago I run agin that youmg doctor, Derry Unthank —"

346

"Oh !"

"Called him out to cure me o' something er other — the blues, maybe — an' he cured the whole world for me."

"He's never said a word to me about your opinions."

"No. Fer a feller that talks a lot, he's powerful close-mouth."

Judy came out and called them to supper. After they had eaten — about twenty of the "dwindled-out" family at the big twelve-foot table — Abraham drove Ishma back to the colony. As they spun along Ishma asked him if he had noticed the queer looking cloud in the west just before sunset.

"I sure did," he said. "I noticed it 'cause it made me think o' one I saw forty-five years ago — the day me an' Judy tied up."

"Please tell me about it."

"You're a crazy gal," he chuckled, but began telling her. "I was a fool boy then, an' that cloud looked like a gathering of the angels to me. I'd left Judy at the gate while I went to the barn with the horse an' buggy. I staid there watchin' that cloud till it faded away."

"Didn't you tell Judy about it ?"

"No. I found her at the gate, an' thought maybe she'd been watchin' it too. She was lookin' mighty purty an' sort o' queer. But when I started to ask her about it, she wanted to know what had kep' me so long, an' then Sally Anderson called us to get to work. We've never stopped yet. I reckon Judy would 'a' laffed at me anyhow, if I'd told her how I'd been wastin' time. That cloud today brought it all back plain as yesterday."

When Abraham said goodbye to Ishma she clung to his big hand.

"Mr. Beasley, I want you to do something for me."

"Lord, you're greedy ! Is that bill in yer pocket lonesome ?"

"No, it's nothing like that. When you get home, you ask Mrs. Beasley what was the loveliest thing she ever saw in her life. The very loveliest, you understand. Will you do that ?"

"If she'll stop long enough."

"You hold her by her apron strings if you have to, and make her tell you."

"Sure ! I'll do my best."

CHAPTER XIV

WEARINESS, enough of it, can break any guard, and Ishma found that youth was not invincible. Across her clear vision there crept, at times, a thin veil of uncertainty. Never a doubt of the rightness of the cause, or the eventual goal. That was fixed in her being as the marrow of her bones. But right did not always triumph, history said. It had been beaten back, and back; forced to burrow under the earth, and wait again and again for its hour. She wanted to reach the goal herself; with her own eyes to see the flowering of the world. Her young years cried out for their due. But youth and time are enemies; one intolerant, one devouring; and the devourer triumphs.

Whether weary or exultant, she moved steadily on, plying her way among the strikers, through the interstices of misery and hope, rebellion and jubilance. Resistance, pressing from far distances, seemed to be everywhere, crawling through every crack and channel, a flood that she made upbear her as a good swimmer is upborne by a conquered current.

There was a difficult day when she almost quarrelled with Derry Unthank. He had joined her in the street, and chose to take one of his abysmal plunges just when she most needed the ascending thrust of his gayety. As they walked along he punctured the conversation, or the silence, with professional diagnoses of the children whom they passed. "Adenoids" — "internal goitre" — "adenoids" — "t. b." — and so on with other terms meaningless to her except for the hopeless finality in them.

"Derry, *are* we going to win ?"

"Yes. Mal-nutrition, with pellagra indicated. We'll win about the year three thousand and thirty."

"You talk like a reformer !"

"Huh ! Maybe the reformers will get their day before we get

348

ours. Rotten teeth. Septic poison. With a generation of work
ers like this coming on in every country of the world — "

"Save *one* !"

" — where are we going to get our fighters ? It's the children
of the reformers and the Established who are being made physically fit. Who cares how many rotten teeth a mill-worker has
so long as he can watch spindles and fix looms ? And how can
a man with a mouth full of decay wash his brain with clean blood
and have a clear thought ?"

"If we had a million dollars — "

"Yeah ! We could give every child in Spindle Hill a good
constitution and a sanitary home. If we had a million million
we could do as much for every Spindle Hill in the United States.
If we had a trillion million we might do it for every worker's
child in the whole tumbling and tooting world. What a race
of efficient slaves we could hand over to the Established ! What
an orgy of rationalization they could indulge in ! They could
show us the speed-up and stretch-out in their fullest bloom, as
the money piled up under their fingers. The unemployed would
pile up too, but what fine, upstanding men and women they
would be, having sucked themselves to maturity on that mighty
sugar-tit, a trillion million ! What a splendid reserve for replenishing the air-fleets and the navy, the cohorts of boot-leggers,
and the clubbed, defeated ranks in the bursting, stinking prisons !
We could give them human material beyond their proudest
dreams of efficiency. For a time, lady. For a time. The next
generation, deprived of its sugar-tit, would have to live and move
under the old conditions. Our ghosts could come back, if they
were silly enough, and walk these streets counting adenoids, red-
sore eyes, and pellagra indications. It's not money the world
needs. It's money-sick now. But brains, brains, dear God !"

"Have you seen Red Shannon, Derry ? I want him to help
me today."

"You'll have to do without him. Two law and order thugs,
full of whiskey and the devil, caught him last night and nearly
beat the life out of him."

"Red ? You don't mean Red ? Happy old Red ! He
couldn't have been doing anything wrong."

"Yes, he could. He was walking down the street. Isn't that crime enough for a striker?"

"But Red! I can't believe it!"

"He's sitting on the porch at head-quarters coughing blood every three minutes."

"Oh, what can we do?"

"Ask me that in the year three thousand and thirty. Good-bye, you lovely idiot. I've got to go into this house and help a woman who is providing a future slave for the Established. Hope it's born dead."

He left her, his lips set in a bitter line, and she went on her errand, her heart under her feet. She could forgive Unthank. He was constantly in contact with suffering, and his nerves were on the jump. But he shouldn't try to fill her with doubt and dismay. She saw enough. Streams of courage, reservoirs of endurance, were daily poured to waste. Every day the picket line, the beating back, the bayonetting, the imprisonments, and they got no farther. But they would. O, they would! It couldn't all be thrown away. Derry had quoted scornfully, "Tomorrow and tomorrow and tomorrow—" But it wasn't so. No petty pace about these determined men and women. These days were not candles lighting fools to dusty death. These days would become glowing yesterdays, lighting the wisest. These days were united in deathless purpose with the future. They were marching together, the future and the present.

With her courage whipped up, she went into the house where Eva Blaine had sent her. An exhausted, bloodless woman was trying to hold herself up in a chair. Three sick children had got out of bed and stared at her from a pallet in a dark corner of the room. The bed was near the window, and burning in the sun at that time of day. If they moved it out of the sun, they'd have to move it back to get the air. It was easier to crawl out and wait for the sun to pass.

The oldest boy was not sick. He wasn't old enough to go into the mills, and he was kept out of school to help around the house. The house needed any help it could get. The family had moved up from Mississippi, bringing their malaria with them. They had been drawn by the promise of work, and the father was in the Greybank. He had more than found work. It had been doubled on him. He was a loom-fixer, and he had displaced two men. Secretly and eagerly he had joined the union, which permitted him to remain in the mill and help feed his family, holding himself ready to come out on call. Despite his double work, a family in health could not live on his wages. A sick one could not half live.

Ishma looked at the filthy bed-clothes. Who was there to wash them ? Her eyes fell on the three skinny children who had crawled from the corner. They were the color of a half-ripe persimmon; their eyes glazed with quinine. Why not let them die ? Why cure them, and fit them out to make more profits that would be turned into a weapon against them ?

The oldest boy, who was acting as nurse, house-maid and cook, seemed unaccountably well. There was a tinge of color in his cheeks, a hint of energy in his eyes.

"I'll be makin' money next year," he said. "We won't need help then." His chest puffed out with prophecy. "The boss says I'll make a good doff boy. They have to run fast up and down the alleys now, they've got such a lot of spools to take off. I bet I could run. I could take off more spools than Jed Gaines."

Good stuff for the Established, Ishma thought, as she left the house, an hour later. Her hope had again slumped, and her feet tried to glue themselves to the pavement. It wouldn't do to meet Derry again. She must get home without sinking any deeper. Then, as she turned a corner, she faced him. His eyes were smiling. She knew before he spoke that the old twinkle would be in his voice.

"Feeling better, dearish ?"

"Wasn't it you who pulled me down ?" she said without a smile, thinking that she would enjoy giving him a good slap.

"Well, I've got news that will pull you up."

"Quick ! I'm needing it. Was the baby dead ?"

"What do you mean ? Oh !" He broke into laughter. "No. A big boy that will make a fighter for us some day. Only we'll win long before we need him. As soon as I could get away from the mother, I went to head-quarters, and Butch Wells came in."

"That nig — negro."

"Comrade, Ishma. Comrade Wells. He had been over to Whitesville working for the union. There are one hundred and twenty-four negroes working in the Whitesville mills, and he got seventy-three of them. Signed up! That's progress, Ishma. That's putting one foot before the other and travelling."

"A few negroes!"

"Is that all you see in it? You, the far-visioned? Don't you know that if every white worker in the South were to join the union, the bosses could still chuckle and pat their paunches? They'd still have a big population of workers to draw from in the unorganized blacks."

"They wouldn't make as good workers."

"Don't be a fool. In three years they could be trained to fill every white man's place in a Dixie mill. The only difference would be a little pigment under the skin, and that wouldn't affect the bosses' money. Equality! I could have hugged Butch when he came in with those names."

"Butch is all right. Nice manners, and he's been to school."

"Went through school and it didn't hurt him. And he's handsome as a chief, and a high yellow. But it didn't keep him from marrying black Gaffie who can't read and write, and who looks as if she were about two jumps out of the jungle."

"What's fine about that?"

"He's had the good sense to unify his nature, instead of spending a life in conflict with himself, as most men — and some women — do."

"I should call Gaffie the visible sign of his conflict."

"Precisely. She's his embodied contradiction, put outside of himself. No war-ground within. He can unify for high purpose. Don't you see?"

"I can guess. When the high air gets too thin for his lungs, he comes down to comfort and Gaffie."

"But goes back higher than before. Nothing like the strong earth-currents for renewal."

"Well, you'll have earth-currents enough when you get all these blacks into the union."

"I'm glad your heart is without prejudice, my dear. Your tongue might deceive me."

352

"Mountain people are always *white.*"

"Yes, and I'm a mountain man. Do you suppose I've not had to struggle with the prejudice that was bred in me ? My mother was Scotch, indomitable, red-haired, and with opinions fixed as Clingman Dome. A dear, beautiful lady, with locked doors to certain parts of her mind, and she'd lost the key to them. Of course she was a Democrat, as all *ladies* were. My father was an easy-going, self-educated mountain-white. One year he dared to vote the republican ticket — the 'nigger ticket.' There were five of us boys around the fireside, three brothers and two cousins. I was the youngest, and the most devilish. That fall, sitting by the fire, I started a new game. I'd nudge the one next to me, and the nudge would be passed around. Then I'd sniff, scenting something unpleasant, and the sniff would make the circle. Mother would be knitting at one corner of the fireplace; father would be reading at the other. Neither would look up, but mother's mouth would be crinkling at the corners. Then I'd say in a low, horrified tone, 'I smell a nigger !' One of the boys would be jumped on as the suspect, and we'd put him out. But the smell remained. There'd be another tumble and tussle, and another would be put out. By this time father would say, 'Mother, can't you control these wild-cats ?' And mother would answer, 'I'm satisfied with their behavior, Jonathan, so long as their *principles* are all right.' When we were all out, the smell still came from the room, and by the time it was focussed on father's side of the fireplace, we would ask permission to make a fire in the kitchen where we could study in purer air. Mother would let us go, and father would keep his face bent over his book. Father wasn't a man to spare the rod, but he never used it when mother was against him. My dear, when a child gets his prejudices from the woman he most admires on earth, he has a long, hard fight before he can leave it behind him. I had ructions and storm before I dropped mine at my mother's grave."

"But you dropped it," said Ishma softly, her perturbed eyes like the water of grey lakes, when the wind is on them and the sun is gone.

"I wish I could be sure. Why, we had a preacher with a smile like St. Francis and hair like the new fallen snow, who used to

353

tell us that the colored man was not an Adamite, blown into being by the breath of God as we were. He had been created a little earlier, along with the experimental beasts. I was only a boy, with an empty brain waiting to be filled, and that was the holy fustian given me. It wasn't strange that my mind was a torture chamber for years before I could say,

> 'Color, a sword, no more divideth Man;
> One race inhabits earth; the sons of God.'"

Derry's head was thrusting upward as he talked — a habit he had come into from thinking much and being with people who thought less. Ishma was annoyed with herself for thrilling to his beauty, as she had done that night on the bridge.

"You look like an archangel, Derry, waiting for orders. But I'm here on earth. I can't talk to you with your chin in line with the North Star."

His gaze fell to her as he said, "Go ahead, dearish."

"You needn't be so patient about it, thank you. 'Sons of God,' you say, but we had to struggle to our stature. Some races have struggled and grown more than others. If we mix them now, won't it pull all of us back? We have a standard to preserve."

"You are making sounds like a Rotarian. But I shan't put my fingers in my ears. The standard which permits *that!*" He waved his hand toward a boy who was passing; a lad with a dead-white face and sore eyes, fiery raw, on his way to night work.

Ishma struggled with her prejudice, but was too honest to deny it. "I don't want to be unfair. But I do wish they were all back where they came from, to go on with their own kind of civilization, whatever it is. We could mend ours faster."

"Perhaps we could. The black people are a handicap that may yet defeat us. We have enough to do to save ourselves without a race question to entangle us. We need wisdom beyond Solomon's, and the charity of Jesus, to help us through, and here we are trammelled with a problem that we can't touch without starting ignorance on the rampage and making prejudice walk abroad in fire."

"But, Derry, you don't think we ought to *mix* ?"

"Biologically, I suppose you mean. Science hasn't answered that question. We haven't enough data on it. And by the time we could get the data, the harm or good would have been done. I don't try to answer that. But, personally, I'd like for racial individualism to continue in the world. When we killed off the Indians perhaps we destroyed in them something more valuable to evolution than we possess in ourselves. They wore blankets and we wear overcoats, but they had a sixth sense more sensitive and active than ours. Perhaps all this materialism that we are passing through is a needless detour. And I hope we'll *not* assimilate the black folk. I'd like to see a black race keeping to its own lines of life, intuitive, rhythmic with nature, building its own shelters for bourgeoning. Why should we think that our method is the only one for returning full-handed into the creative stream ? But that's just my personal preference. All I'm sure about, all I'll swear to, all I'll base my sanity on, is that as workers, of whatever race or color, in these southern United States, we must take hands industrially and stand together. If not, we shall continue to be clubbed, driven and starved. That's as far as I can see. Some day you'll see much farther than that. Yes, it's there in the back of your eyes now, in spite of that little Neanderthal woman you are nursing in your blood."

He paused at a corner, with a sudden, parting query. "Are you going to Yarnboro tonight ?"

"No. I shall try to get some sleep. Everybody else will be there, and I'll not be missed. They're going to take the whole colony, in trucks, except the younger children. Frances Kayle will be left in charge of them. Even the guards are going. Do you think that's safe ?"

"Quite. There'll be no attack on the *children*. The police are going to Yarnboro, to make trouble if they can, and all our men will be needed over there. Don't go to *The Roast Pig* for supper, Ishma. That ice-blanket, Pritchett, is having a party there."

"I'm invited."

"Forget it, and you'll be happier. Goodbye. Sleep a little of that white off your cheeks. It's not becoming to a mountain girl."

As soon as he was gone, Ishma looked into a drugstore to see the time. She had half an hour in which to hurry home, tidy up and change her dress before Pritchett's six-o'clock supper. He was giving it early because any strikers present would want to go on to the big mass meeting in Yarnboro. She didn't admire Pritchett, but she had a weakness for knowledge, and he seemed to know a great deal. She couldn't resist hovering about him occasionally. It didn't matter that the knowledge she picked up was usually depressing. One had to learn.

She put on Virginia's gift, the dress of green and fawn, which had come back surprisingly new from the cleaner's. Virginia, without an accompanying word, had returned the money which Ishma sent her for the dress. Ishma liked it none the less, and wore it happily.

When she reached *The Roast Pig* she went into the little back room through a side door, and was immediately in the midst of a group in confused argument, too intent to take notice of her entrance. Pritchett gave her a half smile and one lifted eye, as his hand indicated a seat. She dragged the chair aside as soon as his divided glance united again on his conversational opponent. She was achingly tired, and wanted to be only on the listening edge of discussion. She didn't want to eat, and was glad to see that she could leave the food alone if she wished. It was a hand to mouth supper. A great pile of sandwiches lay on the table. There was a pot of coffee at each end, and about a dozen cut and uncut pies were scatteringly set out. Cigarette packets were generously present, and about half of the guests were already smoking. Ishma saw that she was late. She had known it as soon as she reached the door and heard Jed Rankin's voice. Jed was a boy from the Smoky region. Normally his voice was a cool, deep drawl, but when he was worked up it shot high and came from a molten fount. The gathering had reached the "worked up" point for Jed.

Pritchett's glance as he talked, drifted to Ishma. Everything about him drifted. His features were unsettled, never quite stabilizing into the finely cut mould for which they were designed. His clothes, of good style and material, were worn hesitatingly, as if he might better have considered something else.

He stood as if he meditated sitting. He sat as if he were on the point of getting up. He walked as if constantly reconnoitering. At twenty-seven his mind had exhausted all enthusiasms and was listlessly old. Born of socialist parents, he had sipped early of Marxian wisdom. Through his High School days he had been the fear and torment of his conservative teachers, and the joy of those who were secretly of his social faith. Before he was eighteen he had spoken on every "red" corner in New York, Brooklyn and Chicago, and had sampled prison life in the three cities. His parents had been able to supply his necessities and rescue him from jails; consequently his experiences had always lacked certain pangs of reality. When the success of the Russian Revolution made the workers' dream more real in all countries, he had retreated to safety with the Socialist party and left the Communists to uphold the Marxian front. The movement, for him, became more or less of a game, and he was enveloped in the boredom that comes from playing any game too constantly. He had tried to get away from it, only to find himself in a bourgeois vacuum that sent him gasping back to the movement. One year he went to London to write poetry, and was dumbfounded to learn that the master at whose feet he hoped to sit, whose mind had played like lightning through the drab fog of poetic mediocrity, had turned back to sink himself in the ecstatic gloom of the Roman Church. Horrified, he had taken an early ship home; actually had taken it instead of drifting onto the deck. He was now in Winbury, because the strike there had promised him something different from all the strikes in which he had been a more or less insulated participant. But the scene had refused him entertainment. Ishma, and a few of her friends, interested him slightly. Some of the more crude and illiterate amused him by their air of equality and naïve assumption. Betters? They didn't know any. It was amusing. But the strikers, as a whole, were colorless. The foreigners of New Bedford, Lawrence, Paterson, were more vivid and alive. American stock! If these scrawny, washed-out creatures were the best it could show, he recommended strong and frequent inoculations from more vital races. In Paterson a starving striker got communitis; in Winbury he got pellagra.

357

Pritchett a month before, had won Ishma's gratitude with a copy of Shelley's *Prometheus Unbound*. She had read it twice in one night; the first time amazed and burning-eyed. Everything in nature that she had known and loved was here given its singing word. In the flush of intimacy after that first reading only beauty and song remained. But the second time she read more slowly, and the lines throbbed against her heart.

> *Peace is in the grave.*
> *I am a god and can not find it there.*

She swirled in that world about him, a world where the good lacked power, and the powerful lacked goodness; where wisdom was without love, and those who loved were without wisdom. She swirled, rose, and billowed on to the great triumph when the freed Titan made the men of earth one brotherhood; on to the "deep truth which is imageless." At sun-up she started out, unwearied and alight.

> *The impalpable thin air,*
> *And all the encircling sunlight were transformed,*
> *As if the sense of love, dissolved in them,*
> *Had folded itself round the sphered world.*

She saw Derry coming to meet her, and remembered that they were to take one of the tent babies to the hospital. Her mind came tumbling back to reality. The Titan was still chained. But she couldn't so quickly lose her luminosity. Derry pretended to be listening as he looked at her rapt face.

"Where's the music ?" he asked.

She hurriedly told him of the book that Pritchett had given her. He looked into her brimming eyes and wondered how he could have left it to Pritchett, the invertebrate, to think of a gift so obviously her due.

"I read all night, Derry."

"I see. 'All things have put their evil nature off.' You look like the Spirit of the Hour yourself. How are your coursers getting along pasturing on vegetable fire ? I've often wondered. And what do you think of the amphisbenic snake ?"

Her face turned a cloudy red. "Of course it's — it's very imaginative," she stumbled, defensive in the broad daylight.

"Striped with inanities. You shouldn't swallow things whole — not even poets, though they take the lightning for a pen and make their ink of morning dew."

She fought for her treasure. "I don't care what you think! I don't care at all! It made me believe. I can feel the earth alive, helping us."

Derry felt a hot stab of shame. How small he could be! What wouldn't he give to feel as she did for one minute? Her eyes darkened with pain, and he ached unbearably, wanting to soothe her in his arms.

"Splendid, my dear," he said kindly. "'We'll not turn down anything that makes us believe."

He began to quote imperfectly, watching her face soften.

> *The painted veil called life,*
> *Which mimicked all that men believed or hoped,*
> *Is torn aside. The man remains,*
> *Equal, unclassed, tribeless, nationless,*
> *Exempt from awe, worship, degree, the king*
> *Over himself; just, gentle, wise; —*

"Like Amos Freer," she cried, glowing.

He hesitated, weighing the statement. "Yes, like Amos," he finally admitted.

Amos was present at Pritchett's supper, but he was saying nothing, tasting nothing. Ishma thought he looked more wise than gentle. The friendly lips were hard set, and she was sure that his round face was thinner than when she had seen it the day before. He was watching Pritchett, who, she became aware, was teasing Jed Rankin to the breaking point. Amos rose and laid a hand on Jed's arm as he spoke to Pritchett.

"You don't care for this strike. Why don't you get out and let us alone? You are not interested in us."

"Not interested? Well, certainly I am not interested in any glorified amœba with a Messianic delusion."

Only one of Freer's friends understood the insult to their

leader. Jason Windrow, a young student of Duke University, jerked off his glasses as if his sudden heat might break them. "You propped up worm !" he said to Pritchett. "Amos Freer doesn't claim to be anything but a man ! The biggest delusion you could have would be to think yourself one."

Pritchett laughed, with big, charitable tolerance, at the little gnat, Windrow, and then ignored him. "Well, Freer," he said, "it happens that your advice and my inclination agree. I'm starting north tomorrow. This supper is my little farewell courtesy. I thought we might get together for an amiable talk, but I see that you will be satisfied with nothing except a discreditable rumpus. It's the fatal weakness of you communists to be always in a row."

Jed clenched his hands, and Amos increased the pressure on his arm. "Don't prove his statement for him, Jed," he said mildly. Then he turned to Pritchett.

"And it's the fatal weakness of you socialists to be always on the run. I don't object to your running, since you feel that way, if only you would go far enough — back into the capitalist camp where you belong, and quit dodging in and out of ours. Our new converts are easily confused. Yes, I've one other objection. I do strongly object to your throwing stink-bombs as you run. Stink-bombs made of the hybrid mess in your brain — a half and half mixture of two antipodal theories of society. Nothing stinks worse than that, and we waste good time having to clean it out. That's your reason for this little supper, Pritchett — this amiable courtesy. You couldn't leave without scattering a few stinkers."

Pritchett had paled, and his unstable figure seemed to knit itself together. The change was becoming. He looked ready to dart on Amos. Professor Beckwith rose to his feet. "Come now," he began. "We have met for enlightenment. We are all sincerely seeking the light. Let us be gentlemen, if we can't be friends."

Pritchett relaxed to his old slouch. "Thank you, Beckwith. Freer may go as far as he chooses. I put no restrictions on a guest."

"I haven't touched your bread, Pritchett. I'm here to get my men."

"Babies, you mean, don't you ? Men usually get about without help."

"Here's one baby with a grown-up fist !" cried Jed, with a lunge forward. Pritchett didn't flinch. He may have been counting on the restraining hand of Freer, but the mountaineer wrenched away from Amos, and halted only when he found Beckwith's bland face in front of him. The Professor was not strong enough meat for Jed, who turned contemptuously away. Freer's hand was again upon him.

"We're leaving, Jed," said Amos. "Don't you see that thug over there waiting for his master's voice. You've arranged your friendly farewell with great care for detail, Pritchett. The police are here, ready to do their duty."

"Not by my invitation. The man was sent by the department when it became known that strikers were to be here. You know they're doing that all the time."

Ishma had recognized the young deputy, Ben Dills, who had helped her with Thelma Rowe. She moved over to him and spoke, under cover of the noisy conversation. "You didn't lose your job."

"Hell ! I wish I had. If I knew where to get another'n it wouldn't take me a bob-tail minute to resign. I've been hearin' a lot o' these strikin' fellers talk."

"Do you know Red Shannon ?"

"Know Red ? Me an' him 's got to be buddies mighty nigh. Say, did you ever hear him whistle 'Turkey In The Straw' with variations ?"

"Then I don't suppose you helped beat him up."

"Beat up Red ? They hain't done that, have they ?"

"They've nearly killed him."

"The dirty rough-necks ! The lousy old — Say, you don't mean they hurt that kid ? He could whistle the blues out of a bag of indigo. Did they hurt him bad ?"

"They've just about killed him. You're in a fine business, friend."

"I'm quittin'. Soon as I can find something I won't starve on. I ain't keen on starvin'. Kain't do with it, like a lint-head."

"What did you do before this?"

"Worked on a farm. An' I'd go back for board an' clothes — jest overalls an' brogues. Anything to get out o' this. How can I go on fightin' these fellers when I know they're right?"

"Ever heard o' Abraham Beasley?"

"Sure. Ever'body has."

"You go to him, and tell him I sent you. Ask him for work. If you don't get it, you'll have a home till you find something. He's not stingy with his bread."

"Lady, I've quit right now. Yes, ma'am, I've resigned. They paid me off today, so they kain't hold out on me. I'll 'phone 'em I'm gone. I won't even go up an' tell 'em. No more dirty work for me! I'll keep my hands sweet with old barn mud an' gwanner."

"Are you the only deputy here tonight?"

"No. There's one over there behind the Perfessor. Cal Buxton. A bad 'un too. He'd stay away from a ball game to get a chance at breakin' a striker's head. There'll be trouble here if he can make it. He's mad because the chief didn't put him on for Yarnboro tonight where the big fun will be. Ma'am, let me tell you something. The strikers ain't goin' to win. They're right, but what's that agin money? You better quit 'fore you're hurt. Money can beat anything. I tell you, money can beat *anything!*"

Ishma smiled. It couldn't beat the spirit of Man. It couldn't beat the tide of Life. One skirmish lost — but they were not going to lose! — would mean nothing. She strained her eyes through the blue smoke to see what was going on in the room. The strikers, she thought, ought to be leaving for Yarnboro, but Freer sat at the table, his elbows resting on it, his eyes staring down. There was boredom and discouragement in his attitude. He seemed to be asking himself, "Shall we never get through with these repetitions?" The strikers were gathered about him and behind him, some in chairs, some standing. All of them were strenuously annihilating Pritchett's cigarettes. They didn't get many in the colony. Jed was going to and fro among them,

362

dropping choice bits of excoriating mountainese. Pritchett was again drifting tranquilly, the master of the hour, enjoying himself.

There were only two women in the room besides Ishma. One was a striker's wife, very young, with sleek, copper hair and dark, well-deep eyes in a starved face. Pritchett, a tolerable artist, had made a sketch of her. Because she was untutored and knew it, she rarely spoke. The other woman had come with Beckwith. She was a grey-haired novelist, hoping to pep up her output for an uninterested public. Ishma remembered having met her. Virginia had brought her to the hospital. "No doubt I'm in her note-book," she thought grimly, but the thought was followed by another which held the spice of exultation. In a little while, a few years probably, the lady's novels would have value only as a sort of historic make-believe. If she wrote "In the Spring of 1928," it would carry as much verity as "In the period when we were dwelling on Mars —" Pick up your shiny bits, she inwardly addressed her; they'll be about as interesting as buttons in a crow's nest. The lady's eyes met Ishma's, and her head bent in graceful recognition. With her little feet rooted in aristocratic ground, she could safely sway and sniff toward the questionable areas of humanity.

"We meet again, Mrs. Bailey," she said, putting out her hand. "I shall see Mrs. Grant very soon, before my annual flitting North. She would like a message, I'm sure."

"I don't think so, Mrs. Owenby."

"O, you misjudge my dear Virginia !"

Ishma had not ceased to think of Virginia Grant with tenderness. Billie Joe always would have her love. When thoughts of the rising storm possessed her, she could see herself befriending her two gentle enemies. But here was this woman, like a well-preened vulture, on the field of actual battle, poking curiously about for titillating pick-ups. Friendship hardened into justice. She saw Virginia Grant wringing her pale, manicured hands, and felt queerly devoid of sympathy. She could only think that such hands would be useful on a spinner's job, after they had won their calluses.

"You may tell Mrs. Grant," she said, "that I grow more grateful to her every day." To herself she added, "And she'll never know why that is the truth."

"O," Mrs. Owenby radiated, "I have told Virginia that you could not be without a sense of gratitude. It was unthinkable! She'll be glad to know I was right."

Ishma gasped away from that vacuous aura, and moved nearer to the one window. It was a large one, in the rear, and wide open. The front room of the restaurant was on a level with the street, but the rear room was built over a basement, and back of the basement the ground fell abruptly away, making the window an actual third story in height from the earth below. Ishma looked down on the spreading foliage of a great Philadelphus in full, sweet-scented bloom, reaching half way up to the window. With her forehead against the heavy screen she tried to breathe. Ben Dills, the deputy, had followed her, and he too faced the screen, as if concerned with the assaulting insects outside.

"I'm goin' to tell you something I know," he said, barely making himself heard. "I'm out of the service now. Clean out. I can talk if I want to. They don't tell us deppity fellers much, but we pick up things. There's goin' to be a lynchin' tonight."

"What? Who?" Ishma's whispering voice choked. Her first thought was of Amos.

"I don't know. But it's not boss Freer. They ain't ready for him yet. They mean to get him, but they've got to work up the mob fer anything as big as that, an' the mob won't start. No, sir, they kain't get the mob started. You fellers have got a lot o' the farmers thinkin' maybe you're half way right, an' they won't start. Some o' the high-ups goin' out an' do the leadin' an' that'll bring in the farmers. They'll foller then, like their own sheep, most of 'em. Say, I heard a mill lawyer talkin' to the chief. He says things are gettin' bad in the country when the riff-raff kain't be swung into line for the dirty work when it's got to be done. Ten years ago, he says, a man like Freer would be lynched an' buried an' fergot in twenty-four hours, just by sendin' the word around. Now it takes lawyers an' preachers an' respectable business men to get 'em started. They'll do it too, with all the lies they're puttin' out steady. They're shapin' up."

"But what about the mob tonight, Ben?"

364

"No mob at all. It's goin' to be quiet, while all the strikers an' most o' the police are over in Yarnboro. If the police are over there, they kain't be blamed for what happens down here."

"But who — who is it ?"

"Who they're goin' to swing ? I don't know. But I've figgered out it's one o' these heah union niggers. They've been sayin' something's got to be done to stop 'em from jinin' up. But I don't know."

"Maybe it's all talk. There's a lot of lynch talk dropped about, you know."

"Well, the deppity friend I got it from is some brag. Maybe he was spreadin' on. But I thought I'd tell you. An' you can put these heah strikers on the look-out, soon as they cut loose from this bunch. Say, I wish you'd get out o' the strike. It's goin' to be bloody — fer the women as well as the men. Us deppities hear a lot that ain't meant fer us. You kain't win. Money can beat *anything*, I tell you."

"No, Ben. You've been listening at the wrong key-hole — a very small one too. Get out of doors and you'll hear the tramp of a hundred million feet. Money can't stop them. Listen to that professor now, if you want to know how small a key-hole can be."

Beckwith had the floor, his cultured smooth voice playing affectionately with his subject. "I don't think that I am assuming too much, Mr. Freer, when I say that whatever your prejudice against the greatly successful, you will not deny that they have used their vast fortunes very generously for the benefit of their fellowmen. They have used them educationally, hygienically, exploratively, and religiously, to our great betterment. I have only to instance the Rockefeller foundation, as one among many."

"I do not deny it. But their great benefits are no offset for the miseries they have inflicted. I have only to instance the world war, as one among many. I also beg to inform you that a classless society could have accomplished vastly more, with no miseries as a necessary accompaniment. Such a society could put in its vest-pocket, so to speak, all the good that the doles of your greatly successful have given us. Education ? Yes. Education with blinders on, to keep themselves in power. Hygiene ?

365

Yes. But not enough to keep their own guarded families safe. While they clear one road of disease, poverty is filling a thousand others. They're after pellagra now. They find it *interesting*. But they won't make it possible to keep fresh, southern grown food where the starving pellagra patients can get it. They won't stop dumping that food in New York bay — tons and tons of it every week — to keep the 'set-up' from being disturbed, while a jobless line is twelve deep before one employment agency in New York City. They'll not stop that imbecility. Intelligence ? Ability ? Professor, I do deny here, now and forever, that the thirty men who control the government of the United States are either able or intelligent."

"And I protest," said Beckwith, still graciously smooth of voice, "that America is not governed by thirty, nor a thousand, men. We have a democracy, and democracy is given to blunders. It might be salutary if indeed we were governed by the thirty most powerful and wise among us."

"Of course you are joking, Professor, about this country being a democracy. And as for your thirty most powerful being also wise, do you know what is their chief trouble at this minute ? What is making them lose sleep, swear behind their teeth, and lift eyes like puzzled sheep ? It's the fact that they have made such a chaotic mess of affairs that their business needs another war when, with all their desperate preparation and scare-mongering, they are unable to supply it. That's where their wisdom has brought them. And able ? Their chief ability lies in doing the one unnecessary thing on earth — making money. Always men will have to go on making shoes, clothes, houses, telescopes, violins, whatever body and spirit hunger for, but they will not have to make money. That will be cut out. Can you imagine a day, Professor, when all values will stand on their own base, having nothing to do with money ?"

"Preposterous, I must say. You confirm my contention that your aim is to sweep away civilization."

"No, my aim is to make civilization possible for everybody. Surely you have heard that maxim that we workers are so fond of. 'Life without labor is robbery; labor without art is barbarity.'"

366

Beckwith's small mind could only cling to stereotype.

"You would propose art for our ditch-diggers and street-sweepers?"

"Most particularly for them, if it should still be necessary in an organized machine age to use human beings for such work. They should have, as all workers should have, the comforts that make life endurable, the arts that make life gracious, the science that makes life a growth. How many, within a mile of where you stand, are blessed with these genuine riches? You have been in most of the homes hereabout, I understand."

The Professor flushed. He knew that Amos knew he was an agent of the Greybank, distributing culture as chosen by Reece-Durkin; snooping around the workers, filling their hearts with fear and their minds with archaic rot.

"Your question, being an accusation and personal, I need not answer. Your statement should have consideration. I observe that your list of benefits does not include religion. If I were to admit all other of your claims, I should yet have to oppose you because you leave out of your scheme the great restoring power of religion. Under no regime can I imagine humanity prospering if cut adrift from divine strength. The spiritual life-blood of a people is a precious thing —"

"Shore it's precious!" Jed burst in. "Precious to *you!* It's *money* to you! You couldn't fool us without that. You take a man an' lash his back an' tell him not to worry about his onery red blood runnin' inter the ash-pan, so long as he keeps his spirchal life-blood goin' good. You tell him to believe in God an' his justice — whack! whack! — an' go to church an' drop his pore little squeezed out dimes inter the plate — whack! whack! — what's a slave's back fer anyhow? — whack! whack! — what's his tongue fer? Pray! pray! whack! whack! **An'** you —"

Amos took Jed by the collar and gave him a friendly shake. "Never mind that now, Jed." He let go, and turned to Beckwith.

"I do deny what stands in your mind for religion. I define it for myself. To me religion means securing for man the finest adjustment possible to the universe in which he must live. It is

367

our enfilade against attack from the stars — the cosmos — the inimical tides of earth — the gorillas, foxes, hyenas within us and without — whatever interferes with that finest possible adjustment. Will you admit that definition into the argument, Professor? Is it worthy of the god you worship?"

"I think I can admit it."

"Then can a religion that accepts war and poverty — the two immediate dragons in the way of that finest adjustment of man to his universe — can such a religion be sincerely upheld by any man capable of logical thought?"

"Are you aware, sir, that many of our churches are taking a stand against war?"

"O, yes! In times of peace there are always some that do that. But let war come and they'll turn rampant as usual — drum-agents for Beelzebub. And as for poverty — "

"I deplore war, and I hold no brief for poverty."

"I understand that. You merely support the religion that upholds them. I don't ask you if it is intelligent, Professor. You must know that answer. I ask you, is it honest?"

Mrs. Owenby had been thrilling and bridling, getting herself erect for a venture. She would open her mouth in a communistic discussion. She plunged over the brink.

"No one can say that Professor Beckwith is not honest! His record is clear! To accuse him — how ridiculous!"

Freer gave a disgusted groan. Pritchett was humiliated. The lady had given his party a toboggan slide to the bottom. Even Beckwith was embarrassed. There was silence in which the roar of the Reece-Durkin mill, converted by distance into a musical hum, could be distinctly heard. Ishma looked through the window at the great building over a block away, with its tiers of glass stories through which the yellow light shone, and having walked there so much and so long, she felt her own body vibrating with its roar and shaking with its pounding looms. Drifting into the room with the subdued roar came the scent of the giant shrub below the window. Elysian fragrance and the hum of peace.

Pritchett rose. He must rush his party uphill again. He would throw a stinker. That would start things. But there was a startling interruption. Jason Windrow was finding the silence heavy. His social specialty was farmyard imitations. Climbing to a chair behind the Owenby, he spread out his arms over her head and gave a verisimilitude of a hen advertising her new-laid egg. The strikers stamped and shouted. Pritchett was ghastly with anger. When the room was reasonably still again, he began to speak, his voice glassily precise.

"You are not altogether wrong, Freer. In fact, I've no quarrel with your principles. But you'll never put them over in these southern United States. You are wasting a truly fine talent. Get out with it ! Go where it will be worth something. Right now one third of your workers that you expect to meet in Yarnboro are off listening to some Holy Roller slobbering about peace beyond the skies. Another third are watching the antics of the medicine man and his crew on Community Green — watching with their mouths hanging open and dribbling gurgles of idiocy. The other third may meet you, as per schedule, but they'll be thinking more about what you are going to give their bellies tomorrow than about the great and glorious march to freedom. The door of revolution doesn't open toward the South. These poor boobs down here will never have the guts to break their chains. They'll be the last of the slave tribes on earth —"

Jed Rankin leapt across the table, reaching for Pritchett's throat. Mrs. Owenby gave a very unaristocratic screech. Lena Allen, the young striker's wife, who adored Pritchett, fell fainting against her husband. Before Jed could land on Pritchett, Buxton was between them, his automatic at Jed's chest.

"Hands up !" he shouted, as if battle were on. There was a slight hesitation. It looked as if Jed didn't have reason enough left to put up his hands. "Put 'em up, Jed," said Amos, and the boy stuck them up, chewing his rage.

"Dills !" yelled Buxton. "Lock that door over there !"

He meant the door to the alley. The connecting door to the other room of the restaurant was guarded by his own body. He was standing with his back to it. "I'll have to arrest you too, Freer," he said. "Come over here by Jed."

Amos crossed over. "You're responsible for this trouble," lectured Buxton. "But you meant to make a lot more for us over in Yarnboro. Guess I've stopped a fine little hell over there.

369

The chief will be glad to know we've got you safe for tonight anyway. That meeting will go like a flat tire without your hot air."

Dills had locked the alley door and slipped the key to Ishma. "I'll 'phone headquarters, Cal," he said, starting out by way of the connecting door behind Buxton.

"I'm not Cal to you," Buxton roared. "Get the chief on the 'phone. The chief, mind you! And have the wagon sent, you little punk! Let the chief know I've got big game!"

"All right, Cal."

The light-switch was near the connecting door. As Dills passed the room went dark. There had been semi-darkness before, but now there was utter black. A whacking sound was heard, and the fall of a body. Then a swirl, a rush, an opening door, another rush. Freer and eight men passed out and down the high steps to the alley. Jim Allen carried his wife. The door was slammed and locked from the outside.

Pritchett found the switch and turned on the light. Buxton was on the floor, in sitting posture, rubbing his head gently. On the floor lay a black-jack. He picked it up. "This ain't mine," he said, still half dazed.

"Somebody has treated you to your own medicine, old boy," said Pritchett. Buxton got up. Oaths poured from his lips. "Ladies present!" cautioned Pritchett.

"Ladies hell! A lady wouldn't come in here to get out of a rain o' rattlesnakes!"

"You — pouf!" cried the Owenby, clinging to knight Beckwith, who was patting her arm with the right degree of assurance.

"Dill 's 'll get the air for this," said Buxton. "He didn't lock that door."

"Yes he did," Pritchett assured him. "I saw him turn the key. But a skeleton key will unlock it for anybody who happens to have one."

Buxton swore again, at unreasonable length. "I've got to arrest somebody. The chief 's coming."

"And the wagon," said Pritchett. "You can ride back."

"For little I'd arrest you!" Buxton spat out.

"Climb down, Cal. You're here to protect me, you know. You don't want the department to get the laugh on you."

"The laugh! What you call this? Not one o' them goddamned hoboes here for me to take in!" Suddenly he saw Ishma, and his eyes gloated. Why in the name of reason hadn't she gone with the others, thought Pritchett. He couldn't know that she had given the key to Freer and he had locked the door from the outside, thinking that she had passed through. She couldn't get out through the connecting door because Buxton was in the way. The eye of the law continued to glare. Pritchett stepped to her side. "This is one of my friends," he said. Buxton's gaze continued fixed. But the woman was dressed like a lady. Maybe he was mistaken.

"You're not that Bailey woman, are you?"

"I am Mrs. Hensley," said Ishma, with lifted head and shoulders.

"All right. I'll put you down for a witness. You'll have to be where I can get you. Ever' one o' them made-in-hell out o' works 'll be in jail tomorrow."

"Mrs. Hensley can go, I suppose," said Pritchett, opening the connecting door. "Come this way, Mrs. Hensley."

Ishma passed through the door. He took a few steps with her and offered a graceful hand. "I'm sorry it's goodbye," he said.

"And I am glad," she answered, not seeing the hand, and turning listlessly from him. "I wish you had never come here."

CHAPTER XV

SHE WALKED home sickened with thoughts of the evening. Was this the bright crusade on which she was bound ? How much of truth was there in what Pritchett had said ? "The door of revolution doesn't open toward the South." Were the workers really braver and wiser in other countries ? In China, in India, in Germany, in Bulgaria, they were fighting and dying in an effort to break their chains. And they were breaking them. Not all were dying. Some would march over the bridge of death. All Russia was on the other side. One sixth of the world ! But here — would freedom have to come from without ? From strong hands reaching to the weak ? She knew that some of the strikers had begun to falter. But for everyone they lost they were gaining ten. What was the matter with her ? This big mass meeting would put courage into everybody. In a few days the second strike would be called. She knew, because she was one of the few who had been taken into the secret. A leak would be fatal. The enemy would do anything to stop it — perhaps attack the colony. But there would be no leak. They would have the Greybank beaten. They were on the verge of triumph. Why wasn't her heart bounding, her blood leaping ? It was because she was so tired, of course. She wouldn't get up in the morning. She'd tell Mildred not to wake her, and she'd sleep until noon.

But when she reached home Mildred was already asleep, in the rear room, with her children. Without speaking to her, Ishma went to bed. Not really to bed, for she slept on a cot, small and short, in the living-room. She lay down, not remembering that she had said nothing to Freer about the rumored lynching. She had herself forgotten it.

On the cot, she half dozed, without rest. There was a lump

in her heart which seemed to be getting bigger and bigger. It was strangely mixed up with Britt and the mountains. Soon she would be going back. Just as soon as the strike was won. Were they going to win ? Three thousand and thirty. Of course they would win ! The lump was growing. Soon it would be larger than 'her body. Britt, and the mountains ! And there was a throb in her brain beating louder and stronger. Soon she would have no brain, nothing but a beating throb, driving out everything else. She kept telling herself to be quiet, to think clearly. Some of the strikers were saying, "It's no use. We're beat. Even if we win, we're beat. They'll keep us in hell till we get out and let the scabs in." She mustn't let them talk like that. They were not beat. In a week they'd bring every worker out of the Greybank. That would show the bosses !

The words of Ben Dills, "Money can beat anything," began pounding with the throb in her head. At last she was actually in sleep. Rebellious sleep. She ought to keep awake. Workers had no time to waste in sleep. They ought to give every minute to the cause. What cause ? Money can beat anything — anything — money can beat — beat — beat —

In her dream a dragon descended on earth and began devouring the inhabitants. First it ate up all the workers and the ruined farmers. It would go to a manufacturing town — textile — steel — rubber — and gorge, shoving out its long jaws and biting entire houses of four rooms at a mouthful. Little children would drop out, and the thing would lick them up as if they were crumbs. It would creep over the farms, crushing houses and overturning barns. Families would rush to the woods, and it would overtake them and curl its tongue about them. After every worker in the world was devoured, it began on the "upper classes." They would hide in great houses like castles, and it would throw its sides against the stone walls and topple them to the ground. Some of the people fled to the sea in yachts, and the dragon made fins of its fore feet and went after them. Soon there was nobody left in the world but the dragon and God and herself. And God was afraid. She could hear him calling him in a tiny scared voice, begging her to help him. "Ishma — Ishma — Ishma Hensley — for God's sake —" Well, that was funny. Why didn't

373

he say for *my* sake ? Why did he keep scratching the door ?

She jumped up, recognizing Leta's voice, and opened the door

"Ishma, I thought you's never goin' to wake up," she said in a whisper. "I couldn't call loud, for I didn't want Mildred to hear me."

"Is Rad sick?"

"He's all right."

"Have you come out married ?"

"We went to Charlotte today. An' tomorrow we're goin' to church an' let the folks know. Some of 'em know already, an' they're goin' to give us a swell party next week. But I ain't got time— Oh, Ishma, you treated me white—an' I've got to tell you, Rad'll leave me if ever he finds out I come here. But you'll never tell. They're lynchin' that nigger, Butch Wells, tonight— 'cause he's workin' fer your union, and—"

"Butch ! Lynchin' him ? Where ? Quick ? Tell me, Leta !"

"Rad thought it was smart, he couldn't keep from tellin' me. Sid Brinn got him into it. Just like he got him into the church. Rad thinks he's goin' to be a big feller. All he's got to do is to stick along with Sid."

"But where, Leta, and when ?"

"Where—I don't know except it's out somewhere on the Big Oak road. Rad was hummin' that song today,

> *Meet me at the lynchin' tree,*
> *When the clock is strikin' three,*

but maybe that didn't mean anything. Only the lynchin' tree is out on the Big Oak road, an' I guess they're takin' him there."

"Have you told me everything you know, Leta ?"

"Everything, Ish. Darn my soul if I haven't."

"Then go home and go to bed."

"What you goin' to do, Ish ?"

"How long has Rad been gone ?"

"He left about five minutes before I did. I waited till I was sure he was out o' the way. He said he'd be back towards mornin'. What you goin' to do, Ish ?"

"I don't know. But you've done your part. Go home now.

I'll remember you for this, Leta. God used good mud in you. Run along!"

Leta ran along. Ishma had dressed herself while talking, putting on, without knowing it, the Virginia Grant dress which had been thrown on a chair. She slipped out, closing the door gently. No use to wake Mildred. She knew she must have a car, and hoped Ed Wallace hadn't taken his old Ford to Yarnboro. It would be just the thing for getting over the rutty road to the lynching-tree, if that was where she was to find Butch, or his body. Sid Brinn had picked his time. With all of the strikers, and most of the rank and file, in Yarnboro, she didn't know whom she could get to accompany her. If she went to Yarnboro first, she would be too late to save Butch, and here in Spindle Hill it would take time to wake people up and persuade them to go. She might try twenty houses before she could find a man at home. Also she might strike just the wrong persons — not many heads were clear on solidarity that involved the negro. Some would be ready to say, "Good enough fer a damn nigger!"

And suppose she *could* collect a posse? That would mean a fight with the lynchers, more men killed, and the poisonous spread of hate.

She didn't believe the lynchers would kill her if she went alone. There wasn't a mob of them. Ben Dills would have known about a mob affair. He had said it was going to be a quiet knock-off, just to scare the negroes, without any public scandal. There had been two cases like that lately, which she had heard of. One was in an adjoining county, where an old negro woman of sixty-five had been hung in her own house by three or four "neighboring citizens," who thought she was a "bad influence." Another negro had been hung not ten miles from Winbury, after an altercation with a farmer from whom he demanded money due him for labor. Both hangings had been carefully kept out of the papers, but the "niggers" had got their lesson. It was likely that only a few men had been selected for the lynching tonight. She had heard Rad say that when you couldn't get a big mob to go on a lynchin' spree it was safer to keep quiet and pick just enough for the job.

They wouldn't kill her. That would be more of a scandal

375

than they would dare to risk. There wasn't likely to be more than four or five men, and she knew three of them. Penn Baxter always went along with Sid Brinn. And there was Rad. They couldn't hide behind black handkerchiefs. She'd call their names and threaten them with exposure if they didn't let go of Butch. She'd go right on, and leave Em Wallace to start the alarm and send help. Maybe she could hold up the murder long enough to give the men time to get there. She made her plan while walking the two blocks to Em Wallace's. Em answered her call. Yes, Ed was in Yarnboro with all the other strikers. He had gone in a truck, and the old Ford was in the back yard. While Ishma was getting the car out she told Em the story, and Em began to jerk on her clothes. Ishma told her to go to the nearest drugstore and telephone Yarnboro. Get hold of anybody who would take a message to the hall where the meeting was being held. Start everybody hunting Butch Wells. Send a group on every road, but start the fastest car they could get out towards Willow Swamp on the Big Oak road. Then Em was to telephone the police and get them to act if she could. The police never hurried on strikers' business, and as for lynchings more than one officer of the law had been heard to say that two or three fine little lynchings would save the department a lot of trouble. Ishma didn't count on the law going on a mad race to save Butch. Em was ready by the time Ishma got through telling her what to do. Em could be depended upon. She was as good a man as ever wore a skirt.

In ten minutes Ishma had left the highway and was chugging along the deep ruts of the logging road that led past the "lynchin' tree." This was only two miles from the highway, but the road had been practically cut to pieces, she found, after a mile out. She trusted to the high axle of the old Ford to keep her off the ground. It was the noise that made her fearful. The lynchers would hear her coming, and might take their victim into the deep woods. But what if they hadn't come this way ? They might not have gone to the lynching tree at all. She could do nothing except go ahead and find out. When her car lights shot forward and fell on a group standing quietly by the roadside waiting for her, instead of panic and fright she felt relief.

376

There were five men standing. Only five! The men kept still, watching her, but she noticed that two of them had their guns lifted and pointed toward the car. There was a half moon giving light enough to outline the gigantic oak tree back of them.

"Halt!" cried one of the men who held a gun. Ishma stopped her car and stood up in it. The top had long been stripped from it, and she rose her full height.

"God! It's a woman!"

"That union bitch!"

"We'll give her the same!"

"An' have the whole United States jumpin' on us? I reckon not!"

"We could bury her, an' nobody 'd find out."

"No, you couldn't, Sid Brinn!" she called out. "There are too many people that know where I am tonight! You can bury me, but you can't hide me. I'll not stay down."

"What you mean callin' Sid Brinn? He ain't here."

"That handkerchief is not big enough, Sid. And Rad Bailey, you step out. I want to talk to you."

"You're the bitch Rad got shet of, are you?"

Ishma saw that one of the men had lowered his gun — Rad probably. He was about Rad's build and height.

"Rad ain't here, an' if he was he's through with you."

"Not here? That's a lie, Penn Baxter!"

There was a simultaneous gasp from the men. Did she know them all? Ishma felt that each man, Rad excepted, was silently deciding her fate. Rad would help her, if he could. The other gun was slowly lowered, and the tall man who held it spoke.

"What you mean — Penn? He's at home asleep."

"Don't hump your shoulders, Penn. Stand up! You can't hide six feet three! You nor Sid either. Ever'body knows the long twins."

Baxter laughed and jerked back his shoulders. "Well, what are you going to do about it?"

"It's you that's got to do, and do it quick. There'll be fifty union men on this road in half an hour. Murderers can't do as they please in this country any more, not even good church members. If you've killed Butch Wells—"

"We ain't killed him. He's gagged, er you'd hear him hollerin' fer his rotten yaller skin."

Ishma jumped to the ground. "Untie him, and put him in my car."

"Say, whad you think you are? Jack Pershing?"

"I'm a God-serving woman, Sid Brinn, though I don't go to church as often as you do. You'll find me saving life instead of taking it."

"A bitch runnin' round with niggers! We ought to skin you alive an' whip you on the raw. An' by God, we're goin' to do it!"

He advanced toward her, and she stood waiting, but her arms were tingling. She would fight hard. They were afraid to kill her. But they might overpower and flog her, which would be worse. Her death would be a reverberating crime, a disgrace to the State, and help the union cause. A flogging, though it should leave her broken for life, could be covered up by the police and condoned by the "best people." An associate of niggers! Behind their screens of respectability, social, legal, churchly, they would smile at the lashes on her flesh. She could see Virginia Grant's delicate eyebrows going up. "And we thought of her as a companion for my innocent child!"

The man that she believed to be Rad, had followed the advancing man and held him by the arm. Rad would help her — if he could. She remembered Em Wallace's pistol, and moving backwards, with her eyes on Baxter, she reached into the car and found it. When she drew it out one of the men had her covered with his gun. The approaching man had halted.

"Don't be afraid I'll shoot you," she said, turning the pistol to her own bosom. "I shall kill myself if you come near me."

Baxter broke into roaring laughter. "You're out to please us, ain't you?"

"You fool! Don't you know it will go harder with you if you force me to kill myself than if you used your own guns? You'll go into court and swear that I killed myself. And why did I do it? Because I'd rather die than be befouled by you. You can't hide that. And you know what will happen to you then!"

378

They were silent. They did know what would happen to them. They might possibly get away with murder, but if they were suspected of the crime far worse than murder, the crime which no southern public can consider without raging, they would be lost. She would be avenged. She wouldn't need the union and the I. L. D. to make hell of it.

Ishma heard Rad's voice. "If you boys can't see we're beat this time, you're purty short o' brains. Butch ain't hurt yet. Just a few kicks and clumps. I say dump him into her car an' let 'em go, if she'll give her word this is the last of it."

"Her word! Lordy God! Whad that be worth?"

"It's worth enough to save your necks," said Ishma. "And you'll have to be quick, whatever you do. You'll have to scatter before the union men get here."

"Why'n't they come along with you, if they're comin' at all? Not let a woman run into a killin' scrape by herself?"

"You ought to know why. All of our men are in Yarnboro tonight. That's why you picked this time for your dirty job. I sent word over there to tell them to come on. And you can be sure they're coming. I came alone because I wasn't going to wait till you'd killed Butch."

"Why'n't you bring the police? Hey, what?"

"You know that too. I was in a hurry. The police walk backwards when there's a lynching ahead of them."

"Did you tell anybody who we were?"

"Yes. One person. I told her she was to let the union know who to make it hot for if I didn't come back. I didn't know how big the devil would swell in you. But she was to keep it secret if I got back safe. I didn't want to hurt Rad unless I had to."

"Reckon we can believe her, Rad?"

"I'll bet my head you can. You can string me up if she's lying to you."

They were now careless of their identity, as careless as if Ishma were a confederate.

"You boys have got to hurry," she said. "You can go ahead with the job, and get yourselves ready to sit in a hot chair till you're one big cinder, or you can put Butch in the car and let us go. If you do that, you'll never be bothered. You know as

379

well as I do that the union don't want trouble right now. We only want to protect our members."

"All right. Let's heave him up."

"Untie him," said Ishma.

"No objection," said Sid Brinn, and proceeded to cut the cords that bound Butch's arms and legs.

"Ungag him."

"Just as you say, kind lady. *He* won't squeal anyway. A nigger knows better."

They saw, and Ishma saw, that Butch was unconscious. "One more good kick won't hurt him," said the one whom she knew was Penn Baxter. He drew back his foot. "No, you don't," said Ishma, interposing her body, and catching Rad by the arm. "Get him into the car ! Help him, quick ! Don't you see how his head is bleeding ? I must get him to a doctor."

She was now violently nauseated, and was afraid she would faint before she could get away. "You'd better help, all of you ! You know what I'll do if you've killed him !"

Two of the men stooped and lifted the negro. "Ketch holt here. Heave his feet !"

"The back seat," Ishma said faintly, and they pitched him in. "There's yer purty boy !"

She started her car, and managed to get it turned. Rad jumped on the running board. "I'll go a piece with you." They drove off, leaving the other men getting out their own car.

"What'll Sid do to you, Rad ?" Ishma asked, after a silence.

"Nothin'. He's a coward. If he cheeps on me, I cheeps on him. He won't risk it. He'll stick to me closer 'n ever. I wouldn't 'a' let 'em hurt you, Ish."

"Maybe you wouldn't. But we'd have been two against four."

They reached the highway. "You'd better get off here, Rad. We might meet the men coming after me. Or the police."

Rad sneered. "No danger meetin' the police !" He stayed on until they entered the town.

"Want me to go by your place, Rad ? It's about as near."

"No. Don't want any car heard around my house tonight."

"You and Leta getting on all right ?"

"Leta ain't you, Ish. I got nothin' to say."

"She'll make a fine woman, Rad."

He seemed struck by a thought. "Say, how'd you find out about us ?"

"The union doesn't give away its secrets, Rad."

"If I thought that Leta—"

"Leta ? Good Lord ! She's a child ! What does she know or care about the union's troubles ?"

"I thought we had ever'thing sewed up. If Leta — "

"You've been a big enough fool for one night, without jumping on a poor kid like Leta. You don't think she'd be the one to do *me* a favor, do you ?"

"N-o," he answered slowly. "I don't reckon she would."

"Then don't stir up a mess with her. Try to be happy, Rad. You've got the chance."

"Leet ain't you, Ish."

"Be thankful for that. I've got a hard life ahead of me — a rough life. I didn't get killed tonight, but the next time it may be different. Better get off here, Rad, and I'll turn toward Butch's house. I know where he lives. See if he's breathing."

Rad got off, leaned over Butch, and whiffed in disgust. "He's too much all right. Think o' you ridin' round at midnight with a god-damned nigger !"

"Goodbye, Rad !" Ishma was driving off. "You'll never hear of this."

He watched the car out of sight, then went home and crept in to Leta. She was sound asleep, just as he had left her. "Little kid," he said. "Of course she's all right." He got into bed, and pulled her arm around his neck.

THERE was a crowd milling in and out of Butch's home. The loudest noise was made by his old mother, who wailed with the vigor of her forest ancestry. The white men who had hurried from Yarnboro were dividing into groups to go in search of Butch and Ishma. The telephone line between Yarnboro and Winbury wasn't working, for some unknown reason, and after long effort Em had succeeded in reaching Yarnboro by relay-

ing through Forest City. There was more delay in getting someone to go to the hall and notify the union men. Only Ishma's
swift action had saved Butch.

The men shouted as she drove up. But she hardly heard them.
Her greatest thrill came from within herself, as she thought of
Derry Unthank. He would know now that she too could act
without prejudice. She could stand clean and clear before him.
It was good to feel so triumphant over that final error in her
blood. She tried to crush down a rising pride in herself.

The door of the house was open, and the light from a kerosene
lamp within outlined the figure of a man on the doorstep. Ishma
recognized Unthank.

"I'm back, Derry," she called, a queer gayety in her voice.
"And here's Butch. Get to work on him. He needs you."

Men swarmed up and began lifting Butch out. There was
silence within the house. Someone had assured the old mother
that Butch was all right, and her wail had ceased instantly. In
a few minutes everybody knew of the rescue. Derry hadn't
moved. When he spoke to Ishma his voice fell like a hammer
of ice.

"You unutterable fool!"

She laughed. He needn't try to be superior any more. "I
took the only safe way, Derry. Would you rather have had a
few men killed, and Butch too? Stop looking at me, and get
to work."

He turned to the bed where they had laid Butch, examined him,
and gave a few orders. The skull wasn't fractured, but he might
be unconscious for another hour or two. "No, aunt Susie, he's
not going to die. Go to the fire and smoke, if you don't want to
go to sleep."

The old woman went to the smouldering fire and took a clay
pipe from her more than ample skirt. Several colored men and
women stood around with their eyes glued on Ishma. She was
feeling happy, and airy light. Her feet wanted to leave the floor,
like feathers. She loved those black and bronze women with
their big, tender eyes.

"Wha' dat wife o' Butch's?" said one of them suddenly.
"She runnin' mad yit?"

"Some yawl go fotch her in. She runnin' round wakin' de settlement, tryin' fo' make evahbody staht huntin' Butch."

"Heah huh howlin' right now ?"

"Yeah, dat's huh !"

A willing contingent rushed to meet the woman. Her howling stopped, and the next moment she had bowled herself into the room, exclaiming, "Wha is she ? Wha' dat angel ob de Lawd ?"

Gaffie Wells was very fat and very black. Her lips were heavy, and her teeth so large that one needed the sure avouch of eyes to believe in them. It was impossible to associate her with woe, though tears were racing down her cheeks. As her fat body moved she shook off an odor that an unwashed collie would have disowned.

"Bressed angel, bressed angel ob de Lawd," she kept repeating, and with a great sweep enveloped Ishma, her fat arms encircling the white neck, her thick lips mumbling at the quivering white throat. "We'll all be in heaben togeddah ! Sistah ! sistah ! Yo' sho' got Jedus in you !"

The fleshy embrace, the murky little room, the smoking ashes, the warm stench, the too eager faces shining greasily at the top of big, black bodies, filled Ishma with uncontrollable revulsion. She thought of a high, clean rock on Cloudy Knob, half covered with sweet moss and red-tipped galax. She shut her eyes and saw a cardinal flying over snow.

The rolling arms lay heavy on her neck. The fat bosom shook against her own. The sickening smell of disturbed animal sweat rose and fell with the black body. Gaffie could not see Ishma's blazing eyes, but she felt the white arms stiffen. Before she could release herself voluntarily, Ishma had thrust her off with a wild blow, followed by another. The first struck Gaffie's face; the second fell terrifically on her shoulder, and she went over backwards. She tried to save herself by clutching at the small table, and the overturned lamp threatened the room with greater tragedy. She went down, striking the hearth cruelly hard, and uttering no cry. The most pitiful thing about her was her dumb surprise. As she fell, a jagged rock in the jamb grazed her temple. Someone caught the lamp and righted it before it reached the floor. Ishma looked at the prostrate woman and saw the blood spurting from her temple. She looked over the smoking lamp and met the eyes of Derry Unthank. There was shock in them that merged in a holy patience. His lips half smiled with his high forbearance. The smile brought Ishma to her senses. With unutterable horror of herself she pushed through the door and stumbled away. As her feet grew firm on the ground she began to run. Derry might be following her. Rage returned as she thought of him. If he looked at her again with that remote and holy smile, she would slap him too! Faster and faster she ran, until she was breathless. Then she stopped. No, she was not followed. Of course not. Who would be concerned with a beast like herself? In the distance she heard an approaching train. She must hurry and cross the tracks before it passed. Half a block away she saw the lights of the station, and pushed toward it, coming up just as the train pulled in. It was a coach train, the 2 A. M. for Spartanburg. At Spartanburg one took the 6 A. M. for Asheville. From Asheville one could go — well, anywhere. She felt in her purse. Yes, she had money. But there was no time to buy a ticket. She was running along the platform —

"Wait — please, wait —"

Nobody heard her, but she scrambled up the steps as the train moved off.

CHAPTER XVI

THE HEART HILL BORN

FOR ENDLESS hours Ishma sat on the train trying to realize who and what she was. She felt that she was travelling with a person unknown. The feeling became so strong that she tried to engage the stranger self in conversation, but no intimacy resulted. With clarity cruel to herself she kept looking back into that dark little room which was "home" to the family of Butch Wells. She saw a creature in her own shape committing an act which she had felt was impossible to her mind and heart. She saw poor fat Gaffie, that no tragedy could dignify, with her broad head on the dirty, uneven hearth, and the rays from the lamp showing the crooked path of blood as it trickled from her forehead down into the cracks between the stones. The silence of the room, as she thought of it, was like a hand on her throat.

The first hour on the train had been the easiest. She was in the flush of flight, resolute, triumphant in a way, her face set to her heart's desire, unconfessed but known. Let the world behind her take care of itself. A flood was driving in her veins, overwhelming thought. Under that flood her mind lay helpless. Against it she had no power.

But the flush had died, her spine had begun to quiver, her eyes had turned back to Gaffie. "Very well," she said at last, behind lips that were pale and regretful, yet still rebellious. "I know what I am now. I'm an animal. I haven't got a little Neanderthal woman in me. She's all of me. I'm nothing else. That's clear. And I'm not going to do a thing about it. I didn't make myself. I'll be as I was made. I wanted to slap that woman and I slapped her. I want to get back to Britt, and I'm getting back. I don't want another thing in this jungle swamp of a world."

As the train began to draw near to Beebread, her mind stirred a little under the flood. She began to think about her probable reception at the station. How many of the old loafers would be there, whittling and spitting ? And wouldn't there be some clacking, some raking about among old smells, after they had recognized her and she had slipped away up the hill ? She couldn't fix her thought on that, and whiffed away the smell of rotten leaves. Nothing ahead of her seemed real except Britt. It would take her an hour to climb the hill. Once she would have felt lazy if she gave it half an hour. But that was in another life, several worlds away. Again there was stir under the flood. She had a sudden muddled picture of Winbury, the great mill, her friends, their fight against starvation and slow death. But the picture drifted into unreality before she could become wholly conscious of it.

Would she find Britt at home ? Gone to a lumber camp maybe, to work out a decent suit of clothes. She couldn't bear it if he were not at home. She would have to go on until she found him. But crops were not laid by. He would have to be at home. It wasn't yet June. Some of the shiftless ones wouldn't be through planting. Of course Britt was at home. She didn't think of Ned. There was only Britt.

She was in the last coach. When the train stopped at the little station she stepped off in the rear, and without a glance at the gathering of men and boys and girls farther up in front of the depot, she turned into the road that led to the river bridge and on up the hill. She knew that every eye was upon her, but they were not living eyes to her. They had no power to hurt.

She didn't know how much she owed at that moment to the dress Virginia had given her. It had been recently cleaned, and on the train she had protected it from cinders and dust by spreading her thin scarf over her shoulders and making an apron of a newspaper she had found in her seat. It looked virginally new to those greedy eyes, and the style of it could not be doubted. Guffaws did not come easily behind that vanishing figure, carelessly imperial and sure of itself.

Ishma pressed on, still without thought, without reflection. She was merely a warm emotion flowing upward to a goal. Ideals, theories, the struggle of a world for breath, had thinned

386

to nothing on the edge of her absorbing desire to feel mountains under her feet and Britt's head on her breast. She put out her hand to touch his hair, and almost she could feel the bright warmth of it.

The mountain air had the honey smell of late May. Leaves were still tender, though the boughs were full. The thickening green of the woods offered a gentle resistance to the unacquainted. But Ishma knew that she could walk into them and old trails would open for her.

She came to Si Welch's scraggly pasture, where white and gold butterflies were idling busily, checkering a gay weft on the sun-blue air. The house was hidden behind the bulge of a piney hill. Lizzie was there probably. She remembered hearing Cindy say that Lizzie had "got her a baby at last, an' it didn't have no home-daddy." Ishma guessed that poor old Si wasn't telling so many jokes these days. She hoped that the dogs wouldn't bark and bring Mandy Welch, or some of her rangy towheads, out on the path. Only silence around the bulge of the hill. She got safely by, not meeting stare or question, and began the stiffer climb that lifted her to where she could look back and get glimpses of the river and valley. At one spot she sat down and tried to think, but only an invasion of nature mixed itself with the inner stream pushing her up to Britt. The breeze touched her with the warmth of new milk, sleepy and drowning. The deep indigo sides of the far hills drew her like thoughts of the sea. The river, here and there visible, made silver pools caught in the swelling fringe of the trees. The sky was as blue as the big closed gentians she used to find in Turkle Gap. No, she couldn't think. Though her mind had come from under the flood, it seemed to have gone out of her, to have thinned itself impalpably on the air for miles around her. Something serious and imperative seemed to be struggling just beyond its horizon, faintly touching it here and there, and she could do nothing to help it over the border. Rising slowly, she climbed on.

Sunset hung over Cloudy Knob cabin. Laviny sat on the porch, finding perfect comfort in her snuff and the knowledge that she could begin nagging Bainie at any moment.

Bainie and Jim had moved to aunt Cynthy Webb's place.

Uncle Zeke was dead, and aunt Cynthy wanted to live with her sister on Larky. Julie, who was now the widow of Tim Wheeler, lived on the little place that Tim had left to her. Aunt Cynthy had invited Bainie and Jim to move down and "keer for her things." Jim was very willing to get a place for nothing, and "no taxes to be pesterin' a man's sleep." They had moved, but Bainie was expected to be at Laviny's call at all times. She was now padding around doing the "night-work," and finally stopped before her mother's chair.

"I've filled the kittle fer the last time outen a bucket, I reckon. Britt 'lowed he'd git the pipe hitched to the Birch spring by night, an' it's nigh that now. Julie can cook supper when she gits done milkin', mommie. I might as well go home."

Laviny took snuff with an air of contentment under injury before she replied. "Suit yersef, Bainie. You always do."

Bainie took the defensive. "Jim hates a late supper nowadays. Sence he's took to workin' better I try to have things sort o' like he wants 'em."

"Jim'll stay good as long as Paddy stayed in the army. He went in at half past one, an' come out at thirty minutes to two."

"Jim's shore workin', mommie."

"Eh ? Well, I'll try to git down an' see him at it. That would shore be a sight."

"You ort to come anyway. Do you good to stir a little. I'm goin' now. An', mommie, I reckon it's no use fer me to come up tomorr'. You don't need me here when you got Julie."

" 'Course I don't. Mighty lucky she come up today."

"She says she'll stay till Monday mornin'."

"Britt an' Julie air two humans that don't tire out bein' good to me."

"Yer own son couldn't be better 'n Britt is," agreed Bainie.

"If he wasn't better 'n most sons I could do without him."

"I wouldn't throw off on Steve if I's you, mommie. Looks like you ain't ever been glad 'bout his comin' back the last time."

"He's done fair well fer hissef since he come in. But I kain't git over his leavin' me twict when I shore needed a helfty hand. Him an' that Ishmalee they's all of a piece. Goin' off an' leavin' ever'thing up to pore Britt."

388

"Steve ain't a bit lazy," said Bainie, with the shadow of courage.

"His daddy all over. Work in the sawmills till his back's broke, an' spend ever' cent 'fore he gits it. He'd better quit hangin' round Julie. That ain't goin' to do him any good."

"She'd make him a fine wife. Jest what Steve needs."

"Julie don't need *him*, Bain Wishart. I want to see a weddin' round here, but it ain't Steve an' Julie. It's Julie an' Britt."

"That would suit *her* mighty well. She's been tryin' git holt o' Britt ever' since that cane-mill knocked Tim Wheeler out o' the way an' left her a widder. She never liked Tim none too good nohow."

"That ain't agin her. Tim was powerful tryin'. Britt an' Julie wuz made fer each other, an' I hope they're findin' it out. I'd like to see two people married fer once that fit in. Here you're workin' yer back sore fer a lazy loafer like Jim. An' you know how that Ishmalee sarved pore Britt. She wuzn't good enough to count his tracks in barn mud. Eh-yes, I'd like to see two people mated up right onct in my life, an' I'll see it when Britt marries Julie."

"Reckon he's thinkin' about it ?"

Laviny was hard put for an answer. "He's thinkin' about *something*. That's plain enough. Fussin' an' puttin' things to rights all over the place, ever' minute he can git out o' the crop. What's it all fer, if he ain't goin' to git married ?"

"Julie would look after you fine."

"They both would. An' not a drap o' my blood in ary one of 'em." It was strange that Laviny should consider this a triumph, but the high note in her voice was unmistakably gloating. "They'll look after me well enough, but that ain't what's settin' me easy. Julie'll be good to Neddy. That's what I'm thinkin' about."

"That kid's rotten spiled now. He won't be worth a snake's egg if you don't quit pomperin' him. Why ain't he home from school ? Fightin' along the road, more'n like."

Laviny cackled her delight. With all her disparagement of her dead husband, there was one thing that she always mentioned with pride. He could hold his own in any fight that ever was. And in this Neddy took after his granddaddy.

"It ain't fightin' this time. I told him to go round by Sally Weaver's an' bring me a poke o' dried apples. I kain't do without 'em fer turnovers, an' I wouldn't 'a' been out ef there wasn't so many people comin' up to hear Britt's phonygraph. I could mighty nigh wish him an' Julie hadn't gone to Knoxville an' made them records. Folks has gone clean crazy about 'em."

"Lordy, mommie, he'd never got anywhere 'thout that bit o' money. He couldn't'a' bought the farm in when it was up fer taxes. You wouldn't have a roof 'twixt you an' the pourin' skies. I always wondered why he didn't stay in Knoxville an' spree around, 'stead o' comin' back here an' settlin' down to a slave's life. I reckon down at bottom he ain't got much sperret."

This was taking the offensive, and Laviny came back with such vigor that Bainie sat down for the battle which she knew was coming. Neither of them noticed a woman moving slowly up the trail.

Ishma's eyes were wide as she looked at the cabin and its surroundings. The cracks in the house had been carefully chinked. The decaying poplars were replaced with sound logs. The new board roof was stained a dark green. A second chimney had been built. The long porch was new, and there were wide steps in front. At one end was a lattice made of curved laurel wood, and a trumpet vine had begun to clamber over it. The yard was covered with short, green grass — that velvet goose grass, probably, that grew in the flat cove above the barn. She had told Britt once that she would carry enough sod down herself from that cove to cover the yard, if she could get rid of Jim's hogs and slop-barrel. There were no hogs in sight now, nor any trace of their devastation. She sniffed, and there was no odor from any barrel. There were front windows in every room, and not a pane missing. About the place was an air, not of plenty, but enough. One could be comfortable here.

Ishma leaned against a tree and listened to the wrangling of her mother and Bainie. That was the same anyway. She couldn't distinguish the words, but she saw that her mother was enjoying herself.

"Poor old Bainie," she thought. "She has to stand a lot. I'll take some of it now. Mommie is in dad's old chair. But it's been worked over. Looks almost smart."

How would they greet her? Her mother of course would use her most violent vocabulary against her, but what would her heart say? She must go on and get it over.

Bainie, with her mouth open on a hot word, looked up and saw Ishma on the trail a hundred yards away. She was still in the edge of the woods.

"Lordy!" cried Bainie. "Who's that? A woman — an' a strange one. Comin' right here. She's walkin' mighty slow. I do believe it's —"

She could say no more. Laviny got up and hobbled forward, trying to identify the visitor.

"What's the matter with you, Bainie? Why'n't you tell me who is it?"

Bainie's words fell like clods on a grave. "Mommie, it's Ish."

Laviny gave a scream and went back to her chair. "Ishmalee! Showin' her face here!"

"Yes," said Bainie, more naturally. "It's Ish."

"Rad's left her, I reckon," said Laviny, shaking with her chair. "He's left her, an' she thinks she'll set down on me!"

"She's comin' awful slow."

"She got any chillren follerin'?"

"No. She's by hersef."

"Hidin' 'em somers, the smarty! Showin' her face to me! I'm goin' to send her down the mountain quicker 'n ever she got down it with Rad Bailey."

"It's gittin' night. You'll have to let her stay till mornin'."

"Don't you be tellin' me what to do, Bain Wishart!"

"Hush, mommie!"

Ishma had come into the yard. She was hesitating, not from concern over a doubtful welcome, but from a rush of feeling that made her sway slightly, as from carrying a weight. She wasn't thinking of how she had left home. Getting back was sufficient adventure.

"Hello, Bainie!" she said, coming close, and pausing. Bainie answered, low but cordial, standing at the head of the steps.

Ishma moved forward and put her foot on the lowest tread, looking down.

"Clean as a table, I declare. You can't be keeping house here, Bainie?" She was smiling, and her tone gently reminiscent.

"No," said Bainie, smiling back. "Me an' Jim's moved down the hill a bit. We've got uncle Zeke's place. Jim thinks maybe he'll buy it."

Laviny snorted at Bainie. Ishma seated herself on the steps and looked up at her mother.

"How are you, mother?" she asked, after waiting a moment for Laviny to speak.

"I ain't ready to say!" Her eyes were sparkling, and she shut her mouth to a hard line.

"Take your time," said Ishma, slightly infected with her mother's hostility. She wanted to cry out, "Where is Britt?" but only repeated, "Take your time, mother. There's plenty of it up here. My, it's good to sit down. I'm not used to climbing now, and I'd forgot how far it was from the station."

"You fergot something else too," cried Laviny, the hard line cracking open. "You fergot this wuz an honest woman's house."

Ishma's face lost all of its wistfulness. She looked hard and superior. "I don't doubt that I've forgotten a good many things that you know, mother."

"'Tain't fer you to act smart an' talk back to yer betters. Where's Rad Bailey?"

"He's married. I reckon that's what you want to know."

"He's got another woman?"

"Yes, mother."

Laviny wriggled excited, started up, and sat down again. "Didn't I say it, Bainie?" she cried. "Didn't I say it? What goes over the devil's back will crawl under his belly, come time." She turned fiercely on Ishma. "You lookin' fer a place to lay up in, I reckon?"

Ishma laughed, not kindly. If her mother kept this up she would have to go and find Britt. "I've got a little money, mother. Enough to pay my way for the night, seeing I'm a stranger."

"A stranger 'd get a bed a sight quicker'n you. I wouldn't tech yer money, not if it 'ud cure my rheumatiz."

392

Ishma softened. "That old trouble hangin' on, mommie ?"

"Ef it is, I don't want none o' yore tears to pizen a poultice fer me. I want to know right now ef Rad took you away an' never ast you to marry him, after I'd pestered Britt day an' night to git a divorce ?"

"Rad wanted me to marry him. He begged me hard. But I wouldn't do it. I couldn't be tied to Rad."

Laviny doubted her ears. This was beyond belief. "Jest out an' out bad you are ! You ain't fitten to set on them steps."

Bainie wanted to hear more. "Who's the other woman, Ish ?"

"A pretty little kid that got crazy about Rad. She was keeping house for us while I worked in the mill. I let her know all about Rad's pet ways, and the better she'd treat him the meaner I'd get, and finally he took her. I told him he had to marry her good and tight, and he did. I was chief witness, and I saw it was done right."

She shattered their consternation with a gay laugh. Laviny managed to speak. "An' you set there tellin' yer own mother ! There ain't a sound bone in ye, Ishmalee. You got tired o' Rad jest like you got tired o' Britt."

Ishma rose. Her cheeks were hot, there was energy in her eye, but her voice was weary and pleading. "Don't say I was tired of Britt. I wasn't. I couldn't go on living like an old cow. Fodder in winter and grass in summer, and a calf every year. But I wasn't tired of Britt."

"It would suit him jest as well if you wuz. He's makin' a good livin' now, an' no hep from you. You think you'll walk right inter it, I reckon."

"No, I don't. I know I'm not due anything from Britt. Not even his steps to sit on. Don't let's talk about that. I see you've got dad's old chair yet." She wanted to talk about Britt, but not in that horrible way.

"Britt fixed the cheer over fer me. They hain't much around here than he ain't fixed over. I reckon you kin see that."

"Yes, I see. I wouldn't have known the old place if it hadn't been for that rock sticking out of the chimney. Does he take care of the flowers too ?"

"He heps. An' Bainie heps. Bainie's got more time now,

with no youngun in her lap. But the flowers air mostly Julie's work. She's here a lot."

It wasn't Laviny's words, but the revealing smirk about her mouth that made Ishma's heart give a queer leap.

"Julie ? Julie Webb ? What's she doin' here ?"

"Gittin' used to her home, I reckon. Her an' Britt's courtin'. They're purty close to the weddin' day ef the signs air right."

Bainie started forward, making a slight noise of denial in her throat.

"Shut up, Bainie," commanded her mother. "You know it's the God's truth !"

"Well, I didn't know it was shore fixed up," Bainie dared to say in spite of her mother's threatening eye.

Ishma was wiping the dust from her shoes on the thick grass around the steps. She had turned about, so they couldn't see her bloodless face. Before she spoke she gave a little cough that might explain any slight choking of her voice.

"I thought," she said slowly, still intent on her shoes, "that Julie married Tim Wheeler. Somebody came down to the mills and told it anyhow."

"They told it right. But Tim got knocked off by a runaway cane mill about a year ago."

A year ago ! Britt must have got his divorce just after that. She felt as if little knives, endowed with life, were running all through her body, cutting the flesh from her bones. Laviny's voice ran on, fondling over Tim's accident, and Ishma was grateful for the refuge of her garrulity. It gave her time to harden. Her fight with herself after what happened in the little room at Butch's was nothing to the pain of this. If only she could crawl off into the woods like the animal she was ! Laviny's voice was a mere rumble in her ears, but towards the end of her tale the words took meaning.

"Then Julie began comin' up here to stay with me times when I needed her. She'd kep' Neddy a lot while Tim wuz alive, an' the youngun wuz crazy about her. Bainie couldn't do ever'-thing up here an' at home too after her an' Jim moved. They didn't want to go, but Britt made 'em see they'd better strike out fer thersevs."

394

Bainie edged in interruptively. "It was Jim wanted to go. He wouldn't stay on here after Britt got the titles. Jim's got to be boss wherever he sets down, an' aunt Cyn don't meddle with him nary bit."

"I ain't talkin' about Jim. I'm sayin' how Julie 's shore been a daughter to me when I's needin' one, an' I ain't afraid she won't keep it up when she comes here fer good an' all."

Ishma spoke, and was surprised to find her voice light and saucy.

"What they waiting for ? Looks like everything around here is ready for the bride."

"They's nothin' more to do that I can think of. Britt's got the pipe all laid from the Birch spring to the house, an' I reckon the water 'll come on any minute. He's up there now, finishin' off. We'll have water from that spring cold as ice the hottest day that comes, an' nobody goin' up hill after it. Set right here an' let 'er come !"

Ishma had leapt to her feet. "He's not gone and spoiled that spring ? The one with ferns and moss all around it and three birch trees looking right into it !"

"It ain't none o' yore business what he's spiled er not spiled."

Ishma dropped back to her seat on the steps. "Of course I don't care," she said, her heart thumping. They all knew that spring was hers. Since she'd been seven years old she had kept it clean and rippling.

"You heard about Steve comin' back, Ish ?"

"Not a word."

"He'll stay this time, I reckon. You'll see him tonight. He's been workin' up on Eagle Creek, but he's gone to Carson tonight to see about gittin' a bonus, er back pay, er something, that he's jest about got his hands on. He'll make the bucks fly. Steve knows how. He's likin' Julie too."

"They's a better man fer Julie, an' you know it, Bain Wishart," Laviny reminded her.

"I've been hopin' Steve would settle down."

"He'll settle down like his daddy did, when he kain't lift his feet, an' not a minute sooner."

"I'll be glad to see old Steve," said Ishma.

Laviny turned on her viciously. "Where at ? You'll not see him here, I can tell ye ! Shorely you're not countin' on puttin' up in *my* house !"

Bainie was troubled. "I'm ashamed o' you, mommie. You go home with me, Ish. It'll be all right with Jim. He ain't ever been hard on you fer leavin' out."

Laviny shook her stick at Bainie and intoned her next remark as from a pulpit. "That woman has been turned out o' the church !"

"Well, well," said Ishma. "And I'm still alive."

Such levity was too much even for Bainie. "It's so, Ish," she said solemnly. "Jim Siler preached an awful sermon about you, an' ever'body was agin you till Britt—"

Bainie stopped, and Ishma smiled. "Well, won't you tell me what Britt did ?"

"He sot outside the meetin' house, an' when Siler come out he lammed him all over the place an' broke down Granny Whitt's tombstone. When it was over they put Britt on a stump an' went round an' round him makin' up a ballit. I'll git Jim to sing it to you, er part of it. Takes about all night to sing ever' bit of it. They kep' piecin' onto it fer more'n a year. It's a mile long shorely. Ain't hardly anybody in Wimble County but's got words in that ballit. Siler's been a lot easier to put up with sence the fight. He was gittin' the swellhead bad, an' that stopped it right off. You come home with me an' I'll tell you ever'thing."

Ishma looked at the softly darkening sky. "It's warm enough to sleep on the ridge. I'd just as soon be out."

Here ended Laviny's self-control. She rose in her chair and screeched in Ishma's face. "The ridge ! You strollop ! You git out o' here ! Git, right now !"

Ishma had come up the steps. She looked about her, her eyes lingering on all that she saw. "All right, mother," she said, and moved down the steps, into the yard.

"I'm comin' too, Ish," said Bainie. "You'll stop at my house."

Ishma went on a few paces and halted suddenly. Britt was coming down the hill. She heard his voice in a soft, happy hum. Happy without her ! He was near the house. She couldn't take

396

another step. He came onto the porch at the end half screened by the trumpet vine. Laviny's chair was between him and Ishma in the yard.

"Well, mother, the water's on!" The same old deep but merry voice. "And tomorrow's Sunday. We'll keep the Sabbath in this house from now on, so far as not carryin' water 'll help us."

Then he came around the chair and saw Ishma. "Hello!" he called, and leapt down the steps. She couldn't lift her hand, but he reached and took it. "You feelin' well enough?"

"All right. How're you, Britt?"

"Above middlin'."

"You don't look surprised."

"No. Si Welch passed where I's at work an' told me you's up."

"What's Si doin' on the mountain?" demanded Laviny.

"The fire warden sent him up. Ever'body's got notice to fight fire tonight. Great help havin' that warden."

Ishma's frozen face became eager. She wanted to know where the fire was coming from.

"Same old place," Britt told her. "Climbin' up from Dark Moon. Cattle fellers set it afire on purpose, but we're goin' to round 'em up this time. It's the worst in four years. That side ' the mountain ain't been burnt over since — "

"Since I went away," Ishma finished for him, and silence wrapped the four of them, though Laviny struggled against it. With Britt's entrance she had felt herself slip from power. Bainie went down to Ishma. She had to get along to start Jim's supper, she said, and she reckoned Ishma was ready to go. But Ishma stood perfectly still.

"You git along from here, Ishmalee!" rasped Laviny.

"Why, mother!" said Britt, seemingly in utter surprise.

"Ain't this my house, I'd like to know?" triumphed Laviny.

"Mommie, it's Britt's," said Bainie. "You know he bought it two years ago when it was up fer taxes."

"He said it was mine as long as I lived. Didn't you, Britt?"

"Yes, but I never counted on your turnin' your own flesh an' blood out of it."

397

"Didn't my flesh an' blood turn hersef out ? 'Tain't me doin'
it. It was done four year ago. I ain't goin' to sleep under the
same roof with that thing, now you know it !"

Britt was ready. "All right, mother. You go home with
Bainie. It's only a little piece an' you'll make it well enough.
If you can't I'll carry you like a feather. Ishma 'll stay here with
me an' Julie an' Steve. I'm lookin' for Steve ever' minute. And
she hasn't seen Ned yet. She'll want to get her eyes on him.
Looks like this is the place for her to stay."

"Maybe Julie won't want me, Britt ?" said Ishma brightly.

"Julie ? I'll say she will ! Don't you be afraid of Julie.
You'll stay here tonight. We've got a lot to talk over, like old
friends."

Laviny gave a grunt of disgust and surrender. "Let's go,
Bainie. I thought Britt had got over bein' a fool, but I reckon
it'll stay with him to the grave."

She began to limp off with Bainie, and Britt looked after her
concernedly. "She'll make it," he said. "It's only a few steps,
and the change'll do her good."

Laviny turned back for one more thrust. "Let me tell you
this, Ishmalee ! You keep yer hands offn Britt. He's a changed
man sence you left him, and all fer the better. That wuz the
best work you ever done fer him — goin' away an' showin' up
what you wuz."

Relieved, she renewed her hobbling, but a little farther on she
stopped and she and Bainie seemed to be in argument. Laviny
turned back toward the house.

"I won't go a step from here," she said, hobbling closer. "I
ain't goin' to be druv out like I was the one that ort to go. Britt,
you drag my cheer out here, an' I'll sleep in the yard, ef you're
bent an' bound to give Ishmalee the house."

"Sure, mother ! Whatever you want," said Britt, taking up
the chair and carrying it into the yard.

"Not way out there," cried Laviny. "I kain't hear nothin' from
the woods."

He laughed, and at the sound of his laughter Ishma's heart flut-
tered. She sank to the steps and leaned against a post. Britt
brought the chair close to the porch, adjusted the back so that

398

Laviny could lie down, then lifted her up and helped her get comfortably settled.

"You're beat out, mother. Now you rest a little."

"Beat out, an' no wonder. I'll nap a bit 'fore supper." Promptly she went to sleep, and Ishma fell into an inward panic. Britt was so near, and that separating voice was hushed. The same tender, smiling Britt, but not hers. "Like old friends," he had said. How was she going to live until morning ? Until she could get away ?

Britt pulled up a chair for her, on the porch, and placed another beside it for himself. Then he sat down. He would tell her now. Tell her that he was going to marry Julie. She glanced at him, but he was not embarrassed, nor was he in any hurry to talk. He sat there as if he were strangely satisfied about something. She had to speak first.

"You weren't looking to see me again, Britt ?"

"Yes, I was. I thought you'd come back sometime." His voice was so free of any claim to her that it aroused her self-respect and she defended it with a denial.

"I didn't come for you anyway."

"No, but you've come."

"I'll tell you what for. I got to craving a sight of the mountains. Craving till I couldn't bear it."

"I counted on that."

"I kept reading in the papers about the fires up here, and I thought of how they'd look. I was ready to leave where I was anyway, and when I got started this seemed to be the road. I was just pulled back. And I got here at the right minute, when there's a big fire on. I'd like to die looking into Dark Moon full of fire."

Laviny, aroused in time to hear her last words, called out, "She's crazier'n a June-bug, Britt !" Ishma never turned her head. "I'd like to die looking right into it," she repeated.

Britt spoke uneasily. "You're stout enough, ain't you, Ishma ?"

Perfectly well, she assured him. The doctors had told her after Vennie's death that her heart couldn't be depended on. She had worried too much over the kid, they said. But she knew she'd be all right, and she was. The baby had been gone a year.

Britt lowered his voice to a whisper, and laid his hand on Ishma's. "It was fine of you, sendin' the little girl back to me. I couldn't write you about it. I counted on your knowin' how I'd feel. You wouldn't have sent her if you hadn't known that."

"She was yours, Britt," Ishma whispered back. "You had some rights."

Laviny's ear was vainly cocked. "Talk louder, kain't you ? I reckon you're ashamed for a decent woman to hear you."

Britt drew back his hand and said aloud, "You were always a great one for being fair, Ishma."

"What about my leaving you ?"

"You had to get out. It was shore bottom here. And you didn't take the boy. You left Ned for me."

"I wasn't afraid you'd think I'd thrown him away, Britt."

He looked at the floor, his shoes, his hands. Then, without lifting his eyes, he said, "You an' Rad — didn't have any kids ?"

He had no right to say that, she thought. He was going to marry Julie. Why should he stab her in passing ? She looked at his profile softened in the dusk. His lowered head seemed waiting and begging too. She lost her resentment.

"No," she said indifferently, "we didn't. I learned how not to. They taught me that down yonder."

Laviny raised her head rampantly. "Sech talk, as I'm alive ! You ain't goin' to set there an' listen to her, air you, Britt ?"

Ishma continued as if her mother had not spoken. "The earth was made for people to live on. I reckon it was." As if struck by a doubt, she repeated, "I reckon it was. And we've messed up things till the best we can do for 'em is to keep 'em off it."

Laviny sat up, stiffened with horror. "You talk like there wa'an't no God ! I never thought I'd live to hear my own child blasphemin'. A gal child too !"

Ishma returned to things more understandable. "You've sure been good to mommie, Britt."

"It was just turn about. She was fine with Ned. We got on all right. I wanted to write you that we were all okay, then it seemed too much like sayin' we didn't need you. I didn't want you to be worryin' about us."

She was silent, thinking of how little she had worried about the hearts on Cloudy Knob, so full she had been of her own despair.

"You looked about, I reckon, an' enjoyed yourself some. Folks down there think they know a lot more than we do."

"They're more mixed up, Britt. They work harder and die faster. But there is help coming. The union — I can't talk about it now."

"You don't have to tell me. I stopped in Elizabethton on my way from Knoxville the last time. You know uncle Ben lives there, and I stayed two weeks. Long enough to mix about with the hands in the Bemberg plant, and they told me a lot. Made me glad to get back to the old plough-handles. You don't have to tell me, Ishma."

"But I'm going to tell you before I go. There's something you don't know. It's sort o' scattered in my mind now, but I'll get it all clear, and tell you before I leave."

"Before you leave? You're not thinkin' o' goin' back, are you?"

"Of course I'm going back. Tomorrow maybe."

Did he think she would hang around him and Julie? She stole another look at him. He was going to say something decisive. She knew that thrust of his chin. But before he was full ready, Laviny, who had been snoring again, lifted her head and screeched, "Rad put her out, Britt! You're talkin' to Rad's leavin's. That's all that thing is!"

Britt rose to his feet. "By God, did he do that?"

"Sit down, Britt," said Ishma, softly. "I fixed it all myself." She pressed her lips together, and her smooth forehead became covered with tight little wrinkles. "I wanted to leave Rad, but I couldn't without knowing that somebody was looking after him. He'd been good to me. And he's got a nice little wife. You let Rad alone."

Britt sat down. "I won't bother him, if that's the way it was. What sort of a hell you been in, Ishma? Good to you! Lord, it was hard on you, after all you'd done to get there."

"All I'd done? You mean — "

"I mean Rad. You didn't love him."

He shouldn't have said it. She turned until he couldn't see her drawn face as she said hardily, "I stood to my bargain."

401

"Course you would. That's all it was — a bargain. But it's off now. And you're goin' to stay up here till you forget it."

Forget it ! Men didn't know anything. "You'd better ask Julie first," she said lightly.

"What I say goes with Julie. But you've got her wrong. She's always talked up for you."

"Much obliged to her. What is she doing now ?"

"Milkin', when I come by the barn. An' there's a lot of little chickens to be tucked in. She always finds more to do than anybody knows about."

"What kind of chickens you raisin', Britt ?"

"Buff Orpingtons," he said ringingly, "and Leghorns for eggs." Then he dropped his head, and they both laughed. Their chairs came closer together after that, and Ishma's voice was softly natural.

"The trail was lovely coming up the mountain, Britt. The ferns are knee-high already, and the tall poplars were sweet as meadows up in the air. Wish I'd got up in time to see them cloudin'."

"Tell you what I saw this mornin', Ishma. That long strip o' saplin's edgin' the old pasture has grown up till there's a regular mist o' poplars in there. I've got rye in the field above, and this mornin' about a thousand o' them little yellow flax-birds lit on the green rye. That was a sight to look at, but all at once they flew up an' covered the tops o' the trees below the field. It looked exactly like the poplars had bloomed out."

"Wish I'd seen that, Britt. We'll look about the place in the morning. If I stay up long enough. I guess you've done a sight of work."

"I've ditched an' fenced, an' got all the old fields in grass, an' enough new land cleared to make all the stuff we need. I've had Si's boy workin' with me for three years. He's strong as an ox, and we make a team. I tried tobacco one year, but I found it took fifteen months to the year to make that crop, because I had to sit up nights with it. I'm stickin' to grass an' corn an' cattle."

"You've learned how, Britt."

"Well, it took some money. A dead man can't walk. That's

what no money means when it comes to buildin' up a farm stuck here in these cliffs. I've spent some."

"You and Julie made your trip."

"That's where the lane turned, Ishma. I brought home three hundred dollars that first time. If you'd only waited a little — "

"Well, I didn't." If he meant to justify himself — to pick up reasons for turning to Julie, she wasn't going to listen.

Britt's face stiffened a little. "When Rad came back that time to sell his timber, he sneaked in when I's gone. Afeard I'd kill him, I reckon. He could 'a' made himself easy. I didn't mean to hurt him so long as you had any use for him. And I'll let him alone now, if you say so. Ever'body knows I could hold Rad out with one arm an' let him wiggle himself to death."

Britt threw out his arm and pantomimed the action, clenching his fingers around the waist of an imaginary Rad. Ishma broke into a laugh that helped her to suppress the burning tumult within.

"You were in Knoxville when he came in ?"

"No. New York."

"You got up there ?"

"Could have stayed if I'd wanted to." He waved New York away with a mild but final gesture. "I didn't keer for it."

Then his voice lowered as over a secret. "I'll tell you, Ishma, I didn't take much to bein' shown off as a freak o' the wilderness. There were some fellers up there who could take a frensharp an' guitar an' play all around me. I wasn't fooled about myself. But the manager who wanted to put me on, said they didn't have the looks. He said the way I threw up my shoulders would take swell with the women. Said I could smile the dollars out o' pockets deep as the Hudson tunnel, an' a lot more spoof that I didn't lap up. Since the war, he said, nobody had any patience with art all polished off. It was genius in the rough that got 'em to the box-office. He'd have a little play fixed up where I could just be myself an' not have to act at all, an' there was no tellin' how fur I'd go. I told him I knowed just how fur, eight hundred miles, an I come on home."

Ishma had grown quiet. For a moment she forget everything except that this was her own man, the man she had chosen to marry, standing up in a gingham dress and borrowed shoes, because love was the only thing in life that mattered. She clasped her hands over her knees, with her gaze absently drifting out in the encircling dusk. And there on the trail, coming out of the woods, stood a boy. He seemed to be a husky lad about ten years old. On his shoulder he carried a little white sack — a flour poke, of course — filled with something. The sack was carefully balanced, while he stood still with his hands carelessly resting on his hips. He was looking toward the porch, apparently much interested in what he saw. The boy was too big for Bainie's Jim, and too little for Andy, who must now be fourteen. She wondered why Britt didn't say, "Hello!" He was absolutely motionless, looking at the boy, and when he turned his eyes to Ishma she knew that the child was his own.

It was Ned. But how was it possible? This big lad! For an instant she could not untangle her eyes from Britt's, and when she looked out again the boy had covered half the distance between the house and the woods. But he paused again, plainly for the purpose of assessing her looks.

"It can't be Ned," she whispered.

"Wait till he gets closer. You'll see."

Britt was whispering too, and neither knew why. But they would have choked if they had attempted to speak aloud.

Britt coughed with vigor and got hold of his voice. "Come on, son," he called. Ned, who was not waiting for an invitation, decided to advance.

"But he's only seven!" Ishma murmured.

"It takes a ten year old suit for him. He's goin' to be big like Steve, even if he has got my hair. Big like Steve, and your eyes and mouth. He helped me a lot when you first went away, havin' those eyes. Sometimes I could believe you's right here."

Ned reached the steps and dropped the poke. "Granmommie's apples," he announced. Then he looked at Ishma and put his question squarely. "You my mother?"

"Yes, Ned," she answered, doubting her own words, and pressing her heart to keep it from her throat. If he would only act like a child! Put his arms about her neck, and cry a little. But he'd never do that. And he was so beautiful that to look at him made her feel that she was melting away. Yet she could imagine his fist doubling up, ready to make it serious for anybody who dared to comment on his beauty.

"I didn't miss a day from school last year," he said, making a seat of the top step and assuming the burden of conversation. "And this year I've had three fights. But Sam Cody has had six."

"We've got some school now, Ishma," said Britt, helping Ned along. "Seven teachers and three busses, pickin' 'em up everywhere. Of course Ned has to walk down the mountain."

"He looks strong enough."

"Can hoe like a man too. You can't trash him in a corn row."

"Teacher calls me Edward. Aunt Bainie told me you's here when I stopped at her house. You ran away. I'm going too. But I'll not run. I'll walk off when I'm ready. I'm going to build bridges."

"He's always building little bridges," said his father. "Got 'em all over the branches. When they's puttin' that big bridge over the Tuckasieg, I had to take him up there twice to watch 'em."

"I'm not going to build river bridges. I'm going to build a bridge across the Atlantic ocean."

"No, son, you can't do that."

"You can if you build high enough. It'll stay right there — clear across the sky, an' people comin' an' goin'."

"Better get through with your feedin', Ned. Old Bill hasn't had any water."

Ned jumped up relieved. This woman looked mighty nice, but maybe she'd want to kiss him in a minute. That's what mothers did sometimes, for he'd seen 'em at it. Just before he passed out of sight around the house he turned and gave an arrogant wave of his hand upward. "Clear across the sky!" he called, and disappeared.

"He'll go, Britt."

"Yes, but it's a long time yet."

"I don't suppose — " she began, her voice struggling — "I don't suppose that he'll ever care anything about me."

"Just give him a chance! Everybody cares about you, Ishma."

"Like mommie!"

"O, she's just blowin' off to hide her feelings. She's harder on Steve than you, and you know what she thinks of Steve."

But Ishma was sunk too low for such comfort to reach her. "I'll be out of everybody's way tomorrow."

"You'll stay right here, like you's at home, Ishma."

"With mommie sleeping out of doors."

"She'll be all right by tomorrow. Julie'll bring her around."

"Julie?"

"She can do anything with mother. She's got her petted out of sight."

Ned put a head around the corner of the house and asked if he might water the mules.

"No, Tom Mix. You let the mules alone."

Ned stepped out. "I thought you's busy tonight," he said, his look embracing both of his parents as he came nearer.

"Maybe I am, but I've got to keep you out of trouble."

Ned came close, looking frankly at Ishma.

"Granmommie said I was just like you."

"O, she did?"

"She got mad once and said I was just like that pig-headed Ishmalee."

"No, no, son!"

"She did. Then she took it back and opened a can of buck-berries for supper. Can you make good biscuits?"

"Sometimes."

"When Julie's up here we have biscuits for breakfast. Daddy can't put on anything but cornbread. How long is Julie goin' to stay this time, daddy?"

"Maybe a long time, son."

"Hooray! Biscuits ever' mornin'!" Ned shouted, and vanished.

Britt stood up. "I'll go and see that he keeps away from the mules. He thinks his head is better than mine sometimes."

He glanced at Laviny. "She sleeps half her time now. A good thing too. Her rheumatism is pretty bad. Hello, there's Steve!"

Ishma went into the yard to meet him. "Ish!" he shouted, and caught her by the shoulders.

"Yes, it's me, Steve. You through travellin'?"

"Shore as rain in Oregon ! What about you ?"

"I'll go further, I reckon."

"Well, I can suit myself now. Go if I want an' stay if I want. The Government 's coughed up at last. Three years' back pay — *and* a bonus."

"He's buyin' Si Welch's place, Ishma. We'll be neighbors."

Ishma couldn't believe it. "Those washed-out gullies !"

"He'll soon have those gullies filled up, an' the fields covered with Korean clover. Cattle on 'em too, fat as lard."

"Finest cold water this side o' the Cascades," said Steve. "A man thinks o' that after dryin' up in the alkali country."

They talked on, about five coves with eighteen inches of black soil never gouged by a plough, of three big benches that you could put a little tractor on, and they'd go partners in machinery. Ishma listened to strange language.

"You won't believe it, Ishma," said Britt, "but I'm takin' a mowin' machine to the top o' Pea Ridge now. You ought to see my haystacks !"

Ishma smiled miserably. He hurried away from the subject. "You'll want a housekeeper, Steve. Got her picked, I reckon."

"Picked ? I've counted her eyelashes !" He began to sing.

> *There's a little gal in Lunnon*
> *Was mighty sweet to me,*
> *But it's fur across the water,*
> *An' there's gals this side the sea !*
> *O, there's gals this side the sea !*

His voice rumbled into silence, and they heard Julie's cry in the distance. She was calling Britt.

"Julie's up here ?" cried Steve.

"Yes. Wants help with that big gate."

Steve pushed before Britt. "I'll take the job, if you've no objections."

"Help yourself, Steve," said Britt, laughing. But Steve was out of sight.

"I'm glad he found out what to do with his money before he got hold of it. He's due to settle down."

"He'll marry now ?" asked Ishma.

"He'll not miss it. They can live right here till he gets Si's place fixed up."

"Live here ? How'll Julie like that ?"

"O, Julie won't grumble. We'll not be crowded. I've put three bed-rooms on at the back. Used all those logs I cut 'fore you left. Mother an' Ned still keep the middle room. Steve can have one at the back. And one is yorn, Ishma."

She thought his face flushed, but it was too dark to make sure. The third room, of course, would be his and Julie's. He ought to flush ! To think she would live alongside of his new wife ! Julie wouldn't be so dumb as that either.

"You're mighty sure about Julie," she said.

"I ought to be, after all she's done. You go in an' see how we're fixed up. I've got to get up to the barn. You look around. Julie helped me plan it all out. If you could brag on it a little to her, it would make her feel good. Wait a minute ! I'll show you this."

He went to a post and turned on an electric switch. Light flooded the porch and yard.

"There's one at the barn too, and one in the spring-house. I'll bet Julie churns there tonight, same as if it was broad day."

He was begging for her approval, and she was too heavy-hearted to give it. "It don't show up now," he said, "like it would if it was black dark. You'll see later. Look at your balsam bush there, Ishma. You can almost see it's blue."

"Yes, I can," she managed.

"We don't have to sit in the dark just because it's come night."

"It must have cost a lot, Britt."

"I could stand it. Got a second-hand dynamo when one of the Ritter mills quit. Me an' Steve an' Si's boy built a little dam an' set it up. Cost mighty little considerin' what we got."

He was starting off reluctantly, lingering for her enthusiasm. "Go in an' look over the place." His voice stumbled. "I want you to — to enjoy yourself. Julie'll be along directly."

Ishma watched him moving off, walking a little heavily for light-footed Britt, then she sat down midway up the steps and covered her eyes with her hands. Her skin seemed drawn and

408

burning, but about her heart was ice. A step roused her. Couldn't she be alone for a minute? It was Steve, too jubilant to notice her weariness.

"You goin' to the fire, Ish?"

The fire? She had forgotten it.

"I'll be along, Steve."

"You'd better. It's worth the climb. I've got to make for the ridge right away. The warden said for me to go ahead and line up the men fast as they came. Julie's goin' to have me a hot supper when I get back around nine o'clock. That will be a good time for you to go up. It'll be black night by then, an' the fire bustin' the heart out of it."

He threw his words back as he walked, and as he ended he was out of sight around the balsam and on the upper trail. At the other end of the porch she heard voices, Britt and Julie, and got up to go in. Britt was expecting her to brag about the house, and she'd have to see it first. They stopped when they came into the light, and she too stopped inside the doorway and looked back. They were standing together, examining something, and soon she knew what it was.

"Yes, it's sort o' purty," said Britt, teasing, and holding it up to the light.

"Sort o'!" exclaimed Julie. "It's the purtiest ring I ever saw. You hand it back here, 'fore you drap it!"

"It's none too good for you, Julie." They came on toward the steps. "Nothin's too good for you, in my opinion. Let's see how it fits."

She held up her finger and he slipped the ring over it.

"I told you it was just right," she said.

Then they both looked at Laviny, and with the same thought.

"You haven't told her yet?" asked Britt. "She'll be mad, but she'll like being mad."

"S'pose you tell her, Britt. She'll take it better from you."

"No, sir! That's one more job for you, Julie."

"An' she'll tell me right now," said Laviny, wide awake. "Come here, gal."

Julie, with a meek, slow step, moved to Laviny. "You truth me now! Air you goin' to git married?"

"Well, yes, I am, aunt Laviny."

"How long will it be ?   You truth me now ?   Out with it !"

"Why — aunt Laviny — we 'lowed we'd step off about Sunday week."

"Thank the Lord ! I been layin' here prayin' fer that. You thought I's asleep. I ain't slept a wink. I been prayin'."

"I's afeard you'd be mad, aunt Laviny."

"Mad ! Lord love you ! I been prayin' fer this thing ! Ishmalee ? Where's that gal ? Ishmalee ?"

Ishma came out of the doorway, and slipped along, half alive, to the porch railing. "I'm here, mother."

"Did you hear that ?   Julie's goin' to be married Sunday week."

Julie ran up the steps and caught Ishma's hand. "I declare, Ishma, we ain't shook hands yet. I'm mighty glad to see you !"

Britt came up the steps. "I told you Julie would be glad, Ishma. She's never stopped likin' you."

Laviny was still chuckling. "Sunday week ! The old woman won't be druv out now."

"Why, aunt Laviny," cried Julie, "who'd ever think o' drivin' you out ?"

"Steve left me twict, an' Ishmalee left me onct, but you won't ever leave me, Julie. I'll have one son an' daughter as long as you an' Britt live."

"Don't you mind her, Ishma," said Britt, almost taking her breath away by laying his hand on her shoulder. "She's just talkin'."

"You'll find out ef I'm talkin'," Laviny screeched, trying to get on her feet. Then something happened that lifted her scream from farce to reality. Ned came rushing into the yard and up the steps. Blood was streaming from his forehead.

"I fell out of the barn loft," he said, wedging the words in between his grandmother's shrieks.

"Hush, mother ! He's not hurt," Britt assured her. "He's not even crying. You hush."

"Neddy don't cry, whatever comes," she whimpered, Britt's command having taken some effect. Ishma, anxious and startled, moved to Ned. Julie, crying that she would get the turpentine, ran into the house.

"Come in, Ned," said Ishma. "I'll fix it up for you."

He gave her a swift look, then his eyes went seeking Julie. He ran past his mother, into the middle room.

"Nothing to worry about, Ishma," said Britt, feeling her embarrassment. "Ned's a tough kid." But he too went into the house, and she could hear the three voices mingling in intimacy that left her cast out. Laviny began to comfort herself.

"Yes," she mumbled, "Julie 'll fix him up all right. She knows how to handle Neddy. Pull that quilt over my feet, Ishmalee."

Ishma's hands struggled with the quilt as Laviny mumbled on. "Pore little Neddy! I'm thankful he'll have a mother that's never had a word raised agin her. He won't be ashamed o' Julie when he grows up. Pull it up, kain't ye? There now, I b'lieve I *will* take a nap fer onct."

She was instantly asleep. Ishma once more sat down on the steps, and Britt came out to say that Julie had dressed the wound and put Ned into bed.

"It's a right bad knock. He struck an old piece of a plough. But he'll be in a black-gum log sleep in a few minutes, and wake up all right in the morning. Julie's in the kitchen. Supper's goin' to be a little late. I'll get you a glass of milk."

"No, no! I'm not hungry. I'd forgot that people sometimes eat."

They both tried to smile. Ned's voice began calling, "Julie! Julie!" and from the kitchen they heard her answer, "What, sonny?"

"Play the banjo for me, an' I'll go to sleep."

"Jest as soon as I start supper to cookin' I'll be right there!"

Britt broke the silence apologetically. "You can't blame him, I reckon, for bein' crazy about Julie."

"Who's blaming him?" she asked sharply, and he made matters worse with, "I s'pose you don't keer. You can't feel much like he's yorn."

Then she was angry. "He *is* mine! Nothing can make that different. She can pet him, and humor him, and make a fool of him, all she wants, but she can't make him hers! He's mine!"

"That's the way I want you to feel," said Britt, his face strangely brightened. When he spoke again he said that he must be getting on to the fire. He wouldn't wait for supper. Steve would be coming down later, and would bring back a snatch of something.

"You're not thinking of going up tonight, Ishma ?"

"Yes, I'm going. I want to see the fire rolling up from Dark Moon. Rings and rings of fire rolling and climbing. I want to look at something that is not a muddle. Something going ahead and going big."

"All right. We'll go. I'll wait for you."

"No, Britt, I'm going by myself."

"It's a steep climb, you know."

"I'm still a mountain woman, Britt. I can make it alone."

"Well, get you a good supper first, then rest before you start. I'll go ahead, if that's what you've settled on. You do just as you like here, Ishma. It's your home, to do as you please in, and as long as you want it. You know that."

He moved off, turning slowly, and she wanted him to go, but when he dropped into his brisk step and vanished she felt that she must run after him. If she didn't, she would never see him again. She had no thought of coming back to the house from the ridge. She would get into Goat Trail and go down through Siler's Cove to the valley. From there it would be easy to reach the little station where she could get a train. She wouldn't have to go through Beebread again.

Her eyes were aching. She went to the light-switch and turned it off. This shiny, new home of Julie's bored her. She was trying to think of something. Something vast and far away. But her mind couldn't reach it. She guessed she was too tired.

Julie came out with a large shawl which she spread over Laviny.

"When Steve gits back I'll ast him to carry her in, an' she won't know nothin' about it till mornin'."

"You'll hear from her then, won't you ?"

"Yes, but she'll be kind o' glad we worked it that way. Whad you turn the light off fer ?"

"There's enough light coming from the house."

"We don't have to be savin' of it. All it cost was settin' it up. I'll have to dowse the light in the room so Neddy can go to sleep."

"That's all right, Julie. Make it dark. The night 's a big thing. I like it for company."

"Well, they's plenty of it."

Julie turned in, but stopped at the door. "Ishma," she began, and her voice was a little troubled. "Neddy sleeps with his granmommie in the middle room. But I can have Steve put her in one o' the new back-rooms ef you want to lay down by him tonight."

Ishma thrilled. Julie's voice, softly concerned, said more than her words. "He's yore flesh an' blood," she added, as Ishma hesitated, swept with longing. What wouldn't she give to have that strong young heart beating by hers for one night?

"Thank you, Julie, but I like for folks to please themselves, young as well as old. Do just like you would if I wasn't here."

Julie went in, and the next moment the light in the room had dropped to a soft glimmer. The tinkle of a banjo drifted out. She was putting Neddy to sleep. Ishma sat on the steps, with the night for company.

CHAPTER XVII

NOT THE SEA

THE BACK-BONE of Lame Goat Ridge was sharp and bare, but not fifty yards below it, on the Wimble side, the woods began to thicken into clots of locusts, poplars, oaks and hickories. Here men, moving like heavy shadows, were raking dead leaves and making a wide swathe of naked ground in preparation for "back-fire." Beyond the ridge, a variable yellow haze in the sky sharpened the brooding height of the land-line and made the woods in the fore-ground more dark and ponderable. The men worked with sweeping, leisurely movements, and the two or three feeble lanterns swung from a limb or a sapling, occasionally made a face or a figure glow into transient life. They laughed, sang and jeered, unconscious of the weird picture they made. All of them had grown up in familiarity with night, woods, and lantern glow. The fear of a "painter," or of a rattler that hadn't sense enough to hole-up when night came, might induce a little caution, but otherwise they felt that the woods were "safe as the meetin' house steps."

"What we workin' 'long here fer?" protested Abe More, the lazy man of the crew, whose expertness in shirking had become a matter for community pride. "Fire 'll never git over them rocks up there."

"You kain't think a hundred yards off," Ben Ross answered. "Right over there to the west, the fire can come below the rocks an' creep round here faster 'n water can run. Keep shakin' that pitch-fork till I tell you to quit."

For reply Abe threw down his pitch-fork and said he was going to the comb to look over. "We got to know how fast that fire is travellin'," he said.

"Don't go to sleep up there an' let it ketch you," called Ben. "We ain't got time to pull you out."

There was a great roll of light from the other side of the mountain, so strongly reflected in the sky that the woods and the men shared the glow. One of them burst into song. The others joined in, and the slope rang with their full, unrestrained voices. It was an old camp-meeting song, one line of the chorus running,

"An' I want to shout in glory when the world is on fire," and the energy they put into it revealed their intention to be on hand at the great day. Industry was vigorously renewed under musical incentive, and soon brought them to a spot where Britt called a halt.

"Here's where Steve's squad started," he said. "You fellers can take a rest, an' make up a bed for Abe. I'll go over to Grape Vine Gap an' see how they're comin' out."

He started off in a westerly direction, saying that he would shout back if help was needed.

"Don't run over that dead-an'-down locus' out there in the dark," Milt Jones called after him. "Hit 'ud snag a harrycane."

"I'm ready fer a set-down," said Ben Ross, picking out a comfortable looking stump.

"This bed o' leaves was made up fer me," said Si, sitting down and taking out his pipe. Others piled near him, and all were soon engaged in an exchange of questionable compliments.

Abe's wife, as the community terror, was a subject that never wearied them. "You notice," said Si, "that Abe is sort o' raw towards me?"

"What you done to him, Si?"

"Nothin'. It's that woman of his, ol' Vin."

"Whad you do to *her?*"

"Nothin'. You don't have to do nothin' to her to make her bile over. She got mad at me t'other day, an' I reckon she went home an' thrashed Abe around till she felt human agin. All I done was to tell her about a dream I had. I met her in front o' the Post Office when about half o' Beebread was settin' around waitin' fer number nineteen. I says you're lookin' mighty well, Vin, an' told her I'd dreamp about her the night before. She jumped on me fer what wuz it, an' I told her, friendly like. I told her I dreampt I's in hell an' was walkin' around to see how they kep' the place, when I saw a big wash-pot in a corner, turned upside down like nobody was goin' to use it fer a while, an' I thought I'd right it up an' fill it with water to cool me off with, an' jest as I laid my hand on it the devil grabbed holt o' my arm, an' screams out 'Fer the Lord's sake, let that pot be!' 'An' what's the matter with it?' I ast him. 'I've got Vin More under there,' he says, 'an' ef she gits out she'll make it so hot aroun' here hell won't be home fer me no more. I'll have to go on new location, an' it'll be a God's trouble to move with all the folks I've got to look after. Don't you move that pot nary inch!' That's all I done to her; jest told her about a dream. An' she got so mad I had to hide down on the river side of the depot till she went home."

Before they could laugh comfortably, Abe came strolling back.

"Hooray fer Abe! He's gittin' here in time to rest."

Abe took on the authority of one who had reconnoitered, though the others knew as much as he did. He dropped down on Si's bed of leaves and began,

"That's an awful bluff over there on the Dark Moon side. Looks fifty miles to the bottom when the fire lights it up. Jest to look down it made my heels hurt."

"How's the fire."

"Pullin' along smart."

"Kain't hurt us now," said Si. He settled back to his banter. "Say, fellers, did you notice that wild hog we skeered up? Had a nose like a meetin' house steeple. Must 'a' been one o' yorn, Milt. You got to quit raisin' them spike-nosed hogs er I got to quit plantin' punkins in my fence corners. They reach through the cracks an' eat 'em all up."

"That's nothin' to what yorn do to me," returned Milt. "I kain't take a jug o' buttermilk to my clearin' an' set it down. They're right there with their nose to the bottom, drinkin' it."

"Look out, Si!" said Ben. "That's my foot. Git off it, will ye?"

"Dunno. Might have to git off the mountain."

"My foot's big, but it ain't as big as yore cheek."

"That's a purty braggable shoe, Ben," approved Milt, as Ben

stuck his foot under a lantern to assess damage. "Git it at Gaffney's ?"

"No. Briartown."

"Britt got a good pair there," said Milt.

Britt ! Every man pricked up his ears. They had been waiting for this moment. Milt lit his pipe disinterestedly. His part was played.

"You's at the station, wasn't you, Si ?" asked Abe.

"Yeah." He cut off a chew of tobacco. "I saw her."

Raz Cody cut in boldly. "What about her comin' back ? Reckon she's goin' to stay in ?"

"The old women 'll run her out," said Ben.

"Shucks," jeered Si. "They'll be astin' her how to wear their clo's. She got off the train lookin' like New York."

This was a real contribution, and was received as such.

"Whad she ever chuck Britt fer anyhow ?" asked Abe. "He was lettin' her tell him right where to set his feet. She could lead him with a sewin' thread."

"Shore !" said Si. "When Britt got married, I thought he's campin' with luck. I'd seen Ish work, and I'd 'a' swore she'd make a wife like Sis Teed over on Larky. Sis could kill an' hang a hog an' her man away from home. Worked at grubbin' er anything. Her hand was rough as a cat's tongue. Teed got mad one day an' knocked her two front teeth out. Then he got her some new ones, long as gourd seed, an' she was so proud of 'em she begun to go to meetin'. She'd never took time before. Teed knowed how to handle her. But Britt didn't take hold right. He let Ish tell him how right from the start. He let her walk all over him. He'd lay flat an' let her walk right up an' down his spiney bone."

"You reckon he's goin' to be fool enough to take her back ?"

"I'll let you ast him that. I ain't got money enough to take me to a horsepittle. What kind o' tobacco you got, Raz ? This is so strong it breaks my teeth."

"Apple-tag," said Raz, handing over his plug. All realized that conversational adventure was over so far as it concerned Britt.

417

"I'll leave you what the dog left when granny dropped her bacon," said Si, biting enormously into the plug.

"Y' all know how Abe ketches rabbits ?" asked Ben. "He goes out an' squats on a ridge an' makes a noise like a cabbage."

"You fellers do the laffin'," said Abe. "I'm thinkin' over that trade Milt 's pesterin' me fer till I kain't git more'n ten hours sleep nights. I've decided I ain't cryin' fer his steers. I ain't makin' a boneyard this year."

"Boneyard ?" cried Milt. "I'll tell you what, Abe, ef you want my steers fer yore mule there's one thing you got to throw in with him er there ain't no trade. That's his crutches. I shore won't 'low you anything on *them*."

The light again flared in the sky.

"I'll bet," said Raz, "the fire has struck that strip o' dead pines about half a mile under the mountain."

"It ain't nigh the pine strip yet," said Abe. "That wuz a bunch o' dead chestnuts with the bark hangin' on. The fire 's bitin' at the bark. You see it's dyin' down already. I know jest where it is, 'cause I caught a black coon under the rocks there one night. It wuz —"

"Say, Abe, you've told that coon story so many times, s'pose you say it back'ards an' make it interestin'."

A sudden clear halloo came from the west.

"They want hep," shouted Ben. The men, all but two, leapt to their feet and set out in a run toward the voice. Si and Abe did not stir.

Ishma drew herself up through the woods; up toward the light in the sky. As she climbed, the blood flowed warmly through her body and her step became firm and light. She could barely see the trail, but her old knowledge of it came back to her, helping her to dodge the thickets and keep clear of the ravine. Action made her heart ache less, and gave her a clearer mind. She began to throb with the old expectation — a little girl following her father to the big fire.

Down at the house below, Julie, with Steve's arm about her waist, was telling him how Laviny had taken the news.

"She shore was pleased to hear it, an' we had our worryin' fer

418

nothin'. I wasn't aimin' to tell her till I had to, but she right out an' ast me. I was goin' to wait till it was over —"

"Till what was over, Julie?"

"Why — you know — the weddin'."

"*Our* weddin', Julie. Git it right, my gal."

"She makes the best o' things when she knows it's too late fer fussin' to hep it."

"I kain't blame her fer thinkin' I'm a no 'count husband fer you, Julie."

"She don't know you like I do, Steve."

"Gosh! Maybe she knows me a lot better. Ain't you afraid, Julie?"

"Not a bit, Steve. An' I want to tell you something. You won't want to hear it, but I've got to tell you. I want ever'thing cleared up ahead of us, Steve. An' the way to do that is to clear up ever'thing behind us."

"Pitch it out, Julie. I can stand a lot now."

"I was in love with Britt once. Awfully in love. Do you keer, Steve?"

"I'm goin' to tell you just what I think, Julie. If you can love me after lovin' Britt, then I'm a darned sight better man than I thought I was, and I thank you for the compliment."

"O, Steve, I'm so glad! With you forgivin' me, an' aunt Laviny takin' it so easy —"

"Wait a minute, Julie. You shore you told her it was me you're marryin'?"

"Of course! Why — I don't know either. She was jest astin' if I was goin' to get married, an' when it 'ud be, an' I told her. Sakes alive! You don't s'pose she thought it was me an' Britt?"

"It don't make a damn bit o' difference what she thought. If she wants to make her own misery, I ain't goin' to let her hurt you with it."

Laviny was not asleep under the big shawl. Ears cocked, she had listened to every word. With the wisdom of the defeated, she made herself as meek under the bludgeoning of fate as her nature would permit. Pretending to wake up, she lifted her head and spoke cheerily.

"Law me, Julie, you'd better be in bed asleep. If Steve's like his daddy, you won't get much chance after Sunday week."

Ishma heard voices above her in the woods, and sat down to wait until the men had passed. She was quite ready to sit down. Her feet had lost their lightness. Her heart had begun it, rebuking her feet. And presently she was all heaviness. She was leaving Britt. She was leaving Ned. Forever. And she knew what she was doing. When she left them the first time, she hadn't known. Now she knew. Ned, so big and alive, and hers. It was her own blood that had dripped from his forehead. It was her own mind that had looked from his eyes. No, it wasn't forever. He would come to her some day. He would have to come. He'd have to know the truth about life, the world, about men trying to live together on one earth, and how they must do it. He would come. They would work and think and march together, she and her strong, young son. Her mind trembled towards activity again. Doors were opening; the clear light was creeping in.

The men above her had stopped to rest. She heard their jokes, their jeers. They spoke of Britt. They were talking of his wife. That was herself. She didn't care. What to her were these trickling streams? She had heard the rushing of great waters. The ocean of life had shored on her heart.

There was a shout, and the men leapt towards it. Two seemed to linger. She heard an indistinct mumbling, then recognized the voices. Si Welch and Abe More, of course. Si would take his rest, because he always fought hard, and Abe because he never fought at all. She smiled with slow recollection, then became still with attention, hearing the name of Bert Wiggins.

"He's up here waitin' fer his boy to die, I reckon," said Abe.

"Yeah. I had a long chow with him last night."

"How'd he say the strikin' folks was comin' out?"

"The mill-bats air goin' to win, he says. But it's mighty nigh starvation. Job Weygood is over in Macon with a truck c'lectin' 'lasses an' hog-meat to take down to Winbury. They'll win if the feed holds out, Bert says."

"Why're them mill-owners treatin' the hands so mean fer, when they's scrapin' the mountains last year, lookin' fer men to work fer 'em ?"

"They say they've got to cut wages 'cause the market 's breakin' up. Bert says they're talkin' round now like nothin' but a war 's goin' to put the market back."

"Well, I ain't got no boy to give 'em this time. He's layin' over in France, an' he's layin' mighty still."

"Bert says it ain't goin' to be that kind of a war, if they git it. Us workin' folks what do the fightin' 'll make it something else. It'll be a war to take over the Goverment an' make the big bosses an' ever'body go to work an' not let 'em have more'n what we git fer ourselves. Me an' Bert set through the haunch o' the night with little Bert, an' we talked it all over."

"Make ever'body work ?"

"Yeah. You'll have to put in steady yersef, Abe."

"We kain't have that kind of a war. We ain't got no army. The Goverment's got it."

"Who 's the army ? Ain't it our boys ?"

"Yeah, I reckon. But pore folks ain't got no chance agin the Goverment. Some o' them folks what's behind it air wuth a million dollars."

"Well, I'll tell you something fer proof. I got it from Matt Weaver, an' he got it straight from Job Weygood. The pore an' the rich air goin' to fight it out."

"You can allers hear that kind o' talk. It's like a he-huckleberry, don't bear nothin'."

"I reckon if it does come to a showdown us mountain folks 'll go with the pore."

"Shore ! We'll go with 'em like the wind a-blowin'. They's our folks."

"Bert said Ishmer was takin' a big hand in the strike."

"Twa'n't the right time fer her to come away then."

"I couldn't git it out o' Bert, but they're talkin' around that Rad left her hangin' high."

"Mebbe she hearn Julie was about to git aholt o' Britt."

"Ay, that brung her in, I reckon."

"Britt couldn't do better 'n take Julie. She's a gal that'll put her head under the fore-stick fer him."

Ishma, listening, felt the doors of light snap shut. Her brain went dark. A warm, black cloud seemed to wrap itself softly about her head, and all her body was again on the rack of yearning. "Britt, oh, Britt!" she called, and lay on the ground, her burning cheek pressed against the leaves and broken twigs, crushed down until it met the coolness of the uncomforting earth.

Half an hour later she reached the ridge, her climb finished. She didn't go to the top of the last cliff, but stood in a gap that opened out over Dark Moon. What she saw held no disappointment. At last life was kind. Here was invincibility, and beauty was its breath. Looking at it, she herself became fire, power, beauty. Like plumed boughs the burning curves rose upward, and she rose with them. Light raced around the horizon, and she was the light. An ocean of white smoke sent its rolling waves against heaven, and she too glided upward to beat at the doors of the sky. In the waves were fiery bits, like splintered stars, and she was those swirling, dancing bits, going to mad, ecstatic death.

Down the steep slope below her, the tree-tops were gilded to the last twig. Oaks, hickories and poplars, strained on their roots as the hot surge caught them. There was no escape. The tall chestnuts crackled and shook. Their young leaves, curling dry and grey, spun from their stems and drifted invisible. Stript boughs became lace-work of glowing white gold. Green pines turned a turbid red, and sent clouds of amber needles into the sky. A cliff was rent wide, and fought the waves of fire with thunderous, flying rocks. The juniper that had crowned it was tossed like an orange mane into the smoking sea. Odors hung hotly in the air, essences of flame, making the senses surrender.

Ishma leaned to the precipice, with upward poise, motionless before flight. When Britt came up to her she merely knew that he was there and forgot him. Alarmed, he started to seize her arm, but he couldn't touch her. He put his lips near her ear and called, "Come away!" She didn't turn her head, but began to talk.

"Oh, there was never anything so wonderful! It's like an ocean of pearls rolling up the sides of the coves, and the fire making it look as if the sun had got under it."

422

"I'm looking at you, Ishma."

She didn't hear him. "I ought to die now. There'll be no other time."

"Ishma !"

"No other time ! Now, now, now !"

Britt's heart lost a beat. He put his hand on her shoulder, but lightly, as if afraid. "Come away, Ishma !"

"Look ! The tree-tops down there !" she cried. "They're clear as dew ! Every twig is shining ! O, it's Jerusalem a-swimming !"

Britt became more frightened. He didn't know that a face could hold so much light. And she was slowly pressing out over that burning sea. He took hold of her arm and leaned close to her ear.

"It's hard on the little birds. It'll take the song out of the air. The music will be gone from the woods. They're nesting now — the nests are full of little ones — "

"Don't think of that ! Don't spoil it, Britt ! Go away !"

"The squirrels too. Their young ones are just coming out — "

"Don't, Britt !"

"And all the green laurel will be burnt white. Just tangled bones warping in the sun, no shining leaves and sweet blossoms — "

"You stop ! What are you holding me for ? Keep your hands to yourself !"

She pulled away from him. The fire rose higher, making a rush up the precipice that surely would bring it to their feet. But there was a sucking of winds and it rolled back, up the sky, on the other side of the world. Ishma clasped her hands above her head and leaned outward as if she must go with the fire.

"It's the night burning up," she cried, "all the darkness — everywhere !"

"It's roarin' hell !" shouted Britt. "Hear the trees a-poppin' ? My throat — " He subsided, clutching his throat. "If I had some water — "

Again he tried to talk. "Ishma, you're as beautiful as — as — there ain't anything like you, Ishma !" He caught her by the shoulder. "Come away from here."

"Don't touch me ! I'm going to that cliff — right to the top ! Don't you come, Britt. I don't want you. I don't want anybody !"

She ran out of the gap and up to the highest tip of rock. Britt felt weighted to the ground. Then he tore himself loose and started after her.

"Don't you come, I tell you !" She was like a pausing wind. No doubt she felt that she could step over that burning gulf and be as safe as the wind. "I want to be alone with it — the fire — night — God — everything. Go away, or I'll jump. I swear I will ! I've wanted to be here for eight years by myself. You go !"

"All right," Britt called up to her. "I'll go."

She watched him start off, then turned to the abyss of fire. As soon as she turned, he ran up the cliff behind her. Before he reached her she sat down. He slipped into a crevice and waited. He couldn't believe she would jump, but he wouldn't take a chance. Not with Ishma and her head going like that. He struggled near enough to reach up and catch her skirt if she should start to jump.

Toward the west, where a mountain spur dammed the valley, the fire reached a sweep of dead pines, and the raging of it, Ishma thought, would have drawn the moon into it had there been a moon. She had sat down because her knees had begun to quiver and crumple with her weight. In a few minutes they had ceased to tremble. She began to get back into herself, to rescue her own shape and soul. But she didn't intend to wait there until the flames drooped and the ecstasy sagged. She must carry that power and fire with her back to her work. For she was going back — not to Winbury, where Derry was, and the comrades who would always remember her moment of defection — but to new places, with new eyes and voices. She would go to a mill-town where the workers had never heard that they could be free, that the world could be theirs; and she would teach them and stay with them until they held her vision. Then she would go to another town . . . and another . . . and another . . . and Ned would come to her. . . .

Toward the west, on that same spur where the fire had found

the acres of dead pines, but higher up than the pines, stood a tall linn. It was now a burning cone shooting up through the white waves that swathed it and rolled about it. The cone shot to the sky, as if the ocean of pearl had found a great golden tongue and must make the universe listen. Ishma rose. She wouldn't wait until that flame fell to earth and the linn stood, a parched wreck, in its own ashes.

Four feet below her, on the fire side of the cliff, the rocks bulged and formed a safe ledge roughly slanting downward. From the ledge she knew she could find Lame Goat Trail and make her way to Siler's Cove. She caught a sudden painful breath, and her hand touched her breast. The ache was still there. It hadn't been burnt away. But where she was going, aches wouldn't matter.

"Goodbye, Britt, goodbye!" she said, waving her hand back to the woods below. Then she turned to leap down to the ledge. The next moment she felt as if a great bear had gripped her and torn her from the cliff. When she saw Britt's face it was so angry and cruel that she felt a bear might handle her more kindly. He dragged her down, not in the least gently, and flung her from him. She fell hard, with a rock jabbing her side and her foot crumpled painfully under her. She could see Britt clearly in the pearly light that fell all about them. He was tramping in circles, kicking the rocks and stamping the earth. Once he stopped in front of her, and she thought that the next minute she might be under his foot too.

"You'd ruther die, would you?" he shouted. "You'd ruther die!" Then he walked away again and resumed his outrageous stamping. Ishma began to understand. Britt thought she had meant to jump into that abyss. He had forgotten about the ledge. No doubt she had been talking insanely, and it wasn't strange that he should think she would do so wild a thing. But why did he care so much? He had no right to care so much, unless he wanted her himself. The hope that swept through her left her motionless.

When she spoke her voice was incredibly gentle. "Aren't you going to marry Julie?"

She had to speak a second time before he heard. Then he

stopped his tramping and looked at her. Again she had to repeat her question.

"What you talkin' about ?" he cried. "Me ? Me marry Julie ? You know she's marryin' Steve Sunday week !"

Ishma was silent and ashamed. Her mind was working in a clear glow. Its rough flash hurt her. Britt lowered his voice to a sort of compassionate contempt for himself.

"No, Ishma, if you want me to marry Julie, that's one more time I can't satisfy you. You could fix Rad, but by God alive, you can't fix *me !* I can pick my own. They're not scarce around my coat-tails either, if I want 'em. Of course Julie would make a good mother for Ned, but that oughtn't to make you want to bust up pore ol' Steve's playhouse. I thought you had more conscience than that."

Ishma uttered an "Oh !" that was a tangle of exasperation, joy and pain.

"What's the matter ?" asked Britt, concerned, but not making a move toward her.

"My shoulder hurts. It struck a rock when you threw me down."

"I'm sorry. I'm dog-gone ashamed o' myself. I went crazy for a minute. You know I was crazy, don't you ? It was so clear all at once what a fool I'd been. Four years just a smooth idiot ! I went crazy when it struck me like that. I couldn't stand it. You see — when you left me — I didn't give you up. I — I knew how it was 'tween you an' Rad. I didn't give you up. All I had to do was to let you alone long enough. Some day I'd see you walkin' up an' settin' down on the porch like you belonged. When I made a little money I couldn't think of a thing to do with it but fix up a home for you, same as we used to talk about. When you came, an' showed so plain you meant to go on takin' care o' yourself, an' told me right out that you didn't come back on my account — I wouldn't believe it. Not all of it. I saw you's low in heart, an' troublin' over something, an' I thought maybe I could get you to stay awhile an' you'd begin to feel different about our teamin' up again. If I'd not set on you about it. And all the time you'd ruther die. It give me a knock. I can't think right yet. I couldn't die as long as you were anywheres a-livin'. I couldn't. Not for no reason at all."

Ishma hadn't tried to stop him. She let the words flow over and through her, like music that broke and bubbled. When he stopped speaking she was still silent.

"You were goin' to jump off an' leave me here just cleaned out. How could you do that to me, Ishma?"

"Come here, Britt," she said at last. "Come closer. I can't talk loud. I — it seems like trying to talk in my sleep."

When he had slowly crossed to her she tried to speak again. "Britt, when I found what I had done — going away — done to myself, I mean. Not you, or mommie, or Ned — just done to myself — every day was as long as a hundred years, and I'd have beat it off the earth right then if it hadn't been for Vennie coming along. And after she came, she needed me. I couldn't go then. Life was hard up here, the Lord knows, but when I looked back at it from down yonder, I thought that if I were in one corn row and you in another, I could hoe and hoe and never get tired if the row was as long as forever."

"Yeah. That's the way a body feels that's got the mountains in 'em like you an' me have."

He was still unbelieving. She would have to say more, and her tongue seemed thick and heavy.

"Then — Vennie died — and Rad — I can't tell you now — I was in such a tangle — I'll explain it all sometime, Britt. And at last I got Rad off — but I was so busy then finding out things — what life meant, and what I — what everybody could do to make it different — then something happened — and I thought there was no harm in my coming back —"

"Of course there couldn't be! But what mixes me up is your trying to rush into the next world after you got here. I know you were all worked up over the fire, but —"

"I wasn't going to jump, Britt. I wasn't big enough for that. Though it would be a dandy old way to go. You forgot about that ledge. I was going to climb down and get into Lame Goat Trail —"

She paused, caught by the misery in his face.

"Just pullin' out. I see."

There was no life in his voice. She jumped up and took him

427

by the shoulders. "Why should I stay here ? You had got along fine. Better without me than with me. You said we'd talk things over like old *friends*. And mommie said you were going to marry Julie."

He shook himself away from her and stared. "Ishma, you don't *keer ?*"

"Like this, Britt !" Her arms were around him. "Oh, like this !" She clung with all her might. "I lied when I said I didn't come back for you. That was all I was thinking about. Just getting to you."

A LITTLE later, when life was again coherent, they lay on the pearl-lit ground and talked. Britt's head was on Ishma's shoulder, and her cheek was warm against his hair. How many, many times she had waked from a dream like that ! Times when she had tried to hold the dream, afraid to open her eyes. And now she could not get them wide enough, could not see and feel enough of the bright reality sweeping through and about her. The fount of her ecstasy was deeper than she knew, for she was profoundly, beneath all else, a giver. With her whole being open to the surge of Britt's love, her joy was complete only in the utter gift of herself, troubled by no withholding.

It was Britt who came first to sober speech. She laughed as he told her not to expect too much of the rocky old place. Living was easier on the mountain than she had known it, but it was still hard enough. The money wasn't coming in any more for his songs. People soon tired of songs. They had to be new always. It was the old farm for it now.

"The new farm you mean, Britt. And don't worry about its being hard for me. I'd be ashamed to come back and find it all easy. I'll have a lot to forget, and I count on hard work to help me."

He drew her to him, his face tenderly solemn. "I'll help you forget it, honey."

So quickly were they thinking of totally different things. She didn't try to explain, but when he added, "What's past is not goin' to hurt you if I can help it," she had to smile.

"It's not the past, Britt. That's nothing now. The terror and

428

the tears are nothing. I can't remember them." She pressed to him, making a home for her head under his chin. "I'm not looking back. It's the future that's going to be so hard to forget. The future of all men and women and little children. You see, I've run away. Three thousand years away." Her head was lifted to answer his puzzled look. "That's what the Chinese philosophers did three thousand years ago. They ran away from life to the farms. I'm back where they were."

"This is life, Ishma."

She gave him a kiss which was all the assent he needed. Explanations could wait. Though her mind was clearer, it was still without energy. Why couldn't love be enough?

"We'll not go down to the house tonight, Britt."

"Great! I was wishin' you'd say that. We'll not be cold up here. That fire's got Wimble County warm. I don't believe I could stand it if anybody else looked at you tonight. I'm a miser, I am."

Her face was a troubled wave. The past was not forgotten. Quickly he began to talk of his plans. There was so much to tell her — all he had done with the farm, all he intended to do. She closed her eyes and listened, seeing Britt as the last farmer in history, safe on his rock ledge with its fertile spots and patches, feeding his family out of his hand; while humanity swirled past him in the wake of great tractors, combines, combustion engines of all sorts, that had released man from the curse of the digger Adam, and set one-sixth of human energy flowing to new fields of freedom.

An old Grange song of Granny's ran through her mind.

> *Here's health to the plough, the brave old plough,*
> *That has fed the nations gone!*
> *May glory as now wave o'er the plough*
> *When a thousand years have flown!*

In a thousand years the plough would be seen only in the corners of museums, and the food-growing process would be imbedded in the earth-wide industrial body. A thousand years? In three generations probably.

Suddenly she saw where she might help. Even on her rock-ledge she could help. Opening her eyes on Britt — sturdy, beautiful, her golden primitive — she leashed him to the new age.

"Britt, you've got plenty of pasture now, haven't you ?"

"Miles of it. I can sell enough calves every year to buy our clothes and things we need."

"And we can have all the milk cows we want in the summer time ?"

"We could. But I'm not goin' to let you be foolin' with milk. You don't need to make a slave of yourself. We'd have to keep a truck an' take the milk to Carson, an' get up at two o' clock in the morning. No, sir ! We'll move along easier 'n that."

"I wasn't thinking about making money. I was thinking about a lot of little kids that I'd like to bring up here in the summer — every summer. I'd like to give them plenty to eat and turn them loose on the mountain to get strong. We could build bark shelters for them, or use your old tobacco sheds, since you're not going to worry with tobacco any more. It will take a lot of milk and eggs. Do you think we could do it, Britt ?"

"It will take a lot of work too, honey."

"Some of the mothers can come up and help me with the hens and cows. And I know men that the mills have scrapped who'd be made over by one summer up here. They'd be crazy to come and help. But I won't push it on you, Britt. The farm is yours."

"If I had a single thing that wasn't as much yours as mine, I'd throw it away. We'll plan out something after you've been all over the farm, and see what we can do. If you can get help there's nothing to keep ever' acre from doin' its share. Maybe we can manage it."

"If I could do that for the kids, Britt, I'd not feel as if I'd run away just to get fat and lazy and old up here."

"That's three things you'll never do nohow."

"Maybe I'll not get lazy and fat, but I'll have to get old sometime."

"You can't. You'll always be pullin' at the world tryin' to get it in shape, same as if you's goin' to live forever. Your heart 'll never put on age. It don't belong to time."

He rose and stood by her. "And I want to tell you what I

think about this helpin' the world business. But I don't mean for you to think the same. It'll be a big turnover from misery to happiness, from ignorance to knowledge, from cruelty to love, and the Lord has got to have a hand in it. We can't do it ourselves. His power must get into men's hearts. 'A new heart will I give you, and a new spirit will I put into you. I will take away the stony heart out of your flesh, and will give you a heart of flesh.' That's the way it will come about. If I thought it depended on us, I reckon I'd be runnin' amuck too, tryin' to do my part."

"But what about this, Britt ? 'Ye that make mention of the Lord, give him no rest *till he establish.'*"

"He will establish when he can come into enough hearts. 'Prove me now . . . if I will not open the windows of Heaven, and pour you out a blessing, that there shall not be room enough to receive it.' Let me tell you, honiest — "

She lay back as he talked, lay on the leafy ground, breathing odors that rolled through the gap from the burning side of the mountain; queer, spicy, heated smells. And there began to mingle with them the scent of an anæsthetic. She shut her eyes, back in the hospital, and the walls stretched out till the hospital was as big as the world. The ether was spreading . . . spreading . . . to the hearts and limbs of the people . . . and Britt was talking . . . talking . . .

"No matter if the rich do hold all the weapons. Love is as impartial as rain. It will creep to them too, and they will drop the spears of oppression. Ay, they will open their hearts and know all men as brothers. They will . . ."

She could hear his voice, and she loved him. But her shut eyes were looking on another face; a face keen, pale, dedicated; framed in dark hair that rippled with the sheen of water. And across Britt's voice ran another voice whose words were a path of flame. "They shall not put out our light. Their sword of power shall be taken away, and as beasts they shall lie down in the darkness they have made. For Man must march, and his heart is a lamp forever."

She looked up at Britt, breathing hard. Britt, the ridin' preacher's son. He was still talking. For him there had been no

431

interruption. "I don't believe that, Britt," she said. "I don't believe it at all. But I love you."

He knelt down and pressed his cheeks to hers. "That's all I want, honiest that ever was !" Then he was laughing. "You know who I'm going to get to marry us ? It'll be the meetin' house this time, an' Jim Siler 'll be the preacher."

His laughter, his eyes, were so young. She would never be as young as that, for all his talk about her ageless heart. And never would she tell him the things that would make him old. So she thought.

When he went to sleep, with his lips nestled against her neck, she lay very still, half awake, half in dream. It wasn't Britt's head whose beloved weight lay so light against her. It was Ned's. Her fair young son was getting strength from her heart. And out on the edge of the dark Derry's voice was no longer a flame, but a half heard monotone. "Yes, you mountain lady, it will be hardest on the young. They will have to put it through. The least we can do is to give them courage and knowledge."

Could she give them courage ? She who had run away ? And knowledge ? What understanding could she have of humanity, who had none of herself ? Twice in three days something unguessed within her had voraciously made itself known. First, that thing inimical to the unity of life; that had left her ashamed and apart, a beast hugging its den, flattened against the walls of separation. And tonight the incredible pain of desire had risen to amaze her. Denied her love, her man, she had been blind with hurt; as dead to vision as a panther on Blackspur tearing the midnight with a cry for her mate.

She opened her eyes, wide-awake, and stared into the night of pearl; night that was nearly morning. A sweet coolness came from it. Her veins partook of it. A squirrel crek-crekked in a tree below her. She heard the soft note of a bird. Wimble-side would be full of birds for a few days; timid, mourning birds. Would it be too late for new nests, new broods ?

She leaned over Britt. He was looking gentle and boyish in the tender half-light. Her lips touched his forehead with a protective kiss, that also held something prophetic. A cup, though full, is not the sea.

432

BIOGRAPHICAL AFTERWORD

Anna W. Shannon

In 1932, when Olive Tilford Dargan was sixty-three years old and had already published nine works under her own name, her first novel, *Call Home The Heart,* appeared under the pseudonym Fielding Burke. Dargan had deliberately sought a pseudonym "like a sword fresh from the scabbard . . . [to] stick in the public mind," a name no one "would jump on."[1] Only a week after the novel appeared, however, a critic betrayed the identity of the novelist in his review in the *New York Sun.* Exhilarated by high praise—even from those who deplored her novel's politics or polemics or both—Dargan forgave the critic's indiscretion. In the deceptive glow of long-deferred success, she wrote Grant Knight, the American literature professor with whom she had corresponded for two years concerning her work on the novel, "You will have to bear in mind when writing your next book that all the New York critics have gone left—glory be!"[2]

Such openness was unusual for Dargan throughout her century-long life. Perhaps that derived from an ingrained sense of privacy, perhaps from the caution imposed upon a person of radical outlook living where and as she did. While Dargan never joined the Communist Party, her allegiances are clear from her associations and her writing. But the details of her life remain screened. She, herself, may have conspired in the destruction of the evidence of her political activities and contacts during two of the periods of political repression through which she lived. Three times, fires consumed the bulk of her papers.[3] That Dargan and her contemporaries were cautious—two letters survive with her cautionary postscripts to destroy them[4]—explains much about gaps and inconsistencies in the biographical record. The desire on the part of Dargan's radical acquaintances and relatives to maintain their anonymity continues even today.[5]

433

Despite the dearth of biographical materials, there are twenty-five collections that preserve Dargan's letters, in addition to letters collected by the family. The letters reveal evidence of a network of women providing one another with their primary source of identity and energy. Olive Dargan drew inspiration from her friendship with and from the work of such women as Rose Pastor Stokes, the controversial and litigious early socialist and founding member of the American Communist Party; Alice Stone Blackwell, daughter of Lucy Stone, editor of *The Woman's Journal,* and engineer of the rapprochement between feuding suffrage organizations before the vote was won; and Anne Whitney, sculptor and patron of feminist causes.

On January 11, 1869, near Litchfield in Grayson County, Kentucky, Olive Tilford was born to Rebecca Day Tilford and Elisha Francis Tilford. They were school teachers who encouraged selfreliance and political awareness in their four children. Her maternal grandfather, Mordecai Day, had exhorted his slave-owning neighbors to give up their slaves and their sinful ways. Both of her grandmothers had been colorful, frontier storytellers, like Ishma's free-thinking grandmother Sarah Starkweather in *Call Home the Heart.*[6]

The suffering of those without class, race, or sex privilege made an early impression on Olive. Having read, at age eleven, in the *St. Louis Courier-Journal* of the birth of a baby in one of the state prisons, she attempted to convince her father to work to change the state constitution to prevent other babies from suffering for their mothers' circumstances. When her father responded by humming his favorite hymn through all its many stanzas, Olive knew that she would have to take action herself, and she composed a suffrage song—a musical retort to her father, the only member of her family who had the vote.[7]

Rebecca Tilford's ill health necessitated the family's move from Kentucky to northern Arkansas, near the Missouri border. Her mothers's invalidism seems to have forced Olive to mature early. She later wrote of her desire to render the full significance of her mother's "broken, unfinished life."[8] Olive began to school herself to take her mother's place as a teacher, assisting her father in his academy until she was fourteen, and then taking independent charge of a school nearby. Here, despite the difficulties of a rowdy class that had defeated her male predecessor, Dargan managed to instruct her thirty to forty students, who ranged in age from six to twenty, in all subjects and through all grades. She also earned their respect and that of their parents. She stayed on until a better position was offered her in Missouri. From Missouri, she moved to Nashville, Tennessee, to enroll in Peabody College, where she had won a scholarship to pay for two years of "rapturous study."[9]

After graduating in 1888 at the age of nineteen, she left for Houston, Texas, where she boarded with an aunt, took a business course, and taught in a business school. Typing skills were to the 1880s what computer literacy is to the 1980s: Olive seized the first opportunity to enter the business world. Her business career, however, was brief. Recalling her first and only job as a secretary in the office of a factory, she emphasized her distaste for this male world of insensitivity and exploitation. An episode that occurred one day at the factory seemed to epitomize her view of capitalism: her employer dictated two letters, the first ordering the immediate closing of a factory employing hundreds of workers; the second, complaining about the quality of the upholstery on his yacht. "I got an education at the factory," she later remarked.[10]

She next sought more formal education, spending a year at Radcliffe College in Cambridge, Massachusetts. It seems probable that she traced the most enduring and influential of her political friendships to the lectures and parlor meetings she attended in Cambridge in 1893 and 1894. Among the distinctions she later cherished was her honorary membership in the Radcliffe Club of New York. In Cambridge, too, she met Pegram Dargan, a minister's son from South Carolina. A senior at Harvard who thought himself a poet, he proposed early in the relationship, but they did not marry until March 2, 1898, when Olive was twenty-nine years old and had already begun to pursue a career in literature. Her first completed play, written in 1898 but later lost, was based on the legend of Joan, the woman Pope.

After their marriage, the Dargans moved to New York City and spent several years there as aspiring authors. Olive Dargan later confessed to a friend that, after a "tiff" with her husband, she had submitted her first poem to be published.[11] Olive was soon sending her poems to other periodicals and seeing them in the pages of *Scribner's, Century,* and *McClure's.* Pegram, in contrast, could hardly have been encouraged with the lack of interest shown toward his

work: his sole publication, *Carolina Ditties* (1904), had to be produced at his own expense. At the same time, Olive was reaping high
praise for her first volume, *Semiramis and Other Plays* (1904); and
her second volume, *Lords and Lovers and Other Dramas* (1906),
was even better received. The critics gave Olive the trousers in the
Dargan household; Jessie Rittenhouse's *New York Times* review, for
example, praised her second volume for an "assurance of touch, a
virile command of plot and form which constantly suggests a man's
hand."[12] *Lords and Lovers* was also well received by Scribner's editor Robert Underwood Johnson, whose genteel hand shaped the
destinies of many of Scribner's authors.

Dargan's extensive professional correspondence with Scribner's during the period 1910–1928 suggests that her view of herself
as a poet was fixed prematurely because of the gentlemanly solici-
tude of William Crary Brownell, Johnson's successor, who encouraged her to continue using "ladylike" obscurity and high flown language in her verse for twenty years. Her tendency to efface her own
personality from her verse must have pleased Brownell, who was
the most Victorian of the major American editors to survive into the
twentieth century. As a consequence, little of her early work holds
much interest for the modern reader except as it reflects on her
narrative fiction.

Pegram Dargan's health deteriorated in inverse proportion to
Olive Dargan's financial and literary success. The sale of the stage
rights to Olive's "The Shepherd," one of the plays collected in *Lords
and Lovers,* made possible the purchase of a farm near Almond,
North Carolina, where they hoped that Pegram's health would mend.
After the move, Olive published nothing for six years. The first series
of Dargan's letters still extant are from this period. "I have been
thinking that I was to have a room of my own . . . but Pegram says
the attic in our cabin can not be made comfortable, so I must wait
another year," she wrote a woman friend who shared her literary
ambitions. She added that she had dismissed a query from Brownell
about this friend's literary plans by saying, " 'Why, she is married
and women don't do anything after that.' "[13]

Such comments seem to be as close as Dargan ever came to
airing her grievances to her correspondents about the way her marriage impinged on her writing. These grievances may have been especially acute when she discovered in 1907 that she was carrying a

"wholly unexpected" child.[14] Now in her late thirties, she feared having a first baby at the farm, far from expert medical care, but wrote Alice Blackwell in confidence that she intended to give Pegram the chance to take responsibility for seeing to the arrangements, since "if Pegram can manage things himself of course it would be wrong for me not to let him do it, even if I am not so comfortable."[15] But Olive soon left for Rose and Graham Stokes's family compound on Caritas Island off the coast of Stamford, Connecticut. Here, where the Stokeses customarily entertained such friends as Emma Goldman and Margaret Sanger, Olive Dargan gave birth in May 1907 to a premature infant daughter, who died only two hours later.[16]

She spent the remainder of the summer on the island, recovering physically, and brooding over the loss of her child. During this period, she declared herself a socialist, writing, "I find that I have been a socialist for some time—all my life in fact—but I didn't know the name for it. . . . However, I [do] not want to get involved in hopes until I [have] fire to spend. It makes one too unhappy."[17] Perhaps she was arming herself for the return to the farm in North Carolina or for relocation in Oregon, where Pegram had been during the summer. "If I go," she wrote, "I shall buy a tent and take [it] with me—one that I can put a stove in—then I shall be sure of a place in which to write."[18]

They did not relocate in Oregon. In 1911 Olive travelled alone to England, perhaps with the financial help of such friends as Anne Whitney and Alice Blackwell, and took up residence there until 1914. Dargan's letters to Blackwell from England outline the continuing development in her thinking as she moved from advocating passive resistance and Christian patience, to a recognition that violence might be necessary to effect social change. These letters also reveal her growing detachment from her marriage, about which she told Blackwell she wanted no detail published.[19]

During her stay in England, Dargan was strikingly silent on the subject of the battles being waged by American women during this critical period in American history, though she received communications from her sister and read *The Woman's Journal* and *The Call,* the latter of which was running Margaret Sanger's series on female sexuality. She supplied detached, yet detailed, descriptions to Blackwell about the bombings, imprisonment, forced feedings of suffragists, and riots that accompanied the British woman's suffrage movement. "The horrors of [the French Revolution] are a bagatelle in comparison with the horrors that are going on yearly in England,"[20] she reported. Although she mentions the privileged women among the suffrage leaders, Dargan writes glowingly of those drawn from the ranks of working women.

While in England, Dargan published *The Mortal Gods and Other Dramas* (1912); *The Welsh Pony* (1913), a work commissioned for private circulation; and *Pathflower* (1914), a collection of poems. None of these volumes was well received. *The New York Times* commented that *The Mortal Gods* was an example of the "strange and dangerous disease" afflicting authors with too much social conscience and too little aesthetic sensibility.[21]

Dargan's homecoming in 1914 brought personal and political disheartenment. Within a year Anne Whitney died. Pegram's mysterious drowning in 1915[22] and the loss of one of her beloved nieces following a ruptured appendix increased her sense of obligation and her actual responsibility for the members of her extended family who remained. During this period, Margaret Sanger, Emma Goldman, and Rose Stokes were imprisoned for telling women about birth control and the nation about war profiteering. Eventually, such foreign-born radicals as Goldman would be stripped of their citizenship and deported.

Dargan's published writing, however, reflects little of the turmoil of these years. Between 1916 and 1922, she published three more works: *The Cycle's Rim* (1916), winner of a Southern Society of New York Prize for the best volume of poetry by a Southern writer that year; *The Flutter of the Goldleaf, and Other Plays* (1922); and *Lute and Furrow* (1922), a collection of poetry. "Burning Bridges," one of the most intriguing poems in *Lute and Furrow*, seems not only a rejection of former means of retreat but may also be read as an allusion to measures the poet may have taken to guard her privacy. *Lute and Furrow* demonstrates that "Miracles . . . happen, common as grass/When bridges are burnt"[24] to allow a poet to venture into new imaginative territory. For Dargan, the burning of bridges in the twenties cleared the way for new political and artistic risks in the decade to follow.

Soon after she returned to North Carolina in 1916, Dargan discovered the compensations of her relatively isolated life. "I thought it would be very difficult for me here on account of the memories," she wrote to Blackwell in 1916, "but since I have taken practical hold of things I find myself busy from dawn until I fall into bed at night. I am getting strong, too, and do anything that happens to be next—mending fences, digging ditches, carrying rocks, cutting poles, and other incredible things."[23] Despite the hard work required to make the farm produce enough to feed her and her family of nine tenants, she now had the leisure to absorb mountain lore, to get to know mountain people, and to begin trying her hand as a writer of prose. Although she purchased a house in Asheville in 1925 in order to spend the winters in relative comfort and safety, she seems never to have freed herself of the responsibility for her tenants or for other people in need.

Dargan's art was strengthened by her engagement in the struggle for survival on behalf of her mountain neighbors. She recognized the importance of joint projects in gaining the confidence of the wary mountain people and wrote repeatedly of new tasks that demanded her attention. In *Highland Annals* (1925), a collection of literary pieces concerning mountain people she had known, Dargan demonstrated her gift for a new medium. The liberating acquaintance with mountain storytellers, whose tales recalled the stories of her childhood, had engaged her latent narrative talents, and she found herself recording and transforming their stories in an effort to capture a way of life already disappearing. By the time she finished *Highland Annals,* Dargan had a model for the heroine of *Call Home the Heart,* but her interest in writing temporarily flagged after 1925 with the passing of the old order at Scribner's. The death of her genteel editor, William Crary Brownell, in 1928, and the accession of the bright, young Maxwell Perkins, who, though he coached Fitzgerald and coddled Wolfe, seems to have cared little for her, ended her long association with Scribner's.

Although her artistic ambition waned temporarily, Dargan also kept up her involvement through reading and discussion in the circle that grew up around Edwin August Björkman in Asheville. Björkman, a Swedish-American novelist, translator, critic, and newspaper editor, introduced August Strindberg, Bjørnstjerne Björnson, and Arthur Schnitzler to an American audience and enhanced the cultural life of Asheville from 1926, when he became editor of the *Asheville-Citizen,* until his death in 1954. Through a local book exchange, Dargan, Björkman, and their friends read widely in world literature. Unlike

Thomas Wolfe, who fled the philistinism of Asheville, Olive Dargan seems to have found there the sustenance she required in order to flourish.

From time to time, however, Dargan viewed her life in North Carolina as a retreat from active involvement in political struggle. In the trickle of letters that have survived, she discusses her writing, the weather, and her health. The only evidence of regret for this retreat was her admission to Rose Stokes that while she busied herself "with all kinds of little local matters," Rose was "remoulding [sic] the world."[25] She maintained contact with the outside world, however, for in the mid-twenties she confessed to Blackwell that she was perusing the *Daily Worker* regularly and "assiduously" and that she was still a "vivid red."[26] Throughout this period, it may be that Dargan's retreat was less complete than it seemed. She was especially sympathetic to young women who married because of romantic notions but found afterwards no escape from poverty and incessant childbearing, and she intended to endow a shelter for such women in Asheville to take the place of the service she had provided in her home while she lived. She comments in 1927 on the indigent who sought refuge at her home:

> This winter I seem to be building up an official employment bureau. There is so much need. And if it is so in this favored region what must it be in other places! I've been helping young girls find work—They come here, so young, so helpless, so pretty, and not a place to lay their heads.[27]

Dargan left an enduring monument to her concern for such women in *Call Home the Heart*'s treatment of the cycle of marriage, pregnancy, and death that defined their existence.

Dargan's increasing identification with the region where she now spent the majority of her time, and her awareness of the fragility of her small literary reputation, caused her to hide her advanced ideas about race during this period. Although she had a warm, forty-year correspondence with William Stanley Braithwaite, a black intellectual and literary critic, for example, she urged her Scribner's editor in 1919 not to mention Braithwaite's praise of her work to a Southern critic who proposed to review her career. "I am covered with shame as I write this," she admits, "because I do feel grateful to Mr. Braithwaite, and I think he is entitled to all I can say in his behalf—but all

I could say in this part of my country would only pull the roof down on us both."[28]

A decade later, Dargan would make Ishma's expression of revulsion toward black people a shocking epiphany in *Call Home the Heart,* acknowledging thereby the persistence and power of racism in the South. Dargan seems to have viewed racism chiefly as a Southern problem when she was writing the novel; she was later forced to confront its pervasiveness when Lillian Smith's *Strange Fruit* (1944), a novel about interracial love and hate, became a *succès de scandale,* after being banned in Boston. For a time, Dargan seems to have believed that Smith's example demonstrated that progress was being made in the South. Dargan saw in Smith's work advances beyond her own reach in the 1920s and 1930s. In 1944 or 1945, she observed wistfully: "Lillian goes right on saying and doing what she thinks should be said and done for the Negroes with no diminution of respect or patronage."[29] Though events would prove this assessment much too hopeful and though her own age limited her ability to take the active risks that the younger novelist was taking, Dargan admired the impulse represented by Smith's novel and her camp and perceived that American racists were the "killers of the dream."[30]

Though we do not know whether Dargan involved herself in the 1929 textile mill strikes, she visited both Gastonia and Marion during the period of the strikes and described being drained by her experiences there. She was encouraged by the work of other women, especially such writers as Mary Heaton Vorse, who were telling the workers' side of the evolving story. With confidence that Vorse and others would write the chapters of the story she missed, Dargan began writing her novel at a brisk pace. Even before she finished the manuscript, she began planning the second volume "to put [her heroine] through the Marion outrage with its incredible murders."[31] By September 1930, she was all but finished with her first draft, having taken almost as long with the last thirty pages as she had with the first four hundred. When the finished manuscript was accepted by Longmans, Green, a publisher she had believed too conservative to handle political fiction by an untried novelist, Dargan mused that Ishma might be less "subversive" than she had intended.[32] She was elated nonetheless. "One of the most stimulating things about this acceptance," she wrote, "is that it shows I really can start out fresh and new and young."[33]

Although there is no doubt that Dargan's strategic problems in presenting Ishma's character and her own political vision alienated both radicals and reactionaries alike, the novel caught on and seemed about to offer its author her first substantial taste of literary prominence. Neither of her subsequent novels, however—*A Stone Came Rolling* (1935) and *Sons of the Stranger* (1947)—met with the reception of the first.

Dargan's activities in the years from 1939 to 1935 are vividly recalled, not by her contemporaries, who are all dead, but by the radical "youngsters" she knew in North Carolina. One of these individuals, a former CIO organizer, recalls Dargan's willingness to allow her mountain cabin to be used as a retreat when things became too "hot" in nearby industrial towns. Another, a former treasurer for the Communist Party, confirms that Dargan was never recruited as a Party member, though she "unhesitatingly agreed" when asked for the use of the cabin as the site for a week-long Party training school in 1941. He adds,

> My first meeting with Olive Tilford Dargan was probably in 1940. . . . She gave me an impression of one who observed the world and her fellow creatures with uncompromising clarity, but yet avoided sitting in judgment. She was passionately humane and felt quite personally the overwhelming injustice in the world, but she seemed to avoid personal animosity against those who profited from it and condoned it. She kept detached, when I knew her, from the immediate political concerns of the day. I think she knew her strength was limited and that she was strongest with her pen. . . . Though Olive was fearful of the FBI and other harassment she was consistently helpful to Communists she knew and she never failed to welcome me when I visited her home. On one occasion when I arrived unexpectedly while she had visitors, she gargled an invented name when she introduced me. For so gracious a lady, it was unthinkable that she not introduce me at all, even though she feared that my public reputation (by 1948) would have made my name readily identifiable. . . . I don't think I ever got a letter from Olive because none survive in my possession and I would surely have treasured them. In all the years I knew her my mail was being watched and often opened by the FBI, so I did little letter writing and Olive needed no warning about writing.

Dargan stopped predicting revolution with assurance after 1947, observing, "I've done my best to 'stand to,' I hope not forgetting art."[34] She left the front lines to others who were younger. When a literary agency in Prague applied for translation rights to her novels, she decided that any publicity was dangerous. "God send another day!" she wrote, "I myself am adopting the discretion of an oyster."[35] In 1955 she wrote of the "shock of having my last and best novel wiped from the public slate . . . [a shock] . . . so cruel and deep that I have not been able to recover from it."[36] Later, she added, "I don't think the inhibition from the fate of my last novel will leave me until I am free of this world."[37] Though she continued to write doggedly, receiving awards for her last volume of poetry, *The Spotted Hawk* (1958), and seeing a final collection of stories, *Innocent Bigamy* (1962), in print at the age of ninety-three, Dargan, like other authors of the thirties, suffered the loss of her audience and of the conviction and courage necessary to sustain achievement. She died in 1968 at the age of ninety-nine.

Anna W. Shannon
West Virginia University

Notes

1. Olive Tilford Dargan to Grant Knight, 12 July 1931, Olive Tilford Dargan Papers, Special Collections and Archives, University of Kentucky Libraries.

2. Dargan to Grant Knight, undated [1932], Olive Tilford Dargan Papers, Special Collections and Archives, University of Kentucky Libraries.

3. Dargan remarks on a 1919 fire in a letter to William Crary Brownell, dated 3 July 1919; she mentions the second fire in a letter to Robert Bridges, dated 21 February 1924. Both letters may be found in the Charles Scribner's Sons Archive, Princeton University Library. A third fire began in an outbuilding on the Georgia farm of a friend to whom she had given two pickup truckloads of her papers for safekeeping during the period of the Red Scare of the 1950s.

4. Robert Underwood Johnson to W. C. Brownell [copy] Olive Tilford Dargan to Alice Stone Blackwell, [undated], Records of the National American Woman Suffrage Association, Manuscript Division, Library of Congress. Dargan wrote, "Burn this at once, if not sooner," to Grant Knight, 17 February 1956, Olive Tilford Dargan Papers, Special Collections and Archives, University of Kentucky Libraries.

5. In addition to expressing my appreciation to those who prefer not to be named, I wish to thank John F. Blair, Olive Dargan's last publisher, for sending me copies of materials in his files; Richard Walser, Professor Emeritus at North Carolina State

University, Raleigh, for supplying me with information on Dargan and for offering assistance in locating others who could supply more; and Wayne Modlin, at the Fontana Regional Library in Bryson City, North Carolina, for providing me with an introduction to one of Dargan's close friends, Mrs. Madeleine Blaine.

The problem of incomplete indexing plagues researchers who seek to recover the documents of women's lives. Only the contributions of alert and knowledgeable archivists enable the work to go on. A case in point is James Hutson, of the Manuscript Division of the Library of Congress, who led me to the sizable, but unindexed, collection of Dargan letters in the Records of the National American Woman Suffrage Association. I also want to thank those at the Southern Historical Collection who made my stay in Chapel Hill to use their Dargan materials a pleasant and productive excursion. I also wish to thank the archivists at the University of Kentucky Libraries, the Princeton University Library, the Amherst College Library, Tamiment Library of New York University, and Houghton Library of Harvard University for sharing with me their substantial Dargan materials. The prompt attention to my queries by librarians and archivists at other colleges and universities holding Dargan letters deserves more than mention, as does the institutional and personal support I received at the West Virginia University Library and in the West Virginia University English Department.

Finally, I wish to thank the members of the Morgantown Women's Research Group, Laura Gottlieb, Anne Effland, Linda Yoder, Clay Pytlik, and Gail Adams, who have shared the frustrations and the joy of my research and writing.

6. A brief biographical sketch by Virginia Terrell Lathrop in the Spring 1960 issue of *North Carolina Libraries* relates stories about Dargan's family. Lathrop makes the explicit connection between Dargan's and Ishma's grandmothers.

7. Typed draft of Biographical Summary, page 1, in the Records of the National American Woman Suffrage Association, Manuscript Division, Library of Congress.

8. Dargan to Alice Stone Blackwell, 30 July 1907, Houghton Library, Harvard University, Cambridge, Mass.

9. Quoted by Virginia Terrell Lathrop, *op. cit.*

10. Quoted by Jane and Thomas Polsky, "The Two Lives of Olive Tilford Dargan," *The Southern Packet*, June 1949, p. 2.

11. Taped interview, 24 November 1976, with Sylvia Arrowood Latshaw, in Sylvia Arrowood Latshaw Papers, Southern Historical Collection, University of North Carolina, Chapel Hill, N.C.

12. Jessie B. Rittenhouse, "Four Books of Verse: The Works of Arthur Symons, Olive Tilford Dargan, Thomas Nelson Page, and William Coningsby Dawson," *The New York Times*, 9 January 1907, p. 30.

13. Dargan to Mabel Hay Barrows Mussey, 2 October 1907, Houghton Library, Harvard University, Cambridge, Mass.

14. Dargan to Alice Stone Blackwell, 18 March 1907, Houghton Library, Harvard University, Cambridge, Mass.

15. Ibid.

16. Dargan to Mabel Hay Barrows Mussey, 1 June [1907], in Houghton Library, Harvard University, Cambridge, Mass.

17. Dargan to Alice Stone Blackwell, 30 July 1907, Houghton Library, Harvard University, Cambridge, Mass.

18. Ibid.

19. Dargan to Alice Stone Blackwell, May 1913, Records of the National American Woman Suffrage Association, Manuscript Division, Library of Congress.

20. Dargan to Alice Stone Blackwell, 10 May 1913, Records of the National American Woman Suffrage Association, Manuscript Division, Library of Congress.

21. *The Mortal Gods* was panned by S. O'S. [O'Sheel Shaenias] in an article entitled "Cacophonic Verse: Mixtures of Controversial Causes and Tinsel Techniques," *The New York Times,* 16 February 1913, p. 79. Obviously, Dargan was now beginning to write more directly about her political views. In *American Women Writers,* ed. Lina Mainiero (New York: Frederick Ungar Publishing Co., 1979), Sylvia Cook says of *Mortal Gods,* that though it is "archaic in form and remote in setting," it is "nevertheless a powerful study of the oppression of the working class in modern industrial society."

22. There are several versions of the story of Pegram Dargan's death. Members of Dargan's family claim that a reunion was in the offing and that Pegram had embarked for England to be reunited with Olive. Virginia Terrell Lathrop asserts that Pegram could not leave his invalid mother to join his wife abroad, but that after Olive returned he left his mother with her and embarked for Cuba. Wife and mother received word that he had been drowned while crossing the channel to the island. Sylvia Latshaw says that Pegram and a brother had once made a suicide compact after a venture in which they had convinced friends to invest failed. According to Latshaw, Pegram had given his brother poison and watched him die, unable to carry out his part of the bargain. Many years later, the memory of this failure still haunted him, and he finally seized the opportunity to end it all during his trip to Cuba.

23. Dargan to Alice Stone Blackwell, 7 April 1916, Records of the National American Woman Suffrage Association, Manuscript Division, Library of Congress.

24. Dargan, "Burning Bridges," *Lute and Furrow* (New York: Charles Scribner's Sons, 1922), p. 101.

25. Dargan to Rose Pastor Stokes, undated [1924], Rose Pastor Stokes Papers, Tamiment Library, New York University.

26. Dargan to Alice Stone Blackwell, undated [1926], Records of the National American Woman Suffrage Association, Manuscript Division, Library of Congress.

27. Dargan to Alice Stone Blackwell, January 1927, Records of the National American Woman Suffrage Association, Manuscript Division, Library of Congress.

28. Dargan to William Crary Brownell, 3 July, 1919, Charles Scribner's Sons Archive, Princeton University Library. Dargan's last extant letters were to Braithwaite.

29. Dargan to Alice Stone Blackwell, undated [1944–45], Records of the National American Woman Suffrage Association, Manuscript Division, Library of Congress. In earlier letters, Dargan discusses Smith's journal, *South Today,* and describes a visit to Smith's famous girls' camp in Clayton, Georgia. The camp, along with the bulk of Smith's papers, was destroyed by fire in the 1940s.

30. The title of Lillian Smith's famous reflections on the psychological cost of racism to the white Southerner. *Killers of the Dream* was published in 1949.

31. Dargan to Grant Knight, 2 October 1930, Olive Tilford Dargan Papers, Special Collections and Archives, University of Kentucky Libraries.

32. Dargan to Grant Knight, 22 March 1931, Olive Tilford Dargan Papers, Special Collections and Archives, University of Kentucky Libraries.

33. Dargan to Grant Knight, 12 July 1931, Olive Tilford Dargan Papers, Special Collections and Archives, University of Kentucky Libraries.

34. Dargan to James Grey, 25 January 1948, James Grey Family Papers, Archives and Manuscripts Division, Minnesota Historical Society.

35. Dargan to Ruth Knight, 19 September 1950, Olive Tilford Dargan Papers, Special Collections and Archives, University of Kentucky Libraries.

36. Dargan to Ruth and Grant Knight, 28 December 1955, Olive Tilford Dargan Papers, Special Collections and Archives, University of Kentucky Libraries.

37. Dargan to Grant Knight, 17 February 1956, Olive Tilford Dargan Papers, Special Collections and Archives, University of Kentucky Libraries.

CRITICAL AFTERWORD

Sylvia J. Cook

Olive Tilford Dargan's *Call Home the Heart,* originally published in 1932, was based, like five other contemporary novels of the early thirties,[1] on the events that occurred during a strike of cotton mill workers in Gastonia, North Carolina, in 1929. It is remarkable that such a literary outpouring should have been produced by a single strike that was neither the most sensationally violent nor the most politically effective in the stormy struggle to organize the textile industry in the South. Even the reporters and journalists who first attempted to distill the meaning of what happened at Gastonia sensed that the events there were the native material of an allegory in which communism and the South were the warring elements. The novelists, too, responded to the grand scale of the conflict that resulted when the Communist organizers of the National Textile Workers Union, preaching revolution, feminism, atheism, internationalism, and racial solidarity, entered a small Southern town whose name, before 1929, was a byword for industrial productivity from its placid, overwhelmingly white, largely female millhands.[2] All of the novelists of the period attempted to capture in their fiction the personal drama in the lives of the mill workers, caught between a rural past that had failed them and an urban future of desperate economic exploitation, torn between their loyalty to traditions of family, church, and race and their dawning awareness that they might be the victims of this allegiance. However, only Dargan, in *Call Home the Heart,* imagined a transcendent, symbolic confrontation that explored vividly the historical situation at Gastonia but was not dominated by it: a clash between intelligence and emotions, principle and prejudice, that the author does not pretend to resolve in any convenient final synthesis.

Dargan wrote out of a long-standing commitment to the power of rationality and science as the best means of reforming the human condition. As early as 1912 she had written a play attacking the horrors of capitalism, and she later used one-act dramas to investigate the evils of child labor and the place of scientific visionaries in the modern world. However, she had also an intimate knowledge of the non-rational propensities and folkways of the Southern mountain poor whites, whose lives she used as the basis for her *Highland Annals* in 1925. In Ishma she created a heroine conscious and worthy of the superhuman task before her, but who is finally driven by the all-too-human passions of love and hate to retreat from the revolution back to her beloved mountains and husband. Though Ishma's personal cup of happiness seems full at the end, she is no less aware than the reader of the sea of human misery that she has abandoned for the call of her heart. The greater satisfaction for Ishma of the triumph of principle is left for a later and less successful sequel to *Call Home the Heart, A Stone Came Rolling* (1935), in which the revelation of the meaning of Ishma's name, "waste," sheds an interesting light on the conclusion of the earlier novel.

Dargan's exploration of the heroic capacities of a poor white woman is not without precedent in Southern literature. Despite a tradition of comic violence and amorality that had accrued around the literary image of the poor white man, his mate had been recognized as more industrious, or perhaps more of a drudge, from her first recorded appearance in the writings of William Byrd in 1728. During the nineteenth century, James R. Gilmore and Joel Chandler Harris created poor white heroines who revealed that their long-suffering was fused with resentment and even the first glimmerings of class consciousness.[3] However, it was not until the 1920s and three novels—by Edith Summers Kelley, Ellen Glasgow, and Elizabeth Madox Roberts—that a poor white woman was given extended and serious treatment as a central character of potentially heroic dimensions. These three novels—Kelley's *Weeds* (1923), Glasgow's *Barren Ground* (1925), and Roberts's *The Time of Man* (1926)—all deal with rural women in rebellion against the values of their society and their individual situation in it. All three are appropriate forerunners of Dargan's Ishma, except that their spheres remain local and rural and their reactions personal—there is no larger sympathetic group like the union to educate or articulate the feelings of these lonely rebels. They are what Ishma might have become without her experience in Winbury and the strike.

Interestingly, in the Darwinian world of these novels, all of the women—Kelley's Judy Pippinger, Glasgow's Dorinda Oakley, and Roberts's Ellen Chesser—are notable first for their physical superiority—not beauty—but strength to survive in a harsh environment. As a child, Judy Pippinger is lithe, active, and bold, compared to the neighbors' "inbred and undernourished children, brought up from infancy on skim milk, sowbelly, and cornmeal cakes, and living on lonely farms where they had no chance to develop infantile mob spirit." Glasgow's Dorinda is tall, determined, decisive: even in repose she appears to be "running toward life." And Roberts's Ellen, who is "hard like spines and sharp like flint," has the rock-like resilience that is necessary to endure the rigors of farm labor and seemingly endless childbearing. Ishma's tall figure is "built for strength . . . larger than the body of most women. 'An' well enough,' said Laviny, 'with all the load she's got to tote.' " The greatest and most inexorable physical demand on these women is the frequency of their pregnancies: Judy attempts to drown herself as the culmination of several unsuccessful efforts to abort an unwanted child; Ellen cries in despair, "Out of me come people forever"; and Dorinda is able to prosper in her farming only because a convenient accidental miscarriage has rid her, not just of her child, but of the need for love and its inevitable consequences for such women. Only in *Call Home the Heart* is the subject of birth control tentatively broached, and even the daring and unconventional Ishma is shocked and repelled when she overhears Derry's advice to Pace Unthank on how to prevent future pregnancies. However, on reflection, Ishma manages to ensure that the information is passed on both to Rad and Britt, and on this subject, at least, she appears to have allowed her intellect a clear triumph over her instinct.

One notable common feature of these three literary ancestors of Dargan's Ishma is a thirst for the meaning of experience and a heightened sensitivity to their environment that sometimes seems to run counter to these women's self-interest, since their lives are so fatally circumscribed by history and society. In her youth Judy Pippinger questions and rejects the opiate of religion with which her country neighbors obliterate their worldly sufferings, but as an adult woman she finds the burden of consciousness so intolerable that she begins to envy men their drunken stupors, and even experiments, unsuccessfully, with some whiskey herself. Ellen Chesser, by contrast, is able to triumph over her narrow experience by transforming and elevating it, in her imagination, into ceremonies and rituals that compensate in intensity for their lack of variety: given the dirty task of planting tobacco, she turns it into a rhythmic procession across a hillside, sun on her head and dew on her feet; at a country dance, she imagines herself turning at the center of the wind. Ellen's unconventional perceptiveness gives her lowly life dignity and significance, if not material improvement. Dorinda Oakley comes a step closer to Ishma by applying her consciousness to scientific and analytical purposes, using her observation of past failures by Southern farmers as the ground for importing Northern technology into Southern rural life, challenging its traditions and taboos; but Dorinda's subsequent prosperity is personal and apolitical. She offers an example to her community of the rewards of common sense and progressive farming, but it has none of the apocalyptic philosophical overtones of Ishma's discovery of Marxian communism and, with it, "the supreme ecstasy, the consciousness of transmuting daily life into an ideal."

Ishma gains the rewards of a questing mind by finding a system of thought and action that gives a public purpose to her life more grand and satisfying than Dorinda's private triumph. However, her awareness of such a system can only come as a consequence of her flight from the country to the city. As long as she was in the mountains, Ishma, like Judy and Ellen, could find in the beauty of nature a panacea for the brutality and degradation that might otherwise have dominated her life. When Ishma abandons the mountains for the cotton mills, she needs more than an improved standard of living to compensate for the loss of this natural world—she has an ice-box, but it proves no match for the water that gushed from the cold spring on Cloudy Knob. She can have consumer goods on the installment plan, but for Ishma they are a poor exchange for the integral quality of rural life, where nature was the source of both trial and reward for farm women like herself. Only in the forge of urban revolutionary ideology does Ishma find an excitement to rival and even surpass that of a forest fire on Lame Goat Ridge.

In the factual history of Southern farm women, the abandonment of the country for the cotton mills came much earlier than the fictional record in the novels of Gastonia. The exodus from lowland farm to town in the South began soon after the Civil War, and within a few decades the mill worker had already become a "type"—a recognizable physical specimen, described with compassion and horror by Mary Clare de Graffenried, an investigator for the Department of Labor:

> Twenty years of vitality sapped by summer heat, eaten out by ague, stolen by dyspeptic miseries! Sickly faces, stooping shoulders, shriveled flesh, suggest that normal girlhood never existed, that youth had never rounded out the lanky figure, nor glowed the sallow cheek. A slouching gait; a drooping chest, lacking muscular power to expand; a dull, heavy eye; yellow blotched complexion; dead-looking hair; stained lips, destitute of color and revealing broken teeth—these are the dower of girlhood in the mills.[4]

Such people were stigmatized as lintheads and factory trash and isolated from the rest of the urban community into mill villages, where, under a system of exploitive paternalism, they were provided with houses, schools, churches, teachers, parsons, and police. Such isolation might logically have led to a sense of class-conscious solidarity among the mill workers, but this was slow to develop in people whose traditional racial, social, and sexual prejudices, as well as their religious acquiescence to the trials of this world, were fostered and reinforced by their employers. A much more volatile element, however, began to enter the mill communities after 1900 when the mills started recruiting mountain people in addition to the lowland farmers. These people brought with them a reputation for both individualism and ready violence: it is estimated that mountain people formed the majority of mill workers in Gastonia. After a boom for the cotton mills caused by the World War, the industry entered a slump in the 1920s, anticipating by ten years the Depression that would devastate the rest of the country. Mill owners tried to reduce their losses by instituting wage cuts and new methods of increasing productivity such as the "speed-up" and the "stretch-out," which required workers to tend many times the number of machines they had been used to. The anger of the Gastonia workers had reached an explosive point by 1929 when Fred Beal, an organizer from the Communist National Textile Workers Union, arrived there to try to weld this fury into collective action.

The strike that began on April 1, 1929, was characterized by a daily escalation of rhetoric and invective from both the Communist organization and the Gastonia establishment that left the workers bewildered. Stimulated by provocative calls to class warfare, they were nevertheless told by the Communists that they might not use their guns during the strike. Bombarded by the mill owners with propaganda about the sexual immorality and bestiality of the Communists, they watched as women in legal picket lines were clubbed and bayonetted by Southern officers of the law. An anti-union mob, singing "Praise God from Whom All Blessings Flow," poured kerosene over cans of dried milk that the union had stored for the strikers' hungry babies. Communist leaders in New York ordered the workers to admit blacks to their union in defiance of their long-standing prejudices, but also in the face of the more logical objection that virtually no blacks worked in the cotton mills. The strike was finally broken, the leaders jailed, and the external semblance of the old system restored, but despite the failure of practical union objectives, what happened at Gastonia had a profound impact on those who followed it and observed its lurid reporting in both the conservative and radical press. It suggested, even before the Stock Market crash of 1929, how close to the abyss a seemingly stable society might be, and how far the traditional values of the past were failing a potentially large proportion of the people.

The course of the strike also directed the attention of fiction writers to subjects formerly unappealing to them: the urbanized Southern workers, who, while perhaps not so picturesque as their rural ancestors in the novels of Kelley, Glasgow, and Roberts, were vital tokens of a political and artistic change for many writers. The shift was marked in Olive Tilford Dargan herself—her 1925 *Highland Annals* was a collection of tales of Southern mountain life, marked by an affection for the culture of the people and the kind of unashamed indulgence in the inebriation of natural beauty that later endangers Ishma's devotion to rational and revolutionary goals. In 1932, *Call Home the Heart* uses this rural world as one element in a dialectic that traces the exhilaration and the anguish of a woman from this background awakening to a new realm of experience.

Dargan's choice of a female protagonist for this process is repeated in two of the five other contemporary novels about the Gastonia strike, Grace Lumpkin's *To Make My Bread* and Myra Page's *Gathering Storm,* and has historical support in the actual circumstances. The millhands included a large proportion of women and girls, who had the most menial jobs and the lowest wages. Despite the mill owners' theory that such employees would be the most malleable and acquiescent, women were in fact the most ardent and forceful supporters of the strike. They were outspoken and active demonstrators, frequently in the forefront of picket lines and parades. They were beaten, bayonetted, and arrested, and on several occasions they themselves used clubs on militia men and deputies. The only striker to be killed at Gastonia was a woman, Ella May Wiggins, the composer of the workers' "ballets"; the twenty-nine-year-old mother of nine children, she was shot by mill gangsters before fifty witnesses, but none of the murderers was convicted. For women like Ella May Wiggins, the union and the strike were a source of hope and vigor; they discovered talents for public speaking, organizing, and committee work, and they acquired a sense of solidarity through loyalty to their fellow workers rather than through the old humiliating group label of "linthead."

That they found the energy to give to the union seems remarkable: one mill woman's description, to a *Nation* interviewer, of a typical day in her life leaves little room for such activities. She rose at four o'clock and began to dress and make breakfast for her husband and five young children. Between five and seven they ate, she cleaned up, the children were taken to their schools or the mill nursery, and she began work in the weaving room. At lunch time she ran home from the mill, fixed dinner for all seven family members, and ran back again. She worked until six at night with a half-day on Saturday. In the evenings, after the children were fed and put to bed, and the dishes washed under the faucet on the back porch, she would sew clothes or iron until she went to bed at ten or eleven o'clock. She did not read, having left school after the third grade to enter the mill, and although she liked movies she had not been to one in six years. She expected that all her children would go to work in the mills, since the only alternative was to go back to the farm, "and there ain't no use doin' that. The farmers haven't got it as good as we have."[5] Though the strike failed in fact to ameliorate the conditions of such women, it apparently altered their consciousness of their lives in a dramatic fashion, although not necessarily in complete accord with the Marxist line of the union. Olive Tilford Dargan, in converting this awakening into fiction, chose to focus with more intellectual honesty than any of the other novelists on the

emotional and conservative impulses of one of these newly radical-
ized mountain women, as well as on her rational and activist attri-
butes.

Dargan establishes from the earliest chapters of *Call Home the
Heart* a split in Ishma's sensibility, between her feelings and her
mind, that is the basis for many of the later dichotomies of the novel—
between its rural and urban worlds, between old prejudice and new
science, between the past and the future, between personal and communal happiness, Britt and Derry, love and intelligence, passion and
principle. The struggle is a difficult one for Ishma because she thinks
and feels with such intensity; despite Dargan's evident sympathy for
a Marxist analysis of society, the novel focuses on an individual in a
conflict with herself that eludes any simple formulaic solution. Ishma's love of Britt and the mountain culture of which he is the best
representative is sufficient at the outset to overwhelm all her
thoughtfully considered objections to marriage and childbearing. She
knows that if she were to listen to his pleadings, "her heart would
surely outride her head," yet she is unable to resist the call of "something wild, sweet and unreasonable within her," and she gives in to
the life of "work and dirt and younguns" that her mind had resolved
against.

However, Ishma does not inevitably bend to her impulses, and
a tension between control and abandonment is maintained throughout the novel. When she discovers in the middle of the night that
the leader of a herd of cows has broken into her painstakingly prepared mountain bean field, she is forced to wrestle with her revulsion
from cruelty to save the fruits of her labor. Knowing that she must
"beat that cow inhumanly," she makes herself "let a murderous
blow fall on the animal's rump." The pattern of triumph over instinct
and retreat at its summons is established long before Ishma flees to
Winbury. Since it is vital to Dargan's design, Ishma must be recognized from the beginning as much more than a passionate mountain
woman who undergoes a dramatic metamorphosis in the city into a
dedicated Marxist revolutionary, and then lapses back again in the
mountains to a more primitive and authentic self.

A false sense of a conversion of Ishma's personality in the novel
led a number of reviewers of the first edition of *Call Home the Heart*,
in 1932, to assert that it shifted from art to propaganda as the setting
changed from rural to urban, only to be redeemed into art again by

the final return to nature. The assumption seemed to be that Ishma was only truly herself in the "artistic" setting of rural poverty, embellished with Indian folklore, pretty scenery, humor, and ballads, while on the mill hill, in the ugly monotony of ten-cent stores and vulgar peep-shows, she became a tendentious tool of propaganda.[6] Yet Ishma's essential character remains unchanged as she moves through these different environments. She is certainly given a drastically telescoped education in communist ideology after she meets Derry Unthank and becomes involved with union activities, and this undoubtedly contributes to a didactic element in the novel, but it can surely be considered neither obtrusive nor irrelevant: what Ishma finds in communism is a philosophical framework for her previous personal and untutored observations. Her private rebellion is given scope and coherence in the writings of Henry George, Bebel, and Marx, and when, in Winbury, Ishma finds that the logic of these ideas sometimes runs counter to her innate prejudices (against blacks, for example), we are well prepared for the consequences of just such a clash, having already seen it repeatedly on Cloudy Knob. The first reviewers of the novel had perhaps more justification in their criticism of the rather rigid endorsement of the contemporary communist line against the AFL, socialists, and liberal academics, all of whom are the objects of at least as much hostility as the capitalist exploiters. However, of those critics who justifiably mocked the formulaic left-wing rhetoric and stereotyped villains, not one objected to Dargan's application of a rather more time-worn formula at the end of the novel, when the reunion of Britt and Ishma is brought to a more powerful emotional climax by having it be the culmination of a conventional trail of lovers' misunderstandings about their true feelings. The provocative politics tended to get a much harsher scrutiny than the satisfied love affair.

Few of the critics of *Call Home the Heart* in 1932 commented on what is likely to be one of the most striking elements in the novel for the modern reader, namely, the pattern of feminist thinking that forms one of the strongest bridges between the rural and urban sections of the book. Ishma does not have to read Bebel's *Woman* in order to rethink her traditional role in society: she has been nurtured in a matriarchal household, where she is the spiritual as well as physical grandchild of the pioneer Sarah Starkweather, who teaches Ishma not only how to read her Bible, but how to skip those passages that do not conform to the old woman's own views. Sarah, who is both superbly competent at her customary farm wife's tasks, and outspoken in defense of sensible deviations from them, sets an important precedent for Ishma at the beginning, by having been stepmother to sixteen children, but mother to only one of her own flesh. This is in immediate contrast to Ishma's sister, Bainie, who presents the household with a new baby every year, even—to Ishma's horror—when there is no longer any scrap of affection left between Bainie and her husband. Sarah Starkweather's freedom from pregnancy until her fortieth year seems providential in a society that believes, "A gal she must marry and a wife she must carry"; but it is the beginning of one quest for control in the novel that ends triumphantly in Winbury, in the whispered spread of Derry Unthank's medical knowledge of contraception among women devastated by the birth and loss of large families.

The advantages of birth control for families suffering from illness and hardships are readily argued by Dargan, but *Call Home the Heart* takes up a more courageous and troubling aspect of the question in the relationship of Ishma to her premature and sickly little daughter, Vennie, for Vennie threatens neither Ishma's health nor her economic security, but is simply a burdensome imposition on the potentially great achievements of her mother. The demands of this child, who winces in strong light, screams if a door is slammed, and shakes with fear if touched by anyone but her mother, make of her a "ball and chain" and her mother "a war-horse pulling a toy sled." The doctor, Derry Unthank, is most direct and brutal when he thinks, "good job if the kid would croak," and indeed Vennie's accidental death does leave Ishma free to use her talents in a broader arena, where she may find a "sense of self-completion" that had not come in her sacrifices for Vennie. Although Ishma does not actually shun the needs of her weak child for the call of her own genius, the release that comes to her, both after Vennie's death and in symbolic dreams of it beforehand, is consistent not only with her later eugenics theories (promising the workers that they will have the kind of children they want, "and not have to sift a hundred to get one we're proud of"), but also with the Emersonian refusal of the novel to accept any conventional obligations without first examining their worthiness. The contrary pulls of obligation and aspiration are most honestly and distressingly confronted in dealing with Vennie, for no easy compromise is allowed between the needs of mother and daughter.

After the child's death, both communist and romantic revolutionary impulses seem capable of being fulfilled in Ishma, for freedom from Vennie means more than the chance to work for the union—it is also the opportunity to reconsider her relationships with Britt, Rad, and Derry—each of whom represents a powerful link to a way of life that Ishma is not wholly at ease with. Although Rad places the strongest material obligations on Ishma, he is the one who can be most summarily dismissed, by her rather manipulative ploys with Leta, because his tie to her is not of mind or heart. Derry, the scientist and radical, who has helped engineer Ishma's intellectual education, is less easily forgotten. Even in the final moments back on the mountain, listening to Britt's voice, "her shut eyes were looking on another face, a face keen, pale, dedicated. . . . And across Britt's voice ran another voice whose words were a path of flame." Yet Ishma recognizes that without Derry, "the world would still be a place for work and hope and the blossoming rod of faith," while without Britt, she herself would become "crippled and incomplete." None of these men, except perhaps Rad, when he defects to the Ku Klux Klan, is treated unsympathetically; even Ishma's brother Steve is granted an affectionate portrait, despite his voicing of the most conservative views about women in the novel: "A woman's a woman. She's bound to carry the baggage in this life. They's no gettin' out of it for her. A man can walk off any time, but a woman kain't. God, or Nature, or something we kain't buck against, has fixed it that way." For Dargan, the feminism of *Call Home the Heart* belongs to a pattern of awakening class-consciousness, aided by a scientific revolution, whose beneficiaries will be all future generations, men and women alike. Any animus between the sexes in the novel is seen as the result of economic exploitation and blind tradition, not as the innate and inevitable result of biology.

Ishma's personal experience in Winbury convinces her of the harmony between her own sense of women's problems and the union's communist attitude toward them. Such convergence is not the case, however, on the question of racial solidarity, where Dargan again squarely confronts a controversial issue that caused a great deal of turmoil in the actual historical situation. Although black workers comprised only an estimated one-half of one percent of the mill workers in Gastonia, *The Communist,* in June 1929, called their presence "the most difficult and at the same time the most vital and fundamental problem we have to solve." This insistence on pursuing an ideological question that was not absolutely germane to the particular situation at Gastonia indicates a split between pragmatic union goals and left-wing eschatology that was central to the immediate failure of the strike. All union leaders in the field in the South struggled with the force of white prejudice, and many wished to compromise, feeling that there were too few blacks and too much bigotry to make the correct ideological stance productive. The novelists of Gastonia, in creating a fictional situation, had rather more freedom to resolve or avoid the question and, with the exception of Dargan, they variously chose to avoid the question of racial tensions or to imagine an idealized Southern proletariat, free of all prejudice and utterly unconvincing.

In *Call Home the Heart,* Dargan attempts to present simultaneously both the anti-racist arguments of the communists and the depth of irrational resistance they are likely to meet, even in so sensitive and intelligent a woman as Ishma. Dargan is also able to subsume the particular issue of racism to the larger moral allegory of the novel, since Ishma's defection on race represents a rebellion of her instinct against her painfully won intellectual conviction, based on Derry's tutoring, of the need for solidarity and comradeship. Despite Ishma's pride in her rescue of Butch Wells from a lynch mob, and her sentimental fantasy of sisterly solidarity with the "black and bronze women with their big, tender eyes," Ishma is repelled by the malodorous embrace of Gaffie Wells and strikes out at her viciously and irrationally. This "Neanderthal" behavior is one of the novel's most daring and shocking moments, since Dargan seems to be endorsing the position so frequently exploited by the mill owners, that the white Southern worker could never accept racial equality. Nevertheless, Ishma's behavior is artistically consistent with her character, and ideologically consistent with the wider betrayal of purpose that occurs with her flight back to the mountains at this point. Her defection on race is a vivid symbol of her general desertion of ideals undermining the perfection of the blissful final reunion with her husband.

The Ishma who returns to the mountains can never fully recapture her former primitive joy there because she is haunted by just such memories and images of the Winbury she abandoned as the bleeding head of Gaffie Wells and the shocked eyes of Derry Unthank. However, the mountain world itself has begun to lose its isolation, and Ishma's newly urbanized sensibility is a token of the industrialized civilization that will inevitably change even the mountains. She is now aware that the future for these farmers, even in as few as three generations, lies in the development of the kind of machinery that will make her life with Britt only a quaint and archaic interlude before the new technological era forever eliminates them. Since such mechanization is inevitable, and since Dargan from her earliest works has evinced a faith in this kind of scientific progress, so long as machines are not used to abuse or exploit people, she presents them as neutral in themselves and capable of becoming touchstones for human achievement. The machines are one of the new forces from the urban world of Winbury that can rival, by their excitement and power, the drama of a forest fire on Lame Goat Ridge, and Ishma responds to them with comparable enthusiasm and respect:

> They could kill, but they could create. That was their first, great function. When she came in to them she felt that she must greet them good-morning, and start the day comradely with the secret force producing so endlessly and enormously for the markets of men. When she left them she caught herself nodding back as she went out the door.

Thus the urban world offers, through this harnessing of natural energy by human ingenuity, a possibility of something beyond material rewards, an opportunity for workers to be no longer victims of nature but sharers in its power. Ishma carries this consciousness back to the mountains, even to the final inferno on Lame Goat Ridge, when she imagines the flames burning up all the darkness of the night. The murderous and creative force of the fire evokes both the machines and the revolution she has abandoned, and gives Ishma a final impetus in the novel to envision an eventual return to the urban world and the future she can help build there.

The fact that the historical circumstances of the novel dictated that the purifying fire for a corrupt society should come in the form of communist revolution, rather than, for example, the resurgence of the Christian spirit that Britt believes in, needs to be taken seriously in any discussion of *Call Home the Heart*. The confrontation of communism and capitalism in the novel is made to serve the larger allegory of the warring forces of reason and unreason in human nature, but the political ideology itself is important. Those American writers, like Dargan, who turned leftward toward communism in the early years of the depression, found in it an epistemology that necessitated a practical program of action. The epistemology offered a method of understanding society that was rational, scientific, and intellectual, even when in pursuit of a seemingly apocalyptic goal: Derry Unthank voices it precisely when he says, "we have to unclog the gate of evolution. We have to sweep out the clutter of unseeing ages. We have to release even spirit through the door of intelligence." The program of action that is the immediate manifestation of this intelligence in Dargan's novel—the rejection of traditional attitudes toward women, blacks, religion, and class structure—has been largely vindicated in the fifty years since the novel was first published. Moreover, the ideas are presented in an artistic context that permits complexity and conflict, and avoids a sense of the rigidly programmatic. However, these fifty years of hindsight have shed a less sympathetic light on other attitudes in the novel—the eugenics theories, the vilification of socialists and liberals, and the endorsement of Stalin—attitudes that are reflected artistically in a certain occasional expediency in the characterization, whereby some people become flattened as characters in order to serve an ideological end. Rad Bailey, one of Dargan's most convincing characters, is suddenly abandoned to the lure of the Klan and Leta when he is getting in Ishma's way; the socialist Pritchett, the academic Beckwith, and the novelist Owenby are all arbitrarily dismissed with sarcasm, in notable contrast to the compassion accorded to Virginia Grant, the wife of the millowner. While the novel is thus not unscathed by Dargan's application of her contemporary understanding of communist ideology in the early thirties, it also derives much of its power from the sense of commitment that led her to explore and vividly recreate a complex urban environment—itself a radically new, and long overdue, setting for Southern literature. The painter Matisse has said that all art bears the imprint of its historical epoch, but that great art is that in which this imprint is most deeply marked:[7] in *Call Home the Heart* it is the immediacy and detail of the fictional milieu of mountain and mill town that give life to the ideas that form the political element of the book.

These ideas are in the tradition of Emersonian optimism in celebrating the life of the mind and the triumph of principle in America, though in the hitherto unlikely person of a poor white mountain and mill woman. They also offer sober reflections on the hazards of such optimism, by insisting consciously on the force of passion, and revealing, unconsciously perhaps, the lure of orthodoxy in qualifying any triumph of pure reason. If *Call Home the Heart* can still create this sense of the power and excitement of the human intellect, poised on the edge of discovering its immense possibilities for enriching experience; if it can still capture the poignancy of the human heart, finding its release in the realm of the senses, searching for comfort rather than comprehension; and if it can embody this dialectic in images that both evoke and transcend its specific occasion, then it is indeed an unusual and valuable American novel.

Sylvia J. Cook
University of Missouri–St. Louis

Notes

1. The other Gastonia novels are: Mary Heaton Vorse, *Strike!* (New York: Horace Liveright, Inc., 1930); Sherwood Anderson, *Beyond Desire* (New York: Horace Liveright, Inc., 1932); Grace Lumpkin, *To Make My Bread* (New York: Macauley Company, 1932); Dorothy Myra Page, *Gathering Storm: A Story of the Black Belt* (New York: International Publishers, 1932); William Rollins, Jr., *The Shadow Before* (New York: Robert M. McBride & Company, 1934).

2. The main books on Gastonia are Fred E. Beal, *Proletarian Journey: New England, Gastonia, Moscow* (New York: Hillman-Curl, Inc., 1937) and Liston Pope, *Millhands and Preachers: A Study of Gastonia* (New Haven: Yale Univ. Press, 1942). My account of the strike is derived largely from these and the following sources: Theodore Draper, "Gastonia Revisited," *Social Research* 38 (1971): 3–29; Vera Buch Weisbord, "Gastonia 1929: Strike at the Loray Mill," *Southern Exposure* 1 (Winter 1974): 185–203; Bertha Hendrix, "I Was in the Gastonia Strike," *Southern Exposure* 4, No. 4 (1976): 74; and coverage of Southern textile workers' strikes in 1929 and 1930 in the *Nation, New Masses, New Republic,* and *Outlook and Independent.*

3. More detailed literary history of the Southern poor white may be found in Shields McIlwaine's *The Southern Poor White: From Lubberland to Tobacco Road* (Norman: Univ. of Oklahoma Press, 1939) and in my book, *From Tobacco Road to Route*

66: *The Southern Poor White in Fiction* (Chapel Hill: Univ. of North Carolina Press, 1976).

4. Mary Clare de Graffenried, "The Georgia Cracker in the Cotton Mills," *Century* (February 1891), p. 491.

5. Paul Blanshard, "How to Live on Forty-Six Cents a Day," *Nation* 128 (15 May 1929): 580–81.

6. See Elmer Davis, "The Red Peril," *Saturday Review of Literature* 8 (16 April 1932): 662, and the reviews by Jonathan Daniels, p. 537, and Amy Loveman, p. 674, in the same volume.

7. Quoted by Terry Eagleton in *Marxism and Literary Criticism* (Berkeley: Univ. of California Press, 1976), p. 3.

FEMINIST CLASSICS FROM THE FEMINIST PRESS

Antoinette Brown Blackwell: A Biography, by Elizabeth Cazden. $16.95 cloth, $9.95 paper.

Brown Girl, Brownstones, a novel by Paule Marshall. Afterword by Mary Helen Washington. $6.95 paper.

Cassandra, by Florence Nightingale. Introduction by Myra Stark. Epilogue by Cynthia Macdonald. $2.50 paper.

The Convert, a novel by Elizabeth Robins. Introduction by Jane Marcus. $5.95 paper.

Daughter of Earth, a novel by Agnes Smedley. Afterword by Paul Lauter. $10.00 cloth, $5.95 paper.

The Female Spectator, Edited by Mary R. Mahl and Helen Koon. $5.95 paper.

First Feminists: British Women Writers from 1578–1799. Edited with an introduction by Moira Ferguson. $19.95 cloth, $12.95 paper.

Guardian Angel and Other Stories, by Margery Latimer. Afterwords by Louis Kampf, Meridel Le Sueur, and Nancy Loughridge. $16.95 cloth, $7.95 paper.

I Love Myself When I Am Laughing . . . And Then Again When I Am Looking Mean and Impressive, by Zora Neale Hurston. Edited by Alice Walker with an introduction by Mary Helen Washington. $7.95 paper.

Käthe Kollwitz: Woman and Artist, by Martha Kearns. $7.95 paper.

Life in the Iron Mills, by Rebecca Harding Davis. Biographical interpretation by Tillie Olsen. $4.95 paper.

The Living Is Easy, a novel by Dorothy West. Afterword by Adelaide M. Cromwell. $6.95.

The Maimie Papers. Edited by Ruth Rosen and Sue Davidson. Introduction by Ruth Rosen. $15.95 cloth, $7.95 paper.

Portraits of Chinese Women in Revolution, by Agnes Smedley. Edited with an introduction by Jan MacKinnon and Steve MacKinnon and an afterword by Florence Howe. $4.95 paper.

Ripening: Selected Work, 1927–1980, by Meridel Le Sueur. Edited with an introduction by Elaine Hedges. $14.95 cloth, $7.95 paper.

The Silent Partner, a novel by Elizabeth Stuart Phelps. Afterword by Mari Jo Buhle and Florence Howe. $6.95 paper.

These Modern Women: Autobiographical Essays from the Twenties. Edited with an introduction by Elaine Showalter. $4.95 paper.

The Unpossessed, a novel of the thirties, by Tess Slesinger. Introduction by Alice Kessler-Harris and Paul Lauter and afterword by Janet Sharistanian. $7.95 paper.

Weeds, a novel by Edith Summers Kelley. Afterword by Charlotte Goodman. $6.95 paper.

The Woman and the Myth: Margaret Fuller's Life and Writings, by Bell Gale Chevigny. $8.95 paper.

The Yellow Wallpaper, by Charlotte Perkins Gilman. Afterword by Elaine Hedges. $2.50 paper.

OTHER TITLES FROM THE FEMINIST PRESS

Black Foremothers: Three Lives, by Dorothy Sterling. $6.95 paper.

But Some of Us Are Brave: Black Women's Studies. Edited by Gloria T. Hull, Patricia Bell Scott, and Barbara Smith. $14.95 cloth, $8.95 paper.

Complaints and Disorders: The Sexual Politics of Sickness, by Barbara Ehrenreich and Deirdre English. $2.95 paper.

The Cross-Cultural Study of Women. Edited by Mary I. Edwards and Margot Duley Morrow. $8.95 paper.

Dialogue on Difference. Edited by Florence Howe. $8.95 paper.

Everywoman's Guide to Colleges and Universities. Edited by Florence Howe, Suzanne Howard, and Mary Jo Boehm Strauss. $12.95 paper.

Household and Kin: Families in Flux, by Amy Swerdlow *et al.* $14.95 cloth, $6.95 paper.

How to Get Money for Research, by Mary Rubin and the Business and Professional Women's Foundation. Foreward by Mariam Chamberlain. $5.95 paper.

In Her Own Image: Women Working in the Arts. Edited with an introduction by Elaine Hedges and Ingrid Wendt. $17.95 cloth, $8.95 paper.

Las Mujeres: Conversations from a Hispanic Community, by Nan Elsasser, Kyle MacKenzie, and Yvonne Tixier y Vigil. $14.95 cloth, $6.95 paper.

Lesbian Studies: Present and Future. Edited by Margaret Cruikshank. $14.95 cloth, $8.95 paper.

Moving the Mountain: Women Working for Social Change, by Ellen Cantarow with Susan Gushee O'Malley and Sharon Hartman Strom. $6.95 paper.

Out of the Bleachers: Writings on Women and Sport. Edited with an introduction by Stephanie L. Twin. $7.95 paper.

Reconstructing American Literature: Courses, Syllabi, Issues. Edited by Paul Lauter. $10.95 paper.

Rights and Wrongs: Women's Struggle for Legal Equality, by Susan Cary Nicholas, Alice M. Price, and Rachel Rubin. $5.95 paper.

Salt of the Earth, screenplay by Michael Wilson with historical commentary by Deborah Silverton Rosenfelt. $5.95 paper.

The Sex-Role Cycle: Socialization from Infancy to Old Age, by Nancy Romer. $6.95 paper.

Witches, Midwives, and Nurses: A History of Women Healers, by Barbara Ehrenreich and Deirdre English. $2.95 paper.

With These Hands: Women Working on the Land. Edited with an introduction by Joan M. Jensen. $17.95 cloth, $8.95 paper.

Woman's "True" Profession: Voices from the History of Teaching. Edited with an introduction by Nancy Hoffman. $17.95 cloth, $8.95 paper.

Women Have Always Worked: A Historical Overview, by Alice Kessler-Harris. $14.95 cloth, $6.95 paper.

Women Working: An Anthology of Stories and Poems. Edited and with an introduction by Nancy Hoffman and Florence Howe. $7.95 paper.
Women's Studies in Italy, by Laura Balbo and Yasmine Ergas. A Women's Studies International Monograph. $5.95 paper.

When ordering, please include $1.50 for postage and handling for one book and 35¢ for each additional book. Order from: The Feminist Press, Box 334, Old Westbury, NY 11568. Telephone (516) 997-7660.